A
FAMILIAR
DRAGON

A FAMILIAR DRAGON

Fanuilh
Wizard's Heir
Beggar's Banquet

Daniel Hood

Contents

SOUTHWARK

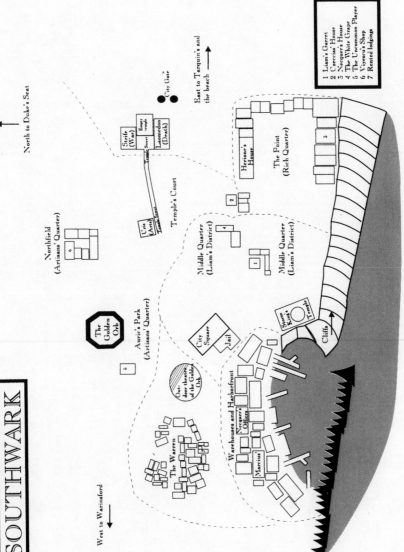

North to Duke's Seat

West to Warminford

East to Tarquin's end and the beach

Northfield (Artisans' Quarter)

6

Strife (War)
Empy temple
Laomedon (Death)
Temple Street

City Gate

Uris Artis
Temple Street
Temple's Court

The Golden Orb

Auriti Park (Artisans' Quarter)

5

Middle Quarter (Liam's District)
4

Middle Quarter (Liam's District)
1

2

Herione's House

The Point (Rich Quarter)

3

City Square
Jail

Out-door theatre of the Golden Orb

The Warren

Warehouses and Harborfront

Exchequer's Offices

Marcus'

Storm King's Temple

Cliffs

1 Liam's Garret
2 Coeccius' House
3 Nercquer's House
4 The White Grape
5 The Uncommon Player
6 Vyvroro's Shop
7 Rented lodgings

Fanuilh

▪ *1* ▪

THE FEAST WAS a thing Liam Rhenford had never thought to see in Taralon and because of that, and his general feeling of being an outsider, he allowed himself a little too much of the hot, spiced wine.

Of course, the merchant Necquer was not really Taralonian; he was an expatriated Freeporter, and their sensibilities were less easily offended. Liam had spent a fair amount of time in the Freeports himself and was not offended, but he found himself wondering if any of Southwark's other merchants, Necquer's competitors, would consider such a feast with anything other than disgust.

Clerks and overseers in their rough best drank noisily in Necquer's home; stevedores and sailors, shorn to the ears in the traditional haircut of Taralon's lower classes, ate his food and sang dirty chanteys in his hall; spinning and weaving girls danced, giggling, to the minstrels Necquer had hired. Even in Southwark, the southernmost city of Taralon's southern duchies, position and the bounds of class distinction were well observed, if not as rigidly as in more northern parts. The merchant, however, had thrown propriety to the wind.

In his own home, Liam could hear other merchants saying, *he let them dance in his own home,* and smiled to himself over the social outrage.

Necquer's home was beautiful in a cramped way; a high, narrow wooden building nestled in the Point, Southwark's tiny rich quarter. Gleaming parquet floors shone under vibrant, imported rugs; light and warmth radiated from countless silver candelabra and roaring fireplaces.

Fine food piled high on trestle tables disappeared almost as soon as it was served, and wine and ale flowed in silver and pewter mugs. Freihett Necquer was entertaining his lowborn workers in a style normally reserved for his social equals as if it were nothing and his workers, in turn, accepted it without question. Glass-paned doors at the rear of the house opened onto a rain-dark stone porch overlooking the harbor; a group of sailors formed a circle there, encouraging two wrestling men with catcalls and shouts. A trio of musicians played loudly, and the sound of Necquer's employees dancing, eating and celebrating was louder than the rain or the surf crashing below.

I had no idea he was so rich, Liam thought, casting admiring eyes about the merchant's home. *I should have charged him more for those maps.*

Ostensibly the feast was in honor of the upcoming Uris-tide, but the real reason was that Necquer was alive and well, and in a mood to celebrate. He had survived one of the worst storms in Southwark's memory and—by a miracle—come home with a cargo of immense value.

When Necquer's workers talked, which they did only rarely between laughing and eating and dancing breathlessly, they talked of that miracle, and many slyly hinted that Necquer had never kept a Uris-tide before, and probably did not know who Uris was.

The miracle was the disappearance of Southwark's Teeth, the towering, jagged rocks that guarded the city's harbor. Rising black and ominous from beneath the sea like the spine of a submerged sea-dragon, they stretched for miles from the west to close off most of the harbor, leaving only a small entrance to the placid harbor. They took a greedy toll for the protection, however, in the form of ships smashed against their unyielding sides, keeping many safe in return for the occasional wreck sent down to the Storm King. A week before, another merchant's caravel, bearing a fortune home from Alyecir, had been crushed into the Teeth. Three men out of a crew of sixty had escaped. Four days later, Southwark woke, blinked its eyes, and saw the Teeth gone. The sea rolled unstopped into the roadstead, and the coast looked barren, for all the world like an old man without his natural teeth. A day after that, Necquer had led four merchantmen limping into port. Experienced seamen declared it a miracle: battered as the ships were by the late season storms, they could never have negotiated the Teeth. And that morning, the day after Necquer's safe arrival, Southwark woke to find that the unknown thief had repented, and the Teeth were back, resuming their posts as if they had never left.

Necquer had more than enough reason to celebrate, and his employees—common sailors, poor clerks, burly stevedores and longshoremen, the girls who spun and wove his trade goods—accepted it wholeheartedly.

Liam listened to everything he could, circulating aimlessly around the noisy, crowded house, taking long sips of wine. He spoke to no one, because he knew no one, and thought more than once of the invitation extended to him by Necquer's wife.

He had arrived almost an hour after sunset, delayed as much by the fact that he would not know any of Necquer's employees as by the rain. The house was already full of people celebrating, and though the music had not started yet, the noise was deafening. He took a deep breath and shouldered his way into the feast.

Necquer had spotted him after a few minutes and jostled his way over.

"Rhenford! It was good of you to come!" The merchant was almost as tall as Liam, but far broader. Almost forty years old, in many ways he was a typical Freeporter, dark of hair and skin, easygoing and unpretentious. He clasped Liam's hand and shoulder, smiling broadly. Over his shoulder, he called out: "Poppae! Poppae! Come over here! There's someone you should meet!"

An expensively dressed young woman separated herself from an obviously painful conversation with a weaving girl and threaded her way through the press. She was beautiful in a quiet way, finely formed, porcelain features framed with a mass of curling, glossy black hair. She was young, barely into her twenties, and she looked almost childlike compared to her husband. Necquer watched her make her way towards them, and it struck Liam as he bowed over her hand that the merchant was carefully scrutinizing their introduction.

"Poppae, this is Liam Rhenford, the gentleman who drew the maps that have made us rich! Rhenford, my wife Poppae."

"Sir Liam," Poppae murmured, a slight smile playing over her lips.

"I'm afraid I'm not a knight, Lady Necquer," Liam corrected politely. He had grown used to the southern habit of indiscriminately applying titles of respect. In the north, where he was raised, the degrees of rank were carefully delineated and scrupulously denoted with countless specific names, each signifying a slight difference in class. Southerners, on the other hand, tended to use whatever title came to mind, as long as it broadly approximated the subject's position.

Necquer suddenly breathed hard, as though disappointed in the conversation, and turned away abruptly. Liam watched him go, slightly surprised. Lady Necquer showed no interest in leaving. In fact, she gazed at him curiously.

"I suppose I owe you my husband's long absences, Sir Liam?"

He let the honorific pass this time. She spoke the southern dialect, but not as thickly as most he had met in Southwark, and her eyes were disturbingly enormous, sad and blue.

"I am afraid you are correct, madam. I did draw some maps for your husband, but had I known they would cause you pain through his absence, I'd never have done it." He had, in fact, given her husband a secret few others knew about. Alyecir and the Freeports, the main trading destinations of ships from Taralon, lay to the west. But to the east and south a number of cities existed on coasts undreamed of by Southwark's merchants, unvisited because of a Taralonian superstition about sailing the Cauliff Ocean. Liam had reached them by traveling overland, but he knew they could be reached from the sea. Late in the summer, it had occurred to him to sell the maps he had made, and he had chosen Necquer primarily because he was a Freeporter, and might not share Taralonian superstitions.

As hoped, Necquer had no objections to trying the Cauliff, and on Liam's assurance that the journey would be short, had departed as soon as he could ready four ships, even though the fall storms were approaching. That had been a little over six weeks before, and already he was back, and if the size of his feast was any indication, the trip had been very successful.

Lady Necquer looked at him with new respect, and edged a little closer, giving in to pressure from the ever-growing crowd.

Liam let his eyes rove over the crowd, nervously refusing to meet her eyes. It had been a long time since he had had to deal with anyone of even Lady Necquer's station, and the social pitfalls their conversation presented loomed large in his mind. On the other hand, he had noticed the discomfort with which she spoke to Necquer's more common employees. He supposed that, clean-shaven and well dressed as he was, he represented a far more interesting companion than longshoremen and tars straight off a three-month voyage. And bowing over her hand had probably not hurt his image.

"You speak passing fair, Sir Liam, and with a Midlands tongue, 'less I'm mistaken."

"You are not, madam. I was born in the Midlands." He could not help feeling that he sounded stiff and stilted to her, but it had been a long while since his breeding had been required of him.

"My husband's tongue was schooled Midlands," she said with a smile, "though a very Freeporter he is. He learned in Harcourt and the other western ports. But tell, how does a Midlands tongue come to speak so far south? And to draw maps of lands even further south?"

Liam dropped his gaze to his boots, taking in the tooled leather, uncomfortable speaking about himself. "When I was a youth, certain . . . family problems forced my departure from home. I have traveled widely since," he finished lamely.

"No first son's legacy for you, then?" she said sympathetically. "You were a second son?"

"Yes," he lied. It was far easier to claim the anonymity of a lesser position than to explain to the curious woman that he was an only child, and that his birthright had been stripped from him in war. And far less painful.

"And so you traveled. But not as a sailor?" she asked, and he detected a note of hope in her soft voice.

"No, madam. Sometimes as a surgeon, or navigator, and twice as captain. Most often merely as a passenger. The charts I drew your husband were taken from my notes."

"Navigator, captain, surgeon, e'en? You are a man of several parts, Sir Liam, though you are no knight." She laughed brightly. Liam caught on only after a moment, and then laughed with her.

"It would very much agree with me to hear further of your travels, Sir Liam."

"Even in a Midlands tongue?" he asked with mock humility, beginning to warm to Lady Necquer's sad eyes and gentle manner. She smiled at him.

Necquer suddenly loomed up behind his wife, smiling as though he had heard the joke.

"Eh, Poppae, we seem to be ready for the minstrels, don't you think?"

The question was asked without any detectable overtones, but Lady Necquer paled slightly, and caught her breath.

"Faith, I suppose we are, lord." She made to move away, but Necquer took hold of her tiny waist and kissed her soundly on the cheek. She snuggled against him, raising one hand absently to his sea-roughened cheek. He smiled at Liam over her shoulder.

"Has Rhenford been regaling you with tales of his journeys, my dear?"

"Boring her, I'm afraid," Liam said with a slight bow.

"Nonsense, Rhenford. You're the most interesting man I've met in a long time, and I'm sure Poppae agrees. Don't you, sweet?"

Lady Necquer nodded eagerly. "I was just asking Sir Liam to tell me more of his travels, lord, but he is a fierce keeper of secrets."

"Well, we'll have to change that, eh, Rhenford? Why not come some night to dinner? You can tell me where to trade next season, and then entertain Poppae. I'm leaving for Warinsford tomorrow, or I'd ask you then, but I'll be back in a few days. You'll dine with us then, eh?"

"Must you leave so soon?" Lady Necquer seemed genuinely upset, but her husband's answer sounded rehearsed, as if they had had the same discussion earlier.

"The snows won't start for another month, and a great deal of what I brought back may spoil, sweet. It must be soon." He kissed her again, and Liam shifted uncomfortably, as though intruding on a private moment.

Lady Necquer returned his kiss absently. "But could not Sir Liam come and entertain me while you are gone? Mayhap just to while away an afternoon?" There was a freight of meaning behind her words, and a plea that Necquer caught, though it flew past Liam.

"Certainly, certainly," Necquer said after a moment's thought. "He shall come tomorrow, then? What do you say, Rhenford? Will you entertain my wife tomorrow afternoon?"

"I . . . of course, of course."

Lady Necquer smiled gratefully at her husband, who admonished Liam to remember his appointment, and whisked her away. Liam stood, confused but strangely happy. He had been in Southwark for over four months, but until then he had spoken—spoken for no purpose other than pleasure—with only one other person.

He smiled to himself and shouldered gently through the throng of celebrating workers to find himself a cup of wine. He drank six more before the end of the evening, eating little, talking no more, and watching a great deal.

Necquer's employees enjoyed themselves thoroughly. They shouted and danced the large group dances favored in the south, encouraging each other with whistles and clapping. The three minstrels kept pace, playing louder and more wildly as the evening wore on. Liam looked on, listening to snatches of conversation about the miracle, and watched Lady Necquer.

As close as they seemed, something was not right between the merchant and his wife. He recalled a comment he had not understood. A clerk at the buffet had told a companion that there might be more than one reason why Necquer had hurried home, and received a wink and a snicker in return. Liam guessed now that they were referring to a mistress. It might explain the strangeness he had detected in the merchant's manner, but he found it hard to believe anyone would be disloyal to a woman as young and beautiful as Poppae Necquer.

Tall as he was, Liam found it easy to keep track of the diminutive beauty as she moved around her home; and it was easy to catch Necquer watching her too, with slitted eyes and an expression that occasionally grew grim. She seemed aware of it, but not disturbed. It was as if she were waiting to show him something, but could not find it in the crowded room.

Towards the bottom of his seventh cup of wine, Liam realized that the room was stiflingly close, and that the feeling was gone in the tip of his long nose. Recognizing an old sign, he prepared himself to go, looking around for his host. He shoved less gently than before through the crowd towards the back of the house, his misjudgement of the gaps in the milling crowd justifying his decision to leave.

Necquer was not to be found in the rear of the narrow house, though several drunken sailors were taking turns walking the length of the rain-slick balustrade that rimmed the porch, ignoring the long drop to the harbor below. *Someone should stop them,* Liam thought hazily, *but not me.* He turned and began threading his unsteady way back through the crowd.

He saw Necquer in the middle of the hall, pressed to one wall by the thick, rowdy crowd. His face was taut and grim, and he was staring across the hall at his wife, who was behind one of the tables that had once been covered with food and now held crumbs and bones. She was staring, pale and unhappy, towards the street door, where a young man stood framed by the lintel. He was brushing rain from long, ash-blond hair, his handsome face swinging to and fro, looking for someone. Necquer followed his wife's gaze, and Liam saw him mouth a curse and begin pushing through the crowd towards the door.

Stung by curiosity, Liam followed after, losing sight of Necquer in the crowd. He did, however, see the young man's eyes suddenly widen, and pushed harder against the crowd when the man spun quickly and dashed out into the rain.

The crowd and his own unsteadiness slowed him, and by the time he reached the door and stepped out into the street, the youth was gone. Necquer stood on the cobbles, his fists bunched by his sides, and Liam almost lurched into him. One fist raised, the merchant spun on him, and lowered his arm reluctantly.

"Rhenford," he said, rain trickling down his face into his beard like tears.

"I thought I should thank you before I left," Liam slurred, wiping rain out of his face with a hand that felt unnaturally hot.

"Rhenford, you're drunk!" Necquer gave a laugh, loud and heartily out of proportion, Liam felt, to how drunk he was, but he said nothing. The merchant seemed to need to laugh.

"Who would have thought a few cups of wine could undo a man who'd traveled the world over?" Necquer laughed, immensely amused and immensely relieved by something.

"I thought I should thank you before I left," Liam repeated, very uncomfortable and feeling very serious.

"You're not leaving yet, Rhenford, not in this rain. At least let me send a servant with you. You'll fall in a gutter and catch your death! Wait in the hall, I'll send a servant for you."

Liam let the merchant guide him back into the house, where he leaned against a wall. Necquer started away, then turned back, looking seriously at Liam.

"You will come tomorrow, won't you?" There was an earnestness in Necquer's voice, but Liam was feeling unnaturally hot all over now, and waved the question away.

"Of course, of course," he mumbled.

"Wait here. I'll send a servant."

Necquer strode off into the crowd and almost immediately, Liam pulled himself away from the wall and walked, stumbling slightly, into the rain.

It was a cold, light rain, and went a long way towards sobering Liam up. He wove only slightly back and forth across the narrow streets, turning his face up to the rain to try to clear his head. By the time he had wound his way down out of the rich quarter, further inland to the neighborhood where his rooms were, his head was far clearer, the haze mostly driven out by a piercing headache, like a spike driven into his forehead.

When he had arrived in Southwark during the spring, he had not looked far for lodging, taking directions from the first longshoreman he met. He had been directed to an establishment run by a captain's widow, and she had been glad to offer him her attic garret, the largest room she had.

Climbing the five flights of rickety stairs, he cursed the choice, and when he slammed his head into one of the room's low-hanging beams, he cursed again, loudly. The room ran the whole length of the house, with a low ceiling and one window at the front, where he had placed a cheap table. Apart from a straw pallet and an iron-bound chest, the table and its attendant chair were the only furnishings. Several books and stacks of papers littered the rest of the room, and Liam remembered how impressed his landlady had been.

"A very scholar, aren't you, sir? Never had no scholar here before," she had said, respect like cloying sugar in her voice.

Most of the sheets of paper were blank, but she had not noticed that. He had wondered if Mistress Dorcas could read, and decided that she was probably illiterate.

He managed to light a candle after several attempts, and finally sat down on the chair, which creaked ominously at his weight. He thought of writing, but dismissed the idea almost immediately, the pain in his head a warning against any attempt at serious work. Instead, he stared out the glass-paned window at the rain and offered a blanket prayer to whichever gods kept the attic roof from leaking, and to those who had kept him from throwing up on his way home.

"No more wine," he muttered, scratching with a thumbnail at the spine of one of the books on the table. "Not for a long time."

The candle guttered, disturbed by a crafty draft that had found a chink in the window. Liam shifted slightly and blew the candle out. He undressed in the dark, tossing his soaked breeches, boots and tunic away, and crawled beneath his two soft blankets. It was cold in the garret, and the smell of mold curled lightly into his nose. Rain pattered heavily on the roof for a while, and he thought he might fall asleep to it, but it tapered off, leaving him with a loud silence.

Restless and uncomfortable, thinking of nothing for over an hour, he finally got off the pallet and searched in the dark for his candle. When it was lit, he opened his chest with the key hung around his neck, and dressed anew, in dry clothes. He started for the door and then, as an afterthought, returned to spread his wet clothes on the chair.

The rain had stopped, but water still gurgled in the gutters, and the clouds had not broken. He hesitated in the street, unsure where he wanted to go. He could simply wander the city, but the Guard frowned on that, and there was nothing in Southwark he had not already seen.

He thought of visiting his only friend in Southwark, and then rejected the idea because it was late.

Then again, he thought, *Tarquin's a weird one, and a wizard; perhaps he's still awake. And it's somewhere to go.*

Tarquin Tanaquil was really more of an acquaintance than a friend, but he seemed to tolerate Liam, and the two got along well enough. The wizard lived outside Southwark, beyond a belt of farms and pasturage on a beach to the east of the city, fifteen minutes' ride away.

Liam set off purposefully through the rain-glistening streets, thinking better of whistling.

It took him almost an hour to reach Tarquin's beach on foot, and his headache was gone by the time he arrived. Happily, lights still burned in the house.

The wizard's home occupied a bend in the high seacliffs where sand had gathered, forming a long, secluded beach. A narrow path cut into the cliffs led down to the waterfront, and Liam stood at its bottom for a minute, admiring the view.

Far out over the sea, the clouds had broken, and the moon turned the horizon silver. Closer in, all was dark, the massive breakwater a looming shadow, the sand black. Only the wizard's home was lit, a warm and cheery presence. It was a villa, a rich-looking house: one-storied but long and deep, white plaster and red tile roof with only a slight peak. A broad, stone-paved patio lined the front with steps leading right onto the sand. The wall of the house facing the sea was almost entirely glass, more glass than Liam had ever before seen in one place. Warm yellow light spilled out onto the patio.

Liam sprinted across the sand, packed down with the rain, and sprang up on the breakwater. Broad as a roadway, it led him along the beachfront to a spot directly in front of Tarquin's door.

It was the breakwater and the beach that had led him to meet the wizard. The coastline near Southwark was almost entirely high cliffs; larger, more stolid cousins to the Teeth. In his early explorations, Liam had learned that there were almost no places where one could swim in the sea, except for Tarquin's cove. Mistress Dorcas had told him about the magician, spouting the normal warnings and superstitions, but one day he had gone down the path, strolled up to the door, and asked if he might swim from the wizard's beach.

The white-haired old man grudgingly gave permission, and from there a sort of suspicious acquaintance began. As the summer wore on and the weather grew hotter, Liam's visits to the beach grew more frequent, and the occasions when the busy wizard recognized his presence grew as well. One time he invited Liam to sit on the patio with him, and they had spoken briefly. From there, it had only been a short while before he was invited in, and their conversations had grown longer.

Standing on the breakwater, alternately looking out to sea and back at the villa, Liam thought that he would never have woke the wizard merely to tell how he had gotten drunk and could not sleep. But since the house was lit, he felt it would be no imposition.

He hopped off the breakwater and strolled across the sand to the patio and the glass-fronted house. He rapped once on one of the thick panes, and waited. There was no reply, so he opened the door, more of a window that slid aside in grooved wooden tracks, and stepped inside.

Though it was chilly outside, the house was warm. Sourceless light filled the entrance hall, bringing out soft highlights in the polished wood of the floor. Corridors and more sliding doors, these of solid wood, led off the room.

"Tarquin?" Liam asked softly, and a shudder ran through him. He had never been further than the entrance hall and one small room off it, a sort of parlor overlooking the beach.

"Tarquin?" he called again. The sound of the waves lapping against the breakwater sounded louder inside than out.

Boldly, he strode down one of the corridors leading towards the rear of the house, and found himself in a stone-paved kitchen, with a huge wooden table and a cavernous baker's oven. No wizard. He noticed that the table was unscarred, the sanded planks unmarked by use.

"Tarquin?" he called again, raising his voice. No response.

He left the kitchen and returned to the entrance hall, choosing the second corridor. Two doors opened off it, one open. More of the sourceless light spilled out, and Liam saw the foot of a bed.

Filled with a dread as sourceless as the light, he approached the door slowly. Then he plunged into the room, awaiting a shock, something loud and frightening. Nothing happened, and he breathed a sigh. Tarquin was in his bed, his hands clasped on his chest. His full white beard spread luxuriously over his scrawny chest.

The room was small, meant to hold nothing more than the bed, which was broad and canopied, carved with dancing figures and covered with a red blanket. There was nothing on the walls, no rugs or rushes on the floor. Only the bed, and its solitary occupant.

"I'm sorry, Tarquin, I didn't know you were asleep."

Liam paused, his relief dissipating. Tarquin had not moved, though his eyes, sunken in the mass of wrinkles that served the wizard for a face, were open, and Liam would have sworn they were not when he first came in.

"Tarquin?" He tentatively put a hand to the wizard's shoulder and pushed. Even through the blue cloth of the robe, Liam could feel the chill.

A trance, he hoped, *let it be a trance.*

He pushed again, this time at the wizard's hands. They fell away to either side in what might have been a gesture of supplication. The palms were stained red. The hilt of a small knife jutted from his chest. The blue robe was dark with blood, and the ends of Tarquin's beard were red, like the bristles of a brush barely dipped in paint.

Liam's eyes narrowed and he leaned over the bed, looking at nothing in particular, taking in the whole. Tarquin looked like he had been laid out for burial, legs decorously together, robe smoothed. The red blanket barely registered his presence, neatly hanging over the edge of the bed, unwrinkled.

The sound of waves slapping the breakwater suddenly intruded on Liam's thoughts, brought into focus by another noise closer at hand. A thin, dry coughing whispered from out in the corridor.

"Fanuilh," Liam whispered. He was thinking of Tarquin's familiar, a miniature dragon. Where was it?

Without a thought, he rushed from the bedroom. Another whispered cough came from behind the second door in the corridor. He pushed open the door and stepped in.

He had a glimpse of a workroom, three long tables, a wall lined with books, another lined with jars of murky fluids and dried things. Another cough.

Then there was a sharp pain in his leg, and a jolt that traveled the length of his body. The pain swelled like blossoming light, flooding to his head. Something within him was being stretched, racked beyond its limits. Pressure built and built, pulling the thing, cracks appearing in its smooth surface. Frozen upright by the pain, he felt the thing in him finally begin to split, torn in two. Absurdly, he thought part of it slipped through him and out the leg where the pain began.

Soul? he thought, and fell.

■ 2 ■

LIAM WOKE AT sunrise, feeling hung over. His head pounded, and ripples of uneasiness radiated out from his stomach through his whole body. He did not open his eyes for a long while, lying instead on his back on the floor, examining his aches internally.

He noted the dull throbbing in his ankle, and remembrance flooded in. Slowly, he forced his lids up and stifled a shout. He gasped silently, turning the shout into a long-drawn breath, and did not move.

Tarquin's familiar, Fanuilh, was lying weightlessly on his chest, its wedgelike head curled between its paws. The little creature stirred restlessly in its sleep, dull black scales rippling, leathern wings flaring briefly to settle back against its gently heaving sides.

"Fanuilh," Liam breathed, and the dragon's eyes flicked open. It heaved itself unsteadily up on its forepaws, slipped slightly, recovered its foothold. Liam could see the dragon's neck and belly, covered with yellow scales as dull as the black ones on its back. For a moment, they were both still, Fanuilh's yellow, catlike eyes boring into Liam's blues. A slim tongue flicked out of the sharp-toothed mouth and ran over the dragon's tiny chin, where the scales gave way to a tuft of coarse hair.

We are one.

The thought intruded in Liam's head, like a flash of illumination. It stayed there, his other thoughts revolving around it. For a moment he thought he might have heard it, but it remained, and did not dissipate. It was a thought in his head, but obdurate and unyielding. He tried to think other things, questions, but they could not force it out.

We are one.

Just as suddenly as the foreign thought had appeared, it went, and Fanuilh shuddered and collapsed again on his chest.

Liam lay on the floor for long minutes, unwilling to touch the creature on his chest. Finally, when its breathing grew even in sleep, he forced his hands up and gently surrounded the form. Slowly, with fear as much as tenderness, he picked up the sleeping dragon and placed it beside him on the floor. The scales, instead of feeling hard or metallic, were like ridged cloth, moire or corduroy, soft and warm. As he moved it, Fanuilh exhaled, and its breath was rank and foul.

Like a dead man's, Liam thought, and repressed a shudder until he had put the sleeping dragon down. Then he rolled away and up to his knees, feeling his stomach turn over. His hangover was well out of proportion to the amount he had drunk.

'*We are one,*' he remembered and shook his head in denial. He stood shakily, and stumbled for the door of the workroom. On impulse, he stopped in the doorway and turned to look at Fanuilh. Sleeping on the floor below him, and not on his chest above his face, the dragon looked harmless, and Liam suddenly bent and scooped up the creature, cradling it against his chest as he looked for a better place to put it.

The worktable nearest the door was empty, and Liam deposited Fanuilh there. The creature did not stir, and, after a moment staring at it, he turned on his heel and walked out of the room.

He limped blindly for the kitchen, ignoring Tarquin's bedroom, his pounding head and raw throat calling for relief. He could think of nothing but cold water, and perhaps bread, or a hot bun. A type of pastry he had once eaten in Torquay sprang to mind, and his stomach rumbled unpleasantly. The sea, when he saw it through the glass walls of the entrance hall, was shiny pink with the new sun, the clouds of the previous evening gone. Morning filled the hall, streaking the shadows of the window panes across the floor like bars.

In the kitchen, the sourceless light still ruled, banishing shadows. He searched bins and cupboards, hoping only for bread and water. Water he found in a jar by the tiled stove, far colder and sweeter than it had any right to be.

Tarquin's magic, he thought, and grimaced, thinking of the hilt rising from the old man's chest.

He lifted the jar to his lips and drank deeply, washing away bile and roughness, gasping with the intensity of the cold. When he put the jar back next to the stove, he felt heat on the back of his hand and stepped away from the stove suspiciously.

Why not? he thought, and yanked open the metal door on the oven's front. Banked coals lay beneath a metal rack, on which rested four small, round buns, piping hot, just like the ones he remembered from Torquay. Hunger took over from caution, and he snatched one of them, juggling the hot pastry back and forth between his hands until he could drop it on the table.

He picked up the jar and drank again, then put his attention to the bun. It was almost too hot to eat, but his stomach roiled, and he forced a bite down. By the time the taste registered, his stomach was quieter.

It was delicious, exactly like the ones in Torquay, laced with currants and nuts, lightly spiced with cinnamon and something sweet and sticky he could not identify. It was wonderful—and clearly magic. The buns were certainly fresh-baked, not reheated, and the coals were as hot as if they had only been lit for an hour. More magic, he supposed, wolfing down the rest of the bun. He had never connected magic with small things like hot cinnamon buns and ice-cold water. Only things of magnificent proportions—calling forth demons, sinking ships, destroying armies. It made him think differently of Tarquin.

Thinking of Tarquin brought him to the corpse in the bedroom, and he frowned. Snatching two more buns from the oven, he went back to the bedroom.

Tarquin was stiffening; that much he could tell by looking. Dead at least twelve hours, as far as his experience as a surgeon and soldier could tell. He leaned against the doorjamb and stared at the corpse, absently eating some of the delicious bread.

"Murdered," he said aloud, and might have laughed at the obviousness of the conclusion.

By whom? Why? He realized he did not know Tarquin well enough to even hazard a guess, and supposed the only one who might know was Fanuilh, and Fanuilh was only a brute beast.

Or was it?

We are one.

The thought had not been his. And the creature had been staring at him so intently. Liam had heard stories that wizards and their familiars were bound in special ways, but that was the result of complicated spells and dealings with supernatural beings, the sort of thing reserved for those who worked with magic.

Swallowing the rest of his second bun, he left the corpse and went to the workroom. Fanuilh was still asleep, curled up with his snout touching his hind legs.

Like a dog, but scaled and winged and clawed and able to send its thoughts into my head. Liam winced and moved away.

The workroom's large windows looked out onto the narrow stretch of sand separating the villa from the cliffs, and let in a gray, shadowy light to illuminate the room. The first table held only Fanuilh, the second a single empty decanter of glass, but the top of the third was completely covered. Liam had not seen it in his brief glimpse the night before, but the morning light showed the table's display, and he wandered over to it.

It was like the sand-table models he had seen engineers make during sieges, but far more complex. It reproduced, in miniature, the coastline around Southwark; but where a mercenary engineer would have been happy with crude representations, the model in Tarquin's workroom was perfect in every detail. The Teeth lay exactly at the center of the table; water on one side, the harbor and city on the other. The town was the most impressive part, completely detailed, right down to the Necquer's harborside porch, and Liam's own garret window. Tiny ships with full rigging rode at anchor, and Liam saw that they actually *rode,* swaying slightly as if on swells. Acting on a hunch, he put his finger down into the harbor. The ships *were* moving, and the water, when he brought his finger to his mouth, tasted of salt. What he had thought well-sculpted whitecaps proved on closer inspection to be real breakers, flowing constantly against the Teeth. The Teeth themselves were rock, and felt as cold and wet as their larger brethren.

Liam whistled in awed admiration and the dawning of an idea.

At the far end of the table stood a lectern, over the edge of which hung a heavy chain. With his eyes fixed on the model, Liam moved around to the lectern. A massive leatherbound book lay open on it, held down with the chain. Tarquin's spellbook, Liam supposed, and read the first few lines on the page that lay open. Abstract, theoretical language, studded with phrases in some foreign tongue Liam had never met; nonetheless, he understood enough of what was written in Taralonian. It was a spell for removing matter to another plane of existence; "translating substance," the text called it.

"He made the Teeth disappear," he whispered. "Damn!"

As a last act, Liam thought, there could be few better. A final testament to Tarquin's power, grandiose proof of his reputation in Southwark as a truly great wizard. Liam wondered if Tarquin knew that it would be his last spell when he cast it.

A paper-thin piece of wood projected from further on in the book, marking another page. Liam pushed the heavy pages aside and scanned the lines of the second spell. Much of the language was the same, and he recognized some of the foreign phrases, but the point of this one was to cloak matter, to make it invisible.

If Tarquin had been trying to decide which spell to use, he must have chosen the one for transforming matter, or else Necquer's ships would have been resting quietly beneath the sea, not to mention Necquer himself.

Could someone have killed the wizard for that?

Liam's eyes lost their focus on the page as he thought.

Who would want to kill Tarquin? As far as Liam knew, the old man had no enemies—at least none that he had spoken about. Then again, he did not know much about the wizard. When they had spoken, it had only been in generalities, about faraway places or things long past. Nothing about each other's lives in Southwark, or their present business. But then Tarquin was a wizard, and they made enemies everywhere. They quarreled among themselves, they had disagreements with those who sought their services, they were marked out by power for the fear and suspicions of the masses. It would not have been hard for Tarquin to acquire enemies, but it was strange that a man who could alter the work of nature in such a way could not defend himself.

I am awake.

It was a thought like the first; hard-edged and stony, brazenly pushing other thoughts away to grab his attention. His head snapped over to look at the table where he had put Fanuilh.

You have eaten. I should eat as well.

There was no doubt the thought came from Fanuilh, and Liam remembered the bite. Why had the thing bitten him?

So that we would be one. I must eat, but I am weak.

Liam crossed the room slowly, eyeing the little dragon. Its yellow eyes never left his.

"Are you doing this? Putting thoughts in my head?"

You do not need to speak. Only think. And I am.

"How?"

We are one. May I eat? The serpentine head nudged at the final bun Liam held in his hand. Liam knelt by the edge of the table, so that his eyes were on a level with the dragon's, and held out the food.

Fanuilh's head snaked out and ripped off a large bite, chewing and swallowing in rapid gulps. Liam watched, fascinated, as the dragon ate more, gulping down the whole bun in seconds. When it was done, it began very gently licking its claws, though it continued to stare at him.

You are confused.

"How are we one?"

You know already. You are wiser than you seem.

"Then—you are like a familiar to me? Bound in that way?"

As you are bound to me. We share a soul now; your soul rests partly in me, and partly still in you.

Liam rose, shaking his head in confusion. "Why did you never speak like this before?"

We were never one before. This can only be done between those who are one. Look.

Suddenly, Liam's sight went black. He cried out, and then his vision returned, but his perspective was wrong. He was looking up into an angular, unlined face, framed with close-cropped blond hair. Pale blue eyes rolled sightlessly on either side of a long, thin nose. It was his nose; he was looking at his own face.

You see with my eyes.

"I want to see with *my* eyes!" he said, and there was another sickening jolt of blindness before he returned to his own perspective. The dragon's head was cocked to one side, regarding him curiously. "Never do that again!" he admonished shakily.

You can do it as well.

"I don't want to!"

Perhaps you will.

There was a long silence. Liam wondered, and then stopped wondering, realizing the dragon could read his thoughts.

"I want you out of my head!"

You can keep me out.

"How?" he demanded.

I will show you, but you must do things for me.

"Do things for you? You've stolen my soul, you little beast! I want you out of my head!"

I am sorry. It was necessary. I was dying. We may—Liam felt the edge of the thought, notched like the blade of a broken sword, as the dragon paused—*We may make a bargain.*

"A bargain! What have you got in return for my soul?"

We only share it. I would not have taken even a small part, were it not necessary. Master Tanaquil thought my gifts worth a small part of his soul. And it does you no harm. But if you help me only a little more, I can teach you things.

"What things?" Liam demanded.

There are things that must be done, and then I will teach you.

"What things?"

How to keep me out, how to see with my eyes. Other things as well.

Despite himself, Liam was intrigued.

"Magic?"

Not much. You do not have the mind for the complicated kinds. But smaller ones, perhaps, and other things. I can help you write your book.

"My book? How did you know of that?" The dragon cocked its head again, and Liam raised a hand. "No, never mind. I understand."

I shared all these things with Master Tanaquil. I can teach you. If you will do things for me. The dragon still looked directly at him, but there was no expression in the creature's eyes.

Liam heaved himself to his feet, favoring his unbitten leg. "What things?"

First, you must bring me more food. In the kitchen, think of raw meat, desire it, and look in the oven.

"I noticed that. An easy enough condition." He limped to the kitchen, and though it was difficult to make himself desire raw meat, eventually the oven produced an uncooked cut of beef, which he brought back to the dragon.

Fanuilh tore into it, biting and chewing in the same convulsive gulps. It did not stop sending its thoughts, however.

Second, the message appeared in Liam's mind, *you must tell the Duke's man in Southwark of Master Tanaquil's murder. His name is Coeccias. Can you find him?*

"The Duke's man? The Aedile? Yes, I can find him. I would have told him in any case. What else must I do?"

Third, you must nurse me to health. As painful as the sharing was for you, it was much worse for me. I almost died when Master Tanaquil was struck down.

"When he was struck down," Liam echoed, and then asked intently: "Do you know who killed him?"

I do not.

Liam mused over this, disappointed, and the dragon did not interrupt him for a while. Then:

I am weak. It will perhaps take a month for me to recover.

Brought out of his reverie, Liam nodded. "Yes, of course. Simple enough. Is there anything else?"

One other. I will tell you when you return with the Aedile.

Liam balked. "Tell me now."

It will be simple enough for you, and there will be time enough when you return with the Aedile. You must be sure he brings a ghost witch.

"A ghost witch? What's that?"

He will know. Tell him that. Is it a—again, the shorn-off thought, as though the phrase was unfamiliar—*a bargain?*

"Yes," Liam said, after a moment's thought.

Then go.

Stung, he turned abruptly for the door, only to turn back.

"Why don't you know who killed Tarquin?"

Master Tanaquil could exclude me from his mind at will. He often did.

"You can teach me to do that?"

I can. I will, when you fulfill the last thing I will ask. Now go.

Still Liam paused, wondering to himself. It was strange to talk and receive the response directly in his head; it was strange to take orders from a tiny, weak dragon; it was strange not to argue—but what, he asked himself, could he do?

It is as strange for me to give orders as it is for you to take them. When you have fulfilled my last request, I will teach you how to be my master.

With that in his head, Liam limped out of the house and onto the beach.

Between Liam's limp and his distracted thoughts, it took far longer to return to Southwark than it had to come out the night before.

Fanuilh had taken part of his soul, but for some reason he felt neither violated nor angry. Liam knew himself to be accepting by nature, taking what was given and making the best of it. There was, really, nothing he could do: he had heard enough about wizards and their familiars to know that the link could only be broken through the death of one of the sharers. He had no idea what would happen to his soul if Fanuilh died, and he had no intention of finding out.

As he thought of it, he reasoned that the experience must indeed have been worse for the dragon. He still had his soul; part of it was simply resting in Fanuilh. The dragon, for a time, had not had a soul. Liam tried, but could not imagine what that would be like.

On the whole, he thought he should pity the little creature, but he could not manage it. It was, perhaps, the nature of the thoughts Fanuilh sent into his head. They were just that—thoughts, without any emotional content. He had never realized just how important the voice was in conveying feeling. Fanuilh's thoughts could not reveal pain or humor or sadness, only information.

Did the little dragon feel emotion?

The tasks it had set out for Liam were relatively simple and, apart from nursing the dragon back to health, would take very little time. It seemed a small thing to do, and when the nursing was over it would teach

Liam to close off his mind, and maybe other things of greater value. It seemed a fair bargain, if the dragon could be trusted.

He reasoned all this out on the long walk back to Southwark, through the still-damp pasturage and stubbled fields. The sun was two hours above the horizon before he reached the city, hanging weak and watery in the fall sky, lending no warmth. It was chilly, and he felt dirty and hungry again. He decided to return to his garret before searching out the Aedile.

Walking up the steep hill to his lodgings, he realized that the pain in his ankle was lessening, and he could place more weight on it. He stopped in the street and examined his boot. There were two punctures the size of large nails in the tough leather. He scowled, wondering what sort of holes had been left in his flesh.

Once in his rooms, he called the landlady for hot water. She brought it up to him in a bucket, with an indulgent expression.

"Overmuch wine, Master Rhenford?" she asked, arching an eyebrow and grinning. "I thought scholars never indulged."

He exaggerated a frown and shooed her away. Sitting in the chair, he tenderly tugged off the punctured boot and checked his ankle, prepared to wash away a crust of blood and bandage a wound.

His ankle was clean, and only two small, circular scars indicated where Fanuilh had bitten him. He gave a short whistle, shook his head, and stripped to wash.

Refreshed by the hot water and feeling much less sick, he dressed in clean tunic and long breeches and felt ready to find the Aedile. He snatched a warm cloak from a peg on the wall and went out.

The Duke in whose lands Southwark lay was a great believer in the very old ways of Taralon. The title Aedile was taken from the language the Seventeen Houses brought with them to the land; so all titles used to be, before the last king of House Quintus died childless and the throne fell to lesser lines.

Even in Liam's Midlands, where they prided themselves on maintaining the old customs, such a man would have been titled colloquially, called Sheriff, or Constable. But Southwark's Duke held to the old ways, and the man was called Aedile.

It impressed Liam, this respect for the days when Taralon was strong under the Seventeen Houses.

He found the Aedile at home, directed there by a member of the Guard who was hurrying home from his shift. It was a small house on the fringes of the rich quarter, neat and well maintained, though somehow out of place beside the larger houses of merchants and rich tradesmen.

A bald servant reluctantly let him in, and bade him wait in a spartan parlor.

A bachelor, Liam thought, noting the decorations—swords and armor, a few hand-drawn maps of the city, the worn but comfortable-looking furniture. He knew little of the Aedile except his name, and a reputation for tough but fair dealing. He had heard that Coeccias would rather break up a tavern brawl with his own fists than take the brawlers into the Duke's court.

Nothing in the Aedile's appearance contradicted his reputation. He was short and broad, heavily muscled, with a thick mane of tangled black hair hanging down below his shoulders. Water beaded in his untrimmed beard, annoyance in his small eyes. Veins and scars ridged the hand with which he curtly waved Liam to a seat.

"Your name, sirrah? And what business," he grated, "that needs must break my breaking fast?"

The Aedile held a buttered piece of bread in his hand, and crumbs dotted his simple black tunic.

"Rhenford, Aedile Coeccias, Liam Rhenford. And there has been a death."

Coeccias laughed loudly. "Come, Liam Rhenford, death is commoner than cheap bawds, and those are very common in Southwark. Surely my breakfast is worth more than mere death!"

"Not mere death, Aedile," Liam contradicted politely, still standing, "but murder. The wizard Tarquin Tanaquil has been murdered."

"Has he? In truth? Now that—*that* might be worth more than my breakfast. That might, in truth."

Liam explained the circumstances, avoiding any mention of Fanuilh, and watched Coeccias take it all in, suitably sober, nodding. When he had finished his brief account, the Aedile nodded firmly once more.

"Well, it seems there's more in it than in my breakfast. I must see the body. Y'have a horse?" Liam nodded. "Good. Collect it, and meet me at the city gate."

"Wait a moment, Aedile. Shouldn't we have a ghost witch present?"

"Aye, that we should." Coeccias paused and regarded him strangely. "It'll little like Mother Japh to be dragged out of her house this early, but we should. I'll fetch her."

The burly man bustled him out of the house into the street, and strode off towards the heart of the city. Liam turned towards the stable where he kept his horse.

It was only a few moments before Diamond was saddled and ready, and Liam was mounted before he thought of his appointment with Lady Necquer. He called the stable lad over and offered him a small sum to take his regrets to the merchant's wife. The dirty boy grinned hugely at the amount and dashed off without a word.

Shaking his head, Liam spurred his mount towards the city gate.

He had a suspicion that Coeccias was not the man to find Tarquin's murderer, unless it could be done easily. And he feared it would not be easy. Honest and competent as the Aedile might be when it came to keeping sailors in line and patrolling the streets at night, Liam did not think he could pry secrets out of Tarquin's corpse.

Which, he further thought, was a shame, since there was no one else in authority to pursue the matter, and he already liked the blunt Aedile.

Southwark had no wall; the steep inland sides of the rise on which the city sat and the jagged Teeth seaward had always been considered protection enough. So it had no gates to speak of, but the beginning of the track to the east that led past Tarquin's cove was marked by two standing columns of worn gray stone, and this was called the city gate.

Liam arrived there before Coeccias and waited on his mount beside one of the pitted stone columns, watching the traffic of farmers' carts and horsemen that straggled along the muddy track.

He had waited far longer than he thought necessary, and for the tenth time was about to go back into the city to look for Coeccias when the Aedile's voice called to him.

"Liam Rhenford! Hark, man!"

Coeccias now wore a tabard over his black tunic, gray linen emblazoned with the Duke's three red foxes, and he rode a mare that looked worn down beside Liam's snorting roan. Two mounted Guardsmen carrying upright spears flanked him, the Duke's foxes on gray badges sewn to the shoulders of their boiled leather cuirasses. Behind them, astride a wall-eyed pony, was an ancient woman bundled in shapeless, faded robes, her face wrinkled as an old apple.

"The ghost witch," Coeccias said, when he noticed Liam's glance. "Mother Japh. This is the man who found the corpse, Mother."

The old woman snorted and mumbled.

"More like the fool saw the master in a trance; he *is* a wizard, all said." Her voice was no more than a whisper, but Liam caught it.

"It may well have been a trance, Mother," he said politely, "but I was not aware wizards cast spells with daggers in their chests."

The woman sniffed indignantly, and Liam arched an eyebrow at the

Aedile, who, it seemed, could not decide whether to laugh or frown. He
settled for taking charge.

"We'd best to't, then."

He booted his mare into a walk, and the Guardsmen followed suit.

■ 3 ■

"NO SPIRITS," THE wrinkled old woman announced in a soft voice, returning to the entrance hall, where Liam and the Aedile waited.

They had waited for her judgement for over an hour while she wandered around the house, humming a little tune to herself, her bright, birdlike gaze darting here and there. She passed through the entrance hall several times, each time favoring Liam with an unpleasant look.

After Liam had satisfied Coeccias that Tarquin was indeed dead, the Aedile had drawn him out into the entrance hall and nodded to Mother Japh, who began her work.

"We mustn't disturb the witch while she searches for spirits," he whispered.

"How does she do it?" Liam whispered back, wondering.

The Aedile shrugged and spoke nonchalantly, his hand resting lightly on the hilt of his shortsword. "Truth, I don't know. But if Tarquin's sprite's here, angered or hot on revenge, she'll feel it, and it may be she can learn something from him."

Liam had never heard of a ghost witch, and the idea interested him. If she could speak with Tarquin's ghost, she might be able to find his killer. He studied the witch closely whenever she appeared.

The two Guardsmen stayed on the stone veranda despite the chill wind off the sea, which the watery sun did nothing to relieve. Coeccias had grumbled irritably when they silently took up their posts, but he did not argue with them.

"And as no ghosts haunt the pile," the witch went on, "and no sprites linger, angry or the like, it follows that the killer's not here."

When the witch had rendered her judgement, she suddenly offered Liam a warm smile, and Coeccias scowled. Liam started and flushed red. He turned on the Aedile.

"You thought *I* did it? You thought *I* killed him?"

Coeccias scowled fiercely at the old woman, who offered him a placid smile. "I suspected, but—"

Liam cut him off angrily. "Then why would I fetch you? Why would I tell you, if I did it?"

"Easy, man, don't rate me. Many's the man's covered his deed thus, and I was only making sure. And y'are Liam Rhenford, are you not?"

"So?" He could not believe the man had suspected him. He prepared to revise the friendly opinion he had devised of the Aedile.

"Truth, it's known that you had traffic with the wizard, more traffic than anyone in Southwark ever had, and who else was there to suspect? And you'd never've known what I thought, if this foolish old woman had kept a still tongue!" He scowled again at the witch, and Liam stalked away, fuming.

A touch on his arm brought him around, and he glared down into Mother Japh's wrinkled, beaming face.

"Take no affront, boy. I thought you'd done it, too. You've an innocent visage," she said, "and that's the worst mark against a man that I know."

Liam did not reply; Tarquin had once said something like that to him. They had been discussing a question of history; Liam had made a point he felt was particularly telling, and the old wizard had begun to laugh. "Get you a beard, Rhenford," he had said. "None'll believe so innocent a face."

"And now, Aedile Coeccias, it likes me to go home, if you can spare one of your frightened soldiers to take me there."

Coeccias shook his head and dispatched one of the Guardsmen to escort the ghost witch back to Southwark. When he returned to the entrance hall, Liam was still thinking over what Mother Japh had said, and how it echoed Tarquin's words.

"She hit the mark, Liam Rhenford. Y'are too innocent for your good."

"Perhaps if I got a hideous scar, or lost an eye and wore a patch I'd be better off, eh?" he asked sarcastically.

Coeccias laughed and clapped Liam on the shoulder, and his anger slowly dissolved. He gave a small smile.

"A scar, a patch! Aye, those'd serve!" The Aedile laughed a little more and went on, still amused. "Unfortunately, Mother Japh's rare wrong, and I can't clap you in for the murder. Which means there's nothing for it but to try and find the killer. We'll search the house."

He led the way with Liam trailing curiously in his wake, eager to explore more of the house. The Aedile questioned him as they went, gleaning details of his relationship with the wizard.

"And you've no idea who might have wanted him dead?"

"None. I didn't really know him well—only from swimming off his breakwater, and the occasional talk. No clues there, I'm afraid."

They stood in Tarquin's library, just beyond the parlor. Books lined every wall; there were no windows in the walls, though a small glass cupola in the roof let in a dim light. Coeccias gave Liam an incredulous look when he mentioned swimming.

"You swam? In the sea?"

"Yes," Liam said.

"No one swims in the sea!"

"I do," Liam said simply, offering no explanation, and the Aedile shrugged in disbelief.

For a moment they stood quietly and marveled at the innumerable books, each impressed in his own way. Liam paced along the shelves, running a finger down leatherbound spines, checking the titles inscribed or painted there. Coeccias stood directly beneath the cupola, turning around in a circle and taking it all in.

"And when did you say you found him?"

"Last night. I—"

"Last night?" the Aedile snapped. "Why didn't you fetch me then?"

Liam goggled for a moment and started to tell about Fanuilh. A thought stopped him.

I was drunk . . .

"I was drunk, you see," he finally said, embarrassed. "And when I saw him, I, well, I fell, and hit my head."

Show him the bump.

"I have a bump, you see." He fingered the back of his head, and noticed for the first time a distinct swelling at the back of his head. "I didn't wake up until early this morning."

"Cupped, eh?" The Aedile smiled and Liam relaxed, though his face was still red with embarrassment. "I suspect that's the only thing that'd make a man bother a wizard in the night."

He left the library, and went across the hall and down the corridor to the bedroom. Liam followed, angry, wondering if the dragon had known they would suspect him.

I thought they might, came the response hard in his mind. He stopped in the corridor. *That is why I told you to bring the ghost witch.*

Coeccias paused before the door to the workroom, looking back at Liam.

"Will y'attend me?"

Liam shook himself and hurried down the hall. The Aedile was looking at the table where Fanuilh lay, its slitted yellow eyes staring balefully back at him.

"Now whatever's this? The wizard's pet?"

He stepped lightly over to the table and slowly extended his hand towards the dragon's neck, trying to appear open and friendly. Fanuilh followed the Aedile's hand, swiveling its head as Coeccias reached for its neck, fingers bent to scratch. At the last moment the dragon snapped weakly, and Coeccias withdrew in shock.

"Little beast!" he exclaimed, rubbing his hand as if the dragon had bitten him, though Liam knew it had missed.

"It's a shame the little creature can't speak. He might tell us everything."

"Aye," Coeccias muttered, then threw a cursory glance around the room. "Naught disturbed here," he said, and left abruptly. Liam stayed a moment, looking at the dragon. Slowly, as the Aedile had, he extended his hand; Fanuilh let him scratch, arching its back in pleasure against Liam's nails. The softness of the scales was still strange to him, and he rubbed them curiously for a moment. No thoughts came, so he patted it once more and left.

There was only one other room, with a cupola like the library but wide windows as well. Motes danced in the weak beams pouring in.

"Anything missing?" Coeccias asked.

"I don't know. I've never been in here before."

Strange objects filled the white-plastered room, hanging from the walls and arranged in free-standing cases of dark, polished wood with glass tops. A collection of thin, elaborately carved wands on a bed of felt in one case; coins with inscriptions Liam could not read in another; jewelry of strange design—rings, bracelets, phylacteries—in another. On the walls, a small tapestry the size of a hearthrug, depicting a stylized eagle soaring powerfully over purple mountains; a stringless, round-bodied lute hung by its neck; a sword and shield, simple and battered, beside a horn chased in silver.

"Truth," the Aedile said, turning to go, "it seems there's naught stolen, so I needn't bother the fences."

Liam reluctantly followed him. "Eh?"

"I needn't bother the fences." Liam's questioning look remained, so Coeccias went on. "Naught stolen, Liam Rhenford. So checking the fences won't discover the murderer."

"Oh, yes, yes. I see." His mind was still on the strange objects on the walls and in the cases, and he wished the Aedile had stayed there longer.

"So, with no thievery, we've only personality. Did anyone hate him? Hate him enough to stick him, that is?"

Liam shook his head. "I wouldn't know. I don't think he knew many people in Southwark—except me, that is."

"Oh, I think many people knew of him, if you see, and there's tales enough of some having dealings with him. I'll see about that, and see if he has a testament."

"A testament?"

"A will." Coeccias instantly supplied the synonym, interpreting his hesitation as confusion over the southern dialect. "He might have left one, registered with the Duke's clerk. Some do, you know."

Liam said nothing; he did not think Tarquin was the kind to leave a will.

"And then there's the interring. Someone'll have to bury him." The Aedile looked expectantly at him.

I will take care of it.

"I'll take care of it," Liam said suddenly, paling at the intrusion. "We spoke of how he'd want it once. Theoretically, of course. I never thought . . ."

The Aedile's expectation turned to puzzlement, and Liam fidgeted. The dragon was arranging things in a way he did not understand, prompting him along paths he couldn't follow. But Coeccias misunderstood his reaction.

"How old are you, Liam Rhenford?"

"Thirty," he responded.

"Thirty," the Aedile mused. He was easily ten years older than Liam, and the harsh lines around his eyes softened. "And never seen a corpse ere this?"

Liam frowned. He had, many times. More times, he guessed, and deaths far worse, than the Aedile had.

Go along.

"No," he said shakily.

"Shall I leave my man to help you?"

No.

"No, I think . . ." He paused, with a convincing gulp. "I think I can manage."

"Well enough," Coeccias said at last. "I'll be about my business, then, if y'are sure."

Liam nodded briefly.

The Aedile nodded as well and went for the door, stopping to ask where Liam was lodging.

"In case I hear anything, or need to speak with you, if you see."

When Liam told him, the Aedile took his leave, collecting the other Guardsman. Liam went out onto the veranda and watched them wend their way up the narrow path. When they had topped the cliff, he went back in.

Fanuilh still lay on the table in the workroom, looking up at him serenely.

The scratching was good.

"And I suppose you'd like some more?" Liam asked sarcastically, but he put out his hand and scratched the clothlike scales. "How much of that did you know would happen?"

I anticipated a great deal of it. The dragon stretched pleasurably, if stiffly, underneath his hand, the simple, happy motion at odds with the cold thoughts.

"Why did you make me lie about hitting my head?"

You know.

Liam was surprised to find he did know. Coeccias had called the dragon Tarquin's pet; he did not understand about familiars, and if Liam had tried to explain he would have presumed that—

"You didn't want him thinking we'd killed him together, you and I."

It would undoubtedly have occurred to him, and it would have made things difficult.

"So now he thinks I'm a weak fop, a man who turns squeamish at the sight of blood. One who's never seen a corpse before."

Do you really care?

Wordlessly, Liam shook his head, and pulled his hand away from the dragon, struck by a thought. He imagined Fanuilh, a dagger stuck in his claws, hovering over Tarquin's sleeping body.

A thought crashed down on the image, blotting it out.

That is foolishness. I could do no such thing.

"Of course not," Liam said hastily, stepping away from the table. It was foolishness, after all. The dragon could not have known he would come along, that there would be another soul for it to share.

There are things to do. You must fulfill our bargain.

"Yes." He shook his head, scattering the shards of his image. "You'll teach me how to keep you out?"

Yes, and more.

"And all I have to do is nurse you to health?"

And the other.

"The other," Liam repeated blankly, then remembered: "The one you said you'd tell me when they'd gone?"

Yes.

"What is it?"

You must find whoever killed Master Tanaquil.

"Find the killer? That's what Coeccias is for," he said doubtfully.

You do not think the Duke's man can do it.

"I don't think he can, no. But if he can't do it, how could I? That's foolishness." He straightened and walked over to the model, his back to the dragon.

You knew Master Tanaquil better than the Duke's man. I knew him better. Between us, we can imagine who might have done it, and find the person. Besides . . . you have done this before.

"Only a few times, and . . ." Liam whirled. "How did you know that?"

We are one. Your memories are mine, and mine would be yours, if you knew how. I know your thoughts everywhere.

There was no special emphasis on the last, but Liam imagined it, and blushed.

"You know what I was thinking, in the city?"

Of course.

He shook his head, trying to drive the thought out. "No matter. Those were a long time ago, and the circumstances were different. I was very lucky."

Nonetheless, you have searched out murderers before. And you think you carry Luck with you.

That much was true, and that was how he thought of it—Luck, personified, like a deity who watched over him. And he had, once or twice, unraveled mysteries.

"Even granting that I thought I could find the killer, why? Why do you want me to? Why bargain for that?"

For the first time, Fanuilh's thought swirled, shapeless. It took what seemed a long time to form.

I do not know.

"What would we do when we found out?"

Again, the thought coalesced slowly.

I do not know.

"Give the murderer to the Aedile?"

I suppose so.

Liam wondered if the dragon was harboring dreams of vengeance, and blushed again when Fanuilh responded.

I do not think so. It is simply something I feel must be done. Master Tanaquil was good to me.

Liam sighed, turning back to the model of Southwark, losing his gaze in the intricate details. He thought of Tarquin, and their all too few conversations. The man had been interesting, if somewhat reserved. Pleasant in his way, seemingly harmless, an eccentric recluse claiming wizardry. But he had made the Teeth disappear, and he had a room filled with strange artifacts that Liam wanted to explore.

I can show you how they all work. They can be yours. Is it a bargain?

He sighed again, leaning forward, resting his hands carefully on the edge of the model.

"See if you can't stay out of my head for a few moments, will you?"

He had already decided to do it, he realized. If for no other reason than that the old man had let him swim off his breakwater. And if the dragon was lying, in any way, about anything, well, then . . .

But he did not finish the thought. He simply let it swirl away, broken off, unsure of what he would do.

"Very well, it's a bargain. I'll need to know everything you can remember about Tarquin."

Four hours later, as the pale sun sank down towards the horizon, Liam rode the muddy track back to Southwark. His stomach was queasy again, and though the ache in his ankle had not returned, he found the lump on the back of his head throbbing.

He had questioned the dragon closely for a long time, dredging up every detail of anyone who visited Tarquin. He was surprised at how many people besides himself had made the trip out from the city and down the cliff path, and, at the same time, how little Fanuilh knew about his master's business. The dragon could remember some names and most faces, and snatches of conversation, but apparently Tarquin had made a practice of excluding his familiar from his thoughts and his dealings. It seemed strange to Liam, to hide yourself from one you had voluntarily chosen to share your soul, but Fanuilh had not thought it out of the ordinary.

It had taken very little time to bury the wizard. He and Tarquin had never discussed their preferences for interment, but Fanuilh assured him that the old man had had no preference, and that simple burial would be enough.

Liam had gone up the beach and found a spot close by the cliffs where the sand was heavier and more like dirt. Using a board, he scooped a deep narrow hole, cursing as the sand ran back into the grave. Finally, sweating through his tunic despite the cold wind off the sea, he decided it was deep enough and returned to the house for the body.

He wrapped it in the scarlet blanket and gingerly put his hands beneath it. Though the old man had been scrawny, his corpse was far heavier than Liam expected, but the stiffness was familiar from several battlefields. He managed to get the body to the grave, cursing his stupidity in choosing a site so far from the house.

When he finally had Tarquin in his resting place, he stood for a moment, looking down at the red-wrapped bundle. It looked pitifully small at the bottom of the sandy trench, like a bright toy lost or forgotten by a careless child. The smell of brine and rotting seaweed filled his nostrils, stinging and cold.

Liam had spent so long among strangers, peoples with strange gods and alien rites, that he could not think of whom to pray to, or how to pray. Undecided, he thought of nothing, listening instead to the slap of waves against the breakwater, and the rumble of the sea beyond.

"I suppose I can only . . ." he finally said, and left the sentence unfinished.

It did not take as long to shovel the sand back in.

He went back to the house only long enough to take his leave of the dragon.

You do not have to go back to the city, the dragon thought as he stood in the doorway of the workroom.

"I can't stay here," he muttered.

It would be easier.

"The answers you want are in Southwark. It'll be easier if I stay there."

There is that. But you will eventually stay here.

Something in the thought—something imagined, Liam said to himself, though he felt it had been there—implied certainty.

"It's not mine," he said. "I'll be back tomorrow morning." With that, he walked away, and the dragon thought nothing more at him.

It was cold, as the year crept into its old age, and Liam folded his cloak closely about him. A procession barred his way briefly as he entered the city; he sat his horse patiently, waiting for it to pass. There was a small number of shaven-headed acolytes in pure white robes, carrying blank wax tablets and chanting sonorously. A gaggle of lay worshippers followed, heads bowed, and behind them came a crowd of solemn children. Liam wondered what it was all about, and then vaguely remembered that a number of processions in honor of the Goddess were supposed to be performed before Uris-tide. He noted that the omnipresent beggars were silent at the procession went past, and that the one-armed man who squatted in the gutter by him only rose to grasp his stirrup and moan when the marchers were out of sight. Tossing the wretch a coin, Liam spurred Diamond away.

He stopped at a stall that sold hot foods after he had stabled Diamond, and bought sausages and steaming bread, thinking of the magic oven in Tarquin's villa. He pushed the thought away. He hoped the sausages would stay hot until he got home, and hurried to his garret.

They did, and the grease had soaked into the bread. He thought they tasted wonderful, after he had carefully cleared all the papers and books off his table. He savored every spiced bite, and sucked his fingers when he was done.

Outside his window, lights showed in some of the darkened streets, flickering torches and lanterns marking inns or temples; orange flames marched purposefully up and down lanes, and he thought of the Guard making their dusk patrol, checking doors and shooing beggars off the streets.

Sighing wearily, he washed his hands in the cold water left from the morning and set about sharpening his quill and preparing ink. Then, with several blank sheets of paper before him, he set to work outlining what Fanuilh had told him.

In the week before Tarquin had died, four people had visited him. It seemed like a large number, but when Liam thought of him as a wizard and not as an eccentric recluse, the visits did not seem so strange. An apothecary Tarquin had known well; a handsome young man who might have been a minstrel; a merchant of high standing with a bodyguard of toughs; a woman heavily cloaked. He dutifully wrote them down along with all that the familiar could recall about them, filling a sheet with his neat, cramped handwriting. All might have an innocent reason for seeking the help of a wizard, dangerous as that was held to be.

"Ask a wizard's help to find silver," ran an old saying that his landlady had sententiously quoted him, "and be prepared to pay him gold."

Liam wondered who made up those sayings, and whether he might be the one who had put a dagger in Tarquin's chest.

Shaking his head fiercely to clear away the thought, he turned his attention to the list he had made, and chose the apothecary to begin with. Fanuilh said the two had had a fight, or at least a very loud discussion, and that the druggist had stalked away grumbling darkly.

It seemed the best lead, not only because of the argument, but because the apothecary was the only person of whose name Fanuilh was sure. Ton Viyescu.

Tomorrow, Liam thought, *I'll go see Ton Viyescu. And what will I say to him? 'Pardon, Master Druggist, but did you murder Tarquin Tanaquil? Or perhaps I should put it this way: are you missing any daggers?'*

He pursed his lips sourly. Fanuilh had read his mind correctly—he *had* searched out a mystery or two, but on those few occasions he had had authority. He had been allowed to ask questions, and piece together facts, and there had been armed men to back him up.

Cursing, he suddenly recalled the dagger. He had not looked at it closely, and it had not been there when he buried Tarquin. Coeccias must have taken it, though Liam had not seen him do it. His respect for the Aedile went up a notch.

I'll have to see it, to know if it's important. And how do I do that? 'Excuse me, Aedile, but could I look at that knife? You see, I've lost mine, and I was wondering if the murderer might have picked it up . . .'

He thought of telling the dragon he could not do it, simply could not search out the murderer, but then he remembered its cold eyes and hard-edged thoughts. Fanuilh would never let him out of the bargain.

A knock interrupted his metal wanderings, and he strode slowly over to the door. It was his landlady.

"Your leave, Master Liam. I knew not you were in, or I'd have brought this sooner. A message from a lady, Master," she added. With a meaningful look and a knowing smile, she held out a folded, sealed piece of paper. He snatched it, almost but not quite rudely, his mouth narrowing at her insinuations.

"Thank you," he growled, and began to shut the door. She would have stopped him, but he stopped himself. "Mistress Dorcas," he began, thinking to ask her what she knew of Ton Viyescu.

"Aye?" Her very eagerness dissuaded him. She was a decent woman, he knew, but entirely too given to gossip.

"No, nothing. Thank you." He smiled warmly and firmly shut the door over her protests.

The letter, when he had finally stopped peering curiously at the intricate wax seal, was from Lady Necquer, forgiving his absence and asking him to come the next day. There was a note of pleading to it, he thought, as though she desperately wanted him to come. She even named the hour, and the comment she added about being deeply insulted if he failed to arrive might have been light, but hinted to him at something more serious. Not that she'd be insulted, but . . .

"Perhaps she's fallen in love with you, you handsome rogue," he said aloud. "Liam Rhenford, breaker of hearts."

He laughed harshly at himself, and felt better for it.

Still, there was something about the letter that made him decide to keep the appointment. The hour she had set was in the afternoon, and he could speak to Viyescu and make whatever other cautious inquiries he needed to in the morning.

As Liam lay in his bed later, trying to sleep, faces circled in his head, their clamoring keeping him awake.

Coeccias, Mother Japh, the merchant Necquer and his wife, his landlady, Tarquin and Fanuilh. In the four months since he had arrived in Southwark, he had counted a day eventful if he had gone to Tarquin's to swim. And suddenly he was drunk at parties, receiving invitations from rich women, investigating murders and losing part of his soul.

It was a great deal for him to think about, after four months of isolation. The faces pressed around him, a rabble of voices and new memories. And above them all, for some reason, loomed the diminutive dragon, and its slitted cat's eyes, and solid thoughts like bricks in his head.

Liam was a long time getting to sleep.

■ *4* ■

EVEN AS LONG as Liam was getting to sleep, he woke shortly after sunrise, the noise of the stirring day rising up through his window. Carters shouted, it seemed, directly below, wagons creaking and oxen bellowing for the sole purpose of waking him. Children had gathered as well, their high-pitched games designed with his ruined sleep in mind.

Grumbling, he pulled himself from his pallet and used the slight dampness at the bottom of his water bucket to wash the film from his eyes. When he felt he could see sufficiently, he searched for and lit a candle.

There was little light in the garret; the window was small and the sky clouded over, filled to bursting with big-bellied rain clouds.

"Rain," he muttered miserably. "And I had such hopes of a ride in the countryside." The joke made him smile a little, though, and he picked up the bucket and went down the stairs two at a time, whistling by the time he reached the bottom.

His landlady was not up, as he knew she would not be, but there was a kettle heating in the huge kitchen hearth. A thin, gray-looking girl, the landlady's only servant, froze when he came down, whistling a sea chantey. Her eyes bulged, and he realized he had not put on his tunic.

Liam let his whistling slide off and grinned wolfishly at her; she took one look at his scarred torso and his whipcord muscles before fleeing wordlessly into another room.

What would Lady Necquer say if I arrived shirtless?

His grin widened, so wolfish the poor drudge would undoubtedly have fainted, and he filled his bucket with hot water from the kettle.

Back in his room, he scrubbed himself thoroughly. While he dried, he scraped away the thin growth of stubble on his face with a pumice stone, wincing at the abrasion. He thought of Tarquin's comment on his beardlessness, and Mother Japh's.

"Hang them," he growled, and tried his wolfish grin again, liking it. Dressing in his best, a forest green tunic with white piping and matching breeches, he felt better than he had in a long while.

Since he had come to Southwark, he realized, and swiped at the dirt on his high boots, managing to bring a shine to a small circle of leather. He looked at the rest of the muddy, stained bootleather, and shook his head.

Not good enough to shine my boots, but better than in a long while.

His hangover was gone, the lump on the back of his head much smaller than the day before. And he had something to do. Not since long before he came to Southwark had he had something worth doing, and the thing he had come to do—his book—had simply not happened. Now he was in the middle of something. He had little idea how to go about it, but it was good to wake with a purpose.

Filled with the wonder of this small discovery, he belted up his tunic and took money from his seachest to fill his purse. As he put the money away, he saw a small knife in a plain sheath and hesitated only a moment before picking it up. The last time he had tried to solve a mystery, a dagger had proven useful.

Liam closed the chest, locked it, and hung the knife on his belt. He put his hand on the hilt and tried the wolf's grin again, laughed at himself, and went downstairs.

This time he did not startle the drudge, who looked at him with relief, as though in his fine tunic he fit the mold of a respectable scholar much better than he had when half-naked and whistling dirty sailors' songs. He did not smile at all when he asked her if she knew where the druggist Viyescu's shop could be found.

She did not, but timidly suggested he try Northfield or Auric's Park, two sections of the artisans' quarter. He smiled very gently at the poor girl and thanked her politely before leaving. He switched over to the wolf's grin as soon as he was out the door, and chuckled to himself as he walked the few blocks to the stables.

The lad he had sent with his message the day before was not there, but a boy who might have been his brother was more than willing to carry a message for him.

"Tell the Lady Necquer I'll be glad to wait on her at the hour she suggested," he said, and then when the boy dashed off down the street, "Hey, boy! The message can wait until you've fetched my horse!"

When the shamefaced boy had retrieved his mount and repeated the message to his satisfaction, he sent him running again, and set off himself for the city gate.

The fat, slate-gray clouds put him in mind of winter, though the breeze from the sea was not very chilly. He remembered his previous winter, spent in a land where the sun shone hot and full all the time, and even the rains had seemed dazzlingly bright. He rode past pastures of cold, colorless grass and fields shorn clean, stripped naked for the coming winter, and smiled. It would be his first winter in Taralon in a long time.

Fanuilh was waiting for him, still on the table in the workroom. The villa was warm, though no fires burned. Liam noticed for the first time that there were no fireplaces where they could burn. This was more of Tarquin's magic, he realized, still working even after the wizard's death. Liam had not known magic could work that way.

The spells are powerful, as was Master Tanaquil.

The dragon was looking at him, and again he found it difficult to connect the placid serpentine face with the stoneblock thought in his head.

"You're up early," he said cheerily, trying to dispel some of the silence that echoed loudly along the gleaming wood and clean white walls.

I need little sleep. Would you get me food?

"Raw meat it is, little master. By your leave," Liam said, bowing deeply before the dragon. It stared up at him with what Liam guessed passed for curiosity, and he hurried off to the kitchen, thinking hard of uncooked steak.

As he watched Fanuilh neatly snap up mouthfuls of meat, he paced eagerly around the room, stopping and starting as one thing and another struck his imagination.

"What are all these things in the jars?" He was looking at one in particular that might have been the preserved head of a dog. He shuddered and moved on, not waiting for an answer.

You are very light today.

"Well, my little master, if you could read my mind, you would know why."

Yes. You have accepted the bargain fully. You are eager to begin. I thought you would be.

"Did you?" This sobered Liam slightly, and he paused before the tiny model of Southwark.

You carry Luck with you, and are checking to make sure you have not lost it.

He laughed out loud.

"True enough! I'm like a man come from the market, patting his purse to see if it still holds his gold. Only I can't feel for my Luck—I have to prove it the hard way."

Fanuilh chewed placidly while Liam chuckled over its judgement. When the last of the meat was gone, it rolled slowly over on its back and exposed the dull gold of its belly.

Scratch? it thought. Liam could almost see the question mark, like black ink in his head. He hastened over and rubbed the dragon's stomach with his knuckles. The feeling like ridged cloth fascinated him.

You will see the druggist today?

"Viyescu? Yes, he seemed the proper place to begin."

What will you say to him?

Liam frowned, concentrating on evening out the area of his scratching, switching to his fingernails. "I don't know," he said at last, flashing his wolf's grin. "I'll find out when I get there, I suppose."

Do not smile like that at him.

He laughed again, and the dragon squirmed impatiently beneath his hand, indicating that it had had enough scratching.

"If Your Highness has had enough, I'll be on my way," he said.

Do not smile like that at him, the dragon thought again, and Liam threw a groan at the ceiling and left quickly.

He frightened his roan by leaping heavily into the saddle and kicking hard with his heels, urging the horse up the narrow cliff path at a fast trot.

He frightened himself with his own high spirits. With the cold and the shorn fields and the lowering gray clouds, with a dragon holding part of his soul and his only acquaintance dead, he should have been depressed.

Instead, he was eager to begin his search.

Viyescu's shop was on the landward side of the city, in a quiet section of the artisans' quarter called Northfield. The rise on which Southwark sat was steep on the south, so that the houses of the rich quarter rose above each other on streets like mountain paths; but the slope was far gentler to the north, and the streets of the artisans' quarter were broader and less steeply inclined. Cobblestoned in the same black stone as the rest of the city, they nonetheless seemed brighter because the houses had fewer stories and more of the gray vault of sky showed beyond the peaked gables.

A helpful washerwoman and a colorful sign directed him to the apothecary. Above the scrubbed doorstep hung a yellow board on which a skillful hand had painted a wreath of ivy over a steaming thurible. The brand was heated by a stooping woman whose breath was flames.

Uris, Liam remembered. Though Uris-tide was not celebrated in the Midlands, he knew enough of her from the sea, where she was honored as the Giver of Direction, the inspirator of navigators and charters. He also remembered her as the patron of alchemists, herbalists, and druggists, though most of those that he knew gave her only lip service.

Ton Viyescu, it seemed, gave her more credit than that.

"A religious man," Liam said to himself and, assuming a grave expression, walked into the shop.

Viyescu looked almost exactly as he had expected, almost familiar in a tantalizing way Liam could not put his finger on, but the state of the shop was unexpectedly different. The druggist was short and gnarled like the roots he sold, with a magnificently tangled expanse of bushy black beard flecked with gray creeping up his cheeks and endangering his tiny, gleaming eyes. He wore a stained leather apron tied over equally stained fustian that might once have been white but was now an ugly yellow-gray. His hands, composed almost entirely of huge knuckles, rested impatiently on the wooden counter. He stood behind it like it was a wall and Liam a spear-shaking raider.

The shop, however, was not the musty, disordered mess he had expected from his other experiences with apothecaries. It was crowded, but each thing seemed to occupy its proper place. Herbs hung in bunches from dowel racks, the spacing between each leafy bundle exact; roots in open boxes filled shelves, their names carefully painted in clear letters on the shelf beneath them. Flasks, pottery jars and heavy glass decanters lined the higher shelves, ranked like soldiers and labeled like the roots. The druggist's protective counter was bare and clean; behind him ran another counter, on which were neatly arranged the tools of his trade. Several mortars with pestles in attendance, a tiny brazier with glowing coals, a thick-bottomed glass beaker for boiling, and a rack of glass and copper tubes of different lengths, jointed and beveled so they could be attached one to the other.

A precise man, Liam thought, as well as religious. It came to him where he had seen Viyescu before: he had been in the procession the day before, at the front of the lay worshippers.

"You are the apothecary?" He managed to achieve a decent Torquay accent, thick and musical.

"I am Ton Viyescu," the druggist growled, eyeing him rudely, and Liam assumed it was his normal manner. His accent marked him from the far northwest, a harsh land by any standards, and not likely to breed politeness.

"I only ask because I have, well, I have important business, and I wish only to deal with a, well, with someone who really knows."

Viyescu squinted suspiciously at him, his beady eyes almost lost in wrinkles. "I know what there is to know about herbs, Master . . . ?"

The question was so pointed that Liam could not ignore it. "Cance," he answered. "Hierarch Cance, from Torquay." He chose a religious title, and it seemed to affect the druggist.

"Ah, well, Hierarch, what can I do for you?" There were no protests of humility, but the hunched man's attitude loosened a little, and he stopped squinting and shifted his hands slightly on the counter, indicating a willingness to serve, if not an eagerness.

"You see, I came to Southwark to meet a man, a *wizard*"—he whispered the word, as though it were dangerous in itself—"and now I find he is dead. Murdered." He nodded somberly, but inwardly he cursed. The druggist was nodding also, not the least surprised, although he seemed a little puzzled.

"And who would this wizard be, Hierarch?"

"One Tarquin Tanaquil," Liam responded cautiously. "Perhaps you knew him?"

"Oh, I knew him. I knew him well enough." His tone indicated that the acquaintance had not been pleasant, and there was something else, a change in his eyes, like the shutting of a door.

"You sound as though you did not like him," Liam said, but continued before the druggist could respond. "I ask, you see, because he was engaged on, well, on certain works for us that are of some importance. Uris-tide is almost upon us, you know." He filled the last sentence with as much importance as it could hold, and let it hang in the air of the shop, competing for preeminence with the musty smell of dried herbs.

"Hm. So it is," the druggist finally said, nodding himself. "He did not seem the sort of man who would care much for Uris-tide. A nonbeliever, he seemed to me, Hierarch."

"Ah, well, the ends of the gods are often served by those who do not know them," Liam said hastily.

"Still . . . Tanaquil was a strange tool for the gods, if you ask me. A filthy man, of filthy habits."

"How filthy? Evil? Did he serve the Darker Gods?"

"No, no, not that," the druggist said quickly, his hands finally leaving the counter to protest the accusation. "Simply not a godly man. A worldly man, like so many, given to his pleasures, and not much bound by the heavens' laws," he continued bitterly. "And proud, very proud. He would not listen to others. I meant nothing else."

"You knew him well, then?"

"Better than most, I suppose. We had reasons for dealings—I sold him certain roots he had difficulty attaining."

Liam gave a sigh of relief. "Then you knew of his business. Tell me, did he—" He got no further, stopped by Viyescu's dark scowl.

"I did not know his business, Hierarch," he said flatly.

"Oh." He did not need to fake disappointment, only a reason. "I had hoped . . . you see, the work he was engaged in was very important, and when I heard he was dead, I thought he might have confided in a colleague."

"We were not colleagues. He was a wizard; I am an apothecary. The two are not the same." Viyescu spoke coldly, crossing his arms firmly on his chest, but Liam sensed something beyond the distinctions of professional pride.

"I know, but there are no other wizards in this benighted city, and I thought, 'Who else would a wizard have dealings with?' and thus came to you. And when I saw Uris on your sign, I allowed myself to hope." He also allowed himself a small sigh.

Viyescu relented a little, letting his hands drop to the counter. "I am sorry, Hierarch, but my business with the wizard extended only to selling him certain roots, and occasionally procuring the rarer types for him. No more, Hierarch, no more."

"Yes, I see, I see." His head dropped, deep in troubled thought. "You wouldn't by any chance have sold him any Percin's Bane, would you?" Percin's Bane was very rare, Liam knew, and only grew in the King's Range; he chose it because it was uncommon.

"No," Viyescu responded immediately. "There is no Percin's Bane in the south."

Liam waited, hoping the druggist would go on, but Viyescu showed no sign of continuing, so he shook his head resignedly and walked to the door. As he was opening it, the druggist's voice stopped him.

"May I ask, Hierarch, how you know Tanaquil was murdered?"

"I was there," Liam answered, and then hurried on: "At his house, yesterday. The morning, actually, after he had been killed. One of the Sheriff's men told me about it. I was quite shaken. The enchantment was so important to us." He let the door close and turned back, trying to inject innocence into his question. "Is the death not common knowledge? I would think the death of a wizard as powerful as Master Tanaquil would be instantly known."

"Tarquin was very reclusive. I doubt if half the town even knew he was alive."

"May I ask how you know of his death?" He arched an eyebrow politely, but Viyescu still stiffened.

"The Aedile—the Sheriff—told me of it when he came to question me. He apparently had the same thought as you."

Liam gnawed a knuckle worriedly. "I can only hope he was not killed by those who would stop our work. Tell me, had he any enemies? Perhaps among the foes of religion?"

Viyescu laughed harshly, like crunching gravel. "The foes of religion were least likely to be his enemies, Hierarch." He stopped and thought, weighing something, and then went on firmly. "Though I cannot imagine any others who would be. He was very jealous of his privacy, as I've said."

Considering this for a moment, Liam gnawed more. "Tell me, if you would, when did you see him last?"

"Only a week or so ago, Hierarch. I went to see him on an unimportant matter."

"I thought you only had business dealings with him?"

"Well," Viyescu said slowly, "yes, only business dealings. Yes." He tugged at his bushy beard, chewing a little at the end of his mustache. He was considering something of even greater importance than before, and finally spoke uneasily, choosing each word with care, measuring the effect on Liam. "There was a woman, really a girl only, who was in trouble." Liam assumed a questioning air, and the druggist went on reluctantly. "Caught in sin, Hierarch. Pregnant." He spit the distasteful word out.

"And so you went to see Master Tanaquil? I don't understand."

"The girl came to me, trying to buy an herb called santhract. It can destroy a pregnancy, Hierarch."

Liam meant only to show curiosity, but Viyescu seemed to misread his expression, and his cheeks burned red with anger beneath his upward-creeping beard.

"I do not sell this herb, Hierarch, and so I told her! I told her only to pray, but she cursed me, and said something about Tarquin, so I went to him to warn him of her sin." He spoke thickly, indignation and righteous anger and something else, maybe desperation, making him slightly frightening.

"You did right, Master Apothecary," Liam said softly.

"Thank you, Hierarch," Viyescu said, still angry, and Liam detected more disappointment than gratitude in the words. He murmured some thanks of his own and headed for the door.

In the street, with the thick door between him and the angry apothecary, he breathed a deep sigh of relief, and offered up an apology to Uris on her sign for impersonating one of her priests. Then he apologized to his fluttering stomach. Though his face felt cool and there was no sweat on his forehead, the back of his neck was flushed, and heat gathered in his armpits and at the small of his back.

His roan was skittish, smelling his disquiet as he swung up into the saddle, and he soothed the horse with a steady hand and a gentle, "Easy, Diamond, easy."

Damned horse is more upset than I am, and he didn't even pretend he was a priest. Which I'll never do again, he thought, urging the horse to a trot through the uncrowded streets.

Viyescu had not been particularly threatening, for all his gruffness and angry talk of sin, and the weird edge of desperation that had hung like smoke around him. But it was dangerous to pretend to be someone he was not, he decided. Though he was a relative stranger to the town, the possible complications were enormous.

Still, for his first attempt, the interview had yielded some results. A cursing girl, deep in sin, who muttered things about Tarquin. She was not on his list, and perhaps she should be.

After all, who might have gotten her pregnant?

He remembered an afternoon early in the summer, drying in the warm sun on the breakwater. The sound of laughter had roused him from his heat-induced torpor, and he had swiveled his head around to look at the stone veranda. Tarquin had been hugging a young woman, who was struggling with him and giggling. She pulled away finally with an embarrassed glance at Liam, and scurried up the path, holding her skirts high. And the old wizard had rubbed his hands briskly together, tipping Liam a lecherous wink before going inside again. It was before he and Tarquin had ever really spoken, and Liam had gone back to the sun thinking only that it was amazing for such an old man. But then, he was a wizard after all, and he had heard of spells. . . .

Who would risk killing a wizard?

An angry husband or father, or even the kind of woman who would try to buy santhract from a worshipper of Uris. Or a druggist who detested sin, and perhaps had a more personal relationship with the young woman than he wished to reveal.

It was not much more than speculation, Liam knew, a kind of day-dreaming; but it might lead to something more, and it was the only clue he had.

Another thought struck him as he rode south out of Northfield, into the narrower, steeper streets of the poorer quarters, where his lodgings were. The Aedile had been there before him. He felt sure he knew far more than Coeccias did about Tarquin's doings, but the idea of having the blunt man precede him around town did little to quiet his stomach. And it was entirely possible that his name might be raised in the course of the Aedile's questioning, which would make his own investigation more difficult.

Being little known in Southwark might have meant he could continue to pretend to be someone he was not, though his own inclination was against it; but if someone caught him out because of something Coeccias had said, it could be dangerous. On the other hand, being little known also meant he knew little. If he had had more information about Viyescu, he might have gotten more out of him.

He tried to think who might supply that kind of information. Barkeeps and the like, of course, though they were often unreliable. His landlady was certainly a great gossip, but he *knew* she was unreliable, and gossip often ran both ways.

His stomach grumbled, and he realized it must be long past noon. There would be time to eat, he hoped, before his appointment with Lady Necquer.

Suddenly, the wolf's grin spread over his face. Lady Necquer very much wished to hear about all the places he had been, and he very much wished to hear about the place they were.

Perhaps they could help each other.

Liam had misjudged the time; it was only a little after midday when he stabled his horse, and he had almost two hours before he had to be at Necquer's home. He ate lightly at a tavern near his garret, taking his time, thinking of polite ways to question the merchant's wife about Southwark.

When he was done, he went back to his room and gathered up a few maps and some books. Then he set out on foot for the Point, climbing the steep streets with his papers tucked under his arm. Bells clanged faintly over the Duke's court, the sound muffled by the heavy storm clouds. A ragged bootblack squatted by the side of the road beside the ironbound door of a merchant, and Liam had the boy shine his boots, tossing him a coin far larger than the job deserved. The boy peered up at him for a moment with what seemed like scorn; Liam shrugged and strode away, up the hill towards Necquer's.

An elderly servant in a simple smock opened the door for him before he could knock, and led him through the house towards the stone porch at the rear. Without its crowd of celebrating commoners, the house seemed hallowed, almost templelike: delicate furniture lightly carven, gilt-framed mirrors and tasseled tapestries from far lands, crystal and silver, rich, dark woods. Traces of Necquer's occupation showed in the distant origins of some of the crystal and the foreign landscapes in the tapestries, but on the whole it was quietly Taralonian, restrainedly opulent. A hush hung over everything.

Lady Necquer was on the porch, looking out at the rough sea. Wrapped in a heavy cloak of dark wool, she huddled in a high-backed cushioned chair; her fine dark hair whipped wildly around her face, which was pointed anxiously westward, at the Teeth. The wind, blocked out of the street by the high, densely packed houses, clawed fiercely at the exposed porch, howling off the whitecapped ocean. The cold had brought crimson spots to her cheeks, and she frowned pensively.

He came level with her chair and bowed politely. The servant coughed.

"Sir Liam, madam."

The concern that had wrinkled her brow lessened, and she started up, a hesitant smile on her lips.

"Sir Liam! I thought you would not come! Lares, hot wine for us, when we go in." The servant bowed and retreated. Lady Necquer returned her gaze to the sea, and Liam looked at her.

"Hard and cruel to look on," she murmured, stepping away from her chair to the stone balustrade. The wind tugged at her heavy cloak. Liam pressed his books and maps firmly beneath his arm, and felt compelled to speak, as though she had invited comment.

"Yes, it is, but at peace the sea can be the most beautiful thing in the world."

She shifted her gaze to look curiously at him.

"I spoke not of the sea, Sir Liam. Those—" She gestured vaguely towards the Teeth, and then suddenly shivered. "It grows cold. Come, let's in." She led the way, shuddering, into the house. Liam followed.

In a parlor on the second floor, with coals glowing in the small grate, the same servant brought them mulled wine. Lady Necquer removed her wool cloak, showing a high-necked gown with full skirts, completely unrevealing in the fullness of its dyed purple pleats and folds. Her moodiness was gone, and she smiled at him.

"You must forgive my distraction, Sir Liam. The cold days like me not. I grow foolish, and I sorely doubted your coming. You wronged me not to come yesterday. I placed much on it." She faltered, and then went on in a different tone. "But I see you've brought books and charts; come, begin your discourse, and I'll attend with a ready ear."

Liam took a sip of the mulled wine, and began unfolding his maps.

Rain was pattering against the thick-paned windows long before he thought of the wine again. Charmed by her interest and attentiveness, he spoke for a long while, finding more to tell than he thought he would. He had been a great number of places that were only rumors to her, and many more she had never heard of, and he detailed strange customs and foreign peoples for her, drawn on by her obvious interest. With the maps and the books, he traced some of the long pattern of his wanderings, and barely scratched the surface of what he had seen.

Fascinated as she was, she leaned towards him, and her eyes sparkled as he described wonders from far away. Sometimes he caught the hint of a sweet scent and remembered her beauty, but she maintained a detachment, a sort of sexual neutrality in the way she pored over the maps with him. He could not tell if she was being wise or merely innocent.

He did not speak of half he had seen, and almost none of what he had done. He left out the wars he had fought in; the crimes he had, on occasion, had to commit; the worst of the horrors he had seen were glossed over without comment; but she asked shrewd questions, drawing inferences and connections he had never considered.

The lecture became a conversation, and though her eyes darted fairly often to a sandclock on the sideboard, her interest never flagged. In fact, it seemed that the more the afternoon wore on, the more questions she asked, the harder she tried to prolong their talk.

Finally there came a pause, and Liam relaxed in his chair, giving his attention to his now-cold wine and the sky outside. It was full dark, the drops of rain trickling down the panes, silver and gold with reflected candlelight.

"I think I must go now, madam. It is dark, and I'm sure you must be tired." He did not move, waiting for her response.

She did not speak for a long minute, and when she did, it was not to excuse him.

"Tell me, Sir Liam, in your travels, have you ever seen a mirror of the Teeth?" The question came from far away, and she seemed to have relapsed into her earlier depression.

"A mirror of the Teeth?" It was the question that put him off, but she presumed it was her dialect.

"Their semblance, I mean. Anything like them."

"Well, I have seen shoals and reefs of great size, and some coastlines almost as rocky as Southwark's, but nothing as impressive as the Teeth, no."

"Impressive?" she echoed, and it was almost a hiss. "Say rather murderous, or Dark—anything but impressive!"

Her eyes were wide and deep with anger, and her cheeks flushed. Liam stood up hastily.

"It is late. I believe I should go, madam."

Lady Necquer's anger disappeared, and she sank back in her chair, deflated.

"It would be well, I suppose, Sir Liam." She stood wearily, as though it were an effort. "I should invite you to dine, but with my lord gone, it would not be seemly." She ventured a wan smile.

"Will he be long in Warinsford?" Liam inquired politely.

"He returns in two days, ere Uris-tide. I anticipate his return eagerly." The smile grew more natural.

"As do we all, I'm sure. Goodnight, madam."

She followed him to the stairs, thanking him for entertaining her.

"A most gentle discourse, Sir Liam, and one I would gladly repeat. Perhaps—" She stopped high on the steps, her smile draining away. From the hall came the sound of voices, the servant's polite husk and another, smooth and refined, but angry:

"I tell you, man, I've an appointment with the lady!"

Lady Necquer clutched Liam's arm.

"Relay to Lares that I am sudden sick, if you would," she whispered, and then continued, more fiercely. "And please, Sir Liam, return tomorrow!" He began to equivocate, but she pressed his arm. "Please!"

He took a deep breath and nodded once. She turned and fled back into her parlor. With another breath and a bemused shake of his head, Liam descended to the hall.

The handsome young man who had fled Necquer's party stood in the doorway, glaring down at the servant. A rain-stained cloak mantled his broad shoulders, dripping water on the wooden boards. With an arrogant flip of his head he looked Liam over, and dismissed him by raking a hand through his sodden mane. He returned his attention to the servant.

"I'll repeat it once more, churl: this is the appointed hour of my meeting, and I mean to have it!"

Liam's eyes narrowed, examining the angry man in detail. A perfectly drawn face, strong chin, nose just sharp enough, widely set, flashing eyes; broad chest, tall, well muscled. His voice echoed magnificently,

eloquent and musical. A golden, leonine hero to Necquer's dark tradesman.

*Now why would a woman like Poppae Necquer spend an afternoon
with the likes of me, and then flee such a one as this?* Liam wondered.

"Lares," he said, "the lady asked me to inform you that she is indisposed."

Both the servant and the handsome man turned to him.

"Aye, Sir Liam," the servant said gratefully, but the young man
glared at him with deep hatred. Liam returned the stare impassively, and
suddenly the other spun on his heel and marched out of the house,
slamming the door loudly behind him.

In the moment of silence that followed, the two men shared a look—
indifferent surprise for Liam, immense relief for the servant. Liam broke
it first.

"I wonder, Lares, if you could find me a piece of oilcloth. I'm afraid
the rain would do little good for my papers."

He indicated his books and maps with a small smile, and the old
servant scurried off willingly to look.

■ 5 ■

LIAM HURRIED HOME through the dark, slippery streets, and found his landlady waiting for him, wringing her hands anxiously. He was soaked to the skin and tried to ignore her, wanting nothing more than to go to his room and dry off.

"Oh, Master Liam," she exclaimed as he brushed past her, "the Aedile was here only an hour gone, conning about for you!"

"Was he," Liam said politely, heading for the stairs with a bright, empty smile.

"Think you it was about the wizard's death?"

That ground him to a halt, and he turned slowly.

"What?"

"I thought, you having passed more than the odd hour with him, that the Aedile might suspect you!" She mispronounced "Aedile" to rhyme with "ladle," but he did not correct her.

"Did he say that? And how did you know Tarquin was dead?"

The stern edge in his voice unnerved her, as though it had confirmed her fears. "No, not so I recall. He mere said he'd have words with you, but I thought that you knowing the wizard—" Liam cut her off.

"How did you hear that Tarquin was dead?"

"Well," she fretted, "I didn't exactly know to be certain until the Aedile came, but's being bruited around the town by some. I heard from one who knows a member of the Guard."

Liam smiled grimly and started up the steps.

"But, Master Liam, what should I do if the Aedile comes again?" she called after him, and he laughed at her worry.

"Show him up," he called back, "and pronounce his title correctly!"

In his room he unwrapped his papers from the sheet of oilskin Lares had given him, and checked them carefully to see if they had gotten wet. When he was satisfied they had not been harmed, he changed to dry clothes, a far simpler tunic and long trousers of gray flannel. He draped his wet tunic over his chair and eyed his boots with displeasure. The punctures from Fanuilh's teeth had let water in, soaking his feet, and he put them aside, hoping they could be repaired. He slipped on a pair of low felt shoes and lay down on his pallet to think.

Coeccias had come looking for him, and if it wasn't already, the news of Tarquin's death would soon be common knowledge to those who cared to know.

The first could mean any of several things. Possibly there were some simple questions the Aedile had forgotten to ask him. More likely something had come up that had caused the man to suspect him anew, despite Mother Japh's judgement. Least likely, of course, was that the Aedile had decided to share whatever information he had. Liam frowned at the thought.

The fact that the death would soon be common knowledge meant he had been right to presume his investigation would become vastly more difficult. It also made Lady Necquer's uselessness more disappointing.

There was something desperate going on with her, concentrating her so completely on herself that she would have little interest in helping him. It revolved around the handsome young man, obviously, and Liam's visit and her insistence on it had been along the lines of a distraction from her greater problem. Or perhaps, he realized, as protection.

Whatever the reason, she was in no state of mind to involve herself seriously in the affairs of a dead wizard. Nonetheless, he found himself curious about her problem. What danger the young man presented Liam could not guess. If he was a lover, she had no reason to fear him. He could not threaten exposure, as Liam had known lovers to do, because it was clear from his behavior at the party that Master Necquer suspected something. It was equally clear that he did not blame his wife.

What, then, could be the problem?

Although he was partly aware that he had a more important riddle to unravel, he gave himself over for a while to considering the distraught young woman.

The heavy tread of boots on the stairs and Mistress Dorcas's voice interrupted him after a while. She spoke loudly, repeating "Aedile Coeccias" several times, and it was painfully obvious that she was trying to warn him. He got up quickly and surprised the Aedile by opening the door before Coeccias could knock.

"Rhenford!" he said, blinking his eyes. "It's well y'are in. I've been conning for you."

"So I've heard, Aedile. Please come in." He smiled over Coeccias's shoulder at his landlady, who was hovering nervously on the stairs and rolling her eyes. "Thank you for showing the Aedile up, Mistress Dorcas." He deliberately stressed the proper pronunciation.

"I'm afraid you've frightened my landlady, Aedile," he continued when he had shut the door firmly in her face. "She thinks you mean to arrest me for Master Tanaquil's murder."

Coeccias ran a scarred hand through his now-trimmed beard and looked around the garret with mild curiosity. "Truth, Rhenford, I may well do that ere long. I've seen some rare parchments this day." He stood by Liam's table, idly shuffling the papers there, occasionally sparing a glance out the window. Liam leaned casually against the door.

"Oh?" he said, with as much indifference as he could muster.

"Oh? Oh, indeed. Rare parchments, I say, rarer than rare. The wizard's testament, booked and noted in the Duke's own court, by the Duke's own clerks, and waxed with the Duke's own seal. A rare testament, that."

"How rare, Aedile Coeccias?"

The burly officer found something that interested him in the papers on the table, and Liam thought belatedly of his list of suspects.

"Y'are a scholar, Rhenford?" Coeccias asked suddenly.

"I have studied," Liam began, wincing over the list.

"Tarquin must've liked scholars, Rhenford. He left you all."

"What?" He could not hide his astonishment, and forgot the list. "Left me all?"

"Seat, fortune, goods—all. Y'are amazed?"

"Of course," Liam stammered. "I hardly knew him!"

"Better than anyone else, it seems. It'd be a strong stroke against you, in the Duke's court."

The return of Coeccias's suspicion hit Liam hard on the heels of the news of Tarquin's will. "You know, in the days when your title was coined, if a man were falsely accused, his accuser was held guilty for the crime," he said coldly.

Coeccias chuckled. "I'd expect a scholar to know that—but I'd also expect him to know that the Aedile's office exempted him from the same statute. How else to uphold the law?"

Stung, Liam flushed. He had not thought the rough-looking Aedile would know the law's qualifier. His hands bunched at his sides, but he said nothing. Coeccias dropped his eyes to the paper that had interested him.

"I'll admit, Rhenford, I came intent on clapping you in. I thought the testament would unnerve you, and if pressed hard, you'd break. But now I think I've erred. Y'are a poor actor, Rhenford, too poor for a killer. And I uncover this scribbling." He held a piece of paper up, nothing but mild curiosity in his voice. "Now, it strikes me strange that a scholar should have a list of a dead man's acquaintances, with notes of arguments and visits all within the last sevennight. Truth, very strange. I'd almost say that scholar was idly scribbling a list of who might have taken off the dead man. Wouldn't you?"

He gave a small smile, and Liam frowned but said nothing.

"Can you think of a reason why a scholar should make such a list?"

"Perhaps," Liam said slowly, trying to control the anger he knew should be directed at himself for leaving the list out, "perhaps he thought the Aedile was too much of a fool to find the murderer, and decided to do the job himself."

Coeccias roared with laughter, filling the garret with the surprising sound. He slapped his knee with the list.

"Truth, perhaps he did! Perhaps he did! Oh, y'are a rare murderer, Rhenford, a rare murderer!" Fresh laughter exploded out of him as he folded the list carefully in quarters and stowed it in his black tunic. Liam had no idea what to do, and simply waited while the Aedile finished his laughter.

"Come," Coeccias said finally. "I'd have you eat with me, Rhenford."

It was drizzling still, but Coeccias chose a tavern nearby, and ducked quickly through the cold shower without a word. Liam sat across the plank table, looking at the Aedile with distrust only half-concealed as the larger man called across the almost empty common room to order beer and food. When the keeper had recognized his order, he turned to Liam with a serious look.

"So, the eyes that scan tomes now con a murderer."

Liam nodded, wondering what the Aedile was thinking.

"Truth, Rhenford, that likes me not. I'm not sure I need you murking the waters with ill-advised questions. Now, I know you think me a clown"—he held up a hand to forestall Liam's denial—"and you may have the right of it. The eagle's eyes are not mine, and I don't see into shadowed hearts. I'm certainly simpler than a scholar, no matter how innocent his face. Yet I'm still Aedile."

"Which means?" Liam had begun frowning deeply at the mention of his innocent face. He found it difficult to contain his uneasiness, and drummed his fingers on the table, looking around the tavern through the smoky rushlight.

"Which means I can't very well allow you to search out an assassin on your own. Yet you have a list of possibles that I'd never have had, and you knew the wizard best. Not well, perhaps, but better than any else. And I can't tell you not to search."

"So?" He was on the brink of being rude when a serving girl came by and placed beer in clay steins on the table, along with a basket of bread, salt and boiled eggs. The Aedile dug in, salting a torn piece of bread and an egg and eating them in big bites. He left Liam waiting impatiently until he had washed down his first egg with a gulp of beer, and then spoke as he set about preparing a second egg.

"So, Rhenford, I'll find you running about the town, as I said, murking the waters and making my work harder. And," he said, gesturing significantly with his egg before biting into it, "you'll find me doing the same to you."

Liam took an egg and nibbled at it unsalted, some of his irritation dissipating as he guessed where the Aedile was headed.

"So we are in each other's way, Aedile. That will be inconvenient if either of us is to resolve this."

"Truth, inconvenient is too small a word for such a large stumbling block."

"What will we do about it?"

Coeccias once again paused as the girl put down two steaming pies on wooden platters.

"I could ask you not to involve yourself," he said, steepling his fingers over the pie and examining Liam's face, and then waved away the suggestion with a laugh. "But I've enough sense to know you'd not. Y'are serious about it? Not merely dabbling to satisfy a scholar's curiosity?"

"Very serious." Liam began eating, cutting into the meat and vegetable pie, highly spiced as most food was in Southwark. He waited for the Aedile this time, who only spoke after he had gone through several bites of his own pie, and then only around a large mouthful.

"I know not why, but I'll warrant you mean it. Then if you'll not keep out of it, and are serious, and my position means I can't keep out of it, and must be serious, then sense says we work together."

It was what Liam had guessed, but he kept his satisfaction from his voice.

"That would seem to be a good idea."

"Good. Then lay out what you know, Rhenford."

Liam eyed him with a half-smile. "How do I know you won't simply listen and then arrest me to keep me out of your way?"

"Truth, you don't," Coeccias said with a wolf's grin that looked far more natural than Liam's earlier one. He must have blanched, because the Aedile snorted and held out his hand, after wiping it on his black tunic. "Would my word suffice?"

"No, no, I'll trust you," Liam said hastily, and Coeccias withdrew his hand with another snort.

Without mentioning Fanuilh, he elaborated on the list the dragon had given him. He had thought it would be difficult to explain knowing so much about Tarquin's visitors, but the Aedile asked no questions, simply nodding as Liam ticked off each visitor and what he knew of them. Finally he came around to his interview with the druggist Viyescu, his imposture of a Hierarch, and what he had learned from it.

Coeccias listened in silence, working his way through his entire pie before Liam was finished. When he was done with the meal, he pushed the platter away and leaned back from the table with a sigh.

"Well, I'll admit you've a great deal more information than I. I did ill not to clap you in yesterday and examine you closer."

"So what do you know? Apart from the will, that is?"

"Only what you've told me, Rhenford. Truth, I knew little enough about the wizard."

"Nothing!" Liam exclaimed. "You know nothing? It looks like I've made a poor deal!"

"I, on the other hand, have made off surpassing well, wouldn't you say?"

Liam massaged his brow roughly, but he had to chuckle at the Aedile's sated-cat grin. "Well, then," he finally said, "the least you could do is try to live up to the bargain."

"It would seem fair," Coeccias grinned.

"What about the knife? You took it, I assume. Was there anything special about it?"

"Only that it was of the sort used by rude players, jugglers and the like. They come in pairs, and have uncommon broad hilts; in one of the pair, the blade retracts harmlessly. For death scenes and the like in entertainments."

"Well, then, that would point to the minstrel—" Liam began eagerly, but caught himself when Coeccias started to interrupt. "Or a clever man who wished to put the blame elsewhere."

"Y'are quick enough. A clever man who wished to point as far away from himself as possible. If he chose a player's knife, that would make him high-born, or at least rich. That would indicate the merchant you saw. And 'less I miss the mark, he would be Ancus Marcius. Oft he travels with the sort of rough boys you described, and is given to the sort of blustering you heard. When did you say he came to the beach?"

Fanuilh's memory had been good, but his sense of time was inexact; the only way to place the date of the merchant's visit was by the weather.

"A day or two after the last of the really fierce storms. I don't remember the day exactly; it was gray and overcast, but didn't rain all day."

Coeccias grumbled thoughtfully. "That would be just after Marcius lost his richest ship on the Teeth."

"The Teeth? You're thinking of Tarquin's model?"

"Truth, it struck me as an interesting plaything for a wizard. Perhaps he failed in some business of Marcius's. The merchant's not very forgiving, I've been told."

"Then maybe you ought to question him."

Frowning, the Aedile poked at the remains of his pie. "Better ask the wind to stand still, or summon the stars to court, than question Marcius. He's high-placed and high-handed, and the offense he'd take would be worth my post. I'd rather you did it."

"Me? If you can't question him, how can I?"

"Make out you're a Hierarch again, or better yet, play the King of Taralon. He'd answer quick enough." Liam grimaced at this reminder of his play-acting with Viyescu, and Coeccias snorted a laugh before going on more seriously. "Best of all, Rhenford, go to him as a scholar seeking employment. Give him your various qualifications, and tell him your previous master, a certain wizard of much power, has been murdered. You seek a new master of sufficient position to protect you from your former's enemies."

"And shock him with Tarquin's name so that he slips up?"

"That'd do."

"And then he has one of his guards knock me out and the next thing I know I find myself a galley slave on one of his ships."

"That'd not do, but if y'are careful, it shouldn't happen. Be meek and mild, innocent as a babe. If he's clever enough to've planted the player's blade, he'll never think a mere pen-nibbler could've found him out. Cleverness and pride go hand in hand."

"Your opinions on human nature pale before the thought of several years chained to a galley seat."

"If you don't return from his offices, I swear I'll personally search every one of his galleys before it leaves Southwark," Coeccias answered cheerfully.

Liam laughed ruefully. "And offer me your best wishes for a pleasant journey, I'm sure. But that'll have to do, I suppose. I'll go see him tomorrow. What will you do?"

"Since you can't go after Viyescu anymore without full religious vestments, I'll search him out again, and maybe trail him with one of my men. Mayhap we'll see if he has any pretty, sinful women in his life."

They left it at that, and Liam let Coeccias pay for the meal, arguing that since he would be facing a possibly murderous merchant the next day, he was doing far more than his share of the bargain. While Coeccias laughed over that, he left the quiet inn and hurried home through the rain.

Sleep was not as long in coming as the day before; in fact, it was all he could do not to drop off as soon as he stretched out on his pallet. There were, however, some things he wanted to think through, and he stayed awake for a few minutes, hands laced behind his head, staring at the pitted wooden beams over his head.

Taken together, the day could not in any way be considered a failure. His visit to Viyescu had provided him with an interesting possibility, and a line of investigation he had not imagined. That a woman of any kind could be involved fascinated him, though he found it hard to imagine Tarquin begetting children at his age. The vague memory of the flushed young thing on the beach that summer morning came back to him, and he turned it over in his head for a while.

He let it go with a sigh, thinking that however interesting it was, as a motive for murder it was less than adequate. More important was his new partnership with the Aedile, which promised him far more of a chance at discovering Tarquin's killer than anything he could have imagined. However simple the burly man looked, he was much shrewder than Liam had guessed, and he knew that Coeccias would make a better source of information on Southwark's inhabitants than Lady Necquer, who had enough distractions of her own to worry about.

In a sense, it was more important that he liked the Aedile. He felt at ease with him, able to joke and talk naturally, unconstrained by the notions and proprieties that kept him almost formal around Lady Necquer.

My luck again, he thought.

Pleased with the alliance, he considered the merchant, Ancus Marcius. From Coeccias's description of his high-handed and often brutal dealings, both in business and in private, Liam thought Marcius considered himself more of a trading prince than a mere merchant. The ship he had lost on the Teeth had been only one of many, but rumor had it that he was taking the wreck almost personally, and had even gone so far as to send threatening notes to several of the local temples, demanding more vigilant prayers and services on behalf of commerce.

Liam smiled in the dark at the man's arrogance, and thought that Marcius's own high self-opinion would make it easy to play the meek scholar in search of a position.

Nonetheless, he was not at all sure that anything of worth would come out of the interview he would have to arrange the next day, unless he could somehow persuade Marcius to take a more than passing interest in him.

Fanuilh, he thought, might be able to help him there. Perhaps there was a spell of some sort. . . .

With a great and sudden yawn, he turned over and began to let sleep claim him, thinking about the dragon. He wondered why it wanted Tarquin's killer found so much. It would have been natural if the creature were enraged, or wildly vengeful, or showing anything approaching emotion, but it betrayed no feelings of any kind. In fact, Fanuilh never seemed angry or amused or depressed or anything at all; it was just there, and following its own obscure purpose.

That night Liam had a dream he had not had in a long time, in which he stood helplessly by and watched his father's keep burned to the ground by the host of another lord. The building that was burning, however, was his landlady's, though the logic of the nightmare insisted it was his father's keep, and the miniature dragon flew crazily about through the smoke and flames, suddenly as huge as one of its larger cousins.

When he woke up to the leaden knocking of rain on his window, he dismissed the dream, which had recurred on and off for most of his adult life, along with its strange new additions.

"I thought I'd left *that* one far behind," he muttered, dragging himself from his warm bed to face the wet and dreary day.

■ 6 ■

IT WAS NOT wise of you to tell the Aedile, Fanuilh thought at Liam, after he had brought meat from the kitchen. Soaked to the skin despite his heavy cloak and unhappy at having had to make the ride all the way out to Tarquin's house in the early morning rain, Liam snapped back.

"Well, there wasn't much I could do otherwise! He could have made it very difficult to go on! He's not as stupid as I thought, you know."

Yes, I know.

Irritably shaking out his cloak, Liam went on. "Besides, I would have had to tell him once I found out, wouldn't I? Unless you were thinking of having me search out Tarquin's murderer just for the personal pleasure of knowing. Justice would have to be served, right?"

The dragon's thought formed slowly. *I suppose . . . perhaps I did not think it out completely.*

"Well, I did, and I think I didn't have any choice about telling him, and I think I have a much better chance of finishing this business with his help. And it's done, so there's no use arguing about it."

The dragon did not reply, lying on the table and giving its full attention to the meat Liam had brought. He tried to wring some of the wetness from his cloak but gave up finally, hooking it over one of the shelf uprights.

"Since you're so interested in giving advice," he said, "I don't suppose you have any idea how I can interest Marcius enough to gain a little of his time."

The thought that came back was interrogatory, like a question mark stamped down on his thoughts.

"I don't know, maybe some spell that will make me irresistibly fascinating, so that he can't tear himself away from me. Maybe a love potion, so he'll confess all his soul's secrets to me. . . ."

I know very few spells, and none like that.

"I was joking," Liam explained. "Have you any practical ideas on the subject?"

I am not sure if Marcius is the proper suspect.

"I'm not sure either, Fanuilh, but there has to be some sort of order to my investigation, or I might as well just send out criers asking the killer to show himself in the town square at noon."

I understand. I simply do not believe it is worth spending the time.

"Well, then," Liam said with an exasperated sigh, "it's a good thing it's not you who'll have to spend the time, isn't it? Besides, he may lead elsewhere, like Viyescu. I'd never thought a druggist could kill, and still am not inclined that way, but he told me about this mysterious girl. I presume you know what I'm talking about?"

The dragon cocked its head and looked at him, as though the question were strange.

Of course. I can—

"Pluck the thoughts right out of my head?" he said ruefully. Another thought began slowly to form, but he tensed and hurried on. It faded away. "Do you remember what she looked like?"

I did not see her. I only heard a voice.

"How did she sound? Young? Old? Angry? Sad? What?"

Seductive.

Fanuilh replied with such certainty that Liam was momentarily taken aback. By the dragon's recollection, the woman had visited Tarquin on the afternoon Viyescu's sinner had stormed out of his shop, but if she had been angry with the wizard for getting her pregnant, would she have sounded seductive? Perhaps Fanuilh had misunderstood her tone.

She cooed.

"All right," he said aloud, "I believe you. She was seductive. But why? Viyescu implied that someone, perhaps Tarquin, had gotten her pregnant, and that she was angry about it. So why coo?"

I do not know. I only heard her coo before Master Tanaquil sent me away.

Liam began pacing thoughtfully around the room, idly picking up glass jars and books and strange tools without paying them much attention. He leaned against the middle worktable, where a single lonely glass decanter stood. Picking it up, he tossed it from hand to hand as he thought. The label, a small square of white paper pasted to the smooth surface, read VIRGIN'S BLOOD, though the beaker was empty and a thick black X lay over the words. Liam grimaced and put the decanter down.

The dragon did not interrupt him, but he found it annoying to know that all his mental processes were constantly open to observation. He itched to be able to keep his head to himself. Despite the irritation, however, he came around to an idea.

"Fanuilh, do you remember a woman who was here during the summer? Sort of pretty, dark-haired, a girl, really?"

Donoé. Master Tarquin called her his 'little barmaid.'

Pleasantly surprised, Liam smiled. "His 'little barmaid', eh? Did she come often?"

Perhaps three or four times, but she was not the one who cooed.

"I didn't think so. Do you know where she was a barmaid?"

You think she might help you find the cooer.

"It's a possibility, you have to admit."

I do not know where she worked.

"Then perhaps Coeccias can scour all the taverns in the city, eh?" He only half-meant it.

Not all the taverns. Only the ones Master Tanaquil was likely to frequent. There should not be so many of those.

Likely to frequent, Liam wondered. "Did he go to the city often?"

Once or twice a week; more often during the summer. I do not know what he did there.

The model of Southwark caught his eye, and he went to it. "Fanuilh, this model—do you know why he made it?"

For a spell. I do not know for whom the spell was intended. He rarely included me in that aspect of his business.

He could think of no other questions, but stayed in the workroom, dipping a finger in the miniature waves with a distracted air. The pattering of the rain on the windows lulled him, and his thoughts wandered and grew unfocused. The Teeth of the model, small though they were, duplicated the grandeur of the original, inspiring a sort of awe and no small amount of fear. With an effort, he eventually shook himself and tore his gaze from the tiny rocks. He took his cloak from the shelf and frowned to find it still damp.

"I have to go," he said, putting the clammy cloth around his shoulders. "Unless you can think of anything else to tell me."

There is nothing.

Liam shrugged irritably. "Fine. If you think of anything . . ."

I will let you know.

"Are you sure there are no spells that would help? Or maybe one of those things in the other room? The one with the cases?"

No. The thought was firm, and brooked no questioning.

Pursing his lips in consternation, Liam left.

From Coeccias's and Fanuilh's description of his manner, Liam had expected Ancus Marcius to be a big man, but the figure on the docks was small, pretentious only in dress.

Ignoring the light drizzle into which the morning's downpour had resolved itself, the merchant stood among a group of stevedores, shouting instructions about the unloading of a battered carrack. Though the rest of the waterfront was empty, Marcius's men bustled along as though there were nothing unusual, stepping briskly in accordance with the merchant's commands. They brought bales and chests down the gangplank and loaded them onto a line of carts drawn by mules waiting miserably in the icy drops. The harbor was quiet except for the slap of bare feet on gangplank and wet stones, and the water was a still and metallic gray, pocked with rain and curtained by a bank of mist rising off the sea. The Teeth hovered across the harbor, vague black shadows.

Marcius was short and slight of build, and his clean-shaven face bore what seemed a perpetually sour look. His clothes, though sodden, were magnificent: doublet and hose of silk dyed a delicate blue, with a heavy cloak of deep purple and low boots of shining leather. Liam thought of his own boots, and the water that was even now soaking his feet through the holes left by the dragon's teeth.

For a few minutes, Liam watched the merchant and the activities he was directing. Then, keying himself up, he crossed the slick stone of the waterfront to where Marcius stood.

"Speed, you knaves, speed! Do you think this wetting likes me?" the merchant shouted. Liam stopped a few respectful paces away and coughed politely. Marcius did not turn, but the man by his side did, showing an ugly face made worse by a long, jagged scar running across his face from ear to ear, bisecting his mouth. A bodyguard, Liam knew, and he made himself quail slightly beneath the man's contemptuous look.

"What do you want?" the guard lazily sneered, dropping a hand to the small cudgel at his belt. Drops of rain gathered on the puckered edges of his scar.

"A word or two with your master, if I might."

"Your name?"

"Liam Rhenford, a scholar."

"Well, Liam-Rhenford-a-scholar, Master Marcius has no time for you now. Be off." The guard scowled and jerked his head to indicate the quickest path of retreat.

Liam cringed and begged. "Please, sir, I've something he might find valuable, if only he'd give me a moment. It's very valuable, on my life."

"Heard you what I—"

Marcius, who, though only a few feet away, had not given any hint that he was paying attention, suddenly spoke without turning to them. "If the fool took a wetting to speak, it's only be right to hear his piece. Speak, scholar."

The guard scowled again and moved aside, letting Liam move up to the merchant's side.

"Many thanks, Master Marcius, many thanks. You'll not regret it, I swear." The fawning sounded ridiculous to Liam, but Marcius seemed to expect it, and he kept it up. "I've come off a bad time, Master, and my situation is not very sound. I'm in a bad way, and I need money somewhat desperately."

"This smacks of a loan, scholar. Where's the value for me?" Marcius still did not look at him, but spoke impatiently. He was much shorter than Liam, who hunched himself abjectly and allowed his hands to grab each other in supplication.

"I'm coming to that, Master, soon enough. I only want to show you my position. My former master, you see, has died," he lowered his voice confidingly, "has been *murdered,* you see, and I am left to a hard lot."

"Murdered?" the merchant said in a normal tone, and Liam bobbed anxiously, imploring quiet.

"Yes, Master, and I'm afraid I may be marked."

"Marked, you say? Who was your master?" He still did not look at Liam, but his voice registered interest.

"Tarquin Tanaquil, Master, but—"

"Tanaquil, you say?" The merchant gave him a hard glance. "The wizard?"

"Yes, Master."

"I did not know Tanaquil had any apprentices." Marcius's eyes narrowed with interest. "How far were you in the art?"

"I was not his apprentice," Liam said regretfully, "just a scholar he employed for certain correspondences."

Marcius lost his interest with a grunt, turning back to the ship and irritably flicking an errant lock of his stylishly long black hair back into its damp place.

"If y'are no mage, what use can you be to me?"

The guard took this as a hint, and laid a rough hand on Liam's sleeve, but he spoke up quickly.

"Before I came into the wizard's employment, Master, I traveled a great deal. I have maps to many places."

Marcius turned slowly to him, his curiosity back, and nodded imperceptibly at the guard, who removed his hand reluctantly.

"Your name again, scholar?"

"Liam Rhenford, Master."

"Rhenford," the merchant mused, looking up at Liam with as cold an appraisal as he might have given a shipment of goods. Perhaps colder, Liam thought, wiping cold streamers of rain off his narrow nose; he would at least know how much the goods were worth.

"Rhenford," Marcius repeated. "I've heard of a scholar who sold Freihett Necquer a set of charts. Could you be that scholar?"

"I am, Master," Liam said nervously.

"Those charts brought him a bulky fortune this season. And now you say you worked for Tanaquil?"

"I was in his employ, sir, yes."

"Have you the charts here?"

"Yes, sir," Liam responded eagerly, and began digging into the satchel at his side.

"No, no, no," Marcius said with evident disgust, "don't be more of a fool than the gods made you, Rhenford. I don't want to peer at maps in the rain. Bring them to my offices, early tomorrow. You know where those are?"

"Certainly, certainly. I'll be—"

"Early, Rhenford. And bring your mappery."

The merchant walked away without another word, ignoring the stevedores, who continued their work. The guard trailed along behind, offering Liam a sarcastic half-bow and a menacing grin, horribly distorted by his scar.

As soon as the merchant was out of earshot, Liam muttered an insult. *I'm no dog, to cringe and cower,* he thought, and let his posture settle back to normal with a relieved grin. It was more fun to be a mysterious, self-important hierarch than a cowardly clerk, he decided, and set off in the opposite direction.

• • •

Liam climbed the steep streets that led up from the harbor to his lodgings. Dirty rainwater rushed whispering through the gutters down to the harbor. He stopped when he was high up in the city and looked back.

The work that still went on around Marcius's carrack might have been performed by ants, and the other ships riding at anchor might have been those of Tarquin's model, the forest of naked masts and spars mere twigs in the distance. He felt as though he might reach out and brush the leaden waters of the roadstead, or pick up one of the ships with his hand. Or, if the mist had not hidden them, take hold of the Teeth and tear them out of the sea, roots and all.

Had Tarquin felt like that when he cast his spell? Like a god on a high mountain with a storm raging unnoticed around him, reaching down a massive hand and rearranging the world to suit his whims? It was a strange idea, and Liam shook rain out of his face and cursed his soaking feet before resuming the climb to his garret.

He smiled gently at the kitchen drudge and greeted her politely. She shuddered and hid her face, remembering his wolfish grin. Shrugging ruefully, he beat a retreat up to his room.

There was nothing more for him to do before his afternoon visit to Lady Necquer. When he had changed into his third and last set of clothing, and spread that morning's wet ones out to dry, he realized he had time to kill, and sat himself with a sigh at his table by the window. His papers were still there, and some of his books. So many blank pages.

When Liam had arrived in Southwark, he had fully intended on filling those pages; had, in fact, bought particularly expensive paper for the task. Hundreds of sheets of it, and in four months he had covered exactly three of them with writing. All he had to show for his intentions were three pages of notes and outlines and, of course, the maps of his travels. He wondered where the time had gone.

Wandering the town, exploring it without noticing the sights. Daydreaming at his window, staring out at the harbor and ignoring the view. Swimming off Tarquin's breakwater.

He shuffled the pages of notes around, debating trying to do something with them. His list of suspects no longer lay beneath them, stowed safely now in Coeccias's pouch, but he remembered it clearly. He now had faces to attach to some of the names.

The druggist, the merchant, the cooing woman, the minstrel. He thought he might as well add the barmaid, Donoé. The last three he had not seen, and he wondered how he could ever possibly find them on Fanuilh's sketchy remembrance. He was getting places, he knew, but if he had to continue running around the town in punctured boots and a perpetually sodden cloak, he thought he might confess to the murder himself.

With an explosive sigh he pushed the papers away and went to his trunk. Beneath a layer of small clothes and trinkets lay a bulging sack made of sailcloth. He snatched it out and upended it on his blanket.

Silver and gold coins clinked together with the happy sound of large amounts, and two or three gems winked dully, their vibrant color only a memory in the shadowy garret.

A fortune by Southwark standards, where a single silver coin was his monthly rent. He had over fifty, and a like number of gold coins, and he knew it little mattered that the faces and inscriptions on them were of kings and in languages that had never been heard of in Southwark. Gold was gold and silver was silver, no matter whose head was on the coin.

He picked out two of the gold coins, and hesitated before picking out a third and dropping them into his belt pouch. When the sack was back in his trunk with its contents replaced, he left his room and walked briskly out into the street.

Liam bought himself a new, heavier cloak that was supposed to be weatherproof, and ordered several suits of warm winter clothes from a tailor in the rich quarter. The man bustled and fawned nicely when shown the gold coin, and promised "eminently satisfactory results" in a few days. Liam left feeling slightly better, and warmer already in his new cloak.

A cobbler repaired his holed boot while he waited, and took an order for two new pairs with gape-mouthed pleasure. A leatherworker yielded up a beautifully tooled belt and a proper scholar's writing case, made to hang from the belt, with pockets for pens, paper and ink, blotter and seals.

His maps rattling around in the roomy writing case, snug in his waterproof cloak and dry toes wriggling in his fixed boots, Liam felt good despite the rain and the blank pages in his room. He bought himself a large lunch in the inn Coeccias had led him to the night before and enjoyed it thoroughly.

When he was done, tolling bells announced that it was time to visit Lady Necquer, and he set out for the merchant's home. The rain still poured steadily down, now gurgling in the overflowing gutters, and the afternoon sky might well have been night, but he whistled, and felt well.

"Master Rhenford," Lares said with unaffected pleasure when he opened the door. "The lady was not sure you'd come."

Liam merely smiled and allowed himself to be let in and led up to the second floor.

Lady Necquer looked pale, but delighted to see him, as though he were a reprieve.

"Sir Liam! I doubted your coming!"

"I could not stay away, madam. It is a great pleasure to enjoy your company." He spoke blandly, the statement only a pleasantry, but her breath caught.

"I . . ." She faltered, and a silence yawned in which Liam fidgeted uncomfortably. He wondered what he could possibly have said, and thought of the handsome, angry young man at the door the other day.

Lady Necquer smiled weakly and fixed her eyes on her lap, spots of color reddening her pale cheeks.

"I beg your pardon if I am skittish, Sir Liam. I thought you were . . . an echo, perhaps." She forced herself to look at him and the smile grew more assured as she gestured him to a seat across from her. "Please, sit, and tell me more of your travels."

He took the offered seat, peering curiously at her. "I'm sorry to be a mere echo, madam. I don't think your husband asked me to come to bore you with repetition."

Something in his tone, or perhaps his mention of her husband, relaxed her, and the unnatural blush faded. Glad of it, he went on.

"If there is anything you need to discuss, madam, or if you'd rather be alone, I would gladly . . ." He let the sentence hang, expressing his readiness to help with open hands. She shifted in her seat, allowing the smile to drop. The look of unhappiness that wrinkled her forehead and pursed her lips seemed very pretty to Liam, and the openness with which she shared her feeling made him feel somewhat special. It had been a long while since anyone had taken him into their confidence.

"Your tendered help is as salve to my troubles, Sir Liam, and I thank you. Yet I am beset by troubles that I may not share with you, much as I'd like. For the time, it is good of you to keep me company. Now," she said briskly, trying to banish the tension with a bright smile, "we'll only have light talk. Tell me such things as you remember made you laugh."

Having set the subject, she sat back and waited, her brow clear and her eyes bright. His mind was blank for a few moments. Nothing particularly funny had ever happened to him, and he found that all he could remember were the faces of other women, one and all in attitudes of sorrow or depression.

Liam did not tell her this, but his look of consternation led her to prompt him a little, and presently he recalled a puppet show he had seen in a caravanserai in a desert country.

Before long, he had a string of stories to tell, half-remembered snatches of the highly stylized comedies popular in his student days in Torquay, the antics of acrobats and clowns from the courts of distant kingdoms, folk tales told by wizened men in a hundred markets, and songs heard in taverns around the world. He even brought out an entire verse of "The Lipless Flutist," a fairly clean one, and half-sang, half-recited it for her in an embarrassed way.

She laughed and clapped her hands when he was done, and he was struck anew by her youth and prettiness. He wondered again what could have upset her so, and thought angrily of the youth. Her unhappiness was obviously connected with him, and Liam cursed the man mildly.

A comfortable silence followed her good-natured laughter at his poor rendition of "The Lipless Flutist," and he only spoke after a while because the question popped into his head.

"When did you say your husband was returning?"

"Your pardon?" she asked, starting from some daydream. "Oh, he returns tomorrow, I hope. He is so often away."

He regretted the question, but she went on, sighing sadly. "So often I sit here alone, and feel his absence strongly. I wonder if he is wracked at sea, or taken by pirates, or bandits—they say there are bandits much abroad this year. On land, bandits wait for him; at sea, giant beasts, storms, the Teeth . . . oh, the Teeth are far the worst."

Shuddering, she dropped her eyes to her lap again, and Liam berated himself for upsetting her, though her returning to the Teeth interested him. So many lives in Southwark seemed to revolve around the grim rocks—Lady Necquer with her morbid fear, Marcius with his sunken ship, Tarquin with his spells. The only teeth in Southwark that had harmed him were Fanuilh's, and a cobbler had fixed that. He almost chuckled, but did not.

"I'm sure he'll return in perfect health."

She drew a deep breath and caught a smile. "Oh, I'm even surer than you, Sir Liam. But you'll grant me the right to worry, I hope." He offered her a small bow from his seat, and she continued lightly. "Now tell me, have you ever left anyone to wait for you? I'd wager you must have left weeping women in a hundred ports."

"No," he said seriously, "I don't think so. I am very easy not to miss."

She scoffed. "I can scarcely credit it, Sir Liam. Surely there is some love who drew you here to Southwark, a beauty who was planted on the docks, awaiting your return with weepy eyes and a kerchief soaked with tears."

Lady Necquer was not flirting, he decided, but teasing. He shook his head, and noticed how dark it was outside. Raindrops still trailed gold and silver on the panes. He would have to go soon.

"Then if it was no woman, what drew you, who've seen the world over, to so remote a corner of it as Southwark?"

"I had been shipwrecked for some months, madam," he lied, "on a desert isle far east and south of the Freeports. The ship that rescued me was bound here, and I was in no position to argue about its destination." He had indeed been stranded on an uncharted island, but the conditions were somewhat different from a shipwreck, and the things he had seen there would have unduly upset her, he was sure.

Even the mention of a shipwreck dampened her spirits more than he would have wished.

"I had no idea, Sir Liam. It must have been horrible." It was clear from her veiled eyes that she was imagining her own husband in such a position, and he frowned.

"Oh, by no means. Very comfortable, really. It did not rain half so much as it does in Southwark, and was warm as summer the year round. I left it with some regret. Of course, I had none such as you to return to, madam. If I had, I probably would have swum the ocean to return."

Lady Necquer smiled gratefully, and he rose reluctantly.

"I'm afraid I must leave you now."

She rose as well, and though she protested that he must not leave, she led the way to the stairs. There she made him promise to return the next day.

"My husband is due to return in the evening. I am sure it'd like him if you waited with me, and dined with us."

She seemed to mean it, and he assented with pleasure.

At the bottom of the stairs, Lares waited with his cloak. With a smile he took it, ignoring the man's attempt to put it on his shoulders, knowing either he would have to stoop or the short old man stretch to accomplish the feat.

"Tell me, goodman," he asked while he tied on the cloak, "who was the young fellow that was here yesterday?"

The servant grimaced with disgust, and probably would have spat if he were outdoors.

"That one! A common player, from the Golden Orb Company, rabble all! Lons is his name, sir, and he plagues the lady unmercifully, all because she let him sing a few songs for her once. Most disgraceful, he is.

He fits the old list, good sir, you know: 'vagrants and sturdy beggars, rogues, knaves and common players.' A very rogue, he is!"

Liam smiled at Lares's vehemence, but the old man did not notice. "He was lurking about earlier, sir, but I happened to mention in a carrying tone that you were visiting the lady, and he skulked off in high dudgeon, I can tell you! A right rogue, that one!"

His cloak secured to his satisfaction, Liam shook his head in proper disapproval at Lons's knavery, and left before he laughed.

Once again he felt good in the rain, daring it to penetrate his snug cloak and patched boots. Even though it was a fair walk from the Point to his garret, he arrived with little more than a few drops on his face and hands, and decided that he had never spent money so well.

Mistress Dorcas was waiting for him in the kitchen, a folded piece of paper clutched in her hands. She handed it to him, apprehension clear on her face.

"It bears the Aedile's mark," she whispered fearfully, still mispronouncing the word.

Annoyed, he tore the paper open and read the note quickly. Coeccias's unruly scrawl invited him to the same tavern they had visited the evening before, the White Grape, and suggested a time.

"Is all well, Master Liam?"

"No," he said grimly, "I'm to be executed tomorrow at dawn." He went up the stairs without another word.

The hour Coeccias had set was only a little while off, but he took the time to put away his writing case, taking out the maps and placing them on the table. When he went downstairs, his landlady was still holding a hand to her chest, breathing heavily.

"Y'ought not to say suchlike," she scolded. "I thought my heart would leap from its seat, to hear of such, even in jest."

"Well, why else would the Aedile summon me if not to execute me?"

"Faith, I know not, Master Liam, but y'are very wicked." He was almost at the door when she regained enough composure to be nosy. "What was his discourse?"

"He wanted to dine with me," Liam called over his shoulder as he left. "The condemned's last meal, he called it."

He shut the door on her leaping heart.

Coeccias was not at the tavern yet, but the White Grape was almost full and Liam was glad to catch the last open table. The girl who brought him the wine he asked for looked at him strangely, recognizing him from the night before and that afternoon.

Sipping the vinegary wine, he rested his elbows on the table and surveyed the customers of the inn. They were quiet, respectable types, not so rich as to belong in the quarter further up the hill, but not given to the noisy dens lower down by the harbor. They sat close to their tables and talked in low voices that suggested sobriety and mildly serious talk, not secrecy. He thought he and Coeccias had probably looked that way the night before and would look that way tonight, and wondered how many more nights they would look so before they had found Tarquin's murderer.

Or before we give up, he mused over a particularly sour mouthful. *If the dragon will let us give up.*

He did not want to think about Tarquin, or Fanuilh, and cast back to his afternoon with Lady Necquer. She was a pretty, refined young innocent, such as he had forgotten existed. Years at sea and in foreign lands had left him unused to dealing with Taralon's well-bred, though he had once been counted high in their ranks. Her problems interested him. They were different from his own, problems of the living, not the dead, and he turned to considering them.

This Lons, a mere player, hounded her, undoubtedly out of passion, because of her pale beauty. A part of him did not blame the man, but mostly he disliked Lons's arrogant voice and handsome face, as well as his rude presumption.

The man was an actor, traditionally one of the lower classes. The list Lares had quoted was from an old law, naming players and the others as undesirables who might be subjected to various fines and punishments just for being what they were. The law no longer stood, but the old prejudices still survived. Though Liam did not share them, he understood them, and knew it must be painful for Lady Necquer to be plagued by one she must consider beneath her.

She must unwittingly have led the boy on, asking him to sing for her and probably showing the same warm approval as she had shown his stories.

Of course, she doesn't think I'm likely to pester her like Lons, because I've such an innocent face.

Liam grinned ruefully into his cup, and looked up to see Coeccias.

"Now what brings such sunny summer to your visage, Rhenford? Have you flushed our quarry?"

Shaking his head, Liam gestured to Aedile to a seat, which he took with a wry smile.

"No, just enjoying a joke at my own expense."

"Then the day has not gone well for you?"

"No worse than yesterday."

Coeccias eyed him curiously and gave his order to the serving girl.

"You should not drink the wine here, Rhenford. The best they have in the house graces the wooden board over the door."

"I'd noticed."

The girl brought Coeccias a mug of beer, and he sipped from it before speaking in a low tone that seemed to fit the quiet tavern.

"Had you no luck with Marcius?"

"I have an appointment with him tomorrow. Very early. I told him I had served Tarquin, and that seemed to give him a start. He asked me if I knew any magic, and was very disappointed when I did not. I'll try to sound him out a little more tomorrow."

"You think he killed the wizard for a failure of magic?" The theory clearly attracted the Aedile; he leaned even further forward with an almost laughably serious expression.

"Well, it was one of his ships that crashed on the Teeth. If he'd had some contract with Tarquin, then it would seem Tarquin did not live up to it." Coeccias leaned back with a small smile of satisfaction, and Liam qualified his statement. "I would not be in too much of a hurry to arrest him, though. He didn't exactly go white and confess when I mentioned Tarquin's name."

"Shrewd ones never do, Rhenford. But I'll grant your doubts. And as it seems you've done your work, I'll report on mine."

He had gone to see Viyescu early in the day, and hinted about a girl who was known to have been an acquaintance of the druggist, and who had bragged in her cups of knowing a certain powerful wizard.

"Though by straight and true I'm not supposed to do such, it was wondrous effective, a great spur to him. There were no bloody confessions, true, but just a few hours later he barred his shop early and found his way to a suite of rented rooms in the lower quarters. A man of mine followed him, and when our druggist left, sore disappointed, he made some discreet inquiries."

The Aedile paused, it seemed, for effect, and leaned back, waiting smugly to be asked the outcome of the questions. Liam waited too, and looked around the common room with an ostentatiously apathetic air. For a few moments, both were silent, before Coeccias's desire to tell overcame his desire to make Liam ask, and he resumed his report with a sour grunt.

The rooms, the owner of the house reported, were rented by a young lady who always arrived masked and cloaked, though the rent was brought to him by a common messenger. The lady was only there a few nights out of every month, but had, on occasion in the past, received a robed and hooded visitor, presumably male. Neither had been there recently, but the rent was still brought by the messenger every month.

"So, what make you of that?"

"Viyescu keeps a mistress."

"No," the burly officer said scornfully. "A hooded, robed visitor? Rented rooms and great secrecy? It's clear we've found the wizard's bawd!"

Liam frowned and shook his head. "Wizards aren't the only people who wear robes, Master Aedile. Priests do too, and some officials, and I've known rich men who affect them to seem sophisticated. What's more, men who value their appearance of virtue have been known to wear disguises when indulging their vices. You think Viyescu went there to warn the girl about your investigation. What I think is far more likely is that Viyescu went there so that his mistress could soothe his fears and worries. You must have startled him a great deal, and he felt the need of her comfort."

It was Coeccias's turn to frown, and Liam pressed on.

"Next month's rent will be due in two days. I'll wager if we wait until then, we'll find that the messenger brings it, which'll prove the girl wasn't Tarquin's. And I'll wager even more that if we trace the messenger, we'll find he gets his money from a man in a neat little apothecary's shop."

The Aedile scowled unhappily, recognizing the validity of Liam's argument.

"Still, it bears searching out," he said stubbornly.

Liam agreed, but only on the principle that they should make the best of what they had.

"There's something else I'd like you to check on. I remember a girl Tarquin once mentioned, a barmaid named Donoé. I think it might be worth our while to talk with her. Can you have your men find her?"

"Seek out a single barmaid? In all of Southwark? Better ask us to find a pearl dropped in the harbor! Have you any idea how many taverns and inns and bars there are in this city?"

"Not that many that Tarquin would have gone into, let alone struck up an acquaintance with a barmaid there. I bet you won't even have to look beyond the rich quarter, and there are none too many bars there."

"All right, all right, I'll send someone round to con for this barmaid. Donoé is her name?" At Liam's nod, the Aedile repeated it with a *humph* of displeasure. "Barmaids! I offer you th' assassin complete in this rented girl and her monthly rooms, and you throw it away on barmaids!"

"Not just on barmaids. There's still Marcius, and the minstrel we haven't met yet." An idea struck him, left over from his thoughts of Lady Necquer. "Say, Master Aedile, what's the Golden Orb Company?"

Confused by the sudden change of subject, Coeccias replied slowly, trying as he spoke to figure out the connection.

"A troupe of players here; they put on a series of entertainments and performances the year round. They've two theaters in the city, a summer amphitheater and a covered one for winter. Often in the winter I close them out, and send them packing to the heath, to perform for the villagers and keep the pest at bay. A close theater in the winter breeds the plague like a she-rabbit coneys." Enlightenment suddenly dawned around the neatly trimmed beard. "You recall the knife, if I guess aright, and think to find your minstrel there! Shrewd, very shrewd, Rhenford! I hadn't thought to comb that rabble for him!"

"No, no, that's not what I meant," Liam said hurriedly. "That's not what I was thinking at all." He began to explain his afternoon with Lady Necquer, but thought better of it. "I just heard the name earlier from my landlady, and I hadn't heard of it before, I thought I might go see a performance."

"Truth, a passing excellent idea! I'll wait upon you, and if you espy the minstrel, that'll be one more way for us to look."

Coeccias smiled happily and dug hungrily into the food the girl put before him. Liam felt a flutter of discomfort. He could not identify the minstrel, because he had not seen him; Fanuilh had, but he couldn't explain that to the Aedile. They might sit through a hundred performances with the minstrel in every one, and Liam would never know it.

He ate his own meal with much less interest.

■ 7 ■

THE COVERED THEATER the Golden Orb Company used in the winter was in the Auric's Park section of the artisans' quarter, far from both the sea and Liam's lodgings. Half-timbered, it towered windowless over the surrounding homes and shops, cut off from them by narrow lanes on two sides and wide streets on the others. High above the street a giant gilt ball hung from a projecting hook, rain sparkling on its surface; the places where the golden paint was peeling were barely visible in the light leaking from the entrance. With only its bottom hemisphere visible, it looked impressive, like a strange moon.

A sizable crowd stood outside the theater's three sets of wide wooden doors, waiting to get in, and more jammed into the small lobby. They were mostly rough-looking men and women, apprentices and seamen, clerks and workers, inured to the rain and cold. With no obvious resentment they allowed the occasional better-dressed patron to move through their ranks directly to the entrance, shoving aside to create a path for the rich or well-to-do that closed up immediately behind them. Liam and Coeccias were allowed to pass this way, like ships cutting a wake through the sea, and came up to a man seated behind a barrel, wearing a tunic of motley, the squares of brightly colored cloth marking him out from the plainer clothes of the audience.

"Good even, Master Aedile. Come to close us out?" His eyes sparkled and his lips twisted with a combination of humor and good-natured malice.

"No, Master Player, only to watch the process. If the play likes me not, belike then I'll send you packing to the countryside." Coeccias smiled as well, and gestured to Liam. "He'll quit us, for a box."

Liam frowned and dug out a silver coin. The Aedile had seen the coin he used to pay for his dinner and, deciding that Liam had done the least work of the day, told him off to pay for the evening. Liam dropped the coin on the barrelhead; the player in motley bowed dramatically over the money and waved them inside.

The small lobby was even more closely packed than the street, but the crowd parted for them again. Before him, between heavy, crudely squared wooden pillars, Liam could see the stage, raised above the heads of the people jostling in the pit, but Coeccias led him away to the left and up a narrow flight of steps. The second floor of the theater was a gallery, segmented into booths by the heavy pillars continuing up from below. The Aedile took one of these booths, and motioned Liam to sit beside him on the cushioned bench.

Inside, the Golden Orb's theater was hexagonal, with the raised stage a disproportionately large edge. Two stories of boothed galleries made up the other edges, while the floor was open and seatless. The poor massed there, a sea of heads talking noisily and gaping impatiently at the stage, while the rich who had cut their way through the crowd filled the galleries; each booth framed expensive clothes and well-fed faces.

Looking around at the others in the galleries, Liam whispered to Coeccias, "I don't think we're appropriately dressed for the boxes." He indicated the Aedile's crumb-strewn shirt of unrelieved black and his own simple cloak and tunic. Coeccias nodded absently, his own attention fixed on the empty stage.

"I suppose not. But those're guildmasters and merchants and high tradesmen in the other boxes, who needs must impress with their wealth their apprentices and drudges below. Y'have neither employees nor servants in the pit, and I hope none of my Guard is down there, or I'll have their heads. And what's more," he added after a thoughtful pause, "they have to impress each other. I think neither you nor I need to do that."

Liam digested this, inspecting the theater with idle curiosity. The huge wrought-iron chandelier reminded him of the great theaters in Torquay, as did the layout of the stage, with its curtained recess and small balcony. He remembered the few plays he had gone to see when he was a student in the capital, and was surprised that Southwark boasted a theater so much like Torquay's. Of course, the roof was thatched, not stone-arched and groined, and the proscenium, balcony and recess were made of plain, undecorated wood, not elaborately carved marble; still, the basic design was the same. And what the Golden Orb lacked in sumptuous decoration and formal sophistication, it made up for in excitement.

The theaters in Torquay had seemed strangely joyless, dark rituals of culture and sobriety; in Southwark, the crowd buzzed and chattered eagerly, excited and impatient for the show to begin. He wondered what the play would be like. He had not bothered to ask Coeccias about it, and as he was about to speak, a sudden wind gusted throughout the theater, cold and foreboding. It rushed outward from the stage with a roar, over the heads of the groundlings, and circled the galleries, rising upward, almost visible in its loud progress, before plunging at the chandelier. Hundreds of candles flickered and guttered wildly, dispersing monstrous shadows before they died. Then the wind died as well, leaving the audience suddenly silent in complete darkness.

"Watch," the Aedile whispered, lightly touching Liam's arm. Liam jumped at the touch in the dark, and peered intently towards where he thought the stage was.

A clean, white light like that in Tarquin's house slowly grew over the stage, evenly illuminating the acting space and limning the expectant faces of the audience, drawing just their features out of deep black shadow. A rowdy groundling called out, "Knave Fitch!" and the cry was taken up with happy applause and whistles from the pit as the growing light revealed a fat man in motley poised in an attitude of thoughtfulness.

With overly dramatic gestures he announced himself to be the Knave Fitch the groundlings had called for, and their loud shouts of approval clearly showed that he was a great favorite. He gave a prologue describing the action of the play, garbling the lines for comic effect, and the groundlings responded with hoots of laughter. Coeccias laughed as well, and Liam smiled at the clown's posturing.

When he was done with the prologue, Fitch bowed grandly, tripping on his cloak in the process, and exited to general applause.

The sourceless light dimmed and then swelled to the quality of a summer day, and a troop of women dressed as princesses skipped on stage, primly gathering flowers in an imaginary forest. After a few lines of introduction, the lead princess called for her ladies to provide music, and a tune suddenly invaded the theater. The lead princess, dressed in a diaphanous dress cut startlingly short, stepped forward and began a graceful dance in time with the music. The lesser princesses ranged themselves around the stage, watching the princess dance respectfully.

She looks like Lons, Liam thought with some amazement. She did indeed resemble the actor Liam had come to see. If anything, she was more attractive than the young man, with shining golden hair hanging below her shoulders and strong, bold features that hinted at sultriness despite her regal attire and almost prurient dance.

Even as he thought how pretty she was, however, the music shifted slightly, the beat faster and the tune wilder. One by one the lesser princesses rose and began dancing as well, keeping behind the leader. She, in turn, changed the style of her dancing, gradually losing all pretense of prudishness. The pure, pastoral aura that had hung around the scene disappeared, and she danced wantonly, the high cut of her dress revealing tantalizing stretches of well-formed thigh. Her dress clung strategically to her breasts and certain other points of interest, blousing over her stomach to pull in around her thighs. She danced with wild abandon across the stage, following the music as it swelled, rising through a series of crescendos to a peak that was clearly meant to be sexual.

Liam watched, fascinated and, he had to admit, aroused by the intentional sexuality of the dance, and blew out an astonished breath when it was over, and the lead princess dropped to her knees, flushed and panting, her hair disarrayed like a golden nimbus around her head.

"Small wonder the guildmasters say the theater is a degenerate influence on their apprentices," Coeccias whispered, as impressed as Liam.

He was going to respond when a figure entered who caught his attention. He hissed in a breath at the sight of Lons striding over to the breathless dancer, and leaned towards the rim of the booth.

"What?" Coeccias asked immediately. "Is that our minstrel?"

Liam waved the question away, focusing his attention on the actor, who walked across the stage to the breathless dancer and helped her to her feet. At first he thought they were supposed to be lovers, but as the scene progressed it became clear that they were brother and sister. When it was over, and the sourceless light dimmed again, he settled back on the bench and frowned. Coeccias poked him impatiently.

"Truth, Rhenford, speak! Is that our minstrel or no?"

"I'm not sure. I'll have to see him again."

The Aedile snorted impatiently, and settled back to watch.

The princess's face and form swam before Liam's eyes, and he compared her to Lons, surer now that he had seen them together that they were related. He thought with displeasure of Lons's haughty bearing and his arrogant handsomeness. Just the sort to plague the poor lady, he thought, a self-involved rake, presumptuous and crude. Liam found he disliked the actor intensely. The sister-princess, on the other hand, drew him powerfully as, he realized, she probably drew every other man in the audience. She was stunning, attractive in an inviting way that was completely foreign to the beauty of Lady Necquer. He compared the two women, and pictured Lons between them.

Scene followed scene, and the play progressed. It concerned the various misadventures of the prince and princess, with the ridiculous antics of Knave Fitch as their court jester thrown in for comic relief. The princess only danced once more, but with the same breath-stopping effect. The sourceless light dimmed often, rising again to reveal different scenes. Several magical creatures made appearances, startlingly real on the stage. Liam thought the makeup and scenery remarkably well done, until a dragon entered to menace the prince and princess, and breathed a gout of fire across the audience.

Coeccias leaned over. "There's a wonderful illusion-maker in those wings," he said, as if he were letting Liam in on a secret with which he was familiar.

Liam smiled faintly, because he had seen the big Aedile flinch at the dragon's appearance. The mention of the illusion-maker who was projecting the marvels that crossed the stage, however, brought Tarquin into his mind. He should have been looking for his murderer, not enjoying himself at provincial theatricals.

Still, Lons's well-shaped and already well-hated face kept revolving through his thoughts, along with that of his enchanting play-sister. She spoke little, but her movements held his attention, and he watched her more than any of the other actors, including Lons, who, as the hero, had by far the most lines.

There was no intermission, and the play lasted for over two and a half hours. The audience, however, never lost interest. Between Lons's heroics, Fitch's obscene jokes, the illusion-maker's phantasms and the princess's sultry beauty, it was a tremendous spectacle, and the eventual denouement was breathlessly awaited.

Lons and his sister confronted the evil duke who had hounded them throughout the play, beating off his minions until they faced the villain himself. There was a long, tense display of swordplay between Lons and the duke, filled with flourishes and narrow escapes, and the crowd gasped and shouted over each pass.

Duel or no, Liam could not take his eyes off the princess, who spent the scene pressed against the proscenium arch, watching in palpable anxiety. Her sheer dress disarrayed to display just enough, her breast heaving with intense fear, she was perfect—or so she seemed to Liam. He believed her completely, and was only vaguely aware of it when Lons finally triumphed. Blood spurted high, more magical illusion, and the hero let fly with a well-chosen epithet on his evil foe, but Liam was watching the princess.

The crowd shouted and cheered madly, but the victory was only conveyed to Liam by the princess, by the delicate way she turned her head at the death blow, and the noble way she forced herself to look on the bloody corpse.

How often he had seen people look on the dead like that! While the rest of the audience noisily celebrated the conclusion, he sat enthralled and deeply impressed. She was magnificent; looks and figure aside, she was amazing, an artist such as he had never suspected the theater to hold. He doubted Lons had carried off his reaction to the death nearly as well.

She was—

Vision died, the theater went black, and for a split moment he thought the illusion-maker must have failed. Then he knew he was blind. His hands bunched convulsively, fiercely gripping the cloth of his breeches. He strangled a scream, and groaned instead.

His breath came in quick hisses, and he knotted the cloth above his knees over and over again.

Calm.

The thought crashed down on his fear, but the terror of blindness rose up again and he groaned a second time . . .

The hero is the minstrel.

. . . and then a third, as the blackness swirled and resolved itself into the stage and the theater, and Coeccias's face. The beard and the reflected illusion-maker's light hid his concerned look in a diabolical mask, but Liam barely noticed.

"Truth, Rhenford! What's amiss?"

"The minstrel," he grated, lurching to his feet in the haze of anger that washed away his paralyzing fear. "The hero is the minstrel," he finished, and bolted out of the box towards the stairs, brushing off Coeccias's hand.

In the street he marched grimly towards his quarter, oblivious to the rain.

"Bastard," he muttered. "Damned bastard in my head." He ground the curses and worse between his teeth, bringing them in and flinging them silently at the dragon.

Blinded me! The bastard!

Fanuilh did not respond, but Coeccias's heavy hand on his shoulder brought him to a stop.

"Truth," he said, honestly confused, "I knew not whether to stay or follow. What's possessed you, Rhenford? Is that minstrel Tarquin's assassin?"

"No, no, I don't know," Liam scowled fiercely, unable to explain. "I'm not sure."

"Is he or no? What know you?" The Aedile's voice sank into suspicion, and he cocked his head to look at Liam from the side. "What aren't you telling?"

"Nothing," Liam hastened to assure him, trying to hold onto his anger. "There's just something I've remembered. I don't know whether it'll mean anything. You'd think it ridiculous." Coeccias started in heatedly, but Liam cut him off. "I've just got to check on it. Look, have one of your constables find out where Lons lodges, and meet me tomorrow at the White Grape at noon. We'll go over and see him."

He winced when he realized he had said Lons's name, because there was no way he could have known it. Coeccias must have caught it too, but Liam did not give him a chance. He swung around and ran off into the rain.

"Rhenford!" He heard the Aedile bellow behind him, and then: "Damn!" But the curse sounded resigned, and he kept on, trotting through the rain.

In the hopes of dredging up his dying anger, he deliberately recalled the sight, or lack thereof, of complete blindness. He had been hung over and ill the first time, in no condition to appreciate the experience. It had been different in the theater. The complete absence of visual input— even the normal phosphorescence of closed eyes—had been terrifying, and the damned beast had inflicted it on him without a moment's hesitation.

By the time Liam reached the stable, the bells were tolling midnight, and he had given up on rebuilding his anger to its first flaming height. Still, he pounded on the door until the night lad woke and grudgingly let him in. A silver coin wiped the sleep from the boy's eyes, and by saddling Diamond himself Liam improved the lad's mood tenfold.

Driven by the last of his ire, he made the cold, wet trip out to Tarquin's, and shuddered as he led his mount down the narrow path in the cliff, imagining the belltowers in Southwark ringing one o'clock.

The sea was an indistinct mass to east and west, though a pier of golden light stretched out from the wizard's home, spilling warm and golden from the glass front over the sand and across the water in a spike to the horizon. The beach was firmer underfoot than usual, condensed by rain. He felt a stab of anger rise up as he stamped into the quiet, well-lit house, tearing off his clinging, damp cloak.

Fanuilh lay in the same position on the table in the workroom, calmly gazing at the door through which Liam stalked.

I will not do it again without asking, the little dragon thought at him, and though the block in his head was as empty of tone as ever, he imagined how it would sound if spoken. As if they had discussed the matter, calmly, and reasonably come to the conclusion the dragon thought to him.

Liam was not pleased by his imagination, and his anger briefly and pleasantly flared.

"You're damned right you won't do it again, you bastard! Because if you do, I swear I'll leave you alone here to starve to death, do you hear!"

He felt better when he had shouted, and though he would have preferred it if the dragon had showed any reaction other than stony calm, it was enough. The last dregs of his anger swirled away.

"Don't the lights in here ever go out?" he asked after a while.

It was important to know. The hero was the minstrel.

"Really? They don't ever go out? How interesting!" He chuckled wryly to himself, since Fanuilh would not do it for him.

I will tell you about the house when you live here. When you have fulfilled your bargain, you will be master.

"And you'll stay out of my head and show me many things I never dreamed of and all will be well with the world," he said wearily. "Let's not go into that again."

You will have to stay here tonight. It is too late to return to Southwark. You should go to sleep now, so that you can meet the merchant in the morning.

"It's not my house."

It is, but for the moment that is not important. You should sleep.

He suddenly felt wide awake. The icy cold was leaving his bones, his numbed fingers and ears were thawing, and he felt more awake than he had in the theater.

"I'll sleep here, but first . . ."

He left the room briskly and went to the kitchen. The house felt strange, full where he had expected it to be empty. There were none of the flat echoes one finds in abandoned rooms. As though it were waiting, he imagined, and drove the idea away with the image of a jug of chilled red wine, beads of moisture trickling down its sides. He was careful not to look at the jug by the stove for a moment, but when he did its sides were slick, and an exploratory finger came up wet with wine. And excellent wine, by the taste of the drops sucked off his finger. Shaking his head, he dispelled the wine and conjured a raw haunch of meat, feeling a little ridiculous as he closed his eyes and bunched his face with effort.

With the haunch on a wooden platter thoughtfully provided by the magic oven and his own imagination, the jug under his arm, Liam returned to the workroom. He dropped the platter in front of Fanuilh and sat crosslegged on the floor by the table.

"Eat up, familiar of mine. I need you to clear up some points for me, and you'll need your strength." He started to go on in the same vein, but stopped and changed tracks. "How is your strength? How are you?" The thought blocked immediately.

Better, but not completely well. I cannot fly yet, though I can move a little. Perhaps a week more.

An image of the tiny dragon skimming over the sand and looping up to dart out over the sea entered his head, and he remembered seeing it fly during the summer, silhouetted by the sun. He had been greatly impressed when he first saw it, but over the course of the summer had come to take Fanuilh for granted, another possession of Tarquin's, like the wizard's fantastic beach house.

Liam nodded as though something important had been decided.

"Well, I think I'll stay here for a week then, and nurse you lovingly back to health."

That would be good. The house is yours. Now you wish to clear some things up.

Toneless though the thought was, it nonetheless conveyed to Liam that the dragon knew exactly what he wanted to discuss. How could it not, when it could read his mind?

"I certainly do. Your memory's far from perfect, familiar of mine, and things are moving a little quickly for me to be wandering around with an incomplete schedule of events. Let's begin from the beginning, shall we?"

There were two events around which to arrange Fanuilh's imperfect sense of time: the death of Tarquin and the disappearance of the Teeth. It had apparently flown over the Teeth the day before, and, returning the next day, noticed their absence.

Between Liam's coaxing and puzzling and the dragon's willing answers and descriptions of the weather, they formed a sketchy timeline, to which Liam added his own observations.

Three days before the Teeth disappeared, Ancus Marcius had appeared at the door of the beach house with his thugs, rude and demanding. He had left after a short time, and his feelings about the interview were not apparent to Fanuilh, though Liam added that only a day before a rich ship of his had been smashed to splinters on the Teeth.

On the same day in the afternoon, Lons sought the wizard out, and remained closeted with him for some time. Fanuilh, told off and bored with waiting, had flown down the beach, and did not see him leave.

Two days later the most violent of a season of violent storms raged all day long, from early in the morning until just after dark. That evening, the woman with the seductive voice had come, and Fanuilh had been shut out again. And she was hooded and cloaked, it explained, so it had not seen her face.

"Even if she had been naked," Liam said consolingly, though nothing in the thought had conveyed regret or a sense of guilt on the dragon's part, "you probably wouldn't have seen her anyway. It was pitch dark all day, and the night was worse." He himself had endured most of the storm wrapped in a blanket in his garret, watching quietly as the Storm King howled and spat his defiance at the world.

Tarquin spoke with her at some length, and Fanuilh was only allowed in the house several hours later. Liam coughed over this, wondering if they had done much talking, but he let it pass. The wizard had been preparing something since the day Ancus and Lons had visited him, and that night he set Fanuilh to watching the house for spirits.

"Spirits?"

They can ruin a great magic. The power draws them from the Gray Lands, like moths. They flutter about it, and get in the way. Master Tanaquil drew them often.

"And you can drive them away?"

I have a form of power that can decoy them away.

"Well," Liam said, impressed by any subject he did not understand. "Well."

They went back to the timeline.

Tarquin remained in the workroom all night, casting the spell. He went to bed at dawn, exhausted, releasing Fanuilh from his watch almost as an afterthought. As a welcome break, the dragon had flown over the Teeth, and found them missing.

"Or rather, didn't find them missing," Liam mused, running a long-fingered hand through his fine blond hair. The dragon snapped down the last of the meat and gazed at him incuriously. He took another gulp of wine, which was still wonderfully cold.

The wizard received no visitors for the next three days, as far as Fanuilh knew. He remained in the house, mostly in his bedroom, ordering his familiar to bring him food.

Removing the Teeth from this world took a great deal out of him.

"So you're sure it was him?"

Who else?

"And he removed them? He used the spell the book was opened to, not the illusion spell?"

I flew down to where they should have been. They were not there. And a mere illusion spell would not have cost him three days of rest.

Chastened, Liam went on.

On the second day of Tarquin's rest, a messenger had arrived from town, bearing a folded, sealed letter. The wizard had read the paper, laughed and mentioned Marcius's name with a chuckle. Then he burned it. That was the day Freihett Necquer made his miraculous return, Liam remembered.

The next day—surprised, Liam realized it was only four days ago—Tarquin stayed in his room till early evening. At dusk he called for Fanuilh to heat water for bathing, and cleaned himself thoroughly. Then he dressed in his most impressive, wizardly robes, the blue ones Liam had found him in, and shut the dragon out for the evening. He had rubbed his hands in the peculiar way that meant he was happy about something, and mentioned extra payments in a deliberately cryptic manner. That was the last time Fanuilh had seen him alive.

He was murdered at approximately midnight. Fanuilh knew this because it had felt Tarquin's death, felt the soul leaving its master, and had collapsed to the sand outside the house. From there it crawled inside, and Liam arrived only an hour after that.

Liam knew the rest. He sat against the wall, sipping at the wine, which was still cool, though he had to hoist the jug high and angle his head uncomfortably to get at it.

Tarquin died at midnight. That would allow Lons enough time to finish whatever performance he was in and get out to the beach. Marcius's whereabouts he did not know, but if the merchant were involved, he probably would have sent one of his hired swords. Viyescu's movements were a mystery as well, and he did not even know who the woman with the seductive voice was. It did not look encouraging when he pieced it all together, and he realized that he had done little more than scratch the surface.

You had not visited Master Tanaquil for a long while. He mentioned your name often. The block erased his own thoughts, and he looked dazedly up from the jug.

"He did?"

Try as he might, he could not understand the portrait Fanuilh had painted. At one moment, Tarquin dismissed the dragon like a mere servant, simply sent the bearer of half his soul away like an inconvenience. Then, apparently, he took the time to wonder about a man less than half his age whom he only saw rarely.

Tanaquil was a good master.

As usual, there were no hidden overtones to Fanuilh's communication, but Liam felt he had offended, and fumbled an apology.

"I meant to come, but the rains had set in . . . and the ride is long. It is a rather out-of-the-way place."

It will not seem that way when you live here.

Did that mean his apology was accepted? That whatever spirit he had offended could rest?

The wine suddenly affected him all at once. His head felt thick but weightless, detached from the rest of his body. He eyed the long legs that now stretched out in front of him as if they were not his.

"I'd better get some sleep."

With an effort, he managed to gain his feet, and the dragon's eyes followed him, the sinuous neck angling up as he rose.

Where will you sleep?

"I'll find a place. Goodnight." Deliberately watching each step, he made his way out of the workroom and around to the kitchen, where he deposited the jug with elaborate care. He even patted it once, to reassure himself that he had put it there.

No more thoughts came from the dragon, and his own were pleasantly unable to form, skipping from one to the other without being able to settle anywhere. With the same measured tread, he sought out the low divan in the library. It did not occur to him to sleep in the bedroom where Tarquin had died.

Curled up on the couch, blinking blearily at the rows of book spines on the shelves, he cursed himself tiredly for not finding a blanket. He knew, however, that he would not need it. The library was warm, just warm enough to sleep in without a blanket. He was perfectly comfortable in his clothes. Only the light was annoying, bright and intrusive, but even as he thought this, it began to dim, dying evenly to a dull glow that was strangely peaceful.

Wrapped in the warmth and dimness of the wine and the magical house, he fell softly into sleep.

■ 8 ■

WAKE.

Liam was not dreaming until a few seconds before he woke, when suddenly he was walking through an ancient ruin that subtly reminded him of one he had seen years before. There, however, the giant sandstone pillars had been inscribed in a sinuous script he could not read; in his dream they were covered with the word *wake* in huge letters, like a command.

WAKE. WAKE.

The stones were in better shape than he remembered, as though they had just been carved, and the message took on an urgency the old ruins had not possessed.

WAKE. WAKE. WAKE.

He snapped away from the desolate city of his dreams, and knew he was in his library.

Tarquin's library, he reminded himself.

You are fully awake?

"Yes," he muttered, then raised his voice. "Yes, Fanuilh, I'm fully awake."

He got up quickly from the couch to forestall any further questions, and scrubbed at his eyes. Then he went to the kitchen and pictured warm water and spiced buns. Mists of steam rose from the jug after a moment, and he found hot rolls in the oven like those he had eaten the first day. He slicked back his unruly hair and washed his face, fingering the stub-

ble. Then he had the stove conjure up another platter of uncooked meat
and went to the workroom to present it to Fanuilh.

"In case you get hungry while I'm gone," he said. "At least it won't
get cold." He laughed at his joke, but the little dragon just cocked its
head. Liam rolled his eyes, and the empty decanter on the second table
caught his attention.

"Why did Tarquin leave that out?"

I don't know.

The lack of expression in Fanuilh's thoughts maddened him; he felt
as if the creature was hiding something from him, using a sort of mental
poker-face. "I don't know," when spoken, could mean a hundred different things, or a thousand. It could carry any significance, different by
shades, determined by tone and pitch, the speed with which the words
were spoken. A wealth of information could hide in the quavering of a
syllable, the length of a vowel.

I am not hiding anything. I simply do not know why he left it out.

"I know, I know. It's just . . . frustrating." It was not fair to blame
the dragon.

*It is strange, though. Master Tanaquil was very neat. He did not usually
leave things lying about unless he intended to use them.*

"Time to go," Liam said abruptly after a moment. "I'll be back
later." He walked quickly outside to his horse, munching on a bun as he
went.

Yesterday's rain had stopped, but the skies were still overcast, and
everything was wet. The trees along the road back to Southwark were a
sodden, lifeless black, stripped of their leaves by the winds of the past
two weeks. Rich, musty smells rose off the muddy fields. The fields and
the sky, and Southwark when he finally came in view of it, looked colorless and leeched out, a painting composed only in varying shades of gray.

Nonetheless, he had slept well in the magic house, and the sweet
taste of the buns lingered in his mouth like a pleasant memory. He felt
good, and he smiled at his landlady's worried chattering over his being
away the whole night. He did not even tease her, stopping only to reassure her and pick up his writing case before stabling his horse.

Marcius's offices were in a warehouse a few streets back from the
waterfront. They were not difficult to find, but Liam walked back and
forth on the cobbles for a few minutes before going in, thinking of how to
handle the interview. His hand dropped to the writing case at his belt,
where his maps were securely settled. Then he slumped his shoulders
meekly and knocked.

The warehouse fronted directly on the wide street, built of salt-stained gray boards, blank and featureless except for the huge wooden doors. His knocking sounded feeble, and he raised his knuckles again when a smaller door, cleverly set into its larger brothers, opened, and a ratlike head was thrust out and snarled lazily.

"What would you?"

"Please, I have an appointment with Master Marcius. My name is Liam Rhenford."

The ratty man looked him up and down disdainfully and then withdrew. A few seconds later the man from the waterfront the day before appeared and gave Liam a mean smile constricted by his puckered scar.

"The scholar comes to serve his time! Enter, good scholar!" He stood aside, motioning for Liam to enter, but when Liam stepped forward he suddenly put himself in the way, so that Liam had to stop short. The rat squealed a laugh, and Scar's eyes gleamed.

"Well, come in, scholar! Why hem? Why haw? Do you wish to see Master Marcius or no?"

"Please, I have an appointment," the Rat mocked in falsetto.

Liam studied Scar, noting the cudgel at his belt and his heavy build. A regular thug, though the scar was from a sword and not a knife. A soldier, maybe? Liam was taller, with a longer reach, and thought he could probably have taken the guard; but he had more important business.

"I swear, sir, I have business with Master Marcius," he whined. "You were there when the appointment was made."

Scar dropped his restricted smile and heaved a bored sigh, letting Liam pass. "Aye, I was there. Come in, you womanly scholar. Marcius cannot see you yet; you'll have to wait his leisure."

Nodding gratefully, Liam eased past him and into the warehouse. It was long and lofty, empty space rising uninterrupted to the raftered ceilings. Crates, boxes, bales, barrels and jugs filled little more than a third of the floor space, clearly the result of a poor year's trading. The cargo of one big carrack might have filled the rest of the room. But that carrack, Liam thought, was just then rotting sixty feet below the sea at the base of the Teeth.

The two guards took seats around a barrel on which a stub of candle flickered. Scar ignored him, settling himself comfortably with his treelike legs stretched out. He ran a dirty-nailed finger along the trench that bisected his face. The Rat kept glancing in Liam's direction and chuckling. Liam chose a barrel several feet away from them and took a seat, focusing his attention on the stairway that ran along one wall of the warehouse.

It was exposed, made of the same weathered gray boards as the building, and ran the length of the wall to a closed-in loft at the rear of the room, illuminated along its way by torches placed in irregularly spaced sconces.

Liam waited for almost an hour. Scar and the Rat carried on a desultory conversation, almost but not quite oblivious to his presence. He did not listen to them, but looked around the room, particularly at the staircase, or at his maps. Impatience grew, and he wanted to get it over with, afraid he would lose all his carefully prepared meekness if he were angry. He prepared himself a dozen times to tell Scar or the Rat to ask if the merchant would see him yet, but always decided against it.

When he was going over the advantages and disadvantages of pressing his appointment for the thirteenth time, the door to the closed-in loft was flung open and he stood up as Marcius called out angrily.

"Is the scholar here yet?"

"Aye, he's just arrived, Master Marcius," Scar called loudly, with an evil grin at Liam. "Just this moment!"

"Send him up immediately!"

The door slammed shut and Scar came over and shooed him to the stairs, trying hard to keep his ruined face straight.

"Heard you the master, scholar? Immediately! Go to, go to!" He fluttered his hands towards the stairway, and Liam hurried over to the accompaniment of the Rat's squealing laughter.

The stairs were dilapidated, creaking ominously beneath his weight, and Liam skipped over them as lightly as he could. The door of the loft had no latch, and swung open beneath his knuckles. He peered into the room as owlishly as he could and inquired politely:

"Master Marcius?"

"In, in! Stand not by the doorway, sirrah! Y'are late enough as it is!"

Liam inched into the room, anxiously rubbing his hands together.

The merchant sat on a high stool beside an expansive secretary laden with papers and account books bound in gold-stamped leather. Open braziers filled with glowing coals flanked him, shelves and pigeonholes stacked with ledgers and scrolls spread around the walls. Wrought iron candelabra bore clusters of candles, reflected as tiny constellations in Marcius's sourly appraising eyes. Dry and perched high on the stool, he was impressive: his oiled, ringleted hair hung perfectly to his shoulders, his clothes hung beautifully from his spare frame, and the height he gained from the stool allowed him to look down his aristocratic nose at Liam.

"Well and well, scholar," the merchant said after peering at him

coldly for a minute. "Report says you've a whole store of goods to vent—
maps, charts, directions, soundings—the rounded whole wanting for a
rich voyage. Report has it you've made Necquer far richer than he's any
right to be."

"I gather he has done well," Liam said guardedly, unsure where the
merchant's elaborately casual conversation was heading.

"I wonder then, why you come to me to vent this mappery? Why not
sell them to Necquer?"

"Master Necquer does not appreciate my services, Master. He won't
even pay me what he owes me, and I must leave Southwark soon enough,
so I need ready money. The whole city speaks well of you, lord, and I
thought to try my luck here."

Marcius considered this for a moment, apparently indifferent.

"Necquer won't pay you, eh?" He smiled dreamily, contemplating
something that pleased him. "Your fault of course, sirrah scholar. 'A
Freeporter's purse is drawn tighter than a crossbow,' they say. Your fault
entirely."

Liam's agenda was not being followed to his satisfaction, and he
tried to turn the talk away from Necquer with a fresh spate of whining.

"Oh, please, Master Marcius, I am in a desperate position. Now that
Master Tanaquil has been murdered, I have no protection in Southwark.
If you'll only buy these charts, I can leave—"

"Why?" Marcius interrupted without heat. "Why should I buy your
charts, when it were just as easy to follow Necquer's ships next season?
Can you tell me that, scholar?" He smiled to himself, as though he had
just made a telling point, but Liam was prepared.

"Ah, now, a shrewd, a very shrewd question, Master," he said in a
flattering tone, "but I've an answer. You see, Master Necquer was impatient. He bought only a single set of my charts in the middle of the
summer, after most of his ships were gone. He only wanted the maps to
those ports he could easily reach. And those are the poorest of the ones I
can guide you to. If he had bought other charts earlier, he might have
reached far richer ports, but as it was he barely made it back by the close
of the season, and only the miracle kept him safe. . . ." He let the
silence draw out, but Marcius did not react to the hint about the Teeth.
Instead, the merchant seemed to consider his words for a moment, then
spat out a question suddenly.

"How do I know you won't sell me your charts and then go speak
with Necquer? Twice as much for you, eh?"

"Oh, no, Master, I'd never deal with Master Necquer again. Why, he has not paid me for the first set of charts! Besides, I must leave South-wark soon."

"Your harping on that theme is most tiresome. Why are you so anxious to part our city?"

"I've explained, Master. I fear I'm in some danger from those who killed my former master, the wizard Tanaquil."

"Know you who took him off?"

"I . . . no, Master Marcius, I don't."

"Then how do you know y'are in danger? You, a mere cowering scholar?"

"I don't know, Master. I'm simply afraid. It was *murder,* after all."

Marcius considered this as well, and Liam wondered if he had gone too far. The merchant had shown no reaction that was clearly incriminating, and Liam felt frustrated. How much of Marcius's suspicion was due to business shrewdness, and how much to guilt, he could not tell, and the uncertainty tempted him to further baiting.

"Well and well, Scholar Rhenford, for all y'are a low time-serving wretch, let's see your maps."

Opening his writing case, Liam burst into exclamations of joy. "Then you'll buy! Oh, Master, you will not regret this at all! You'll be rich, I promise, and I can flee Southwark!"

"I said nothing of buying, fool, only looking. Spread them out."

Chastened, Liam tried to be meek as he laid a few of his maps on the secretary in front of Marcius.

For over an hour, the merchant studied the various papers intently, asking clever questions at every turn. At first, Liam stood by his shoulder, explaining different points, but then Marcius loudly complained of a stench. Liam, remembering that he had slept in his clothes, took the hint and went to the far side of the secretary, though he could detect no odor. More of the merchant's snobbery, he guessed.

Whenever he could, he brought Tarquin into the conversation, using him as a reference and a source of information, bemoaning his death and extolling his virtues. Marcius made no comment, focusing his attention entirely on the maps, and the details Liam supplied about the customs and goods of different ports and cities.

At the end of the hour, Marcius decided to buy three of the maps, with a show of reluctance that Liam knew was feigned. The merchant prince was eager to get his hands on them, but did not want to seem so.

"I suppose I could purchase a few of these, scholar. They'd best be true, or I'll see you suffer for it."

"Oh, Master Marcius, they're true, I'll answer for it! And Master

Necquer's riches will answer for it as well. He's made a huge pile this season, I assure you."

Despite the dig implicit in comparing Necquer's fortune with Marcius's own sunken one, the merchant prince did not rise to the bait, and Liam grimaced inside. He could raise no reaction in the man, which made him think the merchant dangerous, which reinforced his earlier suspicions. A hard, clever, vain man, who would stop at little, Liam judged.

Reaching into the depths of one of the drawers of the secretary, Marcius brought forth a flat metal chest with a key already in the lock. He turned the key and, keeping the lid between him and Liam, opened it. "We've not discussed the cost."

A price was arranged, far higher than Liam would have asked, confirming that Marcius's reluctance was feigned. The merchant prince counted it out in silver coins, a tidy stack of them. Liam reached for the money, but Marcius slapped his hand away and covered the coins with a protective hand.

"Here's more to our deal, scholar. You'll straight leave Southwark?"

"Of course! I cannot stay, not if Master Tanaquil's killers are after me!"

"And you'll not stop long enough, perhaps, to resell your charts to good Master Necquer?"

"Why, no, Master Marcius! I swear—"

The merchant stopped him with an upraised palm.

"Don't forswear yourself, scholar," he said, pitching his voice low and stern. "It'd not like me to find you'd given me the lie and dealt with Necquer. It'd like you to part Southwark, and escape your master's murderers. So take the money, and make short work of your leavetaking. Am I clear?"

"Very clear, Master Marcius," Liam responded, licking his lips nervously. "It will only take me a day or so to arrange my departure."

"Then see to it immediately."

He nodded, and Liam scooped up the money and the maps Marcius had not bought, bowing anxiously. As he was pulling open the latchless door, Marcius spoke again.

"One last, scholar. Where are you lodging now?"

Thinking of the peaceful night he had just spent, he almost said Tarquin's, but a second thought intervened, and he mentioned his landlady's. The merchant prince nodded with a frown of disgust, as though the knowledge were important and the address distasteful but not unexpected.

Liam bowed again and scurried out onto the stairs, shutting the door quietly behind him. Sweat beaded his forehead, and his face was twitching with honest nervousness as he hurried down the staircase, but Scar and the Rat let him pass with no more harassment than their scornful smiles. The high squeal of the Rat's laughter followed him into the gray street, mocking.

Once outside he hurried a few blocks away, not thinking, and then stopped to breathe deep lungfuls of the cold sea air. He almost wished it were raining, to cool down his heated face, and wash away the trickles of hot moisture running down his back and under his arms.

I completely botched that, he thought, though he could not exactly say why he felt that way. His dissatisfaction with the whole interview, he guessed, stemmed from the fact that nothing had come of it. Frustrated with Marcius's nonchalance, he had mentioned Tarquin too many times, trying to get a rise out of the merchant.

His conduct, even the veiled threat about Liam's wanting to avoid Tarquin's killers, was ambiguous. He might have been hiding guilt beneath a facade of snobbery and indifference, or the facade was real, and he was innocent. Liam could not come to any conclusion.

The interview had produced nothing but silver coins he did not need.

It was not until he was within a few blocks of his lodgings that he realized with a jolt what really bothered him about the conversation. He had agreed to leave Southwark.

The idea loomed enormously before him, presenting untold complications. But he would not consider them, ignoring the problems in favor of a second idea that came fast on their heels.

Why was Marcius so anxious to have him out of Southwark? He could not imagine it was solely to keep him from selling the same charts to Necquer. It must mean something more, and there was only one thing it could mean, he supposed.

Feeling suddenly better about the morning's work, he turned away from the narrow streets where his garret was, and headed up to the rich quarter and the tailor he had seen two days earlier.

His clothes were ready, and he spent a few moments admiring them before he had the tailor bundle them up. He paid, and retraced his steps to his garret. There was almost an hour before noon, when he would have to meet Coeccias at the White Grape, so he had the drudge heat water, and washed himself in his room, shaving as well. Then he put on one of his new sets of clothes, a deep blue tunic with soft breeches of owl gray. His good boots and new cloak completed the outfit, and he wished for a mirror to admire himself. There was none, so he went downstairs.

The drudge was the only person in the kitchen, and she stared at his new clothes fearfully. When asked, she stammered that she did not know where his landlady was.

"Well, then, could you tell her that I probably won't be in this evening, so she should not worry. Will you tell her?"

He wanted to laugh at her eager, wide-eyed nodding, and went to the White Grape.

As usual, the tavern seemed empty, though the common room was more than half full. The lunchtime conversations were quiet, and the tables were placed well apart so that sound did not carry. The serving girl recognized Liam, and gave his clothes a second, approving look before coming to his table.

"I doubted you'd come," Coeccias said when he arrived, standing behind his chair for a moment before sitting. "You've tricked yourself up nicely, Rhenford."

"New clothes," he responded, waving a hand in dismissal.

"Well, then, what news?"

"I met with Ancus Marcius this morning."

Coeccias seemed to be waiting for something, edging around a question.

"Anything come of it?"

"Enough to buy lunch, but not much else."

While they ate, he described his conversation with the merchant, and the Aedile listened with occasional murmurs of comprehension.

"I think the warning is genuine," Liam finished. "I think he killed Tarquin over the Teeth, and wants me off the scene because he thinks I may have some information."

"Or he took you for the fool you presented, and played you out your own fears, so you wouldn't deal with Necquer. Your suspicion wilts under that complexion."

It did indeed. Once again he swung back to thinking he had wasted the morning, and his only interview with the proud merchant prince.

"And Marcius expects me to leave Southwark," Liam added gloomily.

"Aye, he does. Naught bettered, Rhenford, and maybe much made worse." The blandness with which the Aedile announced his failure stung him, and he hung his head over his untasted food.

"Well, there's nothing to be done about it," he muttered.

"Truth, nothing. So we'll not nag at it. Let's consider something else,

such as where you flew off to last night, eh?" Frank disapproval rode the
Aedile's heavy brow, and Liam winced.

"I . . . I was not feeling well."

"The play was not so poor as to be sickening, Rhenford. No excuse.
Have you a better?"

"No."

Liam raised his gaze to Coeccias's, and held it against the Aedile's
probing stare. After a long moment of tension, the heavy man sighed and
relaxed.

"I trust y'are feeling better," he said with heavy sarcasm.

"Much, thank you," Liam replied in the same manner.

There was another tension, but it broke when both smiled tentatively. Coeccias spoke first.

"If y'are feeling well enough, we've other business."

He began to describe what he had found out. His men had not
discovered the barmaid Donoé, but they had not been searching the rich
quarter. He had reserved the best taverns there for himself, and expected
to go the rounds the next morning.

"They're good men all," he explained, "but I'd rather they not fright
the poor girl. I'll handle it, and assure the outcome. You may want to
attend me."

It was agreed that Liam would go with him, as he knew what he
wanted to ask the girl, and might think of more questions when he saw
her.

The Aedile had also arranged to be informed if the rent on the
mysterious hooded woman's lodgings was paid.

"We'll know by tomorrow noon whether Tarquin was keeping her or
no. But more than all this," he went on, growing brisk, "is the player.
When we thought him a minstrel, and did not know his face, I was not so
hot to clap him in. Now we have his face and his station, and as an actor,
he'd've had access to the sort of knife as killed the wizard. He seems
most likely to me."

"Then you want to arrest him?"

Frowning, Coeccias tugged at his beard and spoke thoughtfully. "No,
truth, I don't. See him, yes, clap him in, no. Strikes me, all proposed to
the killing were clever enough to fix the blame elsewhere. And of the
choices, the player would be first in my mind to sacrifice—he's the basest.
Viyescu's respected, the woman unknown, Marcius nigh untouchable
without good cause." He stopped, as though there was more.

"And . . ." Liam prompted.

"And . . . he doesn't look the sort. Truth, did you see him stab that villain in the piece? Now, certain it is that duke earned his death more than Tarquin did his, but the pretty boy winced at it—and that only in a play! Did see?"

"I was watching the girl."

"Aye," Coeccias laughed. "Aye. Well, I think he couldn't have done the real deed, if he blanched at its counterfeit."

"I agree. I've seen him elsewhere, and he doesn't seem the type to fight." At the rise of the Aedile's eyebrows, Liam briefly outlined his sight of Lons at the Necquer's party.

"All Necquer had to do was start for the door, and Lons was off like lightning. He wouldn't fight unless he was pushed, I guess. Too afraid his handsome face'd get hurt. And Tarquin wasn't the kind to push too hard."

"Still and all, it'd like me to see him, and maybe fright him a little. If he is our man, he's been cool enough till now, staying the time in town, and acting his plays. We'll talk with him, and set a man to watch him. He may try to take his leave after our little discourse. If he does, we'll have him."

"And if not, we may still scare him enough to make a mistake."

"Agreed. We'll to the theater. The players practice their performances in the morning, and sup just at noon. If we're quick, we'll catch him before his afternoon's work. Attend me."

Liam dropped one of Marcius's silver coins on the table and they hurried out of the White Grape.

A dullness clung to the theater, like a midnight lover in the morning. The golden orb looked gaudy and the doors had a desolate air, as if the building had been abandoned. They opened, however, and Liam and Coeccias went into the lobby, which felt cold and unused. Though there was a broom in one corner, and the plank floors had obviously just been swept clean, Liam imagined they would feel dusty, or perhaps moldy, if he knelt and touched them.

He did not.

In the theater itself a number of actors sat or stood around the pit, eating their meals and talking in low voices. A few candles flickered weakly in the windowless building, and despite the voices and people, it was gloomy.

The man who had greeted Coeccias at the door the night before detached himself from a whispered conversation and came to stand before them, dressed now in a commoner's smock instead of his colorful motley. He executed a grand, mocking bow.

"Your servant, milord Aedile. Have you come to close us out?"

Coeccias frowned, ignoring the actor's bantering tone. "Nay, player. I'd have words with one of your company. Where is Lons?"

The actor widened his eyes in girlish admiration, and spoke with ironic reverence. "Lons? Our great hero? Lons the Magnificent? I fear me his lordship is not here, milord Aedile, but if you stay a moment, I'm sure he'll grace us."

"When?"

"Soon." The actor dropped his joking. "He's gone to sup elsewhere, and'll be back soon. You may await him here." With another grand bow, he twisted away and clapped his hands loudly, calling for the beginning of the afternoon's rehearsal.

Coeccias frowned sourly at the actor's back.

"I'll not be sad to pack *him* off to the heath."

"Who is he?" Liam asked, watching the actor marshall his company on the stage.

"Kansallus. He pens their sorry scripts, gives them their readings. Owns a share of the theater as well, if rumor's to be credited. A very rogue, but with some excellent parts: wit, voice, good sense. He never fusses when I close him out."

There was a small tinge of admiration in the Aedile's voice.

"If you like him so much, why do you shut up his theater?"

"The Duke'd have it so. He doesn't take with the stage, and especially so when they allow women on it. So, a few days after Uris-tide, it's off to the country with them."

Coeccias sighed ruefully, and they fell silent, watching the actors rehearse. It was a pastoral comedy complete with shepherdesses and faeries, in which Knave Fitch played a large role as a drunken farmer. Even with little practice, the clown brought humor to the part, and both men in the lobby chuckled.

Hearing them, Kansallus backed out to the lobby, stopping beside them but leaving his eyes on the stage.

"It pleases you?" he asked, trying and failing to mask his eagerness.

"Truth, it's a goodly thing."

"Yes, very much. It's funny."

Kansallus drank in the praise, bobbing his head happily at the stage, as if to encourage the actors.

"But why," Liam asked during a pause while the scene shifted, "don't you have that girl play the lead shepherdess? The one who played the princess last night? She'd be spectacular."

"That one," Kansallus said, rolling his eyes. "It'd be worth my life and my jewels at once to suggest it. She only plays tragedy, look you, tragedy only. She esteems herself a great actress, a *lofty* actress. No low comedy for her. Mug? Wink? Trip and pratfall? Never! Her feet would rot off before she'd play comedy!"

"A shrew, eh?" Coeccias asked with a wicked grin. "Pity. She's a fair leg."

Liam nodded in agreement.

"Oh, in faith, I cannot deny it. A fair leg, and a fair ankle, bosom and face to keep the leg company. Enjoy what you see on the stage, good sirs, because you'll never see more of Rora anywhere else, least of all warming your bed."

"Rora?" Liam thought he would have done well to find Kansallus long before, when he was searching for someone who knew Southwark and would tell what he knew.

"Rora," the actor confirmed. "No one's bauble is Rora, to be dandled and played with and warmed on a winter's night. Pure enough to hunt the unicorn, our Rora, and too good for comedy—No! No! No! Fitch, you mutton-headed, wool-pated, poxy, dripping . . ." He ran forward, shouting, to the stage, where Knave Fitch was standing with an elaborately innocent face while the rest of the cast collapsed in hysterics around him.

"It is no error of mine, Master Playwright, if my fellow actors cannot restrain their . . ." His voice, rippling with rolled r's, drifted to them from the stage, but the door behind them opened suddenly, and they both turned.

Framed in a wash of gray light from the door, Rora entered, and Liam thought his heart might have stopped. Even bundled in a warm cloak she was stunning, the fullness of her red lips and the perfect beauty of her white complexion etched in the gray light. It turned her hair to dusty gold, and Liam fleetingly compared her to Lady Necquer, dismissing the latter in an instant. She stopped when she saw them. Over her shoulder, Lons loomed curiously.

"Good day, Aedile Coeccias," she said in a rich, musical voice. Her eyes rested on Liam, however, smiling a little mysteriously and arching an eyebrow, clearly aware of her affect on him.

Maybe if I bring my jaw up from my knees, he thought ashamedly, and looked at Coeccias, who cleared his throat.

"Ah, y'are the actor Lons?"

The handsome man, not expecting to be addressed, did not reply at once.

"Aye."

"We'd have words with you, if you can spare a moment."

"But I've a practice—"

"Kansallus will not mind," Coeccias interrupted firmly, crossing his arms on his wide chest.

"Well, then, I suppose . . ." He edged his way in past Rora, who continued to stare at Liam. Liam, in turn, kept his eyes fixed on the other two men, horribly aware of the blush that was creeping up his long neck. He decided that it was a point in Lady Necquer's favor that she did not seem so keenly conscious of her beauty.

"What did you want, Aedile?" Lons seemed a little surer of himself, now that he was out from behind Rora and facing Coeccias. The Aedile gestured significantly at the woman.

"Would you not prefer to be alone?"

Lons stiffened, as did Rora. "Anything you can say to my brother you can say with me as witness," she said coldly.

"Well enough," he said agreeably, turning back to Lons. "Pray you, brother, do tell what business you had with Tarquin Tanaquil?"

Stammering, Lons clenched his hands. "Tanaquil? The wizard? He's called you? The bargain's not fulfilled, the terms not met, I—"

"Lons," Rora warned.

"Still!" Coeccias hissed at her out of the side of his mouth, but the moment was enough for Lons to regain his composure.

"Our business was that," he said formally. *"Ours.* And as it is not finished, there's no need for you t'interfere."

"I doubt but there is, goodman player. You'll have no more business with Master Tanaquil."

"What?" Lons exclaimed angrily. "You can't make me—"

Liam watched Coeccias draw the young man on, and scrutinized the handsome face carefully.

"None'll have business with Master Tanaquil. He's gone beyond business, Lons, sped on his way by a dagger."

Lons gaped, stunned.

"Tanaquil? Murdered?"

Liam had to remind himself that the man was an actor. His astonishment seemed unfeigned, real to a fault. Liam was disappointed, but not surprised. Much as he disliked the actor, he did not believe him capable of murder; Coeccias, however pressed on.

"So you see, sirrah, what was your particular business is now my business, and the question stands. Why did you have dealings with the wizard?"

Licking his lips, the young man looked from one face to another, Liam's and Coeccias's expectant, Rora's wary and warning.

"I needed his help in a . . . in a small matter of the heart."

Rora nodded approvingly, but the Aedile laughed heartily.

"A love potion? You sought a wizard for a love potion? My grand-dam could've made you a love potion!"

"The lady," Lons said with barely restrained anger, "required a great service of me. I lacked the power for it, and sought the wizard's help."

"She needs must have set you a great task," Coeccias said, angling for more.

"The Teeth. She wanted the Teeth removed, to protect her husband," the actor supplied, over his sister's hissed objection.

"You commissioned *that?*" The Aedile was clearly awed. "I hope the lady was worth it."

"She is," Lons replied, with a glance at Liam, who nodded agreement, allowing himself a sidelong look at Rora.

"And the lady's name? Her husband's station?"

"Is unimportant now," Liam said quietly, drawing a surprised stare from the Aedile and a sneer from Lons. "I'll explain later. For now, I've a question." He addressed himself to the actor.

"Tell me, how did you propose to pay Tanaquil? Wizards are costly, and I know the spell took a great deal of effort."

"I proposed no payment. He named a sum, and I agreed."

"What sum?"

"Ten thousand, in gold," the actor said, with a touch of pride.

Rora gasped and Coeccias gave a low whistle, but Liam only nodded thoughtfully.

"And he took you at your word that you could pay?"

"I presume he knew my state. He accepted my compact."

"But you don't have ten thousand in gold."

"No." Lons shifted under the questions, perplexed.

"And so you couldn't have paid him, but he undertook the spell anyway."

"Perhaps he knew he was doing a noble deed—helping true love find its course." Again, there was the touch of hard, wounded pride, the sense of disdain at having his affairs discussed. Liam barked a laugh.

"More likely you dressed yourself up in the richest costume the Golden Orb has and let him think you a rich merchant's son."

The young man blanched, but said nothing.

"And now that he's dead, you don't have to pay, do you?"

"I did not kill him," Lons said thickly, licking dry lips.

With the wolf's grin he had practiced, Liam agreed. "Certainly not, certainly not. No one's suggesting such a thing. It would not be worth murder to catch a beautiful woman, get rid of an unpayable debt, and avoid a powerful wizard's wrath. Certainly not."

The wolf's grin worked nicely, leaving the young man speechless and gaping.

"I think we're done here, don't you, Aedile Coeccias?" Liam raised an eyebrow to the officer, who looked intently at him for a moment, and then nodded once.

"Thank you, Lons, for your time. I don't think we'll be bothering you again." Smiling the wolf's grin again for effect, he ushered Coeccias to the door and let him pass out first.

Rora recovered before Lons did, and began stammering furiously.

"Who are you? How dare you question us—"

He dropped the grin and assumed a polite smile to match his words, which were offhand but firmly interrupted her.

"An interesting thing, Maid Rora. The knife that killed Tarquin was one that players often use. One of a pair, I'm told. It would be interesting to see if the theater were missing any, wouldn't it?"

With a friendly smile, he dipped his head to her, and then turned to Lons, putting his back to the girl.

"Stay away from Lady Necquer," he whispered quietly. "Do you hear? Stay away."

"I'll not," Lons said, trying and failing to sound firm. Liam's remarks had greatly upset him.

"Stay away from her," he repeated. "If Necquer hears—"

"Necquer," the actor interrupted eagerly, as if he had found an attack he could answer, "deserves her not! He's naught but a pandering, strutting—"

Rora hissed a warning and Lons stopped, glaring angrily and desperately at her.

"Just stay away from her," Liam said into the sudden silence, and received a sullen nod from the actor. Denying himself the last look at Rora that he wanted, he went out the door to join Coeccias.

■ *9* ■

COECCIAS WAS WAITING further down the street, leaning against a wall and watching a group of boys scuffle around a leather ball. He looked up with a slight chuckle at Liam's approach.

"It should be branded on your front, Rhenford: 'Take no surprise; I may do anything.' Branded in bold letters, or sewn into your clothes in characters of red."

"What do you mean?"

They started off, leaving the boys behind and heading by tacit consent towards the Point. Coeccias ticked his reasons off on thick, blunt fingers.

"Firstly, you discount the player, and throw your weight behind the merchant. Y'ignore the player whiles we talk, to gawp and stare at his sweet sister. Then, of a sudden, you turn on the player again and fasten your teeth into his throat. You warrant him a motive and an opportunity, and show a familiarity with his affairs I'd have never guessed at. You fair prove him the murderer. And then—then you ask his pardon and go your way! You as much as say 'Y'are a killer, sirrah,' and then leave him at large!"

"You didn't argue," Liam pointed out, and the Aedile threw up his arms in exasperation.

"Oh, no, nor call you the wooden fool y'are, nor clap Lons in as I should! I've grown as wooden as you! And yet I give you my service. That of value I have in this I have from you, and all I see you do makes you out a bloodhound. Y'have an acute nose, Rhenford. Perhaps I'll just give you rein and follow you to the murderer."

Liam shrugged uncomfortably under the praise, and glanced around the street before dropping his gaze to his boots, not looking at Coeccias.

"You could also follow me nowhere."

"I'd wager not. Y'are strange in thought and manner, but I'll be led by you in this, Rhenford, and I doubt not but it'll be to my profit."

They lapsed into silence, Coeccias satisfied and content, Liam wondering.

He *had* as much as said Lons was a murderer, and all the clues pointed that way. The knife, the debt, the timing—almost everything indicated Lons, but he was reluctant to accept that. For one thing, he was afraid his dislike had colored his judgement, that his connection with Lady Necquer made him anxious to find Lons guilty. For another, there was Lons himself—Liam simply could not find murder in the self-involved actor's character. Pride and arrogance, yes, but it seemed the sort he had often found in cowards, men who shrank from blood. And lastly, there was Lon's sister. Rora had taken a powerful hold on his mind, and he found it difficult to remove her. She was an amazing presence, he thought, and though he had felt something cold and disdainful in her, she drew him, her image fluttering around inside his head.

Now that he had warned Lons away from Lady Necquer, he was inclined to find his murderer elsewhere, and he favored the merchant prince. Marcius's motives were muddied, and the evidence did not single him out, but he had the sort of strength of will and capacity for violence that Liam expected to find in a killer. And his threats, even veiled and obscure ones, had the ring of truth.

Liam told none of this to the Aedile. Instead, he thought it out, eyes fixed on his feet as the two men made their way south through the city. Other considerations sprang to mind. He remembered Lady Necquer's comments on the Teeth, and heard now a note of morbid fascination he had not noticed at first. She had been so afraid of them and the danger they presented to her husband that she had agreed to sleep with the man who could remove them.

And Tarquin had been responsible for it; could she be suspected? Or her husband? A series of questions formed themselves in his head, almost involuntarily, that he would ask her that afternoon. He felt instinctively that she was not involved, but her husband might be, if she had told him about Lons's courtship. That Necquer should strike at Tarquin and not Lons was strange, and argued against the suspicion, but the questions interested him in and of themselves, and he resolved to ask them.

"Your face's dark as the sky," Coeccias said finally, with a gesture that took in Liam's wrinkled brow and the cloudy sky. They were back in the neighborhood of the White Grape, and a pall of black hung over the sky.

"Thinking about murderers and rainy days make for a depressing combination."

"Truth, they do. Would a drink help?" The painted signboard of the White Grape hung further down the street, swaying slightly in the stiff, storm-bringing breeze from the sea.

"I think so."

A bottle of the tavern's watered-down white wine sped away the time, and Liam looked up from the dregs to hear the bells announce that it was time for his daily visit to Lady Necquer. He stood up from the table with mixed feelings. Coeccias reminded him of the next day's work, looking for the barmaid Donoé, and they agreed on an hour to meet.

It was strange, Liam reflected as he walked towards the rich quarter, how Coeccias's attitude had changed. Only a few hours earlier the Aedile had been highly suspicious of him because of his abrupt departure from the theater the evening before. Now Coeccias was practically giving up, throwing the weight of the whole investigation on Liam. Had his questioning of Lons been that impressive?

He was not entirely comfortable with the idea of himself as a sort of human bloodhound. He did not picture himself as particularly astute where people's darker motivations were concerned. If he were like that, he could not imagine why people accepted his presence; he knew that he would not want to be with someone who could smell out his deepest secrets.

Yet people did accept his presence. Tarquin had spoken freely around him, the Aedile shared meals with him. Lady Necquer actually seemed to look forward to his visits. Did that mean that, even though they felt he could see into their souls, they felt secure enough with themselves to ignore it?

Was that what Fanuilh had seen in him? The thing that made the dragon entrust him with finding Tarquin's murderer?

Liam Rhenford, human bloodhound. Liam Rhenford, before whom men's souls are laid bare. Liam Rhenford, the perfect investigator.

Suddenly he laughed harshly, repressing the grandiose thoughts.

I'm just asking questions, he thought, grinning, *and they just happen to be good ones. I'm carrying my Luck with me.* He laughed again, and felt better. The narrow street with its border of high walls where the Necquers lived was just ahead.

• • •

"Master Liam, at th'appointed hour, as usual!"

Lare's bow was small out of familiarity and friendliness, not disdain, and the old man ushered him in with a smile.

Well, at least the old man isn't uneasy around me, Liam thought with relief, and offered Lares a smile in return.

"It's becoming a ritual, Lares. They set the tolling of the bells by me."

Lady Necquer awaited him in the same upstairs parlor, and started up with a smile when Lares announced him. She came to him and, taking his hands, kissed him formally on the cheek. Thinking of the questions he wanted to ask and his unfavorable comparison of her with Rora, he coughed nervously and reclaimed his hands as soon as he could.

"Well, Sir Liam," she said, sitting gracefully, "what discourse have you prepared for me this day?" Bright color suffused her pale complexion, and a smile broke out uncontrollably on her face. She seemed intensely happy about something, and he smiled mildly, infected by her mood.

"I'm afraid I haven't prepared any talk for this afternoon. But you, I think, must have some news. If you grin any harder your face will split in two. What makes you so happy?"

Her grin widened until it took possession of her whole face, and she suddenly leapt up and danced around the room.

"Oh, Sir Liam, my husband comes home this day, and will not leave me again for winter entire! My heart is full to bursting!" She hugged herself, and Liam smiled at her childlike joy. He took a breath and spoke heartily.

"When does he arrive?"

"Soon, soon, soon! He'll dine with me this night!" She danced further, twirling around the whole room, and he thought of Rora's dancing in the theater, the exact opposite of Lady Necquer's pure, girlish giddiness. Favoring him with a radiant smile, she danced past his chair, laying a hand briefly on his shoulder.

"He is in the city even now, attending pressing business, but he'll be home soon, and mine for the winter!"

"That's excellent news, madam, and I think I have some other that will increase your happiness."

"Oh?" She came to a reluctant halt, her full skirts whirling around her, and beamed abashedly at him. "You must excuse me, Sir Liam. I'm hardly fit company. I can think of little else but Freihett. But come, your news." Eagerly, she came and sat beside him on the divan, placing a hand on his arm, offering her whole attention with a forced serious look that threatened to break into a wild grin at any moment.

"It so happens," he began slowly, "that I had occasion to speak with someone who I believe was causing you some discomfort."

She nodded, still seriously, but the smile threatened hugely. He went on.

"A young man, an actor, who was presenting unwanted attentions."

The threat of a smile vanished, and she took a deep breath.

"There are some things I know about him that could have caused him a great deal of trouble, and it so happened that I was able to . . . well, warn him off, if you see what I mean. I don't think he will be bothering you again. I did not mean to pry, madam, but the opportunity presented itself. I know it was not my place—"

Taking her hand from his arm, her voice was strained and her eyes downcast on her lap, where her hands were clasped fiercely. "No, it was not your place . . . how did you happen to speak with him?"

Liam stood and took a few steps to stand before an elegant hanging. He fingered its tassels absently, his back to her. "I was well acquainted with a wizard named Tarquin Tanaquil. He . . . died recently, and several things indicated that Lons was involved in the death. I spoke with him about his involvement, and took the opportunity to suggest he leave you alone."

"The wizard was murdered?" The strain in her voice was greater.

"Yes. And certain things indicate Lons was responsible." He turned to look at her, and almost flinched at the pain on her face. "Lons had commissioned Tarquin to make the Teeth vanish, but couldn't pay the price. The knife that was used was a stage blade. His guilt could be established with these."

"He would not do that," she whispered, almost choking on a sob. "He hasn't the strength."

Liam went and sat beside her. "I don't think so either. Tell me, why did you want him to get rid of the Teeth?"

Her words came slowly, with great difficulty. He writhed inside at making her talk about it, but was also grateful that she was speaking freely, and had not chosen to be angry with him. He had feared she would think he had tricked her, had wormed his way into her confidence just for information. But she seemed wrapped up in her sorrow and confusion.

"He . . . he wooed me, professed undying love. The summer entire, while Freihett was at sea. He spoke with such heat, so truly . . . he said he needs must, that he needs must . . . *know* me. I gave him no encouragement, no sign of returning his feelings, but he pressed and pressed. And all while Freihett was at sea, and those cursed Teeth waited to take him down, to crush him beneath the cold blue."

She gasped at the intensity of her vision, at the depth of her fear for her husband, and Liam waited silently for her to go on. Tears brimmed in her enormous blue eyes, but were not shed, and suddenly she smiled bleakly, looking defenselessly at him.

"I thought if I tasked him impossibly, he would give me peace. I claimed the destruction of the Teeth as my price, and sent him away, sure he could not achieve it. It was a fond and foolish thought, wasn't it?" Liam shook his head sadly, and she took a deep breath, steadying herself. "But he did it. The wizard succored him, and he saved my husband's life. What could I do? I could not surrender to him."

After a long pause, she looked earnestly at him and added: "I did not surrender to him, Sir Liam, though he continues to plague me. He was to come to me on the day the Teeth vanished, but I put him off, feigned sickness, and on the day after my husband was home . . . I broke my word, and did not pay him for my husband's life. I have transgressed doubly, in breaking an oath and entertaining a lover while my husband was away. You understand?"

It was important to her, and he nodded again, gravely. "Yes, I do understand. Does your husband know?"

"Yes. I gave him the whole story when he was well. The journey had taken much from him, you know."

"I can imagine. What did he say about it?"

"Naught, or very little. He credited me, and said he would not hold it against me. But he was terribly irked, I know. If Lons had been there, or he'd come across him, there'd have been more than harsh words."

It was time to stop, Liam decided. Lady Necquer's brave smile held, but her lip trembled, and he knew enough for now. She had not thought to wonder about his interest, nor to think that he might connect any of what she said with Tarquin's death. He hated himself for prying, but offered a directionless prayer of thanks that she had not realized what he was after.

"Come," he said, rising, "there's no reason to think on it any longer. Right or wrong, I think he'll stay away, and Master Necquer is back now to stay by your side."

At a sideboard he found wine, and filled two crystal goblets. He brought the goblets back to the divan and handed one to her. She took it gratefully and drank. Tears still brimmed in her eyes, dangling from her eyelashes. He wanted very much to brush them away, but was afraid it

might seem forward. Instead, he walked back to the hanging and examined it, sipping his wine.

After gulping down her glass, Lady Necquer went to the sideboard
and poured herself another, from which she took a smaller sip before
speaking in a deliberately bright manner.

"Now, Sir Liam, enough of all that. Enough and too much. We must
regain our wonted mirth, and find a way to pass the time more in keeping
with my husband's homecoming."

"What shall we talk about? I'm afraid we've covered what I know of
the rest of the world pretty thoroughly."

"Well then," she said with a smile halfway towards her earlier happiness, "we shall cover you. I know where you've been and what you've
seen, but nothing of you. Come hold discourse on Sir Liam Rhenford."

Smiling apologetically, he followed her back to the divan. "That is a
very boring topic, madam. The rest of the world is far more interesting."

"I'll judge that, Sir Liam. You may begin."

Folding her hands in her lap, she assumed a very grave demeanor, as
if she really meant to judge him. He laughed, and she joined him tentatively.

"Come, go to, go to! Tell me about you!"

"Very well," he said, pleased to see her smiling. "What would you
like to know?"

"What you do in Southwark," she answered promptly, and he had to
pause and think.

"Nothing," he said after a while. "Nothing, really."

"Nothing? Naught? I'll not believe that. You certainly don't idle your
time waiting to attend me in the afternoons!"

"Well, I suppose I am recovering. I have been a long time away from
Taralon, and I thought it was time to get back."

"After your shipwreck?"

Had he mentioned that to her? He did not remember, but he was
sure he had not told her the whole story. Now that he thought about it,
he realized once again that he was not sure why he was in Southwark.
The experience on the island had worn him out, and when he had finally
reached Southwark, he was so grateful to be back in Taralon that he had
settled there instinctively. To fill the time, he had half-invented the idea
of writing, but that was not the real reason he stayed in Southwark. It was
safe, a part of Taralon that held no memories for him at all, but that was
a part of his home nonetheless.

"Yes. I'm also writing."

"Stories?" she asked eagerly. "Or a play? Or poetry? I'll wager your verse is passing fair."

"Neither, I'm afraid. History. Or rather, my history, with some of the history of the places I've been." He smiled at her obvious disappointment, and spoke with a hint of reproach. "You seemed to think my stories of where I'd been somewhat interesting."

"Well, and they were," she admitted grudgingly, "when you *told* them. But if you cage them with bars of ink and walls of leather, they'll be stuporous, sleep-inducing, for it was your tongue that gave them life. You'd do better to make of them a romance, or better, a string of poems. Yes! A string of poems addressed to the sweetling who awaits you on shore!"

"But I didn't have a sweetling on shore," he protested.

Brushing aside the objection, she went on. "No matter; invent one! Call her . . . call her Larissa, and pine longingly for her as you view the lusty beauties of the strange scenes you've visited! Mince your words and file your phrase, and harken back to her shining face whenever you mention some far-off wonder!"

They went on in the same vein for a while, as Lady Necquer mapped out the collection of poems she expected from him, and he objected to it every step of the way, laughingly complaining that he was no poet, and had had no girl waiting for him while he traveled.

The idea seemed to inspire her, and though she too giggled at her own high-flown fancies, there was a seriousness as well.

If I were a poet, Liam thought, *it* would *make good verse. But I'm not,* he reminded himself, and reminded her as well, an objection she countered with the suggestion that he perform vigils with the priests of Uris.

"Oh, and Uris-tide is nigh! If you begin tomorrow, you can complete the course of the devotions by midnight of the feast! The goddess'll surely inspire you!"

"I doubt that; Uris is not widely worshipped in the Midlands, and would hardly look favorably on me. Besides, don't men have to shave their heads to attend the vigils?"

"They do," she agreed, and looked at him for a long moment before bursting into giggles at the image of him without any hair at all, with even eyebrows shaved, as was required of supplicants to Uris.

"It sounds a high price to pay for poetic inspiration," he said, but she did not hear, trying to stifle her own mirth. She did, however, hear the heavy tread on the stairs and the voice that came from outside the door of the parlor.

"Poppae! Poppae! I'm home!"

The door swung open, and Necquer entered, still in his dusty travel-ing cloak and mud-spattered riding boots. Her giggles subsided in a gasp, and she leapt to her feet and ran to him, kissing him quickly and often without discretion. He staggered under her affection, and put his arms around her to steady himself, smiling indulgently. Then he noticed Liam, and greeted him with an ironic nod.

"I'd shake your hand, Rhenford, but mine are full at the moment."

Suddenly, Poppae cried out, and ran her hand delicately down Nec-quer's cheek. Just above the line of his beard, a bright purple bruise was blooming.

"You've taken a hurt!"

"It's nothing," he murmured brusquely, taking her hand in his and drawing it away. "An unruly pair of highwaymen, without the sense to be afraid of my guards." She made to fuss about it, but he stopped her with a brief kiss. "It's nothing. You won't even notice it in a few days. Now, Rhenford, I must say I'm glad to see you here. I take it you've been entertaining?"

"Actually, I've just been trying not to be boring."

"Go to, go to," Lady Necquer scolded, shifting so that she could see both men, but leaving her arms around Necquer. "He has kindly borne my maunderings and incessant weeping over your absence, and enter-tained me most regally. He has even promised to pen me a string of poems!"

Necquer smiled at Liam's look of surprise. "Poems, eh? You're more talented than I realized, Rhenford."

"More talented than I realized, Master Necquer. I didn't know I was a poet."

"Well then, you'll stay to dinner and maybe Poppae can instruct you in the art."

"Oh, yes, do stay, Sir Liam!"

Liam was surprised to notice that Necquer honestly meant the invita-tion, though his wife's agreement had been hasty and not entirely heart-felt. And the merchant had not been at all disturbed to find his wife closeted with another man, even though he had recently found out some-one was wooing her. Had he ruled Liam completely out as a threat?

Lady Necquer's obvious desire to be alone with her husband would make that a fair judgement, he thought wryly.

"I'm afraid I cannot. I promised I'd dine with a friend tonight."

Frowning, Necquer accepted the refusal, to his wife's ill-concealed delight. "Another time, then," he said, disengaging himself from his wife to offer Liam his hand.

"Certainly," Liam said, and took the merchant's slim hand, which was warm and moist with sweat. "You really should wear some armor, and a helmet." He pointed with his free hand at Necquer's cheek.

"I do," the merchant laughed, letting go his grip on Liam's hand. "They tried to sneak up on us in the night."

Liam smiled and headed for the door with a slight bow. Lady Necquer, perhaps regretting her fickle change in interest, stopped him and kissed both his cheeks warmly.

"I'll expect you on the morrow, Sir Liam, though earlier. Say noon, if you've no objection. You'll not slip out of that string of poems so easily. We will discuss it then."

"Your servant," he said with a tremendous show of humility and a low bow, and backed out of the room.

At the bottom of the stairs Lares stood gazing reverently up.

"It's no small blessing t'have him back, eh, Sir Liam?"

"No," Liam said with a chuckle, thinking of Lady Necquer ecstatically greeting her husband. "No small blessing indeed. Goodnight, Lares."

A small wave of anger broke over him in the street. He had spent his afternoons entertaining her, turning his own life into an amusing tale to while away her waiting hours, and she had abandoned him the instant Necquer had come back. Necquer, who left her alone for months at a time!

The anger passed into reproach. It was foolish to think that way. Necquer was her husband, and obviously loved her dearly, despite what Lons had said, while he was only a recent acquaintance. And she had not simply abandoned him; she had asked him back the next day, as though nothing had changed.

Smiling a familiar, well-worn smile at himself, he wandered through the darkening streets. It was dusk, the clouds now beginning to shred into tatters beneath the onslaught of the sea breeze. Cold and stinging, the breeze scoured the sky and the rapidly emptying streets, molding his cloak to his back and legs as he walked north. Stars glittered, impossibly distant and small between the rents in the clouds.

Lady Necquer was, after all, almost a child. In her mid-twenties, he thought, and thus only five or six years younger than he, but different, in a way he sought to name.

Sheltered, he eventually thought. The only sorrows she knew were hers, while he had seen those of many others. In ports and lands Southwark had never heard of, on seas her merchants had never sailed, Liam had seen many other people's sorrows, and with an unconscious selflessness, he judged them greater than his. Greater than his burning home and his slain father, greater than being alone in a strange city and alone, for that matter, in the whole world.

It was for that reason, perhaps, that he had not objected to being linked with Fanuilh, or to finding Tarquin's murderer. One was a tie, a bond of sorts, and the other a duty that one might offer to family. He did not delude himself into thinking of Tarquin as a replacement for, or symbol of, his father; no thought could be more ridiculous. But it was a duty he wanted to fulfill, a purpose that went beyond food or shelter or survival, an unnecessary duty, and thus one gladly undertaken.

Liam thought of the house on the beach, and the quiet, dreamless night he had spent there, and decided that though it was not his yet, he would try to make it his.

But he did not want to go there yet. He wanted a drink, and something to eat, and the sound of other people enjoying themselves. And perhaps a glimpse of Rora, to take his mind off the weighty subjects he was now embarrassed to have thought about. He set his feet to the Golden Orb, the wind from the sea pushing steadily against his back, urging him on.

The theater was not yet open, he found when he arrived, his ears and the tip of his nose scarlet with the cold. It was too early for the evening's performance. Exasperated at his own foolishness, he searched the streets around for a tavern. There was no one to ask; the shops were closed and it was so early that the street in front of the theater had not yet filled up with the evening's audience.

He found a tavern on a side street only a few blocks from the Golden Orb, between a house like his landlady's, where the fourth and fifth stories leaned precariously out over the street, and a building with a crudely lettered sign that announced the school of a private teacher of rhetoric and grammar. Liam noticed with amusement that the sign had three misspellings. The tavern was called the Uncommon Player, and the wooden board that swung creakily over the door was painted with a figure in motley juggling three balls of flame. Noise trickled out, like the murmur of the sea from far away.

Inside, the common room was long and narrow, and the noise swelled to a din like battle. The tavern was packed to bursting with laughing, shouting, singing men and women, hectically enjoying themselves. Behind the bar, three men were busy trying to serve enough beer to keep the huge crowd happy. It was hot, and sweat streamed freely down many of the faces, but the smell was oddly pleasant, even with the thick banks of smoke that hovered overhead. Close, but not stifling, and fresh. The evening had only just begun, and the odors and the fun had not had time to sour. He wondered distastefully what it would be like in a few hours, and looked around for a place to sit.

There were only a few tables, inadequate for the large groups that were crammed around them, and all the standing room was taken by the raucous clientele. Even as he stood uncertainly in the doorway, however, four people stood up from the table nearest him, and Liam recognized them as actors from the rehearsal. One of them, a man, shouted loudly and waved towards the rear of the room, while the others settled with the harassed serving girl.

"Fitch! Fitch!" the man called, gesturing urgently. "Call!" Liam followed his pointing and saw Knave Fitch's flushed face nod comprehendingly towards the door and then resume talking with the group gathered around him. The man shook his head and led his three fellow actors out of the Uncommon Player.

Liam instantly installed himself at the vacant table, amazed that the four actors had managed to fit around it. He thought it barely adequate for one.

An earthenware tankard suddenly dropped to the table before him. He caught it instinctively and looked up at the hard-pressed serving girl, who nodded in approval at his quickness.

"I didn't—" he began, pitching his voice above the roar.

"All the drink we serve, master," the girl cut in, and turned abruptly to waltz away into the mass of thirsty customers.

Shrugging, Liam tested the drink and found beer, remarkably cold and far better than merely drinkable. He downed nearly half of it, looking idly around the room. The customers were not the same dour, quiet types as those in the White Grape, but they seemed better off for it, laughing and shouting and drinking hugely, unaffected by the cramped space or the din or the smoke from dozens of cheap tapers and even cheaper pipes. He liked it, assuming a blandly smiling expression while he wondered at the number of people and the pleasure they seemed to take in each other's company.

The serving girl appeared again, dancing gracefully through the unmoving crowd with a huge platter balanced above her head. She slammed the platter down on his table and breathed a huge sigh of relief before holding up her hand to stop his question.

"I know you did not order it, master, but you needs must take it, for that y'are at a table, and at the tables you needs must pay for food, even though y'eat not." She waited for a second and he smiled. She nodded and whirled away again to fight her way to the bar.

He had seen the public houses and taverns and restaurants and saloons of hundreds of cities, and had learned to be comfortable eating alone, so he turned his attention to the platter without a qualm.

Pleasantly surprised, he saw that the Uncommon Player offered nothing cooked, relying instead on quantity to make up for heat. There were three huge wheels of cheese, each spiced differently, and large loaves of flat bread. Cold meat, nuts, apple slices and butter were arrayed around the cheese and bread in workmanlike profusion. There was even a small pot of honey, and he remembered the knife at his belt with relief. The Uncommon Player apparently saw silverware as an unnecessary item.

As he ate, the crowd grew smaller, drifting out in a hail of noisy farewells, until it seemed there was only the small group gathered around Knave Fitch. He held court raucously, shouting witty obscenities and insults at his companions, who rewarded him with gusts of laughter and refillings of his tankard. Liam smiled at some of the clown's jokes, and noticed that there were three musicians at the far end of the room, playing furiously on lute, pipes and a small set of skin drums. They could only occasionally be heard over Fitch's constant stream of filth, mostly when he stopped to take monstrous gulps of beer.

Liam stared at the platter, which was still more than half full, and gave up. His stomach strained uncomfortably, and he felt short of breath; it was by far the most food he had eaten in a long while.

He pushed the platter carefully away, as though afraid some of the food might leap off it and try to run down his throat, and gave Fitch his full attention.

The clown managed two or three more rude jokes before the door of the Player burst in and Kansallus appeared like an angry god.

A *short*, angry god, Liam amended, and watched the proceedings with even more interest.

"Fitch, you bastard!" Kansallus screamed, his face purple with anger. "Call was an hour since! You've less than ten minutes to be on stage, you damned, double-damned, triply-damned ass!"

The little playwright stormed over to the clown, who was draining his tankard unperturbed, and clamped his fingers on Fitch's upper arm in a way that made Liam wince, remembering an old tutor who had done the same thing. With the thumb and forefinger pressing into the meat of the muscle, it could be exquisitely painful, but Fitch took it in stride, handing his empty tankard to a barkeeper and allowing himself to be dragged to the door. Kansallus propelled him through it with a vicious kick to his ample behind, and slammed it closed behind him.

Liam applauded softly, and Kansallus turned, his face suddenly calm and amiable, and bowed deeply. When he rose, he smiled agreeably.

"How now! It's the gentleman of the afternoon that appreciates true art! Might I?" He gestured at the empty chair across from Liam as he sat in it. "I know you not, sir, but you strike me as a man of some discretion, of some taste, if you'll allow me to say so."

"I will," Liam said, and signaled the serving girl.

Kansallus laughed loudly, and then again when the girl brought two fresh tankards to the table.

"Is it a problem when Fitch drinks before a performance?" Liam asked as the playwright downed most of his beer.

"Not in the least," Kansallus answered, smacking his lips and beaming happily. He had sharp eyes, Liam noted, but there were shadows in them, a sort of defensive mask. "He'll outshine the stars tonight, and send the groundlings to their knees weak as babes with mirth. He's best when pickled."

Noting the way Kansallus's eyes dropped to the half-full platter, Liam pushed it across the table and bade him eat, if he was hungry.

"As a rule, I don't sup on the leavings of men to whose names I'm not privy," the playwright said with a smile, though the defensive shadows were thick, ready for rejection. "I'm Kansallus, scripter and part owner of the Golden Orb."

"Liam Rhenford." He held out his hand, which the playwright took briefly and with unshadowed eyes before digging into the platter like a starving man. "You seem hungry, Kansallus of the Golden Orb. Is it not so profitable?"

"Profitable enough," the little man muttered around a huge mouthful, "but not so luxurious that I'll refuse a freely offered meal. Pray you," he said after washing the mouthful down, "if I'm not too bold, what brings a man who walks the day with an Aedile to the Unco' Player at night?"

"I thought I might see your performance tonight. I enjoyed the other one I saw very much."

"Ah, then, y'are as much caught by Rora as any other."

Nettled by the man's amused tone, Liam feigned indifference. "Rora?" The other smirked, spilling a handful of nuts into his mouth, and Liam smiled guiltily. "You must admit, she's a beautiful woman."

"Oh, aye, passing fair, until you know her well. She can be hideous as a witch, if you take my meaning. I'll disappoint you further: she's not on tonight."

"No?"

"She's this night free and the next, for that Uris-tide is nigh. She's a very zealot," he added, with a wink that suggested the opposite.

"No great temple-goer?"

"Not by half. Though no sinner, mind. Pure as the unsunned snow, our Rora." Strangely, he seemed to mean it.

"Then the way she dances is . . ."

"Intuitive," Kansallus supplied with malicious humor. "An imposture of a knowing wench. And all the more impressive for it, if you see."

"I suppose I do."

They fell silent, Liam pondering the idea of Rora's dancing while Kansallus wolfed down the rest of the platter. When he had finished it, he pushed away from the table and began picking his teeth with an immaculately clean fingernail. He was startlingly neat; though his artisan's smock was a little ragged and his thin, reddish hair unshorn, both were clean, and a slight smell of soap arose from him.

"If you do," he said, as though the conversation had not been interrupted, "I'll thank you for the meal with advice: stay clear of Rora. Any fancies you have on her she's sure not to fill, and more like to box your ears or scratch the jelly from your eyes."

"I'll keep it in mind," Liam said, laughing at the transparency of his interest. On the other hand, he imagined that Kansallus and Rora's fellow actors must be used to men showing that kind of interest.

"I'm no wagerer, friend Rhenford, but if I were, I'd have one for you." The playwright was looking at him with friendly appraisal.

"What?"

"I'd wager—though I'm neither snooper nor gossip—I'd wager that whatever else brought you to the Orb this afternoon revolved 'round a certain rich merchant's wife."

Kansallus was indeed the man he should have talked to when he first began investigating.

"And you might have won, had you phrased the bet properly. She was not the focus of the business, but a part of it."

The playwright nodded judiciously. "Lons is an arrogant, silly ass. He deserves to have panted after her, puppylike, for the whole summer. Strange, now, isn't it, that Lons, handsome piece of work that he is, should have such trouble getting what he wants, while his sister has so little getting what she doesn't?"

Liam agreed, and bent forward at the playwright's beckoning finger.

"Though there are some," he whispered furtively, "knaves and cai-tiffs all, mind, but some nonetheless, who say that Rora may get that trouble she wants, but only from a certain individual troubler." He nod-ded again and leaned back, finishing his tankard with an air of having imparted a great secret.

"And that troubler?"

Kansallus shook his head and sighed regretfully. "A cypher, a mys-tery, an unknown quantity of indistinct parts. None of the caitiffs and knaves and vicious gossips who say it can warrant it, and I'm of a mind t'ignore it, but there you are—it's been bruited about."

"I see." He rose to go, and dropped a handful of coins on the table. "It's been fascinating, friend Kansallus, if disappointing as regards a cer-tain dancer. I think there's enough there for another few tankards, if you don't have to go back to the theater."

"I don't, bless you," the playwright said with a broad smile. "And for it, I'll tell you this—have ever seen Knave Fitch scratch at's ear while on the boards?"

"No," Liam admitted. He decided not to mention that he had only seen the clown three times, one of them within the last few minutes.

"Well, he does, from time to time, and the common run think it a pose of comic thought, but's not." Kansallus paused and smiled secretly. "It's a scar he's scratching—from the teeth of a maid."

"Rora," Liam supplied, and was rewarded with a firm nod.

"I know, to look at, Fitch's no rake—but he's a fair number of maids under's belt, and we all at th'Orb give him first crack at any wench. So it chanced when Rora was newly with us as a dancer out of some house on the Point and on her brother's vouching, we stood back and let Fitch go to work. The very next day he appears with a bandaged head, and tells us all she's a hellcat for her virtue, and to stay away. So, that's the dancer—and my warning. Go for tamer flesh."

"I'll bear it in mind. Now I must go."

"Say, friend Liam," Kansallus stopped him again, "one last. I note a writing case at your side. Y'are not, by chance, a scripter as I am?"

"No," Liam answered, looking curiously down at the playwright. "Only sometimes a scholar."

"Excellent news," Kansallus said, the smile deepening. "There's enough of scribblers 'round the Orb, and I'd hate to find this meal a sop for your taking away my livelihood."

Still laughing, Liam made his way through the darkened streets, guided only by the stars and the occasional torch. Kansallus made an excellent source of information, as well as an interesting companion. Not that Coeccias was a bad sort, but he lacked the playwright's good-natured but malicious tongue.

The night was cold, even colder after the warmth of the inn, and he had to fight now against the freshening sea breeze. The doors to the Golden Orb were still open, but he passed them by, wondering what Rora was doing with her evening off.

Sounds were few and far between, the streets empty, and he started once at what he thought was the sound of feet behind him. Then he heard the coo of a pigeon and the flap of wings and smiled with relief. Coeccias might not be very good at searching out murderers, but in four months of frequent night walks he had never been accosted, and that reflected well on the Aedile. The streets were clear of the common run of villains, if private houses weren't safe from the uncommon run.

Nonetheless, he found himself looking over his shoulder more than usual, unable to shake the feeling that he was being watched. Try as he might, he was on edge for the length of his walk, and reached the stables with a genuine feeling of relief.

The boy let him stand inside, out of the cold, while his mount was saddled. Once on Diamond, he felt better, and trotted quickly out of the city towards Tarquin's house on the beach.

My *house on the beach,* he reminded himself, and smiled at the thought.

■ *10* ■

ONCE AGAIN THE house was lit before he arrived, and the warm yellow light spilling from its windows helped him find his way down the narrow path in the moonless night. The surf was unseen but loud, crashing in the blackness like the shouting of giants. He tethered Diamond in the small shed, apologizing for the cramped quarters. He thought about bringing out a blanket to keep the chill off, but noticed that the air of the shed had already grown warmer.

Tarquin planned for everything, he thought, and patted the restive horse soothingly before going back to the house.

You are home early, Fanuilh thought at him as soon as he had closed the door. Liam bit off a retort and waited until he went into the workroom.

"Yes, I'm home early," he said pleasantly when he could see the tiny dragon's face. "I decided that even murderers must sleep, and that if they'd been avoiding me with as much energy as I've been searching for them, they must be tired."

That is not why.

"No, of course not. Why would I bother lying to you, when you can read mind? I'm joking, though that seems to be as useless as lying, since you don't have a sense of humor."

I find different things funny.

"I'm sure you do." There was a long pause. Liam frowned, wondering what Fanuilh would find funny, and the dragon simply leveled its yellow cat's eyes at him. Dragon humor was beyond him, he finally decided, and thought back to his meal at the Uncommon Player. "Are you hungry?"

Yes.

"I'll get you something."

The dragon's head snaked in a sinuous nod, and Liam went to the kitchen and desired raw meat as hard as he could, discovering with a mixture of satisfaction and disgust that it was no longer so difficult.

Fanuilh tore into the meat with its usual gusto, and Liam watched for a few minutes before beginning to wander absently around the workroom. The empty crystal bottle still lay alone on the empty middle table. He picked it up.

'Virgin's blood.' It no longer held the same repulsion for him; it had become simply a relic, devoid of meaning, a jumble of letters that he should have been able to decipher.

He wondered why it was empty, and why the label was crossed out.

What is important about the beaker? It is empty. What can be important about—

"I don't know, but I might if you'd let me think," he said, and though he could not hear the words over the silent block of Fanuilh's thought, the dragon accepted it, and the block lifted. Liam crossed his arms and tipped the beaker at the dragon.

"The vanishing spell does not require virgin's blood, correct? It's not mentioned in the text of the spell. But he had it out on his table, and he never left things lying around; you said so yourself. This must be important."

The number of spells that require virgin's blood is enormous. Tarquin must have over a hundred of them in his catalogues. The uses to which they can be put are a hundred times a hundred.

"How can you read my mind and be so stupid? Maybe one of those was the one Marcius came about," Liam shouted, tired of the dragon's apparent obtuseness. "And Tarquin cast it—the bottle is empty—but not to Marcius's satisfaction!"

Why are you so certain the merchant is the killer?

"Because he *could* be a murderer!" He shouted louder, trying to justify what was really only a feeling.

Many men could be. You could be, the dragon pointed out. Though he knew the creature was incapable of real irony, Liam could not help feeling that its impassive face and toneless thoughts masked a greater sarcasm.

"But you know I'm not!"

Not of Tarquin, yes. But you have killed, and you could kill again. I know, as well as you do. You would regret it, to be sure, but you could kill.

"Enough! I'm in no mood for you to be my conscience. Did you do this to Tarquin? Small wonder he ordered you away so often. And that's not a question you're meant to answer!" he added hastily, and the dragon obliged by staying out of his head. He went to stand by the lectern.

The color and texture of the pages did not match, and they differed in size from spell to spell. Sometimes the inks varied, though most of the writing was in black, in Tarquin's clear, blocklike script. As he flipped idly through the tome, he noticed a page covered with red in a wildly different handwriting.

Another mage's spell, Fanuilh supplied, its back to Liam, still intent on the meat. *They can trade them back and forth, or steal them. It is the instructions that matter, not who wrote them. That book was only stitched together very recently. It contains all the important spells he had collected over his career.*

Liam tried to lift the heavy tome, and found he needed both hands. The chain clanked.

"These are all the spells he collected? What about the books on the shelves? And in the library?"

All the important spells, the dragon qualified. *The books behind you are instructions for mixing and preparing the elements of the spells, and one or two lengthy reports of experiments. The library contains thirty or forty texts on the enchanting of objects; the rest are histories, or poetry, or philosophy or collections of fables. Master Tanaquil liked to read a great deal.*

"I gathered as much from his conversation."

Fanuilh did not respond and Liam turned to the shelf, leaning back against the lectern to examine the books. There were few with marked spines, most of the unadorned leather or wood, many cracked and begining to fall apart from long use.

He wondered which described the uses of virgin's blood. The empty bottle and its crossed-out label annoyed him.

"Tell me, Fanuilh, what spells do you know?"

The thought was a long time in forming.

I know very few. Only those appropriate to an apprentice, as they do not generally require speaking and use few precious ingredients. Master Tanaquil taught them to me from the spellbook he had when he was an apprentice.

"What can you do?"

Put a man to sleep, light a fire, stop blood flowing if the wound is fairly small, cause itching, or uncontrollable laughter. Maybe a dozen others. Useful things, and some that were merely for practice in the discipline.

"You can cause uncontrollable laughter?"

Yes.

Shaking his head with a smile, Liam left the lectern and walked to the door. He stood there and stretched luxuriously.

"How are you feeling?"

Better. The soreness fades. Soon I will be able to fly again.

Liam received the news with an approving nod.

"I'm going to go to sleep now, if you don't need anything else. Wake me two hours after sunrise, will you?"

The dragon's head bobbed gracefully and Liam left the workroom, suppressing a yawn.

He did not go right to the library, but wandered curiously through the house he had accepted as his own. The light was even throughout the house, but the empty, echoing sound was gone. The parlor, the kitchen, the trophy room all felt comfortable, almost welcoming. He did not disturb anything, just entered each room briefly and surveyed the furnishings, smiling the lightly bitter smile that even after ten years of use had not creased his face.

It's not Rhenford Keep, but it will do, I suppose.

Still smiling, as much at himself as at his house, he went into the library to sleep.

Fanuilh woke him precisely at the hour he requested, though there was no accompanying illusion of stone cities from his travels. The call in his mind felt normal, proper in a strange way.

I used to wake Master Tanaquil this way, came the dragon's thought as Liam sat on the edge of the divan, rubbing the sleep from his eyes. He did not comment, but went to the kitchen and imagined another platter of meat for it. He brought the food to the workroom and laid it on the table.

"Eat your fill," he said cheerily. "I want you well and whole soon, so you can begin holding up your end of the bargain."

You think you can fulfill your end soon.

Liam thought for a moment, his eyes on the intricate model by the window, and on the jagged Teeth that dominated it.

"Yes, I do. Today will answer a number of questions."

They were silent for a while, Liam lost in thought, his eyes unfocused on the model. Fanuilh did not eat, but stared at him. He grew aware of the dragon's gaze after a moment, and started with a guilty smile.

"What was I thinking?" he challenged.

Nothing. Your thoughts were diffused.

"What is that like? Looking at diffused thoughts, I mean? How does it appear to you?"

The dragon's stare impaled his, holding it till he grew uneasy, wondering. Finally, the block formed in his mind, and he realized the creature had been searching for a way to express the idea.

Like a flock of birds that explode suddenly from a city square, so scattered and intermingled that you cannot follow any single one. It is confusion.

With even more surprise, he saw that the idea was his, drawn from a memory he had of the birdsellers and their flocks in Torquay.

"I was daydreaming, not confused."

No, but you allowed your thoughts to fly apart. You do that often, letting many lines go their ways, not following any particular one. Master Tanaquil never did that. His thoughts were orderly, like the steps in a ritual. It was easy to follow them.

"Well, then, it's a good thing you won't have to look into my head much longer. We'll finish this business in the next few days, and you can teach me. Now, if there's nothing else, I'll be on my way." The dragon shook its head in wide, sweeping arcs. "Fine. I suggest you study up on what you have to teach me while I'm gone."

The dragon stopped moving its head, and tucked it down between its forelegs, like a dog preparing for rest.

"Good boy," Liam muttered, and went to get his horse.

The morning was colder than the night, and his breath plumed out in clouds that the sharp breeze tore to tatters. Diamond was not cold, but restive, unhappy with the cramped confines of the shed. He tossed his mane and snorted when Liam led him out onto the beach, kicking up spurts of sand that the wind caught and whirled, stinging, into Liam's eyes.

He calmed the horse with a soft word, and once they were up the cliff path, gave him rein. Thundering over the frozen ruts of the road, they passed fields dusted with frost, and Liam had to duck his face down into his cloak to escape the bite of the wind.

Cheeks tingling and scarlet with cold, he gave the snorting horse over to the boy at the stables, and set off briskly for the Aedile's house. The sun was bright and the sky a pale blue that reminded him of summer, but there was no warmth in the light, and a deep chill lingered in the shadows cast by the bleached gray stone and wood of the city.

Coeccias's servant let him into the house and directed him to the small kitchen at the rear. The Aedile was there, using a ladle to stir a large pot hung on a swivel hook over the fire.

"Rhenford, y'are here just in time. I'll have you test this brew, and escape it myself if it's foul." He filled the ladle with steaming liquid from the pot and shoved it in Liam's face. "Go to, go to! Drink!" he commanded.

Inclining his head, Liam sniffed suspiciously and then hazarded a small sip. It was mulled cider, and though it scalded his tongue, it slid down his throat smoothly, to form a warm, spiced ball in his stomach. He nodded appreciatively and took another sip.

"It's not just cider," he accused, to the Aedile's amusement.

"And should it be?" Coeccias pulled two pewter mugs from the mantel above the fire and filled them from the pot, which he then swung further away from the fire. He gestured Liam to a seat at the cluttered wooden table that filled most of the kitchen, and placed one of the steaming mugs in front of him.

"It's a hint of the very water of life, to add the inspirational tone. I've to make a greater batch for Uris-tide, and this is but a test." He took a sip of his own mug and smacked his lips with closed eyes. "It'll do."

A scent of cinnamon rose from the cider, mingled with the hint of liquor, and Liam sipped again approvingly. Coeccias called his servant, and when the man appeared, gave orders for his breakfast.

"You'll eat?" he asked Liam, and without waiting for an answer, told the servant to double the breakfast. Liam smiled into his mug as the heavy man took the seat across from him.

The servant busied himself cutting up bread and bacon and setting them to cook by the fire. The seated men sipped at their mugs for a moment. Liam let the spiked cider warm his hands and stomach, looking around the kitchen. It was messy, but well stocked, with bunches of herbs and vegetables hanging in no particular order from the rafters, pots and utensils scattered everywhere, mingled with half-eaten loaves and scraps of cheese and meat and dirty dishes. Reflecting on the Aedile, it did not surprise him, but it did not bother him either. The suggestion was not of filth, but of comfort and a relaxed attitude towards cleanliness. Liam liked it, in the way he liked Coeccias—with tolerance for obvious faults.

"I thought we were going to look for the barmaid."

"Truth, so we are. But we needs must be fed, eh? And the cider calls for tasting. It'd be blaspheming to offer good Uris an untested brew. It likes you?"

"Yes, very much. But why do you have to make a bigger batch?" Liam gestured at the large pot, obscured by the servant's back as he knelt before the fire, prodding the crackling bacon. "You have enough there to last a while."

Laughing, Coeccias said, "Enough? I'll swear there's little enough for the worshippers, if that was all I put up. Know you nothing about the uses of Uris-tide?"

The servant began laying out dishes on the table.

"No, in the Midlands we never made much of Uris. She was a city god to us, of little use to farmers and husbandmen. There are not many mechanics or apothecaries there."

"What of your vintners, tanners, smiths, armorers, tinkers? Have you no brewers or candlers in the Midlands? Y'are yourself a scholar, and from the Midlands. Uris is patron of all these—how can Midlanders ignore her?"

"I suppose the trades just seemed less important. We paid more attention to the harvest gods."

Coeccias snorted and frowned his way through the rest of his mug. Liam decided not to mention that there were hundreds of places that had never heard of Uris, and that credited her gifts of craft and trade to other gods.

The bacon and toast were ready, and the servant placed them before them in silence, taking their mugs to refill them at the pot. Butter and salt were brought and Coeccias dug in, making huge sandwiches thick with butter. Liam, made hungry by the smell, copied him, and the kitchen was filled with the sound of their chewing.

The Aedile's frown deepened at each bite, and then broke out into a question.

"Truth, you know nothing of the rites of Uris-tide?"

"Very little," Liam admitted.

"And you a scholar," Coeccias marveled. "Well," he went on, carefully putting his third sandwich to one side, "the true rites are complex, and the sole sphere of the priests. Only the divines are allowed in the fane when they are performed, but there're numerous lesser rites for the common run of worshippers."

Solemnly, he described the lay rituals that led up to the actual day of Uris-tide. Daily processions through the streets began six days before, and every true worshipper was supposed to walk on at least one of the days. Some, the very devout, made more than one. Viyescu, the Aedile pointed out with no hint of sarcasm, walked every day, displaying an unparalleled devotion. Each day's procession was led by a progressively higher-ranked priest, and so more worshippers attended the later ones.

The procession Liam had seen was one of the first, and consequently one of the smallest.

"Today's is the most important. I'll be marching, as the Duke's man, and the richest of Uris's images will go forth as well, gilt and jeweled. It was gifted the temple by the Duke himself, and cost a fortune. The Duke subscribes the old ways and worships right strongly."

Beginning at midafternoon in the square at the heart of the city, the procession would go from there around most of Southwark, offering Uris's blessing to all and particularly to artisans and craftsmen. It would be led by the second most important priest in the local temple and include the highest of the city's officials and the richest of her artisans, as well as a large number of commoners. The last procession, scheduled for the next day, would be comprised only of clergy, led by the hierarch of the temple, and carry a very simple image of Uris, an ancient relic handed down from the earliest days of her worship. That night the secret ceremonies would begin in the temple, and the common worshippers would eat only the simplest of foods. Unleavened bread, sauceless meat, milk and water, to symbolize life before Uris gave her arts to the world.

"The cider is reserved for Uris-tide itself. It's a strange brew, liquor and cider and spices, but it goes well with the stuffs served. Look you, on that day, we eat fancifully, with sauces and pastries and dishes that are long in preparation and complex in design, like unto the arts Uris herself gave us, and we offer portions of all to her as grace. I'll bring the pot to my sister, and celebrate with her. She's a large get of children, and many others'll be there from her husband's family, so I needs must make a greater punch than this test here."

Coeccias stopped and picked up his sandwich again. He chewed absently, calculation in his eyes as he looked at Liam, who stared into the rich brown depths of his mug, wondering at his companion's obvious belief.

"Look you," the Aedile said at length, "would it like you t'attend the feast? At my sister's?"

Liam was surprised, but immediately interested. "I suppose, yes, that would be nice," he answered, trying to conceal the attractiveness of the idea.

"Come, come," Coeccias blurted impatiently, "Uris-tide is not time to rest alone. It'd be improper for you to spend it in that empty house. You'll come to my sister's."

There was no room for objection, so Liam simply nodded his agreement.

"Good, then," Coeccias said gruffly. "We'd best get to it, if we're to find this barmaid before I must prepare for the procession."

Gulping down the rest of his cider, Liam followed the Aedile out of the house.

There were seventeen inns, taverns and public houses in the Point, as well as a few private clubs and special establishments that Coeccias thought worth checking.

Though the streets of this quarter were as narrow as those in the rest of the city, the area was much better laid out, with something approaching a plan. They were able, therefore, to follow an orderly route, covering the relatively straight roads one by one. Further down in the city the roads twisted and angled in mazelike complexity, joined by uncountable alleys and hidden courts, all of which could harbor an eating house or wineshop, and Coeccias explained that his men had had to spend a great deal of time to cover a small area.

"I should have thought Tarquin unlikely to frequent the lower haunts, but it struck me not. Happily, there're not so many up here. We'll be through by an hour after noon, and if this Donoé exists, we'll search her out."

Polished paneling and expensive fittings, gilt and silver, foreign hangings and crystal goblets, intricately painted signboards—the inns and restaurants were expensively decorated, the rich accouterments proper for the neighborhood's merchant princes and giants of trade. Some even had their offerings painstakingly painted on large boards, for those customers who could read. The proprietors were quiet, polite men, singularly colorless, who could scarcely be bothered to remember the names of their wives, let alone their serving girls.

It was early in the day, and most of the places they stopped had not even opened yet, but Coeccias's title gained them entrance at every one. It was unfair, Liam knew, to compare these sophisticated restaurants and taverns with the Uncommon Player, but he could not help it. Two hours before noon, they could not be expected to have customers, but they still seemed unnaturally somber, depressing in the stilted formality of furnishings you were afraid to touch and proprietors who acted like courtiers in a tyrant's court. He silently praised the Player, and vowed to avoid the rich quarter if he wished to enjoy himself.

They were most of the way through Coeccias's mental list when they came to a stone building that fronted a stretch of street that was inordinately large for the quarter. It had a full portico with fluted columns a foot thick above which rested a triangular frieze, and broad steps made of carefully fitted blocks of white stone. There was no painted sign or nameplate to announce its purpose, and Liam laid a hand on the Aedile's arm as he started up the steps.

"What's this? It's someone's house."

"No house, this," he muttered, and surprised Liam by flushing. "Come along."

Bas-relief panels adorned the double-leafed doors, but Liam did not have a chance to examine them, because the Aedile pulled one door open hastily and ushered him inside.

White and pink marble greeted them, totally at odds with the gray exterior, and Liam paused, unable to believe what he saw. A sweeping flight of marble stairs curved up and away from a huge foyer, lined with niches holding amorously entangled statues and potted plants. Banks of exotic flowers bloomed in vivid reds and oranges, filling the air with heady scents. Water danced and splashed in a fountain at the center of the room, two stone lovers entwining in the pool. Two young women appeared far away at the top of the steps and then fled, giggling.

"Gods, Coeccias," Liam exclaimed, "it's a whorehouse!"

The Aedile silenced him with a staggering punch to the arm and a frantic "Hsst! Not so loud!"

"Why 'Hsst,' milord Aedile?" The speaker appeared smoothly from behind a heavy arras concealing a doorway. She was tall and bore herself proudly, with an elaborately curled headdress of gleaming black hair and an artfully painted face. "Though we glaze it over with 'house of pleasure' and 'night palace,' we are indeed a whorehouse. The man has the right of it."

She stepped in front of Liam and gazed with imperious amusement at him. "He needs must have seen one before to recognize it so quickly." She held out a ringed hand coolly, and Liam bent over it, suddenly embarrassed.

"Liam Rhenford, lady," he stammered. "Your servant."

Her laughter was loud but not harsh. "Your pardon, sir, but men rarely say that here. In this house, it is more often a woman who gives that office." She turned to Coeccias, leaving Liam crushed and flustering in her wake. "Coeccias," she said warmly, giving him a lingeringly formal kiss on both cheeks. "What brings you to my house?"

"Business, Herione. A few questions for you, if you've the time."

"Ever business, Coeccias," she murmured, and slid her arm through his to draw him towards the arras. "Come along, servant," she called over her shoulder to Liam, who followed along hanging his head.

Behind the arras a corridor led towards the rear of the palatial whorehouse, and Herione went directly into the first room they came to. Walking side by side, arms linked, she and Coeccias seemed matched in size and height, appropriate to each other. Herione was broad, but not fat, statuesque, even in a girl's gown that had no hint of girlishness.

The room was her office, a fact attested by the ledgers in racks on the walls and the tidy columns of coins on a small writing table. A slate board bore a painted diagram of the house, with a woman's name and a blank line chalked into each room; Liam read the women's names and smiled; each was a princess or queen from history or legend. After the lavish entrance hall, the office seemed spartan. Herione gracefully motioned them to a pair of straight-backed cane chairs, and settled herself in a more comfortable padded seat behind the writing table. She traced Liam's gaze to the slate board, and gave a smile that did not reach her eyes.

"Y'are impressed, sir? Blue blood and true, one and all. Only royalty here."

Noting the coldness of her smile, Liam spoke nonchalantly, peering with studied consternation at the slate lists. "I was just wondering if you knew that Princess Cresside was a hunchback in life."

Her smile began touching her eyes. "Well, sir, with no queen worth a whit in Torquay, we needs must take our royalty where we can."

"Well, how can there be a queen in Torquay?" Liam responded, grandly flinging a hand at the slate board. "You have them all here!"

The smile reached her eyes finally, and Liam thought he might have made up for his gaffe in the hall.

"Tell me, Coeccias," she said, turning to the officer, who had fidgeted through the exchange, "is this your business? T'upbraid me for the naming of my stable?"

"A scholar, Herione. It's his business to know such things. He meant no offense."

"Coeccias, y'are wooden," she sighed. "I know't, he knows't; why make you amends? Now come, your business." She steepled her hands before her on the table among the coins, and became serious.

"Have you a girl named Donoé here? A barmaid, or serving wench?"

"None such," she replied instantly.

"Not perhaps one of your empresses?" Coeccias asked, raising an eyebrow at the slate board. Herione shook her head definitely.

"None such. Why do you ask?"

The Aedile glanced at Liam, who shrugged absently, still looking at the slate board. "We're looking for a girl of that name, who may've known the wizard Tanaquil."

"The murdered wizard." She did not seem fazed by the news, but she did look curiously at Liam. "Do you always string along a scholar when you con a murderer, Coeccias?"

"No," the Aedile rasped at the playful tone in her voice. "He knew the wizard best of any, and's proved helpful. So, no Donoé, and we're to't again. Come, Rhenford."

He stood, but Liam waved for him to stop.

"Wait a moment, if you would. I've a question or two the lady may be able to answer, if I may ask."

Coeccias muttered, " 'Take no surprise' " to himself, but remained standing behind his chair. Herione shifted polite interest to Liam, who moved his gaze from the slate board to her.

"Your questions, sir?"

"Has Ancus Marcius ever come here?"

"Ever? More than ever, sir. Quite often. Twice, thrice a moon. And's good for a solid gold each visit," she added meaningfully to Coeccias. "I'd hope this won't reflect on him."

"If he's a murderer, bawdry won't soil him any more."

Herione offered a slight nod in agreement.

"Truth," she exclaimed softly.

"One other question, if I may. Has Freihett Necquer ever come here?"

"Necquer?" She frowned into her memory.

"A Freeporter merchant."

"Oh, yes, yes. Necquer. Once, perhaps, a long while since, over two years. He took a wife not long after, and has not returned since."

Liam nodded, gratified. "Thank you, lady."

Coeccias muttered his thanks and the two left, going unescorted through the empty foyer with its gurgling fountain and out into the cold street.

Liam paused for a moment on the steps to look closely at the bas-relief panels set into the doors. They depicted strange scenes, large groups of people engaged in uncertain acts. The carvings were not explicit and, in fact, were strangely tasteful, almost artistic. He tried to trace the intricacies of one scene with the point of a long finger, and then gave up and went down the steps to join Coeccias.

"An acquaintance?" He phrased the question as casually as he could, though he was more than a little curious. There had been undercurrents running rampant in Herione's office that went beyond Coeccias's responsibility for keeping tabs on the local houses of pleasure. Yet he could not imagine the stolid, bulky Aedile having anything to do with the quick-witted madame.

"What's Necquer in this?" Coeccias shot back, ignoring the issue. "Is his wife Lons's taskmaster?"

"She is, but I don't think Necquer's involved. I asked for . . . personal reasons."

Liam took it as a measure of how little the Aedile wanted to talk about Herione that he did not press about Necquer. That was all right; it was Coeccias's business, after all, and the visit had dispelled his suspicions of Necquer. If the merchant had been unfaithful to his wife, as Lons had suggested, he would have done it in Herione's house, clearly the most expensive in the city and, from its unassuming front, the most discreet.

So discreet, Liam thought, *that in four months I never heard of it. What else is there in this city that I've missed? The Golden Orb, the worship of Uris, Herione's house—so much I've missed, and so little I can say I've seen.*

Preoccupied with his own morose thoughts, he did not hear Coeccias the first time, and had to ask him to repeat his statement, which he did after clearing his throat.

"I said she was somewhat of an acquaintance. The Duke requires a man to register the houses. The office is mine."

Liam accepted the tight-lipped explanation with a noncommittal sound and remained prudently silent. Coeccias strode along the street with a heavy thunder in his thick brows.

The owner of the second-to-last inn on their list somewhat nervously said that yes, he did have a serving girl named Donoé. When Coeccias had allayed his fears that the girl was a criminal, and convinced him that they only wanted to ask her a few questions, he bustled off, shouting her name.

"Fortune bears us only a small grudge," Coeccias growled at the innkeeper's retreating back. "She saved us from one last house; quite generous of Her." Liam nodded absently.

The inn seemed appropriate to Tarquin. It was comfortable, without the ostentation of the others in the rich quarter. The woods were blond, and light flooded in from a large window, and it reminded Liam slightly of the wizard's home on the beach. For a man who had chosen to live outside a city, it would be a good place for a quiet drink when he had to be there.

Donoé, when she was dragged from the kitchen by the anxious proprietor, was the girl he remembered. Hiding her fidgeting hands in a wet cloth, flushed and eyeing Coeccias subserviently, she was a far cry from the laughing young woman Tarquin had so gallantly sent on her way in the summer, but he could not mistake her looks. She was very young, perhaps only sixteen, and had the sort of prettiness that is mostly youth and innocence, and only really noticeable when informed with happiness. At the inn, confronted with the Aedile's bearlike scowl, her prettiness faded into fear, and she was not worth a second look.

Liam regretted it, recalling her happy smile in the summer, on Tarquin's veranda. Coeccias made it worse by snorting as soon as she appeared, which frightened her even more than her employer's peremptory summons.

"Herself?" Coeccias asked him, and when he nodded, went on gruffly: "Well then, to't. You wanted her."

Wincing at the words' effect on the wilting girl, Liam cleared his throat and spoke to her as pleasantly as he could, indicating one of the tables.

"Perhaps you'd care to sit? Coeccias, could you get us something to drink?"

The Aedile trudged grudgingly off to the proprietor, and the girl reluctantly took a seat at the empty table, staring wide-eyed at Liam, who smiled reassuringly.

"Do you remember me?"

She shook her head vehemently.

"You're sure? On the beach, maybe? You were there a few times."

Though her eyes could not get any wider, they changed expression from fear to recognition, her hands clapping to the tabletop to emphasize it. "From the beach! You were at the wizard's!" Recognition changed back to fear, and she practically wailed. "Oh my lord, is that the matter? I swear I'd nothing to do with his taking off, I swear!"

"I know, I know," he assured her hastily, aware he was handling it badly. "I only want to ask you a few questions, Donoé. I know you haven't done anything."

"I was sore sad to hear he'd died, sore sad, my lord!"

"Yes, yes, I know, but I have to ask you a few questions."

He patted her hand gently, which seemed to calm her a little, and Coeccias brought two cups of wine with ill grace, which gave her some time to collect herself. The Aedile retired to the bar, leaving them alone.

"Now, Donoé, I have to ask you a few questions," he repeated, when she was more sure of herself. "About Tarquin. I need to know if you knew anything about his affairs."

"Oh, no, my lord, I never pried nor gossiped, my lord, I swear!"

"Let me ask that a different way. Do you know if he saw any other women?"

"Other women?" She was clearly puzzled.

"Did he bring any other women home that you know of? Any, maybe, that he met here, or elsewhere?"

She thought for a moment, and suddenly looked full into his eyes in shock.

"My lord!"

"What?"

"You think I . . . I . . . you think he *knew* me!" She whispered it fiercely, in disbelief and accusation, and Liam colored instantly. He was handling this very badly, he knew, but took comfort from the fact that Coeccias probably would have bungled it worse.

"Well, I suppose, I—" he stammered.

"He did no such," she stated indignantly. "I'm only a poor serving girl, I know, but I'm chaste, and Master Tanaquil was a true gentle! He'd an oath of purity himself, he said!"

Momentarily stunned by her vehement defense of her virtue, Liam sought for words, and finally asked tentatively, "Then what were you doing at his house?"

It was her turn to color, and though he had thought the question natural, it seemed to deflate her rage at his insinuation.

"He wanted blood," she whispered, lowering her head in shame.

"Blood?"

"The blood of a virgin."

He had to strain to hear the words she spoke into her lap, but they disappointed him deeply. The empty decanter had held *her* blood, and Tarquin had probably crossed out the label because he had used it all. A hundred uses for virgin's blood, Fanuilh had said. Tarquin might well have gone through gallons of it, and the clue he had thought so much of was nothing.

Donoé lifted her head and glared defiance at him again. "But it hurt not a bit, and Master Tanaquil was a true gentle, and paid me well, and there's naught wrong with what I did! I'm chaste, you, and Mater Tanaquil was a true gentle! He'd an oath! I tell you, you've no right to slander me nor him, serpent!"

She was standing by the end of her tirade, though he thanked all the gods he could remember that she did not raise her voice. She did, however, turn on her heel after labeling him a snake, and stalked back to the kitchen with all the terrible dignity of an affronted and wrathful teenage girl. She even shouldered her employer aside.

Though he had not heard all of their exchange, Donoé's abrupt exit and Liam's chastened expression told him enough, and Coeccias laughed loudly, coming to the table.

"Come along, 'serpent.' Y'have insulted enough of Southwark's maids." He propelled Liam out of the inn to the street, leaving the cups of wine untasted.

"That," Liam sighed, "was very bad."

"Y'have no talent for searching into the innocent," Coeccias commented cheerfully, drawing him along the street, "and if that's a murderer, I'll scale the Teeth. Now, if she'd been a killer with blood on her blade and it at your throat, you'd have battered her to her knees with questions. No shame not to hone your wit on girls, Rhenford. Now, what'd she relate?"

Still unhappy with the way he had conducted the interview, Liam told what he had found out: the origin of the virgin's blood, the purpose of Donoé's visit to the beach, and most importantly, the oath Tarquin claimed he had taken.

"A vow to remain chaste, eh? I've heard wizards do stranger," the Aedile said. "It fair puts Viyescu's mystery maid out of thought."

"And leaves us with Marcius, and Lons."

"It leaves us with Lons," the Aedile said. "There's naught that's proved against the merchant."

"Hmm."

Coeccias rolled his eyes in exasperation, but Liam did not notice. A piece of Donoé's story had lodged itself irritatingly in his head.

"If you were a wizard," he suddenly asked, "wouldn't you have to test to know if your virgin's blood was good?"

"What?"

"Do you think Tarquin had a test? A way to know if she were still a virgin?"

"Truth," Coeccias answered with a smile, "I scarcely know her, but I'd wager that trull'll be a virgin on her deathbed."

Liam ignored the Aedile's joke; he had not been thinking about Donoé at all. He pushed the idea to the back of his head, and took up considering more immediate questions. They walked towards the outskirts of the rich quarter, the Aedile smiling at the warmthless sun bright in the sky, Liam staring at the cobbles, tracing his thoughts there.

Why had he mishandled Donoé so badly? Was the other man right, he could only be sharp with people he truly suspected? In a certain way, it was comforting to think that he was not completely suspicious, that only those who deserved it called out the bloodhound in him. And in the end, he had gotten the important information.

On the other hand, they were left with Lons, a conclusion he could not believe.

They left the confines of the rich quarter without saying a word, passing into an area of smaller buildings of poorer construction and pushed closer together. Suddenly remembering his appointment with Lady Necquer, Liam stopped.

"I just remembered; I am supposed to meet someone soon, back there."

Without a trace of anything more than casual curiosity, Coeccias said, "Poppae Necquer?"

"Yes," Liam answered shortly, refusing to be surprised by what the rough-looking man picked up.

"Then we'll part here. I'm to prepare for the procession. We ought to meet later, to see if there's any current news."

"The White Grape for dinner?"

"No, the Grape grows stale for me, and I've all that cider to finish. Come to my house after the procession. You'll know it's done by the bells. The priests'll toll all when the procession gains the temple."

"Your house, then," Liam agreed.

Coeccias smiled and suddenly stuck out his heavy hand, and Liam took it firmly.

"Though y'are only a scholar, y'are a good hound, Rhenford, and a better man. Don't fret so over a silly girl, nor over the player. We've got to see justice done—I for my office, and you for the wizard. Whatever we do, whatever we've done, is to a higher end."

Liam fidgeted, but Coeccias would not let go of his hand until he relented.

"I suppose so. I suppose you're right."

His hand was released, and the two men bid each other goodbye diffidently, as if embarrassed by their words and thoughts. Coeccias went down the street to the city's heart and his procession. Liam turned around and traced his way back towards the Point and the Necquers' house.

■ *11* ■

LIAM WAS NOT far from the Necquers' when he left Coeccias, and the bells had only just begun to announce noon when he knocked on their street door. Lares received him as usual, but did not usher him up to the parlor. Instead, he motioned for Liam to wait and, avoiding his eyes, hurried up the stairs himself.

A few minutes later, Lady Necquer came down in a whirl of skirts, her face drawn and pale. She stopped on the bottom step and shot a fearful look back up before coming quickly to him.

"You must away, Sir Liam," she whispered anxiously. "I cannot receive you this day." Her eyes kept returning to the stairs, as though she were afraid something horrible would come down them.

"May I ask why? Are you ill?"

She laid a hand on his arm, and quickly withdrew it. "My apologies, Sir Liam, but I beg you not to press. I simply cannot receive you. You may come tomorrow, at this hour, if y'are careful."

"But—" He did not move, not understanding, and her face screwed up suddenly before she burst out:

"My lord would not have you so much about! Now please, Sir Liam, do not ask the wherefore; only go!"

Bewildered, Liam hesitated in the face of her distress, shifting from foot to foot.

"Please," she begged. "Come tomorrow, and let none see you."

His thoughts scattered, and he retreated, sketching a hasty bow. She

shut the door firmly behind him. Standing in the street, he stared at the
closed door and blew out a heavy breath.

"Necquer won't have me around so much," he wondered aloud, then
turned away down the street, shaking his head and muttering. "And just
the other day he asked me to dinner. Freeporters. Hah."

The afternoon stretched emptily before him, with nothing to do. He
had hoped to fill a large part of it with Lady Necquer, listening to her
outline the series of poems he could not write. The odd hour he could fill
with wandering, or maybe a visit to the Uncommon Player. Now there
was nothing, and it was far too early to go to a wineshop.

A long lunch was a poor second, he decided, but it was all he had.
Over the course of the morning, he and Coeccias had been into every
tavern in the Point but one, and he chose this last one to eat in, solely
because it was the farthest from the Necquers' and would take the lon-
gest time to reach.

It did not take as long as he wished to get there, but the service made
up for it by being extraordinarily slow. He could almost feel the minutes
creeping away.

In a way, his impatience for the afternoon to be over amused him. It
had been quite a while since he had anything to wait for, and he had
watched so much time slip profitlessly away that it was strange to be-
grudge the hours.

He was anxious, he saw, for the whole business to be over. For
Tarquin's murderer to hang, for Fanuilh to be shut out of his mind, to
resume his quiet life. The activity that had brought him bouncing out of
bed only a few days before was now tiresome. It had brought him the
contact with other people that he belatedly realized he needed, but the
investigation had begun to color the contact.

Lady Necquer had sent him packing, after all, and he had grown
used to their daily conversations.

So much so that now my afternoon seems empty as a keg after a feast,
he reflected ruefully. Heartily sick of the search for Tarquin's killer, and
even sicker of his own maudlin thoughts, he gratefully turned his attention to the lunch he had ordered.

The meal was huge, and the cost equally large. Just past the soup, a
thick broth delicately spiced, and into the fish, sole with a fiery-hot sauce,
he managed to put his concerns away and keep them at bay for the rest
of the meal. The afternoon light crawled slowly across the front of the
nearly empty tavern, and when he was done, over an hour had passed.

"Not late enough," he cursed. Hours still lay in wait before him, and
like stubborn crows, his thoughts swung back to pick at what he had

learned from Donoé. By her report, Tarquin had sworn an oath of chastity which, if true, effectively destroyed any theories about the wizard having gotten the hooded woman pregnant.

Or did it?

He had a happy inspiration concerning the rest of his afternoon, settled his score quickly, and set out for Northfield. His stomach groaned for time to deal with the heavy meal he had put down, but he gave it as little thought as possible.

Viyescu was in his shop, and clearly wished he hadn't been. He twitched when the door opened and Liam walked in, and set down the mortar and pestle he had been using with a heavy thud.

"Hierarch Cance," he grated unhappily.

"Master Viyescu. I'm sorry to bother you again."

The druggist shrugged to indicate that it did not matter, but there was no fluidity in the gesture: his shoulders were a single block of tension.

"I wanted to ask you some more questions about the wizard, and the pregnant woman who mentioned him."

"I'm afraid I can't spare the time, Hierarch," the druggist said, in a strange tone that bordered on pleading. "I must prepare for the procession."

"Ah, the procession," Liam answered airily. "Of course. You'll be marching?"

"I always do, Hierarch." Viyescu sounded almost miserable, and Liam fixed his gaze squarely on the man's eyes.

"Of course. I only wish more followed your example. But I must detain you for only a few moments, and as you know, the business with the wizard is quite important to the temple in Torquay."

"As you wish," Viyescu acceded nervously. Liam noted with mild astonishment that the druggist had actually begun to sweat.

"It has to do with the woman who mentioned Tarquin to you. I think I misunderstood you when last we spoke. I thought you implied that the wizard had gotten her pregnant, but I have it on the best of information that he had sworn an oath of celibacy."

The words seemed to strike Viyescu with physical force. He stammered for a moment, and then controlled himself with visible effort. "I apologize, Hierarch, I did not mean to imply that. *He* did not get the girl pregnant; *he* did not sleep with her."

"I see. So some other man was the father, then? Not Tarquin?"

"No, Hierarch. Not Tarquin."

"You see, I've been trying to figure out what has happened to him, because he was important to us, if you take my meaning. Tell me, did this woman ask you for any virgin's blood?"

The question drew a complete blank from Viyescu, who shook his head as if he might have misheard. "Virgin's blood, Hierarch?"

"Never mind. She only asked for santhract?"

Viyescu nodded eagerly. He was being more cooperative than he had been before, and Liam wondered why.

"How does one take santhract?"

"Powdered, Hierarch," the druggist said instantly, "in wine or cider to cut the taste. But I never sold her any," he added quickly. Indecision suddenly flickered behind his eyes, and he began to add something before cutting himself short. Liam waited for a moment and then went on, disappointed.

"And she wanted it to terminate her pregnancy?" Viyescu nodded again. "She must be very deep in sin, Master Apothecary. Very deep." He intoned the words deeply, with as much of the piousness of a Torquay priest as he could remember. It sounded silly to him, like a poor imitation from his student days, but the sound clearly hit Viyescu another way.

He began to speak, faltered, and gazed deeply into Liam's face, searching for something. Liam willed himself to remain impassive, hoping that whatever was sought would be found, but apparently he disappointed the apothecary because he only said, "Yes, Hierarch, very deep," before snapping his mouth shut.

"Did you know the woman when she came to you?"

"No, Hierarch," Viyescu said, firm once again, but Liam knew he was lying. "I had never seen her before."

The sound of a horn echoed out over the city, and Viyescu looked up in alarm.

"The procession! I must go now, Hierarch, if I'm to be on time. You'll excuse me?"

Liam gestured graciously, though inwardly he was angry and frustrated. The druggist had been on the verge of telling him something of importance, something about the woman. Watching him pull off his stained apron, Liam cursed himself mentally. It had been very close. What was Viyescu hiding?

"I must go upstairs to change," the druggist said when he had hung his apron on a peg, pointing vaguely towards the rear of his shop. "Don't you have to prepare for the procession, Hierarch?"

"I have a dispensation for this Uris-tide," Liam said smoothly, and allowed himself brief mental congratulations for having thought it out earlier. "I will be watching, of course, but the business Torquay has sent me on is terribly important."

"No doubt. I, on the other hand, must prepare myself."

Liam understood the dismissal. "Certainly, certainly. Perhaps we can talk again?"

"I do not know what else I can tell you, Hierarch."

"Of course. Well, then, I'll be on my way." He turned and started for the door, and then stopped, his hand on the latch. "Master Viyescu," he said, smiling pleasantly, though he wanted to shake the man until he spoke. "My prayers will go with you in the procession today."

If it was not what the druggist had been looking for in his face a few moments before, it was certainly very good. Viyescu's expression softened, and he nodded once.

"Thank you, Hierarch," he said, his voice suddenly thick.

"Perhaps you would do me two small favors, Master Viyescu," Liam risked. "Perhaps if you see this woman again, you would not mention my interest in her? And perhaps you would pray for me as you go in the procession?"

"I am not worthy," Viyescu said, his eyes dropping to the floor.

What does that *mean?* Liam wondered.

"Who is? Nonetheless, I would appreciate both."

"As you wish," Viyescu mumbled, and then quickly left the room.

Liam paused for a moment in the empty shop, wondering about the man's strange behavior. The sound of the horn being winded again called him back to himself, and he went out into the street.

The horn sounded twice more, and he noticed a few people hurrying towards the center of the city. Towards the forming procession, he guessed, and set his steps to follow. He had, after all, told Viyescu that he would watch.

Ordinarily the square at the heart of Southwark bustled with people, selling goods or buying, gawking at jugglers or clowns or musicians. Rival birdsellers sent their disciplined flocks charging into each other from either side of the square, the object to confuse the other birds into joining the strongest flock. It was a game Liam had never tired of watching, and he had never passed through without stopping for a moment.

There were no flocks that day, however, and no men with elbow-length gauntlets urging on their feathered soldiers with whistles and high-pitched cries.

The squat stone bulk of the jail and the imposing, columned facade of the Duke's court on the western side of the square did not usually deter the chattering crowds, and on most days the wineshops, cafés and stores scattered around the other sides did a brisk business.

The square seemed less active today though it was thronged with people who spilled into the sidestreets and approaching lanes. Hundreds obscured the pavement, most dressed in their brightly colored holiday finest, but they were hushed, expectant.

By discreet pushing and taking advantage of his thinness, Liam managed to edge his way into the square proper, but the crowd was so thick that he found it uncomfortable, and shoved his way along the fringes of the square until he came to a two-storied wineshop. It was empty, and his footsteps echoed loudly as he entered.

All of the staff of the wineshop were at the galleries on the second floor, gazing in reverence out over the square. Liam coughed politely, and the barkeep whirled in fury at the interruption, then stopped himself when he saw Liam's expensive clothes.

"Ah, my lord," he fawned, "you'd grace us to share the process with us. If it please you, sit here." He shooed a crowd of serving girls and tapboys from the table in front of the central gallery and installed Liam there, cheerfully ignoring his employees' sullen looks.

"Something to go with, my lord?"

"Just wine," Liam said.

The barkeep brought it quickly, smiled obsequiously, and dashed to another gallery, forcing a spot for himself between two angry serving girls.

Liam sipped at his wine, turning his attention to the square below.

A platform had been erected at shoulder height against the grim stone steps of the jail, and Liam noted with a wry smile that there were fixtures that would allow it to be changed to a gallows. Around the platform, a small space had been cleared by members of the Guard, resplendent in black surcoats emblazoned with the Duke's three foxes and polished, ornately useless ceremonial armor. Inside the circle of armored men several people had gathered. A small knot of shaven-headed acolytes of Uris talked quietly amongst themselves; Ancus Marcius held silent court over three other prominent merchants; and Ton Viyescu stood alone in a blindingly white full-length robe, his face screwed up in a sour expression beneath its encroaching beard. Coeccias, his shaggy hair painstakingly combed, his own surcoat and armor crumb-free, scowled at a man dressed in the everyday uniform of the Guard. The man was speaking at length about something, and in the middle of his speech, Coeccias began scanning the crowd impatiently. As Liam watched from the gallery, the man finished his report and the Aedile dismissed him offhandedly, his eyes still searching the crowd. Then he looked directly at the second floor of the wineshop, started, and grabbed the departing man, pointing in Liam's direction.

The man nodded and pushed his way into the crowd, crossing the packed square towards the shop. The gathered worshippers parted silently for him, their attention still held by the empty platform. Liam, however, watched him with interest until he disappeared below. Then he turned his gaze to the stairs, expecting the messenger to appear at any moment.

When he finally heard footsteps on the stairs, he rose himself and walked towards them, meeting the man at the top.

"Are you looking for me?"

The messenger stared at him, obviously not having expected to be met at the head of the stairs.

"Y'are Liam Rhenford?" he asked suspiciously.

"Yes. Coeccias sent you?"

"Aye, to carry you these news. The rent's paid on the lodgings, sir, and so not by the wizard. Someone else keeps the hooded woman."

"That's all?" Liam said after a moment. It did not surprise him— Viyescu had just told him that Tarquin had not kept the woman.

"Well, sir, just that the owner said the coins used were the most fantastic he'd seen, though neither clipped nor light. Good gold, but strange."

Liam raised an eyebrow in politeness, but was not interested. He was more concerned with figuring out Viyescu's strange behavior. What had the druggist been about to tell him? More importantly, was it connected with Tarquin's death?

The sound of the horn called him to his surroundings, and he turned back to the gallery, the messenger following behind wordlessly.

The horn was winded only once this time, and Liam saw that one of the shaven-headed acolytes was standing on the platform, raising a silver-chased ram's horn to the sky. He sounded it twice more, and a clash of cymbals answered the third, at which he hurriedly left the platform to join his fellows below. All eyes in the crowd turned to the north, where the main point of the procession was approaching.

Two young boys led the way, crowned with wreaths of laurel and dressed in short white tunics despite the cold. They spread rushes in the path the crowd cleared for them, walking solemnly. Behind them followed a single man in complicated flowing vestments of white sewn with pearls and gold and silver threads. He wore a tall scarlet mitre and carried a golden lantern and an oversized book bound in tooled, painted leather. His massive belly bobbled beneath the vestments, and his beard straggled over three extra chins, giving rise to Liam's blasphemous thought that Uris's second-highest priest would not enjoy the next day's fast.

The priest did manage to look grand, however, pacing measuredly on the carpet of rushes strewn by the pageboys, aloof and proud under the silent scrutiny of the crowd.

Behind him, borne in a litter carried on the muscular shoulders of eight bald acolytes, came Uris's image, shrouded in a snowy tarp. Last in line was a group of musicians, piper and drummer and the man with the cymbals, marching unobserved in grave lockstep. The attention of the crowd was divided equally between the fat priest in his magnificent clothes and the covered statue.

Only the rustle of sandals on rushes and the sigh of the wind could be heard as the procession moved into the circle of Guardsmen. The pageboys went up the narrow steps to the platform, leaving rushes behind, and the priest followed them, moving to the edge to face the crowd. The litter bearers brought their load to rest in front of the platform, neatly turning around so that Uris, when uncovered, would face her worshippers like the priest. Coeccias, Viyescu and the merchants stood in ranks to the left of the litter, looking up at the priest; the other acolytes knelt to the right. Finally the musicians took up their position at the bottom of the steps leading to the platform.

When they were ready, the piper nodded to the priest, who handed the lantern to one boy and the book to the other. Liam was struck by the awe with which they received their burdens, and the way they held them firmly in their hands but away from their bodies, as if afraid to soil them.

Just a book and a lantern, Liam thought. He had never had much use for organized religions, though he knew the gods were there. Meet the Storm King face to face, he thought somewhat scornfully, and see how much you care for a book and a lantern.

The ceremony was interesting, he had to admit, if only for its aesthetic and historical value. Once rid of his book and lantern, the priest raised his hands and began a chant in a high-pitched voice that swept over the silent square. Rising and falling in a stately, cadenced rhythm, the chant described the wondrous gifts Uris had bestowed on the world in an obscure, highly refined dialect of High Church Taralonian. Liam vaguely recognized it from his student days in Torquay, and was able to follow haltingly along, despite the complex syntax and the strange, inverted poetry. He wondered if anyone there besides the priest, the acolytes and himself understood a single word of it.

After several verses lauding Uris in general and her two major gifts—medicine and writing—the chant broke into song. The shaven acolytes raised their voices with the priest's, ranging around his high tenor in a complex and surprisingly merry harmony. At first the drummer was the only musician playing, giving the singers a simple beat, but then the piper began, and the man with the cymbals joined in as well with carefully muted crashes. They were, however, only the framework of the music, a steady undercurrent for the voices of the celebrants.

The singing went through two repeated verses, and then subsided into just the priest's chant, though the drummer continued to beat out a more subdued rhythm for the chanter to follow.

It went on for almost an hour, breaking from chant to song back to chant, going into detail about Uris's contributions to almost every civilized craft, illustrating the gifts with old myths and legends. First the piper wove into the chant and then the cymbalist as well, until the only way to tell chant from song was by the participation or silence of the shaven chorus. The crowd of worshippers remained silent, and Liam gave a moment's admiration to their stoicism, packed closely into a cold square listening to a long service in a language they could not understand. For his own part, he was too absorbed in translating it to himself to notice the length, and he grudgingly admitted to himself that it was beautiful in a strange way.

Finally, with the sun little more than an hour above the western horizon, the singers and musicians brought their last burst of song to a halt, and an imposing silence descended on the square. Flushed with his exertions, the priest on the platform retrieved his book and his lantern from the pageboys and raised them high for the adoration of the common worshippers. He let a suitably dramatic pause go by, and then pronounced a blessing they could understand.

"Uris, Light of Our Dark and Teacher of the World, bless this city and this gathering!"

A muttering of "So be it" rose from the assembled crowd, and every person in the square and the wineshop galleries where Liam stood bowed their head. On cue, two of the acolytes caught hold of the immaculate tarp that covered the image on the litter and pulled it back, so that it slid up the front of the statue and then fell back from its shoulders.

Liam almost whistled, but checked himself. The statue was incredible, an eight-foot-tall woman bearing a book and a lantern and a benign expression. Uris had been rendered in exquisite detail, but what struck Liam was the obvious cost of the image. Carved of wood, barely an inch was free of some expensive decoration, from the cloth-of-gold robes to the chips of jade that were inset in her fingers to stand for nails. Her eyes were multifaceted diamonds, her hair uncountable wires of beaten silver; the book and lantern were gold, and in the heart of the lantern, representing the flame, was an enormous winking ruby. Countless smaller gems glittered from her robes, sewn into the cloth-of-gold.

Absurdly, Liam thought of a thief he had once known who would then and there have resolved to steal the statue, and then made good on the resolution. Thievery, however, was far from the minds of the worshippers in the square, who could not decide whether to gaze devotedly on their goddess or hang their heads in humility.

Once he judged the people had had their fill of the statue, the priest walked down off the platform and allowed the procession to form behind him. Without any discernible scurrying, everyone found their places; the pageboys once again in front, joined by the acolyte with the horn, followed by the priest, the litter, the rest of the acolytes, then Coeccias and his Guardsmen dressed in their ceremonial armor. As the only layman who had made all the processions of the week, Viyescu walked alone next, with the musicians behind him. Last in the official procession came Marcius and his gaggle of prominent merchants.

The horn sounded again, the musicians struck up a tune, and the procession began to move fairly quickly out of the square to the south. As soon as Marcius and his group were past, the general crowd fell in behind them, beginning to raise up songs and shouts. Instruments appeared among the hitherto silent worshippers, and the noise swelled into a happy celebration, loudly heralding the unveiled Uris through the city.

The procession was headed down towards the harbor and moving rapidly, the hundreds of worshippers pressing hard after, bearing their noisy celebration with them.

Liam watched until the last had straggled out of the square, leaving a loud silence in their wake. A long pent-up sigh escaped from the messenger, calling attention to him.

"Where will they go?"

"To the harbor, sure," the man said, as though it should be obvious. "And then they'll up through Auric's Park and Northfield, and so back to Temple's Court."

"I've never seen the celebrations for Uris-tide before," Liam said, thinking with pity of the litter bearers and their heavy cargo.

"They're every year," the man said, looking at him like he was an idiot. "How could you not?"

He began to explain, but then decided not to bother. If the man couldn't figure out from his accent and his name that he was a Midlander, why bother enlightening him? Instead, he simply shrugged and sat down at the table, pulling his unfinished wine to him.

The messenger stayed for a moment to bestow a pitying look on him, and then left.

Liam stayed at the wineshop for another half an hour, reflecting on the ceremony through two more cups. Few other Taralonian gods required processions, even in Torquay, which was noted for its zealous maintenance of ancient rituals.

At length, however, he could not keep his thoughts from the investigation, and he felt compelled to do something, even if it was just to walk—which he did, at length.

The procession's taking a long time, he thought as he strolled the nearly empty streets, with even more pity for the litter bearers.

He walked west from the square, past the outdoor theater he now realized was the summer home of the Golden Orb's company, and into the Warren, the sprawl of narrow, twisted streets and tortured lanes that housed most of the city in ramshackle houses that stretched impossibly high. They seemed to rely on each other for support, leaning forward across the streets, almost touching as they reached four and five stories.

Ordinarily he would not have gone there, but the spirit of the celebration must have taken hold, and there were few people in the streets, some of whom looked like they might actually have been cleaned to honor the goddess. Even the ranks of the beggars were thinner, many undoubtedly gone to try their luck with the processors.

And besides, Coeccias had told him that the apartment rented by the hooded woman was in the Warren. He pondered Viyescu's strange behavior once again. For some reason, his questions about the woman had upset the gruff druggist, but Liam found it difficult to understand why. It might have something to do with Tarquin, but it might have been that the druggist was simply unwilling to discuss the intricacies of sin with a priest. He might well have tripped himself up again with his religious imposture, closing off an avenue of investigation with an ill-chosen ploy. Or maybe Uris herself was frustrating him, as a punishment for pretending to be one of her Hierarchs.

Still—Viyescu had wanted to tell him something, and had not. Until he knew what it was, he could not dismiss the inkling at the back of his mind.

His thoughts as aimless as his footsteps, he was well into the Warren before he heard the bells tolling from far to the east in Temple's Court. On hearing them, he pulled up short and immediately turned around.

There was little for him and Coeccias to talk about—the news about the rent being paid made little or no difference, and his impressions of his conversation with Viyescu were better kept to himself—but at least his afternoon of waiting was over.

Liam began to hurry through the city to the Aedile's house, and had to concentrate to slow down, to give Coeccias time to get home from the Temple of Uris. He even managed to make himself stop to buy a jug of wine, thinking it appropriate to bring something with him.

He need not have bothered. Coeccias opened the door himself when he knocked, and there was a steaming mug of mulled cider in his hand.

"Ah, y'have brought a small something, have you?" Relieving Liam of the jug, he ushered him in and then led the way back to the kitchen, which was considerably neater than it had been in the morning. Noticing Liam's appreciative glance, Coeccias laughed. "Burus was busy all the day, setting straight for the morrow. Cleaning's forbid on the eve of Uris-tide."

The servant looked up from stirring the steaming pot of cider and smiled sourly, handing Liam a cup without preamble.

"If it please you, Rhenford, we'll save the wine for another time, and finish this batch of cider. I'll not drink it tomorrow, and by the next it'll be fairly undrinkable." He sat at the table, motioning Liam to sit opposite him, and raised his mug. Liam touched his mug to the Aedile's, and they drank in silence for a moment.

"Truth, it's a blessing to be out of that infernal armor," Coeccias said after a moment. He had changed into his usual stained black tunic, though his hair had stayed perfectly in place. As though reminded of it, he ruffled it with his free hand. "I'd just as soon make a trifling donation than march that process again. It's a passing trouble."

"I imagine it must be worse for the men who have to carry the statue."

"Oh, aye," the Aedile agreed. "I'd sooner wear the armor than carry the goddess, but I'd even sooner just worship from afar. Not for me are pomps and displays, I'll tell you, though I'm as deep in for Uris as any other."

Burus apparently decided the cider was sufficiently stirred, because he stood and left the room.

"Now say, Rhenford, what think you of the moneys handed out?"

"The rent? It's paid, so we know for sure that the woman was not Tarquin's—though I never really thought she was. We're still left with Lons."

"Ah, I note y'omit Marcius from your accounting, at last. Y'are convinced, then?"

"I can't imagine or prove anything else, though I still think Lons doesn't have it in him."

He did not mention Viyescu. What he had discovered—what he *thought* he had discovered—he could not put into words. He thought the druggist wanted to reveal something, wanted to come forward, but it was only a fleeting feeling, a hunch. Not worth bothering Coeccias with.

Coeccias shrugged. "I'd agree, for argument, but thinking's no place here—the *knowing* is all. We know the player had a right good reason, and the knife was that of a player. All points to him, though why he's not fled is beyond me." For a moment, the Aedile stared into the depths of his mug, then looked up and spoke in a different tone.

"There's another thing, though, that'll interest you. The druggist recommended himself to you."

"Viyescu? He mentioned me?"

"Aye," Coeccias nodded. "At the fane, after the procession. He must have seen me post the messenger to you, for he came to me when all was done, and asked if I knew the hierarch. It took a moment, but then I recalled your imposture, and said I did. He said there was something he'd thought of to tell you since your last talk, something that might interest you."

"Well?"

"Truth, he mumbled and muttered and jigged around it, saying he'd only come to tell it through pure meditation on Uris and a lot of other pious rambling, but the pure and straight of it is that 'the woman' had come to him again, just the other day, and begged once more a dram of the poison from him. Now this is our woman, is it not?"

"Yes, but we already know Tarquin wasn't keeping her," Liam said, shaking his head.

"Remind me: what was the herb?"

"Santhract, but it doesn't matter. Tarquin was dead, not pregnant."

"That's true," Coeccias admitted. "Though here's more on it: this hooded and cloaked beldame must've put a mighty fright to our druggist, for that he was shaking leaflike, and pale, and looked around him oft."

"So?" Liam could barely restrain his frustration. Viyescu's information was scarcely to the point, gone the way of his interviews with Marcius and his decanter of virgin's blood. Wasted breath and effort poorly spent. He was annoyed with the business, and with Viyescu. The puritanical druggist's problems had nothing to do with Tarquin's death, of that he was suddenly sure. Lons was the killer, though he did not want to believe it. "So some temple-soft fanatic is frightened by a woman? It's not proof, it's not *knowing*, and the *knowing* is all, isn't it?"

Was that what Viyescu had wanted to tell him? That he was frightened of the woman? It did not matter.

He regretted his tone, but fortunately the Aedile did not take it amiss.

"Truth, you've the right of it. More like Viyescu was afraid to talk with me, or to utter ungodly thoughts in Uris's fane. The knowing is all, and we know it's our player. Perhaps we'll clap him tomorrow." He fell to pondering his cup of cider, and when he saw it was almost empty, lumbered over to the fire to refill it, taking Liam's cup as well. Bending over the pot, he muttered heavily. "I'll say, though, that I'm wondering wherefore he hasn't fled. If I were him, I'd to the heath before we were a street away."

Liam accepted his refill. "He has probably guessed you have someone watching him, and that the proof is circumstantial. It is circumstantial, though damning."

"Enough to hang him, if need be, though I'm loath to do't," Coeccias said ruefully, resuming his seat. "A confession'd do my heart good."

"He probably guesses that as well, and is hoping we'll give up. Or maybe he thinks my warning was all the punishment he'd get."

"Ah," Coeccias said, his eyes lighting with malicious humor, "then that was the matter you had when you let him off! To keep him off the Lady Necquer!"

Nodding miserably, Liam cursed himself. He had bungled it, bargaining with their best suspect for an unimportant tangent.

"Y'have a soft spot for the gentler sex, Rhenford, that much is clear. Perhaps he thinks we'll not take him for the murder because you're overfond of his sister, eh?"

The jibe stung, though a smile lit Coeccias's eyes, and Liam hung his head.

"Well, on the morrow we'll clap the player, and the matter'll be done."

Liam drank unhappily to the resolution. Strangely, he thought of Fanuilh. With Lons's arrest, he would have fulfilled his part of the bargain, regardless of his numerous missteps; he wondered if the dragon would carry out his part as ineptly.

They sat for a while, drinking the cider. Coeccias refilled the mugs twice, and Liam's face flushed with the spiked drink.

Suddenly the Aedile boomed out a laugh and slammed his mug to the table.

"Why sit we here like maudlin old crows?" he shouted, his teeth beaming hugely in his black beard. "We've conned and caught our killer! It's done! We're done with it! On the morrow he'll take up residence in the jail, and I'll to clearing drunken tars out of taverns, and you'll to your books! We're clear! Come! Bring the pot!"

The Aedile jumped to his feet and careered out of the kitchen. Liam stood more slowly, and felt the blood rush dizzily in his head. He had drunk more than was good for him, but he had the sense to use a rag to hold the hot ring of the pot he took from the fire. Coeccias's sudden good cheer both surprised and amused him, and he gratefully allowed it to distract him from his melancholy mood.

Calling for Burus to light a fire in the parlor and to bring food, Coeccias then saw to the fire himself, and cursed the servant good-naturedly when he appeared.

"Damn your slowness, Burus! I've the fire in hand! You to the food, and mind you bring your pipes as well, and a third mug! Now, Rhenford," he called when Liam came in, carefully carrying the pot, "hang it on the fire, and see yourself to another mug!"

Burus came back with a huge tray covered with cold meat, cheese and bread, and a flute under his arm. Liam perceived through the rapidly descending haze of the cider that the servant's smile was sour by a trick of his face, and that he was well acquainted with his master's sudden moods. He left the food on a chest that stood by the fire, and stood back to check his flute.

Though his lunch had been large, Liam attacked the platter, both because the spiked cider had given him a new appetite and because he was afraid of the haze it had imposed.

"Now, Burus," Coeccias said while Liam stuffed sausage, cheese and bread indiscriminately down his throat, "it's not yet Uris's appointed fasting time, and Rhenford and I've finished up a business the like of which I've never seen in my office, and there's most of a pot of cider to down. So, you'll have a mug, and we'll have a tune." Gesturing imperiously, he filled the extra mug and thrust it at the servant, who took a deep draught before setting it down and commencing a high, lively air on his flute.

Coeccias burst out laughing and applauding at once, and stamped his feet in a ragged approximation of time.

"Go to, go to, Burus! He knows," the Aedile bellowed confidingly to Liam, "that that's my favorite." Liam was busy with the food he had heaped in his lap, but he managed to look up and nod appreciatively, though he had never heard the tune before.

By the end of the song, Liam had finished a large portion of the food on the platter, refilled his mug and begun beating out the rhythm on his knees. Burus was more than a fair musician, and Liam recognized his next song with a bright grin and an emphatic nod of approval. The servant had started in on "The Lipless Flutist" over the strenuous objections of Coeccias, who wanted to hear the first song again. As soon as he saw that Liam was engrossed in the song, however, he stopped shouting for the old one, and came and sat by him, slurring his question slightly.

"It likes you?"

"Very much," Liam replied, running over the obscene words to the song in his head and noticing the mischievous glint in Burus's eye as he cocked his head over the plain wooden flute. It seemed as though the servant was daring him to sing.

"Then sing it," Coeccias roared in his ear, swaying perilously.

"I can't sing."

"Play?" When Liam, wanting only to hear the song and recall its lyrics, ignored him, the Aedile grabbed him and shouted his question again. "Can you play?"

"Yes, yes."

"The lute?"

"Yes, the lute, a little," Liam said, willing his friend to be quiet. To his great disappointment, however, it was Burus who was quiet, laying aside his flute and looking at his master with an unvoiced question. Coeccias lurched to his feet and went to the chest. Dropping the platter on the floor, he flung the lid open and rummaged for a moment, coming up with a much-battered lute case. He opened it tenderly, and revealed a rosewood lute of tremendous craftsmanship, with ivory pegs and silvered edges. He presented it to Liam and then took a seat on a caned chair off to one side of the room.

"Will you, sir?" They were the first words Liam had heard Burus say, and he was surprised to hear a courtly voice issue from the sour face. He noticed suddenly that Burus was older than Coeccias, the thin hairs that straggled across his bald head a dirty gray.

"I suppose, yes, just let me tune it."

"It'll need no tuning, sir."

Shrugging, Liam picked out the first few notes of "The Lipless Flutist," and heard that Burus was right. Encouraged, he went on more confidently, and the servant joined in soon. After a few minutes, the rust in Liam's fingers wore away, and the two matched each other. Coeccias started singing the most common verse once they had run through the main theme twice. His range was poor, and he shouted more than sang, but the words came out clear and loud, and the words were the most important part of "The Lipless Flutist." Liam entered the singing almost right away, and though the mix of the two men's voices was hardly pleasant, it was not outright offensive, and seemed to fit the ruder lines quite well.

The variations on the song's basic theme—the adventures of a flute-player with no lips—were almost endless, and Coeccias and Liam diverged radically after three verses. The Aedile tried to return to the beginning, but Liam went on, into a verse he had once heard in Harcourt. Coeccias joined him on the refrain, though, and they brought the song to a rousing finish, shouting and laughing, with the heavy official jigging across the parlor.

Laughing, Liam flexed his fingers, pleased that he had remembered how to play. Another thing he had not done in a long time.

"Y'have a fair hand for the lute," Burus commented, cheeks red from playing the furiously paced song.

"And y'have a saucy, impertinent tongue, rascal!" Coeccias shook with laughter and clapped his servant on the shoulder, rocking the slighter man.

"I only learned because of that song," Liam said. He had indeed learned to play because of "The Lipless Flutist," taking up the lute to fill long hours on deck and as a way to remember the countless verses that had amused him in taverns and wineshops and camps in a hundred lands. He smiled at the pervasiveness of one song, and recalled a particular version.

"There's a variation to it, if you'd like to hear it."

Coeccias loudly left no doubt that he was in favor of it, and Burus smiled indulgently.

He led them through the variation, called "The Lipless Flutist and the One-Armed Lutist," laying out each new line for Coeccias to roar along. He included a few of the special rills that went along with mention of the Lutist, and found Burus accompanying him easily, while Coeccias clapped with drunken joy. They sang the new verse twice, and then paused, drinking much more cider and laughing with the Aedile as he tried and failed to remember the lines Liam had just taught him.

"You'll write them out for me, Rhenford," he said angrily, and then called for another song.

Liam began one of the few others he knew, a sailor's song, high-spirited but relatively clean for the normally filthy genre. Burus picked it up effortlessly, and added a number of flourishes that enhanced the simple melody. As he bent his head to check his fingering, Liam marveled at the gnarled old servant's skill. He was a true musician, not a dabbler like Liam, who had only learned individual songs and not the theories or ideas behind them. He could play the songs he knew, but Burus could learn a new one easily, and make it better.

They played two more songs that Liam knew, and Coeccias remained silent, staring fixedly at a space between them. When they were done, Liam bowed over his lute at Burus.

"You're a fine player, Burus. A really fine musician."

The servant flushed and scowled, and the Aedile roused himself from his stupor to take another gulp of cider and fix his attention on the lute Liam held.

"And so he should be, Rhenford! My father had the teaching of him, and my father was the rarest that ever served the office of Duke's Minstrel!"

Burus's scowl deepened, but he did not speak angrily. "That lute was his," he said, pointing with his flute, "and though you do it no disgrace, he was as far your master as a king is a swineherd's."

"Aye, a rarer there never was, a rare man for a song," Coeccias muttered morosely, and then suddenly burst out laughing. "And the rankest time-server and flatterer the Duke's court ever saw! How think you I came to my own office? Son of the Duke's favorite, and good for naught but chucking tosspots into the street—so off with him to Southwark, and create him Aedile!"

"Y'have done credit to it, Coeccias," the old servant said mildly, and the Aedile nodded firmly.

"Truth, I've done my all, and few could do better. But go to, another song!"

Burus began a slow, mournful song, a dirge to Laomedon, the God of the Worlds Beyond. He peered questioningly over his flute, but Liam shook his head and smiled, carefully putting the beautiful lute back into its case before refilling his mug.

The pot was finished by the time Burus had gone through four more songs, three of which Liam did not recognize. Finally, the servant put aside his flute and drained the last of the only cup he had taken.

"If there's nothing else, I think I'll to my cot."

"No, naught else, good Burus, beside my thanks." Coeccias seemed to be over his earlier wild drunkenness, and nodded gravely at his servant's bow.

Liam whistled after the old man had gone, now far worse off than his friend. The haze was fully extended now, and he was glad the pot was empty, because the thought of even another sip made his stomach ache.

"He's a fine musician," he whispered in awe.

"Truth, a fine man as well."

Unsteadily, Liam made his way to his feet. "It's time for me to go."

Coeccias did not argue, but he did stand and open the door for him with a wide smile.

"Y'are no poor player yourself, for all Burus's roundabout way of saying it. Y'ought to come again, and let him teach you some other tunes."

"That would be good," Liam said thickly, trying forcefully to regain control of his reluctant legs. Their talk of Coeccias's father had brought to mind his own, and he felt inexpressibly sad beneath the numbness of the cider.

"On the morrow, then," the Aedile said, as Liam went out the door.

"Yes, tomorrow," he muttered, waving a hand over his shoulder.

There was a cold breeze in the street, and it thinned the haze enough for him to realize that trying to ride out to Tarquin's would be pointless, if not dangerous. With that muddled thought, he forced himself to start for his garret.

The stairs seemed to stretch interminably ahead of him, but eventually he reached the top, bumping from wall to wall. Sad, fuzzy thoughts of his father and muddled curses for Coeccias's wickedly spiked cider echoed in his head. Fully clothed, he collapsed onto his pallet and into sleep.

■ 12 ■

AS USUAL WHEN he was even slightly drunk, Liam slept poorly, plagued by nightmares.

In Tarquin's house, which the dream meant for his father's keep, a wild revel was going on, and he, as a crippled jester, was being baited like a bear. Hounds snapped savagely at him, biting his legs and hands. Blood streamed down his legs, but he could not move to defend himself. This greatly displeased the revelers who circled him. The wizard himself, Donoé at his side, his face a demon-mask with the flickering orange candle-light, laughed disdainfully at Liam's pitiful gestures. Coeccias tossed a seemingly endless supply of lutes at his head and growled encouragement to the dogs. Lons and Lady Necquer, lying together on the same couch, shrieked with delight as a particularly large bite was torn from his leg. Others he had met—Viyescu and Marcius, Kansallus and his actors, even Mother Japh the ghost witch—gorged themselves on wine and roasted meat, screaming for the dogs to dispatch him.

Weaker and weaker, Liam tried to avoid the pack, but the laughter and the hatred of the revelers discouraged him, and he allowed himself to fall.

The dogs pounced on him from all sides, rolling him over with the pressure of their attack, and he gazed up into Fanuilh's eyes. The dragon was hovering high above him, gazing imperturbably down on the dog's feast. Suddenly, it flapped its wings gently, and at each downstroke a sound like thunder echoed through the suddenly silent chamber. The revelers stopped indulging themselves, and looked in awe at the dragon as more peals of thunder rang out. Liam looked helplessly into the creature's eyes, searching for something he could understand.

Knocking at his door, subtly like thunder, woke him up, and he left the dream with a muffled gasp. He jumped to his feet, disentangling himself from his blanket with difficulty. He could not have slept very long; it was still dark out, his candle was still burning, and he was still slightly drunk. There was another knock and he jumped, then took a deep breath to steady himself and hurried to the door.

Rora stood there, a concerned look on her flawless face. Liam recoiled in surprise and her concerned look grew troubled.

Must be a dream, Liam thought; *where are the dogs?*

"Master?" she said, taking his sweating palm in her own cool one. "Is all well? Your face's a fright." Her voice was a wellspring of good intentions and honest worry, and her hand felt wonderfully cool and smooth, but he pulled away roughly and turned into the room, suddenly aware that it was wrong for her to be there.

"Nothing. Just a dream." He scrubbed at his hot face and swiped his hair back, knowing enough to know his wits were not with him. He did not hear her come up behind him, and jumped again when she laid her hand on his shoulder.

"Master, is all well?"

He saw his chair by the window and, convinced it was a refuge, threw himself into it.

Rora followed, dropping her heavy cloak on the bed, and knelt by him. Her skirts ballooned out from above her waist in a black mushroom, and he focused on them, sternly forcing himself to ignore the low cut of her bodice. She laid a light hand on his knee.

"Master Rhenford, y'are not well, I fear." Her hair was held away from her face by a simple clasp, and rippled down her back. A sweet perfume crept like a thief behind what was left of the cider's haze, and he stirred and shoved at her hand.

"I'm fine, fine. What do you want?"

She took his bluntness in stride.

"Faith, Master," she said, rising smoothly and pacing a few steps away, "I must beg a boon." She turned on him, her eyes sparkling with tears, pressing her hands tightly palm to palm.

I'm not up to this, Liam thought, feeling very stupid.

"You'll clap my sweet brother in for a crime he had no hand in, Master, and I must plead his innocence! On my body I swear his soul's free of taint!"

Oh, gods, why did she swear on her body? I'm going to regret this.

"Plead to the Aedile," he snapped, shaking his head in wide arcs he almost could not control. "I can't do anything for you."

"The Aedile! Even I can see y'are his genius! I pray you, Master, speak with him! Plead my brother's half, bespeak his innocence, I pray you!"

She knelt again squarely in front of him, claiming his wandering attention. He could not look at her for longer than a few seconds; the only thoughts that came to mind were dangerous.

If only she'd go away, he thought vainly, *I could stop worrying about looking at her breasts.*

Two tears welled up, and then traced perfect courses down her fair cheeks, and he knew he was going to make a mistake.

"I'm only a common player, I know, Master, but I've as much honesty as a gentle! Lons is guiltless in this, I swear! By Uris I swear, Master!"

"Don't call me that; I'm not your Master," he protested feebly, waving his hand at the entrancing vision, hoping it would go away.

"Y'are, Master," she cried, and her hands flashed spontaneously to his knees.

Much higher than before, he thought with alarm, and though he tried to move them, could not. She tried to bury her head in his lap, beginning to weep in earnest, but he managed to fend her off.

I can't let this happen.

"I pray you, Master, bespeak the Aedile as you can! You know you can turn him off that track! I'd do anything to prove Lons honest!"

Anything? No.

She managed to get her head onto his lap, and continued to plead, though her sobs were muffled.

This is so wrong, he thought, and tried to stand up, which was a mistake.

Rora came up with him, and somewhere in the confusion of rising, her lips met his. The cider and conversation had left him flushed and hot, his lips dry, and hers felt cool and moist, tasting slightly of salt from her tears.

Damn cider, damn Coeccias, damn Lons and Poppae Necquer. I'm making a mistake.

"I'd do aught," she whispered, her voice suddenly low and throaty in his ear.

Damn me.

• • •

Sometime later, she stirred beside him on the pallet, and then, even later, Liam rolled over and found her gone. The cider, too, was gone, and his head was clear enough to allow him to curse himself soundly.

"Damn, damn, damn, damn," he chanted into the darkness, with his hands knotted behind his head. He had made a mistake, he knew, and tried to console himself by cursing Coeccias's cider and thinking about how long it had been since he was with a woman. It did not work. Would she expect him now to leave her brother alone? That was ridiculous, of course; Lons had had every reason to kill Tarquin, and despite his alibi, everything pointed to him. There was no way he could convince Coeccias otherwise without some new piece of evidence, and it was entirely unlikely that one would come his way. If only Marcius had done something, or if Donoé had told him a different story, then he might have supported his belief that Lons was not the killer. As things stood, though, there was no other conclusion.

But Rora would not see it that way, naturally. With his foolish, stupid, damnable drunken acquiescence, he had as much as told the tearful, pleading innocent that he would help her brother.

Innocent? Her perfume lingered, and he imagined his blanket and mattress still held a hint of her warmth. Naive, perhaps, but not innocent. She had been . . . *amazing*, he thought guiltily, so that even a half-drunk man might look back on the experience and shake his head in wonder, and regret that it was over. And doubly regret that it had happened at all. Kansallus had only partly guessed about Rora. No virgin, certainly.

Liam groaned out loud, trying to express the mix of sensual reminiscence and self-condemnation, or at least drive it away.

Poised over him at one point, she had looked down on him, flushed and deeply involved in what she was doing to him with her body, her hair in wild disarray.

"You're going to get fat," he had murmured, running his hands over her silky, sweat-damp skin.

"Too much wine," she had laughed. "You know players. . . ." The rest was lost, spoken into his throat as she arced downward to begin again.

The memory was so vivid that Liam had to sit up in bed and rub his eyes to keep from actually seeing it.

It had been so long that he only wanted to revel in it, but he could not allow that. He had to do something, anything, to avoid remembering, or it would only strengthen his guilt.

He had effectively pledged to help her brother, and racked his brain for a way to do it. He went over the investigation point by point, rethinking every clue, reexamining each possibility. Was there something he and Coeccias had missed? Some old idea they had put aside that might be dusted off?

The sky outside his window had taken on the deep royal blue of predawn before he thought of even one thing he might check. Viyescu's hooded woman, and her desire for new poison. It was almost surely pointless, but the druggist had for some reason thought it worth telling. And there was Coeccias's report of Viyescu's nervousness and, more important, his own strange meeting with the druggist. What if the mystery woman had threatened him? What if they had gotten closer to the truth with Viyescu, and then passed it up for the easier explanation that Lons afforded? What if, what if. Since Marcius had not seen fit to confess, it was the only thing he could imagine as a possibility, however slim. He decided to visit the apothecary again, to ask the questions he should have asked before, and just then noticed the color of the sky.

It was far too early to go to Viyescu's, he knew, but he was afraid to sleep, afraid that Coeccias would arrest Lons before he could unearth a new clue to protect the player, and his sister. He shifted uncomfortably on the pallet, wondering how to occupy the time before he could go to Northfield and, worn out by the hard cider and his exertions, fell instantly asleep.

Panicking, Liam woke all at once, jumped up from his pallet, and ran to the window. The sun was still low; he had only been asleep for a few hours. Still, he felt a tremendous pressure to be out and on his way to Viyescu's. He stripped and splashed the entire contents of his washbasin over his body, then dried himself patchily with his blanket.

Lying directly in front of his door was a folded piece of paper, pure white and of good quality, one of the sheets he had bought on his arrival in Southwark. Sunlight from the window slanted onto it, and he frowned as he knelt to pick it up. It was too far into the room to have been shoved beneath the door; Rora must have left it. There was no name on the outside of the paper, and he opened it as if it might contain a dangerous animal.

Wincing, he read the short note through twice. The writing was crude, the letters poorly formed, the spelling atrocious, and the message painful.

I know you won't fail me, Master, not now. Pray you, bespeak the Aedile on my sweet brother's part. I swear his innocence!

There was no signature, but the note did not need one.

Growling, he almost crumpled the page, but instead threw it towards the table. He did not wait to see it flutter to the ground like a wounded dove, several feet short of the table.

He hurried past the shrinking drudge and out into the street, buckling his belt as he went and haphazardly tucking his breeches into his boots. Outside, the sky stopped him for a moment. It was a fine morning, just cold enough to chill the wet spots left by his uneven toweling, and the vault of the sky was unbroken blue, pale and bright. A line of black clouds, however, like waves in the sky, were building up far out over the sea, and he knew that by afternoon the day would be shattered by storms.

It made little difference to him. He was concerned with his own stupidity, and the obligation he had foolishly assumed. He found he was grinding his teeth, and he strode through the streets like an ill wind, cursing himself. Beggars, seeing his clenched fists, did not try to stop him, but he did not notice.

Gods, let the druggist have something.

Liam was grasping at straws, and knew it, but when he allowed himself to consider the fact his mind dropped back to the night before, and to what he had tacitly agreed. So he tried to reorder what he knew, and cast about for new constructions that would, if not find another murderer, at least clear Lons.

Viyescu turned white beneath his untamed beard and began shaking when Liam entered. Dismissing it as the product of his own undoubtedly grim appearance, Liam crossed to the counter.

"Hierarch," the druggist whispered anxiously, "what brings you here again?"

"I spoke with the Aedile yesterday, and he gave me some news from you."

"Yes, certainly, but surely there's no need to—"

Liam cut the strangely distressed apothecary off. "The woman who mentioned Tarquin came back?"

"Yes, Hierarch." Viyescu was subdued, accepting questions much more easily than before.

"And asked for more santhract?" Viyescu nodded. "You didn't sell her any?"

"I've said, I don't sell it; it likes me not."

"But she frightened you?"

Startled, Viyescu goggled at him.

"She frightened you. The Aedile said you looked frightened."

"Oh," he hemmed, "it was naught; I just—"

"Did she threaten you?"

"Perhaps she spoke some in anger, but it was naught, if it please you, she—"

The apothecary was lying, Liam felt sure; the woman had threatened him, but he did not want to admit it. Liam let it go.

"I see, I see. I've just one more question for you, then." Viyescu was visibly relieved, and Liam wondered at his change of attitude. His stern, puritanical righteousness was gone, as well as the subtle hinting of their meeting the day before. Viyescu clearly regretted having said—or having begun to say—anything. "Santhract is used only to . . . terminate pregnancies, correct?"

"Yes, Hierarch."

"And then only in small doses?"

"Yes, Hierarch."

"What if someone was given a larger dose? Could it kill a man, say?"

Sweat broke on the druggist's brow, and Liam had to try hard to keep calm. What was making him so nervous?

"Could it?"

"I have so heard," Viyescu stammered softly. A hot stab of hope and relief went through Liam. He had latched onto something.

"How much did the woman want?"

The druggist leaned forward with wide eyes, as though he had not understood the question.

"I'm wondering if she wanted enough to kill a man," Liam explained.

"But—but Master Tanaquil was stabbed, was he not?"

Liam shrugged, as though the question meant nothing. "It doesn't matter, of course—you don't sell santhract; it likes you not, eh?" Here was something much more than he had hoped for, and he could not avoid lacing the question with acid irony. Viyescu shook his head instantly.

"And of course, you still don't know who this woman is?" Viyescu shook his head again, obviously unwilling now to speak, not trusting his tongue.

Liam did not care. New ideas crowded out the druggist's worried face. A hundred possibilities spun half out of the few small revelations he had gotten and half out of his guilty need to exonerate Lons.

"Of course," he murmured. "Thank you, Master Viyescu. Your help will not go unnoted." He turned and left the druggist behind his counter.

The black line of clouds was noticeably closer but Liam paid them no attention, his thoughts fully occupied with the web of suppositions he was weaving. He ambled out of Northfield back towards his garret, staring with unseeing eyes at the cobbles. Beggars let him go again, frowning at the tall, distracted figure.

What could the poison mean? And what had Viyescu so upset? It must have to do with Tarquin, or the druggist would not have sent the news to him through Coeccias. So the woman and her poison must be connected with the wizard's death. That was a thorny problem, because if Donoé's story was to mean anything, Tarquin could not have gotten the woman pregnant, and besides, he had been stabbed, not poisoned.

A thousand new questions rose from that. If Tarquin had not gotten her pregnant, who had? And why was the wizard involved? Could the murderer be a person he and Coeccias had never considered, namely the hooded man who came to the unknown woman's sometime lodgings?

Too many new questions. The neat fabric of their solution seemed likely to unravel beneath the weight of his new thoughts. And to further complicate matters, he suddenly wondered if Rora might perhaps have been far less innocent than he thought. The encounter could easily have been planned as a sort of blackmail, to try to turn him away from Lons.

She could not have known he would be drunk and thus vulnerable, but his admiration for her had been obvious. If Coeccias had commented on it, she must have noticed it, and Kansallus had said that she was used to being sought after. What if Lons had sent her there? If he had, it put the guilt firmly on his shoulders.

"Gods," he groaned, "I've been so stupid."

There was nothing for it, though, but to go on trying to clear the actor. Rora might have come to him on her own, unsure of her brother's innocence but determined to protect him in her own way. Again, the possibilities were enormous, and a hundred lines of thought stretched away into uselessness. He and Coeccias had settled, however reluctantly, on an explanation that now seemed simple-minded.

Looking up, he saw that his feet and his musing had carried him to the street where his lodgings were. He stopped uncertainly at the corner and gazed with mild distaste at the high, dark house and the tiny window that fronted his garret. He thought how much better it would have been if he had gone to Tarquin's the night before. Remembering the house, he remembered Fanuilh. He had given no thought to feeding the little creature and, feeling guilty, headed for the stables.

The mass of new and complicated questions weighed heavily on him as he rode, and he attempted to sort it out by going over the information he had, and poking holes in it.

The mystery woman was still looking for poison, and Viyescu some-how connected it with Tarquin's death, and was frightened about something. Lons had not tried to escape, but his sister had tried to turn suspicion from him. The decanter, his treasured decanter with the crossed-out label, suddenly seemed a clue again, unreadable but nonetheless a clue. And the illusion spell Tarquin had marked in his book might hold significance. Marcius had done nothing, but Liam would not dismiss him. Despite his inactivity, he might still fit into the puzzle's unexpectedly wider dimensions.

All he needed was a way to fit everything together. His mind revolted at the new complexity, somehow feeling that simpler explanations were better. Still, he juggled the pieces around, hoping for a way to clear his conscience.

He saw the mounting clouds from the beach, and put Diamond in the shed. The wind had picked up, scouring the beach with cold, stinging sand. He let himself into the house.

I did not think you would come.

Liam waited until he was in the workroom before answering.

"I almost forgot. I've been busy."

I know. Fanuilh's flat cat's eyes and toneless thought stung more than the wind-flung sand. *Sleeping with the dancer was not wise.*

"It was the cider," Liam muttered abashedly, unable to meet the dragon's gaze. "Are you hungry?"

Yes.

He hurried out to the kitchen and fixed his thoughts on the oven. When the raw meat was ready, he brought it back and laid it silently on the worktable.

Coeccias thinks the player killed Master Tanaquil, Fanuilh thought after several large mouthfuls. It moved more easily, and Liam wondered how long it would take to recover completely. *But you do not think so. Your thoughts are scattered on the subject.*

"That's because I'm not sure now why I think he didn't do it," Liam admitted. He went to the second worktable and picked up the empty beaker with its obliterated label. "I don't think Lons is the sort who would kill, but now I have to wonder if I think that because of Lady Necquer, and because of Rora. That's why my thoughts are scattered. If you'd let me tell you things," he said more strongly, "instead of picking them out of my head at random, this might be easier."

Even as he spoke, he knew it was foolish. The dragon would know— because he knew—that his thoughts would be scattered whether or not it invaded them. Fanuilh let it pass, putting all its attention to the meat.

Staring at the beaker, Liam suddenly struck his forehead with his free hand and cursed. It was such a simple question, but he had never thought to ask it.

"Fanuilh, when did you first see this decanter?"

Master Tanaquil had it for many years.

"No, I mean, when did you first notice it here, on the table? Empty?"

The morning after Master Tanaquil removed the Teeth.

"The morning after the woman visited him."

Yes.

Liam set the decanter down on the worktable and went to the book of spells on the lectern. It was still open to the spell that had caused the Teeth to vanish, and he ran his finger along, looking for a list of ingredients.

Symbol components, appeared the thought in his head, and he looked over at the dragon, which had its back to him and was busy gnawing bones.

"What?"

They are not called ingredients; they are called symbol components, and there is no list. Where they appear in the text, they are underscored.

Shrugging at the unresponsive scaled back, Liam rechecked the spell, and saw that the dragon was right. After the initial abstract paragraphs came the actual instructions, and several words were underlined: pitch, purified water, a white-hot brazier of coals, and others, some of which he could not identify. But there was no listing for virgin's blood. Disappointed, he scanned the spell again and found nothing, then flipped through the book to the illusion spell.

There, to his relief, the words "an ounce of virgin's blood" were underlined. He barked a triumphant laugh that brought Fanuilh's head around.

What have you found?

"Well," he said, repressing his grin and going over the words of the spell, "virgin's blood is not called for in the vanishing spell, but it is in the one for invisibility. And since the decanter wasn't on the table until after the woman came, we can reasonably suppose that she requested the spell."

That does not necessarily follow.

"Not necessarily, no, but for the sake of argument—"

It might have been for Marcius.

"Yes, it might," Liam said impatiently, "but we're not going to work that idea just yet. We're going to focus on this woman."

It would help if you knew who she was.

Liam closed his eyes and massaged his brows. "Fanuilh, how is it that you can read my thoughts and remain so impenetrably stupid?" His eyes snapped open and he held his hand out, palm up, to stop the dragon. "Don't answer. Just be quiet."

In blessed silence, he checked the ingredients—symbol components, he reminded himself—for the spell of invisibility, and then compared them with those for the other spell. Both called for pitch, water and coals, and two of the unidentifiable items from the latter were required by the former. The only difference was that virgin's blood was listed under invisibility, while there were three items underlined in the vanishing spell whose names he did not recognize.

The theory behind each spell seemed the same; the difference in effect was accounted for by the three unknown components in the more powerful one. Intrigued, he checked the texts with more care. The vanishing spell often referred to a "representation" or "model" as the focus of the spell, while the casting of invisibility centered around a "homunculus" or "mannikin."

"Fanuilh," he began, but the dragon's thought cut him off.

Invisibility is usually cast on a person, hence the homunculus; a doll, really. Vanishing is for objects, hence the model.

It was looking at him, the long neck twisted sinuously over its shoulder.

"So Tarquin would have had to have a little doll of a person to cast the spell—or could he use this?" He pointed at the model, and Fanuilh's wedgy head shifted to look on the miniature Southwark. No thoughts came for a while, and Liam began to fidget. Finally, a tentative thought snaked into his head.

He might have. I believe the spell can be cast on an object. Before Liam could say anything, another thought came in. *But I am not sure.*

"Of course not," Liam said, "nor am I. But I've one more question. Did Tarquin have a test for Donoé?"

For her blood? No. He trusted Donoé. He trusted people often.

"As he trusted Lons," Liam mused. "To take a man's word for that much money. . . ."

The player did *look like a rich merchant.*

"Yes, yes, but what man—no matter how rich a merchant—will pay that much gold for a woman? Why just take his word?"

Master Tanaquil was a powerful wizard. He had no need for money—he called the fees he charged "gauges of need." How much someone would pay, or what they would be willing to do, for his spells indicated how much they needed them.

"So when Lons agreed to 10,000, he showed his need. Now the question is, what did the woman agree to? How great was her need?"

I do not know. I cannot follow your thoughts on this. They are very scattered.

"Of course they are," Liam agreed, smiling broadly, already on his way out. "It's a tenuous connection at best, very tenuous." He stopped to stroke the dragon's clothlike scales, and feel the creature arch happily under his hand. "I'll be back tomorrow morning."

Do not forget.

"I won't," he called from the hall.

Do you really think this is important?

He stopped in the doorway and shouted back. "I hope so. I'd hate to think I came all the way out here just to feed you."

Diamond safely stabled, Liam went back to his garret to get his writing case and the letter from Rora. He did not really need his writing case. The letter was more important. He did not want it lying around for his landlady to see and, thinking of the way Coeccias had gotten hold of his list of suspects, he did not want the Aedile to find it. They had become friends, to a certain extent, and he was ashamed to think of the things he had to hide.

His landlady was holding court in the kitchen, ordering the drudge around when he walked in. She smiled broadly and began speaking at once, almost as though she had been expecting him.

"Master Liam! Uris bless us, you've just missed some gentlemen who came calling for you."

"Really? Who?"

"None I'd ever seen," she said, pitching her voice in a whisper that seemed to invite the exchange of confidences. "And they'd not leave their names, or business," she added significantly.

Liam grunted noncommittally and went up the stairs, glad to frustrate her and thinking of the letter and the rest of the day. There was still an hour before noon, when Lady Necquer had told him to come back. He was not sure if he would bother. First he had to see Coeccias, and find out what he thought, and then he would decide if he could spare the time to go up to the Point.

With the letter secure in his writing case on his belt, he started back down the stairs.

"Master Liam," his landlady called peevishly from the kitchen. "The men who're asking after you are here."

He thought more of her irritated tone than of the visitors she had announced. *I really shouldn't go out of my way to annoy her,* he thought. *She's just a harmless old gossip.*

The man who stood just inside the kitchen door was a stranger, though Liam knew the type from his short-cut hair and the way he smacked his fist into his palm. The Rat stood behind him, and as Liam came off the last step into the kitchen, Scar stepped through the door, his ghastly smile wide and unpleasant.

Damn, Liam thought. *At least they're not armed.*

The three toughs began moving in, the Rat around one end of the table and the unknown tough around the other. Liam waited until all three were away from the door, and then moved.

"Run and fetch the Aedile," he shouted at his landlady and her drudge, and ran at the Rat. The drudge, young and smart, dodged past Scar, but the older woman found her way blocked by Scar's widespread arms. She backed away, gaping and goggling like a landed fish.

The Rat was not prepared to be attacked, and Liam hit him twice in the stomach, doubling him over. Liam was surprised how easy it was; the Rat was obviously no brawler. The man he did not know, however, was, and came up behind him before he could turn and caught his arms.

Scar grabbed the terrified landlady and thrust her angrily at the gasping, teary-eyed Rat. "Hold fast, jack; the woman'll not harm you," he sneered, and shoved past the other man to confront Liam.

With his arms tightly held behind him, Liam could only kick at Scar, but the bigger man swatted his leg away easily. The man who held him wrenched at his arms and hooked one foot around his, drawing him off balance. Scar snorted with laughter and waded in, slamming his fists into Liam's stomach with a sound like the thump of heavy sacks.

Liam's face mottled with pain and sickness, his sight grew blurry, and he became aware that the man behind him had eaten onions. The strong smell washed over his neck and face.

Onions, gods, he thought, and closed his eyes against two more punishing blows. Then he felt himself slipping to his knees, let go, and a rough hand grabbed his hair and jerked his head back. He opened his eyes weakly. Scar's face was only a few inches away, and he focused with difficulty on the puckered edges of the man's disfigurement. It was a livid purple, a shallow trench across the face.

"There's a man we both know of that's not pleased you've been to another man we both know of," Scar said, "and this man fears y'ought to part Southwark soon. Y'understand?"

He shook Liam's head by the hair he held, which did not help Liam's concentration.

"I haven't been to anyone else," he managed over the roaring ache that was his stomach and chest.

Scar stood up and let go of his head, sending him straight to the ground. The stone floor of the kitchen was wonderfully cold.

"You lie, Rhenford."

"Aye, and at full length," the man who had held him laughed, and aimed a perfect kick directly between his legs. Liam tried to curl up, but his stomach screamed in protest and he simply lay prostrate. Somewhere in the room, the Rat giggled.

"Remember," Scar's voice came to him, close to his ear, "part Southwark soon. This day." A rough hand cuffed his ear, but the stinging was nothing compared to his other pains.

He heard a number of footsteps hurrying out of the kitchen, and then the slamming of the door, but he did not open his eyes. The floor felt good against his burning face, and his muscles would not allow him to move much.

"Oh, Master Rhenford, what've they done!" His landlady was kneeling over him, tentatively touching the back of his head, but he was aware of it only as an annoyance.

Well, he thought dimly, *at least Marcius has done something.*

▪ *13* ▪

BY THE TIME Coeccias came bustling in with the drudge, Liam was sitting up on the stairs, hugging his stomach. Mistress Dorcas hovered, pestering him with unwanted attention.

"You're awfully quick," he said sourly to the Aedile, moving an arm to wave away the piece of steak his landlady was shoving at him, and wincing at the movement.

"You don't seem to've taken much hurt," the Aedile said. "The girl had you drawn and quartered three times over." He gestured with a wry smile at the drudge, who was staring unashamedly at Liam's pallor. "Who was it?"

"Some of Marcius's playfellows." He finally pushed the landlady gently aside as she tried to probe a particularly delicate area. "Please, madam, I'm fine. And steak is only good for black eyes." He wondered where she had gotten the steak; she never served anything so good to her boarders.

"Y'are all right, then?" Coeccias moved to his side, and Liam quickly nodded, not wanting the Aedile's blunt fingers added to his landlady's.

"I'll be fine. Just winded."

He was much more than winded. Bright yellow and dull blue bruises blossomed in his imagination, counterparts to the ones he knew would soon appear all over his torso. Still, Scar had done his job remarkably well, for all the apparent indiscriminateness of his blows. No broken ribs, nothing damaged internally. He had checked himself over as thoroughly as possible, and saw none of the telltale signs he remembered from seeing more badly beaten men.

"And soon to bruise," he added. "But then, I bruise easily."

"I've heard scholars do," Coeccias said in a strange tone, as if something else was occurring to him. "So, Marcius has thrown's hand in?"

"It seems so. Why don't we discuss it upstairs?" He nodded significantly at his landlady, who was wringing her hands and clucking with sympathetic concern as well as watching them greedily and pricking up ears for every word. Amused, the Aedile bent forward to help him up, but Liam forestalled him with a grunt.

He made it to his feet and then began to sway, seized with dizziness. The Aedile casually steadied him, and gave him his arm to lean on as they went slowly up the stairs.

"Our thanks, madam," he said over his shoulder, "if you'd send up some wine?"

Liam lowered himself gingerly into the chair by the window and slumped slowly over the table, unspeakably happy he had not eaten that morning. The nausea was receding, but bright points of light still squirmed at the edges of his vision. They merged with the motes dancing in the mild beam of light lancing through the window, and he closed his eyes and leaned into it, trying to warm away the dull pain.

Coeccias paced silently around the room, waiting, apparently, for the knock at the door that revealed Mistress Dorcas herself with a jug and two mugs. He took them and pressed a coin into her hand with a stern look.

"For the girl," he warned. "A good lass, and quick-legged. Our thanks again."

The landlady let him shut the door in her face without so much as a word.

With his own cup filled, he put one down by Liam's open hand, and began pacing again.

"Truth, I'd have never thought Marcius to be so open in his businesses."

Liam gave a questioning grunt and tilted the mug to his mouth without raising his head. The wine slid coolly down his ragged throat, and quieted what was left of his dizziness.

"It surprises me that he'd only beat you, and leave harsher measures by. If I were Marcius, and I thought you could finger me a murderer, I'd've had my roughs beat you more than senseless."

What started as a laugh turned to a drawn-out "oh" of pain, and Liam gave it up. "Marcius didn't have his roughs beat me senseless because Marcius isn't worried about being connected with Tarquin's death. One of them said that Marcius was terribly unhappy with me for having seen a man we both knew."

"And what of it? The man's me, and Marcius wanted to fright you from helping me."

"No," Liam smiled limply, his head still on the table. It would have been ridiculous, if his stomach and chest did not hurt so much. "Marcius wanted to fright me from helping Freihett Necquer. Remember the maps I used as such a clever pretext for seeing him?"

Coeccias's face went blank, and then broke out in a sheepish wince. "It liked him not that you might sell the same over again, to another merchant. We misjudged how slight a thing would draw his ire. For mere mappery he'd beat a man; but think what he'd've done to a man who failed him in an important spell. It argues against him with the wizard."

Speaking was less of an effort now; even as Liam listened to the Aedile his body was reconciling itself to the beating. "It does, a little, but I don't think it's in any way we've imagined, if at all."

Coeccias glowered and crossed his arms.

"Pray you, Milord May-Do-Aught, how not? What news have you to change your mind and redraw the whole argument? No, don't tell, I'll guess—now you think the player's the man, accompliced by the high priest of Uris. Well? Do I hit the mark?"

"Not even close," Liam laughed, and regretted it instantly. He quickly told what he had learned that morning from Viyescu, and what he had figured out from Tarquin's spellbook. The Aedile pursed his lips at the new information, as if he had just sucked a lemon.

"And so we're not done. You'll want to search out this woman, and hope to substitute her for the player. You never gave him up as guilty, did you?"

"No," Liam admitted, annoyed that Coeccias had struck so close to home. There was no need to mention Rora, he figured. It would only lessen Coeccias's confidence in him.

"Then what would you? How do we gather her in? Do we set a crier out, begging all cloaked and hooded women gather in the square this day week?"

"I don't know," Liam said, ignoring the sarcasm. "I think we could talk with Viyescu again, and maybe have him followed. I think he knows her better than he lets on; perhaps he'll lead us to her."

"And what with the player? Do we take him, or leave him loose?"

"That's up to you." He forced himself to say it, though his conscience firmly admonished him. "Take him if you like. He's still the best suspect."

Throwing his hands up in a familiar gesture of exasperation, Coeccias began his heavy-footed pacing again. "If you'd your way, I'd have to leave him forever, while you con the town for some unfaced woman who, by reason of some broken clues, only *may* have a hand in this. You see what you put me to?"

"Are you satisfied that Lons killed Tarquin?"

"Truth, satisfied enough!" He was clearly not satisfied however, and let his anger fall away, deflated. "If you'd a plan, it'd be easier to let this play on. Have you any plan?"

"I still think Viyescu knows more than he says. He's frightened of her, though."

Coeccias snorted. "Of a maid! Ha!"

"Not of violence, obviously, not from a pregnant woman. But she may know something about him, some secret sin, that keeps him from telling."

"The threat of revelation?"

Liam shrugged. "Maybe. He was all bluster the first time I went to see him, and changed his tune when I said I was a Hierarch in disguise. He accepted it right off, as if he was expecting me to pronounce divine judgement on him."

"And he so devout," Coeccias breathed. "It would mock his pious marches and professions. An interesting turn."

"If there were a way we could find out more about him, something about drink, perhaps, or women . . ."

"Herione'd know it, if it's to be known, or she'd know who might know. I'll to her now. Is there anything else I should ask?"

"Oh, anything that comes to mind," Liam said airily, drawing a grin from the Aedile.

"Perhaps I should ask if she knows who killed the wizard."

"It couldn't hurt."

"Truth, it couldn't! I'll do it." Chuckling, he paused in the doorway, and looked back thoughtfully. "Perhaps I'll send some men to look for Marcius's roughs to boot. We can't have our poor, milky scholars beaten in their own homes. What were they like?"

Liam described Scar and Ratface vividly, and gave what he could remember of the third man.

"A scar so big should shout itself about the city. We'll have them in soon enough."

"Tell your men not to be too gentle with them," Liam called as the Aedile closed the door behind him.

Less than twenty minutes later, Liam was closing the door himself. Much to his landlady's dismay and the drudge's obvious admiration, he managed to clear the kitchen without falling over.

The clouds, and with them a bleak chill, had reached the city from the sea; the blue sky was only a thin memory to the north. Still, the cold air cleared his head and took the edge off his aching. He kept to the side of the street, trailing his hand along the walls of stone and wood, unsure of his wobbly legs.

On reaching the Point without collapsing, he counted it a minor victory. It was undoubtedly stupid to go out, but he felt less sick. Leaning against a wall a hundred yards from Necquer's house, he caught his breath. The stone of the wall spread numbing fingers through his cloak and around his back, reaching to dull his throbbing muscles. The cold would feel even better if he turned around and let it touch his chest directly, but that would not do. People were already giving him strange looks as they passed.

Can't have people making love to walls in the Point, he thought, and kept the laugh in his head to save the pain. Maybe in the Warren, or even Auric's Park, but certainly not the Point.

The wall he was leaning against was a real wall, not just the side of a house, high and smooth, the stones closely fitted. From Tarquin's model he knew that inside the wall lay a small garden, lovingly tended. The miniature in the workroom was perpetually in bloom, with two tiny rose-bushes and three flowerbeds like intricate needlepoint. Now, the real thing would be on its last legs, drawing in on itself for the approaching winter.

Idly, he wondered who owned the garden. It might be the woman he was looking for, a pregnant woman who casually asked for poison and frightened fanatic apothecaries and might think nothing of murdering a powerful wizard. He imagined her like some warrior-queen, tall and broad and spectacularly pregnant, her belly swollen to the size of a cauldron, with a dagger in her hand shaped, for some reason known only to his imagination, like an icicle. The picture was surprisingly vivid, and he closed his eyes and sculpted more, a face stern and without beauty, shrewd eyes blazing thunder. A chin ships could be wrecked on. He smiled. She might own the garden he rested outside.

Or she might not.

He shook his head and forced himself slowly away from the wall.

Though twelve bells had rung half an hour ago, he did not hurry, shuffling the last yards to Necquer's door at a comfortable pace.

Lares was long in answering the door, and he allowed himself to slump against the door frame while he waited.

The old servant's face screwed up when he saw Liam, and he ushered him in reluctantly.

"Good day, Lares."

"And to you, Sir Liam."

They stood facing each other in the foyer, Liam bracing himself with his legs spread wide so he would not fall, Lares shifting his weight uneasily and studiously examining a small section of the floor.

What's wrong with you? Can't you see I've been beaten by a merchant prince's toughs and can barely stand up? Isn't it obvious? Liam's face twitched at the questions he left unasked, stifling a laugh.

As Liam cleared his throat, Lares finally spoke, and he sounded miserable.

"If it please you, you should not've come, Sir Liam. I know I'm a mere pantler, and y'are a very gentleman, a good and noble, and you mean no harm. And Uris knows you've kept the lady's spirits high and diverted. But you should not've come. The Master's said he'd be gone the most of the day, but if he were to spy you here . . ." He left off, shaking his head woefully, and Liam spoke soberly, his lightheadedness effectively crushed.

"I won't stay long, Lares, I promise."

The servant looked him full in the face for a moment, as if judging how much his promise was worth, and then nodded.

For once, Liam did not mind the slowness with which the old man ascended the staircase. It covered his own weakness, and gave him time to think. He probably should not have come; but had not Lady Necquer told him to? And he wanted to know why her husband did not want him around. If she would just tell him that, he would leave.

Lady Necquer did not rise to meet him, but heard Lares's introduction in silence and waited on her couch. She sat in a simple, unaffected beige frock, her hands folded in her lap, and Liam was surprised by the depth of unhappiness on her face.

Maybe Marcius had her beaten as well, he thought, and instantly felt distaste for the joke wash through his mouth. Her eyes were puffed with tears barely restrained, she was unnaturally pale, and her voice caught when she spoke.

"Sir Liam."

She was not being cold, he knew, but keeping her reserve in order not to lose control completely. Necquer must have impressed his wishes quite forcefully.

"I won't stay long, madam," he replied, and remained standing.

"Pray you, Poppae," she blurted, and then regained her composure. "I think you might call me Poppae."

"Very well, Poppae." He wanted to sketch a bow to accept the intimacy, but had to settle for a nod. "I won't stay long, and I certainly don't want to cause any trouble between you and your husband. I just wondered . . . well, I wondered why Master Necquer would so suddenly want me kept away."

Her eyes fixed on the patterned carpet at her feet, she took a deep breath. "He says I've been too free with my confidences."

Liam pretended to take his time digesting this, though he knew exactly what she was talking about. "You mean about Lons," he said at length.

"About the player, yes."

His long silence this time was genuine. "But I helped! He won't bother you anymore."

"You misconstrue, Sir Liam," she sighed heavily. "My husband feels th'affair more than you can fathom, and so attaches more import to its every aspect than he should. He . . . he introduced Lons to our home."

The sentence came from her mouth like lead, a bare recital of facts. Liam found nothing to say, and she went on in the same way.

"Before he left for the ports on your charts, he went to the Golden Orb, and there saw a spectacle that he said had amused him no end. He commissioned a number of the players to give a private performance here. Lons was among them, as well as the clown, Fitch, and the beautiful dancer, and the other chief actors. Some two days after, Freihett parted, and Lons commenced his calls. I thought it no harm at first. . . ." She stopped suddenly, and then resumed quickly: "But you know the rest."

"Yes," he murmured.

"And so my husband feels it partly his shame that all this has come about. He was most grieved that I took you into our secret. He guards his privacy jealously, Sir Liam, you must understand."

"I do, I do." Liam stood, torn. She looked extremely young, and unhappy, and he compared her unwillingly with Rora. The two were probably the same age, somewhere in their early twenties, but while the dancer was a mere actress, the lowest of the low, she faced her problems with fire and determination. She had sought him out, and gained his assistance, while Lady Necquer, her superior in wealth, breeding and position, allowed him to be sent away. Strangely, he felt only a grudging admiration for Rora's spirit, but he pitied the woman he was with, and wanted somehow to console her.

He would have gone to her on the couch and tried, not out of any desire to be near her, but because he sensed that was the way it was done, with quiet words and innocent caresses. However, he was not sure how she would interpret it, and moreover he did not know if he could carry it off. A lifetime in the company of men, a widowed father and scholars locked in musty books, and then rough mercenaries and sailors, had given him little chance to practice. The few women he had known would never have submitted to Lady Necquer's lot, and had never needed that kind of comfort.

So, he cleared his throat and managed a small bow, despite the twinge it sent through his bruised body.

"I will leave you then, madam."

She did not move, so he turned and moved slowly to the door.

"Sir Liam!"

He stopped and turned around, to discover her on her feet right behind him. Before he could say anything she brushed his cheek with her lips and then backed away.

"You are so very kind," she said wistfully. "I would I could hear more of your stories. Perhaps when you've written them?"

"When I have finished them, I'll send you a copy," he said, bowed again in haste, and left.

A last, thin strip of blue sky limned the northern horizon and, as Liam walked back to his garret, the clouds were rushing down to blot it out. They were coal black, roiling and angry, but the cold wind that bore them felt good. The clean salt smell supplanted the odor of Mistress Necquer's perfume.

He walked a little faster, but not much, and still kept close to the walls. The streets were emptying rapidly in anticipation of the approaching storm, and even the beggars were throwing foreboding glances at the sky. Imagining the purple bruises soon to appear over most of his upper body, he allowed himself a groan, and when he reached his house, sank into one of the kitchen chairs.

Mistress Dorcas was nowhere to be seen, but the drudge edged up to him and shyly inquired if there was anything he needed. Touched, he got a coin from his pouch and asked her if she could get him something to eat. She snatched the coin and disappeared out the door before he could specify what he wanted.

The drudge was back quickly, with a covered pot and a few loaves.

"Broth," she explained, laying the pot and the bread before him. "All that can be got on Uris's Eve, but best if y'are ill about the stomach," she added, biting her lip, afraid she might have gone too far.

He nodded. "You're wise, girl. I've known warriors who showed less sense."

She blushed and brightened at once. "Y'have?"

Dipping a spoon into the broth, he laughed. "I once knew a prince—the envy of armies, the hope of his country—who won a great battle, though he took a wound to his stomach. Afterwards, he stuffed himself full of wine and roast meat, though I advised him not to, and was so sick that he missed his own victory celebration."

"Then he died," the drudge whispered, fascinated.

"No, he just lay in his bed for a day, moaning and groaning, sure someone had poisoned his food. They had to postpone his triumph, and his reputation was greatly diminished. The defeated army sent a present to the cook."

She giggled, and stopped, remembering his money. From the pocket of her smock she produced a sweaty handful of coins.

"Your money, Master," she said, and laid the change down beside his pot. He eyed it for a moment, and tasted his soup. It was only lightly spiced, not too hot, and the warmth soothed his throat. He waved his hand at the money.

"Keep it; you've done me a great service. The broth is just what I needed."

"Oh no, Master, I daren't." She shook her head and backed away from the table as though he had suggested something indecent.

"Go ahead, take it. Consider it my thanks, please."

She only shook her head and gazed fearfully at the street door, through which suddenly stalked his landlady. The thin, angular woman shot the drudge a commanding glance that sent the young girl scurrying away.

"Y'are better, then, Master Liam?"

"Much, madam, thank you. Your girl has been good enough to get me some soup, and I took a short walk that has cleared my head a great deal."

"Huh," she sniffed, and Liam sensed that she was unhappy about something. "I only hope the Aedile has nabbed the monstrous roughs who did this shameful thing."

It was not a question, but he answered it anyway. "He is looking for them right now."

"Then he'll have them, that's sure." She frowned again, but he was busy with the soup, which was doing wonders for his stomach. She puttered aimlessly around the kitchen while he ate. "Perhaps it's none of my affair, Master Liam," she said at length, "but, might I ask, why did they assault you?"

"A small disagreement, of no importance," he said, waving his spoon airily.

"If it please you, Master Liam, I think it could be of some note, for my part at least."

There was a tone in her voice he had never heard before, and it surprised him; it was firmness. She had always been such a sycophant, flattering and sucking up to him because he had money and had allowed her to believe him a scholar. He set his spoon down and steepled his fingers, looking at her curiously over the tips.

"It was a disagreement over the terms of a sale. I sold their master some information, and he thought I had sold the same to another man. I had not."

"Well," she said doubtfully. "Well, you needs must see my position, only a widow, and with my name to protect and this house to manage. I can ill afford any smirch to be attached to this house by the general opinion, you see."

"It won't happen again.'

"Faith, how can I be sure, Master Liam?"

If he hadn't been conscious of his tender sides, Liam would have laughed. She was trying to find a way to throw him out—him, her star boarder, the eminently respectable scholar. Then he thought about the last few days, and realized how it must look to her. Tarquin's murder, the Aedile suddenly calling, fights in her kitchen.

And midnight visits from beautiful young dancers, he thought with dawning comprehension. She must think he had grown depraved.

He decided to make it easy for her.

"You can't be sure, madam, and I see your point. Your house's reputation must be protected, and even though I haven't done anything in the least improper, I can see my presence is disturbing. I'll pack my things, and leave in two days, after Uris-tide."

She was taken aback, clearly not expecting this sudden capitulation. He allowed himself a small smile, and returned to his soup.

"You may keep the deposit for the room."

"Faith," she stammered, "I meant not that—"

"No matter," he interrupted with his spoon, "I wouldn't dream of damaging your reputation. Consider me gone."

For a few moments she lingered while he studiously ignored her in favor of his broth, and then she skulked off unhappily.

Liam could not tell why she should be unhappy. He had agreed to leave in order to protect her "reputation," or what little she had. Near the bottom of his broth he thought of an answer. She would probably have been willing to sacrifice her good name for an increase in rent. Shaking his head at her malleable virtue, he pushed aside the empty pot and tried to make himself comfortable in the rigid wooden chair.

The money the drudge had left caught his eye. The rungs of the chair's ladderback pressed into a sore spot, and he leaned away from it to pick up one of the coins.

A small silver piece, stamped with the face and name of Auric IV, dead a hundred years but still well-defined on his currency. The noble profile and the laurel wreath were easily made out, despite a century's use, and most of the inscription of his name and title could still be read. The other coins, mostly copper and of more recent minting, showed age, worn smooth, simple discs of cheaper metal. They made better coins in the days when being King in Torquay meant something.

Someone had mentioned coins to him recently. Who? He moved the coin over the back of his hand, from finger to finger, wondering, a trick he had learned in his youth. It helped to have thin fingers. The silver piece made the trip from index to little finger and back three times.

He had it: the messenger Coeccias had sent him in the wineshop above the square, who had told him about the mystery woman's rent being paid. He had said something about the coins being strange, the strangest he had ever seen. Why would he say that?

Southwark sent ships as far as any other city in Taralon, trading in lands as far apart as Alyecir and the Freeports. A certain amount of foreign currency could be expected to come in from those places; besides, since the decline of the monarchy, any local lord could mint his own, thus adding to the mix. Provided the coins were really of the metal they claimed, no one would be interested in the origins. The coins would have to be strange indeed to arouse comment. So why had the landlord mentioned it to the messenger?

If the gold was good, it would mean the engraving was strange, which must mean that it was not impressed with the profile or head of the minter. One head on a coin was much the same as another, Liam knew, and he had seen a greater variety than most. So the coins must have been carved with a different image.

Some of the lands he had been to engraved their coins with local animals or buildings or landscapes that would seem strange to the people of Southwark.

To most of the people of Southwark, he thought, except for Freihett Necquer, whom Liam had sent to some of those lands in search of trade.

Perplexed, he missed his fingering and the coin slipped to the floor, where it rolled away under a heavy cupboard. He ignored it, cautioning himself against his own thoughts.

Just because Necquer had been to lands no one from Southwark other than Liam had ever heard of did not mean that the coins were his. They might have come from a member of his crew, or from some tradesman to whom he had paid them. They might not even be from one of the cities on Liam's maps, but from the mint of a Taralonian noble with strange tastes. It might mean nothing, and Necquer might not be involved at all.

But it might mean that Necquer kept the hooded woman. Lons's comment came back to him. He had said that the merchant did not deserve fidelity.

It could not hurt to check. If he was right, he could tell Coeccias who the hooded woman was, and that would settle a great number of things. With trembling fingers, he gathered up the coins, shoved them in his pouch, and left.

The bells were tolling three as Liam passed the city square. The sky was alive with writhing black clouds, but he did not think about the imminent storm. Coeccias had told him where the woman's apartment was, deep in the Warren. He would look there, and try to find out what made the coins strange.

He walked faster, and though he still kept close to walls, the dizziness was almost gone. The soup had settled his stomach, and all that was left was a steady, uniform aching. It was relatively easy to ignore.

The Warren was less uninviting than usual, the poor being smart enough to clear the streets well in advance of the storm. The lodgings he was looking for were located off a court that was approached from two separate streets by long, narrow alleys. His footsteps sounded like the slithering of wet snakes on the slick, gritty stones, slipping on mounds of sodden refuse. In the summer, he knew, he would not dare enter the hidden court for fear of the stench, but with the rains the smell was held down, and all that reached his nostrils was mildew. He hurried into the court, gazing wistfully up at the thin ribbon of gray sky far above him.

Even on a sunny day, little light would have filtered down to the tiny courtyard, ringed in by topheavy buildings. With the clouds, he had to squint to make anything out. Fragile porches climbed the walls like ivy, hung with washing. There were few windows in the walls, and those were small and showed no lights. A heap of broken furniture and staved-in casks took up nearly half the floor of the courtyard. Two thin children, a boy and girl as far as he could tell, clambered over the jumbled pile with the agility of mountain goats.

Liam called to them, and they approached silently, arm in fearful arm, with wide, respectful eyes. The girl, no more than ten, took in his clothes and attempted a clumsy curtsy. At a pinch from her, the boy knuckled his forehead. Liam asked them if they knew the owner of the building at the east end of the courtyard, the one whose entrance was almost blocked by the wooden junk they had been playing on.

The girl shoved the boy, who turned and ran, nimbly climbing over the pile and disappearing into the building.

"My brother'll fetch'm m'lord," the girl said, curtsying awkwardly again. Liam nodded and looked around the courtyard. There was nothing to see, so he turned his eyes back to the girl, who still stood before him, staring with unabashed greed at his rich clothes. He blushed under her scrutiny. She was no more than ten, with dirty, colorless hair and a child's smock, but her eyes seemed to take him in and dissect him, weighing every piece of him for value. Apparently she rated him high, because she shared a confidence with him.

"He's a fat rascally knave, m'lord, is th'owner. For that he's so long in coming."

"Mmm." Liam did not know what to say. He had never penetrated this far into the Warren, never left the larger streets, and he had never felt at ease talking with children. He was relieved to see the boy clambering back over the pile and to hear behind him the cursing of a full-grown man trying to make his way around.

The girl had told the truth: the owner was fat, and sweating heavily despite the chill. He had the poor man's haircut, shaven until just below his ears, and he cursed like a sailor until he caught sight of Liam. Then he stopped and wiggled his way past the last projecting piece of garbage and bowed as deeply as his belly would allow. He knuckled his forehead as well, with the ease of much practice. The boy and the girl drifted back to their playing.

"How now, my lord? If it please you, what office can I perform?" He was obsequious in exactly the manner Liam disliked, rubbing his hands together with an oily smile.

"The Aedile Coeccias sent a man to you recently, about one of your lodgers."

The fat man nodded eagerly, dropping his grin for an expression of considered interest.

"You told him the rent had been paid this month in foreign coins."

"Faith, m'lord, the strangest coins I ever saw, most strange."

"Can I see them?"

The man stiffened, and his face alternated between suspicion and contrition. "No, if it please you, my lord, for that I've spent them. On wood, my lord, and warm clothes, with winter almost on us, my lord."

"Well, never mind; can you tell me why they were strange?"

He scratched his bare neck and shuffled. "Strange indeed, strange indeed. They showed beasts the like I've never seen, even in the menageries as travel down from Torquay and can be seen for a copper. Great beasts, my lord, like—well, like naught so much as a bull, but with a whip in place of a muzzle, and so large that a city stood on its back."

"Were there others?"

"No my lord," the man said regretfully, "only those."

"Well, thank you."

It did not matter; he knew the coins to which the man was referring. They came from Epidamnum, one of the ports on the maps he had drawn for Necquer, and represented what were called elephants. The Epidamnites used them for war, and put towers on their backs. He had only seen elephants on coins from that land, which meant that it was likely that only people from Necquer's crew could have them.

The man still shifted from foot to foot, as though expecting something. Liam cleared his throat and dug into his pouch.

"Thank you again," he said, pressing a coin into the owner's hand. The fat man smiled and knuckled his forehead, then retreated behind the mound of junk where the children played, bowing his way.

Liam called to the girl, and she reluctantly climbed down from her playground to stand before him. The boy stayed perched atop the pile, poised and watchful.

"Thank you," Liam said and held out two coins for her. She snatched them, dropped a quick curtsy, and ran back up the pile to the boy, holding the coins high like a prize. The boy smiled shyly.

It had grown darker in the courtyard, and Liam hurried out one of the alleys. The street it opened on was broad, marking the edge of the Warren and the beginning of the waterfront district. A row of brick warehouses stood across the way. Necquer's offices were only a few streets away.

The clouds had grown angrier, agitated by the harsh wind from the sea; it would rain soon, but there was time to visit the merchant before it broke. Necquer would not be happy to see him, certainly, but what did that matter? He would simply ask a few harmless questions, and make sure Epidamnum had been one of the ports the merchant traded in. And since Necquer was already displeased with him, he could afford to annoy him a little more.

Necquer's warehouse was more attractive than Marcius's, red brick and long-fronted with a wide strip of clean windows near the roof. There was a large sign as well, painted in elaborate letters, announcing "Freihett Necquer, Factor and Merchant." Liam had been there before on three occasions, while selling his maps. There were no guards, only an old doorkeeper who seemed to recognize him. He let Liam in, and bid him wait while he went to announce him.

There were more goods in the warehouse than in Marcius's, kegs and boxes and bales reaching to the raftered ceiling in tidy stacks, and they filled most of the floorspace. Between the stacks at the center of the warehouse, an aisle had been left that led back to the offices. The doorkeeper appeared again after a moment, and waved Liam on.

"He'll see you," the old man called.

Liam went down the aisle and passed the doorkeeper into the merchant's offices. There was a large area with tall secretaries and the high stools that went with them. The other times he had been there, clerks had perched precariously on the stools, busily scratching away at ledger entries and bills of lading, making jokes and speaking among themselves. Now there was no one, all gone for Uris's Eve, Liam supposed, and the silence was eerie. Necquer's private office was beyond the clerks' area, behind a stout wooden door. He knocked at the door and then went in.

Necquer sat at a simple table, papers piled neatly before him, pen and inkpot and blotter arrayed with military precision. Sea charts and maps of Taralon hung on the walls, but Liam did not see his own charts. Too valuable to be displayed, even for Necquer's own clerks.

"Rhenford. What may I do for you?" He spoke formally, sitting rigid in his chair, his affability replaced by a brisk, businesslike demeanor.

"Well, Master Necquer," he said, smiling brightly, "I had the afternoon free, and it struck me that we never really discussed the outcome of your journey."

"Yes?"

"Naturally, I'm interested to know more about it. The maps, after all, were mine, and I'm glad to have heard you did well by them. But I'm really more interested to know how you found the lands themselves. Some of them I have not visited in a long time."

"Really?"

"Yes. For instance, I was wondering how things were in Domy—I spent six months there, and found it a very pleasant place. Did you find it so?"

"The trade was good."

The merchant's apathetic answers were exasperating. He decided to simply ask.

"Ah. And Sardis? And Epidamnum?"

"We did not make Sardis. Epidamnum was fairly profitable." He mentioned the second port without hesitation.

"I would like to discuss your journey in more detail, Master Necquer. Compare notes, you understand. Perhaps if you could spare an hour or so?"

"I am occupied at present, Rhenford. I have work to fill the afternoon."

Liam could sense that Necquer was getting impatient, but he wanted to know how far he could push him. It couldn't hurt, as the merchant's attitude towards him was already obviously negative.

"I see. Maybe this evening, then? Only an hour or so, I promise."

"Tonight is Uris's Eve, Rhenford. I will be working until eight, and then I must attend the vigil at her fane. I cannot spare you any time."

He spoke the last in such a way that the word "ever" was clearly attached, and Liam decided to take the hint.

"That's too bad. I would have liked to hear what you thought. Well, perhaps some other time."

"Perhaps," Necquer said coldly, and pointedly picked up his pen and began writing.

Liam nodded and left, still smiling brightly to show that he had not taken offense. The merchant paid him no attention. The doorkeeper was waiting outside the clerks' room, and escorted him out.

A fat drop of rain stained Liam's cloak. The storm was only a few minutes away, and he walked as quickly as he could towards the city square and the jail.

Lay worshippers were not allowed into the Uris's Eve vigils, Coeccias had told him. Necquer knew he was a Midlander only recently arrived in Southwark, and would not expect him to know that. But why then say he was going to attend the vigils? A convenient lie to avoid meeting with him, or did Necquer have somewhere to go at eight? More likely the first, but it was just possible that the merchant had a rendezvous scheduled. And if it were in the Warren, with a certain hooded woman . . .

Liam hurried faster, happy Scar had left his legs alone. The drops of rain began to fall sporadically, spotting his cloak, and by the time he reached the jail, it was a solid drizzle.

Coeccias was not there, but the Guardsman on duty let him sit on a hard bench in the small, cold antechamber.

"Th'Aedile's to be back soon," the Guardsman said, and left him alone. As he waited, he thought through what he had found, and how he would present it to Coeccias.

If the hooded woman was Necquer's mistress, then he had gotten her pregnant. It would make sense, in a way, for her to want to get rid of his child—it would not do for a prominent merchant to have an illegitimate child in the Warren. Therefore the santhract, which Viyescu had presumably sold her, though he denied it. There was nothing, however, that tied the affair to Tarquin's death, except the fact that the woman had mentioned his name and had, perhaps, visited him.

What did the virgin's blood mean, and the second spell for invisibility instead of total disappearance? It seemed as though he had stumbled on a separate mystery altogether, in which Tarquin's death was only a secondary event. There were too many extras for them all to revolve around one set of circumstances. The hooded woman, he feared, would turn out to be nothing more than a pregnant mistress, and worse, a dead end.

For a moment, he thought about ignoring Necquer's appointment and letting Lons stand guilty. The player's knife and the motive were enough to damn the young man, and Liam could explain to Rora, if he had to, that there was nothing he could do.

He rejected the idea at last, though not because of any debt he felt he owed to the dancer. He admitted he owed her the effort, but the real reason he was interested was because he wanted to know who Necquer's mistress was. He wanted to compare the hooded woman with Lady Necquer, and even more with his own image of her.

When the Aedile tramped grumpily into the antechamber, soaking wet, Liam had figured out what he would tell him.

"The very sky's cracked, and the gods weep themselves dry in wetting the earth," Coeccias complained, spraying sheets of water from cloak, hair and beard, and taking Liam's presence for granted. "You were not at home when I called. Should you be walking, after your heavy exercise of the afternoon?"

"It didn't turn out to be as bad as it felt," Liam replied, standing up. "I found something interesting."

"Truth, I've news as well, if you'd hear it."

Liam nodded over-graciously for Coeccias to precede him.

"Come in first," the Aedile said. "I've need of something, for it's cold and wet."

Liam followed him into the headquarters of the Guard. It was essentially a barracks, with a couple of rough cots and a number of pegs on the wall, some holding cloaks and hats. Halberds huddled in every corner, and there was a huge keg in the center of the rush-strewn floor. A door in the far wall, bound in iron and barred by a thick wooden beam, hid the jail proper. Two cavernous hearths flanked the room, and the Guardsman who had kindly allowed him to shiver in the anteroom was busy building a roaring fire. He barely nodded at Coeccias, who nodded back and went straight to the keg, catching up two tin cups from one of the cots. He filled them at the keg, and handed one to Liam.

Expecting beer, Liam drank deeply. It was some kind of hard liquor, and he almost coughed it up before it burned out his throat. Coeccias sipped appreciatively, and his eyes twinkled at Liam's distress.

"You'd be wise to drink small, Rhenford."

Liam coughed and spluttered his agreement.

"Now, for what's been discovered to me. Herione relates that Viyescu had indeed been to her house, perhaps twice, but it was long since, perhaps two years. She did not remember what he wanted, or what he did—she sees the whole book and catalogue of vice there, so the sins of a wretched apothecary would not impress themselves strongly on her mind."

"Still, even a single visit would impress itself strongly on a fanatic prude like Viyescu. Particularly if he enjoyed it, or maybe went somewhere else afterwards. Herione's women are expensive, aren't they?"

"To bed a princess or a queen should be," Coeccias laughed, but he was following Liam's thoughts avidly. "Y'are thinking he found out a form of entertainment less dear, and the memory plagues'm?"

"Anyone who knew would be able to hold it over his head. It would destroy his little part as Uris's prime lay worshipper, wouldn't it? At least in his own head, and that's where his devotion carries the most weight."

Coeccias laughed again, this time in half-mocking wonder at Liam's conclusion. "Y'are a seer, Rhenford, better than a bloodhound. Y'are an eagle, peering down into the puny souls of men, and reading their hearts like open books. So, we've some proof that Viyescu may be led by the hooded woman—what of it?"

"Nothing, yet. We have to know what she wanted of him, other than santhract, and why. And we'll know that when we find out who she is." He paused, he admitted to himself, for effect. "And I think I know how we can do that."

With the cocking of a bushy eyebrow, Coeccias invited him to explain how.

"I may be wrong, but I think the woman will be meeting her benefactor tonight. I'd like to be there." He did not say how he had guessed at the rendezvous. If there was no connection between the hooded woman and Tarquin's death, there was no reason for anyone to know of Necquer's infidelity.

"To peer deep into her soul and pry her inmost secrets to light? You'll want company, then, I'd guess."

"No," Liam said slowly. "As I said, I may be wrong, and I'd rather be wrong alone, with no one to see."

Coeccias laughed hard and walked over to the Guardsman, who was still tending the fire. "Truth, well said, Rhenford, well said! 'I'd rather be wrong alone,' that's well said. Withal, the Warren at night in a storm's no place for even a bloodhound. You'll take Boult here with you," he said, indicating the kneeling Guardsman with a thick forefinger. Liam began to object, but the Aedile ignored him and began talking to his underling, who had looked up sourly. "And Boult, my lad, if you see anything that Master Rhenford tells you to forget, say, if you see a man going somewhere he oughtn't, you'll clean it from your mind, like a forgiven score on a tavern board, wiped away. Won't you, my good Boult?"

The Guardsman nodded with ill-disguised displeasure, and the Aedile grinned up at Liam. "What time should my good Boult join you?"

"A little before eight." Once again, Coeccias had anticipated him and had understood Liam's sensibilities better than he had himself. Why the Aedile did not solve the mystery on his own was beyond him. The blunt, rough-looking man could be as perceptive as anyone Liam knew.

"Well then, Boult, can you make the schedule?"

Boult acquiesced with ill grace to his commander's lighthearted question.

"Then you'd best to your garret, Rhenford, before the storm waxes too great to walk the streets, and await the ever-cheerful Boult there."

Liam agreed, and left the rest of his liquor untasted on the keg.

∎ *14* ∎

THE STORM HAD moved beyond mere drizzle when Liam left the jail, but it did not achieve its full strength until after he had reached his garret. As he shook out his cloak, thunder exploded and the patter of rain on the roof swelled into a constant drumming, then one continuous rumble, like the passage of a herd of horses. He cursed Necquer soundly for choosing a night like this for a meeting.

It was warm in the garret, and he looked at his bed, thinking how little he had slept the night before. Ignoring the reasons why, he decided to make up for it. He carefully spread out his cloak to dry and threw the rest of his clothes onto his chair, pleased that the new cloak had kept out most of the wet. When he blew out his candle, a flash of lightning lit the room, and he stopped for a moment before settling down on his pallet. The rain was coming down so hard that it was difficult to tell it was rain at all in the darkness, falling like a curtain across his window. It was quite a storm.

Even with the constant rumble on the roof, or maybe because of it, and his own missed sleep, he dropped off almost as soon as he crept beneath his blanket. The last thing he managed to do was turn onto his back, to spare his abused front.

A slackening in the rumble overhead woke him. The worst of the storm's fury had spent itself. Having been unable to wash Southwark away, it gave up, and wasted itself in a rain that seemed almost gentle in comparison with its previous power. The change woke him, and he thought for a moment as he sat in the dark that the storm had stopped altogether.

He felt more clearheaded for the nap, but his body was a solid ache from neck to waist. He debated dressing in the dark, to avoid seeing the damage Scar and his friends had done, but fumbling for his clothes without a light would undoubtedly lead to bumps that would aggravate his bruises. With a wince at every movement, he fumbled around in the dark for his tinderbox, and got a light the first time.

Bruises had bloomed all over his chest and stomach, a dark purple that was intriguing and revolting in the flickering yellow light of the candle. His body looked like an abstract tattoo, and he shuddered at the thought while he climbed gingerly into dry clothes.

Boult had not arrived yet, so he presumed it was before eight, and he was glad he had not had to be woken by Coeccias's surly Guardsman. He wondered what time it was, and a knock at his door satisfied him. It would be Boult, and it was time to go to the Warren. He went to the door.

Not expecting Rora, he stood for a moment in shock while she slipped into the room. Her cloak left a trail of water behind her, and beads of rain gleamed in her thick golden hair.

"Master," she said breathlessly, nestling close to him.

Speechless, he backed away, holding her shoulders to keep her at a distance.

"Forgive me, I could not stay away," she pleaded, ignoring his shock. "Have you bespoke the Aedile?"

What was she doing there? He forced his frozen jaw to open, and to speak. "No—yes, in a sense. I've spoken to him, but—"

"You've not!" The fury in her eyes at his betrayal, and the accusation in her tone, frightened him.

"Yes, yes I have, but in a different way." He hurried to pacify her. "I couldn't just tell him not to arrest Lons; he'd have been suspicious. I have to find out who really did it, or at least come up with enough evidence to suggest that it might have been someone else." He wanted to shout at her, to push her out, but the anger in her eyes stopped him; and yet she was pouting in a way that was irresistible. And the memory of her, panting over him in the dark, rose like an ugly ghost in his mind. What time was it? When would Boult get there?

"But what if you can't find the killer? What then?" She spoke with an effort, though he could not tell if it was because of her anger or the fact that the possibility frightened her.

"Then I'll make Coeccias leave Lons alone," he lied, unable to say anything else. "But not till I've tried to find the real killer."

"Who did it, think you?" The question, and the intense way she asked it, startled him.

"I don't know," he stammered. "I have an idea, but I need time to prove it." That was a lie as well: he had no ideas, only clues that did not lead to conclusions. What would Boult say if he saw Rora there? Would he tell Coeccias?

To his immense relief, she relaxed. "It was wrong to come, I know," she said sorrowfully, then looked at him with forlorn hope. "But you'll help, will you not?"

"Of course I will," he assured her, and began herding her to the door. "Now you must go; I'm expecting someone who must not see you."

"I'll go. I must to th'Orb in any case." Without warning, she flung herself at him and kissed him soundly, feverishly, letting him go reluctantly. "Grace you, Master," she said, and slipped out the door, her large, promising eyes turned over her shoulder at him until she was out of sight down the stairs.

Liam let go an explosive breath, and walked shakily over to his chair to collapse. While she was there, he had been aware of her closeness only because of the stupid desires it had raised. Now his chest throbbed painfully where she had hugged him. He could not slump, because it bent tortured muscles, so he had to sit upright. Instead, he heaved several sighs.

Gods, I'm a fool, he thought, *a lucky fool, but a fool nonetheless.* He offered several undirected prayers of gratitude that Boult had not walked in on the middle of the conversation. He had no idea what he would tell her if he could not prove Lons innocent, and could only hope it would not be necessary.

To avoid wondering about it, he forced himself to think about the night's business. If he could find out who Necquer's mistress was, it might give him a start. He doubted it, but would not allow himself to consider the doubt.

The hooded woman was pregnant, most likely by Necquer. She had told Viyescu she would go to Tarquin, and then done it, speaking to the wizard in a seductive voice. She had presumably commissioned a spell, an invisibility spell that would have been cast on the Teeth, because there was no other model in Tarquin's workroom.

That, he thought with consternation, made little sense. Whether Lons had intended it or not, it was the spell cast for him that had saved Necquer's life. If the hooded woman wanted Necquer dead, why not just entice the wizard to cancel the spell entirely? Why choose another spell that would make it look like Lons's had worked? And where had the virgin's blood come from? A pregnant woman would obviously not have any virgin's blood around her. He imagined the woman as he pictured her, nine months gone, handing Tarquin the decanter over her swollen belly and calmly proclaiming it virgin's blood, and her own.

Liam listened to his own laughter, and was scared to detect a note of hysteria in it.

Two hard knocks on his door steadied him, and he took a deep breath before granting entry.

Boult came in, dressed in a heavy riding cloak and high boots, as unconcerned with showing his unhappiness as before. "There's still a heavy storm, and the gutters run like a river in spate. Y'are sure you wish to attempt the Warren this night, Questor Rhenford?"

"Questor?" He was used to the indiscriminate way the people of Southwark flung titles about, but he had never heard this one attached to himself before. Questor was an old name used for special agents of the king in Torquay; it had lain unused for decades. As long unused, Liam realized, as the title Aedile.

"Aedile Coeccias said I was to call you that, for that it signified you were an officer of his, and gave you the right to command me." Boult could not possibly have cared less, and Liam found he liked him for it. He was almost perfectly average for Southwark—black hair shorn to just below his ears, neither short nor tall, skinny nor fat, with a blank face and heavy-lidded, black eyes. He looked bored, in a way that suggested he could be put to better use.

"Well, I'm afraid there's nothing for it, Boult. There's something I need to see in the Warren, and the good Aedile doesn't think I should go there without an escort."

Boult shrugged, with more than a hint that Coeccias might be right.

"I appreciate your confidence, Boult," Liam said sarcastically. "Let's go." Secretly, he was delighted with the taciturn, insolent Guardsman. He would not be the sort to talk about what he saw.

Boult had exaggerated his report of the weather: the gutters were full, but not overflowing, and the storm had resolved itself into a steady, icy downpour. The drumming gave rhythm to the gurgling melody of the rushing gutters. Snug in his cloak, with the Guardsman at his side holding a shielded lantern, Liam was strangely elated. The prospect of discovering just who the hooded woman was filled him with excitement. He began to feel confident that it would solve the mystery to his satisfaction, and he would be able to fulfill his obligations to Coeccias, to Rora, and to Fanuilh. He envisioned the explanation in vague terms, and saw himself giving it to each in a suitably modest way. He smiled behind the hood of his cloak.

The rain, though still thick, allowed the light of the lantern and the glow from the occasional window to play over the street. There was no one to be seen, and the hissing and drumming of the water closed in on his ears, shutting off all other noise, but twice he faltered, an itch between his shoulder blades. He felt watched, but put it off to the rain and the dark, and submerged the anxiety in thinking of what was to come.

Once they reached the Warren, Boult let him take the lead and the lantern, winding through the streets heading for the courtyard. It seemed to take longer than he remembered, and he was afraid he had gotten them lost in the maze of streets, when suddenly the swinging beam of the lantern showed the mouth of the alley he remembered from the afternoon. Breathing his relief, he turned down the alley, Boult at his back.

Lights showed in many of the windows surrounding the courtyard, but none on the ground floor. The yard was left in darkness, which suited him well. He had not given much thought as to how they would wait for Necquer and the woman, and he began to plan.

Beckoning for Boult to follow, he squeezed around the left side of the pile of wreckage, jabbing his sore body several times, and once walking hard into a piece of wood at chest height. He had to stop for a moment, tears springing to his eyes, before he could go on. It had looked much easier in the dry daylight, and the lantern did not help much, illuminating only a tiny section of the heap. Finally, however, he was around, and standing before the door of the tenement, which sagged on leather hinges. He handed the lantern to Boult and pushed at the door, which moved a few inches and then ground to a stop. He could see from the gap between door and jamb that it was neither locked nor barred, so he grabbed at it and shoved up and back. It moved easily, lifted over a pile of unseen rubbish. A single candle flickered high on a wall in the room beyond, casting suggestive shadows over a railless staircase and more rubbish, heaped against the walls like talus at the foot of a cliff.

Not the most likely place to house a mistress, Liam supposed, but convenient to Necquer's warehouse, and well out of the sight of his social peers on the Point. He only took a few steps into the room, to look up the stairwell. It rose in flights far up the building, to the top floor as far as he could tell. There seemed to be no other entrance to the stairs. Boult prodded at a large, unidentifiable mound with his toe, and muttered, "The Warren," with disgust.

"All right," Liam said in a low tone, "here's what we'll do. We wait outside. When the person we're looking for arrives, you follow them inside, at a decent distance, and go up the stairs with them. Find out which door they go to, and pass them. As soon as they're in whatever room they're headed for, come back and tell me. Clear?"

"Most obvious, Questor," the Guardsman said with only the slightest trace of irony, "except, if it please you, how'm I to know who we're looking for?"

Liam grinned, and Boult granted him a small one in return. "I'll let you know when he arrives. Now come on."

Boult shrugged and followed Liam back into the courtyard and beyond the pile. They settled themselves between the wall of the court and the right side of the high tangle of used furniture and rubbish. Liam could see the doorway of the building, and hoped that with the garbage and the rain, they would remain unseen. As a precaution, he took back the lantern and hooded it completely, leaving them in the dark.

They waited interminably, but Boult said nothing, and Liam tried not to allow his high spirits to ebb. It was difficult, with the rain seeping slowly through his cloak, the wet chill setting his bruises to aching, and the mental itch returning to his back. He thought hard on the clue he was about to get, and succeeded at least in pushing the last worry away. There was no reason for anyone to have followed him, or to be spying on him. There was no way for anyone to know how close he hoped he was to catching Tarquin's murderer. He thought of Marcius, but dismissed the idea. Having delivered his warning, the merchant would surely wait at least a day to see if it was carried out.

So he convinced himself that the suspicion was merely his nerves, and began to turn over his clues again.

Why the second spell? If Tarquin had cast it, it would have meant Necquer's death; surely his mistress would not want that. But what if she had? Ignoring the why, which he hoped he would understand when he knew who she was, he focused on the how. She had gone to Tarquin for the spell, but the wizard had not cast it, and Necquer had made it to port safely. Was that reason enough to kill him? Again, he would know better when he knew who she was.

The waiting dragged on, and several times Liam was sure he heard the bells tolling eight, though he knew hearing them through the rain was impossible. They both shifted their positions several times, trying to minimize the discomfort of rain and projecting garbage. Liam was in the middle of an extensive rearrangement when Boult laid a hand upon his arm and he froze, one leg raised, searching for a secure spot in the unseen mess underfoot. Boult steadied him without a word.

A figure glided out of one of the alleys, shrouded in a voluminous cloak and hood. The woman, Liam knew at once, and squinted at her through the rain, willing her hood to fall away. It did not, and she came on, slipping around the pile like a ghost, mere yards from them. She was shorter than he had imagined her, but the cloak billowed so much that it could easily have hid the prodigious belly he had given her. Only when she had gone through the door did Liam realize she had not carried a lantern, and had negotiated the streets easily in the dark. The idea disturbed him.

Beside him, Boult let out his breath, and Liam did the same, allowing his weight to settle back on both feet with relief.

"That our man?" the Guardsman whispered, touching Liam's arm again for his attention.

"No. Wait."

It did not take as long the second time, and Necquer announced his presence well in advance with the light of a lantern. He came hurrying down the same alley the woman had used, but with none of her weightless grace. They heard a distinct ripping sound as he negotiated the rubbish heap, followed by a curse, startlingly loud. Liam placed a restraining hand on Boult's shoulder, and waited while the merchant opened the door. He stood in the doorway, threw back his hood, and examined a large tear in his cloak, shaking his head and spitting in anger. Liam recognized his face for certain, and gently shoved Boult.

Necquer entered, and the Guardsman disappeared around the pile, to reappear seconds later at the door. He paused a second, listening, and then went in. Liam waited as long as he could stand it, and began creeping around the pile himself. By the time he managed to cross the garbage, Boult was back, leaning with crossed arms against the doorsill.

"In th'attic," he said, gesturing up with his thumb. "I near followed him up, but stopped in time."

"Did someone greet him?"

"He knocked thrice, in a peculiar way, and a woman's voice bid him enter. You can hear through the walls as through the thinnest kerchief."

"Better and better." He would not be able to see the woman, but he could hear her at least, and their conversation might give something away. "Shall we?" He started for the stairs. Boult obediently followed with an apathetic shrug that seemed his only method of expression. At least it was dry indoors.

The stairs creaked ominously as they walked, and Liam winced even on the first flight. Going slowly and planting his feet carefully only seemed to make it worse, and the cries of old, creaking boards flew straight up, he was sure, to the attic where Necquer waited. He was struck by what he was doing—spying, basically, invading the most private moment of another man and woman. The parallel with Fanuilh did not escape him.

There was a candle on the second-story landing, but none beyond. Light showed from underneath some of the doors on the floors they passed, but this only emphasized the pitchy blackness of the stairwell. Liam's heart began to beat faster, and his skin was damp beneath the cloak. Sounds came from some of the apartments they passed, bodiless in the dark: a young girl singing to a crying child, a hissed argument between two men, the sounds of a meal in progress. The two men crept on, and the sounds died away as they reached the fourth floor, accompanied only by the creaking of the treads. Above him, Liam sensed space, a black void where the stairs to the attic would be.

Boult stopped him, and leaned close to whisper. His breath was warm in Liam's ear.

"It's the next flight. Your boots, Questor. The boards fairly shout here. The quarry made Hell's own clatter going up."

Did the Guardsman think Necquer was his quarry? He did not bother to correct him. He was after the hooded woman, and what she knew about Tarquin.

She tried to get Tarquin to substitute Lons's spell, he thought, bracing himself against the unseen wall to pull off first one boot, then the other.

"Wait here," he whispered to Boult, and wondered if he nodded in the darkness.

Switching spells would have meant Necquer's death. Why would she want that? And why would she kill Tarquin when he didn't perform the spell?

The darkness was absolute, palpable in a sense, like warm water pressing around him. He put his stockinged foot on the first step, and hesitated. His heart beat loud, his mouth was dry. It was just spying; he had done it before in a dozen places. In wars. This was not a war; this was the merchant Necquer betraying his wife in adultery, which was entirely his business, and none of Liam's.

And why didn't Tarquin perform the spell? He had the virgin's blood, and if he had been stupid enough to believe Lons would pay him, he would certainly have believed the seductive voice.

He forced his other foot to move, and gained two steps. There was a thin line of orange above his head, the bottom of the door to the attic. It was a goal. He made two more steps with only a single stifled squeal from the decrepit wood. Suddenly he imagined the door above swinging open, and Necquer glaring angrily down at him.

I'd piss my breeches, he thought, and had to clap his hand to his mouth to stifle a giggle.

The door stayed closed, and he forced himself up three more steps. Sweat trickled down his face. He heard a voice from above and stopped, his heart hammering.

It was Necquer's, from the sound of it, though he could not discern the words.

Had she killed him because he did not cast the spell? Was that reason enough? Or had he figured out why she wanted the spell cast, and threatened to reveal it? If he knew why she wanted Necquer dead, he could understand.

If she wanted Necquer dead. If that was what the spell was for. If—

He cursed himself viciously and silently. He would never know if he did not go further. Three more steps, stooping, his hands groping for the treads in front of him, the wood brittle and ridged beneath his fingers. Traces of wet from Necquer's boots, and whatever shoes the woman wore.

He could hear Necquer's voice now, suddenly very clear, as if he were right next to him. His heart lurched, and he swayed in the darkness. The line of warm orange was on a level with his eyes, and he brought his legs up with infinite care, so that he was squatting on the step.

"You should buy better wine," Necquer was saying, apparently just beyond the door. He heard a clink. Goblets? His mouth was dry. "I certainly have enough money to afford some decent wine."

There must have been a reply, because the merchant was silent, but Liam could not hear it.

"No expense too great for my sweet chuck," the merchant laughed.

Your sweet chuck would have been happy to see you rotting in the sea, he thought, grinding his teeth, and wanted to shout to the woman to speak up. The woman in his imagination had a stentorian voice, a voice like a trumpet, a voice that carried across miles as well as attic rooms. She did not even whisper when she stuck daggers in wizards. Why was he so sure?

"You're not going to start that again, are you?" said Necquer, exasperated. "I've told you, she's my wife. There's nothing else for it. You're looked after well enough."

She wanted him to leave his wife. She was pregnant, and he would not leave his wife.

"That's a good girl," Necquer said after another pause, reassured and magnanimous. "No more arguments, then. I've only got one other cheek." He laughed.

One other cheek? One other cheek to bruise. She had hit him, not some nonexistent bandit. When he came back from Warinsford, he went to see her first, before his wife. And she had hit him, hard enough to leave a mark.

"Then you'll be rid of it?" The merchant's tone was more serious; there was uncertainty in his voice, and a shade of apprehension. "There are herbs, I know. See Viyescu, he can get them. You're not so far along, are you? It's not even showing."

Rid of the child he had sired. That was a reason to kill a man, Liam supposed, because he had gotten you pregnant and would not marry you and ordered you to get rid of it. But she had already gone to Viyescu for the santhract. And after Tarquin's death she had frightened him enough to get it for her. So why try to kill Necquer, if she was prepared to do as he wished?

He clearly heard the rustle of skirts across floorboards. She was moving, and, by the sound, towards him. For a moment, he thought irrationally that she was going to open the door and find him, and then he caught hold of himself. She was coming to Necquer, and he heard another sound, the brushing of cloth against cloth. Was she embracing him? Then a loud kiss. Yes. He prayed with all his might, squinting his eyes in the dark with effort. *Please, please, please, speak.*

"I'll attend to it soon," she said, and his eyes sprang open and his mind reeled. "Soon. For now, drink your wine and let's to bed."

Gods, what have I done?

"A fine idea, my sweet," Necquer said, the smug smile practically audible.

Liam heard the merchant's words, but they were meaningless to him.

He knew the voice, though he had never heard it used seductively, the way Tarquin had. A dozen revelations fell on him with stunning force, and his arms trembled so much that he had to lower himself to the stairs, resting his forehead against the damp wood.

She wanted Necquer dead for his betrayal, for refusing to spurn his wife, because she was fierce that way. She had killed Tarquin, he was sure, because he had threatened to reveal her.

"Finish your wine," she said with an indulgent laugh.

And he had done that because he had discovered that the virgin's blood—so hard to come by, so useful, and Donoé couldn't possibly supply enough, however willing she was—had not been real. How could it be, when she was not a virgin? So when the illusion spell failed because of the faulty blood, the wizard had cast the spell Lons wanted instead and threatened to reveal her. And for nothing, nothing at all. She had agreed to lose the child, to reconcile herself to his wishes, to go to bed with him again.

Liam did not want to move. Self-reproach held him in an iron grip, and he wished the dark would surround him and become complete.

Gods, I have so completely bungled this whole damn thing. His mistakes were beyond repair.

He could not tell Coeccias, he could not tell Fanuilh. He could not tell them, because then he would have to tell them what he had done in his weakness and imbecility.

"When I've more of a thirst, after." After what was clear. Necquer gave the word a lecherous weight. There were footsteps, moving away.

After, Liam thought miserably. *After I've crawled back down these steps and ridden as far away from Southwark as I can.*

"Careful, it'll spill," the beautiful, musical voice laughed. "You'd best drink it now, or it'll end on the rugs."

Would she not shut up about the wine? He did not want to hear her anymore. He wanted to get Diamond from the stables and ride north, to Torquay, maybe, or the Midlands, or maybe further.

"You want me drunk, do you?" Necquer laughed aloud.

Drunk, of course, drunk, Liam thought, shaking his head bitterly, *drink the wine, drunk if she can't have you dead. Drunk is—*

His head jerked up in the dark, and he gaped at the door. Drink the wine—

Because you powder santhract and take it in a cup of wine or cider to hide the bitter taste, and the right amount of santhract will terminate a pregnancy and too much will kill a man.

He scrabbled to his feet and jumped forward, stumbling on the stairs but gaining his balance again as he hit the door.

It burst open and he slid to a halt in his stockings.

"I didn't think—" he began, and stopped, because what he had not thought of was what to say.

Necquer and Rora stood in the middle of an expensive carpet, swaying close to each other, shocked, the merchant's hand on her exposed breast, the cup in his other hand at his lips. A broad bed, with snowy sheets, a wide window to the right. A huge number of candles, shocking after his time in the darkness of the staircase.

"Poison!" Liam shouted. "Santhract!" He pointed at them, and Necquer dropped the cup, still staring. Only a little wine spilled out. Rora's face twisted in rage.

"Questor," Boult gasped hesitantly from behind him. When Liam had suddenly burst open the door, he had hurried up.

Rora lunged at him, her teeth bared in an awful snarl, but Necquer instinctively grabbed her arm and pulled her up short. The momentum carried her around toward the window, but she turned back with a dancer's grace and lunged again, snarling furiously at Liam. No one heard the soft thump that came from the roof above.

"She's trying to kill you," he shouted at the merchant, afraid to let her speak. What would she say? He felt guilty, terribly guilty, as though he had used her. It never occurred to him to think of it the other way around. So he shouted, trying to drown out denunciations she did not try to make. "Santhract in your cup. She killed Tarquin Tanaquil, because he would not help her, and would have told you about it."

He went on, shouting disconnected facts at Necquer, who hauled the hysterical dancer to him. The merchant held her roughly by the shoulders, trying to see her face, and she suddenly spat furiously at him. Her nails flashed up toward his eyes. Liam and Boult both started toward the struggling couple.

The large window shattered, and a dark shape hurtled towards Rora in a shower of broken glass and wood. It lit on her back, water gleaming on the scales, and a single beat of the wings drove Necquer back. Blood fountained from Rora's neck, where the wedgelike head had buried itself. She screamed.

Fanuilh rose off her back and darted in the air around in front of her to plunge at her face. Shouting now, she flailed her arms at the creature, but it came at her like a whirlwind, biting and scratching and pushing, silent except for the flap of its wings. It pulled back for a moment and then leapt again, forcing her back against the windowpane with its remnants of glass and wood, and then over.

She fell, and the dragon disengaged itself, hovering in the window. It turned its head over one shoulder, between the lazily sweeping wings, and fixed its gaze on Liam.

Done, Master.

Then it dove out the window after Rora.

For long seconds, the three men remaining in the attic room stared at the shattered window. Gusts of rain blew in, spraying successive patterns of moisture on the rug, darkening it.

Numb, Liam could only think of Fanuilh's weakness, its constant protestations of *soon, soon.* But the dragon had killed her.

Silenced her, he thought, and stirred to drive the idea away.

Boult moved as well, and the spell that held them was broken. "Questor," the Guardsman said shakily, his voice uncertain.

Liam shook himself, like a dog shedding water, and looked at Necquer. The merchant's face was white, his eyes bulging and his lips moving without producing any sound. Even when he slipped bonelessly to his knees in the broken glass, Liam took it for shock, but when the merchant heaved convulsively and clasped his stomach, Liam rushed to his side.

"Go get Coeccias," he barked at Boult. "Get him and make him bring Viyescu. Tell him to tell Viyescu that the Hierarch said he needed an antidote to santhract. He'll understand." He knelt by the contorted merchant, and found the Guardsman at his side. "Go now," he shouted angrily. "Tell him it's santhract—he'll understand. Go!"

After a second's gawking, Boult shrugged—his all-purpose reaction—and darted out the door.

The merchant was feverish, his skin slick and gritty and radiating unnatural heat. He crouched on his knees, one hand splayed out on the ground while the other clutched at his stomach. He took in great lungfuls of air with croaking sobs, as if he was desperate to breathe. His head swung in wide arcs, like a frightened cow.

Glass was digging into Liam's knees and stockinged toes, and he could see trickles of blood run, mingled with rainwater, from beneath the merchant's outflung hand. Grimacing, he put one hand around Necquer's waist and took hold of his chin with the other, probing a long finger between the clenched teeth.

"Stop fussing," he muttered as Necquer tried to roll his head away, and managed to shove his finger down the merchant's throat. Necquer's teeth closed momentarily, and then his mouth and throat opened, and vomit gushed out, lukewarm and thick on Liam's hand and arm.

As he held the spewing merchant, mechanically urging him to get rid of the contents of his stomach, he looked vacantly out the window.

Fanuilh killed her. No recriminations, no heaping on of guilt. She could never reveal what he had done, what he had allowed to happen.

He could not decide how he should feel, and, for safety's sake, felt guilty.

■ *15* ■

BOULT RETURNED QUICKER than Liam had expected, but without the Aedile. Coeccias, he explained, had gone to get Viyescu, and sent him back to help, if he could.

There was little for him to do. Necquer had gotten rid of everything in his stomach but was wracked by dry heaves, and his breathing was still labored. Liam held him around the waist and shrugged at the Guardsman, who set himself to brushing the broken glass and wood into a pile with his foot. The window had no shutters, and the rain still blew in.

Taking the lantern, Boult edged towards the windowsill, and risked a soaking by leaning far out. He dangled the lantern below him, turning his head this way and that. When he ducked back in, Liam was looking at him.

"She lit not on the ground," the Guardsman said in simple explanation, with yet another shrug.

The idea horrified Liam, but he did not let it show. What would Fanuilh do with her?

Coeccias arrived then, followed by Viyescu, who was carrying a bulging satchel. He did not seem in the least surprised when he saw Necquer's state, but darted ahead of the Aedile and took charge of the situation. They laid Necquer out on the bed at his orders, and then Liam stood aside as the druggist removed several flasks and twists of paper from his satchel.

Concentrating on Necquer, Viyescu kept his head down, as though unwilling to recognize the others around him. Liam kept his eyes and thoughts on the merchant as well, though he spoke a little to Coeccias.

"Boult explained?" he asked without turning his head.

"Some, not all. The maid, though? I'd've never credited it, had you told me before." There was a note of admiration in the Aedile's voice, as if he thought Liam had suspected Rora all along. It set Liam's teeth on edge, but he only grunted noncommittally.

In order to get his antidotes down the merchant's throat, Viyescu needed him upright, and he called Liam to help him. He spooned semi-liquid pastes into Necquer's slack mouth while Liam held him behind the shoulders.

Boult had returned to looking out the window, and suddenly called for Coeccias. The Aedile went to the window, and their voices were drowned out by the rain. Viyescu took the opportunity to speak.

"Hierarch Cance," he said in a voice so quiet Liam almost did not hear, "I needs must beg your forgiveness for my sins." He did not look up, staring rigidly at the spoon he was inserting between Necquer's teeth.

Liam had been expecting something else, and it did not help that he had almost forgotten the name he had used. How could the apothecary still think he was a Hierarch? But it seemed he did, because he waited for a moment, and when Liam did not answer, went on, tight-lipped.

"There're things I've done, Hierarch. I'm sure you know—the woman and I—I beg your forgiveness. The woman and I . . ."

Not able to stand anymore, Liam spoke, more harshly than he meant to.

"Save this man and all is forgiven." It sounded silly to him, melodramatic and, worst of all, unpriestly. He cringed, but Viyescu merely paused, and then nodded.

"My thanks, Hierarch," he said after a moment. "Uris grace you," he added. He gave the merchant a few more mouthfuls, and then motioned for him to be let down. Then he waved Liam away and set to checking under Necquer's eyelids and taking his pulse.

At the window, both Coeccias and Boult were leaning out, careful of the jagged glass still left in the sill. The Guardsman was pointing something out. Liam wandered over as the two men pulled their heads back in.

"Something?"

"The maid," Coeccias said. "Caught on a gable, I think."

Liam blanched. Fanuilh had not taken her, of course. It was ridiculous to think he could have. Still, the thought unnerved him. He asked if he could go, and Coeccias nodded after a moment's thought. He and

Boult could handle getting her up, or they could get another member of the Guard.

"Will y'attend me at my house? Burus'll let you in. There's still the Uris's Eve fast to break."

Liam refused, as politely as he could, but the Aedile pressed him to come to the feast the next day at his sister's.

"There're matters," he had said in a gruff, strangely gentle tone, "that require our discourse, if not this night, then tomorrow." He was obviously concerned about Liam's distracted air and pale face. "Come to my house at midday tomorrow."

Liam agreed, and left as quickly as he could, ignoring the glance Viyescu threw at him. He sat in the dark on the stairs and pulled on his boots. Miraculously, the broken glass had not cut his feet, but he did not think of this.

He knew that Coeccias had let him go because he thought him a weak scholar who had never seen blood before. It did not bother him: better to appear a coward than face Fanuilh's handiwork, and the corpse to which he had unwittingly led the dragon.

The rain pelted him as he walked slowly back through the Warren, but he only hugged his cloak closer to him. Perhaps the worst of it was that he had not expected anything like this, that the adventure he had so blithely embarked on only a few days before had turned out so very different.

Unable to face the ride out to Tarquin's in the rain, and unwilling to face what might be waiting for him there, he went to his garret. Mistress Dorcas was not in the kitchen when he entered; he heard her conducting the Uris's Eve meal with the other boarders in the dining room. Relieved, he slipped upstairs, not bothering with a candle.

He threw off his cloak and sat in his chair in the dark. The window bothered him, however, with the rain pelting it, and he decided to try his luck with sleep.

His luck held, and he only had time before he slipped off to think one thought three or four times.

I'll have time to think about it tomorrow.

A weak, underwater light filled the room when Liam woke. The rain had stopped sometime in the night, and the clouds, now only light gray, had retreated much higher into the sky. It was almost ten, he guessed.

He was stiff and sore, much sorer than the day before. The tattoo on his chest had begun to turn a sickly yellow at the edges.

Healing well, he thought, and turned a groan of pain into a laugh.

Moving slowly, he dressed and packed his few belongings into his seachest. It was light, even with all his possessions in it, but he managed to bring it downstairs only at great expense to his aching muscles.

The boy from the stables brought Diamond round to the kitchen door, and helped him lift the chest to the horse's withers and tie it tight. The boy's generally merry air and the nonchalant way he accepted a large tip reminded Liam that it was a holiday. It also explained the small number of people in the streets, and the fact that Mistress Dorcas was not up yet. On Uris-tide, she obviously believed she could sleep in.

This suited Liam well; he did not want to see her. He mounted Diamond slowly and set him to a gentle, easy pace. It took almost an hour to reach Tarquin's house, but Liam was not unhappy with the ambling gait. There was plenty of light, even with the clouds, but he knew even if it had been a beautiful, sunny spring day he would not have wanted to approach the house.

Fanuilh, however, was nowhere to be seen, and no thoughts crashed into his head as he walked tentatively from room to room, calling the creature's name. Bemused, he went out to the beach and let the trunk tumble off Diamond onto the sand. Then he half-dragged, half-carried it into the entrance hall.

Feeling he had pressed his luck enough, he left it there, mounted Diamond again and started back for Southwark.

He did not want to see Fanuilh, and was glad he had not. He did not want to see Coeccias at the moment either, but he had promised, and there were things that he would have to explain. He purposefully dawdled on the way back, because he did not want to arrive early.

Coeccias was waiting for him, opening the door himself and ushering Liam in.

"How was your sleep?"

"Good," Liam said, surprised to find it was true. "I'm sore."

The Aedile laughed. "Your friends'll be in hand soon." He led the way to the kitchen and put the finishing touches to a positively monstrous cauldron of cider while they talked.

Liam outlined the story, filling in the details he had learned or figured out the night before. It was remarkably easy.

Rora was pregnant and Necquer would not support her. Kansallus's talk had hinted at a certain pride and vengefulness in her; if anything, he had underestimated them. She had obviously been much more fierce than Kansallus had guessed, even with the evidence of Knave Fitch's mangled ear. And the way she had used Viyescu to get her the poison to murder Necquer and then threatened to reveal whatever had passed between them indicated the depth of the ruthlessness hidden behind her beauty.

"I don't think she was altogether right in the head," Liam commented, and Coeccias grunted his agreement.

So she was set on killing Necquer. Lons must have told her about his deal with Tarquin, and she convinced the wizard to switch the spells, in return for some of her blood. Why she chose the illusion spell was not clear; perhaps she did not want to ruin her brother's arrangement, and thought that as soon as the Teeth disappeared, Lons could claim his reward. It would not matter if Necquer tried to enter the harbor the very next day and was smashed to pieces. Perhaps she thought it would be fitting, a sort of double revenge: give his wife to another man and then kill him.

"She was clearly somewhat mad, for all her cunning." Liam amazed himself with his own tone of voice. He sounded cold and analytical, describing the events from a pitying distance. He wondered how he was able to do it.

Tarquin had tried to cast the spell she wanted, but it had failed—Rora had had no real virgin's blood to give him—so he cast Lons's original request, maybe as a kind of revenge. When Necquer returned unharmed, she went to see Tarquin, most likely to upbraid him for not casting the spell, not knowing he had figured out her deception. He threatened to reveal her plot to Necquer, so she killed him.

"Of course," Liam said finally, talking to Coeccias's expansive back as the Aedile crouched over his boiling pot like a gnome or dwarf from a story, "there's little pure proof. Much of it's only circumstance, and motive. The santhract she put in Necquer's wine proves something, I guess, and she was pregnant. Really, it just fits best." He paused, reflecting. He knew she had done it. "And Tarquin's familiar certainly thought she did."

"Truth. Curious, that," Coeccias said at last, rising from the pot. "But I grant you all—she must have done it. There's naught else that makes sense. And I've something from Herione, as well: Rora used to dance for her—just dance, you mind—nigh on two years past. We'll say that's when Viyescu met her, and Necquer as well."

For a moment, the stout man regarded Liam intensely, as if trying to pry a secret from him; then his features softened into admiration. Liam realized Coeccias had been wondering how he had figured it all out. In telling the story, he had left out both Rora's visit to him and Fanuilh's part. Thinking back, he realized he had sounded like quite the natural investigator, and the cold, confident tone he had assumed had not hurt. It was Luck, again, the Luck he carried with him, that allowed him to handle something incompetently and somehow come out looking all the better for it.

It made him feel very uncomfortable, and he hung his head to hide his guilty blush. He suddenly thought that he had not said Rora's name once while telling what he knew. He had said "she" or "her." Not her name. It made him feel worse.

"When do you want to tell Lons?"

"I've already done it, last night," Coeccias said. He and Boult had brought Lons his sister's body, recovered from the gable where it had lodged in her fall. Liam was shocked by this, but the Aedile hastened to explain. Fanuilh had not been vicious—scratches on her back, and a single bite at her throat. He and Boult had washed away the blood from her face and hands, and covered the wounds pretty well. "The Golden Orb's company parts Southwark tomorrow for the heath, and Lons'll with them."

There was nothing else to say about the investigation, and Coeccias suggested they go to his sister's. Liam wondered how they would get the cauldron of spiked cider to her house, but it turned out that she lived only a block away, and Coeccias simply filled a smaller pot to bring with them.

"One of the whelps'll run back for more when we've drained this one."

Coeccias's sister was like him, broad and short, with weight to spare but a warm, matronly face. She kissed her brother warmly and made much of Liam. Her husband was a cooper, and they had an uncountable swarm of children. They held Liam, as a stranger, in awed respect, but mobbed Coeccias affectionately at first, and then Burus when he appeared.

Several relatives of Coeccias's brother-in-law soon arrived, bringing huge amounts of food and an army of small children to the feast. The tables groaned under the weight of the food, and afterwards, stuffed to bursting, the whole family gathered around to sing to Burus's piping. They were merry, and Liam felt out of place. There were things he wanted to think about, and though he would have liked to stay, he knew he could not contribute to their celebration, and left soon after the music began.

He spent three days alone at Tarquin's, exploring the house and thinking about all that had happened. He slept on the couch in the library and spent the days idly leafing through the books or examining the items in the wizard's trophy room.

Many times the image of Rora floated in his mind, cursing him, saying all the things he had been afraid she would. She reviled him, called him a betrayer and a fool, a heartless monster. He knew he was not these things, that she had used him, and that he was not responsible for her death. He knew them, but he could not shake a feeling of responsibility.

At other times he thought of Viyescu, whose darkest, deepest kept secrets he had effectively exposed in the guise of a priest. He hoped that the druggist might have taken his hasty absolution in the attic to heart, but did not think that even that excused his deception.

And there were Freihett and Poppae Necquer to consider. He would not be able to see them, to deal with the husband or pass an idle afternoon with the wife. What he knew of them, and their awareness of some of his knowledge, would make such encounters extremely uncomfortable.

Still, what else could he have done? He could not have known things would turn out the way they had.

In the end, he simply acknowledged that he had not handled the whole thing well, and vowed to leave it at that. In time, he thought, he might well be able to.

On the second day, Boult appeared at his door, rousing Liam from a book of history he had found in Tarquin's library. The Guardsman had brought a copy of the wizard's will, as proof of ownership. The diffidence and hang-all attitude Liam had liked in the man was gone, replaced with a sort of uneasy respect.

Coeccias had been telling stories about the investigation, Liam knew, and portraying him as some sort of omniscient seer into men's souls, whose only weakness was a certain queasiness at the sight of blood. He was surprised to find that he did not mind the picture as much as he might have. He felt a little guilty because the result was more Luck than omniscience, but at heart he was secretly pleased.

Boult also brought a note from the Aedile. It was very short, scrawled wildly across a piece of paper. In it, Coeccias invited him to dinner the next day, and mentioned that Necquer had recovered completely from the santhract. Finally, he wrote that Scar, Ratface and their friend had been caught, and were currently residing in the Aedile's jail awaiting judgement.

Liam asked Boult to tell Coeccias that he would come to dinner.

• • •

Between all of this, he stood on the beach, or sat on the balustrade of the veranda, and scanned the sky for signs of Fanuilh. The little dragon did not return for three days.

His feelings were mixed about the creature. It had lied to him when it said it was still too weak to fly, and he knew that it had followed him to Rora. That bothered him, but he reflected that there was little he could have done about it. The dragon could see into his head at will.

That, really, was what bothered him most, and he thought angrily of their deal. And he had thought of something he had to attend to, with which the dragon might help.

Wake. Wake.

On the morning of the fourth day after Rora's death, he was wandering in a dream through the old temple, and the walls were inscribed again with the single word:

Wake. Wake.

He woke on the couch, and looked deep into the dragon's glittering cat's eyes.

"You're back," he muttered.

Yes, Master. I had to hunt, and I thought you would be angry with me.

Sitting on its haunches, neck bent, Fanuilh looked like a dog awaiting a well-earned whipping.

"I was," Liam agreed, putting his feet to the floor and running a hand through his tousled hair. He was much calmer than he had thought he would be. "You didn't tell me you were going to kill her."

The thought was a long time forming: *It seemed appropriate. She killed Master Tanaquil.* Another idea formed, very quickly, and just as quickly disappeared. *When we joined, it came to me that it was something you would do.*

"Me? You mean you got the idea from me?"

Yes. You did such a thing once.

Liam laughed, but it was bitter, the kind of laughter he directed at himself. "Yes, I did. But I was much younger then. Much younger. And I've paid for it as well." He had an insight into the creature's nature, how little it understood of men, and how it must pick and choose its ideas from its master.

I am sorry, Master.

There was a long pause.

"Then you recognize me as your master?"

Yes.

"And you'll fulfill your part of the bargain?"

I will serve you as you wish. I have done what I . . . There was a
break in the solid thought, as though Fanuilh had never used the concept
in connection with itself before. . . . *what I wanted.*

"You'll teach me how to keep you out of my head?"

Anything you wish, Master.

"Do you know what I want to do now? What I want to take care of?"

Yes. The dragon lowered its head, as if ashamed to admit that it
could still read his mind.

"Can you help me with this thing I have in mind?"

Yes.

"You'd best tell me how. I want to do it today."

With Fanuilh's help, it was easy. Liam rode into Southwark alone
that afternoon and left Diamond at the stables. He told them he would
be keeping the horse with him after that night, and settled his account.

Then he strolled down towards the harbor and the one thing he
needed to make sure of. The clouds had rolled away a day before, leaving
a bright sky out of which a cold, invigorating wind blew. His soreness was
gone, and he felt well.

The harborfront was busy, men and animals straining to move the
last of the season's cargo. He walked alone to Marcius's warehouse, and
knocked at the smaller door. An unknown face appeared, and ordered
him off. There was no activity around the building, and Liam smiled to
himself spitefully. There was no activity because Marcius's best hopes
were at the bottom of the sea. He found he could not muster much
sympathy.

"I think your master will want to see me," he said, and pushed his
way past the ugly face into the warehouse proper.

Two new men waited behind the doorkeeper, who now thrust his
face into Liam's and growled.

"I think you—" he began, and then his eyes rolled up in his head and
he slumped heavily to the ground. Liam stepped back, startled, and saw
that the other two guards had dropped as well.

Fanuilh fluttered to the ground behind them.

"They're all right?"

Asleep. It will not last long.

"Then we'd better hurry."

He walked to the stairs, and with a lazy beat of its wings, Fanuilh
rose and settled on his shoulder like a bird. It was large, the size of a dog,
but Liam barely felt the weight, and he imagined he looked quite fear-

some. Fanuilh rocked gently to keep its balance as he hurried along the creaky steps.

Marcius's perfectly coiffed head snapped up as his office door slammed open, and a shout of anger died on his lips as he saw Liam stride into the room with Fanuilh on his shoulder.

From the merchant's sudden pallor, Liam judged that he did indeed look frightening with the tiny dragon in tow.

"Master Marcius. Do you remember me?"

"Yes," the merchant stammered, and before he could recover himself, Liam plowed on, as much to keep Marcius off balance as not to laugh at what he was saying.

"It was not wise of you to fool with a wizard, Marcius. Do you understand that?"

Marcius nodded once.

"The things that can result are unpleasant, you see."

Marcius nodded again.

"And I would not want to have any unpleasantness. Your men are in prison, now, and will remain there. I allow them to escape lightly, because I know they acted on your orders. You will rescind any such orders you may have since given, and will leave me in peace. Do you understand?"

Marcius nodded several times, his eyes on Fanuilh, who was yawning widely, revealing needlelike teeth.

"The maps I sold you are good, and will not be sold to anyone else. I suggest you put them to good use, and forget about me. Is that clear as well?"

The merchant was still nodding when Liam left, because Fanuilh stayed behind.

I will leave here in a few minutes, Master, and wait for you at the beach.

Not used to thinking to the dragon, Liam simply nodded and walked out.

Once on the street, he indulged in a broad smile. He had achieved the effect he was looking for, and knew the merchant would not bother him again. He was pleased with his own performance, absurd as it seemed in retrospect, but knew that most of the merchant's fear had stemmed from Fanuilh's presence.

And the dragon had acted completely in accordance with Liam's wishes. It was truly his servant. The thought buoyed him up, inspiring another secret smile.

Wondering what else it could do, he let his imagination play with the idea as he walked to dinner at Coeccias's.

There was still a great deal of cider left from the Uris-tide batch, but between the heavy meal Burus served and a misguided attempt on the part of the three men to go through all the verses of "The Lipless Flutist," they finished it by midnight.

Wizard's Heir

■ *1* ■

THE GODDESS BELLONA had only recently sprung upon Taralon, her worship at first heralded only in the mountain city of Caernarvon, a place well suited to her grim pursuit of the martial arts. But there were wealthy men in Caernarvon, and when they decided to share their goddess with the rest of the kingdom, they spent the money necessary to do it in style.

From the outside, the temple they had purchased in Southwark was undistinguished, a square block of plain masonry at the end of Temple Street, wedged closely between the crenellated home of the old and well-established worship of Strife and the appropriately dark one of Laomedon. The three formed a cul-de-sac, graced by a simple fountain, and the only thing Bellona's temple added to the scene was a modest cupola and a row of small, circular windows.

The inside was different. The decoration of the newly dedicated temple—it had once housed a sect long dispersed, whose name and god few remembered—belied its drab exterior, and revealed the wealth of the goddess's followers. There was no statue of the goddess herself, but there were expensive suits of armor and stands of weapons in the niches between the half-columns that lined the walls. Light from the windows in the cupola glanced off hauberks rendered useless by elaborate gold scrolling, swords encrusted with gems and sheaths of rare silk bound with silver wire.

Liam Rhenford, standing in a dark corner by the door, his breath smoking in the cold air, wondered why they had not built an entirely new temple instead of renovating an abandoned one, then shrugged the question away. *Temple Street's crowded as it is,* he thought, and shifted his gaze from the expensive arms to the middle of the large chamber, to the empty fire pit. He pointed discreetly at it and whispered to the man beside him.

"No fire?"

"No burnt offerings for Bellona," his companion, the Aedile Coeccias, answered. "Only that straight from smoking execution, if you take me."

Liam refrained from even smiling. It was all well for Coeccias to make puns—he was the Aedile, and had been invited to view the temple because of his position as the Duke's representative in Southwark—but Liam was only a guest, brought along at his friend's request. He did not want to appear disrespectful, though there were only two acolytes in the temple. They stood to either side of the altar, tall young men in chain mail suitable to battle service, broad-bladed spears grounded firmly at their sides. They had not moved since Liam and Coeccias entered the temple.

The altar itself was rather dull, a simple block of stone fit with a shallow bowl and blood gutters for sacrifices. The real heart of Bellona's temple lay behind it, on a shelf cut into the stone of the wall: a war chest of dark oak, bound in iron. It was a plain piece of furniture, as functional as the altar or the mail worn by the acolytes, but rumor in Southwark held that it contained a greater treasury than all the city's temples put together.

Liam studied it for a moment, imagining the wealth supposedly inside. Rumor had elaborated on itself, and mentioned not just gold and jewels, but unsigned notes-of-hand on the great Lowestoft mines in Caernarvon. He thought of the parchment, foot-wide squares representing the labor that dug treasure from the heart of distant mountains.

A passing ray of light played on the surface of the chest but could draw no glimmer; the oak was old, the iron blackened. The light moved on a little, up and behind the chest, and reflected off a chain bolted to the wall. Liam followed the chain up to a staple near the base of the cupola, then at an angle to the center of the cupola, where it slid through another staple and down to a cage.

It was plain, like the chest, the bars set close together, but Liam's eyes were keen enough to make out the figure inside, the lion's body, the broad wings, the eagle's head.

Gods, it's a gryphon! Where did they get a gryphon?

The creature stirred, setting the barred perch swinging. The chain clanked dully. The faint sound of its wings rustling reached the ground, and Liam frowned. He pitied the beast; confined as it was, it could not even stretch its wings. He had seen a gryphon once, free in the air in the far north, and he could still remember the excitement and beauty of it. The gryphon in the cage looked gray in the poor light, like a figure cast in lead. He shook his head, and decided he had looked enough.

"I'll be outside," he whispered to Coeccias, and made to leave.

"Attend a moment," the Aedile whispered back, catching his arm. He gave Liam a stern glance. "We'd do well to show our respects. And I needs must thank that Alastor." He was referring to the priest who had welcomed them to the temple and, after a very brief description of Bellona, had left them alone to inspect the building. Liam was not sure if their being unsupervised was a mark of indifference on Alastor's part, or a sign of tact. He could not tell; he had never understood priests very well.

Liam nodded briefly, and along with Coeccias bent his knee toward the altar. He did not bow his head, though, as the other man did, letting his eyes wander over the temple again, resting at last on the gryphon's cage. After a few long moments, it began to seem as if the Aedile would never break the obeisance.

When Coeccias finally rose, Liam jumped to his feet and went out the large wooden doors, leaving his friend to find and thank the priest for the visit.

It was cold in the cul-de-sac at the end of Temple Street, and stray winds, baffled by the closeness of the buildings, battered themselves back and forth across the square. Liam paused on the steps to pull his cloak close around him.

There was no one in the street, though he could hear voices from Strife's establishment. Someone was shouting orders in the courtyard that lay between the outer wall and the temple proper, which sat like a castle keep at the rear of the compound.

The building to the left was silent, a silence Liam imagined was ominous. Those black walls hid the rites of Laomedon, whose special domain was death and the Gray Lands. Rumor—an older rumor than the one about the wealth of Bellona—said that there was a book inside each of Laomedon's shrines, in which was written the exact time of every man's death. Liam shuddered; though he prayed occasionally, he would never be able to reverence the gods of Taralon the way his friend did—and he was conscious that his seeming lack of respect might have annoyed the Aedile.

When Coeccias came out onto the steps, Liam tore his eyes away from the dark temple and gestured vaguely.

"It'll snow soon," he said. The sky was a uniform gray from horizon to horizon.

"Truth," Coeccias said. Frowning now, he asked, "Have you no conceptions of what's proper, Rhenford?"

Stopped on the shallow steps of the new temple, they made a strange pair: Liam tall and thin, clean shaven, his blond hair cropped close, a long weatherproof cloak hanging to his ankles, and the Aedile shorter, much broader in muscle and bulk, for once wearing a clean jacket of quilted gray wool.

Liam gulped, a little surprised at his friend's vehemence, and the strange, appraising look the shorter man was directing at him.

"Are you so careless of your gods in the Midlands, then? As to leave to a temple with no obeisance?"

"I'm sorry," Liam apologized, "I meant no disrespect."

"Here I'm invited to view the temple," Coeccias went on, barely mollified, "invited ere it's even been consecrated, and I cart y'along, as a thing of interest to a scholar, and you want to part without even a glance at the altar!"

"I'm sorry," Liam repeated, meaning it. "I saw the altar. I was impressed. I just . . ."

He could not really explain what he had been thinking. He had long been separated from the gods of his youth in the Midlands, which were mostly similar to those of Southwark. In long travels he had encountered a thousand strange gods, with stranger rites, and had become insensitive to what they meant to those who believed. But he could not say that to the Aedile. There was no way to explain that, to him, one god was much the same as another.

"It was the gryphon," he said finally, by way of a lame excuse. "It shouldn't be caged like that."

Coeccias grunted and offered a wry smile. "It likes you not, eh? Sacrifice? Do Midlanders have no custom of it?"

"No," Liam said slowly, recalling the occasional deer offered to the Black Hunter, or farm animals given up to the Harvest Queen. "No, they do—but nothing like that. Gryphons are . . . special. Not like a steer or a cock. And they shouldn't be caged like that. They can fly, you know. Their wings work."

Starting down the steps, the Aedile barked a laugh. "Truth, Rhenford, y'are passing soft. What is it if their wings work? All the better for them to wing their way to the Gray Lands, and bring message to the gods."

They strode across the square, Liam shaking his head but making no comment. The fountain was dry, and the trapped wind scoured its stone with a whispering sound. Temple Street was almost deserted as they walked west; one or two acolytes sweeping steps and porticos, and a number of beggars. It was not Godsday and, with winter upon the city, there were no sailors in search of blessings.

Liam was silent until they passed the temple of Uris, at which time he ventured a comment on the plainness of Bellona's treasury.

"Aye," Coeccias said, "a right old war chest. But as I told you, rumor vouchsafes a high stack of drafts, direct to the Lowestoft mines. Old Bothmer Lowestoft is high with the new goddess, they say, a passionate convert."

"That'll make trouble with the others—a new banker in town. And with drafts on the mine, it won't matter that Bellona hasn't many temples." Ordinary drafts could only be redeemed at a temple of the same god that had originated it, while one from Lowestoft would be honored anywhere in Taralon, or even in the Freeports. The wealth of the Caernarvon mining family was legendary.

Stroking his beard, Coeccias considered this. "That's the right of it. You've nosed it out, Rhenford. It'll make for fierceness in the spring, when the merchants are drawing funds." He chuckled to himself, amused in advance at the competition among temples for the lending business. "Trust you t'ignore the proper ceremonies, but strike the heart of a different matter."

"I didn't mean to ignore it," Liam protested again, but the Aedile was not listening.

"We'll have snow this night," he said, cocking his head and squinting one eye at the sky. Then he recalled something, and put a hand on Liam's arm, stopping him in the street. "Faith, I forgot! Did see the messenger last night?"

"Messenger?" Over the past few months of living among southerners, Liam had grown more or less used to their dialect, but he missed this word.

"The messenger," Coeccias repeated, "the bearded star!"

"A comet?"

"Aye, a comet! Did see it?"

"No," Liam admitted, "I didn't. When was it?"

Coeccias's face grew childish with wonder, an expression Liam found funny. "Last night, an hour, perhaps two, after dusk. It blazed out of the north, like a rule across the city to the sea. Did you truly not see it?"

"No. I was inside at the time."

For a moment the Aedile frowned, realizing that most people would have been indoors at that hour. "I was posting the Guard, and saw't with these very eyes, like a torch across the sky. I swear, Rhenford, such a thing I've never seen!" He looked again at the sky, as if the trace of the comet still lingered behind the clouds. Liam looked as well, smiling lightly. He had never seen his friend so excited.

"I wonder what news it brings," he said.

"As for that," Coeccias said, walking on again, "for myself I have no faith in that. We term it a messenger, but sure the gods have better ways of revealing their news to us. Why else have temples and all the omen-readers and foretellers?"

"Still," Liam persisted, "what if it did mean something?"

"Pray it doesn't," Coeccias said, crossing his fingers. It was a gesture common in Southwark, and it had taken Liam a while to understand that it was what southerners used to ward off ill fortune. They used a different sign in the Midlands, where he had grown up. "I've no need of new things breeding in Southwark. With a new fane to welcome and the winter, I've enough to worry on. Winter's worst for me, I tell you, Rhenford. I'd rather the summer, even with all the tars ashore, kicking up demons in the wineshops. With the cold and the confinement, people are fractious, like to murder and such. There're three corses already this week cooling their heels for burial. No, it'd little like me to have a new wonder."

They walked the rest of the way to Coeccias's house without speaking. Liam thought on his friend's position in Southwark, impressed anew by the range of responsibilities entrusted to the rough-seeming man. As the Aedile, he was like the captain of a ship, entrusted with the helm of the city—but he had little of the autocratic power normal at sea.

He worries over it, Liam thought, *like a mother hen.* And yet Southwark ran well, particularly when compared with any number of the larger cities Liam had seen.

The Aedile lived in a small house on the fringes of the Point, the rich section of the city. They stopped outside the door.

"Will you not come in? Burrus'll make a quick cup, hot, something to warm you."

"No," Liam said, looking again at the sky. The clouds had darkened perceptibly. "I think I'll ride out now, before the snow starts. It looks like it'll come sooner than we thought. Thank you, though."

"No mention," Coeccias assured him. "Burrus'd be happy to do't."

"No, thanks. And thanks for taking me to the temple. I really meant no disrespect."

The Aedile smiled. "I know't, Rhenford. Y'are just stranger and stranger, the more I know you."

They parted with a handshake, Coeccias going inside and Liam around to the back to fetch his horse.

He was glad to get out of the city, though it was colder. The wind howled straight off the sea, stinging his cheeks, tearing at his cloak like a clumsy thief. But the countryside, though gray and lifeless, was less oppressive than the narrow streets of Southwark. The cold seemed to leech the color from the buildings, and made the cobbles seem more like metal than stone; Diamond's hooves had rung on them like clashing swords. Beyond the city gates, at least, they thudded normally.

Giving the horse its head, Liam hunched himself against the wind and thought back to the look Coeccias had given him outside Bellona's temple. It had reminded him of something, though exactly what eluded him at the time. The answer came to him as the roan settled into an easy lope, and his body relaxed naturally to the rhythm.

The two men had met only a few months before, in connection with the murder of an acquaintance of Liam's, a wizard named Tarquin Tanaquil. Their friendship had grown out of the search for the murderer, but at first it had been only a partnership, and a not entirely willing one at that. Liam knew the details of the wizard's life, but Coeccias knew Southwark, and had the official standing to pursue the investigation.

The look reminded him of the one Coeccias had given him while they were searching Tarquin's house the day after Liam had discovered the body.

When he thought I'd done it, Liam realized. *He looked at me as if I were guilty of something.*

He brooded on that for a moment, and then shook his head with a laugh at himself.

As I was—guilty of disrespect to his goddess.

Though Bellona could hardly be considered Coeccias's goddess yet. It would be years, Liam knew, before she was fully accepted into the Taralonian pantheon. Years and miracles and a gradual accretion of followers.

There was more, though, of which Liam thought himself guilty. "Soft," the Aedile had called him. Liam was not against sacrifices in principle or in fact, and the blood did not make him squeamish. But he had not corrected the Aedile, as he had not corrected him on the day they looked at Tarquin's corpse, when the officer assumed he had never seen a dead body before. Coeccias entertained a number of misconceptions about him, Liam knew; some he had let flourish because they smoothed the course of the search for Tarquin's murderer, and others he had simply been powerless to stop.

And I never told him about Fanuilh, Liam thought, adding the wizard's familiar to the list. As his ride went on, the list grew longer, things about his past—battles fought, places visited, crimes considered and committed—and even some of the details of the investigation into Tarquin's death. Though he had found the killer, it had happened mostly through luck—but the Aedile believed him to be a kind of human bloodhound.

Diamond's easy lope shifted, and the movement jarred him from his musings. They were on the edge of a high cliff, the sea below them, and a small cove reached by a narrow path.

In the cove was his home, a small villa in the southern style, low and long with white plastered walls and a red tile roof. From the top of the cliff he could not see the front of the house, but light spilled from its many windows, warm and welcoming on the sand and the breakwater and the gray, choppy waves beyond.

He started Diamond down the path, watching the house the whole way, trusting the horse. It was still strange to him, to think of the house as his own. Often, on returning to the cove from the city, he expected to discover that it had vanished in his absence.

It never had, of course, but he was still unaccustomed to the idea of a permanent home.

Sharp wind picked up sand from the beach, and Diamond's hooves flung up more as Liam urged the roan to a quick sprint from the end of the path, and then reined it in sharp in front of the patio.

Smiling at the quick stop, he jumped briskly from the saddle and led the horse to its stall, a small shed to the side of the main house. It was cold inside, but while he unsaddled the roan and brushed it down, the shed grew warmer, magic responding to their presence.

With the horse fed and bedded down, Liam left the shed and walked around the house to the patio, and the front door, a glass-paned affair that slid along wooden grooves.

He paused there, rubbing his hands and blowing on them, and thought, *I'm home.*

He closed his eyes, concentrating on the thought, forming it into a block and pushing it out and away. Suddenly the thought vanished, and a similar block filled his head.

Welcome, master.

He formed another thought, molding it more carefully, crafting the interrogative.

How was that?

Excellent, came the return thought. *It was easy to pick up.*

"Good," Liam said aloud, "then I'm coming in, because it's freezing out here."

The door slid open easily, and a blast of warmth struck him. He stepped in quickly and shut the door, though he knew the magic of the house would keep out the wind, as well as any sand the wind might care to bring with it. His boots, though, were another matter, and he took them off by the door, so as not to track wet sand across the shining wooden floors.

Walking down the corridor to the right of the entrance hall, Liam hung his cloak on a convenient peg, and reveled in the warmth of the enchanted house. He turned into the second door and smiled down at Fanuilh, his familiar.

The creature lay in a small basket on the floor, underneath the first of the three worktables that filled the room. It was a dragon, complete with leathery wings and a wedgelike snouth filled with sharp teeth, but it was tiny, the size of a large cat, or a small dog.

"Like a puppy hound," Liam said aloud, and laughed when the dragon reared back its head.

I am not a puppy, it thought at him.

"You might as well be," Liam joked, indicating the basket, with its padding and blanket. Fanuilh's reaction pleased him; for a long time after their meeting, he had wondered if the dragon had felt any emotions at all. And while there was no emphasis in the thought that followed, there was no way he could avoid thinking of it as indignant:

I have eaten puppies, Fanuilh thought. *And you should practice with your mind.*

"I've told you before," Liam said, squatting down and scratching the dull black scales of the dragon's back, "I think that's silly. There's no point making the effort to think at you when you're right in the room." The dragon rolled over, exposing its dull gold belly for scratching, but its thought seemed reproving.

Master Tanaquil always did.

Before the murder, Fanuilh had been the wizard's familiar. It had joined its current master by a process Liam preferred not to remember—a painful bite and an even more painful splitting of his soul, so that part resided in the tiny form he was scratching.

"Well, I am not him. Get used to it, familiar mine. And while you're at it, think about when you're going to teach me how to keep you out of my head."

One of the drawbacks to having a familiar, Liam had learned early on, was that it had access to his mind whenever it wanted. The dragon had promised to show him how to cut it off, but they had not yet reached that point in the lessons it was giving him.

You are not ready. You can barely project a thought to me from the top of the cliff. You must practice.

"But if you can read my thoughts, why do I have to project?"

To cut me off, you have to be able to project. And you have not yet seen the silver cord.

Liam frowned, but continued scratching. "You and your silver cord. I'm not sure it exists."

It does, the dragon insisted. *It is the ethereal bond that joins us. You must practice seeing that as well. Master Tanaquil could see it effortlessly.*

"Fanuilh," Liam said sharply, "understand this." He poked the dragon in the belly for emphasis. "Tarquin is not your master anymore. I am—and I am not a wizard. But you promised to teach me this, and you will."

It stared at him for a moment, no readable expression in its cat's pupils, and then ducked its head once, low, in submission.

Of course, master.

Liam nodded severely and stood up. "Now, I'm going to eat. Do you want anything?"

The dragon nodded, bobbing its head on its long neck.

"Something raw again?"

Its head moved rapidly up and down.

"Come along, then. Though you really should be hunting. I think. You're going to get fat, lounging around the house all the time."

I fly every day, the dragon thought, trotting after him, out of the workroom, across the entrance hall, and down another corridor to the kitchen. Its claws clicked on the wood as it walked, the noise shifting slightly as it crossed onto the flagstones of the kitchen.

"Fat," Liam repeated.

There was a large baker's oven set into one wall, and he stood by it with closed eyes, imagining the food he and Fanuilh wanted. From experiment, he knew there was no need to close his eyes. He found it easier, however, to envision a meal that way—and it seemed appropriate, in any case, like he was wishing and having the wish granted.

The oven was magical, a small part of the magic that pervaded the house. It was a strange sort of magic, one Liam had never considered before—a very practical wizardry that took into consideration small things such as keeping sand out of the front hall, or heating Diamond's shed, or preparing meals. It even kept the small privy by the bedroom clean and sweet smelling, an amenity that never ceased to delight Liam.

The house was his, but it had been built by Tarquin. The wizard had left it to him, in a will signed and registered only a few weeks before his death. When Liam thought of it—which he tried not to do—the legacy bothered him. He had known the wizard for only a few months before his death, and only as a passing acquaintance. It was an extravagant legacy, entirely out of proportion to their relationship. But then, Tarquin had been the perfect model of an eccentric old wizard, with his long white beard, his sigyl-sewn robes and impenetrable, often pompous conversation. Liam occasionally missed their meandering talks.

Opening the oven, he removed the two platters he had imagined, and set them on the table. He hooked a stool with his foot and drew it over, while Fanuilh crouched and sprang up, landing lightly in front of its meal.

This had become something of a ritual for the two of them over the past two months, eating dinner together, the dragon crouched over a platter of raw meat and Liam tucking into some dimly remembered dish from his long travels. The oven could produce whatever he could imagine, and he made a practice of calling forth things that had never been made in Taralon. Some, indeed, like the one he ate that night, could not have been made there, because the rice and vegetables in it grew only in lands far to the south.

Where is that from? the dragon inquired, at the same time as it delicately tore a chunk from its cut of meat, and snapped the piece down whole.

"Originally, I'm not sure. I first had it in a place called Mahdi."

A Freeporter colony?

"No, though the Freeporters trade there. It's about two months' sail west of Rushcutters' Bay."

Far.

"Hmmm."

What was the new temple like?

Liam described it briefly. It was a polite fiction he had enforced on Fanuilh—the pretense that the dragon could not just search his memory at will.

The gryphon was gray?

"It looked that way, though the light was bad. The cupola is strange;

the light angles down and leaves the dome shadowy. Gryphons aren't gray?"

No.

It had finished its meal and, after a quick stretch, clicked across the table to Liam's plate, watching him. When he was done, he pushed the plate away and smiled.

Are you finished?

"Yes. Go ahead."

This, too, was a ritual. The dragon wanted to try whatever he called up from the oven, and now it ducked its head into the stew of rice and vegetables.

"I'm going to read," Liam said, standing.

Do you wish to practice? Fanuilh asked, its head deep in rice.

"No, not tonight. Tomorrow."

Too wet, it commented, as he left the kitchen.

"You wouldn't like it dry," Liam called over his shoulder, with a laugh.

Too cooked.

He did not go to the library, despite his announced intention. He lingered in the entrance hall, looking out at the dark beach, and then entered a room on the same side of the house as the workroom.

Magic, sourceless light swelled up as he came in, revealing a series of waist-high wooden cases with glass tops. Assorted jewelry and wands lay inside, bedded in black velvet. There was a hanging on one wall with a stylized eagle on it, rising powerfully in flight over purple mountains; on another were a sword, a shield and a horn that would have fit in Bellona's temple, as well as a stringless lute hung by its neck.

Fanuilh called this the trophy room, and assured him that all the items were enchanted, though it had yet to explain exactly what each did. Liam had found that he was not particularly interested—they were all Tarquin's, as far as he was concerned.

In fact, most of the things in the house were Tarquin's. Liam owned few personal possessions and had left most of the wizard's things where they were. He had thrown away only the stock in the workroom, which included all things needed for casting magical spells: herbs and roots, countless glass jars and flasks containing stranger things (including the severed head of a dog and a human hand), for which he had no use. They wre the "material components" of spells, Fanuilh had told him, and he could not cast spells. As it was, he had felt guilty about throwing them away, and had actually gone and apologized over Tarquin's grave. He had buried the wizard himself, in the heavier soil where the beach met the cliff.

After a few minutes he grew bored of the trophy room. Until Fanuilh explained them, they were little more than curiosities.

The dragon emerged from the kitchen as he returned from the entrance hall.

I will fly tonight, if you do not mind, master.

"Go right ahead," Liam said, feeling magnanimous, and a little ridiculous. He could not imagine a reason to mind. "Though it's going to snow."

It will not bother me.

"Good. You need the exercise."

I am not fat.

"Yet."

Fanuilh made a little sniffing sound and slid the front door open with its paws. Liam closed the door when the dragon was out, and laughed to himself.

I really shouldn't make fun of him, he thought. *He doesn't understand my humor.*

Which, he realized as he went to the kitchen, was why it was fun to joke with the little dragon.

In the weeks when he first moved into the house, platters and plates and cups from the oven had accumulated around the kitchen, piling up until there was no room to eat. In despair, he had asked Fanuilh what to do with them, and the dragon nonchalantly suggested he put them back in the oven, which was what Tarquin had always done. Since then, dirty dishes had not been a problem—they simply disappeared in the oven between meals—but Liam had been strongly tempted to strangle his familiar for weeks afterward, whenever he cleared the table.

He thought of that as he put the empty dishes into the now-cold oven, and then went to Tarquin's library.

The wizard had been a man of wide interests, and his library reflected it—an eclectic selection of texts, from convoluted discussions of the esoterica of magic to equally convoluted philosophical texts, with collections of poetry, fiction and history in between, as well as a number of volumes of travelers' tales. There were three different bestiaries and, thinking of the sad creature in Bellona's temple, Liam pulled down the thickest.

The entry on gryphons began with an intricately illuminated capital G and an elaborate picture of a group—*Pride?* Liam wondered, *Flock?*—of the magical animals. It told him little he did not already know: that

they were rare, most often found in the north of Taralon, in the King's
Range. That they grew rarer the farther south one went, that they were
unknown in the Freeports. That they were fierce and proud, that they
were beautiful. He had not known that their hearts were useful in a
number of powerful spells, but it did not interest him and he had already
heard that they had a language of their own.

The last paragraph of the entry, however, was entirely new to him.
Written in red ink, as opposed to the black used for the rest of the text, it
began with the heading: STONE GRYPHONS.

"Though bearing a distinct physical resemblance to the creature described above in all particulars except color," the paragraph read, "STONE
GRYPHONS should not be confused with their earthbound kin. Of a slate
gray color, these beasts are magical creatures of an entirely different
complexion. They haunt battlefields and graveyards, and eat the souls of
the dead, as opposed to the fresh meat favored by the common gryphon.
It is also held that they can walk the Gray Lands, and move freely
through the ethereal, astral, earthly and heavenly planes. Little else is
known of them, though no living man has ever recorded receiving a hurt
from them."

Liam frowned over the page. Could Bellona's acolytes be holding a
stone gryphon for sacrifice? He paged through the other two bestiaries;
one had no entry even for normal gryphons, and the third mentioned the
normal kind, but not their gray cousins.

With a dissatisfied *hmph* he replaced all the books on the appropriate shelf, and drew out the book of philosophy he had been working on.

While he tried to puzzle out the strange arguments the book presented, it began to snow, softly at first, then harder. He looked up in the
middle of a particularly inane digression and noticed that the library's
skylight was covered with a light dusting. Putting aside the book, he went
out to the entrance hall and slid open the door.

The patio had a dusting of snow on it as well, and the light from the
house made it glitter prettily. He breathed deep, enjoying the salt cold in
his lungs.

"Fanuilh!" he called. There was no answer. He called again, then
bent down, made a snowball, and lobbed it out toward the sea.

He was wearing only stockings, and the snow quickly soaked them.
He hopped back in, stripping them off and dropping them on his boots
by the door.

He can let himself in, Liam thought, and went to bed.

There was a bedroom down the hall on the right, but he did not
sleep there—it was where he had discovered Tarquin's corpse. Though

two months had passed, and he had buried the wizard in the bedclothes and bought a new mattress filled with cotton ticking, he could not bring himself to sleep there.

Instead, he went into the library, where there was a divan long enough to hold him. The room darkened as he took off his clothes and wrapped himself in a light sheet, and he fell into blackness quite comfortably.

■ *2* ■

WAKE, MASTER.

In his dream, Liam was reading a giant bestiary, filled solely with pictures of Fanuilh. He turned the pages one after another; each entry was accompanied by a picture of his familiar. And all began with two illuminated words:

WAKE, MASTER.

He closed the book and woke up.

A pure white light suffused the library, a combination of the house's magic and the sun shining through the covering of snow on the skylight.

"What is it, Fanuilh?" He groaned and sat up, stretching leisurely.

You must come see. There has been a robber.

Liam checked in midstretch.

Come see.

He threw aside the sheet, jumped into a pair of breeches and ran out into the entrance hall, where he skidded to a stop.

Fanuilh was crouched by the door, its snout close down by the floor, examining a set of sandy footprints. It reminded Liam absurdly of a dog sniffing out a trail, though he knew the dragon's sense of smell was not as keen.

They go into the trophy room, and into the workroom.

"Ahh," Liam groaned. "Robbers. Wonderful, really, wonderful." He cursed, once, with feeling. "All right, let's see what they took." With a resigned expression, he crossed to the trophy room, careful not to step in the sand and puddles of melted snow left by the robber's feet.

The flying rug, Fanuilh noted, *and something from the cases.*

Liam nodded: the hanging with the eagle was gone from the wall, and the lid of one case was open. He looked in—one of the wands, a slim ebony stick, was missing.

"Very particular thieves," he murmured. The dragon leapt up onto the cases; its claws clicked on the glass. "Nothing else missing?" Fanuilh's head swayed from side to side. "All right; the workroom."

He caught his familiar around the middle and hoisted it up to his shoulder; perched there, it rode him into the workroom. The shelves were empty—his own work—and the intricate, perfectly detailed model of Southwark was still on the third worktable, by the window. Tarquin had made it for the last spell he cast before his murder.

The wizard's book of spells, however, which had been chained to a lectern in front of the third table, was gone. The chain was looped neatly on top of the lectern, one link snapped.

Liam and Fanuilh both stared for a moment at the pile of chain.

"Very particular thieves," Liam said again.

Only three things—the wand, the carpet, and the book.

"Go check Diamond," Liam said suddenly.

Without hesitation the dragon sprang from his shoulder, flapping its wings gently, and flew out of the workroom.

When it returned, its master was dressed and back by the lectern, kneeling to examine the footprints.

The horse is there. But with the rug, the robbers would not need the horse.

"Wait," Liam said, touching the sand with one finger. In a strange way, he was not upset by the robbery. Instead, he was excited, in a purposeful way. Without being aware of it, he was responding to the robbery as if it were a call to action—and the opening of the sort of mystery the Aedile thought him so good at solving. There were steps to take, he knew, a logical course of action. First, a set of questions. "Hold on a moment. One thing at a time. First, when did you find this?"

I returned from my flight only a few minutes before I woke you.

"Out all night, eh?" He kept back the joke that occurred to him. "So they could have come anytime after I went to sleep. Now, what did they take? I mean, besides the spellbook. I know about that—but what's the rug? And what's the wand?"

The rug flies. It can carry a person. The wand levitates objects.

"Objects?"

Things too heavy to be carried by a man.

"Very good." He stood up, brushing his hands on his knees. "We have to assume our thief knew what he wanted."

One of Fanuilh's thoughts began to form in his head, but Liam held up a hand, and it disappeared. He scratched the back of his head for a minute, pursing his lips, then caught what he was after.

"Didn't you say the house was protected?"

Yes. The thought formed instantly, as if it had been ready. *No one could enter without the owner's permission.*

"And the spell still holds, even though Tarquin's dead?"

You are the owner now.

Liam sucked at his lower lip for a moment.

"Who could break the spell, and get in?"

A wizard of sufficient power.

"So our thief is a wizard."

There are no wizards in Southwark powerful enough. And I would have noticed the expense of energy necessary to breach the spell.

"But it was done," Liam pointed out reasonably.

Yes, but not with a spell. I would have noticed.

"Are you sure?" He knew little enough about how magic worked, and would have to trust the dragon's judgment, but he wanted it to be sure. "No doubts?"

None.

"All right, then, any other possibilities? A common housebreaker shouldn't have been able to open the door."

A breaching spell could have been laid on the thief, or an amulet or ring or wand.

"And that you wouldn't notice?"

Only at the moment the spell was laid. I would not notice the use of the enchanted item—only the original casting.

The discussion was moving into realms Liam did not understand, and he decided to cut it short. He wanted to move on to his next obvious step.

You are going to report it to the Aedile.

"Of course. As soon as we clear up a few things. The protection on the house could have been broken only by a wizard, but you say there are no wizards in Southwark."

None.

"Or a breaching spell could have been placed on something—almost anything, correct?—which would have let the thief enter."

Anything at all.

"So we have either a careful wizard, or a thief with access to enchantments. And in either case, we have someone with a very limited list of desires—just the wand, the rug and the book. The book argues for a wizard, because a thief would probably be unable to use it. But the lack of a spell used indicates a thief with magical assistance."

There were thieves, he knew, who specialized in stealing enchanted items. Most often they worked on commission. But he could not imagine such a thief in Southwark—the city was simply too small to warrant such specialization and, if Fanuilh were right, there were not enough wizards around to make it pay.

None at all, the dragon corrected. *No wizards.*

"Well, we'll let Coeccias sort that out. I just want to have the right information to hand him."

The dragon cocked its head at him, its yellow eyes slitted in puzzlement.

"Well?" Liam said after a minute of his familiar's scrutiny. "What?"

You are going to report it to the Aedile.

"Yes," he replied, "what else would you have me do?"

You could find the thief yourself. He stole your things.

Liam shook his head. The dragon had persuaded him—forced him, really—to investigate Tarquin's murder, and although he had eventually found the killer, he could not say that the process had been pleasant. Not pleasant in the least.

"No," he said at last, "not this time. This is Coeccias's work. He's best suited to it—I'd only make a mess of things again."

The dragon had no shoulders to speak of, so it could not shrug, but Liam could tell that it would have.

As you will, master.

"Exactly," Liam said. "As I will. I'm not going to get beaten up or involved with murderous women or go creeping around in the rain again. We'll let Coeccias handle it."

As you will.

Nodding suspiciously, Liam backed out of the room and took his cloak from the peg.

On the ride into Southwark, Liam had time to compose his thoughts. Diamond enjoyed the snow, kicking up great gouts, prancing and blowing. The barren fields were suddenly pretty, mantled in white.

It's not my place to pursue this, Liam decided. Robbery was not murder, of course, not as likely to turn dangerous.

Stop that, he told himself. He would not pursue it. Finding sneak-

thieves was Coeccias's responsibility. There was no need for him to go in
search of his stolen possessions.

They're not even mine, really. They're Tarquin's.

Sighing, he admitted that this was not true. The wizard was dead; he
had named Liam his heir. The book and the rug and the wand were his.

But that doesn't mean I should try to find them. Coeccias can do that.

Then why, he wondered, had he asked Fanuilh those questions? And
more important, why was he so keyed up? Why had the little dragon's
announcement made him jump from the divan, not in fright or anger, but
with excitement?

And why was he letting Diamond amble that way, curvetting about in
the newly fallen snow, instead of spurring him hard for the Aedile's
offices? Why was he in no hurry to report the crime?

It is not your place, he told himself fiercely. *That's why there's an
Aedile.* Pulling his cloak forward to protect his face, he startled the roan
by booting it in the ribs. The horse sprang forward, racing for the city.

Fanuilh had woken him only a little after dawn, and their discussion
and his ride had taken less than an hour. Liam trotted into the city
square, reined in sharply and stared about him.

The square was practically deserted. At that hour, despite the snow,
it should have been filled with people, buying and selling, passing the
time, crossing the expanse of cobbles to any one of the five major streets
that fed into it. Now there were only a few forlorn hawkers, huddling
around a tiny brazier.

Liam clucked his horse on, noting even as it clopped along that the
snow was trampled and scattered everywhere.

"A lot of tracks," he muttered to himself, "a lot of milling about."

He dismounted in front of the squat bulk of the city's jail, the headquarters of the Guard, and looped Diamond's reins through an iron ring
on the wall. The cold metal stung his hands, and he reminded himself to
get gloves.

The Guard at the door, rubbing her bare hands miserably, recognized him as a friend of Coeccias.

"Good morrow, Sir Liam. Come t'attend th'Aedile?"

"Yes. Is he here?"

Her face brightened, a smile spreading across her frostreddened
cheeks. "Nay, but gone over to Temples' Court, for the hurlyburly."

"Hurlyburly?"

"Have you not the word?" She grinned, and Liam knew that she was making up for not being a part of whatever was happening in the nearby neighborhood. He shook his head. "Truly?"

"Truly. What's happened?"

"Uris take me, who could 'scape it? It's bruited all the town over!"

Although Liam had a certain amount of sympathy for the woman, left behind to guard the empty jail while the Aedile—and most of the Guard, guessing from the tracks in the snow—were off at whatever had happened, his hands were cold.

"What happened?" he repeated, enunciating carefully.

"There's been murther!" She slurred the last word, as southerners tended to do. "One's tried to take off the hierarch of the new fane!"

"Murder?" This was news, certainly, worth more than his mere robbery. And of a priest, as well. He had noticed the tendency of natives to ignore the difference between Temples' Court, the neighborhood, and Temple Street proper, where the homes of the gods were.

"Oh, aye, vicious, too, in the dark of night, a dozen masked men—"

The Guard stopped abruptly, snapping to attention, catching up the halberd she had leaned against the wall. Liam peered over his shoulder and saw Coeccias crossing the square. Thunder stood out on his forehead, and his fists were clenched.

"Rhenford!" he bellowed. "Rhenford, praise all the gods there are, just the wight I've need of!"

Liam froze. While they investigated Tarquin's murder, the Aedile had acquired an exaggerated sense of his skills as a bloodhound. In a flash of intuition, Liam knew his friend was going to ask him to look into whatever had happened over in Temple Street.

Coeccias took his time over it, though. He gave Liam a slap on the shoulder and the Guard a glare as he came up the steps, then stumped on into the jail. Liam followed him in. There were cots along the walls, and weapons piled haphazardly about. Fires roared in twin hearths, set at each end of the room, but the Aedile went straight to an open barrel in the middle of the floor. He dipped a tin cup in and tossed down the contents.

Wincing at the sight, Liam loosened his cloak. The barrel held a local kind of hard liquor that left him gasping and choking. The stout man, though, only sniffed and dipped his cup again.

"Truth, Rhenford," he said, "that's like life. And it scarcely daybreak!" He turned, his thunderous expression slipping away, replaced by a frank look of exhaustion. "I'd swear Old Man Sun dawdled in bed a day, to keep Mistress Night abroad. I'd warrant I've never passed a longer."

"I can imagine," Liam said, settling on his haunches by a fire and warming his hands. "Murder, eh?"

"Murder?"

Liam nodded at the door. "She said there'd been a murder over at the temple of Bellona."

Anger swept away Coeccias's exhaustion, and he took two steps toward the door before stopping himself. "Damn her!" he shouted instead. "Next it'll be the Duke's been taken off and the sea's turned to blood! Rumor! Gods, Rhenford, it likes me less than . . . less than . . ." Words failed him, and he spluttered on for a moment before Liam interrupted.

"No murder, then?" The idea, strangely, did not relieve him much. If the Guard had exaggerated the emergency, then Coeccias might be able to focus on his robbery—and he found that a small part of him wanted just the opposite.

"No! What's passed is bad enough, and I'd not be surprised if there were blood in the end, the way Cloten's carrying on, but no, no murder." His beard wagged as he chewed his lower lip, and Liam had to prod him again.

"Then what?"

The Aedile shook his head, as if remembering the other man's presence. "What? Oh, aye, what. Only that some thief's tried to rob Bellona's treasury, and given Cloten a knock on's head while at it."

Liam gave a startled laugh. Coeccias glared at him. "The treasury? We were just talking about that yesterday!"

"Aye, we were—but while we were talking, another was plotting, and tried to lift it late last night. Cloten caught him at it, but he got away."

Holding back another incredulous laugh—he could not imagine anyone fool enough to break into the temple of a warrior goddess—Liam only shook his head, and caught up a poker. "Who's Cloten?"

"Only the greatest ass ever to grace Temples' Court—or all of Southwark, for that. Do you know that he actually tried to challenge the Hierarch of Strife, to his face? Old Guiderius came in to wish him well, had heard the news, and Cloten, that ass, gave the man the lie outright! In his teeth! Can you imagine?"

Liam could not, because he knew neither man. But he qualified his earlier thought—he had known a thief years before who might have broken into Bellona's temple. He smiled briefly at the memory.

"My Guards had to pull the old man out," Coeccias went on, pacing the stone-flagged floor. "He was that enraged! I've posted most of my men down there to keep the peace, but Cloten only laughed!"

"Who," Liam asked patiently, "is Cloten? And who is Guiderius?"

Coeccias whirled on him, astonished for a moment, then relaxed. "Aye, aye, I forget. Truth, Rhenford, it's as if I were speaking to myself." He took a deep breath, marshaling his thoughts and his calm. "Cloten's Hierarch of Bellona, and Guiderius of Strife, an old and regular fixture in Temples' Court."

"Wait—who was the priest we met yesterday? Alastor—I thought he was hierarch."

"No, no," the Aedile said, waving away the question. "He's but second; 'Keeper of Arms,' they title him. Cloten's hierarch."

"All right, then, why would Guiderius want to rob Cloten?"

Coeccias rolled his eyes. "Truth, I could warrant no reason, though Cloten's fixed on it. And thinks it more an attack on his self than a robbery—as if any'd worry themselves with his worthless life, and it weren't clear the thief was after the treasury!"

Liam stirred the fire, thinking. There was an obvious reason, of course: Strife was a war god, and there would be no love lost between competing sects. Still, feuds among churches were few and far between in Taralon, and Coeccias seemed sure it was just a robbery.

"So," he said, "why am I just the wight you're looking for?"

Coeccias stopped pacing, a guilty smile twitching on his lips. "Truth," he faltered, "I was hoping you'd, ah, that you'd . . ."

"Help you? Help you find the thief?"

"Rhenford," he said, opening his hands and speaking frankly, "I'd not ask if it weren't trickish. It's as much this Cloten I need a hand with as the thief. He's difficult."

"Difficult?"

"Prickly, a headstrong horse with his own mind and the bit between his teeth. I fear me he'll pursue this with Guiderius."

"Well, all you have to do is find the thief. Then he can't blame Guiderius."

Coeccias rolled his eyes. "Oh, aye, just find the thief. I'll snap my fingers and make the rounds of the usual cutpurses, and one'll confess, eh? This is no ordinary thief, as well you know, Rhenford. This is a passing job, and called for a passing thief."

"I suppose that's true," Liam said, recalling his own thought on the thief brave enough to try a temple dedicated to war.

"Truer than true—and the reason I ask your help. You've a penetrating eye, and a head for this. Come, will you?"

There was hope in the Aedile's eye as he looked at his friend, and

Liam knew he would have to put it out. The man had put too much stock in his success in finding Tarquin's murderer.

"I can't," Liam said simply. "I've got my own robbery to worry about."

He gave a quick account of the burglary, mentioning both the wards the thief had passed and the things he had taken. When he was done, Coeccias was wincing.

"Passed through the house while you were abed, did he?"

"Yes."

"And took only magical things?"

"Yes. That's why I came in this morning—to tell you about it. I'd hoped for your help."

Coeccias ran a thick hand through his unruly hair, frowning. "It likes me not to have things magical in the hands of a thief. But with this in Temples' Court . . ."

During his ride into town and his discussion with the Aedile, Liam had realized an important thing about himself. He was bored. Not the boredom of an hour, or of an afternoon. It was deeper, a dissatisfaction with the placidity of his life over the past two months. For over ten years, his life had been constant movement, a whirlwind progress that had led him halfway around the world, only to drop him in Southwark. In Southwark, where, except for the brief week when he sought Tarquin's murderer, he had done exactly nothing.

Not true, he told himself at the fire. *I've had my work with Fanuilh, and Coeccias and I are now friends. That's worth something.* He was not sure, however, how much, and he was now sure that it was not enough.

"With this in Temples' Court," Coeccias finally said, picking up his earlier statement, "my cup's full."

There was one thing to check before committing himself. "Well, are there any thieftakers in Southwark?"

"Thieftakers?"

"Yes, men who catch thieves for a living," Liam explained, though he could tell from his friend's puzzled look that there were none. Southwark was undoubtedly too small to need them.

"There's me," Coeccias said, "and the Guard."

"I know, but in some cities—Torquay, for instance, and Harcourt and most of the Freeports—there are men who do it for money. They're hired to solve a particular crime, usually small things like housebreaking."

Coeccias sniffed at the idea, and Liam turned his head so that his smile fell into the fire. If there were no thieftakers, and Coeccias had his hands full dealing with the trouble in Temple Street, then . . .

"In that case, I imagine I should try to find the thief myself."

"Truth, Rhenford, that'd be grand," the Aedile said, as if he had forgotten his earlier request for help. "If you'll track your thief, I'll track Cloten's."

Liam paused. "Agreed." After all, he told himself, tracking a thief could not lead to as many complications as tracking Tarquin's murderer had. And it would certainly be easier than placating an irate hierarch. "Can you give me the names of some pawnbrokers—ones who are used to handling expensive items?"

With a pleased smile, Coeccias bustled about, finding pen, ink and paper in a cupboard, laying the sheet out on top of the liquor keg. "There's not so many as fit," he said as he wrote, "only two, when all's said, if y'are thinking of fences. Y'are?" Liam nodded. "There're others who'll take lesser items, but only these two for things the like of yours." He blew on the sheet of paper to dry the ink, then handed it to Liam. "And while you're conning your thief, keep your ears pricked for word of mine, eh?"

"My pleasure," Liam said, taking the paper and noting the two names and addresses in the Aedile's unruly handwriting. He did not really think his thief would be fencing his goods; he needed the names for something else entirely. "I trust you'll do the same?"

Coeccias offered him a mock bow. "What say we meet on a schedule and exchange information?"

They decided on dinner the next day, at a familiar inn, and Liam pulled his cloak close around his shoulders, preparing to go.

"There's something else," he said, standing by the door. "Where can I find Mother Japh?"

The Aedile considered for a moment. "I'd think her in her morgue now. Why?"

"I need to ask her a little about magic. Where's her . . . morgue, did you call it?"

"Aye, that's her word for it—a place we keep unclaimed bodies. Next door, beneath the courts. Though I'd not seek her there, 'less corses like you."

Liam took in the Aedile's warning with a sober nod; sooner or later he would have to disabuse his friend of the notion that he was blood shy.

"Right. Perhaps I can send in a message."

"That'd be best," Coeccias said solicitously.

Once again hiding a smile, Liam stepped out of the Guard barracks and into the cold morning. There was an oddly familiar itch between his shoulder blades, and his hands flexed on their own. He recognized the feeling.

He had something to do that was worth doing.

■ *3* ■

A BRIEF WORD with the Guard on the steps assured him that she would watch over Diamond, and Liam walked over to the building next door.

The Duke's courts were large for a city as small as Southwark, filling most of the western side of the square. The squat Guard barracks looked like a poor relation huddled up against their side, their rude stone clashing with the neatly dressed blocks of the courts, rising in three massive stories pierced by rows of narrow, widely spaced windows. A thin, square tower rose another two stories from the middle of the building, housing the bells that tolled the city's hours. Torch brackets had been riveted into the stone front, and Liam knew from experience that at night the courts flickered with firelight, its long shadows stretching and dancing across the facade and up to the bell tower.

There were no torches now and the courts looked deserted. Liam went up a broad staircase to the wooden doors and pulled at the heavy knocker. Rubbing his hands to keep off the cold, he examined the coat of arms hung above the doors: three red foxes on a gray field, without subdivisions or signs of intermarriage. The Dukes of the Southern Tier kept their line apart from the general nobility of Taralon, marrying among the petty landowners and merchants of their duchy. It had done little to endear them to their peers, but it had kept their interests firmly rooted in their own lands and left their coat simple.

A withered old porter eventually cracked the door and demanded his business.

"I'd like to see Mother Japh," Liam told him, and was rewarded with a sour grunt and a slight widening of the crack. He slipped inside, blinking at the sudden darkness. However brilliantly illuminated they were on the outside, the Duke's courts were ill lit inside. The grumpy porter held up a lantern and grumbled.

"Come along, then," he said after squinting at Liam's face for a moment. "She's below."

They went along a broad hallway in the heart of the building, the porter's lantern throwing distended shadows on the chilly stones. Thin lines of orange light stood out beneath the doors that lined the empty hall, and Liam barely made out the words painted on them: Wills and Deeds, Shipping Registrar, Ducal Imposts, Births and Deaths. He shuddered a little at the last word, and picked up his pace to catch the porter, who had gone on without stopping.

Liam found him by his light and his misshapen, monstrous shadow, several steps down a narrow circular staircase. They descended, Liam growing colder as they passed below street level. The courts themselves, he guessed, were on the higher floors—and he further imagined each, as well as the tightly shut offices on the first floor, with its own roaring hearth and a snug official warming his toes by it. The porter's breath steamed as he led the way from the bottom of the staircase.

There was a long, low-ceilinged corridor, with solid-looking doors on either side. No light escaped from under them, including the last one, at which the porter left him without a word.

Bemused, Liam knocked once, then twice more, quickly, as the porter's light dwindled, then disappeared.

"Who's it?" he heard, from the other side of the door.

"It's Liam Rhenford, Mother Japh. Aedile Coeccias sent me."

He heard a light laugh and the door scraped open, revealing a wizened old woman in a light shift, a rug in one hand.

"In, in, Rhenford, let not the cold in!"

He jumped into the room and she slammed the door, tucking the rug around the bottom of the jamb. It was stifling in the small pace, so hot he could remove his cloak, so hot the windows were unshuttered, mists of condensation across them.

"It's warm," he said, draping his cloak over his arm and tugging at his collar.

"And so it should be," the old woman chuckled, gesturing at the huge fireplace that filled one end of the room. It was easily the largest Liam had ever seen, suited to a foundry or a large smithy. Only a fraction of the hearth was used, but it was enough to set him sweating. "It was supposed to be the base of a . . . oh, the word goes from me—you'll know it—it was to heat the whole pile, through chimneys in the floors and such."

"A hypocaust?" He looked with new appreciation on the huge stove, noting the breadth of the flue.

"Aye, that's the very word, only it doesn't work as it should. The masons mistook the plans, and laid the whole awry, so that," she said, with a wink and mischievous grin, "it only serves to warm me, and the rest make do with braziers and the very smallest of hearths."

Liam smiled back. A hypocaust was no mean trick of architecture; he was not surprised that it did not work, only that it had been attempted. "But how is it," he asked, turning his gaze from the fire to the foggy glass, "that you have window here, in the basement?"

Mother Japh cackled and, taking his arm, led him over to one of the windows. She rubbed a spot clear of condensation and bade him look through it. "That's Narrow Lane," she said, pointing down at a snow-filled road that earned its name, barely ten feet from side to side. "Behind the building, you see? On the front there's the square, but behind, there's Narrow Lane, and a much lower thing it is. So there's my windows, that I had them unshutter and glass when I came here. And how they carped! But they're there, and give good light toward the end of the day."

With another smile, Liam turned from the window and surveyed the room. He had met Mother Japh only once, really, on the morning he discovered Tarquin's body. She had seemed friendly then, once she had made certain that he was not the murderer. They had exchanged a few words on the rare occasions since then, whenever they passed each other in the street, but had never gone beyond that.

Now he looked at her room, noting the numerous pots by the furnace of the would-be hypocaust, the jars and bins, the worktables with tops battered and scarred and burned. Mother Japh, he knew, was a ghost witch, but he had no real idea what that meant: he knew even less about witches than he did about wizards, which was precious little.

"Do you live here?" he asked, careful to keep any tone of judgment out of his voice. He had not noticed a place to sleep among the clutter of items, though there was a door in one wall that might lead to a bedroom.

"Faith, no," she laughed, a happy, amiable chuckle that screwed up her already-wrinkled features. "Only work, and stay when's cold, for that the wood and coal are free, grace of the Duke." She laughed again. "Faith, living in the morgue!"

"What is that, exactly, a morgue? Coeccias mentioned it as well."

"Why, it's where we keep corses, do you see, those unclaimed, tars, thieves, beggars, and so on. When the Guard finds them, eh?" His questioning look around the room provoked her to a stormy laugh. "So he looks for 'em! Oh, that's strong, it is! They're not *here,* Rhenford, they're *there"*—she pointed at the second door—"and precious few at the moment, so there's no worry."

"No worry," he agreed, wondering if Coeccias had communicated his misconception about Liam's squeamishness to the ghost witch.

"But now, you've not come to see my corses, nor to repair the hypothing, have you? You've a question, eh? Or two?"

He had more than two, and those that came first to his mind—*What exactly is a ghost witch?* was prominent among them—he put aside, remembering the real purpose of his visit.

"I do, and I hope you can answer them."

"With a will, if I can," she interrupted, "though mind, I'm no scholar."

As briefly as possible, he explained the theft of Tarquin's things and the magical wards the thief had overcome, and she clucked in sympathy.

"What I want to ask you is, whether you know anyone in Southwark who could do that. Anyone who could break one of Tarquin's spells."

"Don't you know?"

"Me? No, that's why I'm asking you."

"But I'm a witch—you're the wizard!"

He looked at her, stunned. "I'm not a wizard!"

"Go to," Mother Japh said, waving a hand at him. "In course y'are. You live in a wizard's house, don't you?"

"Yes," he admitted.

"And you've befriended his familiar, haven't you?"

"Yes, but . . ."

"And now you want to search out a spellbook and a magic wand and carpet. And you say y'are no wizard! Pshaw!"

"But I'm not," Liam insisted. "I don't know anything about magic." While this was not exactly true, it was far closer to the truth than the idea that he was a wizard.

"Truth? Nothing?"

"Nothing."

She accepted his avowal grudgingly, as if she did not wish to believe it. "The whole city's sure of it. It's bruited about everywhere."

Swallowing an angry impulse, he reflected that it made a certain amount of sense. If they followed Mother Japh's logic, then the rest of Southwark would have come to the conclusion that he was a wizard.

"Not a very forward wizard," the old woman amended, "but a wizard for all that."

"Well, I can assure you I'm not," he said reasonably. "And that's why I came to you. I know witchery and wizardry aren't the same—"

"More than most can say," she interrupted.

". . . but I was hoping you could tell me if there were any other wizards around."

"As it happens," she said, "I can. Can tell you that there aren't, that is. Apart from you, that is. And since you say you're not, there aren't any."

"Are you sure?"

"As sure as I can be," she said, with no trace of affront. "Wizards don't come to Southwark, see you. Tarquin Tanaquil was the only one as did, and see how he was served! No, wizards don't come here. There's no Guild branch—Southwark is too small—and the Duke's court is deemed unfriendly to 'em."

"Unfriendly?"

"It's not, but's seen that way. He only follows certain old rules and ways, that curb wizards in ways that like them not."

Liam was aware of the Duke's penchant for the ancient laws of Taralon, and vaguely remembered an old set of regulations that prescribed the activities of wizards—those "engaged in the arcane arts," the code said, "or pursuing said knowledges and applications."

"Apart from Tanaquil, no wizard's visited Southwark since I was born, though I know they're thick as flies by a bilge to the north—in Torquay and Harcourt. If one were to come, I'd warrant, even disguised, the word'd go out."

"So there's no wizard in Southwark?"

"I can't say it for fact, but so I'd guess. Wizards have a . . . smell about them, eh? A feel, like a great lord or lady, eh? They can't help but seem like wizards."

"Do I smell like a wizard?" He asked only in jest.

She stared at him for a moment. "Aye, you do, or something strange, at the least."

"That's nice to know," he said, and the irony was not lost on her.

"Don't take it so, Rhenford. It means only that you don't resemble the common run—and for that, I'll show you something."

She bustled over to the second door, touching his arm. He followed, frowning heavily over her comments. The first time they met, she told him his face was too innocent to be believed; now she was telling him he smelled like a wizard, and that the entire city thought that was what he was. He had not liked being told he was too innocent—he liked it even less to be thought of as a wizard.

The room beyond was larger by far than the one they had left. Its end was shadowy, the windows stopping halfway down, with the light from the door barely reaching that far. But what Liam saw was enough.

There were a dozen tables in view, and more in the dark part of the room. The tables were stone slabs raised on squat blocks, barely waist-high, and there were corpses on three of them.

"This is your morgue?" he asked, bothered not in the least by the sight of the bodies but by the fact that Mother Japh spent so much time near them.

Like living in a graveyard, he thought, and must have grimaced, because she laughed.

"Oh, it's not so bad, Rhenford. There're not always so many, and they come and go with frequency; never here more than a se'ennight. And I needs must be near, to keep the spells going."

"Spells?" He walked to the nearest body, a naked man with bluish skin under a coating of tattoos, and a bloated face. The morgue was cold, but not cold enough to keep corpses from rotting; some of the heat from the hypocaust's furnace had to seep through the intervening wall.

"For to keep them fresh, see you? It'd fair clear the whole square if they was to rot." The notion set her laughing again, and he noted the little bundle lying between the feet of the corpse. He pointed at it, and she nodded. "Aye, that's my work. It'll keep the body from rot for almost a month, with attention. A simple witchery, but I didn't bring you here for to show you that. See you that last?"

She pointed at the third corpse, separated by a few tables from the others, and he walked over. It was a man, small and lightly built; a weak man, it would seem, judging from the thinness of his arms and the general paucity of muscle. There was a look of vast surprise on his face, his mouth agape in a silent shout; a gash in his chest showed where a knife had gone in.

"What do you make him?"

Liam looked at the face, the thin arms. Then, to prove to himself that the atmosphere of the morgue was not getting to him, he reached out and rubbed one of the man's hands. A chill reached him from the dead skin. "A clerk?"

Her face lit up. "Why?"

"No calluses except on the pads of his fingers, no muscle, no scars. Not like the sailor over there." He gestured to the tattooed blue corpse.

Mother Japh nodded happily. "Aye, y'are as sharp as Coeccias says, and more." He ducked his head, both pleased and displeased with the praise. "But that's not what I wish to show. There's more beyond. Now watch this."

She shut the door, leaving the morgue with only the dim gray light from the windows. Her thin brown shift rustled over the floor as she paced to the center of the room and raised one hand. A flat circle of brilliant blue light burst in her palm, then spread to the walls in a shimmering plate. Liam was considerably taller than the ghost witch, so the plane of light broke around his neck—and for all the world he could have sworn that he was treading water in a cobalt blue sea, coruscating with little phosphorescences.

Mother Japh lowered her hand, the plate following, trailing down Liam's chest, then past her own face and down, until it rested a foot or so above the tables.

"Face about," she told him, and he turned, dazzled by the way the blue light played around his waist, flashing and sparkling.

"What—" he began, and then saw the breath of the first two corpses in the room.

Single flames burned above each corpse's mouth, tiny whirls of fire just by the mouth, straighter jets farther up. No more than a foot tall, they reminded Liam of the breath of dragons.

An irrelevant thought came to Liam: that Fanuilh could not breath fire.

"Their souls," the ghost witch said, and her voice was hushed, almost reverent. "Till they're called—buried, or burned, or fetched by whatever'll take them to the Gray Lands—their souls burn above their mouths. But now turn about again."

He did, and saw immediately that there was no flame above the mouth of the third corpse.

"See you?"

"No flame."

"No flame—no soul. Which is as saying there's a ghost roaming Southwark now."

She suddenly closed her fist and the blue field shredded in an instant. Liam started, then rubbed his eyes for a moment. Blue sparks swam in his vision.

"The spirit can't find its body, and so it'll wander, until it comes upon it. This corse was found in Narrow Lane," Mother Japh went on, pointing out the window, "just a few yards from here, and I've been hoping the spirit'd find the body, but it hasn't." She heaved a deep sigh, clearly touched by the plight of the lost spirit.

"Does this happen often?" Liam asked, staring in wonder at the surprised face.

"It's rare enough—true ghosts are, see you—but's a murder, eh? The wound in the chest, most like a theft, and Narrow Lane's dark and dangerous at night, for all of Coeccias's work and that it's right by the Duke's courts. With a strong taking off like that, losing the spirit's possible."

Liam breathed hard and backed away from the spiritless corpse, leaning against an empty table.

"It seems winter is the time for strange events in Southwark. Two major thefts—or a major theft and an attempted major theft—a spiritless body, the comet . . ."

The ghost witch's gray head bobbed up and down. "And a new goddess, mind you." Her nod took on a judicial quality, and she pointed one gnarled finger at him. "A new goddess. There's something there, I'll tell you. More than the messenger, or your thieveries, or this corpse. There's something there."

A brief silence fell on the morgue, and Liam suddenly found that he wanted to leave.

The ghost witch accompanied him up the stairs with a shielded candle, a shawl thrown over her shoulders. She opened the main door of the court, but blocked his way for a moment.

"Thank you, Mother Japh," Liam said. "At some point, if you would, I'd like to talk to you about witchcraft."

He expected a pleasantry or, more likely, a joke. Instead, the old woman's face creased worriedly.

"Be you careful searching out your thief, Liam Rhenford. There's more at work here than meets the eye."

A chill wind cut through her thin shift and she ducked suddenly down the corridor, clutching her shawl tight, headed for her furnace room.

Mother Japh's warning in his ears, Liam remembered the way Coeccias had winced when he heard that the thief had been wandering around the house while he slept. He had planned to head straight back to the beach; instead, he asked a question of the shivering Guard in front of the barracks, and guided Diamond north, to the section of the artisans' quarter known as Auric's Park.

In a narrow alley begrimed with smoke and ash he found a swordsmith, and bought a matched hanger and dirk. There were few armed men in Southwark's streets—it was a small city, too small for the political rivalries that sent swordsmen roaming Harcourt or the Freeports—and he had not felt the need of weapons before. But he had been a soldier on occasion, and the feel of the hanger's hilt in his hand was oddly comfortable.

With his purchases tied to his saddle, he set off, out of the city.

The snow had settled over the fields outside Southwark, and though the sky was uniformly leaden, the empty expanse and the open country lifted Liam's heart. After the closeness of the Duke's courts and of the city in general, he threw back the hood of his cloak and was pleased to let the cold wind bite at his face.

A certain, undefinable thrill ran through him; the nearest he came to it was a sense of purpose. Finding the man who had robbed him was no earthshaking enterprise, he knew, but it gave him something to do, and he discovered for the first time that he did not like having nothing to do.

It was something he had never had a chance to learn before. Born the only son of a minor Midlands nobleman, he had grown up amid the constant chores and duties of his position—and the battles and rumors of war that swept that turbulent region. He escaped them only briefly, to study in the great city of Torquay—and was then called back urgently, only to see his father killed and his home burned in one of the Midlands' pointless feuds. From that point on he had traveled, never stopping in one place for more than a few months, seeing the world as soldier, clerk, sailor, scholar and merchant captain. His residence in Southwark was due only to the fact that he had been shipwrecked on a voyage out of the Freeports, and the ship that rescued him hailed from the small city. Why he had stayed so long—almost six months—was sometimes a mystery to him, and while he did not want to leave Southwark, he knew now that inactivity was not his natural element.

He reined Diamond in above the cove, the lonely sail of a fishing smack just visible at the extremity of vision. There was a strong breeze up out to sea, and the small boat scudded westward, toward the roadstead at Southwark.

Too strong for him, Liam reflected, noting the power of the wind and the height of the waves. *Hope he makes port.*

The thought sat in his mind for a long moment, and then he formed another, and pushed at it.

I'm home.

The dragon's thought came almost instantly.

I hear you. You are projecting very well.

Liam allowed himself a self-congratulatory smile.

There is a man here to see you. He is waiting on the patio.

He turned his eyes to the beach, but the house cut off his view, and he started Diamond down the path warily.

What is he like?

He wears a long cape, the dragon reported, *and a hood, and he carries a sword. But he is not hiding.*

His own sword was not hung from his saddle properly, but he loosened it in the sheath and laid it across his legs anyway. The trail switchbacked, and it was not until he reached the sand that he saw his visitor, a tall, ominous figure in a long black traveling robe. He was pacing back and forth rapidly as Liam urged his roan across the beach.

At Liam's cough, the stranger whirled, apparently startled, dropping into a fighter's crouch with one hand on the sword at his waist. Liam found his own hilt, but did not draw. It would have been awkward, anyway, and he was glad when the other relaxed. The stranger's speed was disconcerting.

"Pray, sir, are you Liam Rhenford?" The voice was low and polite, but with a wet burble to it, as if the stranger were sick. The dark hood covered his face, and Liam saw that there was a piece of cloth sewn across the neck of the cloak to fully hide the wearer's face.

"I am," he answered, keeping his face calm. He did not like the professionalism of the crouch he had seen, nor the way the other's hands clenched rhythmically at his sides.

"The wizard?"

Something in the way the stranger's voice cracked when he asked the question made Liam cock his head.

"No," he said, carefully. "That's my name, but I'm not a wizard."

"But you have a familiar," the stranger said, and Liam recognized the crack in the man's voice: he wanted a wizard. "And only wizards have familiars, and they said in the town you were."

The wind was strong on the beach, plastering the stranger's thin robes around him. His whole body was quivering, like a spring wound too tightly, and his hands continued to make fists in rhythm. The skin looked slightly scaly. Liam saw, but kept his face clear and his voice even.

"What do you want a wizard for?"

The stranger's hood tipped up, and Liam knew he was being examined. Then, with a ritual slowness, the scaly hands came up and pulled the hood back.

Liam blinked once. Diamond skipped suddenly, and he quieted the horse with a low word and the pressure of his knees.

It might have been a mask, sewn from the imperfectly cured skin of some albino snake. Fine cracks laced the scales around the man's eyes and mouth, larger ones on his neck and brow. His eyes were surprisingly deep, blue wells in the desert landscape of his face. It was not a mask, though, and Liam could even remember the name of the disease.

"Low-root," he whispered. "That's low-root fever, right?"

The mask tightened only a little; the stranger's eyes did not move. "Yes."

"You're from Caernarvon?" Low-root, he had been taught, appeared around that city only, and was named after a plant that grew there whose roots looked like the skin of the stricken.

"Yes."

"Oh, gods," Liam said slowly, eyes widening. "Did you come all the way here for a wizard?"

The sick man shrugged, a jerky motion. "I serve Bellona. When the opportunity came to travel here, I took it. I had heard there was a wizard here who could help me."

"I'm sorry," he said, meaning it. "There was, but he's dead. He died only two months ago. This was his house." He looked away from the ravaged face to Tarquin's house, and understood the crouch and the sword, and the service to Bellona. Sufferers of low-root were notoriously fast; the disease gave them speed and reflexes that were the envy of the healthy. To compensate, the affliction killed them early—and made them look like monsters.

"I see," the stranger said stiffly, shrugging again. "Then I will go."

"Please," Liam blurted, sliding from his saddle and taking a quick step forward, "please, I'm sorry. You must be cold—it's cold here—come inside and have something warm."

The other man only shook his head, a bitter smile cracking his cheeks. "I have waited too long. We are on double watches today."

"Look, I mean it. Something warm. You must be cold."

"I am not cold."

With an insight that chilled his heart, Liam realized that the man was young. It was impossible to tell from the disfigured face, but he was sure the other was no more than eighteen. Too young to accept death so easily. Liam felt a wild urge to do something, anything, for this sick man.

"Something to eat, then. I can fix something quickly. I can't imagine they feed you well in the temple. And it must have been cold. I hope you haven't been waiting long."

He was babbling, and knew it, but he felt the other's disappointment keenly, as if he had failed in some ill-defined responsibility. Tarquin had once told him that people were forever pestering him for spell: spells for love, spells for revenge, everything from small cures to full-blown miracles. Now, Liam realized, they might look to him for those spells—and he would have nothing for them.

"I would have something to eat," the other said.

"Good! Just let me put my horse away. It won't take a moment."

Liam ran Diamond to the shed and sped back, sure the stranger would be gone. He was waiting by the door, however, staring out at the sea with a bleak look. He blocked the entrance for a moment.

"I never thought the sea was so big."

Liam laughed, a little too heartily. "Big? This isn't big. Why, there's land less than eighty leagues away on the other side. The Cauliff's big, and Rushcutters' Bay—not this."

Caernarvon was landlocked, though, a mountain city, and the stranger only nodded gravely.

He waited in the entrance hall while Liam ducked into the kitchen, reappearing a moment later with a typical Southwark pie and some plates. He led the way into the parlor at the front of the house, and set the dish down.

He felt the sick man's eyes on him as he cut out two pieces and laid them on the plates, and the weight of the stare made him hesitate as he handed the stranger one.

"Low-root is not catching," the other said, hesitating himself from taking the plate.

"I know," Liam answered, holding the plate out with a firmer hand. "You're born with it, aren't you?"

The other man nodded once, and took his meal.

He ate with surprising appetite, well more than half the rich pie, laden with fish and vegetables. He spoke sparingly, but Liam learned a little. His name was Scaevola, and though he was born with the fever, his very poor parents had not strangled him, as most did. Not that that was any great kindness, Liam gathered, as life was not easy in Caernarvon, even for the healthy. The rise of Bellona's temple had literally been a godsend for him—they accepted anyone, at the insistence of Bothmer Lowestoft, to whom the goddess had revealed herself. He had learned swordcraft, and though he was only a low acolyte, the temple had treated him well.

When he was done eating, Scaevola stood and bowed, the motion graceful and fluid, with none of the jerkiness that had marked his eating.

"Grace you, Liam Rhenford, for the food. I must go now."

His host could find nothing to say, and settled lamely for: "Double watches, eh?"

"Since the attack on Hierarch Cloten, yes."

Liam walked him to the door, and when Scaevola shyly put out a scaled hand, pleased himself by taking it instantly. It was warm, almost hot, and he felt a heat rising off the acolyte, but he held the grip for long enough, and it was Scaevola who broke it.

"Grace you."

"And you," Liam said, then cleared his throat. "Tarquin left many books here. I could look through them; perhaps there is something there."

A pained grimace rippled across Scaevola's face. "Perhaps. Perhaps not. I doubt it."

"I do, too," Liam admitted, blushing, "but it doesn't hurt to look, does it?"

Scaevola considered this, a furrow running across the scales of his forehead. "Sometimes it does," he said, and before Liam could respond, he slipped out the door.

He was a swift black shadow on the gray sand, and he flew up the path in a smooth run.

It was still early afternoon when Scaevola left, but Liam wasted the rest of the daylight in wandering moodily about the house. He had checked Tarquin's books thoroughly—he was already familiar with most of them—and found nothing about low-root fever that he did not already know.

The visit had depressed him, and Fanuilh kept out of its master's way. It approached him only later, after the sun had set, when he lay on the divan in the library.

Master? it thought. *Did you speak with the Aedile about the robbery?*

"You know I did, Fanuilh," Liam said glumly, "and you know what happened. I'm in no mood for pretending that you can't ransack my head at will tonight."

I do try not to look. But it would be easier if you knew how to block me out.

"Yes, yes, yes," Liam said, dragging himself to a sitting position on the divan and focusing on the dragon. "You're right, of course. We'll practice."

It was a surprisingly successful session. Liam almost caught the hazy outline of the silver cord Fanuilh said bound them, and he managed to project his thoughts to his familiar for almost half an hour.

Later, the dragon sent a thought from deep within a bowl of rice and red beans usually served two oceans away from Taralon.

You have a plan for finding the thief.

"Yes," Liam said. He was massaging his temples. The practice had given him a headache. "I do."

Are you sure that is the best way to find thieves?

"If there is a guild in Southwark, yes. Much the best way."

But as he stretched himself out in the library a few minutes later, he found he could not muster much enthusiasm for the idea he had come up with in Coeccias's office. Scaevola's parting words echoed in his head, and he lost them only when he finally fell asleep.

■ *4* ■

LIAM FELT BETTER about his plan in the morning. The sky was still gray, the waves outside his windows short and choppy, but the depression he had felt after Scaevola's visit had lifted, and he was able to eat his breakfast with something approaching high spirits.

Fanuilh came into the kitchen, talons clicking on the stone floor, and hopped onto the table.

"Good morning," Liam said around a mouthful of bread.

Good morning, master, the dragon replied.

"Breakfast?"

Yes. You will look at pawnshops today?

"Indeed I will." He went to the oven and imagined his familiar's usual breakfast of raw mutton.

And this will help you find thieves?

"I hope so. I'll need your help."

What will I do?

Liam explained. He found he did not mind the dragon's resumption of the pretense of separated minds, and detailing the plan helped him clarify it in his own head.

It seems a circuitous way to find them.

"It is," he admitted, going back to the oven and pulling out a wooden platter heavy with mutton. "But is there really another way? I can't very well go into town and start calling out for thieves." He smiled a little at the idea. "And it should work."

It should, the dragon thought, tearing off a small piece of mutton with its needlelike teeth and swallowing it whole. *But what if it wasn't a thief? What if it was a wizard?*

"If it's a wizard," Liam said with a frown, "we're sunk. But neither you nor Mother Japh thinks there's one in Southwark right now—and if there was, how would I find him? I suppose you can keep your eye out for any flashes of power, but if our hypothetical wizard didn't use any magic to get into the house, then why would he use it afterward? Which means we can only hope it's a thief."

What will you do if you catch him?

"I'm not sure. The big guilds actually forbid stealing from other thieves, and punish offenders quite harshly. But a small one—who knows? If I can convince them I'm a thief, I may be able to buy the things back."

And how will you explain that to Coeccias?

The dragon had finished most of its mutton before Liam answered. "I don't know. I don't think he'll like what I'm proposing."

Then do not tell him.

Liam chuckled. "I may not, at that. Now, tell me, do you think you can do what I asked?"

It raised its head from the last of the mutton and licked the tuft of hair on its chin. *Certainly,* it thought, and Liam imagined a hint of affronted pride. Imagined it, because he had never known the dragon to display any emotion, beyond curiosity—and he was not sure that was an emotion.

"I never doubted it," he told his familiar. "I think we should go."

The riding does you good, Fanuilh thought at Liam. *You do not look so fat.*

At the edge of Southwark, by the worn pair of pillars that were called the city gates, Liam checked his horse and frowned up at the sky. He could barely make out the thin dot against the clouds that was his familiar.

What are you talking about? he projected. *You're the one who is fat.*

That was good.

I mean it, Liam thought. *I am not fat.*

Very good, was the only response; Liam snorted and gave Diamond a thump on the ribs to get him going.

"Fat," he muttered to himself. He had never been fat, and even the two months of plentiful food from Tarquin's magic oven had not put any weight on his thin frame. The muscles in his arms, he had to admit, were not as dense as they once had been, but what did he need muscular arms for?

"Nothing," he said under his breath, but he touched the hilt of his hanger and offered a quick prayer to his Luck, to make sure of it. He personified it that way—his Luck; it was the only god he ever specified in his prayers, and it almost always repaid his faith.

Coeccias had given him the names of two fences and, after he had stabled Diamond at a convenient hostler's, he walked leisurely to the shop of the first. The sun had made the streets clearer, though there was still snow in the gutters and slush in the deeper ruts. He was glad for his thick boots and his warm cloak, and the sword at his side hung comfortably. His pace acquired a little swagger, and he was whistling by the time he came into Auric's Park.

The first pawnshop was in a cramped alley near the smithy where he had bought his weapons. It was wedged between a wineshop and a grungy stall that sold hot sausages and what looked like moldy bread. There was nothing written over the shop, but there was a board with a symbol painted on it: two squarish pieces of wood with jagged edges clearly meant to mesh. A ticket.

Liam kicked some of the snow and slush from his boots and went in. Once his eyes adjusted to the dim light, he took in the crowded shop and its proprietor.

A jumble of goods filled every available inch of space, piles of seabags and faded clothing, furniture broken or merely old, a barrel of rusty swords and spears, a glass case filled with a riot of jewelry. Unguessable shapes hung from the ceiling, one of which Liam tentatively identified as a loom, and one other as a section of ship's railing, complete with belaying pins and dangling rope ends. There were tapestries on the walls, layers and layers of them, of unguessable value. What might have been intricately woven cloth-of-gold peeped from behind a crude thing of wool. Tied to each piece were claim tags, the broken halves of wooden lozenges marked with numbers. A thick layer of dust cast a gray pall over everything—goods, floor, and owner. The last stood behind a stack of three sea chests, approached by a narrow lane through the stacks of pawned items.

The dust seemed thickest on him, and Liam could have sworn there were cobwebs in his hair. He was old and stooped, with an expression of vague bewilderment which only grew vaguer when he recognized his customer's fine clothes.

"Hail, milord," he mumbled, "welcome to my humble shop."

"Good day, my friend. I wonder if I can help you."

The pawnbroker raised his arms helplessly.

"Help *me*, I mean," Liam corrected himself with a smile. "I'm looking for some goods."

The old man looked around his shop, as if noticing the clutter for the first time. "I hope so, milord." He paused, clearly daunted. "What did you wish?"

"Some of this one's things have gone free," Liam said carefully, "and this one wants them back. They're green things, and this one believes they may have been enslaved."

He received only a wide-eyed goggling in response; the pawnbroker shuffled behind his counter of sea chests.

"They're green," Liam repeated, emphasizing the second word.

"Milord?" the old man said, gumming his upper lip and looking absently at a pile of clothes to his right. "I . . . I'm afraid I don't have any green things. There are some passing pretty colors among these, I think." He began to pick through the clothes.

Liam touched the pawnbroker on the arm and gave him a gentle smile. "It's all right, my friend. I'll try somewhere else."

"There were some pretty colors here," the old man said. "I was sure of it. . . ."

He was still poking through the pile when Liam left, breathing deep to get the dust out of his lungs.

Did he say anything, master?

Liam jumped; he had forgotten Fanuilh, and now he scanned the sky, noticing that the dragon was perched on the roof of the sausage stand only when the creature flapped its wings. A quick glance showed him that no one was near; the sausage seller's back was turned.

No, Liam projected. *I think he may be too old. Stay near, though. Follow him if he goes out. And don't let anyone see you!* He was proud of the way he managed to give the last sentence an imperative accent in his head.

Very well, Fanuilh thought back. *You will go to the other fence now?*

Liam nodded. He could feel a prick of pain at his temples; he had projected too much. Risking a wave at Fanuilh, he walked out of the alley, in the direction of the second address Coeccias had given him.

On first viewing it from the deck of a small coastal trader, he had decided that Southwark looked like an amphitheater. From the placid roadstead, the city spread up in a semicircular fan of buildings. The highest seats, though, were the best: the Point, Temples' Court, Northfield and Auric's Park all sat on a high ridge of ground, looking down on the rest. The city square and the homes of the large class who dealt with shipping needs—chandlers, clerks, small shopkeepers, trade agents and factors—were in the middle and steepest part of the amphitheater; while the lowest part held the Warren, as well as the manufactories and warehouses that fronted the harbor.

Liam left Auric's Park, heading down the progressively narrower streets, passing the city square by a wide margin and eventually reaching the blurry high border of the Warren. Shrill, piercing winds shrieked through lanes that were made into tunnels by overbuilt upper stories. More than once his cloak flared about behind him, caught by a mischievous wind and flapping like the wings of a crippled bird.

The snow in the gutters was turning black, and he carefully kicked the filthy slush off his boots outside the second pawnshop. It was on one of the area's wider streets, which led down to the harbor. A sign similar to the first hung over the door, the ticket halves painted white this time.

Inside there was the same clutter of goods, but there was less dust, and the woman who owned it stopped her vigorous sweeping, sizing him up immediately.

"Good day, milord! Have you come for something special?" She reminded him of a fox; her red hair encroached on her face in pointed sideburns, and her long nose twitched as she faked a curtsy.

"Actually, I was. Some of this one's things have gone free, and this one wants them back. They were green. I thought they might have been enslaved." The phrasing was not perfect, he knew, but he wanted to be able to deny the words, if necessary.

The pawnbroker's long nose twitched furiously, and he saw her pupils draw into tiny beads and then expand, along with her smile.

"Green things, milord? I fear me I do not catch you."

She did, though, and he saw it.

"Now I come to think of it, I doubt you would have these things. I'm sorry to bother you."

He offered her a slight bow and she nodded back primly. Her nose twitched once again, as she walked him to the door.

"If there is aught else I can do, milord?"

"No, thank you."

He walked more than twenty feet before he heard her close the door.

There was a corner only a hundred feet farther up the street, with a rain barrel under a low-hanging gutter. The cobbles ran relatively straight; he took up his post by the barrel, and found he could look down on her door easily.

Slipping his cold hands through the slits of his cloak and into his breeches pockets, Liam made a mental note to buy gloves, and began his wait.

The fox, he was sure, would go to ground soon. The old fence in Auric's Park would probably amount to nothing—he was so old, Liam figured, that he probably would not notice the sky dropping on his head, much less the hints scattered in his shop. He had left Fanuilh there for the sake of thoroughness, but he laid his hopes on the fox.

The red-haired pawnbroker did not disappoint him. Liam's feet were beginning to ache from the cold and his back was hurting before she came out, but come out she did, bundled up in a long scarf and a ragged fur. There were more people in the street now, but he had chosen his spot well. The street descended so steeply that he had no trouble picking her head out in the crowd. She was heading down toward the harbor.

Twice he was sure he had lost her—at a corner, blocked by a pair of recalcitrant oxen with plumes of steam rising from their nostrils, and in a cramped lane nearly choked with stalls selling charms and fortunes—but both times her coppery hair gave her away.

It was only a short trip, despite the anxiety he felt each time he lost sight of her, and her final destination disappointed him. She stopped in front of a stall where hot food was sold, and received a heavy pot over the counter from a woman who, judging from her red hair and long nose, might have been the pawnbroker's sister.

Liam stood with his back to the stall, pretending to examine a collection of sailor's scarves and listening to their conversation. They shared a barked laugh about a man named Raker—and that was all. The pawnbroker did not mention his visit, and left the stall with the pot.

Disappointed, Liam trailed along behind the fox, following the smell of stew from her pot. *Rabbit*, he noted. *Of course it would be rabbit.* He did not lose her on the way back, but she only went to her shop. He trudged up the street, glancing sourly at the door as he passed, and resumed his position by the rain barrel.

There had been no guarantee the plan would work immediately, he told himself, or at all, for that matter. She would not necessarily run right out and tell the Guild. He had hoped, however, that she would, guessing that Southwark was small enough that a stranger dropping chant around would be picked up immediately.

The pawnbroker is leaving his shop.

Liam had so far dismissed the old man that Fanuilh's thought came as a surprise.

Where? he projected, ignoring the instant throb in his temples.

He is heading out of Auric's Park.

Follow him. Show me when he stops.

Yes, master.

He had not expected the old man to do anything—but then, he reminded himself, he might only be going out for rabbit stew. Nonetheless, Liam quickly grew impatient with his watch. The red-haired woman did not emerge from her shop, and no one went in. Again the cold was seeping into his boots.

In his mind's eye, he saw the dusty pawnbroker shuffling slowly along, and willed him to hurry.

He is going to the Point, Fanuilh reported at last, but Liam only nodded, forcing himself to concentrate on the woman's door. The Point made a certain amount of sense, he realized, though exactly where the man would end up would certainly be interesting.

He is going into a house, Fanuilh thought.

Show me, Liam projected back.

Are you sure, master? Liam had never enjoyed using Fanuilh's eyes—he found the experience disturbing. But this time he nodded, and closed his eyes quickly. There was a flicker in the darkness, and when he opened his eyes again, he was looking down on an entirely different street, apparently from the roof of a building. The old pawnbroker was just approaching a run-down town house. He checked to the left and right, then opened the door and ducked inside.

If that isn't it, Liam projected, *I don't know what is.* The town house's windows were all shuttered, and its general air of disrepair made it look like a rotten tooth among the healthy, occupied homes to either side.

He closed his eyes—Fanuilh's eyes—and when he opened them, he was looking into the concerned face of a beggar.

"Pray, master, is all well?"

Liam smiled with delight, and dug into his pocket.

"All is perfect, my friend," he said, and set off for the city square, leaving the astounded beggar behind with a handful of coins.

Coeccias was in the barracks when Liam stopped by, though he said he was going out immediately.

"Truth, Rhenford, that Cloten'll be the death of me, if I'm not his first. Now he's given the lie to the Death herself, in front of Laomedon's own fane!"

Liam knew that Laomedon's highest priests had no names of their own, but were referred to simply as Deaths; he had not known, though, that Laomedon's Death in Southwark was female.

"It's a she? The Death is a woman?"

The Aedile waved away the interruption. "To her very face, I say! Can believe it? I've to go there now and calm him, before he tasks the Duke with it." He was wearing a clean black tunic with the Duke's foxes on it, proper for an official visit.

"Calm him? I thought it was a she."

"Not the Death," Coeccias explained, "she took it all in course. Very cool, she is. She did not even deign to answer him, and that liked Cloten not. He vowed that if I do not find the thief soon enough, he'd start looking on his own."

"Can't have people looking for thieves on their own," Liam muttered, but the Aedile caught it, and laughed.

"Truth, not often, Rhenford! But tell me, how goes your search? You'll have conned and caught yours by now, eh?"

Once again, the display of unwarranted confidence made Liam wince. He hastened to correct his friend. "Not at all. I have an idea or two, but very hazy ones. In fact, that's why I came—I need a little information."

"Ask then, but quick. Only the gods know what Cloten'll do next."

"Is there a thieves' guild in Southwark?" If there was no guild, then he had just wasted his morning. It was a question he should have asked the day before, but it had never occurred to him that there would not be one.

Coeccias's head jerked up and he stopped the pacing that had taken him from one end of the long barracks to the other ten times in as many minutes.

"Why ever would you ask? Y'are not thinking of contacting them?"

"No," Liam lied blandly, thinking of his earlier conversation with Fanuilh. If he could buy back his things, he did not want the Aedile to know about it. "But it would give me some help in figuring out how to approach the thing. Guild thieves have different ways than rogues—they spend more time together, for one thing, and they often frequent the same wineshops and taverns."

Coeccias thought for a moment, stroking his beard. "There is," he said at last, and slowly, "but how t'approach them is beyond me. They're a close band, and I have heard they're short with outsiders."

That was no surprise to Liam; all guild thieves were short with outsiders. "Do you know anything else?"

The look Coeccias gave him was composed equally of uncertainty over telling him more and curiosity at what he already knew. In the end, he covered both, and added a warning. "Here's all: they name their princeps—that's how they style the guild leader—they name him the

Werewolf. I know not if it's the man's name or a general title. They are a close group, all said, and lay low, unlike one of your big-city guilds. I catch the individual thief from time to time, but have never tied them to the whole. And I don't try, Rhenford. However much of a hound y'are, they're wolves. The princeps's name says it."

Liam nodded, accepting the information and the warning. "I'll be careful," he promised.

"As you were with Ancus Marcius and's toughs, eh?" Ancus Marcius was a merchant Liam had wrongly suspected of murdering Tarquin; the suspicion had cost him a beating from the man's bodyguards.

"More so. Much more so."

Coeccias smiled briefly at the memory, then heaved a sigh, recalled to his duty. "Now I needs must go. Waiting will not like Cloten in the least."

The two men crossed the square together. The normal crowds were back: hawkers and street performers, customers and beggars. The snow was gone, trampled beneath hundreds of feet, leaving only a dark, wet sheen on the cobbles. They parted at the far corner, Liam heading north to the stables where he had left Diamond, Coeccias heading east for Temple Street.

Once on his horse, clattering toward the city gate, Liam remembered Fanuilh. He formed the dragon's name in his head and projected carefully, ready to stop at the first hint of a headache. To his relief—and pleasure—there was none, and the dragon responded immediately.

Yes, master?

Return to the house. I'm finished in the city. Until tonight.

Yes, master.

No stab of pain in his temples yet; he projected again.

I'm getting better at this.

Yes, master. I will see you at the house, and we can practice more.

Liam nodded happily to himself and spurred diamond to a trot. He was getting better at communicating with his familiar, and he had a plan.

Once beyond the pillars at Southwark's eastern edge, he urged the roan into a flat-out gallop.

Scaevola was waiting on the patio; Liam saw him from the path, and eased back the wild grin etched on his face by his cold gallop to a smile of greeting. In the back of his head, though, he scolded himself. The sick man had been right; there was nothing in Tarquin's books to help him.

"Hail, Liam Rhenford," Scaevola said, his disfigured face expressionless.

"Hello," Liam replied, dismounting and putting out his hand. He was happy—and a little ashamed—to see that the other man was wearing gloves. "I'm afraid I do not have anything for you. There was nothing in the library."

Scaevola grasped his hand firmly, waving away the apology with his other. "I expected nothing," he said, and a shy smile cracked the scales on his cheeks. "There never has been anything."

Liam nodded, unsure what to say. He pitied the younger man, but did not think it right to express his sympathy. After an awkward pause, Scaevola pointed to the bundle at his feet.

"I saw—yesterday, you were wearing a sword—I thought . . . All of the other acolytes at the temple are exhausted, and there has been no practice. . . ."

He flushed, the blood lining the edges of scales; the whites of his eyes stood out brightly. Kneeling fluidly, he unwrapped the bundle and stood, holding two wooden practice swords.

"You want to spar?"

"I thought, perhaps . . ." Scaevola let the sentence trail away, put off by Liam's unfeigned astonishment.

There was another heavy pause, which Liam struggled to fill.

"I don't—I'm not much of a swordsman, I'm afraid."

"Of course," Scaevola blurted, kneeling again to put the practice swords away. "I understand."

"No," Liam said quickly, "don't put them away. I'll go a round with you. It's just that I really am not much of a swordsman. Just let me put Diamond away."

He led the horse to the shed behind the house, leaving the acolyte on the patio, kneeling by his bundle. He was being honest when he said he was not good with a sword; while he had often been a soldier, his experience in combat was small, and he had never developed much skill. Most soldiers did not, he knew. War was more a matter of having enough men in the right place at the right time, of feeding armies and keeping them paid and healthy, than of the individual warrior's prowess. The battles he had been in were all crude things, where victory came from brute force and sheer numbers, not the finesse of single swordsmen. Only a very few experts—some warrior monks, members of the Society of Heralds, and, of course, devotees of war gods—ever became masters of swordsmanship. The average soldier was more concerned with being fed and keeping his footing on a field made slippery with blood.

So when he returned to the patio, he repeated his warning, even as he picked up a practice sword and made a few tentative cuts in the air.

"As I said, I'm not very good."

"No matter," Scaevola said, taking the other sword. "You'll want to remove your cloak."

The cold bit through his tunic, but he brought his sword up and saluted.

They fought four brief matches—not as brief as they might have been, but Liam saw after the first few passes that Scaevola was holding back. Even so, he was amazed at the other's speed. The wooden sword flickered practically unseen, dodging past his rather feeble guard, whispering around his ears or flicking at his legs. He jumped and twisted as well as he could, but Scaevola was everywhere, gracefully pushing him around the patio as if he were a child. He never came off the defensive, desperately putting up his blade to try to ward off Scaevola's lightning blows. Soon—far too soon, he thought—he had no thought but for the clatter of sword on sword and the next pointless attempt to parry. At the end of the fourth match, he breathlessly called a halt.

"Enough," he said, dropping the sword. He had forgotten the cold; sweat ran down his face and soaked his tunic, but the other man looked unruffled, his breath coming easily. He looked at Liam with concern.

"I'm sorry. Are you not well?"

"No," Liam wheezed, "just out of practice."

Fat. The echo of Fanuilh's words rang in his head, a counterpoint to the pounding of blood. He was not fat, he insisted to himself, only out of practice.

He caught his breath. "It's too cold. Let's go inside."

Scaevola bundled up the swords and followed him into the house.

Liam was exhausted; he slumped at the kitchen table, wiping sweat from his face and breathing hoarsely. "Are you hungry? There's something in the oven." He managed to focus for a moment, imagining a pie.

The sick man hesitated, looking at him with something close to pity. Liam shook himself and straightened in his chair.

I can't be that *tired,* he thought. "Go ahead," he said aloud. "And get me a glass from that jug, would you?"

Scaevola hastened to pour a cup of wine from the jug by the oven, and placed it solicitously in front of Liam, then retrieved the pie. He sat opposite his tired host, picking uncomfortably at the food.

"I am sorry, Liam Rhenford," he said at last. "I should not have asked you to spar."

Liam shook his head. Three greedy swallows of wine had given him a little strength, and his hands had stopped shaking. "I am out of practice, that's all. I have not worn a sword in some time. And when I did wear one," he added, "that was really all I did. Wear it. I can count on the fingers of one hand the number of times I have drawn a sword."

Neither was true: he had drawn more times than he could count—he had simply never gotten good at it. But the excuses seemed to make Scaevola more comfortable, and he began eating with a will.

After a few minutes, when he was completely sure of himself—that his hands would not shake, or his breath whistle in his throat—he put his thoughts to the man across the table. The symptoms of the fever did not bother him much, though he had to admit that they were awful. Instead of revulsion, he felt curiosity at the strange mix of benefits and disadvantages conferred by the disease. Scaevola was practically a monster to look at, but without a doubt he was the fastest swordsman Liam had ever seen.

The sick man felt his scrutiny and looked up from his pie expectantly.

"Are you the best in the temple?"

"Yes," Scaevola admitted, without a trace of modesty—a simple fact. "I teach the others. Though now, with the double watches and all the excitement, there is not much time for practice."

"Ah," Liam said, "the excitement. The robbery. I understand Hierarch Cloten is greatly . . . agitated by it."

Scaevola rolled his eyes, the leathery scales around them not moving at all. "Agitated is no word for it. He has accused everyone of the crime. I cannot imagine why he would make trouble with our dear goddess's father, but he does."

"Father? Bellona's father?"

The acolyte put his spoon down. "Some of us believe," he said thoughtfully, "that Strife is Bellona's father, his get by . . . well, we differ on Her mother. It is a cause of discord in the temple. Alastor, the Keeper of Arms, says Uris is her mother, though I am not sure of that. Cloten says she has no mother or father. That she merely is." His tone indicated what he thought of that.

"I had no idea."

"Her worship is but young," Scaevola explained. "Many details are to be determined, though most are coming to believe Her divine parenthood."

"But Cloten does not?"

"No. He has arguments, sometimes heated, with Alastor, and I have heard that he has ignored certain instructions from Caernarvon. But he is Grand Hierarch Lowestoft's nephew, and cannot be naysayed."

Liam listened carefully. Temple politics had never caught his interest much, the gods of the Midlands being old, well-established and placid, but the information might be of some use to Coeccias in his investigation. And there was something he was interested in himself.

"Tell me about the gryphon."

"A sacrifice," Scaevola said diffidently. "Hierarch Cloten says we will offer it up when we open the temple officially."

"Where did you get it?"

"We caught it on our way here from Caernarvon. There was a fight, just as we were coming out of the mountains. Some brigands." His eyes lit up at the memory, and for a moment he was silent, as if reliving it. "When it was over, and we were dedicating the combat to Bellona, we found it at the edge of the field, among the dead. It was strange, though, it was scavenging, only looking at the fallen, and it made no effort to flee."

Liam frowned; the gryphons he had seen and read about were fierce fighters, jealous of their freedom.

"We chained it easily," Scaevola went on, "and it has not given us any trouble since."

"How do you feed it?"

"We do not," Scaevola said, avoiding Liam's eyes. "On our way here we tried to, but it refused all we supplied. Keeper of Arms Alastor would bring it something different every day, but it would have none of it. By the time we got here, Hierarch Cloten forbade him to try anymore."

"Let me guess," Liam half joked, "Alastor didn't listen, so Cloten hung it from the ceiling so he couldn't get at it."

Scaevola did not share the joke. "There was a great argument over that. Those who built the temple before us had hung something from the dome. I do not know what it was—Keeper of Arms Alastor says a large image of their god—but the chain was there when we moved in. Hierarch Cloten decided it immediately. Many of us do not like the idea."

"Really," Liam said, for lack of anything else. Bellona's worshipers seemed to have quite a few points of contention.

They were quiet, brooding for a while. Finally, Scaevola pushed away his plate and stood up.

"I must return now. Thank you for the meal—and the practice."

"Not at all," Liam replied. "I only wish I could have been more of a match for you." He got up and led the way to the door.

"You are untrained, that is all. You could be quite a warrior if you tried."

Liam laughed at the comment. "I don't think so."

They shook hands, and once again Liam watched the acolyte run across the beach and up the path.

He stretched leisurely and went back to the kitchen, where a thought at the oven soon produced a bucket of warm water. He stripped and washed the dried sweat from his body, thinking about what he had learned.

At first glance the theological differences among Bellona's followers did not seem like much, but as he thought about it he saw a potential hint or two. If Cloten was Bothmer Lowestoft's nephew, he would be doubly interested in protecting the notes on the Lowestoft mines, particularly if his orthodoxy was in question. That might explain his extreme reaction to the attempted robbery, as well as his wild accusations of Guiderius.

A string of questions gradually occurred to him, things he would ask of Cloten, of the Keeper of Arms, Alastor, of Guiderius and the lower followers of Bellona.

As he put on a clean tunic and breeches, he stopped the ideas.

"Tell Coeccias," he muttered to himself. "You've got your own thief to catch." He turned his thoughts to his own search and what little headway he had made.

The abandoned house in the Point was a good starting place, and the plan he had made the day before still seemed the best way to approach it. He would take care of that later that evening, after his dinner with the Aedile. But apart from that, he had done little. If his thief were not a thief at all, but a wizard, he still had no way of proceeding.

How do you find a wizard? he wondered. Fanuilh could find one, if he performed a magical act, and Mother Japh had assured him that if there was one in Southwark, word would spread quickly. But those were hardly sufficient; he needed a more concrete way.

With a heavy sigh, he went into the library and began picking books off the shelves.

■ 5 ■

AN HOUR LATER, with fifteen tomes on magic piled at his feet, Liam was no further along toward a method for finding wizards than when he had begun. The books dealt with the details of working magic or the theories behind magic or reports of magics that had worked and some that had rather spectacularly *not* worked, but never with the people who worked, theorized or reported. There were no biographies of wizards or descriptions of their habits, no quick and easy list of characteristics to look for, and after leafing through the last book that even vaguely mentioned wizardry, Liam set it down on a teetering stack, leaned back and closed his eyes.

He did not sleep, though; only slipped into a pleasant torpor, tired from the sparring with Scaevola and an hour of reviewing books he did not understand.

Some wizard I am, Liam thought, a frown settling onto his face. *I don't even know half the words.* He knew he was better educated than most people, and had some skill with languages, but the jargon of magic had often proved far beyond him.

With a sour grunt he rolled over, wincing at a bruise from Scaevola's wooden sword, and began reviewing his plans for the evening. He was to meet Coeccias for dinner, and after that he would be free to follow up on the house the old pawnbroker had visited. The prospect excited him, not least because it was his only idea. If it did not lead to his thief, then he would be forced to start over, and he guessed that would mean giving up.

The problem was that he knew too little. When he had looked for

Tarquin's murderer, Fanuilh had been able to give him names and, to a certain extent, motives, concrete starting points. With this robbery, he had only questions: why had the thief taken only the rug, the wand and the book? A proper thief would have taken everything that was not nailed down, even if he had been commissioned to take only those three items. And what if it hadn't been a thief? The breaching of the house's magical wards suggested a wizard, but both Fanuilh and Mother Japh were convinced there were none in Southwark.

Except me, he noted, rolling over with another grunt. There were simply too many questions and only one place he could imagine to find answers.

Liam forced himself to sit up and open his eyes. A weariness was settling over his limbs, and he stretched to be rid of it. *No sense walking into the local guild sleepy,* he told himself, and went to the kitchen to splash cold water on his face. Coeccias had made the thieves sound extremely dangerous, and he wondered for a moment whether he ought to bring his sword.

Bring it, came Fanuilh's thought, a heavy imperative in his head.

"They might take that the wrong way," Liam said out loud.

Project, the dragon ordered.

He sighed heavily, but found that it was not as difficult as before. *They might take offense if I go armed.*

Bring the sword.

The dirk, he suggested. *Just the dirk.*

I will come, too.

"Oh no," Liam said, leaving the kitchen and walking toward the workroom. "They'll definitely take you the wrong way." Fanuilh lay in its basket, curled up nose to tail, and offered him a brief glance. "They'll think I'm a wizard."

And if they do?

"Thieves aren't terribly fond of wizards, and these don't sound like the kind you want angry at you. The big-city guilds have strict rules about violence, but from what Coeccias says, the southerners may have their own ideas."

Then I will hide nearby—on the roof or in the street.

Liam considered the suggestion. "All right. That would make sense. But you're not to interfere, unless I'm clearly in danger. Understand?"

Yes, master. Will you practice now?

"I don't think so," he said, looking out the window at the rear of the workroom. The narrow space between the back of the villa and the cliffs was already filled with dark shadows. "I think it's time for me to meet Coeccias."

They had chosen to meet at the White Grape, a small inn on the border of the Point and the middle section of Southwark, not far from the city square. It had no stables, and Liam was forced to find a hostler some distance away, but the walk to the inn and the ride into the city, not to mention his earlier exercise, only served to sharpen his appetite. Coeccias was not there when he arrived; he chose a table and drank a beer, patting his rumbling stomach every few moments.

The serving girls knew the two of them, and when Coeccias finally threw open the door and stumped in, one of them jerked her thumb at where Liam sat. The Aedile threaded his way through the crowded tables.

"You're late," Liam noted, a little sharply. "I ordered two of their sea pies."

"Truth, I'm lucky to get away at all. I needs must've done something very ill, to be saddled with that Cloten, but for my life I know not what." He fumbled off his padded wool coat and dropped heavily into his seat. A serving girl brought him a mug before he could ask, and he drank half of it in one gulp. "Rhenford," he went on, wiping foam from his beard, "that's the best of a bad day."

"So Cloten is still making trouble for you?"

"Aye. He has set a day, by which if I don't have his thief in hand, he'll—I quote here—'see to the matter himself.' See to the matter himself! He'll to war, he means, and lay siege to both Strife and Laomedon, the fool."

"I take it you've made no progress, then?"

"None," the Aedile admitted with a rueful grin. "Not the least. And how to? Cloten swears it was a dozen men, if not more, all armed and armored, but his guards say they heard nothing."

"You've spoken to them all?"

"Aye, though Cloten seemed to think that a waste of time. 'Why do you ask them?' he says. 'I was there. I was the one who was attacked. Ask me, ask me. I've told you all you need to know.'" The Aedile's impression of the Hierarch made him sound like an angry fishwife, and Liam smiled. "It's not so funny, I warrant, when he's in your face. And he spits when he talks, as well." He swiped a large hand across his beard, and then laughed. "I spoke to the guards, though, in the end, and only one heard aught. A queer fellow, all muffled and jerky, as if he crawled with fleas, but said he'd heard something like spurs in the street outside."

"Muffled? Hooded, you mean?" Coeccias nodded. "I think I've met him, too. His name is Scaevola, and he has low-root fever."

"Low-root? The Caernarvon plague?" The Aedile groaned and covered his eyes with his hands. "Bad enough they send me Cloten, but the plague as well!"

"It's not catching, you know. You're born with it."

Coeccias slowly drew his hands away from his eyes. "Y'are? Y'are sure?"

"Yes. No one's ever caught low-root fever, that I know of."

"Hm. Well, if you say it, I'll warrant it, but it likes me not, all the same. Bellona's brought more trouble to Southwark than I'd like, goddess though She is."

Liam studied the worried expression on his friend's face for a moment, then spoke hesitantly. "I think she may have brought something else." He described Scaevola's two visits to his house, and the theological dispute about Bellona's parentage. "He didn't seem to think it was terribly important, more of a minor disagreement, but if Cloten is arguing with his second in command, and ignoring orders from the main temple in Caernarvon . . ."

"It might go far to explaining his strong reaction," Coeccias mused, picking up the thread of Liam's thoughts. "But what does it tell us about the attempted robbery? Precious little, as I see it."

"Well," Liam answered slowly, "this is only a thought, but what if your thief wasn't after the treasury? That is, what if he wasn't a thief at all?"

Coeccias's mug paused halfway to his mouth, and his jaw worked soundlessly for a second. Then he put his mug down softly. "I take it," he said carefully, "that you're suggesting an assassin."

Liam shrugged. "Not a real assassin, in the sense of money for a life taken. But a disaffected believer, someone who disagrees with Cloten, or thinks he's promoting blasphemy. After all, he did say it was a group of men, not just one thief. And you say Scaevola heard spurs in the street."

"Aye, aye," the Aedile murmured, tugging now at his beard, his food forgotten. "But then, why in the street? Why not in the temple? Bellona has no real worshipers in Southwark yet. All Her acolytes are in the temple—so why the street, outside? And I have my doubts about cloten's 'armed band.' More likely one or two, given the time it took them to get away before his own guards arrived. A dozen couldn't escape in a minute."

"All right, but would a thief go armed? Most don't. And they certainly don't wear spurs. Though you are right about the noise being outside. It doesn't make any sense."

The same thought occurred to both men at the same time; it made Coeccias rock back in his seat, while Liam whistled.

"Guiderius," the Aedile suggested.

"Or the Death."

"It could be, though more likely Guiderius. Bellona threats Strife more than Laomedon."

"For that matter, She threatens every temple on the street, given that treasury. I must say, though, that I can't see anyone trying murder over moneylending."

Coeccias snorted. "Y'are new in Southwark, Rhenford. It's been done. But you've the right of it—most likely Strife or Laomedon." He heaved a deep sigh. "Which means now I needs must start a whole new line of questions, and very trickish ones at that. Truth, trickish isn't in it. 'Pardon, Keeper of Arms Alastor, but do you disagree with Hierarch Cloten enough to take him off?' "

"It does seem a little complicated," Liam admitted.

"Complicated? Like crossing a room full of black cats under a new moon without a candle, Rhenford. 'Pardon, Hierarch Guiderius, but did you try to kill Hierarch Cloten, for that his goddess also practices war?' A little complicated!"

"Don't forget that some of Her acolytes think she's Strife's daughter. I don't know how Guiderius would feel about that."

Coeccias sipped at his beer, frowning miserably. "Truth, Rhenford, this goes from bad to worst. One thief was bad enough, given Cloten . . . but now you make a religious war of it!"

"I didn't make a war of it! Somebody else did; I'm just giving you ideas."

"In future," Coeccias grumbled unhappily, "keep them to yourself."

It was strange, Liam reflected in the lull that followed, how much they both disliked asking questions. Both were good at formulating questions, and knew it—though Liam thought the Aedile placed entirely too much faith in him on that score, as on many others—but they hated the process of asking. Perhaps, he decided, the problem was not the questions, but that the answers were all too often the ones they did not want to hear.

Coeccias had resumed his interrupted meal. When he shoved his empty plate away he settled back in his chair and gave Liam a long stare.

"So. Now that y'have muddied the search for my thief, pray tell me about yours. In hopes that I can make it difficult, see you."

They both smiled a little. "It's not good," Liam said. "I checked on those two fences, and neither had any idea what I was talking about. And I've looked through all of Tarquin's books, but there was nothing there about how to find a wizard."

"Mother Japh said she'd told you there were no wizards in Southwark."

"Yes, she did, but she might have been wrong. And if there are no wizards, how would a thief get the spells necessary to break the wards on the house?"

"She also said she showed you her morgue."

Liam nodded, and then realized what he had admitted. Coeccias thought he was squeamish around the dead. "Yes," he said noncomittally, and felt the color rising to his face. "It was helpful."

"She said," the Aedile went on, a little smile playing on his lips, "that you warranted her one of the corses had probably been a clerk, for that you felt his hands."

Liam stammered out that he had, his face burning red. He had not thought that Mother Japh would talk to Coeccias, nor that he would ever be caught in his lie. It had merely been something about which he felt vaguely guilty, a small secret that he hid from his friend for the sake of convenience. Now Coeccias's smile was growing.

"I've a theory, Rhenford, and I would that you'd help me with it. Do you recall asking me about thieftakers? Was that the word? Thieftakers?"

"Yes," he answered, wondering where Coeccias was going. He felt like blurting out the truth—that he had seen a thousand corpses, been in a dozen battles, seen and heard and been things the Aedile would never believe—but the confident expression on his friend's face held him back.

"Y'have always presented yourself a scholar, Rhenford, but I think not. Know you what I think?" Liam shook his head and waited. Coeccias smiled with satisfaction, and leveled a finger across the table as he pronounced: "I think you were one of these thieftakers."

Liam laughed harder than he had for months. He liked the Aedile, and had more respect for his ability as an investigator than the man did himself, but he could not imagine a more outlandish conclusion. A thief, yes, and a spy once or twice, but a thieftaker? His laughter annoyed Coeccias.

"It fits, does it not? With your nose for a villain, and what you know of thieves? Come, tell me how a man would know such things if he weren't one of your thieftakers?"

"It could be," Liam managed, wiping tears from his eyes, "and I admit that it would seem to make sense. But I can assure you that I wasn't."

"Then how do you know all the things you do?" his friend demanded.

"By listening," Liam explained, "and asking questions. Sooner or later, if you listen enough and ask enough questions, you learn a little about everything. For instance, from listening to you I know a great deal about being the Duke's man in Southwark, but that doesn't make me the Aedile, does it?"

Coeccias grudgingly admitted that this was true, and for just a moment Liam worried that his friend was truly angry with him. Then he realized that the Aedile's frustration came from disappointment: he had hoped that Liam was a thieftaker, because it would explain him. Most people had a rightful place and position in Taralon—sailor or merchant, soldier or priest, what it was did not matter—and that place made it clear who they were. Liam, on the other hand, had no place. He lived in a wizard's house and had a wizard's familiar, but he was not a wizard; he called himself a scholar, but he neither wrote books nor took pupils; he hunted thieves, but was neither thieftaker nor Guard. He defied understanding to a certain extent. It was a sobering thought.

"In any case, if I were a thieftaker," he said, "I'd be a rather poor one. It's already two days, and I haven't found my man."

"But y'have an idea, I warrant." The Aedile seemed resigned to the fact that his guess at Liam's past was a failure, but his old faith in Liam's skill was still showing in full force. "What will you next?"

"I'm not sure. I have to give up the idea of wizards for a bit, and follow up on thieves. The fences weren't much help, but I think I may know a way to get in touch with some thieves."

With a wave of his hand, Coeccias indicated that this was as much as he had expected. "In course, but what then? Are these thieves yours, or will they only know yours?"

"Again, I'm not sure," Liam said, though he was. If the Southwark Guild was as vicious as Coeccias claimed, they would not stand for an unlicensed thief in the city, which meant they would have to know his thief. The question was, what would happen from there? "I'll have to see. And as far as what I do then, I think that will be up to you," he hedged.

"How so?"

"It may happen that these thieves won't tell me who my thief is, but they may take him a message."

"Ah, I see you now. The message will say you'd be willing to buy back your goods." Sometimes Coeccias surprised him with the quickness of his perceptions.

"Well, yes, it would—if that does not bother you."

"Bother me? Why should it?" The Aedile seemed genuinely puzzled, and Liam breathed a mental sigh of relief.

"I thought you might object to my dealing with them."

"I have no objections. If it's the only way to recover your goods, then so be it. Look you," he said seriously, leaning over the table and ticking off his points on blunt fingers, "I tell you this in confidence, Rhenford, though I guess you already know it. There are things in Southwark I can do. I can patrol the streets, and prevent or sound out the grossest murders. I can break up riots and bar brawls. I can see that the taverns on the waterfront do not vend paint for wine and poison the tars. I can keep tabs on the brothels and close the theaters and bear-baiters. I can keep the scales in the markets honest and, as a rule, I can keep the number of cutpurses down to a few. But there is much I cannot do. I cannot question the great merchants or the gentry, I cannot interfere with the temples, and—most to the point—I cannot break the Guild. I have not men nor time, nor inclination."

It was a long speech for Coeccias, and he sat back when he was done, vaguely embarrassed at having made it. Liam nodded, though; he had known or guessed at most of it.

"Then that is what I'll try to do—buy them back."

"Fair as fair can be. Though mind you, if y'have the chance to clap your thief, do it. It'd like me to take in a housebreaker. Who knows where he'd lead me?"

They finished their beers, each wondering where it would.

By the time they left the White Grape, a cold, clear night had covered Southwark with a dark sky, punctuated only by the hard, brilliant points the stars made, and their breath trailed away in white plumes. They parted outside the door of the inn, Coeccias back to the barracks in the city square and Liam ostensibly for the hostler where his horse was stabled.

He had not been honest with the Aedile when he told him he would be going back to the beach. His intention was to visit the abandoned house on the Point, but he judged it too early, and he wanted a little time to go over the finer details of his plan.

After walking a few blocks, he discovered that these were not many, and that the finest point he had to go over was whether he would carry out the plan at all. If Southwark's Guild was as dangerous as Coeccias said, it might prove foolish. They might not be bound by the rules that held in other guilds—they might not be bound by any rules at all. And they might look askance at an uninvited visitor. An unpleasant image occurred to him: his own body laid out in Mother Japh's morgue, one of her preservation bags between his feet and a little blue flame dancing over his mouth.

Unless my soul goes wandering off, and there is no flame, he thought, and pulled his cloak closer. Could his soul go wandering off? Part of it rested with Fanuilh, he knew. Would that keep it in place? He could have asked the little dragon, but refrained. He did not really want to know.

Instead, he wandered through the city, out of the middle district, north of the square and into the artisans' districts. The streets were dark, illuminated only occasionally by candlelight from windows and irregularly placed torches on the walls; he imagined himself a shadow, gliding through the city outside the warm pockets of life. The feeling disturbed him even more than his earlier image of Mother Japh's morgue, and he began to cast about for something to occupy his time.

His feet took him of their own accord to the Uncommon Player, but he stopped at the door of the rowdy tavern. The Player was his favorite in the city, a meeting place for minstrels, actors, the more adventurous artisans and a general crowd of interesting types that never failed to entertain him. He chose, however, not to go in that night; he wanted his head clear for his work later on, and the Player had a rule about the minimum number of drinks ordered.

As he stood at the door wondering what to do, he saw a bright pool of light from around a distant corner, where the entrance of the Golden Orb was. It was Southwark's only theater; he had been introduced to both the Orb and the Player while looking for Tarquin's murderer. There should have been no lights there; by the Duke's law, it had been closed since the beginning of winter, as a precaution against the spread of disease.

Hoping for something of interest, Liam left the light and noise of the Player behind and turned the corner. The gold-painted wooden globe that usually hung over the theater's doors was gone, replaced by a series of boards painted with various fantastic animals; the cheap smoky links beneath each tended more to obscure than reveal the paintings, but Liam recognized a lion and a giant boar. The others he gave up on.

A forlorn-looking boy hopped from foot to foot by the one open door, clutching a sheaf of pamphlets. His cheeks were bright red with cold; a ragged scarf hung around his neck and trailed down to his knees.

"What's inside, boy?" Liam asked, looking at the painted signs.

"Animals," the boy said sarcastically, indicating the boards. "Pictures of 'em, aren't there?"

"I thought the theater was closed."

The boy looked at the open door, frowned in concentration for a moment, then looked up at Liam with a sneer. "Doesn't seem that way now, does it? Seems passing open to me."

"Right. How much to go in?"

"Ask the keeper," the boy said, jerking a thumb at the open door and resuming his hopping.

Smiling, Liam entered the Golden Orb, and behind him he heard the boy mumble at the empty street: "Come see the animals. Come see the menagerie. Come see the blasted animals, you idiots."

The lobby was empty, so he opened one of the doors to the groundlings' area and poked his head in.

"Hello?" he called.

A voice answered him from the far side of the theater: "Get back out there and get me some customers, you little bastard!"

Liam cleared his throat. "I am a customer."

The Orb was octagon shaped, with galleries and private boxes on seven sides and the stage on the eighth, and longer side; from the roof, high above where the groundlings stood, hung an enormous chandelier. Normally it held hundreds of candles, but only a dozen or so now flickered, so that Liam could only hear and not see the voice's owner jump up, trip over something and then come running over to the doors.

"Your pardon," the woman said breathlessly, stopping with a rushed curtsy. "I thought you were that wretched boy, come to complain of the cold. You're here to see the menagerie!"

"Yes," Liam said, smiling. The woman wore a strange mix of clothes: a long skirt so broad and shapeless that it had to hide a few more skirts underneath it, a man's boiled leather vest with metal studs on it and a hawking glove on one hand. Her steel gray hair was pulled back tightly from her pocked face, which was covered with vividly colored, inexpertly applied makeup. In her ungloved hand she held the skinned carcass of a rabbit.

"Well, first is first, sir," she said cheerily, "and I needs must ask you th'entrance, which is a silver crown or its equal—though not its better, for I've no change—and well worth it, you'll see, I'm sure."

Liam produced the coin, but the woman, realizing her hands were full, laughed. "Oh, you'll have to hold it for now, sir, 'til I'm rid of this coney. Now just do me the favor of lighting one of those lanterns, and I'll show you the greatest menagerie to grace Southwark since . . . well, since last I was here with it, and it's better now by far!"

There were two rusty lanterns by the door, and flint and tinder, and when he had one lit, the woman led him across the theater floor, talking all the while.

"I'm wont to be closed now, sir, you see, but with the snow and the cold, the trade is down, and I need to be here at all hours, on the off chance of someone like yourself—mind that cage"—of which there were several, large and small, scattered across the groundlings' area, all covered with patched tarpaulins of sailcloth—"seeing the wisdom and stopping in." She led him up to the stage, climbing nimbly with her skirts bunched up in the hawking glove. He followed, and they stopped in front of the largest cage, where a bucket with the bloody rabbit skin inside stood.

"I'll show you this last," the woman went on. "I shouldn't show it first, for that it's the main attraction of the menagerie, and the true claim to greatness. But I've this coney, and it to be fed, and it must be fresh or it'll not eat. So." With a deft twist of her wrist, the woman flipped up the edge of the tarp and tossed the meat inside. A slow rustling issued inside the cage, and as the sound of powerful jaws crunching through bone filled the area, the woman smiled happily.

"Now," she said, taking off the hawking glove and proffering her clean hand, "we can be introduced. I'm Madame Rhunrath, proprietor and keeper of Taralon's Greatest Menagerie."

Liam started to take her hand, then, realizing she was holding it palm up, pulled a silver crown from his pocket and handed it over. She bit it quickly and smiled again. "No offense meant, sir, none at all. Mere precaution."

"None taken, I assure you."

"Good! Then we'll see Taralon's Greatest Menagerie!"

It did not take long to see the whole thing. Madame Rhunrath led him from cage to cage, pulling off the tarps and displaying her animals, most of which were not pleased with the idea. She had three wolves, a bear cub that could balance a ball on its nose, a very large and very sleepy snake, a mountain goat with enormous, doubled-curved horns, four long-tailed monkeys that wore matching vests and could juggle, and three large hawks. It was not an impressive collection, but Liam enjoyed the woman's patter; once she realized that he knew something about animals, she cut out most of the obvious fictions and displayed a remarkable knowledge of the habits and characteristics of her stock.

"The monkeys, now, poor things," she said, "are too cold. They're from the distant jungles, south of the Freeports, and the weather here likes them not. In the summer, they chatter and juggle like little demons—I taught them myself—but just now they're rather useless."

There was a cage of sparrows near the rack on which the hooded hawks stood perched. "But I'll warrant an educated gentleman like yourself has seen hawks hunt, eh? I let a sparrow and one hawk loose at a time, and it gives the city folk no end of a thrill to see the hunt . . . but I imagine you wouldn't care for it."

"I've hawked," Liam said politely, "though I can imagine it must be interesting to see it in a building. Still, no need to waste a sparrow for just me."

Madame Rhunrath breathed an open sigh of relief. "Sparrows are expensive."

There was only the cage on the stage left, but she mentioned it somewhat diffidently. "I'm afraid you'll think it rather poor now, knowing all you know of animals, but there it is—it's the best I've got." She led the way up to the stage and pulled back the tarp. "Just a lion, I'm afraid."

Though not natural to Taralon, the lion had taken on a certain mythical status in the kingdom; they featured regularly in heraldic devices and in stories, and for the average Taralonian, seeing a live one would be a once-in-a-lifetime event. For Liam, who had traveled more than most and seen a number of the creatures, it was still a pleasure. He had seen enough to know that Madame Rhunrath's was a fine specimen, in good condition, and he told her so.

"I take good care of him," she said proudly as the lion stalked back and forth in its cage, lashing its tail against the bars. "A big cage, plenty of fresh meat. He's the best in Taralon, even better than the ones in Torquay. If I could get but one other passing attraction, I could leave the Southern Tier and head north."

"What sort?"

"Sorry?"

"What kind of animal? What would you prefer?"

Madame Rhunrath shrugged, as if the possibility were remote. "Oh, a unicorn, or a salamander—though keeping the fires high would be a problem, so no, no salamander—and manticores are too dangerous, with their spikes. Wyrms, as well. A sphinx would pass. I heard tell once of a menagerie that had a demon, but it got loose one night and ate them all. In the south, they say, there are animals bigger than houses with noses like tails that can do tricks. One of those would be nice."

"Elephants," Liam said. "They're called elephants."

The menagerie keeper's jaw dropped. "Have you seen them?"

Liam was not paying attention, though. He was watching the lion pad around its cage, a half-snarl on its face. "They have a gryphon in Bellona's temple."

"A gryphon," Madame Rhunrath sighed. "What I wouldn't give for a gryphon. That'd bring them in."

Thinking of the gryphon reminded Liam of his business, and he turned from the cage. "Thank you, madame. It was well worth the crown."

She walked him to the door, apologizing for her meager display and asking him to tell all his friends to come. "None of those who know as much as you do about animals; it's sure to disappoint. But those who're ignorant or city bred—and your servants! Sure, your servants would enjoy it!"

Liam, reflecting on his staff of personal attendants, smiled and said he would mention it to them.

■ *6* ■

THE SURLY BOY was still hopping from foot to foot and muttering to himself, but Liam ignored him and strolled down the street. The musky smell of the animals hung about him for a moment, and he breathed deeply of it before the cold wind tore it away. When he was far enough from the theater that the boy could not see him, he formed a thought and projected it.

Well, servant? Would you like to go to Madame Rhunrath's menagerie?

Fanuilh answered almost immediately, *I do not have a crown for entrance.*

Perhaps you could be an exhibit, Liam thought.

Fanuilh did not respond.

Liam walked slowly; it was not quite late enough for what he intended. Despite having been reminded of the gryphon in the temple, he had enjoyed the menagerie. Madame Rhunrath clearly liked her animals, and treated them as well as they could hope for in a cage. He wondered how she managed—it had to be difficult to keep her stock in food if the crowds were as thin as they seemed. He was also curious about her location—the Orb was supposed to be closed to prevent large gatherings, where disease could spread. Coeccias had been strangely inconsistent in enforcing the Duke's law.

There was no one in the street; the windows of most of the houses he passed were dark and the rare torches had almost all burned out. He wished he had borrowed one of Madame Rhunrath's lanterns.

Look up.

He glanced skyward immediately, more in search of Fanuilh than in response to its command.

"Where are you?"

Look south.

He could see only the diamond-hard stars at first, but then, as he swept the southern sky, he saw the moving flicker and the hairy white tail.

"A comet!"

There was a perceptible lightening, the sky shading from black to deep royal blue, as the comet moved. Liam stared at it with childlike awe; he understood now why Coeccias had been so excited. It was like the first long mark on a blank slate, a splash of white paint on black velvet. He had seen falling stars, but none compared to this.

"If it isn't a message from the gods, then it ought to be," he said to himself, then tore his gaze from the heavenly sign with regret and resumed his walk. The glow from the comet cast an eerie half-light on the streets, catching on the snow that had not been swept away, turning blacks to grays and whites brilliant. He found his eyes jumping to left and right constantly; doorways and alleys and sidestreets that were earlier invisible were suddenly filled with vaguely threatening shapes.

Fanuilh? he projected.

I am at the house.

Good, he answered, not meaning it. He wanted the dragon with him in the disquieting streets, not perched at his destination. Steeling himself, however, he picked up his pace and stopped looking from side to side, focusing himself on the quickest route to the Point.

The streets there were wider, and there were more lights in the houses. He realized that he was practically jogging, and forced himself to slow down when he came to within a block of the abandoned house. Having seen it only through Fanuilh's eyes, and that from above, it took him a moment to recognize it at street level.

A leathery rustle drifted down to the street, and Liam saw Fanuilh briefly fan its wings from the rooftop.

I am here. I will wait.

Good. Follow my thoughts—don't interfere unless I ask you to.

I will not, master.

Liam nodded his approval to himself, but made no move for the door of the abandoned house. He distracted himself from his task by thinking of how easy his communications with the dragon were becoming, and how wonderful and strange the comet was.

What finally stirred him to approach was an unbidden image of himself standing in the middle of the street in the dead of night, staring like an idiot at an empty house.

Get moving, he told himself, stepping off the cobblestones onto the stoop. *It doesn't matter if it looks like it's haunted.*

In the faint light of the comet, with snow dusting the windowsills and the tops of the shutters and the steps to the door, it did look haunted. There was nothing in the architecture—plain stone, well cut and neatly laid, though unadorned—that would inspire fear, and when he had looked through Fanuilh's eyes the place had been merely a little sad, something discarded. It was different at night.

Which is what they want, Liam scolded himself. *Why would thieves choose a place that looked inviting?* He gripped the hilt of his dirk, went up the rest of the stairs in three quick steps, and pushed at the door. It did not give, and for a moment he felt a wave of relief wash over him, quickly quelled by a firmer grip on his dirk.

The knob, idiot.

It turned easily under his hand, as if it had recently been oiled, and swung open without a sound. A dark corridor lay before him, at the end of which he could just make out a black curtain. Liam took a deep breath and walked quietly down the hall, his hands spread out to touch either wall, conscious of the thick carpet beneath his feet and, strangely, beneath his fingertips. By the time he guessed that they were there both to muffle sound and warm a house that could not allow smoke to appear from its chimney, he had reached the end of the corridor.

He listened for a moment, but heard nothing, so he pushed aside the heavy curtain and blinked in the light of a single candle.

Then he was falling, shoved violently from behind, being picked up and slammed against the wall. There was a knee in his stomach, a grimy hand over his mouth and a cold steel point against his throat. Two bright, feverish eyes caught and held his glance; the wickedly smiling mouth, inches from his, spoke.

"Hello! Coming in the middle of the night! All unannounced! Bad manners!"

"Hey," said someone else from the corridor, a woman, "he's left the door open!"

"Well, then, close it, you stupid whore!" said the man who was holding Liam.

Master?

Liam shook his head once, but could not project. The knife at his throat pressed a little closer, and the man clamped his hand harder on Liam's jaw.

"Leaving the door open! Bad, bad, bad!" With each "bad" he banged Liam's head against the wall and dug a little with the knife. When the man had finished, he screwed up one eye and examined his prisoner. "Now I wonder," he said, "will it talk? Will it shout? If I take my hand away—though not my knife, no, no, not that—will it make a noise?"

Liam shook his head steadily, as steadily as he could manage with the pressure on his stomach and the man's hand on his jaw.

"I closed the door," said the woman somewhere to Liam's left, "and I'm no whore!"

"Shut up, slut," the man said, and jabbed a little with his knife. "Now, ere I kill you, I'm going to take my hand away, and ask what your business is here. And you'll not make a noise, eh?"

Liam nodded slowly. The thief withdrew his knee and took his hand away, but kept the knife in place.

"Well—your business?"

"This one wants to drink the *princeps,*" Liam said and, with a confidence he did not feel, added: "So hie the *gladia* from this one's breather."

"Uris!" the woman exclaimed, and Liam's eyes flashed to her for a second. She was only a girl, no more than twelve, dirty and dressed in a ragged smock. "He chants!"

"Shut up!" the thief hissed. When he returned his attention to Liam his eyes squinted meanly. "Where'd you learn that, eh? Eh?" He dug again with his knife, and a warm trickle went down Liam's throat, beneath his collar and further down his chest.

Forcing nonchalance, Liam ignored the cut and tried to look bored. "This one chants for this one's a chanter. *Momenta* hie the gladia. This one would drink the Werewolf."

The chant was little more than a slang, more a set of parallel words and archaic phrases than its own language, but just the few words he had used had a great effect on the man holding him. His gleaming eyes screwed up, then widened.

"Japer," the girl whispered.

"Go tell the Werewolf," Japer ordered.

"But, Japer—"

"*Go!*"

The girl scampered out, ducking beneath another black curtain. Japer eyed Liam nervously.

"Where'd you learn that?" he asked again, this time with a degree of uncertainty.

"A far *carad,*" Liam replied, which was not true. He had not learned his chant in a far carad, another guild, but from a solitary thief who had once belonged to a guild. There was no need to reveal that; he could provide enough details to get away with the lie. With a slight frown, he peered down at the knife. "The gladia?"

"Not yet," Japer growled, and then the girl returned, breathless. "He says bring him."

In a series of swift motions, Japer pulled Liam's dirk from the scabbard and tossed it to the girl, who fumbled with it, then jerked his prisoner forward by the front of his tunic.

"Watch the door," he told the girl, who was searching for the dirk on the floor.

"But, Japer—" she protested, standing up.

"Watch the door, bitch!" he said, then spun Liam around and jabbed the knife at his back. "Through the curtain."

Beyond the curtain a set of stone steps led down to the cellar of the abandoned house, and Liam went down them with an approximation of a saunter.

Master? Fanuilh asked. *Is this wise?*

Of course, Liam projected. *Perfectly wise.*

There was light at the bottom of the stairs, an uneven orange glow, and when he left the last step Liam saw that it was coming from a small brazier, banked with nuggets of coal. Around the brazier were four men, each holding a skewer, cooking chunks of meat over the coals. They all looked up when he entered.

"*Avé,* brothers," Liam began, but was interrupted by a kick from Japer that sent him to his knees.

"So this is the stranger who chants," said one of the men, handing his skewer to another and standing up. He wiped his hands on his dirty breeches and walked over to Liam.

"This one is the princeps," he said, and offered Liam a hand up. It was easy to see why he was nicknamed the Werewolf: grizzled salt-and-pepper hair welled up from his chest and over his face, up his cheeks around his eyes, which were a luminous green. And his incisors were disproportionately long.

Liam hesitated before taking the Werewolf's hand, then allowed himself to be drawn up. He did not know why, but he was grateful to see that he was taller than the head of the Southwark Guild. The shorter man smiled, a deliberately feral smile, but Liam refused to let it shake him.

The teeth and the eyes must take him far, he thought.

"Avé, princeps." Liam waited.

"Avé," the Werewolf responded at last. He should have called Liam "brother"; the omission was not good. "Carad Southwark plays no rogues."

That was all right. Liam had anticipated that the Guild would not allow thieves who were not members to practice in the city.

"This one is not operanding," he said. *"Sola* larking." He was not working, only visiting.

"What carad?"

"Badham Wood." This drew the attention of the men around the brazier, and a curse from Japer, behind him. The Werewolf smiled.

"Badham, eh?"

"Doh." Yes.

"This one has drunk the princeps of Carad Badham."

"Stick," Liam supplied, the name of the thief he had known, and waited patiently for the next question. He knew roughly what it would be.

"Wings tell this one Carad Badham liberates much momenta." Gossip told him that Badham Wood was doing well now.

Liam shook his head and smiled, feeling the expectant gazes of the other thieves in the cellar, and the heavy gaze of the Werewolf. "Carad Badham is long broken." The Badham Wood Guild had disbanded a decade before. It had been more a loose association of bandits and highwaymen than a proper guild, but it was accorded that status out of respect for its princeps, Stick. A legend in the Harcourt Guild in his youth, Stick was exiled for an unknown offense and took up with the brigands in and around Badham Wood, a vast stretch of forest near the King's Range, far to the north. "Stick is long no princeps. Last this one heard, he chanted in the Freeports."

There was a distinct change in mood in the cellar. Japer took his knife away from Liam's back, and the thieves by the brazier resumed their cooking. The Werewolf's smile grew less feral, became almost friendly—almost. There was still an edge of wariness to his voice.

"Doh," he said. "Wings told this one that, too. So, a chanter, eh?"

"Sola larking," Liam answered. The word could mean many things, from visiting to loafing to being retired—anything but actively stealing.

"No chanting?"

"None," Liam assured him. "Sola larking."

The Werewolf was silent for a while, studying him, undoubtedly trying to unnerve him with his fierce green stare and the way he rubbed at his cheeks, pulling his lips back to reveal his abnormally long teeth. Liam guessed that he was out of danger; the question now was whether the visit would be of any use.

After a minute of unbroken quiet, during which Liam became aware of a slight draft through the cellar carrying a sewer stink, the Werewolf spoke again.

"*Peir* drink the slavers momenta? Peir drink the carad momenta? An not chanting, peir?" Why had he gone to the fences? Why did he want to meet the Guild? If he was not stealing, why?

Of course they had been waiting for him, Liam realized. Ever since the old pawnbroker had come that morning, they had been expecting the stranger who chanted to appear. That explained why three men who were eating seemed to ignore him with such calm—though he could see that they were paying keen attention to his conversation with the princeps. He wondered why Japer had not known about him.

"Some of this one's portables have gone free, and this one would reslave them."

The Werewolf shrugged. "Portables, eh? Open window. Drink the slavers."

"Closed window. They're green."

"Ah." The princeps nodded sagely and pulled at his cheeks again. The glow from the brazier caught on his teeth. Green things were enchanted; few fences even in large cities would handle stolen magic. "Locked window. This one can't abet." He could not help. Liam sighed. If they would not help him simply because they thought he was a fellow thief, he would have to call on something higher. He sighed again, for effect, and crossed his arms.

"Does Carad Southwark not *connit* the *Legium?* Does the Werewolf not connit the Legium?"

Liam had met Stick just as the Badham Wood Guild was breaking up, and despite the fact that there was a good twenty years between them, the two had traveled together for almost a year. During that time the legendary thief had, for no good reason that Liam could understand, made it his duty to teach the younger man everything he knew about thievery. It had been a considerable amount, not much of which Liam had ever had a chance to practice. The basics—picking locks, moving and climbing quickly and silently—had been useful, and he had even picked a pocket or two when desperate, but he had never thought he would need to know about the Legium.

A body of law created centuries before, the Legium was an oral code for thieves to follow, rigidly enforced by guild disciplinarians in the larger cities of Taralon and the Freeports. The code varied slightly from city to city, but was generally based on that maintained in Harcourt, where it

was supposed to have originated. The Southwark Guild looked fairly
rudimentary, but he hoped they held to it.

The Werewolf looked offended, drawing up his chin and sniffing
haughtily. "This one connits the Legium."

"Then connit the *pre legio.*" The first rule of the Legium was that
thieves did not steal from other thieves—at least, not when they would
be caught.

"The carad did not connit a larking chanter in Southwark."

"*Unum,*" Liam said, agreeing. It was a fair argument—the Guild had
not known he was a thief, and thus stealing from him did not break the
pre legio. He began to smile, though, thinking that the Werewolf had as
much as admitted that one of his thieves had robbed Liam. The princeps,
however, spoke on.

"And how connit it the portables were freed by a carad chanter?"
How did Liam know he had been robbed by a Guild thief?

"Carad Southwark plays no rogues," he answered with a smile, which
brought a laugh from one of the eating men. The Werewolf had just said
there were no non-Guild thieves in the city.

The princeps smiled grimly; a point for Liam.

"An the portables were freed by one of this one's chanters, this one
does not connit it." If Liam's things were stolen by a Guild thief, the
Werewolf did not know of it. "But Carad Southwark is *magnum;* this one
can drink the chanters, and spy."

If your Guild is so great, Liam wondered, *why are you all dressed in
rags and hiding in an abandoned building?* But he did not say this; instead
he shrugged.

"This one will not splinter the pre legio. The legio slaver is a fair
split." He would not insist on the pre legio, which would require the
offending thief to return the goods and make some reparation. The
fence's rule meant that a thief had preference over fences in buying
things stolen by another.

The Werewolf tugged at his lower lip thoughtfully. "A fair split,
vertas." "Vertas" was a modifier, like "indeed" or "truly." "An this one
can spy the chanter with the freed portables, can part *lux?*" If he could
find the thief who had the goods, could Liam pay cash?

"Doh," Liam assured him.

"Unum," the Werewolf said. It was done. "This one will spy the
chanter, and make the split. What portables, and when liberated?" He
would find the thief, and arrange the deal; he needed to know what had
been stolen.

"A book, a wand and a rug, all green," Liam said. The chant had no

words for these. "Two *ombers* past." Two nights. He held up a finger,
forestalling the Werewolf's smile. "Bar this one wants to drink the
chanter's soul." He wanted to meet the thief himself.

The princeps's incipient grin faded, leaving a crestfallen look behind.
He had obviously been thinking of what he would skim off the top of the
deal; he would tell the thief one price and Liam a higher one, then take
the difference. Liam thought of this, but that was not really why he
wanted to meet the thief who had robbed him. More important to him
was knowing how the thief had gotten past the wards on the house, and
what he planned to do with the magical things he had taken.

Still, he wanted to laugh at the hurt look on the Werewolf's face.
"An will wing this one the chanter's *cognom* and *caster,* this one'll part a
gift for the carad." If the Werewolf would tell him the thief's name and
where he lived, Liam would make a donation to the Guild. The grizzled
princeps's smile returned, and one of the men around the brazier tipped
Liam a wink. They had finished eating, and were passing around a clay
jug of wine with a jagged shard broken out of the rim.

He was suddenly aware that the sewer stink had grown stronger, and
was mixing most unpleasantly with the lingering smell of cooked meat.

"Unum?" he said quickly.

"Unum," the Werewolf said. "What's the gift?"

Liam considered only for a second. "Not momenta. An this one
drinks the thief and reslaves the portables, then the gift. It'll be magnum." How great, he did not know, but from the way the Werewolf's eyes
gleamed, he could tell the man was hoping it would be vertas magnum.
Magic was expensive and unique; the Legium had a number of specific
rules about it, none of which, Liam was grateful, applied in this case.

"Unum," the princeps said, sticking out his hand. "This one will spy
it out and wing it to the caster. The caster?"

Liam took the man's hand, but shook his head. He did not want to
tell the Werewolf where he lived, even though the man could probably
find it out easily. "Not this one's caster. We will drink in the *iter,* in the
glare." He wanted to meet in the street, during the day.

The Werewolf shook his head and laughed, a little nastily. "This one
is the princeps. This one does not travel in the iter, sola on the iter. In
the ombers." As princeps, he did not go out *in* the iter, the streets, only
on the iter, the rooftops. Iter meant both, *in* or *on* made the difference.
And he only went out in the ombers, at night.

"Then another chanter," Liam suggested, and a little maliciously
jerked his thumb behind him. "Japer."

Laughter from the three men drinking wine, and a curse from Japer.

"No," the Werewolf said, "not Japer, bar Mopsa. Japer, hie Mopsa."

Grumbling, Japer clumped up the steps and returned a minute later with the young girl from the entrance.

"Pickit," the Werewolf said, "drink this chanter." A pickit was a small tool for opening doors; it also meant an apprentice thief, someone inexperienced. "That one's cognom is Liam Rhenford. Drink that one. Will drink him again."

Liam nodded at the girl, who stared sullenly back at him.

"Avé, Mopsa."

"Avé," she replied, and then burst out: "But, Wolf, do I have to? I'm—this one—is no frog!"

All the men laughed, Liam, too. She was clearly a very new pickit, and her chant was weak. She was being told to bring him a message, which made her in chant a croaker, a kind of bird that was supposed to have its own language. She had used the word for informant.

The Werewolf cuffed her lightly on the side of the head. "As told, pickit. Drink the chanter when told, and where." He looked at Liam. "When and where?"

"Next middle glare, in Narrow Lane, behind the Duke's courts." Noon the next day should give him plenty of time to find the thief; the place had popped into his head unbidden.

The Werewolf seemed to think neither strange.

"Unum," he said, and shook Liam's hand again. "Then the magnum gift."

Liam nodded. "Avé, princeps. Till the middle glare." He took one last look around the cellar, received a nod or two from the other thieves, and headed for the stairs. Japer blocked his way for a moment, then stepped surlily aside.

Walking slowly up the stairs, he did not allow himself to think; he concentrated only on getting past the two curtains, past the street door, down the stairs and into the cold street. Then he took a deep breath, cleaning the sewer smell out of his nostrils and noticing suddenly the patches of sweat beneath his armpits and down his back.

Perfectly wise, he told himself, and, shuddering, began jogging away from the Point.

A block away, Liam made to pull his cloak close around his neck, and brought his hand away tacky. Japer's blade had not cut deep, but there was a thin trail of dried blood from his throat down beneath the front of his shirt. He cursed, licked his fingers, and tried to scrub it away,

all the while continuing to put distance between himself and the Southwark Guild.

Thousands of thoughts crowded through his head at once, a situation
Fanuilh, who could see his thoughts, had once described as watching a
flock of startled birds leap into the air and mill violently about.

His plan had worked; the pawnbroker had led him to the Guild. His
chant had held up, his knowledge—and the Guild's application—of the
Legium had been sufficient. Carad Southwark struck him as a singularly
poor affair; the guilds Stick had described to him had led him to expect a
sort of underground court. Of course, he had been talking about the truly
big guilds, in Torquay and Harcourt and the Freeports and even Caer
Urdoch, where membership could number in the hundreds. Even so, the
Southwark Guild seemed pitiful. The Werewolf, for instance, had
seemed a little stupid, for all his cunning, no match for the godlike pictures of the princepses Stick had talked about.

The one in Torquay, for instance, always called the Banker, regardless of whether it was his real name or nickname, was supposed to have a
pleasure barge the size of a grain ship. And the princeps in Harcourt,
whose name Liam could not remember, was rumored to be in regular
consultation with that city's ruling council. Liam could not imagine the
Werewolf doing anything more than the occasional housebreaking.

Straw in his hair, the night boy at the hostler's made it more than
clear that he resented being awakened to perform his duties, and Liam,
with the difficulties entailed by holding his cloak closed with his fingers to
hide the blood at his throat and trying to keep the cloak from touching
that blood, forgot to give the tip which he would normally have felt the
boy deserved. The boy's grumble reminded him of the tip, but also made
him decide to forgo it.

Liam was already past the city gate when Fanuilh made its presence
known by dropping lightly onto Diamond's neck. Though at first the
horse had been frightened of the dragon, it had come to accept it, and
only showed that it recognized the extra rider by rippling the muscles of
its neck and snorting once.

Fanuilh sat staring at him, and Liam slowed Diamond to a walk.

"So, you see . . . perfectly wise," he said.

Your throat is cut, the dragon thought.

"Only slightly—a nick. I've done worse shaving."

He could have killed you.

"Yes," Liam admitted readily; the thought had not been far from his
own mind throughout the whole visit. "But I did not think it likely. They
are thieves, not assassins."

There was no hint in Fanuilh's next thought to show what it felt, no indication of why it changed the subject, but Liam imagined it might have followed a *hmpph* of exasperation. His father had often made abrupt changes in subject when, as a boy, he had insisted on following a line of conversation that was inappropriate—and he had always preceeded them with a *hmpph.*

There is no word for "you."

"Eh?"

In the chant, there is no word for "you."

After a moment, Liam confirmed this. "No, no word at all. More than that, thieves don't use "you" at all. When there is no chant word for something, they usually use the regular word, but they just drop the pronoun altogether. And that's strange, because almost the first word you learn in any language is 'you,' as opposed to 'me' or 'I.' "

They discussed the chant for the rest of the ride home, Liam trying to explain it and Fanuilh asking a series of alternately pointed and pointless questions. As Diamond ambled down the cliff path, Liam summed the language up: "It's not really a language, you have to understand. There are all sorts of things for which it has no words. It is more of convention, a secret sign, a way for thieves to recognize and communicate with one another to the exclusion of others. They can talk about all the various aspects of a job, but not how to cook a meal, or mend a shirt. There are sixteen different words for locks—sixteen!—but no word for pot or horse."

I have only one more question, the dragon thought, clearly realizing that its master was tiring of the discussion.

"What?"

Diamond broke into a jog, sensing home. To the east, the black of the sky was shading to blue, as the day approached. The evening had lasted far longer than Liam expected.

How did the Werewolf know your name?

■ 7 ■

THE QUESTION WAS still in his head a few hours later, when Fanuilh woke him from a deep sleep. The dragon was still sending the image of a bestiary into his dreams, the illuminated W of WAKE growing more and more elaborate each time, twisting intricate traceries of vines in vivid colors.

He had tried to puzzle out how the Werewolf had known who he was, but without success. He knew he had not mentioned his name, and Fanuilh agreed. He could not remember telling the old pawnbroker his name, either. There was no way the princeps could have known it. Sleep had overcome him a little after dawn, while he was still wrestling with the question.

Yawning and bleary eyed, he slumped at the kitchen table with a mug of hot coffee, a drink he had encountered in a land far to the south. Fanuilh sat on the table opposite him, eating raw mutton with gusto. It hated the taste of coffee but enjoyed the smell, so there was a steaming bowl in front of its platter; after every few bites it would raise its head and sniff deeply. The sound made Liam smile, and the coffee was helping to wake him up.

"There's no way he can know my name, no way that I can imagine. . . ." He let the sentence trail off, watching the thin slits of his familiar's nostrils expand and its eyes close in appreciation of the rich scent. An idea struck him, and it seemed obvious. "Unless . . . unless what Mother Japh says is true, that everyone thinks I'm a wizard."

Fanuilh cocked its head. *Everyone knew Master Tarquin.*

"Exactly! Because with only one wizard in the whole city, everyone would at least have heard of him. And thieves, particularly guild thieves, would be particularly interested in local gossip. And they had almost half a day after the pawnbroker told them about me to figure out who I was."

You are somewhat distinctive.

"No I'm not."

You are taller than most, and your nose is long and thin, and your hair is blond and you dress better than most. You are distinctive.

Liam did not agree, but he let the point go. It did not matter much, anyway; Southwark was small enough that any competent group of thieves should have been able to figure out who he was from a description. With the simple riddle solved, he felt able to start his day, but there was a little coffee left.

"The Werewolf," he mused, cupping his hands around his mug, "was probably trying to impress me, do you see? To show that he was clever, that he knew my name even though I hadn't offered it."

If so, you disappointed him.

"That I did," Liam said with a chuckle, "that I did." Then, a little nervously, he touched the base of his throat and stopped laughing. The cut there had scabbed over completely. He touched it once more, then forced his hand away.

And even if you had reacted with astonishment, the dragon thought on, *would he really have been being clever? How difficult could it be to identify the only wizard in Southwark?*

"I'm not a wizard," Liam began heatedly, and then stopped himself. "Oh. I see what you mean. It doesn't matter if I am or not, because people think I'm a wizard. That's annoying."

Why?

The last of his coffee disappeared in a long gulp. "I don't know. I don't like being taken for what I am not. I don't want people to expect more or less from me than I can offer. And before you say that I allow Coeccias to do just that, you can stop and reflect that that's a different situation entirely."

Is it?

"Not at all, but I want it to be, so it is, at least as far as you're concerned. Now, it's time for me to go meet the girl."

On the ride into Southwark, he thought about what he had said to the dragon. Whether or not people in the city believed he was a wizard, it was different from what Coeccias believed him to be, but only in degree, not kind. Just as there was no feasible way to disabuse the entire city of the notion that he was a wizard, there was no way he could see to show Coeccias that he was neither a blood-shy weakling nor a brilliant thieftaker. Or at least no way to prove it without revealing that he had, to a certain extent, lied to his only friend. He could simply tell the truth, of course, but he feared his friend's reaction.

How the Aedile managed to hold two such contradictory opinions about him was another riddle he could not even begin to fathom.

As he rode into town there was more activity in the city than on the previous two days: the sun was shining and the worst of the snow was gone, trampled to a thin black slush underfoot. People filled the streets, busy on errands neglected; carts from the countryside thronged the city gate and blocked countless intersections; children threw sloppy handfuls of snow from rooftops and the mouths of alleyways. It took him longer than it should have to reach Narrow Lane, in part because of the crowded streets and in part because he did not really know how to get there.

With Diamond safely stabled, he crossed the city square just before noon. He had assumed that Narrow Lane could be entered by way of Chandlers' Street, which entered the square just south of the Guards' barracks, but when he went around that corner, there was no sign of other streets. He went back into the square, up past the Duke's courts and turned into Butchers' Road, but there did not seem to be an opening there, either. As he came back to the square, the bells in the tower began ringing noon, and he hurried over to the barracks and asked the Guard on duty how to find Narrow Lane.

The Guard looked at him as if he had grown another head, and practically refused to give him directions.

"You don't want to go there, Master Rhenford. It's not fit for you, sir, I swear it's not."

"Look," Liam fumed, "I do want to go there, and I want you to tell me. Now."

At last he prevailed, and the Guard explained the rather complicated route he would have to follow. Narrow Lane was a horseshoe whose apex touched the back of the courts and the barracks: he had to go down Butchers' Road, through Tripe Court, make a left into the alley at the first bath house, pass three dead-end alleys, then turn left again at Narrow Lane. Noon was almost half an hour gone by the time he reached that section of the lane that touched the Duke's courts, and he bitterly regretted the choice of meeting place.

Narrow Lane was more an alley than a lane, and more a tunnel than an alley. Overhanging balconies and overbuilt stories cut out the sunlight, leaving only chill shadows; in a number of places the buildings on either side of the lane actually met. A few obscure shops were scattered along its length, but for the most part it was residential, with doorways leading to interior courtyards or steep, dark flights of stairs. It was only slightly less dirty than the Warren, the slum area by the waterfront, but it felt more oppressive. The few people in the road eyed him suspiciously, and once he dodged a stream of liquid that arced down from the sky, looking up to see a laughing boy doing up his breeches in a window four stories above.

He could not help shaking a fist at the boy, but he also could not help laughing a little himself. He did not belong there.

If he'd hit me, Liam thought, *that would be different.*

Mopsa was waiting for him at the very top of the lane, where the cellars of the Duke's courts formed a blank wall of stone, at the foot of which had accumulated a talus slope of refuse, thrown out at the curve of Narrow Lane. He recalled from his childhood a bend in a river, where improbable things had washed ashore while the current hurried on in a different direction. Mother Japh's windows were a good fifteen feet above his head.

"Avé, brother," Mopsa said, as though doubting whether he were really a brother at all. "Y'are late." She was squatting by the blank wall, up to her ankles in slush and dirt, and looked even more ragged in the daylight. Her hair hung limply down to her shoulders, cut unevenly and clotted with mud, and he could not tell what color it was. A blanket was thrown around her shoulders, but she clutched herself beneath it.

Liam hated being late, and because he felt foolish for suggesting a rendezvous he did not know how to get to, her reprimand stung him. But he did not like being scolded by a twelve-year-old, particularly a foolish one.

"First off, *pickit,*" he said, emphasizing the word heavily and leveling a long finger at her, "you never talk like that in the street, understand?"

"Like what?" she said defiantly, thrusting out her chin.

"In chant," he said quietly. "It's a good way to draw down the Guard on you. Do you think they don't know what the chant is, or can't recognize a few words of it?"

Mopsa's eyes narrowed skeptically, and she stood up, crossing her arms. "Not the Guards here, brother. They're fools."

He closed his eyes for a moment, summoning patience. He did not get along well with children. "Pickit," he said quietly, "don't chant in the streets. And don't call me 'brother.'"

"Why not?"

"Because you're just a pickit, not a full chanter. You should call me 'uncle.' And besides, no one would believe you were my sister anyway, if they should happen to overhear you being so foolish as to chant in public."

Mopsa grudgingly accepted this. "All right, Uncle. Now, do you want to hear Wolf's news?"

"Yes."

As she spoke, Liam began to regret what he saw as his rather harsh correction. She was thin, too thin, and he wondered about the Southwark Guild. Stick had always told him that apprentices in Harcourt were fed and fussed over so much that they often turned out fat and useless. He recalled the way Japer and the Werewolf had treated the girl, and his regret grew.

"He says it could only be Duplin, for that my other uncles"—she weighted the word with disdain—"were all otherwise occupied. More, he's the only one of my uncles that would treat with green things. And none have seen Duplin in two days."

"Since he robbed me," Liam figured. "Do you know where I can find him?"

"He has many hidey-holes, and might be in any of them." She paused, balancing the advantages and disadvantages of her next sentence. "Wolf said I was to help you find him. I know most of his places."

Liam began to smile, and then a gust of wind swept down Narrow Lane, setting Mopsa shivering and bringing her smell to his nose. She reeked of the sewers, and he thought of the smell in the cellar the night before. He angled his head away.

"Tell me, Mopsa, when you leave the Point by the sewers, do you never wash after?"

The girl's teeth stopped chattering, and she looked at him in stark amazement. "How did you know about the sewers?"

"Because—oh gods"—another whiff reached him—"because you stink of them, just like that miserable cellar."

She took an exploratory sniff, and shook her head. "But that doesn't mean . . . I mean, we could use the roofs."

"There's not a lot of shit on the rooftops, Mopsa. How many places does this Duplin have?"

"Six or seven," she said, still puzzled both by his assertion that she smelled and his knowledge of the sewers.

"Close together, or far apart?"

"Passing scattered. Duplin ranges the whole city. A great one for artisans' homes, he is—he can pick a lock anywhere from here to Auric's Park."

The wind died down, and the smell fell away, but Liam made a quick decision. "Come on," he said, turning back down Narrow Lane, "if I have to go anywhere with you, you're going to have a bath."

"A bath?" she said, then hurried after him. "I can't have a bath."

"Why not?" Liam asked, busy checking the upper stories for mischievous boys.

"I've no coin to pay for one, to start."

"I'll pay," he said absently, still on the alert. "Any other reason why you should stink?"

She could think of none, and trotted after him in silence, trying to keep up with his long-legged pace. He led her to the bath house he had passed earlier. It was an unpretentious building, long and low with tiny, grilled windows billowing steam. The foyer was a small room; two doors led to the interior, with two wooden counters flanking them. The floor was cold tile, wet and slippery, and he stepped carefully up to the counter by the door marked with a figure wearing a dress.

"My niece would like a bath," he said to the woman there, who looked over his shoulder and blanced at the site of Mopsa, cringing a little by the door.

"Mother Uris," the woman exclaimed, "she's filthy!"

Mopsa snarled a ferocious curse at the woman, and Liam had to bite back a grin.

"She's been playing in the street, I'm afraid, and my sister is coming for her today—she's been visiting—and I can't let her see her like this."

Color was disappearing rapidly from the counterwoman's face as she wilted beneath Mopsa's baleful stare.

"I can't let her in the baths like that," the woman stammered, then blinked and took control of herself, turning her attention to Liam.

"A private bath, then," Liam suggested, pulling a handful of coins from his purse for effect. "She really does need to wash."

The counterwoman weighed Mopsa's language, state of disrepair and angry glance against Liam's polite tone, expensive clothes and obvious resources.

"Private baths are dear," she warned him.

"Nothing's too dear for my dear niece," he assured the woman, and in a matter of moments she was herding Mopsa—careful not to touch her—through the door to the women's baths. A minute or so later, she was back.

"Her clothes," the counterwoman said, "should be burned."

"Burn them," Liam said cheerily. "Do you know where I can buy some others quickly? Nothing showy, though, just a plain frock and a warm coat."

The woman did know a place, and after he had paid her the exorbitant fee for a private bath, he went to the shop, a few streets away. He returned a half an hour later with some decent clothes and a pair of shoes, and handed them over to the counterwoman. Then he waited. And waited. And waited. He chatted a little with the men's attendant—there were apparently a number of excellent clubs that met at the bath, one of philosophers, one of ships' captains, one of chandlers—and he waited some more.

It was over an hour before Mopsa returned, bundled in her new coat and shining clean. Her hair, Liam saw, was mouse brown.

"Good bath?" he asked, opening the door.

"Three of them," the apprentice thief said with some satisfaction. "I got the water in the first two so dirty they had to change it. Said they were going to melt down the tubs."

Liam waved good-bye to the counterwoman and closed the door.

"I would think, though," Mopsa was saying, "that you could have gotten some better clothes."

"Want to stand out, do you? Good practice for your line of work."

The sarcasm was not lost on the girl, who looked up at him from where her head was sunk in the collar of her new coat. "I guess they're warm enough. But don't you mean *our* line of work?"

"No," Liam said, "I'm retired."

"Just larking?"

"Retired," he insisted. "Watch your mouth. And now, where do we find this Duplin?"

Of the six places Duplin usually frequented, two were in the Warren. Liam wanted to visit those first because the afternoon was growing old, and he did not want to get stuck in the area after dark. Mopsa, surprisingly agreeable, led the way down to the waterfront. Being warm and clean seemed to have taken much of the edge off her, and Liam guessed that it had been some time since anyone had done anything nice for her. He thought to ask her about it, then decided not to. Instead, he asked her to tell him more about Duplin, the man who had robbed his house.

"No one said he did it," she reminded him. "Only that all the others were busy, and he hasn't been seen since the night your things were set free."

He nodded; the point was moot. It had to be Duplin; everyone swore there were no wizards in Southwark, and everyone swore there were no thieves but Guild thieves, and he was the only one unaccounted for on the night Liam was robbed. And he had not been seen since.

Probably drinking himself silly with the money he got from my things, Liam thought sourly, realizing that it was entirely possible that Duplin would already have sold them.

Never mind, he told himself. *Duplin will tell us who he sold them to, and we can follow them from there.*

The more Mopsa told him, the more he was sure Duplin had done it.

"An overweening type, a passing grandee, he is. Full of himself. Rightfully, though, to some thinking—a great one for locks and windows and chests, and smooth on the roofs. He taught me how to climb a sheer one, says I'm good at it for that I'm a girl, and small."

"It helps," Liam said, remembering a roof that had collapsed under him. It had been foolish to try to climb on thatching, but nothing much had come of it.

"I should say," Mopsa boasted. "I'm the fastest on the iter in all of Southwark!"

"Mouth," Liam said, and she clapped her hand over hers.

"Sorry," she mumbled.

"Go on."

"He's always freeing—taking—big things. Jewelry or plate, unique things. He had a silver teapot, a time, that was shaped like a swan. It was a monster, and no slaver—fence—would take it, so he had to melt it down. And he likes to plan. Plan, plan, plan. He does half as many jobs as anyone else, he spends so much time planning, but his jobs always give more, much more, because he thinks big and he thinks ahead."

By then they were in the Warren, with its crowds thinner and poorer, its buildings and streets dirtier, dirtier even than those in Narrow Lane, and its layout far more confusing. Mopsa threaded her way through the alleys with ease, though, and Liam simply tagged along. She spoke to a number of people on the way, mostly urchins as dirty as she had been. Her new smock and coat were plain, and a little too big for her—she had to hold a fold of the smock in her hand to keep it from dragging in the slush—but she conspicuously stroked the material whenever she met a child she knew, and they reacted appropriately, eyeing the clothes with envy.

"My uncle," she said to one of them, nodding her chin at Liam with a smug expression.

"Yes, dear," Liam said the second time she tried this, "and uncle grows tired. Let's hurry."

The friend darted off and Mopsa resumed their walk with a sniff.

"You might at least let me show a little. Do you know how long it's been since I've had a new coat?" She began calculating, counting time on her fingers.

"Never mind that," Liam said. "I don't want to know. And besides, didn't I tell you? I'm taking those back once we find Duplin."

She froze in the street, shocked. "You're not!"

"No, I'm joking, now come on."

"You're not!" she repeated, this time a warning.

"I said I was joking. Now come on!"

"You'd better be," the girl said, "because they burned my other clothes."

Wishing he had not made the joke, Liam gestured down the street. "Can we, please?"

"Swear you were joking."

"I swear."

In the end, they got to Duplin's hideouts only in the Warren that afternoon. The first was just a wineshop, where messages were often left for him. The barkeep knew Duplin, but had not seen him in over a week.

"Gone up the hill," he said, jerking a thumb toward the Point. "Vowed never to come here again. Wish he'd come back, if just to keep his punk from coming in and weeping and shouting every night."

The "punk" lived at his real hideout in the Warren, a single room off a dark courtyard. She was in her forties, and long faded; the wattles of her neck wobbled as she bemoaned her fate and Duplin's inconstancy.

"Said he was off on a big job," she whined, "the biggest. His last, he said, sure to set him up for good, and he'd be gone a week and then be back for me and we could set up a carriage and live like lords and ladies."

When it was clear that that was all she knew, Liam beat a hasty retreat, as the woman appeared to be working up to a good strong cry—one, he suspected, that might put the whole rickety house in danger of collapsing.

In the street, Mopsa giggled and tugged at Liam's arm.

"If Duplin was going to set up a carriage with one, it wouldn't be her. He's got another up in the Point, and a better one than that in between. He's probably holed up with one of them."

Duplin's informal polygamy amused her to no end, and as they walked back up the slope from the Warren, she regaled him with stories of the amours of various thieves in the Guild. Her commentary was often interrupted by yawns, and Liam realized that she could not have had much more sleep than he had the night before. Furthermore, he had not eaten anything all day, and his stomach rumbled a warning as they neared the city square.

"Are you hungry?" he asked suddenly, cutting her off in the middle of a meandering story about a thief and three prostitutes.

"Hungry isn't in it," Mopsa replied immediately. "You paying?"

He was, after extracting a promise from her that they would visit Duplin's other hideouts early the next day.

They found a small eatery near the square, and the girl had ordered a broiled sole, a bowl of fish chowder, a sea pie, a jug of wine and a loaf of bread before he could stop her.

"And mind you the bread's fresh," she told the astonished serving girl.

"You can't eat all that," Liam told her.

"If you can pay for it, I can eat it. You just watch."

Shaking his head, Liam told the serving girl to water the wine and bring him a sea pie.

Mopsa was almost as good as her word, stowing away the vast majority of her meal in starving gulps, complaining between mouthfuls at the watered wine and working in bits of thief stories during her brief moments on the surface.

"How many are there in the Guild?" Liam asked at one point.

"I don't know," she replied offhandedly. "Maybe twenty, maybe thirty."

"And are you the only girl?"

"Me? No, there's another. But she's a real chanter," Mopsa paused to debone a strip of sole and eat it, "the best, after Duplin and the Wolf. And she can read, too, whole words and books and things."

"Can't you read?" Stick had told him that all apprentices were taught how, as one of their first lessons. It came in handy, he had said, in all sorts of situations.

"Me? Read? Ha! Not hardly. And who would teach me? I don't think the Wolf can read, and I know Japer can't, or Vellus or Lightfingers or Dancer."

Liam had finished his pie, and sat back to nurse the rest of his wine, leaving the girl to gorge herself in silence. He was surprised once again at how disorganized the Southwark Guild was, how far below Stick's high standards it fell. Small but relatively rich, the crumbs from Southwark's tables ought to be able to support a prosperous group of thieves, but these were hardly better than beggars. Of course, the city had no branch of the Wizards' Guild, either, a fact to which he had never given much thought. Torquay and Harcourt had one, as well as Caernarvon and Caer Urdoch and even Carad Llan—and all had decent thieves' guilds. There might be some connection, not obvious, a combination of age and wealth and population that gave those cities the base for a well-established set of guilds. Perhaps in a hundred years, the Werewolf's ragtag group might come to resemble its better-developed counterparts in the other cities.

Or perhaps not, Liam thought, unsure if that would be good or bad. Certainly it would be better for apprentices like Mopsa.

The girl had by then eaten as much as she possibly could, which was more than Liam would have believed. She lolled in her chair, breathing heavily and clasping her stomach as if she were pregnant.

"Gods," she exclaimed heavily, "but that was good!"

"Are you sure you couldn't eat a little more? A whale, perhaps? A roast ox?"

"A sweet, maybe," the girl suggested, then rejected the idea. "No. Might throw up."

"And we don't want that," Liam said, dropping some coins on the table. "When you're ready, starveling, we'll go."

She was ready remarkably quickly, though she walked slowly and groaned from time to time as they headed for the square. They parted there, Mopsa waddling off into the crowd and Liam pacing aimlessly. When he could no longer see her, he strolled over to the Guard barracks and asked if Coeccias was in.

He was, and invited Liam to sit with him by one of the hearths in the long, low room.

"Truth, Rhenford, it likes me to see you," the Aedile said, warming a cup of liquor over the fire. "Things grow from worse to worst, and I've little idea what to do."

People were piling problems on Coeccias's plate: rumors of a ghost in the Warren, complaints from a group of chandlers about a ship called the *Heart of Oak* that had left harbor without paying several large bills, and concerns, ranging from the curious to the hysterical, about the meaning of the two comets—all of which he was supposed to address.

"Though no one suggests *how,*" he said, shaking his head in bemusement.

His biggest problem, however, was still the affair in Temple Street, and Liam winced when he heard of the trouble that had sprung from his suggestions. The Aedile had put questions about the banking business to both Cloten and Guiderius; the first had refused to talk about it, declaring that it was a poor excuse for an investigation into attempted murder, and any fool could see that they were dealing with assassins, not thieves,

let alone bankers. Guiderius had grown equally heated, asking if Cloten
had raised the question, and what business was it of the Aedile's in any
case, did he not have more important things to do. Keeper of Arms
Alastor, Cloten's second in command, had vehemently refused to discuss
any matters of doctrine, and rather rudely terminated their conversation.
Coeccias actually looked woeful while reporting this, and Liam sensed
several times that he was on the verge of asking for direct help again.

"And the worst, Rhenford, the worst is yet to come, in two parts: the
first, that a gang of Cloten's men clashed with a gang of Guiderius's.
Nothing serious, mind, a broken bone or two—but fighting! Fighting in
Temples' Court! Can imagine? The second, though, is what likes me
least." He beckoned Liam closer, dropping his voice to the sort of hush
most people reserved for naming the Dark Gods, for fear that naming
them would invoke their presence. "The second: you know of the messengers, eh? The comets?"

Liam did, and mentioned the one he saw.

"Exactly! Two! And has Mother Japh told of her friends' two-headed
calf?"

Liam did not remember a two-headed calf, but he understood the
significance ascribed to such a monstrous birth, so he nodded.

"Now, look you, I tell you this in confidence, and y'are not to mention it to a soul, but last night, just after the second messenger appeared,
all the candles in Temples' Court—all!—blew out. No wind, the priests
said, just winked out, like a snuffer put over all at once."

Liam rubbed at the bridge of his nose, trying to fathom the meaning
behind the signs. As a rule he did not much believe in omens and
portents, but he remembered Mother Japh's words, and wondered.

"And more on it," the Aedile went on, and Liam heard with some
surprise a genuine note of fear in his friend's voice, "I spoke with the
priests of Uris today. They're the best at hieromancy and scapulomancy
and all the other 'mancies, and had been casting and reading entrails and
throwing runes all day—and they absolutely refused to say a word about
what they'd seen. Refused me outright and sounded frighted about it.
What do you make of that?"

Ordinarily he would not have made much of it, but Mother Japh's
warning stuck in his head, and he could not help but give it some weight.
Coeccias fell silent, brooding over the fire and his cup of wine. After a
minute Liam shivered and stood up, pulling his cloak around his shoulders and saying he had to go.

"Must you?" the Aedile asked, a little desperately. "Have you eaten?
I'd hoped to talk a little more with you. How goes your search?"

"Well enough," Liam said briefly, knowing that he had not thought
enough about what he could tell his friend. He could not come out and
admit that he had penetrated Southwark's Guild, and though he was
fairly sure Duplin was his thief, he felt an obscure desire not to speak too
soon. There was his Luck to consider, and it did not care to be taken for
granted. "And I'm afraid I have eaten. I have to get some sleep. It was a
late night last night."

Coeccias smiled wanly, a sorry excuse for his normal broad grin. "I'll
warrant it was. Y'are close to your man, eh?"

Liam tipped his hand back and forth, temporizing. "I'm not sure.
Tomorrow, I hope, will tell. I'll be in the city all day. Do you want to have
lunch?"

By lunchtime he could figure out what to tell the Aedile and what
not.

"Aye, that'd like me. Noon, then, here?"

Liam agreed, and left his friend in the barracks, staring moodily at
the fire.

Liam was uneasy on the ride home, looking about him first in the
city, searching for signs of strangeness in the streets, the people, the air.
It seemed the same, the same thinning crowds as the night drew on, the
same torches and candlelit windows, the same patrols of Guards. But it
felt different, smelled different, like the smell just before lightning
strikes. It was expectant.

He breathed easier in the fields, with Diamond galloping smoothly
beneath him and the wind cutting at his face and hands, but his thoughts
slipped to more personal matters, and became confused.

What to tell Coeccias about his search loomed large, a question he
was now not sure he could answer. If he told him about the Guild, he
might be obliged to help Coeccias break it, and that would not necessarily be a bad thing. There was a part of him, though, that rebelled at
the idea, a part that did not like having gained the thieves' trust only to
betray it. If he had only found their hideout in the Point, and turned the
knowledge over to the Aedile, it might have been acceptable, but he had
met them, and used them for his own narrow purpose. He would not feel
right now in turning them over to arrest.

That led him to the fact that he had not even thought to ask them if
they had had any part in the assault on Bellona's temple. The same
problem applied as earlier: if he asked them about it, they would tell him
because they thought he was a thief, and telling Coeccias would make
him an informant. Apart from the possible danger of reprisals, the idea

was distasteful to him. He could draw a fine line between spying and informing, and had done so in the past.

A very fine line, he reminded himself, *but still a line. Gods, how do I get myself into these things?*

He cheered himself, though: his Luck seemed to be holding. Luck capitalized, personified, Liam Rhenford's Luck, as he thought of it. The mixed fortune that threw him into the frying pan and brought him out only slightly singed, with a meal in his hand. It was a strange image, but that was how he saw it.

In this case, his Luck had brought him close to Duplin, whom he strongly believed to be his thief, but left him with nearly insoluble questions about his friendship with the Aedile and his loyalty, however tenuous and misguided, to the Southwark Guild.

The house on the beach beckoned like a refuge, and he entered it happily.

I'm home, he projected, almost without thinking.

Welcome, Fanuilh thought back.

I'm going to sleep. Wake me an hour after dawn.

An hour after dawn, the dragon echoed, but Liam was already halfway undressed and did not respond. More tired than he had known, he crawled onto the divan in the library and was asleep before the lights had dimmed.

■ *8* ■

AN HOUR AFTER dawn, Fanuilh dipped into Liam's sleep and brought him out, leaving him to stretch luxuriously on the divan for almost fifteen minutes before:

You really should get up now.

"Why?" Liam asked loudly, then jumped when the dragon thought: *I am right here,* and he saw the creature crouched at the foot of his make-shift bed.

"Why?" he repeated, a little more calmly.

Because you have things to do.

"All right," Liam grumbled, and swung himself upright. His sleep had been long and deep, and he felt good. A short, bone-cracking stretch, then he stood up and made for the kitchen.

Will you have coffee? Fanuilh asked, trailing after him like a hungry dog.

"No, but you may have a bowl if you like."

The dragon ducked ahead of him and jumped up on the table; he did not need to repeat the offer. Steam rose from the jug in the oven as he imagined coffee, and he filled a bowl with it, picturing meat for Fanuilh and sausage and bread for himself in the oven.

They ate in silence, but Liam wondered what a stranger would make of the scene: a man and a miniature dragon seated opposite each other, breakfasting (one on raw meat and an aroma) with perfect composure.

You will find the thief today, Fanuilh predicted when it had finished its meat, and was sniffing in the last of the chilling coffee's scent.

"I hope so."

You are sure this Duplin is the thief?

"If he's not, then we're sunk, aren't we? I have no way of finding a wizard and, if he's not of the Guild, no way of tracking a rogue. It has to be."

Because you want it does not make it so.

"Who said I wanted it?" Liam retorted, without anger. The dragon was only giving voice to his own worries. "And anyway, what does it matter? If it's not Duplin, then what do I lose? A book, a wand and a rug that I don't know how to use. I'm more concerned about what to tell Coeccias."

Tell him nothing.

"That's easy for you to say. He's my friend, and he's the Aedile. Here I've gone and found the Southwark Guild, a thing he said was impossible, but I can't tell him. And I can't tell him because the only reason I found them was because I was once a thief, and now I feel a stupid obligation not to turn them over."

He will understand. He knows his limitations, and accepts them. He will understand—or at least accept it—if you say there are things you cannot tell him.

"I know that," Liam said. "That's the problem. He'll take it as another sign that I'm an expert thieftaker, and a man of 'deep parts,' or something else ridiculous, when all I'm really doing is protecting a bunch of thieves who ought to be locked up."

You were a thief once.

"Only for a little while," Liam protested, "and certainly not dirty and disorganized like these." It sounded stupid even as he said it, and he knew that the well-being he had felt on waking up had been false. There were, as usual, too many questions to answer, too many dilemmas to solve. Life was never easy, particularly when he had things to do.

He pursed his lips and blew, a gesture of resignation. "Righ. Forget that. I'll figure out something to tell Coeccias."

You are leaving now?

"Yes. As you said, I have things to do."

I will follow you, his familiar thought, then added, a quick block forming in his head before he could answer: *To guard your back.*

Liam did not refuse the offer.

The ride into Southwark, he realized that morning, was becoming something of a respite for him, a chance to think things out, to resolve thorny issues, to plan his day or, on the return, to mull it over.

Between the top of the cliff path and the city gate he decided what he would tell Coeccias, and what he would do if Duplin was a false lead. First, he would be open with his friend. He would explain what he had done, even how he had done it, and simply say that he could not give Coeccias any information that might be damaging to the Guild. On the other side, he decided that he could tell Mopsa to ask the Werewolf if any of his thieves had taken a hand in the attempted robbery of Bellona's temple. It did not strike him as the handiwork of a set of chanters as disorganized as the Southwark Guild, but he would ask. And if by chance one or more of them were involved, he would insist that Coeccias use the information only to placate Hierarch Cloten. After all, nothing had actually been stolen, and if Coeccias said that he knew who the thief was, but that he had fled Southwark, that surely ought to assuage the priest.

As for Duplin, if he turned out not to be Liam's thief, then that was all there was to it. It would mark the end of his investigation, and he would consider himself no worse off for his trouble. The book, the wand and the rug were useless to him, and though he did not like the idea of having lost some of Tarquin's things, there was little else he could do about it.

Sorry, he told Tarquin's shade, *but there reall is nothing else I can do about it. If Duplin is not our man, then we both lose.*

He had meant it as a joke, a small thing to lift his own spirits, but even as the thought trailed away in his mind, he remembered the grave on the beach with a shudder, and apologized to the wizard's spirit for the disrespect.

The shudder followed him into Southwark, though, and colored the way he saw the city. To the north of him lay Temple Street. A pregnant silence hung over the area, and the streets nearby were unnaturally quiet. People seemed to whisper, scurrying on their errands and avoiding the eyes of those they passed. Even the beggars looked apprehensive.

Cities, Liam knew, were like that, especially small cities, and most especially small port cities. People thought country folk were superstitious and easily frightened, but in reality it was city dwellers who became agitated at the slightest provocation. A base of common sense and healthy skepticism ran through the countryside of Taralon, while her cities were hotbeds of rumors, faceless fears and sourceless worries. Here, in Southwark, everyone would have seen or heard of the comets, most would have gotten wind of the attempted robbery of Bellona's temple, some few would know of the tensions in Temple Street, and almost none would have learned of the priests' disturbing discoveries there.

Nothing but gossip, yet the townsfolk acted as if Southwark were under siege.

A cold winter, Liam thought, *and nothing to do but sit and shiver.* The trading season was over, only a few coasthuggers were still sailing, and the small manufactories that supplied Southwark's goods were on half-time. The theater was closed, the menagerie that replaced it hardly worth the time. It was no wonder winter was Coeccias's busy time.

Liam was in a gloomy frame of mind when he finally met Mopsa, this time on the corner by the bath house they had visited the day before. As he approached, the girl produced two apples from the pocket of her coat and, with no small amount of ostentation, threw him one. He caught it one-handed.

"Breakfast," she announced with pride, the apples obviously stolen.

"Thanks," he said, his gloom lifting a little. "Not from a stand near here, are they?"

"No, up the hill a ways. The grocer'll never miss it."

"Where to, then?"

"Duplin had four more haunts; three quite near—one in Narrow Lane, as happens—and one up the hill. Can't go there till we've finished the apples."

"The nearest, then."

They walked unhurriedly through the streets toward the first two of Duplin's hideouts, munching on their apples. The sun was out and, though not warm, gave the pleasant illusion of warmth. Closer to the harbor, further from Temple Street, the city lost some its furtive aspect, seemed almost normal. People bustled a little more, hurried less, dallied in the streets to exchange greetings.

Duplin liked women, Liam decided after they had seen two more of the thief's hideouts, but they did not seem pleased with him. In the first hideout—two small rooms looking out on a dirty courtyard near the Storm King's temple—a girl of no more than eighteen years was installed. She pounced on them as soon as they had entered, demanding information about Duplin. The rent was coming due, and she was running out of pocket money.

"Actually," Liam said, "we were hoping you could help us find him."

"Find him?" the girl shouted. "How could I find him? I've lost him—or he's lost me, the bastard, more to the point—and haven't seen him in over a se'ennight. He's off on one of his jobs, he is, and's probably spending all the coin elsewhere ere coming back to me!"

"Did he say what the job was?"

"To me? Not likely," the girl said with scorn. "I'm just a toss for him—no talking, no loving, just a toss and a snore, that's Duplin."

Liam frowned at the girl's coarseness, and shot a glance at Mopsa. The two were no more than five years apart in age, and while he knew the young thief was no innocent, he was not comfortable having her hear such things. He could have spared himself the worry; she was leaning idly against the doorjamb, hardly listening.

"Nothing at all?"

"Not a word," Duplin's girl assured him.

"And when did you last see him?"

"A se'ennight, I told you, and look you, if you see him, you can tell him not to come bothering me without he's got coin in his pocket." She seemed prepared to go on, but he thanked her quickly, and ushered Mopsa out.

The second hideout was a few blocks away and much like the first, only the woman there was older and knew more.

"Aye, he told me of his job," she said suspiciously, "what's it to you?"

"We were supposed to work something together this week," Liam lied smoothly, having prepared on the walk over, "and I haven't been able to find him."

The lie paid off, far more than he had expected it to.

"So y'are the one, eh?" The woman snorted her disbelief. "Funny, you don't look like a tar."

"Well . . ."

"I know, I know, you're in disguise. Right. Look, if he's ducking you, it's no more than he's doing to me. You were supposed to do that job, what, three days ago? He's probably gone and done it without you, and left us both in the lurch."

"Gods, I hope not," Liam said, feigning worry and trying to be as vague as possible. "It's pretty dangerous."

The woman laughed loudly. "Dangerous, he says! A little ride in a boat and a simple break-in! Dangerous! Y'are just worried about your share!"

He smiled sheepishly. "I suppose I am, yes."

"Well I'm afraid you've lost it, tar, because Duplin must have gone and done it without you."

Liam tried to prolong the conversation, but there was little he could do without admitting that he knew nothing of the job Duplin had planned. He and Mopsa left then, promising to let the woman know if they ran into the thief.

In the street, Mopsa nodded at him with judicious approval. "Well lied, uncle."

He bowed. "Next."

"His next is in Narrow Lane," she said, and began leading the way there, rhapsodizing on the various great lies she had heard in her time. Liam, however, was not listening: he was struggling with the information he had just learned.

Duplin had planned a big job for the night his house was robbed, which made perfect sense to him, but he was puzzled at the inclusion of a sailor and a "little boat ride." The break-in was obvious, but how did the boat ride fit in? And where was Duplin?

Celebrating, Liam thought, answering his second question. *Sitting somewhere and drinking up the money he got from selling my things.* That in and of itself was problematic—he had resigned himself to Duplin having already fenced the book, the rug and the wand, but he wanted them back. Having tracked Duplin, he would then have to track down the fence, or the client for whom the robbery had been committed. The idea of a client raised a number of issues, but he put them aside for the moment; his first question interested him much more than either the hypothetical client or the more probable fence.

Why had the boat been necessary?

The answer, when it came to him, was so plain it was painful. Duplin had decided not to brave the cliff path at night and had left Southwark by sea, rowing or perhaps sailing out of the harbor, past the Teeth, and down the coast to Liam's cove. That explained the sailor—someone to handle the boat.

Mopsa was still rattling on about a huge lie she had told to get out of some punishment or other, but he interrupted her.

"Did Duplin ever accept commissions?"

The girl stopped in midsentence, confused. "What?"

"Commissions. Did people ever pay him to steal things for them?" It was a question he should have asked much earlier, because even though he had convinced himself that Duplin had been the thief, and even imagined he knew how he had gotten to the cove, he still did not know how he had gotten past Tarquin's wards. A client—almost certainly a wizard—was required. More, it would explain why Duplin had restricted himself to just the three things. Without specific instructions, the thief would probably have emptied the whole house.

Mopsa's answer was not quite what he hoped.

"No," she said firmly, "the Wolf won't allow it. See, there was a time a long whiles ago, when some merchant or other—some say it was Ancus

Marcius, and some Master Goddard, still others some Freeporter—hired one of the Guild to steal the account books of another, and it led to all sorts of troubles. The Addle came close to breaking us, it's said, so the Wolf's hard against taking jobs from outsiders.

"Duplin, though," she went on, as if considering an idea new to her, "he just might. He and the Wolf are always arguing about the Legium and what's in it and what's not. He's got all sorts of fancy ideas."

"Who's 'the Addle'?"

She looked at him to see if he were joking. "Who's the Addle?"

"Yes."

"The Addle is . . . the Addle. The Ladle. The Big Dog, the head of the pack."

Dog was chant for thieftaker, the Big Dog. . . . "The Aedile? Aedile Coeccias?"

"Who else?" she snorted, then pursed her lips disdainfully. "As if you didn't know who the Addle was."

There was something strange in the way she said the last that made him frown, wondering what she meant. Aedile was not a common title in Taralon, and neither Addle nor Ladle, though they made sense for Southwark, were part of the chant. How was he supposed to know who 'the Addle' was?

They had reached Narrow Lane, and the second to last of the places Duplin frequented. Liam looked skeptically at the run-down wineshop Mopsa indicated, just beyond the bend where the road touched the back of the Duke's courts. It was a cramped little place, barely two yards wide at the street but delving deep into the heart of the building. Shards of glass and clay from shattered bottles and jugs crunched underfoot as he and Mopsa entered, and the air was thick with the smell of smoke, sour wine and other, less pleasant things. Liam picked his way carefully across the open floor, to where a thickset man slept in a chair, his feet propped up on another. A dog, a dimly seen shadow with flashing teeth, snarled from behind the man's chair, and he jerked awake, bellowing: "Get out! Get out, you bastards!"

Then he saw Liam and Mopsa, frozen stock still, the daylight at their backs. He spat, ran a hand over his completely bald head. "Sorry. Who are you?" His second greeting was only marginally more friendly.

Liam cleared his throat. "I'm looking for a fellow named Duplin—" Liam began, but the bald man twitched, startled.

"Never heard of him," he said immediately. "Don't know him."

Mopsa nudged Liam, shook her head. "Are you sure?" Liam asked. "He comes here quite often, sometimes gets messages. He was telling me just a few days ago about your place, how much he likes it, and that I could leave word for him here."

The bald man pinched his nose between two fingers, and looked suspiciously at Liam. He began to say something, and then the dog behind him growled. He reached back and swatted at it.

"Shut your hole, mutt," he ordered, then turned to Liam. "Can't take a message for a man I don't know." He sounded sullen, like a child asked to wash behind his ears. "Couldn't even if I wanted to. Never heard of your friend. Got enough trouble here without taking messages for people I don't know."

Liam glanced around at the mess of the wineshop, the remains of bottles, the puddles of vomit and urine, and nodded. The place smelled like it had been festering for days. The bald man, however, was staring at the floor, chewing on his lower lip, considering. A troubled look passed over him as he absently reached one hand down to pat the dog.

"Friend," Liam said softly, unwilling to intrude upon the man's sudden reverie, "if you should see Duplin, could you—"

"I won't see him!" the bald man shouted, jumping up from his chair and setting the dog to barking. "I won't see him, I don't know him, now get out!"

The dog lunged between his legs at Liam and Mopsa, and they ran, not waiting to see him catch the beast by its spiked collar.

Halfway down Narrow Lane they stopped to catch their breath, the dog's deep-throated barking still barely audible.

"Duplin has nice friends," Liam commented. Mopsa frowned in the midst of her panting.

"He knows Duplin. He's lying."

"I gathered."

That much he had understood. But why? Nor did he understand the man's quick, irrational anger, or the vaguely sad mood that had preceded it. It was hardly to the point, however, and he put the question away at the back of his mind—adding to the pile already there—and focused on the important issue.

"All right, let's get on. There's only one more, eh? Then he's got to be there."

The last of Duplin's hideouts was as much of a disappointment as the others. In the neighborhood just next to the Point, it was a set of rooms on the fifth floor of a building with a large courtyard, and the owner told them that he had not see Duplin in five days.

"Nor, his wife," the man added with an angry shake of his head, "but that in four days. And of course, that with her 'brother,' and the two of them cozier than a brother and sister should be, if you take my meaning."

"Cozy?"

The man laughed, a little bitterly. "I'll warrant Duplin's wife is now at sea with his brother-in-law." He laughed again, and Liam understood that he found Duplin's being cuckolded some consolation for the loss of a tenant.

"Ran out on him, did she?"

"My guess," the landlord said, shaking his head again and smiling ruefully. "And me not likely to see the rent for another month."

"What did you mean by 'at sea'?"

"Oh, that," the landlord said. "Her 'brother' was a sea captain, a passing tar, no land legs, even. Pray you," he said, changing the subject suddenly, "you wouldn't be looking for rooms, would you?"

"No," Liam said. "Sorry to bother you."

Mopsa held herself in until they were back in the street, the landlord safely out of earshot.

"She wasn't—" the girl began eagerly.

"Duplin's wife," Liam finished for her. "I know. Duplin isn't married."

Mopsa pouted a little, but Liam did not notice. He was thinking about Duplin's woman and his "brother-in-law," the sea captain, presumably the tar for whom Liam had been mistaken earlier. If she had run off with the man with whom Duplin was planning his job, what did that mean? No one had seen the thief since the time just before the night Liam was robbed, and now one of his women—his favorite, judging from the better neighborhood he kept her in—had disappeared with his accomplice.

He was making much of it up, piecing it together from inadequate clues, but if the story he was imagining held true, it was entirely possible that Duplin was dead, with Tarquin's enchanted things on their way to some distant port. He cursed.

"What?" Mopsa asked, driven out of her pout by curiosity. "What's that for?"

"That is for the fact that Duplin may well be dead, which means I'll never get my things back."

"Duplin dead? Nah, can't be. He's canny, I tell you. If you're thinking the sea captain and his punk . . . well, forget it. Not likely, not in the least. Duplin's too careful for that."

The way she said this, though, only planted the idea more firmly in Liam's head. She spoke as though Duplin were a hero, however, and the death Liam had suggested were unwelcome feet of clay on her idol. He did not press the idea.

"I think that's enough for now," he told her.

"No lunch?" she said, placing her fists on her boyish hips. "I got breakfast."

"Here," he produced a coin. "Buy yourself lunch."

"What about you?"

"I'm not hungry."

She rolled her eyes. "That's not what I mean, uncle. I mean, what are you going to do?"

"Not eat lunch," he said, puzzled.

"About Duplin," she prompted. "What are you going to do about Duplin?"

"Nothing," he said, though that was not true. He thought he might go down to the waterfront and look around there, but he did not need the girl for that. "I think I'm finished with Duplin."

"He's not dead," Mopsa insisted. "You should revisit his haunts tomorrow. I'll with you. What time will we meet?"

"We won't," he said, not wanting to tell her how sure he was that Duplin was dead. "I know where they are now. If I want to, I can find them myself."

"Ha! I doubt it! You couldn't find your way around the Warren, I warrant, let alone down on Narrow Lane. I'll with you."

Looking down at the girl, he was suddenly reminded of how young she was, and how hard it must be for her in the Guild. She probably wanted to continue helping him because it meant she would not be cuffed by the Werewolf or kicked around by Japer.

And because you buy her clothes and food, Liam told himself. He remembered a half-wild cat he had once given food to, that had developed a persistent attachment to him. He had eventually had to take it along with him on a sea voyage—it refused to be left behind—and they had found it in the hold halfway through the trip, dead in the midst of a pack of giant rats.

He did not plan to take Mopsa to sea with him, though.

"All right," he said at last. "We'll meet at the same time tomorrow, but down on the docks. Do you know where Duke Street comes out on the waterfront?"

"I can find it," she said confidently. "No worry. I'll meet you there."

"Don't be late," he called out, but she was already hurrying off down the street, his coin clutched tightly in her fist.

● ● ●

Coeccias was seated by one of the hearths when Liam came into the Guards' barracks, staring at the fire there, and for a moment he wondered if the Aedile had moved since he left him the night before. Seeing his friend's face, he thought of the name Mopsa had given him and bit back a guilty grin; Coeccias indeed looked addled, and his lips moved soundlessly, as if he were working some complex calculaion in his head. Liam remembered then, with a pang of regret, that he had forgotten to tell the girl to ask the Werewolf if the Guild was involved in the business at Bellona's temple.

"Hello, Coeccias. Have you forgotten our lunch?"

The Aedile jumped as if stung, flushing, and clutched Liam's arm.

"Truth, Rhenford, you near frightened me to death. My mind was wandering far and abroad—but I'd not forgotten. I'm here, am I not?" He smiled, as if he had made a feeble joke. "Then, where else would I be?"

"Trouble?"

"Say 'More trouble,' or the 'The same trouble twice over with a new trouble added for spice,' and you come close." Liam's presence seemed to have invigorated him; he took a deep breath and snatched his jacket from a peg, bustled Liam to the door. "But we'll have more on it over lunch. I'm passing sick of this room."

He stamped across the square, Liam trailing in his wake, into a large tavern. The owner knew him, made a deferential bow; Coeccias hardly acknowledged it, leading the way up a narrow, twisting staircase to the second floor, where a number of tables stood by windows looking out over the square. They took a table by a window that looked out on the Duke's courts, the owner fussing over their chairs and gushing a list of specialties he was pleased to offer "Your Eminence, Master Aedile."

"Enough, Herlekin," Coeccias growled, "two pies, two pints, and some privacy."

Herlekin hurried away, not at all put off by the Aedile's gruff manner. When he was gone, Coeccias gave a long, exhausted sigh and rubbed briefly at his eyes.

"As bad as that?" Liam had rarely seen his friend so harried, and felt bad for him.

"Worse." He launched into a description of Cloten's latest tantrums, the increased pressure the Hierarch was bringing to bear, the heightened tensions in Temple Street. Three more chandlers had come, demanding action on the *Heart of Oak,* the ship that weighed anchor without paying its bills—"As if I could whistle up a squadron and hunt them down!"—

and someone had broken into a number of apothecaries' and herbalists' shops the night before.

"Not one, mind you, or two," he explained, "but seven—all the ones in the city! No money taken, in course, that would make too much sense. Just a mess made, and some different herbs and things taken, some with value, some without. Most likely vandals, but passing thorough vandals, to hit seven different shops in seven different places, and take no coin and an odd assortment of plants."

Liam thought of his own very particular thief, and began to wonder.

"Oh, but there's more . . ." Coeccias paused as Herlekin returned with their meals and fulsome wishes for their enjoyment. When he had left, the Aedile pushed aside his plate and leaned close over the table. "Remember the omens the priests wouldn't tell me about, and the lights all down Temples' Court being snuffed?"

"Yes?" Liam felt himself falling prey to Coeccias's conspiratorial tone, leaning in himself, speaking in a hushed tone.

"No more on it, of course, no details, no telling points, but a deputation from Temples' Court to ask me to petition the Duke for the right to a cleansing."

Liam gestured to indicated he did not know what a cleansing was. Coeccias had a definition ready; he knew that Liam was not familiar with Southwark's various rites and rituals.

"Do you remember Uris-tide Eve? The rite here and the procession and blessing around the city?" Liam did remember it; he had sat at that very table to watch the ceremony in the square. "It's much like that, only more so. The whole pantheon participates, priests and acolytes from all the gods in Temples' Court, and there's a great number of sacrifices— little boats burned in the harbor, calves and goats on all the altars, a general fast for a day. There's usually one before the trading season starts, to propitiate all and sundry above in hopes of a good return. But they want one now, and they have to get the Duke's permission, for it fair shuts the whole city down for a day and a night."

"All the temples participate?"

"There y'have the thorny part. The Duke'd be glad to have a cleansing—he's strong for the old rites and ways—but will Bellona be included? Cloten has made himself so noxious to the others that none know if She'll be allowed in. Her worship is new, Her godhead unproven to many. While the cleansing might make things right with the gods, it might make things worse among Their priests."

"And Temple Street is not a very comfortable place as it is," Liam pointed out. "I passed near it this morning, and it felt like there was a pall over the whole neighborhood."

"Aye, I don't doubt you'd notice it, sharp as y'are. I swear it's colder there than anywhere else in the city. The air fair freezes in your lungs."

"So what did you do?"

"What could I? When the Hierarchs of twelve temples ask you to ask for a cleansing, you ask. What's more, I think it wise, if it can be worked. It'll take a day for my courier to reach the Duke, he'll make a quick answer, a day to return. The temples have promised to reach a decision on whether to include Bellona, and have agreed that I can cancel the cleansing, even if the Duke approves it."

Liam was impressed. "They said that?"

"I stand well with the priests," Coeccias said, without trace of pride; rather as if it were an unpleasant burden. "They trust me to do what's fit." What exactly was fit was left unexplored, and in a heavy, contemplative silence the two men picked at their meals.

It was a complicated set of affairs, and Liam could understand the distracted look he had seen on the other man's face in the barracks. He was sorry he had not sent a message to the Werewolf, and sorry he could not be of much help to the Aedile. On the other hand, his own business had grown far more complicated than he had envisioned four days earlier riding into Southwark and realizing he was bored. Something to do was one thing; a million things and a practically unsolvable crime were another. A small, cringing part of him was glad that Coeccias was so distracted with his own worries he did not think to ask Liam about his.

They sat that way, eating disinterestedly, for almost a quarter of an hour, and then Coeccias pushed away his plate and glanced out the window. Something caught his eye and he leaned closer, his breath fogging the glass. He wiped impatiently at the spot, craning his neck to look down into the square.

"What is that idiot doing?" he asked, more of himself than Liam.

"What's going on?"

"It's that Boult, waving his arms like a madman. I've never seen him like that." He stood, fumbled with the window latch, swung it open. "Boult!" Then louder, a roar that turned heads across the square: *"Boult!"*

Liam saw the man, a Guard who had helped him find Tarquin's murderer and was as completely unflappable as anyone he had ever met, jumping up and down on the stairs of the barracks, shouting at the Guard here.

"Boult, you ass!" Coeccias bellowed, and the Guard spun around so

fast on the stairs that he almost fell off. Then he was sprinting across the square, skidding to a halt beneath the window and gasping up at the Aedile.

"Fighting—fighting in Temples' Court!"

With a curse, Coeccias dashed away from the table and down the stairs, his speed surprising in so heavy a man, leaving Liam alone at the table.

Liam himself, a little stunned, sat at the table for a few seconds after Coeccias's heavy footsteps had faded down the staircase. Then he shook his head and stood up quickly, dropping coins on the table and running after his friend.

Fanuilh? he projected from the stairs, remembering that the dragon had said it would follow him into the city. *Where are you?*

On top of the inn, master.

Go to Temple Street, Liam ordered. *Wait for me there.*

He came out of the inn just as Coeccias emerged from the barracks, a small buckler in one hand and two wooden truncheons in the other. Boult and the Guard from the door were right behind him, bucklers and truncheons ready.

The Aedile saw him, pointed toward the way to Temple Street. They met at the northeast corner of the square, and Coeccias tossed Liam his extra truncheon.

Master? Fanuilh asked.

Go, Liam projected, falling into step next to Coeccias. He mouthed the word to himself: "Go."

■ *9* ■

WHAT AM I doing? Liam thought, loping alongside the grimly puffing Aedile, in front of the two Guards. He clarified his thought for himself: *What do you think you're going to do?*

Temple Street was like a drain, like a sinkhole that had opened up in Southwark and was drawing the city inexorably toward itself. As they ran, others joined them, little tributaries mixing into the main flood that coursed down the crooked street, past the staid fronts of the established temples toward the cul-de-sac where the fighting undoubtedly was.

Vendors, beggars, shopkeepers, even women and a crowd of children became part of the group led by Coeccias, and Liam was relieved to see at least ten more Guards, drawn by the shouting, fall in behind them. He clutched the heavy truncheon, had a moment to notice the button of metal at the base of the handle—*An iron core?* he wondered—and then the entire mass rumbled to a stop at the entrance to the cul-de-sac, halting raggedly behind the Aedile's outflung arms.

Almost thirty men struggled around the fountain, a tangled mess of writhing, flailing figures, pressed too close for real sword work and mostly striking with pommels or fists. Bellona's men wore chain shirts, Strife's only brown robes, but it was not clear if either had the advantage. Liam could see two men calmly surveying the scene from the steps of Bellona's temple, presumably Cloten and Alastor; another man, presumably Guiderius, raged and shouted in the gateway to Strife's walled compound. The noise was what Liam remembered of battle—confusion made audible, a hundred wordless shouts, the clang and thump—and for the better part of a second, he wondered whether Strife and Bellona should meet in so common a manner, like feuding lords. There was no style to this fight, only a milling, mindless brawl.

Then Coeccias was calling out instructions: "Half the men with Boult, to the left, half the men with me to the right, and for truth's sake don't hit each other!"

A second of confusion among the Guards, and then they split smoothly, running into the square as Coeccias had ordered, only twelve to separate thirty. Liam ran after the Aedile, his knuckles white on the truncheon, sparing a second to glance at the steps of Laomedon's temple, where a woman in a close-fitting hood and black robes stood smiling, as black-robed acolytes clustered about her.

Master.

The thought was a distraction; he was running, he had no time to answer.

This is not safe, master, Fanuilh thought to him again, but by then he was following Coeccias into the whirl of fighting men, dodging a sword at its edge. He whirled, trying to catch the blade on his truncheon, missed, hit the owner in the side of the head, stumbled backward into another man, bore him to the ground.

He was disentangling himself from the man's legs when another sword flashed above him. He thrust the truncheon forward by both ends, praying, *An iron core, please,* and the sword hit his stick, jarred his arms practically out of their sockets and threw him back onto the man he had knocked down a second before. The sword came with him, lodged in the wood, and a Guard decked Liam's disarmed opponent with a shrewd blow to the head from the haft of a pike.

And it was over.

The Guards were pushing the men apart, kicking and shoving with pikes and truncheons, angry blows and loud curses. Wounded men—there was blood in the fountain, blood on the cobbles around it—staggered to their feet, some were helped up by their companions. Liam scrambled upright, stepped away from the man he had knocked down, and looked around, breathing a vast, happy sigh.

From the corner of his eye he saw Coeccias's truncheon flash out, and just after the Aedile's curse heard bones cracking; a follower of Bellona howled and dropped his sword.

"Back off, you bastard!" Liam had never seen his friend like this—so angry. If he could have, he would have warned Cloten not to shove his way forward, through his retreating men, to confront the Aedile.

"Well, Master Aedile," the Hierarch said, his thick, half-swallowed

Caernarvon consonants making him almost unintelligible. "I hope you are happy!"

Coeccias twitched—visibly twitched, the truncheon jerking an inch like a reflex—and Liam turned away, wondering which of Cloten's bones would break first.

He found himself looking at the Death, the hooded woman on the steps of Laomedon's temple, and she was staring directly at him. He could tell she was staring at him, had singled him out from all the men around the fountain, all the men in the cul-de-sac, and when she was sure he knew, she smiled and bowed. It was a knowing smile, and a very slight bow, but it unnerved him more than the whole fight. He turned quickly back to Cloten and Coeccias.

"What . . ." the Aedile was saying, struggling for control of himself, "what do you mean, Hierarch?"

"I mean," Cloten said, tilting his chin up, "that if you had arrested only the men responsible for the attack on me, none of this would have happened." He was wearing a long purple robe under a steel breastplate, but his hands were empty. His hair was cropped in a bowl shape just above his ears; his lips were thin and bloodless; the chin he tilted at the Aedile was sharp. Liam disliked him instantly.

"I trust," said a new, cold voice, "that y'are not referring to my brothers." It was Guiderius, a tall man in a simple brown robe. He had a neatly trimmed, graying chin beard and a heavy mace in one hand. He bowed to Coeccias. "I must apologize for my brothers, Master Aedile; they were provoked."

Coeccias was grinding his teeth, glaring at Cloten, who spoke immediately: "I am referring precisely to your brothers, Guiderius, who first attacked me in my temple—"

Master. There was an emphasis to Fanuilh's thought, a hint of urgency, but Liam shrugged it off.

"—and have now called for open battle in the street!"

Master!

"Hush!" Liam said aloud, meaning Fanuilh but drawing the attention of the two Hierarchs and the Aedile.

Guiderius almost smiled, but Cloten goggled.

"Can you not restrain your . . . your constables, Aedile?" he demanded.

"He's not of the Guard," Coeccias grated, flashing Liam an irritated glance, "he's a Quaestor, the Duke's servant, and you, sir, will remember it. More," he went on, his voice gaining volume, "you will all go into your temple and not leave it without my permission. No man is to enter this

street armed again, or I'll clap him in. And you"—he jabbed at Cloten
with his truncheon, making the Hierarch jump back a step—"you'll await
my pleasure. Is it clear? You'll wait on me, and not say a word, nor stir
forth from the fane, until I've come to you. Is it clear?"

Cloten gasped like a fish out of water.

"Is it clear?" Coeccias asked again, a dangerous low rumble.

"It is clear," the Hierarch stammered, and stalked off to Bellona's
temple.

Coeccias turned to the other priest, his anger hardly abated, but
tempered a little by his apology. "It ranks me, Guiderius, but I must ask
the same of you. No armed men in the street, and I'll have to come to
you with questions. If you'd wait on me . . ."

"Certainly," the old priest said, not easily. "I understand, Coeccias.
I'll wait on you." He bowed and turned away, calling for his men to
follow him. The brown-robed acolytes moved as a unit, bearing their
wounded with them, and disappeared into Strife's crenellated compound.
Bellona's men, however, straggled back into her temple in some disarray,
their Hierarch already gone. Liam caught a glimpse of Scaevola helping a
man with a deep cut on his leg, practically carrying him up the steps.

I didn't see him in the fight, he thought. *Was he there?* He decided not:
he did not think Guiderius's men would have stood long against the sick
man. *Not with his speed,* Liam thought. *I'd pit him against a score any day.*

He had a vision, for a moment, of Scaevola dancing through the cul-
de-sac, his sword flickering like lightning, men falling behind him like
reeds. Then Coeccias barked a laugh at him, and Fanuilh thrust a dense
block of thought into his head.

"Truth, Rhenford! 'Hush,' indeed!"

MASTER!

What is it? he projected, trying to shape the question to include his
exasperation while forcing himself to smile sheepishly at the Aedile—no
mean task, he discovered. It was not easy to divorce his outward expression from his inward thought, like holding two conversations at once, on
wildly different subjects. Which was exactly what he was doing.

Coeccias shook his head, as if he were not sure whether he was
amused by Liam's outburst, or annoyed by it. "Now what made you do
that, I wonder?"

I have found the rug.

"What?" Liam could not help it; the word slipped out just as "Hush"
had a moment before. Fortunately, Coeccias had already turned away,
putting off his judgment and his question, barking orders to the Guards,
who were the only people left in the cul-de-sac.

I have found the rug.

Liam took a deep breath, reminding himself to keep this conversation silent.

Where?

On the roof of Bellona's temple. Do you wish to see?

Yes.

The Guards had been dispatched on various errands—gathering the scattered weapons around the fountain, clearing away the crowd farther up Temple Street, taking position by the entrances of the two fighting temples—before Coeccias sought Liam out.

He was sitting on the edge of the fountain. By the time the Aedile came to stand before him, he had already seen the rug through Fanuilh's eyes. It lay flat on the roof of Bellona's temple, next to one of the windows in the dome, invisible from the street. Fanuilh had flown up and switched its own sight for Liam's, and he had experienced a dizzying moment, hanging above the street, peering down at the splash of purple on gray stone, the tiny figures—himself included—far below.

Are you sure it's Tarquin's rug? he projected, when his vision was restored. He could see his hands, clutching at the fabric of his pants.

There is the eagle, and the color is correct.

"Stupid question," he muttered to himself; it was obviously Tarquin's rug, and just as obviously stuck up on Cloten's roof.

Can you bring it down?

Then Coeccias was in front of him, concern on his face.

"Rhenford? Is all well?"

He realized he must have looked strange, perched on the fountain, lost to the world. He jumped up quickly. "Yes, I'm fine, fine. Just tired. The fight—"

Coeccias's jaw dropped, making a round O of his mouth. "Gods, Rhenford, you should not have been in that! What were you thinking? Y'are no bruiser!"

Liam brushed the Aedile's hand from his shoulder. "Don't worry about it. I'm fine. But I have to talk to you, now."

"In course, in course. Y'are sure all is well?"

"No," he said deliberately. "All is not well. We need to talk, right now. It's about this whole business." He gestured all around, at the temples, the blood on the cobblestones.

Master, is this wise?

Never mind, Liam projected, faster and with more assurance than he had ever displayed before, *I should tell him, and I should tell him now, before he goes to meet the Hierarchs.*

Aloud, he said: "Is there someplace we can go that is private, and has access to a roof?"

Coeccias's look of concern grew careful and placating.

"Certainly. Certainly."

"Don't look at me like that," Liam snapped, "I'm not mad, and I haven't gone battle crazy. The rug that was stolen from me is up on top of Bellona's temple, and I'm sure it was used in the robbery."

"Rhenford," the Aedile began, then stopped and shrugged. "I'll not argue. Y'are sure?"

"Yes."

"And you want a roof? Any roof, or Bellona's roof?"

"Any roof, but it can't be seen from the street."

"Right, then, the Duke's courts would be the place, Milord May-Do-Aught."

It was a name he had given Liam during the search for Tarquin's murderer, and by it he meant that he had decided never to be surprised by anything Liam did. So with no further argument, he started walking out of Temple Street.

Liam walked beside him, projecting to Fanuilh.

Can you bring the rug?

Yes, though people might see.

Let them see. They've seen enough strange things—a dragon with a carpet won't seem out of place.

As you wish, master.

Exactly, Liam finished, though he found he could not give the mental phrase the ironic twist he wished. *I'll work on that,* he added, more to himself than to Fanuilh.

Coeccias was mumbling to himself as well, and Liam caught only a few of his phrases, but the irony in them was clear. "Charges into a fray like he's berserk . . . finds his rug where my thief should be . . . can't be seen from the street . . . Milord May . . ."

Liam was only half listening; he was revising the list of things he had promised himself he would tell his friend that morning. There was little point explaining his experiences with war or corpses: they were not relevant to the fact of Tarquin's rug and Bellona's temple. His relationship with Fanuilh, on the other hand, was completely relevant. He could not explain how he knew where to find the rug without exposing the link between them, nor the fact that the little dragon was about to bring the rug to them.

There might have been an easier way to do it; he could have had Fanuilh bring the rug back to the house on the beach after dark, and tell Coeccias the next day that he had found it on a tip from an anonymous thief. But that would take too long, and the Aedile was going to speak with the Hierarchs that afternoon. If he knew about the rug, it might change his approach.

Their approach, Liam realized, because it seemed plain to him now that their two thieves were connected, if not one and the same. Though why a thief who could break through Tarquin's wards would need the rug to break into Bellona's temple was beyond him.

Still muttering, Coeccias led the way through streets buzzing with the news of the fighting, shrugging off questions and shouts from the townsfolk with a gruff: "Naught to worry on, all over, out of the way."

They crossed the square and mounted the steps of the Duke's courts; Coeccias pounded a fist on the oak boards and, when the surly porter appeared, shouldered him aside.

"We're going upstairs and don't wish to be disturbed. Give me the key to the bell tower."

"The bell ringer has it," the porter shot back.

"He's up there?"

"It's almost the hour, isn't it?"

Coeccias growled and hefted his truncheon; the porter jumped back. "Let's up, then," he said to Liam.

Fanuilh, Liam projected, *do you know where we're going?*

I am already there, master.

Liam glanced up at the ceiling of the hallway instinctively. *I did not see you.*

I saw you, Fanuilh returned. *You were looking at your feet.*

They were on the stairs, climbing up.

Did anyone see you?

I do not think so.

They passed three landings, the stairs changing at the second from stone to wood—dark, massive beams. Thin arrow-slits threw narrow beams of light into the stairwell.

And you have the rug?

It is here. But the bell ringer is here as well. He has not seen me, the dragon added, before Liam could ask.

They reached the top of the staircase, and Coeccias opened a door onto a small passageway. It broadened after a few yards into a long attic with steeply pitched sides, rough plank floors layered in dust. A set of footprints ran from the passageway straight to a rack of bells, which a man was polishing. His legs were crooked, so he appeared to stoop even when standing upright, but his arms and torso were thick with muscle, which made him look top-heavy. He did not respond to Coeccias's calls until the Aedile touched his back.

Then he turned slowly from his bells, a smile creeping across his face when he saw who it was.

"Master Aedile," he said, recognizing a friend.

"Yes, Tundal," Coeccias shouted. "I need you to leave the bells for a minute."

Tundal was only deaf, not slow, and he pointed to a sand clock attached to the rack. The mound in the lower half almost filled the glass.

"It's the hour soon, Master Coeccias. I have to ring them." He spoke in a barely audible whisper.

"I know, Tundal, but this will only take a moment. The bells can wait."

The bell ringer shrugged and walked off, nodding politely to Liam as he passed. His twisted legs gave him a peculiar up-and-down gait. When he had closed the door at the top of the stairwell, Coeccias turned to Liam.

"This won't take long, will it?"

"No," Liam said, looking quickly around the attic. *Come in, Fanuilh.*

The bell rack stood in the center of the attic, where a tower pierced the roof, rising an additional two stories. Open shutters allowed the sound to reach the city. The dragon flew in through one of these, the rug clutched in its claws, rolled up now. It turned smoothly and fluttered down to land in front of Liam and the astonished Aedile.

How did you roll it up? Liam projected.

With my claws, the dragon answered, and Liam was again sure that there should have been a qualifier to the statement, something along the lines of *How else?*

"Tarquin's familiar?" Coeccias said, pointing at Fanuilh and waiting for an explanation.

"My familiar," Liam corrected.

"Then y'are a wizard!" To Liam's surprise, his friend looked triumphant, as if a long-held suspicion had proved right.

"No," Liam hastened to say. "Not at all." He quickly outlined the beginning and extent of his link to Fanuilh—how he had found the dragon the night Tarquin was killed, how it had bonded to him against his will, taking part of his soul with a bite, how they communicated, could share sight—as much as was necessary to explain the finding of the rug.

"So he found it?" Coeccias asked at last, to clarify.

"Yes. And that's why I wanted to tell you right away, because—"

"Because then our thieves are one and the same," the Aedile finished, and a sly smile lit up his face. "Which means that I did no wrong to label you Quaestor in Temples' Court, for that you'll now help me to sort out Cloten!"

Liam was at a loss for words for a moment. He had expected to offer his help, not have it taken for granted. That did not bother him, though; what puzzled him was how quickly Coeccias had understood, how quickly he had connected the crimes and known that Liam would be willing to help.

He knew the other man considered him a human bloodhound, a master thieftaker, but he thought he had made it clear that he was not any of those things. Now he wondered if he really had those skills, or if he just seemed that way to others.

"Y'are sure y'are not a wizard?"

"Positive," Liam said at once. "I am definitely not a wizard."

"And he," Coeccias asked, pointing at Fanuilh, "he is not a wizard?"

"I . . . I don't know. I'm not sure. Are you a wizard?"

The dragon peered up at him for a moment, a quizzical expression in its slit eyes. *You know I am not a wizard, master,* it told him.

"No. Fanuilh is no wizard."

"More's the pity," Coeccias said. "A wizard could solve this in a moment. For us to do it will require at least another lunch. Come, I'm hungry."

With the rug tucked under his arm, Liam followed Coeccias down the narrow staircase. Above them, Tundal rang the bells as quickly as he could, trying to make up for their lateness with speed. Above Tundal, Liam assumed, Fanuilh would be flying back to the house on the beach, there to wait for him to return home.

They went back to Herlekin's restaurant, and their table on the second floor. New pies were brought, and new mugs of beer, and both men made significant inroads before they began to speak.

"I won't ask," Coeccias started, "about your joining the fray in Temples' Court. I won't ask about the way you handled your truncheon, and I won't ask why you didn't tell me about Fanuilh when we were conning out that woman."

"That woman" had killed Tarquin, and Liam was happy not to have to explain; he had kept the matter secret for fear that suspicion would fall on him. He said nothing, though, waiting for what Coeccias would ask.

"I needs must know, though," he continued, "what you've learned about your thief. You can see that, eh?"

"Yes," Liam said gravely. "It makes sense." He had realized that as soon as Fanuilh told him where the rug lay, and had hastily organized his thoughts, seeking a way to tell what was necessary without exposing the Guild.

"You've made contact with the thieves here, then?"

Liam admitted that he had, and started in on his roundabout explanation. Coeccias stopped him.

"No. I'll ask, and you answer. If there're those you wish to protect, it'll be easier."

Liam nodded eagerly, surprised again at the Aedile's comprehension of his dilemma, and relieved by his delicacy.

"Do you know your thief?"

"I think so," Liam said, "but I can't find him."

"And it'd not do to have the Guard searching for him?"

"No, it wouldn't, but that's not the real problem. The real problem is that I think he's dead."

With as little detail as possible and no names, Liam told what he had learned with Mopsa: the outlines of Duplin's plan, the fact that no one had seen him since the night before the twin robberies, the disappearance of the woman he kept near the Point and her "brother," the sailor.

"So your thief takes a boat from the harbor with this sailor, steals your rug, and then returns to Southwark to use the rug to get to the roof of Bellona's fane. He drops onto the altar, tries to lift the treasury, and is surprised by Cloten. He drops Cloten and flees, the rug left behind. And then you think the sailor killed him and fled with the girl?"

"That's my guess," Liam said, "but there are problems with it. First of all, why leave the rug?"

"Easy enough—they weren't with him, or couldn't get to it. He left it on the roof in his haste."

"Possible, but why would he need the rug in the first place? From what I've heard, he was an excellent thief, so he should have been able to climb that wall easily."

"He needed it to take that heavy chest from the altar," Coeccias suggested, but even he could see the problem with that. "How did he plan to get the chest off the altar?"

"Exactly. He might have used the wand—Fanuilh said it was for levitating objects—but then why have the rug at all? And what did he need the spellbook for? Only a wizard could use it. For that matter, I don't think anybody but a wizard could use the rug or the wand. I know I couldn't. But at the same time, everyone tells me there are no wizards in Southwark now."

"I'd warrant it."

"Then why didn't my thief take everything in the cases?"

"Or naught at all? Why visit your home if nothing there was of any use to him? No, we needs must assume that your thief could use what he stole."

"Or that he was put up to it by someone who could. And that brings us back to how my thief got past Tarquin's wards. Fanuilh says they are still in force, and will only open for the owner of the house."

It was a very strange conversation for Liam, and different parts of his mind stood at different distances from it. On one level, he was perplexed and frustrated by the intricacies of the puzzle at hand, the competing and often contradictory facts, the general lack of important information. On another, he was both concerned about what he said, avoiding any specific mention of the Guild, and a little skeptical as to the need for doing so. And on another, final level, he was amazed by the whole conversation, the things he was saying about Fanuilh, about whom he had never spoken to anyone, and the ease with which Coeccias accepted the situation.

Finally, after they had pursued the mystery for almost half an hour, they both agreed that further discussion was pointless.

"We need a solid path, Coeccias. We're going in circles."

"Aye, that's the truth. A solid path, and a direction to take on it. But what path? What direction? I've the Hierarchs waiting; perhaps we can start there."

"All right," Liam said, though inwardly he cringed at the idea. He did not want to have to face either priest, given the questions he thought he would have to ask. "And there's another thing: the sailor and the woman. I think we can safely assume that they've left Southwark."

"Can we?" Coeccias objected. "Is it so sure?"

"I think so. Or at least, I think we can safely assume it as a place to start. We have to start somewhere." With the Aedile's grudging acceptance, Liam went on: "From there, I think we can assume that they left by ship. The snows recently would make travel overland difficult, and since this other man was a sailor, it would make sense."

"Agreed, but what then?"

"We need to check the docks, to know what ships have left recently. There can't be many, in winter."

"No," Coeccias agreed, reminded of his other problems. "There's that damned *Heart of Oak*, though they could hardly have planned to passage on a ship that fled its creditors in the middle of the night. In any case, what will that tell us?"

"It might give us a name—something, anything. I don't know. Perhaps a clue as to what happened to my thief. And I think I will go down to the docks and find out if anyone saw my thief. One of his women mentioned a 'little boat ride,' and people in Southwark know the difference between a boat and a ship. So perhaps he tried to hire one, before he met the sailor. Or perhaps the sailor is known down there."

"You'll look for that? If you will, I'll have a man look into ships that have weighed anchor recently."

"Good enough. Now, there's one other question we have to look into, but I have no idea who might help us. It has to do with magic."

Coeccias grimaced. "There's none in Southwark can help us." He brightened then: "But there is one I know of, though he's not in the city now. Acrasius Saffian—he might be able to answer a question of magic. Though what question?"

"We need to know if theurgy can work with wizardry." Theurgy was religious magic, the power of the gods as channeled through their priests. Wizardry was an open book compared to theurgy; the secrets of the power were jealously guarded by the priests and never discussed outside temple walls.

"Y'are thinking that Guiderius worked a miracle to get the thief into your house?"

"Not necessarily Guiderius—perhaps some other priest—but yes. I don't know anything about theurgy, but I know it can be powerful. And if it's anything like wizardry, a priest against whom it was practiced would know it. So that if Guiderius used power from Strife to enter Bellona's temple, Cloten would know."

"But if he used it to enter your house, then used some of Tarquin's enchantments to enter the fane, Cloten wouldn't." Coeccias nodded judiciously. "It sings, Rhenford, it fair sings—though it would like me not if Guiderius were in it."

Liam shrugged apologetically. He knew the old priest of Strife had an excellent reputation, but that did not mean he could not be a thief. "Who is this Saffian? Can we get in touch with him?"

"Acrasius Saffian. He's a scholar, and the judge of the Areopagus, the Duke's circuit court for magic. The Duke's laws include a mass of statutes on offenses involving all types of magic, though mostly they touch on black magic, demonology, the like. Not many are ever invoked, so Saffian only rides the circuit once a year. For the rest he's a scholar, a delver into deep wells of all sorts. He summers in Southwark, but he winters with the Duke in Deepenmoor. If needs must, I can send a rider this day, to task him with your questions. We'd hear back in a day, more like two."

"Too long," Liam said.

Coeccias agreed. "I've a feeling things will turn even uglier in Temples' Court. And with the odd mood of the city these past two days, it might spread. Still, there's nothing for it. We'll send the word, hope for an answer, and in the meanwhile proceed as if the answer were yes."

"You mean, 'Yes, a priest could overcome the wards on Tarquin's house'?"

"Aye."

"All right. Then we have a plan."

"No, Rhenford," the Aedile said, picking up his mug to drain the last of his beer, "we have too many plans."

They stopped at the barracks briefly, long enough for Coeccias to send a Guard down to the waterfront to ask after ships and for Liam to write out his question for Acrasius Saffian. Coeccias signed it, and told another Guard to see that it was sent by courier to the Duke's Seat at Deepenmoor. Then they set out for Temple Street.

■ *10* ■

THERE WAS A disturbing lull in the streets, a quiet and tense aftermath to the fight between the temples. The news was disseminated in whispers, which grew excited as Coeccias and Liam passed.

"Word has spread," Liam commented.

"Aye," the Aedile said, worrying at his lower lip, "they'll note our passing into Temples' Court and make much of it." He cast a speculative eye at the sky. The earlier brightness was gone and the sun slowly began to sink behind gray clouds. "It'll be dark soon, and the story'll be over the whole city how I bearded Cloten in his own den—regardless of whether I do it or not.

"I tell you, Rhenford," he said after a pause, "these days like me not. There is too much to do, and too little to do it with." They had reached the cul-de-sac; an old man in the brown robe of Strife was using a bucket to splash water over the bloody cobbles, and six Guards stood in a tight knot near him, talking among themselves. One noticed the Aedile as he gestured at them, and alerted the others. "That's a half dozen men that'll not be of use elsewhere in the city this night. Which means the patrols in the Warren'll be smaller, and there'll be complaints from those wights that I'm ignoring their woes to the benefit of the rich in the Point."

"But this isn't the Point."

"I know that, as do you, but to those in the Warren, it's always the Point. The Guard entire could die of the plague, and they'd say it was a trick of mine to pander to the rich."

The Guards now stood roughly to attention, and the one who had noticed Coeccias's approach now came over to them. It was Boult.

"Not that I much blame them," the Aedile said ruefully. "I've never enough men for patrolling there at the best of times, and now they've a ghost—did I tell you?—a proper ghost, haunting the ways."

Boult knuckled his forehead to Coeccias and nodded politely to Liam, but he managed to inject a sense of familiarity into both gestures. "Master Aedile, Quaestor Rhenford."

"All quiet here, Boult?"

"Aye, sir. Just the elder with the bucket abroad, though we heard the Hierarch raising a fuss." There was no need to ask which Hierarch; Boult jerked a disdainful thumb over his shoulder at Bellona's temple. "He's quiet now."

"Grand," Coeccias said sarcastically. "I'm sure he'll be the soul of reason now."

"We could postpone this for a year or so," Liam suggested.

His friend smiled briefly. "Aye, or until the man died of old age—but I don't think he'll oblige. We'll be going in, Boult. Try and have the men look like soldiers, eh? Not a gaggle of gossiping fishwives."

Boult saluted again with a lazy grin, and returned to the knot of Guards. Neither Coeccias nor Liam, however, made any move toward Bellona's temple.

Liam was thinking about the ghost in the Warren, and a word Mopsa had used. She had called Duplin's hideouts "haunts."

"Coeccias," he asked diffidently, unsure if the idea was worth broaching, "where is the ghost seen in the Warren?"

"Eh? Where?" The other man had been glaring at the tall doors to the temple at the end of the street.

"I mean, does it stay in one place, or does it wander around?"

"Truth, Rhenford, I've no clue. It's a ghost, it doesn't have a fixed address!"

"In all the ghost stories I've ever heard, the ghost haunts one or two special places—a favorite room, a particular castle, the place it died. . . ."

"Y'are thinking of Duplin," Coeccias guessed, and sighed. "I'll send a man to ask." He singled out a Guard, called him over, and explained the mission. The man looked uneasy, but on seeing his master's menacing frown, saluted quickly and dashed off toward the Warren. Coeccias shook his head in disbelief. "Do you know, half the men have asked to be switched to the day watch? But enough—we dawdle. We'll never beard the lion standing outside his den."

Liam could not imagine Cloten as a lion—a bleating sheep, perhaps, or a weasel—but his steps were no quicker than his friend's as they crossed the cobbles to Bellona's temple.

The differences from their first visit were legion. The gray gryphon still hung in its cage, far up in the dome, the supporting chain angling down the altar, behind which the temple treasury sat untouched. But on the altar itself, red-stained swords lay in a heap. The fire pit, cold the last time Liam had seen it, was now roaring, and water was being boiled by its heat. Bruised and bloody men were scattered around the temple floor, propped against the walls, hobbling back and forth for hot water and bandages, cleaning armor.

It seemed to Liam like an armed camp, not a temple, and he was a little surprised to notice how familiar it all was. He had seen a hundred such camps, and this one differed only in being indoors—that, and the fact that he was not part of the camp. A dozen pairs of eyes jumped suspiciously to the doors as he and Coeccias entered, and two guards, untouched in the fight, sprang to bar their way with spears.

"Stand aside," the Aedile growled, "or fetch Hierarch Cloten here. I would speak with him."

The guards shared a look and one of them began to answer back, when Scaevola appeared behind them.

"It is all right," he said in his hoarse, wet whisper, and lightly touched one of the guards on the shoulder. "Ask Keeper of Arms Alastor to come here."

When the men had stepped away, Scaevola bowed. "I apologize, Master Aedile, Master Rhenford. They are no longer in Caernarvon, and have not realized it yet."

"No matter," Liam said, intrigued by the quickness with which the two men had obeyed the sick man.

Scaevola spread his hands and shrugged. His face was hidden within the depths of his hood, but the blasted skin of his hands showed in the light from the fire pit. "I have wanted to speak with you, Liam Rhenford. I did not think you would come here, but if I may?"

Liam heard a strange note in Scaevola's voice, an edge of weariness and, he guessed, desperation. "Of course," he said, then saw a man wearing a solid breastplate much like the one Cloten wore hurrying toward them. "As soon as we've spoken with the Keeper of Arms."

Bowing again, Scaevola stepped back to allow the priest to come forward.

"Aedile Coeccias," the Hierarch said with a slight bow. Alastor's face was flat and almost perfectly round, which made him seem fat, despite the leanness of his body. His head bristled with stubble; Liam guessed it was a soldier's haircut, not a priest's, shaved for comfort under a helmet and not a religious principle. The Keeper of Arms' gaze was direct, and frankly troubled.

"Hierarch." Coeccias offered a civil nod, but he was clearly displeased. "Is Hierarch Cloten not able to attend me? I specifically asked him to be available."

Alastor frowned. "Hierarch Cloten is closeted at prayer just now, Aedile Coeccias. He is trying to receive guidance from the Mistress of Battle."

Liam detected a hint of sarcasm in the way the priest said "trying."

Crossing his arms, Coeccias pointed at Liam with a finger. "Quaestor Rhenford has been seconded to me by the Duke to assist with the investigation into the attempted thievery. It was my wish that Hierarch Cloten meet with him, to go over the details of that evening. You can well see that his indisposition will make that difficult, and slow the investigation."

The casual lie—he had certainly not been seconded by the Duke— did not suprise Liam, but the formality of his friend's little speech took him aback, and he was not sure what direction Coeccias was going in.

"Yes," he stammered in the sudden pause, as the other two men looked to him. "It will make things difficult. Without Hierarch Cloten's comments, I do not know if I can form a clear understanding of the events."

"I believe I can help you there," Alastor said smoothly. "I have heard all Hierarch Cloten can remember, and can tell it to you somewhat less . . . heatedly than he could. And Scaevola here was the man on watch when it happened. He can add his part himself."

"I suppose that will have to do," Liam said, with a shrug to indicate that it might not be enough.

"For the moment," Coeccias added significantly. "I'll still have to speak with Hierarch Cloten later, at the very least about today's incident, if not about the other matter."

Alastor nodded acceptance of the condition. "Shall I begin?" At a gesture from Liam, he recounted Cloten's story of the night.

Unable to sleep, the Hierarch had been in his room, reading, when he heard the sound of footsteps and the clanking of metal from the main temple. His room was midway along a corridor that ran from the rear of the temple, where a door opened onto the alley behind, to the entrance to the hall they stood in. Cloten went down the hallway, drawn by the sound, and entered the temple proper through the door by the altar.

Alastor indicated it, in a recessed alcove off to the left. By the dim light
of the few candles, he saw a man by the temple treasury, gripping the
chain that held up the gryphon's cage and tugging at the chest. He was
about to call out when he was struck from behind and fell to the ground.
When he regained consciousness a few moments later, he heard the
sound of the front doors of the temple clanging shut.

"At first we assumed it was the thieves leaving," Alastor said, "but
we later discovered it was only Scaevola, going out to look for them."

"I had come in only a moment before," the sick man volunteered,
stepping forward to join the group and directing his comments at Liam
with a new respect. "I was the guard on duty that night, and I had
stepped outside for some air. I came back after almost fifteen minutes
and found Hierarch Cloten lying by the altar. I ran out again, to look for
his attackers, but they had already gone."

"They must have escaped out the back," Alastor said, "through the
corridor Cloten had just come down. But then, Aedile Coeccias already
knows that—and knows that that is strange, since we found the rear
entrance locked."

Liam and Coeccias shared a brief, somewhat embarrased glance.
"Actually," Liam said, "we now know that they entered from the roof.
We can assume they left the same way."

"And how do you know that?"

"We found the, ah, instrument they used." He was being forced to
revise his thoughts on the attempted robbery. If Cloten had been looking
at the man by the treasury chest, and had been hit from behind, there
must have been at least two of them. Duplin and his sailor brother-in-
law, then, he decided. In the scramble to escape, they might have left the
rug behind, though how they got down the outside of the building without being seen was beyond him. There was something else, though, that
disturbed him.

"You said Hierarch Cloten was knocked down from behind?"

"Yes."

"And that knocked him unconscious? Was he hit in the head, or did
he hit his head when he fell down?"

Alastor looked briefly for support at Scaevola, who spread his hands
to show he did not know. "I'm not sure," the priest admitted.

"Well, did he have a bruise on the back of his head, or the front?"

"I am not sure," Alastor said after a moment, "that he had a bruise
at all."

"Truth," Coeccias said, barely restraining his anger, "you can see
these are the kinds of things we needs must ask the Hierarch himself."

"Yes," Alastor agreed thoughtfully. "I can see that. But I am afraid he is praying at the moment, as I told you."

"Very well," the Aedile said. "Quaestor Rhenford, have you any more questions?" Liam shook his head. "In that case, we will leave you, but I must insist that as soon as Hierarch Cloten is available, word be sent to me. We will need to speak with him. You may tell one of my Guards outside, and they will inform me."

Alastor bowed and turned away, moving among the wounded men; Liam and Coeccias had started to leave when Scaevola tugged lightly at Liam's sleeve.

"Quaestor Rhenford," he said, the title stressed. "May I have a word with you?"

"Oh, yes, Scaevola, I'm sorry. I forgot." He had been thinking of the dome and a quick experiement he wanted to make.

The hooded man indicated Coeccias. "Alone, if the Aedile does not mind."

Coeccias snorted with ill grace, but left; the doors of Bellona's temple were too heavy to slam, but he shoved them closed anyway.

"Actually, Scaevola," Liam said, "I wonder if you wouldn't mind stepping outside with me. There's something I want to see."

The other man agreed, and followed Liam out of the temple. They turned left, around the corner of the building to the alley on the south side. The walls of the temple were simple squared blocks of stone; the traces of an old facing of marble were still visible in places, and Liam lightly ran his hand over the pitted surface, calculating. The rug had been near the southeast corner of the roof, and there were enough irregularities in the wall there. It could be climbed, but that made little sense. Why climb down when the rug was there? And how could the thieves have escaped notice?

"Quaestor Rhenford?" Scaevola murmured politely.

Liam turned from his inspection of the wall, a little embarrased. "Sorry. What did you want to talk about?"

"I wanted to ask you if you knew anything about visions."

"Visions?" Liam asked, confused. "You mean dreams, or hallucinations?"

"No," Scaevola said firmly, "visions. I . . . I have had one, I think. I had hoped you might help me understand it."

There was a not of pleading in the sick man's voice, an expectation of assistance. Liam frowned. He had been worried about Mopsa coming to expect things from him, and now Scaevola was looking to him for help, no doubt because of his rash extension of sympathy. On one had he did not mind: he wanted to help the man, and he knew it could not hurt to have the confidence of someone in the temple, especially given the evident respect with which Scaevola was treated. On the other hand, he was a little annoyed with himself for getting involved. There was nothing he could really do for the other man, and he hated the idea of people having unduly high expectations of him.

"Shouldn't you talk to the Keeper of Arms about it, or even Hierarch Cloten? I think they might be more help than I could be."

"I cannot speak to them—or anyone else in the temple," Scaevola blurted, then whispered hurriedly, as if eager to get it out: "Last night I saw Bellona, Quaestor, but I do not know why."

"You dreamed it."

"I did not dream it. I do not sleep, Quaestor; people in my position do not sleep."

Liam considered the strange pride with which Scaevola said this; he had not known that low-root fever stole sleep from its victims.

"You never sleep?"

"Never."

There was a long pause while Liam digested this. Then he gave a low whistle and shook his head. "All right. Tell me what you saw."

In Tarquin's library there was a book on visions and visitations; Liam had leafed through it once or twice, reading passages at random. Scaevola's account matched many of the ones he had read.

He had been in his cell (he had one to himself; though they accepted him, none of the other acolytes would share a room with him) lying on his pallet, when the walls suddenly shone with an unbearable light. He threw his arm across his eyes, and when he removed it, the goddess was standing before him.

Liam pressed for details on her appearance, but Scaevola merely shook his head. "She was beautiful," was all he could say, his hoarse voice trembling with awe. She carried a breastplate and a sword, which she laid at the foot of the pallet where he cowered. Then she put her hand to his forehead and blessed him.

"She smiled at me, Quaestor, and then She disappeared."

"And the sword? The armor?"

"Gone as well—but they were a Hierarch's."

Then Liam understood why Scaevola could not mention the vision to his superiors in the temple. If it was true, Bellona had singled him out to be one of her high priests, which he could hardly tell the present high priest and his second in command without some sort of evidence.

"That could be difficult," he said. "Honestly, I can't imagine Hierarch Cloten believing you."

"Nor I," Scaevola said as the euphoria with which he had recounted the visit faded into misery. "But if She has called me, how can I not answer?"

"You need proof, some open sign to convince them."

"But dare I . . . dare I ask Her? Should I pray for one?"

Liam sighed. "I don't know, Scaevola. I don't know much about the gods in general, and still less about yours in particular."

"I was afraid of that," the other answered, his disappointment well masked. "I had to ask, Quaestor, because you are the only person I know here, besides my brothers in arms."

"I'm sorry. I can't tell you whether prayer is proper or not. But I can tell you that you will need solid proof of Bellona's intentions, if you mean to act on them."

It was difficult to read Scaevola's expression; his hood covered most of his face, and what little was visible was scarred and cracked. However, there was no mistaking the abrupt change in his tone, the false note of nonchalance with which he asked: "Have you seen what you wanted to see, Quaestor?"

"What? Oh, yes, yes, I have, I think." He had not, but it could wait.

"Then I will leave you." With a quick bow he was gone, jogging back to the doors of the temple as if, in standing still for so long, he had accumulated energy that had to be expended.

Liam leaned back against the wall and ran a hand over his long face. *Visions,* he thought, *now there are visions. Robberies and fights between temples weren't enough, and ghosts and comets, too—now there's going to be a power struggle inside the temple.* For he was sure that Scaevola believed his vision, and would eventually be driven to act on it. The question was, would he get the proof he needed to make it easy? The vision seemed to indicate that Bellona had chosen Scaevola as her Hierarch as a way to settle the squabbles over doctrine, and Cloten did not strike him as the type to step aside with good grace.

Coeccias cleared his throat, bringing Liam out of his reverie. "Something about the wall interests you?" the Aedile asked, without a trace of sarcasm.

He expects me to do strange things, Liam thought, *so he can watch this.*

"Yes." He took off his cloak and handed it to the Aedile, and then pulled off his boots. "Hold these, will you? I want to climb up."

Cold from the cobblestones seeped immediately through his stockings, and he turned to the wall before Coeccias could argue.

In theory, climbing walls was simple; Stick had taught him, explaining the method in detail, and then made him practice until he was sick of it, and then a little more. The secret was in the fingers and toes, and not staying too long in one position. "Fast," the thief had told him, "go fast and don't think about it."

But with the iron cold of the stones alternately numbing and tearing at his fingers and toes, and the sharp wind that plucked at him once he was ten feet up, he cursed Stick and resorted to a trick he had devised himself. He pictured a lizard in his mind, a green, light lizard, swarming effortlessly up the wall, its digits splayed out. The image helped, took his mind off the pain in his hands, the small cuts from the sharp fragments left from the marble facade.

No lizard, he knew, would have panted quite as hoarsely on reaching the top of the wall, nor hauled itself up onto the roof there with quite as much relief. His hands were red and raw, prickles of blood on the fingertips, and he thrust them under his armpits to warm them up; his stockings were torn, and a dampness spread among his toes that he knew was not sweat.

So it can be done, he thought, and groaned a laugh. *Now all I have to do is get down.*

He crouched uncomfortably, resisting the urge to stand and stretch the cramped muscles in his calves and shoulders; the wind was stronger on the roof, and he did not want to be plucked off his narrow perch. He was on a triangular wedge at the southwest corner of the temple, where the rectangular body of the building met the base of the dome; three of the windows could be reached from the ledge, each a good six feet tall and frosted with ages of grime. He slid forward to examine the window directly in front of him.

Years of accumulated rust and dirt had been chipped away from the metal frame, and when he pused at the glass, the window opened inward a few grudging inches.

Satisfied, he turned around and, with his hands braced against the frame, stood up, pressing his back flat to the dome. It was, he had to admit, a breathtaking view of Southwark: he could see the city square, the temple of the Storm King, all the way down to the harbor, to the jagged range of rocks called the Teeth, which formed the outer wall of the harbor, and beyond to the slate gray sea, choppy with whitecaps. He did not look long at the panorama, however; he was more interested in the neighboring buildings.

The roof of Laomedon's temple was a mere ten feet away, a relatively easy jump, but there was no room for a running start on his ledge.

It would take a very brave—or a very desperate—man to make the leap, and though either description might have fit Duplin and his companion after Cloten discovered them, Liam did not think it likely. It had been snowing that night, and the ledge would have been slippery, even further reducing the chance of a good start. *And who would jump there, anyway?* Laomedon's home was just as eerie from the roof as from the street. The thieves would have to have been very desperate to brave the black temple.

They might have left by another window, and tried to cross the alley behind the temple, or the one to the north, but how would they have opened the window from the inside? If the windows there were as dirt-encrusted as the ones near his ledge, it would have been impossible.

Could they have used a spell? he wondered, and then nearly jumped from the ledge himself as a clanking noise and a muffled squawk from behind him set his heart thumping and dragged a shout from his throat.

Slowly, he twisted himself around, the blood roaring in his ears, and knelt before the window, looking into the temple. Through the grime, he could dimly see the gryphon's cage, swinging in wide arcs on its length of thick chain. It was oscillating toward him, the cage just on a level with the base of the dome, and the creature was staring at him, its giant black orbs above a sharp beak.

When it saw that he was looking at it, the gryphon simply stared back, occasionally bunching its hindquarters and thrusting against the cage when the arc of its swing shortened. It was gray all over, he saw, a dozen shades from tail to head, as if it had been cleverly carved out of stone from different quarries.

"Hello," Liam said, and tapped on the window. Then the creature squawked again, but it was not a challenge. To Liam, crouched shivering on the roof, it sounded like an appeal.

He shook his head slowly, finally breaking eye contact with the gryphon through force of will. *Get down,* he told himself, and quickly lowered himself over the edge without a backward glance.

The descent was, strangely, much easier. He was not thinking about the climb, and he had grown somewhat used to the cold. Nonetheless, when he reached the ground, having jumped the last ten feet, he fumbled hastily to put on his boots and his cloak. Coeccias crossed his arms and waited while Liam beat circulation back into his hands, and stomped his feet warm.

"Like a very spider," the Aedile commented approvingly. "Think you that was how our thieves got in?"

"Lizard," Liam corrected. "And yes, I do. At least, they got into the building by the window up there. I don't know if they climbed—it wouldn't make much sense, since they had the carpet. But I do know they didn't leave that way."

At the Aedile's questioning look, Liam explained about the distance between buildings. "They could have reached only those windows so they couldn't try the other alleys around the temple. Since they didn't use the rug to escape, they would have had to climb down, or jump across—which I don't think they did. It's too far. And it also seems unlikely they climbed down—with all the noise and alarm in the temple, they couldn't have just come down off the wall and walked out through Temple Street."

"Aye, probably not," Coeccias agreed, "but then, how did they escape? They couldn't have just stayed up there till the search slackened . . . so how did they get away?"

Liam shook his head. He had no idea, but he was thinking more of the gryphon's black, depthless eyes and the squawk it had uttered, which had struck him as a cry for help.

It was getting late, the sun slipping away behind the clouds, an imperceptibly gradual darkening of the sky to herald the merging of afternoon into night. Liam's feet felt slippery in his boots, and he suggested to Coeccias as they left the cul-de-sac that he might buy some new socks and then go to the bathhouse. They were passing Laomedon's temple, and Liam paused to consider the empty portico, where the Death had stood only a few hours before and smiled at him. He could not see the doors through the shadows thrown by the pillars, and for a moment imagined that there were none: that there was nothing but darkness.

"Nonsense," Coeccias said, clapping him on the back and breaking the illusion. "No Quaestor seconded to me by the Duke'll go to a public bathhouse. You'll come home with me, and Burrus'll see to your feet."

Liam accepted the offer readily; Coeccias kept a small but comfortable home nearby, and his servant Burrus was a friendly man who played the flute well. In a companionable silence, Liam limping slightly, the two men made their way out of Temple Street. Night had taken hold by the time they reached the Aedile's home, and Coeccias threw open the door, calling loudly for candles and hot water.

"And stockings as well, Burrus, clean ones, if there are any!"

Burrus appeared from the kitchen, greeted Liam, and disappeared again, to follow Coeccias's instructions.

"I'll just wander around to the square," Coeccias said, as Liam slumped into a chair and started pulling off his boots. "Word should be back on what ships have parted Southwark, and on the haunts of your ghost."

Chuckling at his own wit, the Aedile left Liam to remove his tattered stockings, wincing at the crust of dried blood around his toes. Coeccias's joke brought to the fore his idea that the ghost in the Warren might be Duplin, and reinforced his conviction that the thief was dead. There were a number of ways to find out, but the surest did not appeal to him, and he put off considering it to deal with his battered feet.

"What have you been doing?" Burrus asked when he returned, a bowl of steaming water in his hands and towels thrown over his shoulder. "Fishing for sharks with your toes as bait?"

"Climbing temple walls," Liam replied, grinning. As he gingerly cleaned his feet, he was happy to see that there were only a few serious cuts; most of the blood had come from scrapes. Still, his own stockings were ruined, and he accepted a clean pair from the bald servant with a grateful smile.

"More trouble with that new goddess," Burrus guessed.

"Yes. There was a fight in Temple Street this afternoon."

"And you were climbing the walls to escape it?"

Liam laughed; he liked Coeccias's servant, his sense of humor and his familiarity. He was like Boult in his easy manners, and Liam was struck by the type of people the Aedile attracted. There were few fawners and scrapers in the Guard, and Burrus never failed to speak his mind, though he was by turns tactful or funny about it. He had been apprenticed to Coeccias's father when the latter was court bard at Deepenmoor, and had known the Aedile since he was a boy. For reasons Liam could not fathom, he had given up on his life as a bard to serve Coeccias when he was created Aedile of Southwark.

"Exactly. I stayed up there until Coeccias had it all sorted out."

"Which he did by boxing a few ears."

"More or less."

"But now you are helping him, I imagine." It was a shrewd guess, and Liam wondered how he had made it.

"Yes, I am, as a matter of fact. In what little ways I can."

Burrus offered a mysterious smile. "Coeccias lays great store in what little you can, Master Rhenford. I wonder if you know how much. Just the other evening, he explained to me at great length how sure he was that, if you would only help him, the problems in Temples' Court would be solved like that." He snapped his fingers, and Liam snorted. It was exactly what he did not want to hear.

"Hmm. Do me a favor, Burrus. When you hear him talking like that, try to talk him out of it."

The older man only laughed and went off to the kitchen, returning a moment later with a cup of wine.

"You are a young man, Master Rhenford, and for all that you have seen, you have not seen enough of yourself. You do not know your value."

The conversation was uncomfortable. Liam did not know his own value, but it did not interest him very much, and the wise smile on Burrus's lips made him fidget.

"Nicely put," he said, by way of shifting the discussion away from the personal, "but what man knows his own value? What man would want to know it, for that matter? Nine out of ten ignore all evidence of their real nature, or confuse it with what others perceive it to be."

"But not you," Burrus countered, refusing to be drawn into generalities. "Coeccias told me how distressed you were to hear that many in the city think you are a wizard. Nine out of ten would encourage that, not protest."

"Nine out of ten fools," Liam muttered. Tarquin had been a wizard, and what did it get him, other than a knife in the chest?

"Yes, they are, but again: not you. You should have more faith in yourself, and drink your wine."

It was impossible to think of Burrus, with his rich, bardtrained voice and knowing smile, as a nag, but Liam came close. "I'll drink it, if we can talk of something else besides me and my value."

"As you please," the servant said, but he still smiled confidently, as if he had scored an important point.

■ *11* ■

COECCIAS RETURNED BEFORE long, going straight to the kitchen to get a glass of wine. When he had settled himself in a chair opposite Liam, he told him what his men had found out during the afternoon:

"Only one ship's parted Southwark in the past se'en-night: the *Heart of Oak,* the one that cheated the chandlers—and that on the first tide five days ago."

Liam nodded; the morning after he had been robbed, and Cloten attacked.

"Now, for your ghost," Coeccias went on, swirling his wine thoughtfully, "he's been seen in four places."

There was a map of Southwark hung on the wall, which Liam approached as the Aedile listed the spots. Two of the four he mentioned were in the Warren. The map showed the twisting sprawl of tiny alleys and courtyards, but it did not give all their names; nonetheless, they were able to determine that the ghost had been seen outside the wineshop where Duplin often received messages, and at a corner only a block away from one of his hideouts. The other two sightings had taken place in Harbor Street and Coopers' Row, both roads that led up from the Warren toward the Point.

"What does the ghost do?"

"Do? What ghosts are wont to do, Rhenford—scare those that see them witless."

"But nothing specific? I mean, did anyone say what the ghost looked like, or wore, or said?"

"Not that I know," Coeccias replied. "Have you seen your thief?"

"No."

"Then what does it matter? You couldn't recognize it from a description, could you?"

He could not, but Mopsa could. If someone had said what the ghost looked like, he could have checked it with her or, better, with the Werewolf or one of the older members of the Guild. He did not want the girl involved, but that was beside the point in any case, because he did not have a description. Which meant he would have to get one.

"How often does the ghost appear?"

"Every night in the Warren, a few hours before midnight. It's been seen outside the Warren only twice, in Harbor Street and Coopers' Row."

A question occurred to him that he should have asked before: "When was it first seen?"

"It was reported two days ago," Coeccias said, "so it could be your thief, if he was taken off after the botch-up at the temple."

"Yes," Liam said thoughtfully. "And it appears every night?"

"For the past two."

"Can you lend me a man tonight?"

Coeccias shook his head and chuckled. "Milord May-Do-Aught wishes to go ghost-hunting, is that it?"

"Not willingly, but I have a feeling it would be worth our while to know. The sightings are all near my thief's hideouts, and it seems very strange that he should have disappeared."

"Perhaps he fled with his punk and his sailor friend on the *Heart of Oak*."

"I don't think so. I told you I spoke to some of his friends, and they all seemed to expect him back."

"Well, then, I can lend you Boult. He's the man to have if you needs must hunt ghosts."

The suggestion pleased Liam. He had encountered a few ghosts in his travels, and had little physical fear of them. Most were tied impotently to a specific spot, and could do nothing to harm the living. Still, they were frightening, and the Guard's unflappable calm would be nice to have at his back.

The two men sipped at their wine for a while, quiet, content not to talk. The low crackling of the fire barely intruded on Liam's thoughts, as they jumped from one idea to another, back and forth fruitlessly. There were too many unresolved questions. How had Duplin gotten past the wards? How had the thieves gotten away from temple? Why had they taken only the book, the rug and the wand? Why did Cloten not have a bruise?

There were other thoughts, unwelcome things that cropped up in the path of clear thinking, Scaevola's vision and the Death's smile chief among them. He did not want to mention the first to Coeccias, because he considered it the sick man's secret, but the other was his own, and he could share it.

"This afternoon," he began hesitantly, "during the fight, something . . . strange . . . happened."

"Some *things* strange happened," the Aedile corrected. "Did you have a special one in mind?"

"Yes, I did. Something apart from the other strange things, an extra one. I'm not sure what it means, or if I'm just imagining it."

"Well?" Coeccias prompted after a moment. Liam had fallen silent, considering.

"I'm probably imagining it."

"Rhenford!"

"All right. Just as we were going in, as we were running, I saw the Death on the steps of Laomedon's temple. Now I know this will sound strange—"

"You've said that already; go to, go to!"

". . . but afterward, I'd swear she smiled at me. At me in particular. She caught my eye, and she nodded and smiled at me."

He had hoped Coeccias would laugh at the idea, or at least put it down to the heat of the fight. The other man, however, tugged at his beard, twisting his mouth as if he had tasted something sour.

"Truth, did she?"

"I think so, though I might have been mistaken. There were other things happening at the moment."

Coeccias disagreed. "I doubt it. Y'are sharp, and the Death is not given to throwing smiles and nods to the wind. If you saw it, you saw it, and that worries me. We've enough to trouble us without another temple thrown into the mix. And certainly not Laomedon." His fingers crossed on the outside of his cup, then uncrossed as he remembered something. "Though now I think of it, the Death was not among the Hierarchs who requested the blessing."

"Great." Another riddle. "Should I do anything about it?"

"Aye, I think you should. I think you should attend the Death tomorrow, at her temple."

"Call on her? 'Excuse me, Death, but why did you smile at me yesterday?'"

"Something like," Coeccias said, ignoring Liam's sarcasm. "Y'are a Quaestor now, and can do it. Present yourself in that office, and pose a few questions about the robbery. If she meant anything by her smile, she'll tell."

"Or not."

"Or not, perhaps. But what else can you do?"

Liam frowned; he did not want to visit the black temple. Of all the gods in the pantheon, Laomedon was the one with which he was least familiar—and he would have preferred to keep it that way. He had met the Storm King face-to-face once, and lived not to tell of it, but he balked at the idea of approaching a place whose priests were called Deaths.

Nonetheless, he would go. There were simply too many unresolved questions to ignore it, and a feeling was growing on him that the thing they faced went beyond the robberies. Finding Duplin might not put an end to it.

Burrus tentatively suggested a little music, but neither Liam nor Coeccias was much in the mood, and they sat in silence for over an hour, locked in their own thoughts. The Aedile grunted from time to time, twisting in his chair as if there were nettles in the seat.

The bells in the Duke's courts struck nine, jerking both men to their feet.

"I should go," Liam said.

"Aye. Boult'll be at the barracks. Tell him I said to attend you. And take care, Rhenford—if not of the ghosts, then at least of the Warren."

Since both worried him, Liam promised to do so before leaving.

The streets were empty, and a sharp wind blew off the land, pushing him seaward. It whistled and keened over the rooftops, hooting on the myriad chimneys.

A perfect night for chasing ghosts, Liam thought, and until he reached the city square, he seriously considered calling his familiar. When he saw the torches by the barracks and the reassuring presence of the Guards there, he gave up the idea. *Boult will be as good as Fanuilh—I hope.* He realized, then, how much he had come to accept the little dragon's presence in his life. Since the day his father's keep was burned, Liam had never been in one place long enough to develop permanent relationships—moving from camp to ship, from port to mountain fortress, from Taralon to the Freeports and beyond—and he was surprised at how often he thought of the dragon.

Boult was inside the barracks, a pile of battered truncheons at his feet and a sanding stone in his hand. He accepted Coeccias's orders without question, but without enthusiasm, dropping the stone next to the truncheons and grabbing a coat from a peg. When he reached for a halberd, Liam stopped him.

"You won't need that."

"We're going to the Warren?"

"Yes."

"Then I'll take it. Things are not so easy there as the last time we ventured in, Quaestor Rhenford."

The last time they had been looking for—and inadvertently found—Tarquin's killer, and Liam did not like to think about it. The object of their search this time, however, was scarcely better, and when Boult asked after their quarry, he was slow to divulge it.

"We're looking for a man," he said, taking an unlit torch from a barrel by the door. He occupied himself with catching a light for the torch from one of those burning outside the door, and waited until they were walking past the Duke's courts before xpanding his statement. "A dead man."

To Liam's relief, Boult lived up to his expectations.

"The ghost, eh? I suppose I really don't need the pike, then." He did not pause, though, or try to turn back. "Can you tell me why, Quaestor, or is it secret?"

"No, no secret," Liam answered. "I think one of the men who tried to rob Bellona's temple has been killed, and I think the ghost in the Warren may be his."

They turned down Butchers' Road, now deserted. The shops were closed and barred, awnings rolled up, stands taken down. Offal lay frozen in gutters, flickering grotesquely in the erratic torchlight.

"And if you see the ghost?"

"I'll know if the thief is dead."

The answer satisfied Boult, and he lapsed into silence, but it did not satisfy Liam. What good would it do him to know if Duplin was dead? It would only put an end to his investigation. He did not think they could catch the ghost and put it in jail for Cloten's benefit, and even if they could, what sort of information could a ghost provide?

Enough of that, he told himself. *Stop trying to talk yourself out of this. It's just a ghost—what harm can it do you?*

That unfortunate question plagued him as they passed through Tripe Court and followed Butchers' Road to where a bend in the street marked the beginning of Coopers' Row. He hated his imagination then, as a picture of himself and Boult floated through his head, both of them addled with fear, their hair gone white.

Stop that, he ordered, and picked up his pace, marching down Coopers' Row so quickly that Boult had to jog to keep up with him. The buildings on either side of the street quickly grew seedier as they approached the edges of the Warren, but there was still no sign of life. Windows everywhere were shuttered tight, or empty, like eyeless sockets, opening on pitch black, abandoned rooms. These bothered Liam the most, and he carefully avoided looking too deeply into them.

He remembered his trip with Mopsa, and guided them to the wineshop where Duplin used to receive messages. A feeble glow slipped underneath its tightly shut door. Liam stopped in the street and heard a faint murmur of voices from inside.

"Do we go in?" Boult asked.

"I don't think so," Liam said. "We had better wait in the street. There wouldn't be people inside if the ghost came there, and Coeccias said the ghost appears here every night at ten."

Boult shrugged indifferently and positioned himself against the wall of the house opposite, only a few feet away. Liam leaned back beside the door of the wineship, the torch held out in front of him, and they began to wait.

It seemed like an eternity, and Liam spent it questioning the wisdom of what he was doing. The torch hissed occasionally, the murmur of voices inside the wineshop died away, the wind rose up, whistling, then faded. Boult shifted position once or twice, coughed.

This is stupid, Liam thought again, and then they heard the distant tolling of the bells in the Duke's courts. Liam counted each chime, absurdly hoping that they would total nine, or eleven, that somehow they might have missed ten, missed the ghost.

It was ten, and there were no more. Liam caught Boult's eye, and knew that the Guard was holding his breath, just as Liam was holding his. The sound of the bell lingered in the clear winter air, trailing on unbearably, then died. A full second later, both men exhaled, and Liam gave an embarrassed grin.

Then they heard the weeping.

It was a low sound at first, barely distinguishable from the wind, from their own breathing. It rose, though, catching their attention, freezing them where they stood, erasing Liam's grin. It rose, a child's sobbing, then a man's, deep and broken, a rasping cry that raised the hackles on Liam's neck.

It went on, loud now, easily heard over the wind, and when Boult spread his hands, Liam put a finger to his lips, urging him to silence, to immobility.

The glow rose out of the street, seeping through the gaps between the cobbles, rising up as if it were following some invisible pattern, spreading upward to delineate legs. It moved smoothly, like paint trickling down only up, past the legs, to the waist, to the torso, a white glow haloing a man, his back to Liam, his head down, clutching himself with luminescent arms and sobbing.

Liam could see Boult past the ghost's shoulder; the Guard was wide eye, but he did not look afraid, only amazed, stunned by the glowing, crying ghost.

"Boult," Liam whispered, and then the ghost looked up, saw the Guard, whose head jerked back as if he had been struck. Then the ghost was moving, spinning around and running down the street. It wailed a long, desperate moan and Liam, stung into action, ran after it, thinking only that he had not seen its face.

He heard Boult's pounding footsteps behind him, heard his own, but he could hear nothing of the ghost's, and was not sure it even touched ground. The eerie glow that encased it made such things difficult to tell, but it was moving quickly, far faster than he was, dodging down the streets of the Warren, trailing its wail like a banner.

The torch flared wildly, fanned by the wind as he picked up speed, and Liam dropped it so that he could run even faster. The ghost was a block away, but he could see it clearly by its own glow, turning onto Harbor Street.

He burst onto Harbor Street seconds later, saw it receding up toward the Point, and ran as fast as he could after it. His throat burned with each gasp, the cold air searing deep into his chest, and he was running in blackness, unable to see his feet or the road before him. All he could see was the glow of the ghost, loping up Harbor Street past the closed shops, howling as though it were in pain, like an animal unable to understand its hurt.

It disappeared.

He had lost it, and as he stumbled to a stop, he cursed himself hoarsely for dropping the torch. The moon was hidden behind clouds, and he was blind, doubled over and gasping for breath, a stitch in his side. He forced himself to straighten up, stepped uncertainly to the side of the road, stretching out his hands in front of him, finally touching stone. With his hand lightly brushing the wall, he started jogging, following the dim wail of the ghost as it faded in the distance, determined, though it was pointless.

Once he stumbled, barking his shin on some unseen obstacle, but he regained his footing and inched forward, creeping now, both hands on the wall like a blind man. He was amazed at how dark it was.

If only that damn ghost would come back, I could see. He could hear it, still wailing, and then, after an eternity of groping, there was no more wall, and he was standing at the corner of an intersection. But what intersection?

"Quaestor!"

He jumped, frightened, and below him, an immeasurable distance down Harbor Street, he saw a torch bobbing along, a pinprick in the blackness.

"Boult!" he shouted, and blessed the man for picking up the torch. "Up here!"

The torch began bobbing violently, and a minute later the Guard ran up, awkwardly holding both his pike and the fitfully burning brand.

"Gods, Quaestor, I thought I'd lost you." He sounded nervous, but Liam paid no attention.

"Where are we?"

The flame, no longer moving, grew, the circle of orange light expanding to reveal the corner at which they stood. Boult held it high, then pointed to the left.

"Spice Court, and up there, Coopers' Row again."

Liam took the torch. He could barely hear the ghost's cry, somewhere to the east, up the hill. If it was Duplin, it might be going to his apartment in the Middle Quarter, but suddenly he did not think so; he was thinking of the barkeep in Narrow Lane, who had lied about not knowing the thief—and the corpse in Mother Japh's morgue, which he had thought that of a clerk.

"Come on," he said, and started jogging up Spice Court, tired from his sprint but with refreshed determination. Boult sighed behind him and then followed, not wanting to be left in darkness again.

Through Spice Court, onto Coopers' Row, going uphill this time, turning right at the bath house, past the three blind alleys. Neither man spoke, saving their smoking breath, and they were at the beginning of Narrow Lane. The wailing had stopped but Liam pressed on anyway, hoping now to meet the ghost, to get a look at its face. The street was even more like a tunnel at night, with the torchlight catching on the overhanging stories, throwing weird, elongated shadows all around them.

Liam slowed down as they approached the bend, moving close to the wall, the foundations of the Duke's courts just ahead. Motioning Boult to stop, he handed over the torch and edged around the corner, feeling his way again.

The ghost was standing outside the door of the bar Liam had visited with Mopsa, its white radiance playing around it, a fuzzy nimbus of light that pooled on the cobbles around it and sparkled on the dirty snow heaped in the bend of the road. It stretched out a hand and pawed at the door.

"Please, Faius, let me in," it begged. "It's bitter cold out here, Faius, and they're after me."

Liam paused, struck by the misery in the ghost's voice, and its thin frame. A thief could have calluses on the pads of his fingers, just like a clerk.

"Go away!" shouted a voice from behind the door, the voice of the lying barkeep. "Leave me alone!"

Why didn't I think of that before? Liam berated himself. *I wouldn't have to be here now.*

"Gods, Faius, you can't do this to me," the ghost moaned. "There's animals after me, and the Guard, and it's so cold, cold, and y'are my friend, Faius. Just look what they've done to me, Faius, they cut out my goddamned heart." It started weeping, hitching sobs that made the white glow jump and dance.

"Go away!" Faius bellowed hysterically.

"My heart . . ."

"Duplin," Liam whispered softly. "Duplin!"

The ghost turned its head slowly and saw him, poised a few yards away.

"Look what they've done to me," it said, facing him now and gesturing to its chest, where a dull purple stain lay beneath the radiance, a knife wound and a face like the corpse in Mother Japh's morgue, whose body had been found in Narrow Lane the morning after Liam was robbed.

"Who did it to you, Duplin?"

"It's so cold," the ghost said, looking down at its wound, "and the birds won't leave me alone, but I can't help them, and someone's cut out my heart."

He's gone mad, Liam thought, with some pity. *And so would you.* "Who cut out your heart, Duplin?"

Duplin's ghost, though was not listening; it was staring at the broad purple stain and starting to wail again, the forlorn cry growing louder and louder even as the ghost started to sink, dropping into the cobbles. Faius was shouting wordlessly behind the closed door, trying to drown out the sound, and Liam jumped forward.

"Duplin!" he shouted, even as the ghost disappeared. He cursed and stomped his foot, then turned sharply. "Boult!"

The Guard ran around the corner with the torch, shaking his head. Faius was still shouting, and Liam kicked viciously at the door, gratified at the splintering of the lock and the thud as it hit the barkeep, silencing him.

He pushed inside, Boult coming after with the torch held high, and found the bald man huddled behind the door, holding his forehead with one hand, the other stretched out. He was weeping and pleading, but it did not deter Liam.

"Oh, gods, Duplin, I'm sorry, don't hurt me."

Liam reached down, grasped the man by the front of his shirt and hauled him roughly to his feet.

"How did he die?" Liam demanded, shoving the barkeep against the wall. "Who cut out his heart?"

"The sailor," Faius spluttered, "the sailor did it."

"When?" It was strange; from what he knew of him, Liam did not think he would have liked the living Duplin, but the sight of his ghost, pleading futilely at his friend's door, had roused in him an angry sense of injustice.

"Four, five nights ago, the night after the messenger." The bald man looked as if he were regaining his composure, so Liam pushed him hard against the wall again, making sure to bang his head in the process.

"Here?"

"No, in the street," the barkeep said, wiping at his teary face. "I swear I didn't see it, didn't know it, 'til the Guard found the body in the morning. I swear."

"Shut up," Liam told him.

"I swear it, master—"

"Shut up!" Liam growled, shoving the barkeep again. "Did they say anything? Do anything? What did they act like?"

"I don't know," the barkeep said, beginning to cry again. It seemed faintly ridiculous—he was big and mean looking, and the crying only made Liam angrier.

"Think, you idiot!"

"I don't know, master, I swear I don't. They might have been arguing, but the place was crowded—don't bang me again, please, master—I swear, I don't know anything, and he's been haunting me every night since!"

For a long moment Liam glared at the cowering man, his fists twisted in the cloth of his shirt, and then he relaxed his grip, as if he had just discovered that the shirt was dirty.

"Come on," he said to Boult, suddenly disgusted with Narrow Lane and eager to be gone.

The Guard once again had to jog to keep up with him, awkwardly managing the torch and his halberd. "We could clap him in," he suggested as they passed out of Narrow Lane. "For not telling what he knew."

"Better yet," Liam said viciously, "we could just leave him be, and let Duplin haunt him for the rest of his days."

"There is that," Boult agreed. "Seems fitting."

"No," Liam said after a long pause, his anger receding as quickly as it had sprung up. "There's no point. He's not responsible, and I think he's had enough of a scare. I certainly wouldn't want Duplin haunting me."

"Nor I," Boult said fervently. "So it was your man?"

"Yes," Liam said. They had reached the city square, and he looked thoughtfully at the Duke's courts. It had been stupid not to connect Duplin with the corpse in Mother Japh's morgue, but even belatedly it settled some questions. "Do me a favor, will you? Leave a message at the courts for Mother Japh, saying that I would like to speak with her tomorrow, and hope to find her in sometime during the morning. And also leave word for Aedile Coeccias about what we saw tonight, and that the ghost was Duplin."

"Y'are going home?"

"Yes. No, no, wait. Don't say the ghost was Duplin. Just say it was my thief. And forget the name yourself, will you?"

"No fears there," Boult assured him. "Once I leave your messages, it's me for the barrel in the barracks 'til I forget the whole damn evening."

Liam smiled grimly. "Don't get too drunk, Boult. There'll be work for you tomorrow night as well."

Taking the torch, and leaving the Guard to puzzle out what he meant, Liam set off for the stables.

By the time he reached home, his body felt drained, worn out by the long day, but his mind was curiously alert. He ran over his growing list of answers, and found that his list of questions had grown faster.

On the surface, he had found his thief, and presumably Coeccias's as well. With Duplin dead and his accomplice and murderer off at sea, the investigation should be at a close. He had his rug back, and would simply have to give up the wand and the spellbook. Coeccias could try to mollify Cloten with the information, and though Liam did not think it would work, what else was there?

The problem, he knew as he kicked the wet sand from his boots and entered the house, was that he felt there was something else, and it irritated him.

"Fanuilh," he called. "Where are you?"

In the workroom.

"Come into the kitchen. I want to talk to you."

He went there himself, tossing his cloak on the back of a chair and conjuring up a meal in the magical oven.

The dragon padded in, blinking its eyes sleepily, and flapped its wings once to rise onto the table.

Good evening, master, it thought.

"Good morning to you, familiar mine. Were you sleeping?"

Yes. There was no hint of reproach in the thought, but Liam apologized anyway, pulling a bowl of coffee from the oven with his meal.

"Sorry. Smell that. I want to tell you a story, and I want you to help me figure it out."

Very well, the dragon thought, arcing out its long neck to sniff daintily at the coffee.

"All right," Liam began, around a mouthful of food, "you know this story, I assume, but I want to tell it to you whole. We start with Duplin and his sailor friend. They have been planning this job for at least a week—we know from Mopsa that Duplin is a great one for planning—and then they do it, correct?"

Apparently.

Liam held up his spoon to show that he agreed. "Exactly. Apparently. They sail out here, and Duplin comes in and steals three of Tarquin's enchanted things."

Your *enchanted things,* the dragon corrected.

"Whatever. We know only one person came in, because there was only one set of footprints." He paused to take another mouthful, and the dragon sent in a thought.

How did he get past Tarquin's wards?

"Leave that. Just the story as well as we can figure it—the problems will come later, and believe me, there are more than enough problems. Now, only one set of footprints."

He went on, describing the night in as much detail as he could. Duplin, with Liam's things, returned to the boat, and the two men sailed back to the harbor. From there, they went to Bellona's temple, presumably using the rug to get to the roof. They opened the window and somehow got down to the floor, where one of them tried to get at the temple treasury, stuffed with unsigned notes of hand on the Caernarvon mines. Cloten interrupted them, and the other thief knocked him out. They then escaped by the roof—the back door was locked, and Scaevola was out front—leaving the rug behind.

"Sometime later," Liam concluded, "they went to Faius's place in Narrow Lane, where the sailor stabbed Duplin, and then fled with his supposed sister-in-law on the *Heart of Oak* the next morning. We have one thief's body in the morgue, and the other thief is at large, at sea, and out of reach. Story told."

The problems . . .

"Yes. Can you name them?"

Liam counted them off on his long fingers as the dragon listed them.

1. How did Duplin get past Master Tarquin's wards? 2. How did the thieves get to the floor of the temple? 3. How did they escape? 4. Why did they leave the rug behind?

It looked like a list in Liam's head, complete with the numbers. He smiled. "Excellent! But you missed some—the most important ones."

Fanuilh cocked its head. *Which?*

Liam did not bother to count off his own points. "Why did they sail back to the harbor? It's easier to get from here to Bellona's temple by land than by sea, and even easier by air. Why didn't they use the rug? We have to assume they knew it was here—they chose what they took very carefully. So why come by sea at all? It's not a long walk, and they would know they could take the rug back. They must have known how to use it, because it was up on the roof. How they got to the floor of the temple doesn't interest me so much—they might have used a rope, and a sailor could climb a rope as well as a thief, probably better.

"The question is, why didn't the gryphon make any noise? I was only standing outside, and it nearly shouted me off the roof. How they got off the roof after Cloten found them is an excellent question, but so is the fact that he didn't have a bruise, or at least not one anyone can remember. And the last specific question, of course, is what did they want the spellbook and the wand for?"

There was a long silence; Liam toyed with his food and Fanuilh sat back on its haunches, the coffee grown cold and the odor stale. At last, it suggested, *A wizard hired them?*

"But who? Tarquin was the only wizard in Southwark that we know of, but he's dead. And you yourself said that you would know if a new one arrived."

He might have given Duplin an enchantment to break the ward's magic elsewhere.

"Yes, so that you wouldn't have noticed. But why bother? Why conceal wizardry, when there are no wizards in Southwark?"

You thought it might be one of the priests.

"Yes," Liam conceded, "I did. And it's still a possibility, but we won't know that until Coeccias gets a reply from this Acrasius Saffian."

Then we must wait until then.

"But I don't want to wait," Liam said irritably. "I want to know now."

Because there are other questions you have, the dragon observed. *Not "specific" questions.*

"Lots of them," Liam admitted. "For instance, what did the Death's smile mean? And I want to know if Scaevola really had a vision, and if he did, what it means—and whether it has anything to do with what's going on. And then there's the comet, and the candles in the temples blowing out a few days ago. And while we're discussing the bizarre and unnatural, what did Duplin mean about there being animals and birds after him? The gods only know the tortures of being a ghost, but that seems beyond even them."

Suddenly he was sick of talking, and of thinking. He was tired, and his feet hurt in his boots. "Are you finished with your coffee?"

Yes, master.

"I'm going to bed. Will you wake me early?"

Yes, master.

"No more pages from the bestiary, all right? And no ancient temples, either. Something simple—a pretty girl, with long brown hair." He closed his eyes and thought hard, imagining a dark-eyed beauty from a distant land. "Can you see her?"

I can, the dragon answered, and when Liam opened his eyes, he laughed. Its tail was curled around its legs, and its eyes were directed at the ceiling; it somehow looked the picture of prim disdain.

"Wake me with her," he ordered lightly, and went to the library to sleep.

■ *12* ■

NIGHTMARES TROUBLED LIAM'S sleep, and when Fanuilh dutifully sent the exotic beauty into them to wake him, she was quickly incor-
porated. She cried "Wake!" from the cage of the gryphon in Bellona's
temple, while Scaevola sat astride the creature as it flew around the
dome. She called "Wake!" from the roof of the temple, holding the rope,
slick with blood, that Duplin was using to climb down the outside of the
building, beneath a sky swarming with thousands of brilliant comets. She
called "Wake!" from the portico of Laomedon's temple, wearing the
skullcap of the Death and the sheer robes of a dancer, while Cloten's
men marched in a precise circle around Guiderius's men, who did the
same, the two lines weaving in and out but maintaining an impossible
integrity.

Finally the dream righted itself, and she was kneeling by the divan in
the library, cooing "Wake!" at him, and he did.

"Gods," he grumbled, hauling himself out of bed and scrubbing at
his face. Cold sweat clung to him, and he shivered. "Let's not try that
again, shall we? At least not until you're better at it."

They are your dreams.

He could not think of a response, and slouched out of the library,
rubbing his eyes. It was just past dawn, and the sun shone weakly out of a
mackerel sky. He shaved and washed perfunctorily, dressed and got
breakfast before he was truly awake.

Will there be coffee, master? Fanuilh asked, padding curiously into the
kitchen.

"Yes, there will be coffee, master," Liam muttered. "You know, you call me that, but I seem to do all the serving around here. Why can't you conjure up breakfast once in a while?"

The magic works only for the owner.

"But you have part of my soul. That makes you a part owner—or do you just want the part where the food is eaten, and not where it's made?"

Even if I could conjure the oven, the dragon objected, ignoring Liam's comment, *I could not get the food out. I have no hands.*

"Quite right," Liam conceded, retrieving their breakfast from the oven and setting it on the table. "We can't have you dropping the plates and making a general mess. I wonder if I could train you to balance them on your nose."

I do not think I would be good at it.

"Naturally. The question is, what would you be good at? The house cleans itself, I take care of Diamond, and there's nothing else to be done around here. Perhaps I should sell you to Madame Rhunrath's menagerie."

You would miss me.

"Not likely," Liam said, but he said it lightly, because he knew it was true. He would miss teasing the dragon, using it as a sounding board for his ideas, and as a comforting presence in the house. It filled a gap for him, somewhere between a pet and a friend, and he seemed to be aware of the fact.

"Would you miss me?" The dragon cocked its head and peered at him, as if the idea were alien to it. "All right, never mind that. Do you miss Tarquin?"

Master Tanaquil was a good master.

Liam puzzled over this equivocal answer for a moment, then gave it up. He was never sure if he should give up hope of understanding the little dragon.

You will meet the pickit today.

"Yes, and the Death, too, and Duplin's ghost again."

Why the ghost?

Liam searched for an answer. "I'm not sure. I have to talk with Mother Japh about that. Since she has the body in her morgue, there might be a way to lay him to rest. That at least would be something done, and it would get the 'wights' in the Warren to leave Coeccias alone."

You feel sorry for him—Duplin.

"Don't you?" He studied the dragon's reaction, the way it paused in the middle of a bite to consider.

I do not think so. He is dead, but does not know it. It is foolish.

"Foolish," Liam echoed. "You are very strange, Fanuilh." He said it fondly, though, and scratched the dragon's head as he left the kitchen.

I am single-handedly making that hostler the richest man in Southwark, he thought, frowning at the diminished pile of coins in his palm. Then he tossed them in his pocket and walked away from the stables, heading for the waterfront. He had more money at the house, enough for a long while, considering that he paid for food only when he was in the city. He had more money, in fact, than he had had for years, but the times he had been without had not taught him to be careful with it. As long as it was there, he would spend it as he saw fit, and when there was none left, he would see fit not to spend any more.

Harbor Street was crowded as he strolled down it, people taking advantage of even the weak, watery sunlight to open stands and hawk their various wares. It was heartening to see the mounds of fish and barrels of oysters, the crates of lobsters, the fishermen hauling their catches up from the docks and the shoppers bustling down from all over the city to buy. There was a cold, salt smell to the air, and he marveled at how much different the street was during the day.

How many of them know, he wondered, *that just a few hours ago there was a ghost running here? And a fool running after it?*

He came onto the docks and turned to the east, to the far end, where Duke Street trickled out, winding down a steep incline from the temple of the Storm King, and was content to wait there for Mopsa.

The docks were busy as well. Almost fifty ships sat at anchor in the harbor, or tied up alongside the wharves, but they were mostly quiet, settled in for the winter, decks stripped and masts denuded. It was the fishermen who filled the waterfront, maneuvering their small boats in and among the larger trading vessels, manhandling their catches up slimy water stairs and onto waiting wagons, which boomed on the foot-thick planks of the piers and jetties and rattled on the cobbles. It was a happy scene, for all the cursing and shouting, and it pleased Liam immensely, a pretense of normality in a city where ghosts ran the streets and temples clashed.

He knew Mopsa was behind him even before she slipped her hand into his pocket, and he let her grab his purse before touching her wrist. Then he frowned and shook his head at her.

"Is that the best you can do? No wonder you're still a pickit."

She handed back the purse with a sheepish smile. "I wasn't really trying, you know, just testing you."

"Of course not. And they wouldn't really cut your hand off for stealing, either."

She gave a superior smile. "Not in Southwark, Uncle. I'm too young. A few days with the Addle, then I'd be out." At least she knew the law; still, she was too complacent. When Stick had taught him thieving, he had made the dangers clear.

"And have the Guard spreading your description, and every stall-keeper and merchant and hawker looking at you. Every time you get caught, it makes it twice as easy to get caught again."

She digested this soberly, and apparently did not like the taste. With a grimace, she changed the topic.

"Have you thought about where y'are going to start?"

He had not, he realized. Southwark's waterfront was not terribly big, but there were an awful lot of people about that morning, and he could not just work his way through all of them. He had been thinking more about the fact that he knew Duplin was dead, and the girl did not. Should he tell her?

"Well I have," Mopsa said impatiently, after about a second's delay. "I think you should go ask Valdas what he knows."

"Who's Valdas?"

"Just an old man who spends his time on the docks, but he knows more of what goes on than anyone else."

That made sense to Liam. Every port, no matter what its size, had a man like that, usually a retired sailor, who could recount the history of every ship, every sailor and every coil of rope. Bigger harbors usually had more than one; Harcourt had at least a dozen, and the giant roadstead at Dordrecht probably supported twice that.

"Do you know him?"

"Know him?" the girl said, as if he had insulted her. "Didn't he used to give me bread every Godsday?"

"Then lead me to him," Liam suggested, throwing out his arm and bowing over it.

She did, marching confidently through the crowds of fishermen and fishmongers, checking over her shoulder every now and then to make sure he was following.

They found Valdas in the middle of the docks, unofficially supervising the unloading of a boat filled with eel pots. He was ancient but cheerful, long years at sea etched in his round white face, with a sunken mouth from which jutted three proud yellow teeth. He was practically swaddled in clothes, four layers visible at his neck, where a bright red scarf easily three yards long had gotten loose. One of his sleeves was empty, and Mopsa tugged at it.

"Valdas," she said, tugging again. "Can I talk to you?"

He turned, and delight crinkled his doughy face. "By the gods, if it isn't . . . no, it isn't either, not Tarpeia, nor Dorcas neither—but it is! It's little Mopsa, though grown now, and dressed like a boy!"

"I'm not dressed like a boy!"

His delight undimmed, the old man beamed on. "Your hair's cut short, like a boy's."

"But I'm not dressed like a boy!"

"Aye, but your hair is. Now come, little Mopsa, and talk with old Valdas. Y'are not as much about the docks as was your wont, nor with a clean jacket and shift, neither."

The girl stifled a sigh, and indicated Liam. "My uncle would like to talk to you."

"Ah! And you've an uncle now—how fine!—and a gentlemen, too! Good day to you, master, and good days. And a fine wind, too, for you, sir. Buying Mopsa a clean coat—that's good on you, sir, for that she's usually a dirty little whelp, though I haven't seen her in over a year, and get to wondering where's she's gone."

He continued to smile, bobbing and bowing at Liam with befuddled amiability.

"Good day to you, Valdas," Liam said. "Mopsa was telling me that you know a great deal about what goes on down here."

"Oh, aye, one way or another, I throw my net wide, and pretty near everything comes into it," the old man said happily, "though not as wide a net as yours, sir, I'm sure, you a gentleman and all, with such fine clothes. I mostly sit in my old shack there"—he pointed vaguely down the waterfront—"and I hear what there is to be heard. Not that such would be of interest to you, a gentleman and all. And sure, isn't it a cold day?"

"It's not that cold," Mopsa protested, but Liam quickly agreed. He had seen the open, almost innocent, appraisal in the old sailor's eyes.

"It is very cold," he said. "Perhaps, if you have the time, we could go somewhere and have something warm to drink, and you could see if you can answer my questions."

"Well!" said Valdas, apparently greatly surprised. "Well! That would be a rare honor, and a passing pleasure, and would do a man's heart good! Why we could go to the Green Eel—no, we couldn't, either, it's closed at this hour—and the other, the Freeporter's Wife, why that's not been open in years—no, not the Pot and Mess, either, he never sells a drink before noon—why, sir, I don't think there's a decent place for

something hot that'll be open for hours!" He scratched his head, indignant at this state of affairs, and then winced. "And come to think of it,
sir, I'm busy at the moment, with the unloading, you see"—he jerked a
thumb over his shoulder, where most of the eelpots had been removed
without his indispensable aid—"for all that I've only one arm, I've two
eyes and twice as many brains, and the morning's not for wasting in
taverns."

"I see what you mean," Liam said, smiling politely. "Perhaps we
could forgo the drink and speak here. I'd be immensely grateful if you
could spare just a minute—and perhaps you would be good enough to
accept a token of my gratitude, and have a drink on me later, at your
convenience." He put a hand meaningfully into his pocket, and jingled
the purse there.

"Oh, sir, I don't know how I could," Valdas protested, lying with a
sincerity that Liam found strangely refreshing. "A token, at most, sir, a
mere token—for your sake and the girl's, not my own. To drink your
health with, only, sir, and only if you were to insist."

Liam produced a silver coin and pressed it into the old man's hand.
"I do insist, Valdas."

"Sir, you are too kind, a gentleman, sir. Mopsa, your uncle is a
gentleman, as any can see by his bearing and his fine clothes—and the
fine clothes he's bought for you. Sir! Your health! Now, your questions?"

It took some time, because of Valdas's roundabout manner of speaking and his digressive habits, but they managed to discover that he had
indeed seen a man and a woman go aboard the *Heart of Oak* the night of
the two robberies, and had seen the ship put to sea the next morning with
all haste. But when Liam suggested that the man and the woman had
bought passage, the old sailor cackled long and hard.

"Ha! Bought passage! Oh, sir, y'are a passing jester, fair—no offense
meant, sir, but what I mean—bought passage!—why, do you see? Why
buy passage?"

"Why not?" Liam said, unable to see the humor but smiling anyway.
"How else would they get on board?"

Valdas's cackles faded away, stopping with a brief coughing spell.
"How else, sir? Why, by walking up the gangplank of his own ship, is
how! For the man was the captain, and the captain the man, do you see?"

"Are you sure?"

"Sure as the sea is wet, sir. I don't sleep as much now as I used to,
and I saw them board her myself—Captain Perelhos, and his woman. I
remember it well, sir, very well, for that he was storming and swearing,
and ordering all things well, and kept me up half the night, though that

was no great loss, do you see, for that I don't sleep neither sound nor deep, being old."

"And they were the only people to go aboard, this Captain Perelhos and the woman? There were no other passengers?" He waited tensely for the reply; this was not news he wanted to hear, though he had half expected something like it.

"None, not a one, sir," Valdas beamed, "and how could there be, on the *Heart of Oak?* She's but a poor schooner, sir, only the one mast and no great weight of sail, though sturdy, and one for a storm. She carries no great cargo, either—a regular packet ship, letters and small parcels and, of course, the pay."

Things were changing rapidly in Liam's mind, lists rearranging themselves, chronologies shifting, and then the word *pay* hit the whole structure like a hammer, shattering it.

"Pay?"

"Aye, sir, coin, two or three heavy chests of it. For that any number of merchants use the *Heart of Oak* to pay their factors—the little merchants up and down the coast who vend their wares. She carries an extra complement of soldiers, and is reliable—not likely to founder in the heavy seas—so every month or so Perelhos takes aboard the money from different merchants and guarantees to distribute it to their outposts or their creditors or what have you, and returns with accounts and reports and sometimes revenues, though it's mostly going out that he has any money."

"Two or three chests of it," Liam murmured absently. "Close to a fortune."

"Aye," Valdas said, chuckling, and held up a finger. "Which, mark you, is what makes it passing strange that he should fleece his chandlers, do you see? Chests of money on the *Heart of Oak,* and he leaves the port with a host of unpaid debts! And him no doubt needing to come back in a month for supplies!"

"I doubt he'll be coming back," Liam said slowly, sifting through the wreckage of his ideas. Perelhos had not fled his creditors, but the Guard, afraid because he had stabbed Duplin in Narrow Lane. The reason for the murder could be almost anything; they might have argued over the woman, for instance, or the plan or the division of the loot—but he was sure it had not involved the rug, the spellbook or the wand, or Bellona's temple. With a sinking feeling, Liam concluded that the robbery Duplin planned had nothing to do with the crimes he was investigating.

Going out of the harbor in winter was no "simple boat ride," and he berated himself for not thinking of it earlier; the currents outside the

Teeth could be vicious, and the winds were unpredictable. Inside the harbor was a different thing altogether, and any man born in a seaport could row a dinghy out to an anchored ship, particularly if the captain of that ship was willing to help. And with two or three chests of money there, it would be well worth the trip.

Instead of two connected crimes, Liam suddenly found himself facing three, and the one he knew the most about was the one he was least interested in. Duplin had not planned to rob him, or Bellona's temple; he and Perelhos had concocted a scheme to steal the captain's own cargo. Perelhos would express his sincere regrets to the merchants whose money had been stolen, and then split it with the thief.

"Sir?" Valdas asked. "Are you sick?"

"No, not at all," Liam said quickly, the concerned expression on the old sailor's face and the disapproving pout Mopsa wore telling him how stunned he must look. *I am stunned,* he thought, *and very, very confused.* "I'm fine, thank you. And thank you for taking time to speak with me, Valdas. You have been a great help."

He found another silver coin for the old man, and turned away in the midst of his thanks.

No, he corrected himself, *I'm not confused at all. I'm just at a dead end.* He could not prove that Perelhos and Duplin had planned the crime he imagined, but he did not want to. He wanted to know who had stolen Tarquin's things and then tried to steal the temple treasury, and now he had no one to suspect, no clues, and nowhere to begin.

"Hey! Uncle!" Mopsa appeared at his side, running next to him as he paced along the waterfront. "Hey, where are you going?"

Liam stopped, and the girl went on a few steps before stopping herself.

"Where are you going? What's wrong with you? You look ill."

He wondered that his disappointment should show so much on his face. And yet he was not as disappointed as he might have been. Valdas's words had made sense only of the questions he had raised with Fanuilh the night before. There had been too many holes in the supposition that Duplin was his thief; the old sailor had helped him discard an unsuitable hypothesis.

"Where am I going?" He did not know; he had not gotten as far as thinking out his next step. To Coeccias, he imagined, but he could not tell the girl that. And what would he do about her? He ought to let the Werewolf know that Duplin was dead, but he did not want Mopsa to hear it from him. He could write a note—she could not read—but then she had said she was not sure if the princeps could, either. "I have to meet someone," he said, "and I want you to send word to the Werewolf. Duplin is not the man I was looking for, but I need to see him tonight." A vague idea struck him, the merest outlines, but it seemed fitting. "Ask him to meet me in Narrow Lane at ten. Tell him I'll have his gift then."

Mopsa looked suspiciously at his small smile. "Why?"

"To give him my gift. The one I promised."

"Yes, but why Narrow Lane, and why tonight? And what if he won't come?"

"Don't ask, pickit, just do as you're told. Ten in Narrow Lane, where it bends. All right?"

"All right," she said sullenly.

"And buy yourself a lunch," he said, but though she took the offered coin, she did not seem pleased.

"Can't I come with you now?"

"As told, pickit," he repeated, and made a shooing gesture.

She walked off, pouting over her shoulder every few steps.

When he could no longer see her, Liam started up Chandlers' Street for the Guard barracks.

Coeccias was not there when he arrived. "More trouble in Temples' Court," the Guard told him at the door, and Liam groaned. As he walked over to the Duke's courts, though, he had a consoling thought: the trouble the day before had led Fanuilh to discover the rug. If the newest trouble yielded a clue even half as significant, he would welcome it with open arms.

He knocked at the tall doors of the courts for five minutes before trying the handle, and found them open. The porter was nowhere in sight, so he slipped quickly down the hallway to the staircase. The darkness after the first twist of the spiral was complete, as it had been on his last visit, but he cursed the creeping fears stirring in his imagination and groped his way down to the cellar.

Just like last night, he thought, and squeezed his eyes shut, shuffling hastily down the corridor to Mother Japh's door. The old woman opened it almost immediately, and he stepped in.

"Rhenford! What would you? I had your message from the Guard," she said irritably, "and have been attending you all the morning."

The morning was not old, but Liam ignored her frustration. "I've found your ghost."

Her expression changed; he had caught her interest. "The one in the morgue? The clerk?"

"Not a clerk—a thief, and he wanders past here every night just after ten."

"Does he?" Mother Japh asked, excited. "To where he was taken off?" Liam nodded. "There's a fortune for you—the time and the place. If I can get his body there, he'll find it himself! That'll like Coeccias no end!"

He had expected just such a reaction, and stopped her. "Before we do that, I want to ask you something. Is it possible to trap him?"

"Trap him?" The old woman's eyes narrowed suspiciously. "For what?"

"Not really trap him," Liam said hastily, "but just hold him for a minute. I want to ask him some questions."

Her expression softened, and she nodded sagely. "Ah, I see now. You said he was a thief in life. Is this your thief?"

"No, not exactly. Actually, not at all. But when I saw him last night, he said some things that I did not understand. I was hoping we might, well, lure him somewhere with his body, ask him a few questions, and then let him go."

Tapping at her chin, she spoke thoughtfully: "Aye, it's possible . . . a bit of lead over the mouth and nose, someone outside . . . aye, it could be done. Though not for long, see you. Most ghosts are stupid, do you see? Addled a little. They can pass through walls like nothing, but they often forget. With lead over the face, we could hold him, at least until he thought to go through the wall."

"Would you help?"

"Help? With a will, Rhenford, with a will! It'd like me to see him properly buried."

"And you can arrange it? I mean, put lead on his mouth and nose? And why lead?"

"In course I can. Spirits cannot pass through lead, for that it's a gross metal, a base element, and withstands their airy nature. Though it would be best if we had someone he knew in life on hand."

"A friend?"

"Aye, a friend would do us nicely."

"I can arrange that." He could probably arrange two friends, he realized, and decided he would with a mean little smile. It was petty, but he thought Faius deserved it, and the Werewolf, too.

"Rhenford," Mother Japh said suddenly, "are you being careful?"

"What?"

"Mind you, I told you to be careful. Just then, you did not look like you were being careful."

He remembered her warning, and protested feebly: "Of course. What do you mean?"

She leveled a short finger at him. "There's more here than this ghost, Rhenford. I said it before, and'll say it again. This morning's news only proves it."

He was confused. "What news?"

"Have not heard?" She waited, and when he shrugged, spoke soberly. "A host passed through the city this morning, at dawn. Thundered out of the north, clattered like Hell through the streets, and drew rein in Temples' Court."

A host? "An army? In Southwark?" Was that the trouble the Guard had referred to? "That's impossible! How could there be an army in Southwark? I didn't see any soldiers!"

"That," she said pointedly, "is exactly it. No one *saw* soldiers—they only *heard* them, a noise like legions in the streets, and shouted orders and horses and all the trappings, but nothing to be seen at all. And all camped in Temples' Court."

Liam whistled. "In front of the temple of Bellona?"

"Where else? I told you there was more here, and that new goddess is at the very heart of it."

"No doubt," Liam said, wondering how hard Scaevola had prayed, and if this was his sign. "Did they do anything else?"

"No, they didn't. My house is down the hill aways. I didn't hear that they did anything other than wake all of Temples' Court, but isn't that enough?"

"No," he said, "it's not enough. Thank you, Mother Japh. If you would arrange those things for me, I would be grateful. I'll come back around nine."

She raised her eyes to the ceiling. "Y'are not going to be careful, Rhenford, I can tell."

"I don't need to be careful," he told her, "I'm very lucky."

Liam did not feel lucky five minutes later. His head full of the phantom host that had paraded down Temple Street, he walked out of the Duke's court and called out to the Guard.

"Is the Aedile back?"

"No, Quaestor Rhenford," the Guard replied.

Liam turned, meaning to head for Temple Street, and saw Japer across the square, lounging against the wall of Herlekin's restaurant. For a moment their eyes locked, and the thief touched his forehead, smirked, and disappeared into the crowd.

"Damn!" Liam exploded, and when people stared at him, he clenched his fists and headed off in his original direction. There was no chance of catching Japer.

It had been bound to happen: his precaution of waiting until Mopsa was out of sight before going to see the Aedile had been silly, if not completely careless. It had never occurred to him to be more circumspect, but his few experiences as a spy had been brief, forthright things: sneaking into an enemy camp, scouting out unknown territory. He wondered that he had not been spotted before, and then realized that he probably had.

Then why didn't they do anything about it?

There was no satisfactory answer, but he knew that he had underestimated the Southwark Guild. What the price might be, he had no idea, so he ignored it. After scolding himself thoroughly for his stupidity, he put thoughts of the Guild aside, and concentrated on Temple Street.

◾ *13* ◾

IF WORD OF the nighttime host had not spread as far as Harbor Street and the waterfront, it had at least completely infected the neighborhood around Temple Street, exaggerating and, perhaps, justifying its already fearful mood. Many of the shops in the nearby streets were closed, and a group of old women stood by the entrance to the row of temples, some still in their nightclothes. They had been awakened by the passing of the invisible army and now they hung by the corner, glancing down the row of columned facades, as if desperate to enter and pray but afraid of what they might find there.

Liam passed them without a second glance, his boots echoing in the empty road. The temples loomed on either hand, their doors shut. It was early yet; the sun had not penetrated into Temple Street, and in the shadows the houses of the Taralonian gods were mute and unhelpful. Greasy smoke oozed from the dome of Pity, burnt offerings creeping humbly to the heavens. He noted it, strode on.

The six Guards in the cul-de-sac looked pathetic, too tiny a force in the empty space, huddled in a circle and warily eyeing the walls around them. Liam did not know them, but one recognized him.

"The Aedile," he said, as if he did not expect to see his commander again, "is in there." He pointed at Bellona's temple.

No one answered Liam's impatient knock, so he pushed open the door himself, and stepped inside.

Now it looks like a temple, he thought, and it did. All resemblance to a military camp was gone; acolytes littered the floor in uneven ranks as though stricken, some kneeling, a few lying prone, with their arms flung out and their faces pressed to the cold stone. A fierce whispering reached him from the altar, Coeccias and Cloten facing each other, Alastor off to one side, and then the Aedile's voice boomed through the temple: "And I tell you you will not!"

Cloten hissed a reply, and Liam hurriedly picked his way among the praying acolytes. There were tears on many of the men's faces.

"No! I'll not have it!" Coeccias insisted. His face was red.

"It is not your will," Cloten said icily, stepping behind the altar; it did not seem that he was retreating, but more as if he were taking up his official position. "It is Her will." He jabbed a finger toward the ceiling.

"The Duke's will rules this city," Coeccias said.

"Then send word to your Duke," Cloten replied disdainfully, "and while we wait his answer, I will have satisfaction!"

Alastor saw Liam approaching, and stepped away from the altar to meet him.

"It would not be well to interrupt them, Quaestor," he whispered.

"What are they arguing about?"

Looking quickly over his shoulder, the Keeper of Arms explained: "Hierarch Cloten has challenged Strife to a duel."

"He challenged Strife?"

"His temple," Alastor clarified. "A champion from each, to do battle tomorrow. Hierarch Guiderius has accepted the challenge. It is Bellona's will," he finished, but it was clear from his tone that he had his doubts about that.

"Did something happen here this morning?" Alastor was a man he could speak to, Liam had decided, more reasonable than Cloten and more disposed to cooperate.

The Keeper of Arms glanced at him, startled. "What do you mean?"

"When the host arrived, what happened here?"

Alastor was quiet for a moment, considering, then shook his head with regret. "I cannot say, Quaestor. It is a matter for the temple to deal with, not the Duke."

"Does it involve Scaevola?" Liam pressed.

Again the priest was surprised, his hasty denial serving only to confirm Liam's suspicions. "Not at all, Quaestor. As I said, it is a matter for the temple, not the Duke."

"Then you would not mind if I spoke with him?"

"With Scaevola?" the priest asked uneasily. "I am afraid that is not possible. He is . . . in retreat. He will be Bellona's champion in the duel tomorrow." Alastor's tone was ambiguous, and Liam guessed that Scaevola's retreat involved guards at the door of his cell.

"Alastor!" Cloten snapped from the altar. "Who is that?"

"Quaestor Liam Rhenford," the priest answered quickly.

"Seconded to the Aedile by the Duke," Liam added politely, with a deep bow in Cloten's direction. "I am here to help find the men who assaulted you, Hierarch."

Cloten sniffed, taken aback by Liam's good manners. "There is no need. They will be discovered tomorrow, on the field of honor."

"Of course," he said smoothly, walking over to the altar. "But perhaps in the meantime you could spare me a moment, Hierarch. There are just a few things I hoped you could clear up for me."

Unsure of himself in the face of Liam's apparent deference, Cloten stammered.

"It will take only a moment," Liam assured him, "and I would greatly appreciate it. For instance, perhaps you could describe the man you saw standing here." He put his hand on the shelf where the temple treasury sat, and smiled expectantly at the high priest.

"I have already gone over this with the Aedile—" Cloten began, and Coeccias started to speak, until Liam overrode him gently.

"I know, Hierarch, and I regret the inconvenience, but it is different to hear it from the person directly involved. Could you just describe the man?"

"Very well," he said with an exasperated sigh, "he was of average height, with a beard."

"Could you say what color beard, or what he was wearing?"

"No. It was dark."

"Of course—forgive me. But could you guess the shape of the beard, for instance? Was it like the Aedile's, or Hierarch Guiderius's?"

"Neither," Cloten said, his face flushing at the mention of the high priest of Strife. "It was full and long—it reached to his chest."

Liam nodded approvingly, trying to keep the man talking and cooperative. "Now, could you tell me what he was doing?"

"I have already been through all this!"

"I know," Liam said sympathetically, "but please, exactly what was he doing?"

"Oh, very well. He was tugging at the chest, trying to move it."

There were leather straps on either side of the chest, Liam took hold of one and pulled experimentally. "Like this?"

Wood grated on stone as the chest slid an inch on the shelf. Behind the chest, he could see the bolt stapled into the wall, the chain running straight up the wall to another bolt, where it angled across the dome. He ran a finger around the edges of the staple; the mortar there was old and thick, sunk deeply in the stone of the walls. There was no way he could see to lower it.

"How do you feed the gryphon?"

"We do not," Cloten said, irritated by the question, as if there were no reason to feed it. "We are going to sacrifice it to the goddess." He looked at Alastor meaningfully, and repeated himself: "We are going to sacrifice it."

"But how will you get it down?"

"With ropes," the priest said shortly, rapidly growing impatient. "Now, if that is all—"

"Just one more question," Liam interrupted. "Did you see the man who knocked you down?"

"I did not. The coward struck me from behind."

"And where did he hit you? He hit you in the head, didn't he?"

"No," Cloten said, suddenly stiff. "He shoved me in the back."

"But you lost consciousness?"

"I must have hit my head when I fell."

"Ah, you had a bruise, then?"

"I do not recall," Cloten said, and Liam knew he had pushed the priest to his limit. "Perhaps I was only stunned. I fail to see the importance of these questions, sir, as the cowards will be exposed tomorrow. Good day."

His purple robe swirled dramatically as he spun on his heel and stalked off to the door in the alcove.

"It will not!" Coeccias shouted. He had kept silent until then, for which Liam was grateful, but the high priest ignored his comment, slamming the door behind him. The Aedile ground his teeth with rage, and turned on Liam. "Did see? Did see that? The man is a fool!"

Alastor, who had watched his superior's departure with a worried frown, cleared his throat, and Liam hurried to quiet Coeccias.

"We should discuss this elsewhere," he said. "I have to tell you some things."

Coeccias lowered his voice. "Truth, Rhenford, I've heard too much—but I'll attend you." He forced himself to nod politely at Alastor. "I apologize for shouting. Yet you must make him understand that there can be no duel."

Alastor shook his head. "It is Her will," he said, this time with a hint of resignation. Then he too retreated to the door in the alcove.

Liam and Coeccias made their way out of the temple, moving quietly through the rows of praying men. Only a few raised their eyes to note their passing, and Liam noticed that none seemed resentful: only curious, or confused. If that indicated an ambivalence toward Cloten, Liam would not be surprised. On the other hand, between the theological and hierarchical disputes, the visions and visitations that plagued her temple, Bellona's worshipers had more than enough reasons for confusion.

Something had clearly happened when the invisible army arrived in the cul-de-sac, something that almost certainly involved Scaevola, and it had set almost the entire community of Bellona's worshipers to serious praying.

Once outside, Coeccias vented his rage by shaking his fist at the closed door and cursing Cloten vigorously. He finished his opinion with: "The arrogant, blind, pox-ridden bastard!" and then stopped, out of breath, huffing his anger when new curses failed him.

"You can't stop the fight?"

"No," the Aedile said. "It would take the Duke's written hand, and that cannot be had for at least two days. There's no ban on dueling in Southwark, though there should be. The Duke has a faith in the field of honor, and's not above applying it himself. Mind you, it would be no large affair, were it not that the champions will each have one or two score of seconds, all armed to the teeth. And I can't tell them to go unarmed, and Cloten knows it, for that their very weapons are holy to them, and I can't interfere with their 'worship.' Now just think you, what will Cloten do if his man loses? Will he take it like a man? It doubts me—he'll order a general massacre!"

"I don't think Cloten's man will lose. Alastor said it would be Scaevola, and he's one of the best swordsmen I've ever seen."

"Truth, these are good news. I think I can trust Guiderius not to rage if he loses. I'll just have to hope that Cloten'll take his satisfaction from winning, and demand no more." He rolled his eyes to show how much faith he placed in the likelihood of Cloten demanding no more, and blew out a heavy sigh. "But come, Rhenford, do you have more news?"

"I do," Liam said, "but it's not good." He briefly explained what he had learned the night before in Narrow Lane, and on the docks that morning: the identity of the ghost, and the fact that he had almost certainly been chasing the wrong thief. "So now, at the very least, you know why the *Heart of Oak* slipped anchor so quickly, and we can get rid of the ghost in the Warren."

Coeccias smiled grimly. "Aye, that's something. Though now I have to tell all the merchants who had money with Perelhos that they're like never to see it more, and you have to trap a ghost. And we've no direction to take here at all."

"There is still the possibility of one of the other temples being involved. We have not heard from your judge, Saffian."

"That we'll hear tomorrow, I think, though I would not put much faith in it. It makes little sense for another temple to have done it. They're all old, well rooted. Even Strife has little to fear in the poaching of worshipers—not with Cloten presiding for Bellona. None'll approach. And even if he weren't a complete ass, there're enough mysteries and split hairs at work in her rites to keep all but the most learned away. And what do the learned need with a warrior goddess?"

"Still, you have to admit that it's all we have. Who else would have done it? The only thief who might have been involved is dead, and the only wizard who has been near Southwark in years is dead, and buried right by my house."

Coeccias turned a pensive look at the fortress walls of Strife's temple compound, and Liam wondered how much of his reluctance to suspect the other priests in Temple Street sprang from his own personal bias. These were the gods the Aedile had grown up with, and from what Liam could see, he was friends with many of their priests. It must be difficult for him to imagine them as sneak-thieves.

Nonetheless, the possibility remained, and really was their only avenue. Who else could it be? With the best thief and the only wizard in the city both safely out of the question, who else would have the power to break the wards on Tarquin's house and want to steal Bellona's treasury?

Even as he thought that, something in the formula nagged at him; some awkward phrase, something out of place. He wondered if he was framing the question correctly, but could not conceive of another way to put it.

"I wonder," he said at last, "if we should go speak to Guiderius."

"I already have. He's accepted the damn challenge—had to, he said, for the honor of Strife, and I must say I see where he stands—regrets it, but has accepted. There's no moving him." He looked at Liam, who was chewing lightly at his lower lip, and rolled his eyes again. "Truth, what am I thinking? You don't want to talk him from the duel; you want to put him to the question, and sound him as to whether he could play the thief."

Liam blushed. "You have to admit—"

"Aye, aye," Coeccias said, waving aside his protests. "You've the right of it. We needs must be thorough. And I suppose it's only fair to try

Guiderius, after the way you prized the facts from Cloten. I haven't seen the man so open since he came to Southwark."

"Can we go now?"

With a shrug, Coeccias led the way across the cul-de-sac and knocked at the gate of Strife's temple. A brown-robed acolyte with a naked sword in his hand let them in, and asked them politely to wait while he informed Guiderius of their presence.

There was a courtyard inside the gate, and the temple proper stood at the far end of it, a square structure with four towers rising from the corners. Sheds and wooden buildings lined the inside of the courtyard, plain, sturdy barracks, a small smithy, a number of pens and stalls for different animals. There was even a mews for hawks. It seemed more like the manor of a rural nobleman than a temple, except for the blood red marble of the temple itself, and the richly detailed carvings that covered its walls.

Guiderius came out of one of the small buildings, dusting his hands on a brown robe like the gatekeeper's. There was a fletching feather stuck in his goatee; he bowed with a patient air.

"Again, Coeccias?"

"No," the Aedile said, managing a rueful smile. "If you must, you must, Guiderius, and I cannot change that. But it would like me if you could spare a moment for my friend, Quaestor Rhenford. He is helping me to try and sort out this mess."

"I believe I saw him doing just that yesterday afternoon. Good day, Quaestor Rhenford. You wield a cudgel well."

Liam blushed again. "Thank you, Hierarch. I am more lucky than skilled, but the two are often mistaken."

The priest smiled his appreciation of the joke. "Very true, especially in battle. Y'are much a soldier?" He sounded like Coeccias, the same southern dialect, the slurring together of words.

"No, more a scholar than anything else. There are a few questions—"

"Rhenford," the priest said suddenly. "Liam Rhenford? The wizard? Old Tarquin Tanaquil's apprentice?"

Liam goggled at the older man for a moment. "No," he stammered, then got control of himself when he saw Coeccias trying to hide a smirk. "No, Hierarch, I am not a wizard. My name is Rhenford, and I do live in Tarquin Tanaquil's house, but he left it to me because we were friends. I was never his apprentice, and know nothing of magic."

"Ah, I see," Guiderius said. "I apologize. One hears these things bruited about, and they take on the color of truth."

"Not at all," Liam said. "It seems everyone thinks I am a wizard. But there were some questions. . . ."

"By all means, Quaestor. What would you know?"

The priest folded his hands and smiled expectantly.

Liam realized he did not know where to begin.

"First," he began, and then a question occurred to him. "First, can you tell me, are there any in your temple who resent the appearance of Bellona?"

To his surprise, Guiderius chuckled. "I can assure you," he said with perfect confidence, "that Strife has no grudge against Bellona. While it is surely false that She is His daughter, our temple accepts Her happily. Coeccias knows this—we were among the first to welcome Cloten to Southwark."

"A great mistake," the Aedile muttered, drawing a rueful nod from the Hierarch.

"It would seem so," Guiderius concurred.

"I understand that," Liam said, "officially, of course, and personally for you. But perhaps not everyone feels the same way. There might be one or more of your community who do not feel the same. Is that possible?"

Guiderius shook his head, and said flatly: "No. Not in the least. We are a warrior cult—we all take a vow of discipline. The man who violated a stated principle of the temple would be liable to expulsion. It is inconceivable."

"And yet some of your men participated in the fight yesterday. Surely brawling in public is not a mark of discipline."

"They were attacked," the priest pointed out reasonably. "Of course they may defend themselves. But as for the possibility of some of mine breaking into Bellona's temple, it is not even remotely possible."

In the face of the man's iron bound certainty, Liam could not think of any more questions. He did not believe that Strife's discipline could extend so far, but he could not contradict the Hierarch, for Coeccias's sake.

"Well, that is good to hear. But perhaps another temple? Laomedon, for instance, or the Peacekeeper?"

The idea amused Guiderius. "I hardly think the Peacekeeper would be happy to have His priests breaking into other temples, let alone assaulting other priests. And Laomedon is little concerned with the doings of the other gods."

Liam frowned. "Then perhaps some of your lay worshipers?"

"I can't imagine that, either. The people of Southwark are passing tolerant, Quaestor; short of human sacrifice and worshiping the Dark Gods, we'll allow almost aught."

"What about the money lending?" Liam asked, switching to his last suspicion.

"You mean those notes-of-hand on the Caernarvon mines? I would not bother with that, Quaestor. Trade is high in Southwark, and next season promises to be rich, no temple that I know of is unduly worried about Bellona's wealth."

All his questions neatly deflected, Liam spread his hands and smiled. "Well, Hierarch, I think that is all I wanted to ask. It seems as though no one in Southwark could possibly be involved."

"No one of Southwark," the priest said. "Have thought that it might be someone from Caernarvon?"

"Yes," Liam said, thinking of Scaevola and the doctrinal disputes he had heard of within Bellona's temple. "We have thought of that, but unfortunately it seems as unlikely as anything else."

"It truly is a mystery."

"Aye," Coeccias said sourly. "Sorry to pester you, Guiderius. We'll part now. You'll keep your men on a tight rein tomorrow?"

"In course. Though there'll be no need: on the field of honor, the righteous will always triumph."

He smiled and bowed, then returned to the outbuilding from which he had come.

"The righteous almost never win on the field of honor," Liam commented. He had seen a few duels, and they always went to the better fighter. "Guiderius's man will lose."

"Truth, y'are a doomsayer, Rhenford. Have you no faith?"

"Not in this," he answered. "You wait."

Coeccias yawned suddenly, stretching tiredly. "I am hungry. Come, let's get something."

It was early, an hour or more to noon, but Liam did not object. He was at a loss, and a feeling of futility swept over him. Thieves, wizards and now priests seemed beyond the reach of suspicion; there was no one left. He began to wonder if there was any point to continuing, but still the few facts he had fluttered through his mind maddeningly, like flies on a hot summer day.

They left Temple Street, passing a new group of people waiting there, who stared at Coeccias as the two men went by, but did not approach. The Aedile led the way to a small tavern nearby, and called for food. When the meal arrived, he attacked it with more fierceness than hunger. Liam sipped at a mug of cider and drummed his fingers on the tabletop, running over and over his basic assumption.

Someone had bypassed Tarquin's wards, stolen his book, wand and carpet, and then broken into Bellona's temple to steal her treasury.

He played with the phrases, rearranging them, deleting some, keeping only those he knew were absolutely true.

Someone had definitely bypassed Tarquin's wards. Fanuilh insisted they were still intact, and that it had not been done by another wizard, which meant either theurgy or a thief with the proper enchantment.

They had stolen the three items. That was undeniable, as was the fact that at least one of them, the rug, had later ended up on the roof of the temple, which meant that his house had been robbed first. He toyed briefly with the idea that the two were unconnected, but decided that would get him nowhere.

Then they had broken into the temple. That, too, was undeniable, because Cloten had discovered them in the act of stealing the treasury.

"Hold on," he muttered to himself.

What if they were not trying to steal the treasury?

Coeccias heard him, and looked up instantly from his meal. "Hold what?"

It was the only one of his assumptions that he could safely discard, the only event in the whole night that had not actually happened. Cloten had seen a man tugging at the treasury—not a man taking the chest out of the temple, or opening it to take out the notes-of-hand.

"I had a thought," Liam said, not sure if he should share it.

"Out with it," the Aedile demanded, and the hopeful look in his eyes made Liam wish he had kept silent.

"What if—and this is just a guess—what if our thieves weren't thieves at all? What if they weren't trying to take the treasury?"

Coeccias snorted, the hope going out of his eyes. "What if they were just there to pray? What if they were just taking a stroll in the middle of the night? What if I suddenly grew wings and flew to the moon?"

Perversely, his friend's ridicule increased Liam's interest in the idea. "No, wait, just listen. All Cloten saw them doing was tugging at the chest—and only one man at that. I tried to pull that thing, and believe me, it would take at least two strong men to carry it."

"So? There was another there."

"I know," Liam said patiently. "Indulge me for a minute. Have you got any better ideas?"

"We could book passage on the next ship out of Southwark," Coeccias replied, but he pushed aside his plate and prepared to listen. "Go to,

Rhenford. Spit it out. What do the men want, if they don't want the treasury?"

"What's on that shelf?"

"Nothing."

"Vandalism, then. Like those people who broke into all the apothecaries' shops in Northfield. Maybe they wanted to smash up the place, to discredit Bellona, because they don't want her worshiped here."

"Laypeople, you mean—not priests."

"Probably, yes. I'm willing to take Guiderius at his word when he says no one on Temple Street disapproves of Bellona."

"It seems a great deal of trouble just for a mess—stealing your things, going up to the roof. A pot of paint, good red paint, splashed on the door, a dead cat on the steps, both'd be easier, and more visible to the world at large."

Liam admitted this, and then thought of something else. "You know, there is something else on the shelf." It was, perhaps, even more improbable than vandalism.

"And that's?"

"The chain that holds up the gryphon's cage."

"There is that," Coeccias said slowly, considering the idea, and then rejecting it. "But who in Southwark would care about the gryphon?"

Liam thought of Madame Rhunrath, who would have been delighted to have the creature, but she did not have a beard, and what would she have done with it anyway? She could hardly exhibit it.

Still, when he said, "No one," he qualified the statement: "But then, no one could get past Tarquin's wards, either."

The Aedile studied him intently for a moment. "Y'are thinking of something, Rhenford. Is it of value, or just a fancy?"

"A fancy, I think. But worth looking into, if only I knew how." Who would be interested in the gryphon? What if it was a stone gryphon, the rarer type mentioned in one of Tarquin's bestiaries? He tried to call to mind the brief passage: they were rumored to eat the souls of the dead, and they could walk in the Gray Lands, the places where dead souls went. That seemed a contradiction, because the Gray Lands were supposed to be a place of peace, except for those small sections reserved for the punishment of the evil.

No one would be interested in an ordinary gryphon, but Laomedon might be interested in a stone gryphon. The Gray Lands, after all, were his domain.

"I think I will go visit the Death now," he said.

"Then it's not a fancy," Coeccias accused. "Y'are thinking of something, and it involves the Death. And do you know, Rhenford? I've no interest. It'd like me not to know. If your visit is fruitful, I'll be happy, but otherwise, I'd rather let you be wrong alone."

Liam was not surprised at his friend; his attitude only mirrored Liam's own. He had no desire to speak to the Death, but his aversion to entering the shrouded temple of Laomedon was weaker than his frustration at their dead end. Where else could he go?

And besides, he reasoned, *you met a ghost just the other day. How much worse can the temple be?*

▪ *14* ▪

LIAM REPEATED THE phrase to himself in the cul-de-sac while he
stared up at the grim portals of the temple of Laomedon, and summoned
his nerve. For no reason, he was afraid, more afraid than he had been
outside the Guild's abandoned house in the Point, more afraid than in
the Warren, waiting for Duplin's ghost.

There had been no temple to Laomedon in the Midlands. The dead
there were simply burned or buried, with a few observances and sometimes a funeral feast that was more melancholy than frightening. In the
city of Torquay, where he had been a student, however, there had been a
temple, and it was the focus of any number of ghost stories and dark
rumors. He did not try to remember them, but they came to mind unbidden as he hesitated in the cul-de-sac, and he had to force them down.

The Southwark temple was smaller than the one in Torquay, but it
maintained the same sinister appearance, like an outsize mausoleum.
The walls were of a black, dull stone that drank in light; the columns of
its small portico were smooth cylinders of the same stone, without fluting
or capitals, and they cast thick shadows on the single door.

This is silly.

He took the steps two at a time, with a jauntiness he did not feel, and
knocked three times quickly, before he could stop himself. The door
looked like that of a tomb, but it did not creak when the black-robed
man opened it.

"My name is Liam Rhenford," Liam said in rush, "and I would like
to see the Death."

The man nodded, as if this were the most normal thing in the world, and ushered Liam in.

"If you'll wait here, I'll bring her word of you."

Without waiting for a reply, the acolyte slipped away, leaving Liam alone in the long hall. It was dark at his end, near the door, and at the far end, but in the middle of the hall the walls were pierced by wide arches open to the sky, letting light in. A row of columns of the same unreflective stone ran down either wall, and between them were statues, dimly seen in the shadows by the door, crouching like dogs or lions. He fidgeted for a moment, then stepped to one side and peered closely at a statue, put out his hand and touched the head of a carved gryphon.

"Ha," he breathed, most of his apprehension draining away, and then the acolyte was behind him, his approach unheard.

"If you will come with me, sir?"

Liam stood quickly, and for a moment considered making his excuses and leaving. But he was there, and there were questions he could ask.

"Yes, thank you."

He walked next to the acolyte down the hall, the gryphon statues between the columns revealed as they neared the light from the arches.

"Those statues," he asked, "what are they?"

"Gryphons," the acolyte answered easily. "The servants of Laomedon, Whom all serve."

Was it that easy? Liam could not believe it. *It looks like Cloten and I were barking up the wrong side of the street,* he thought.

The arches opened on identical cloistered gardens; the acolyte turned into the one on the left. The bushes were withered with winter, the beds were covered with straw, but Liam was sure that in the spring and summer the gardens would be beautiful, which surprised him. He had not expected gardens in the temple whose Hierarch was called the Death.

She was waiting for him just off the arcade that ran on three sides of the garden, in a low-ceilinged room with a large fireplace. It was a cheerful place, with vivid tapestries on the walls and comfortable chairs.

"Please sit, Sir Liam," she said, rising as he entered and dismissing the acolyte. "I have been expecting you for some time."

The greeting was odd, but she did not seem threatening. She wore a long black dress, buttoned from her neck to her feet, and a snug skullcap covered the nape of her neck and ended in a point like a widow's peak on her forehead. Her features were too finely cut for prettiness, with wide and childlike eyes, and her voice was high and girlish. She was not at all what he had expected, and it put him on his guard.

"I have been meaning to come since yesterday, Death," he said, standing behind the chair she had indicated. "You smiled at me during the fight."

"I did," she affirmed, smiling again. "I thought you would come much sooner."

"I was not sure it was meant for me." This was not at all what he had anticipated, and he was impatient to ask her about the gryphons in her hall, but he was unsure of himself, put off by her easy, open manner. Her next statement threw him even more.

"It was, Sir Liam. The gods are much interested in you these days. Please sit."

He choked briefly. "Me?"

"Yes, you. Do sit, please."

He sat gingerly, as if the chair might be a trap. "Why are they interested in me?"

"Things are happening in Southwark, Sir Liam, important things, and you have a part in them."

This was so far from the interview he had imagined that he abandoned his planned questions entirely. "I'm sorry. I don't understand."

She steepled her fingers and looked to the fire, as if searching for inspiration. "There are four ways the gods reveal themselves in this world," she said, carefully picking her words. "Really, there are more than four, but for the moment we can say that there are only four. Do you know them?"

"I can guess," he said, but he did not want to; he did not, in fact, want to hear any more. He had been in the presence of a god once, and thought it once too often.

"Do not trouble yourself; I will tell you. First, there are signs—messengers, the flight of certain birds, omens, and the like. Second, there are those to whom the gods speak directly—prophets, some madmen and, occasionally, priests—who do the bidding of Heaven by express command. And then there are those who, without knowing it, follow that bidding—by accident, as it were. Do you understand?"

"By accident," Liam repeated. He had a strange feeling, like the world was telescoping in on the room where he sat, telescoping inward, so that there was nothing beyond the room and the girlish priest who smiled and nodded at him. Nothing but words and mysterious smiles, no arcade, no gardens, no temple, no city.

"You do understand, Sir Liam. You have done the bidding of Heaven before, by accident. Have you not?"

He shook himself, the feeling gone but the glimmer of comprehension remaining. "The Storm King thought so," he said, and remembered that it had not seemed that way when he cowered before the cloud-wrapped god, begging pardon for the crime he thought he had committed.

"So He did. Have you been to His temple here in Southwark?"

"No." He had been in the city for over six months, but had chosen to avoid the edifice that brooded over the harbor, separate from the other temples. "It did not seem proper."

She waved the question of propriety aside. "It is not to the point. That is the past, and we are discussing the present. There is something I am permitted to tell you, and you may make of it what you will. It is this: no one will die tomorrow in Southwark."

The change was too abrupt; he was still absorbed in his memory. "No one will die?"

"No one."

"How do you know?"

She giggled, and he was struck again by how young she seemed. "How do you think, Sir Liam?"

He raised his eyebrows, then lowered them. "Ah. Of course."

"That is all I am permitted to tell you. As I said, you may make of it what you will, but I should think it will effect how you will proceed from here."

How he would proceed? How *would* he proceed? He had no idea, and her vagueness stirred a spark of rebellion in him. "I was hoping you could tell me something else."

"There is nothing else," she said, with a hint of sadness.

"Yes, there is," he persisted. "You can tell me what service stone gryphons perform for Laomedon."

For a long moment she stared wide-eyed at him, and then burst out laughing. "Oh, Sir Liam, I can assure you, no one in this temple had anything to do with that."

"With what?" he asked, as innocently as he could.

"You know very well what," she chided him lightly. "With the attempted theft at Bellona's temple, if you insist that I say it out. For one thing, there are no bearded men in this temple."

How did she know the man had a beard? And why had she so quickly made the connection between his question and the incident in the other temple?

"In that case, you should have no objection to telling me what service they perform." He was excited now, suddenly more interested in the investigation than he had been in days; even though it might be tied to broader events in which he did not particularly want to be involved, he was at least beginning to see their outlines.

The Death wagged a finger at him, but conceded the point. "Y'are right, Sir Liam. I should have no objection. The question is, would anyone else?"

"You would know better than I."

Her eyes turned to the fire then, and he was suddenly aware of a maturity in her that had not been apparent before. His sense that she was inappropriate for her position faded; Laomedon might weigh a question as soberly as she did at that moment, he imagined, and with just such a pensive look.

She roused herself eventually, after nearly a minute. "What do you know of stone gryphons, Sir Liam?"

"Only that there is one in the temple of Bellona, and two dozen statues of them here."

The Death did not smile. "No more?"

He hesitated. "I read that they haunt graveyards and battlefields, and eat the souls of the dead."

"A misconception. Battlefields sometimes, but never graveyards. And they do not eat the souls of the dead. They are the most special servants of Laomedon, more so than I or any acolyte in this temple. They carry the souls of the elect to the Gray Lands, those marked out by Fortune or greatness to dwell in the most beautiful quarters of those lands. Auric the Great went to the Gray Lands on the back of a stone gryphon, and Ascelin Edara, and the poet Rhaeadr, and many you would not know, nameless in this world but blessed beyond. Does that answer your question?"

Scaevola had said they caught the gryphon after a battle with bandits, and that none of the worshipers of Bellona had been hurt; he wondered which bandit had been among the elect.

"If they are the most special servants of Laomedon, surely he would not like to see one sacrificed?"

"No," she agreed, "He would not." She left implicit the contradiction that no one from her temple had done anything about it. There was a long pause, in which he gathered together and reordered his thoughts.

"I suppose I will go," he said finally.

"There is nothing more for you here," the Death said, spreading her empty arms. "I will see you out."

She led him through the wintering garden and down the hall of columns and gryphons to the street door. He stopped there, and gestured at the statues.

"Does no one ever see them?"

"The statues, or the real ones?"

He had meant the statues. "Both."

"There is a real one on view in Bellona's temple," she said, with no trace of emotion. "But the statues? No. The dead are brought in by a separate door, purified, and sent back out for burial. No one but His servants have been in Laomedon's home—and now you."

Liam was not sure how much of an honor it was. "I see." He reached for the door, then stopped. "The fourth way—the fourth way the gods reveal themselves. You didn't say."

She might have smiled, but it was dark, and by the time he opened the door and let the light in, her face was serious.

"They reveal themselves," she said. "Good day, Sir Liam."

At least she didn't think I was a wizard, he thought as the door closed behind him, and he looked out at the cul-de-sac. He realized then that, though it had been a busy place in the last few weeks, before the arrival of Bellona it would have been secluded, the neglected end of Temple Street—an appropriate place for a temple that admitted none but the dead.

There were more important things, however, than how the cul-de-sac might have been before Bellona came from Caernarvon. What he had learned—he corrected himself: what he had been told—put a completely new spin on all of his and Coeccias's investigations and, while he was not sure what they could do with the information, he knew he should tell the Aedile at once.

Temple Street was still quiet as he went out of it, and the unnatural hush seemed to have infected more than just the immediate neighborhood. The city square was almost deserted, a few men huddled near the entrance to a wineshop, a lone woman hurrying across, her skirts billowed out in front of her by the wind, like a ship carried uncontrollably across the surface of the sea. He wondered how far beyond the square the mood of uneasiness had spread. *Soon enough,* he thought, *the whole damn city will be hiding under their beds.*

Coeccias was in the barracks, crouched over a table and rapidly filling a sheet of pure white, expensive paper with his unruly handwriting. He looked up when Liam came in, laid aside his quill, and held up another, cheaper sheet of paper, folded in quarters.

"One of Cloten's boys gave this to the Guards by the temple—fair demanded they deliver it that very moment."

Liam took the note, turned it over; apart from his name, misspelled, there was nothing on the outside.

"Go to," Coeccias urged, "read it. You can tell me of the Death when I've finished my missive to the Duke."

Liam stopped in the middle of unfolding his letter. "You are writing to the Duke? What about?"

"To tell him I've taken it upon myself to stop this damned duel. I've thought it through, and there's no chance of it turning out well. If I halt it, Guiderius and Cloten can both maintain their honor, and I can avoid a passing mess." His tone was defiant, as if he were daring Liam to disagree.

"I don't think you should do that."

"And why?"

Liam held up the letter. "Let me read this, and then I'll tell you."

Coeccias gave an exaggerated shrug, picked up his quill and threw it in the inkwell.

The letter had been written in block capitals, with the elaborate care of the near illiterate, and contained many misspellings and crossed-out words.

Master Liam Rhenford, it began, *I am writing this to you for Hierarch Scaevola, who begs you to come see him next morning before the duel. Hierarch Cloten has said he will allow it. The time will be just at dawn. Again, he urgently begs you to come.*

There was no name signed to it, but Liam imagined one of the praying acolytes laboriously printing out the message. If he needed any proof that something had happened in the temple after the arrival of the phantom host, Scaevola's new title was more than enough. The question was whether Cloten had authorized it, and he doubted the obnoxious priest had. More likely the temple was split, with some accepting whatever sign had come that morning, and others, certainly Cloten, denying it.

Liam handed the note to Coeccias, and when he had read it, explained what he thought. "And what's more, I would guess that that's why Cloten pushed ahead with the challenge. Scaevola would be the obvious choice, but he may be hoping he'll lose, and get rid of him. That would put an end to any discord in the temple."

"And leave that knave safe as its head," Coeccias agreed. "All the more reason to cancel the duel."

"It would be, but there is something else."

"The Death."

"Yes." He recounted his conversation with Laomedon's priestess, omitting nothing, not even the mention of his own past. He had considered skipping over it, but decided not to; he did not want to have any more secrets from his friend.

Naturally, it was that part that intrigued Coeccias the most.

"And what was it, then, this task of the gods you performed by accident?"

"It's not important now," he said, and then, at a twinge from his conscience: "I'll tell you later. What should concern us more is what she said about no one dying tomorrow, and all those gryphons in Laomedon's temple. I'm not sure I believe her when she says no one there was involved."

Coeccias was staring intently at him. "But you do believe her about tomorrow, eh?"

Liam started to answer, then paused, frowning. "I am not sure. I think I do—but you are right, it does not make any sense. Why would she tell the truth about one thing, and not the other?"

"Truth," the Aedile said, shrugging, "I know not. Perhaps she's telling the truth about both. In either case, let me ask you: should I send this letter?"

The burden was unfair; if Coeccias did not stop the duel, and there was trouble, Liam would feel responsible. On the other hand, he knew his friend would not blame him; in fact, he would take the responsibility himself—but that would not lessen Liam's guilt.

Cross your fingers, he told himself, *and hope your Luck is with you.*

"Let the challenge stand."

Crumpling the letter he had begun, Coeccias let loose a heavy sigh. "Aye, I thought you'd say that." He threw the wad of paper into the fire. "So now, how do we proceed? Will you follow this with the gryphons? I suppose I should apologize for being so short with the idea earlier."

"Who would have guessed? I certainly did not think I would find Laomedon's temple decorated with them. The problem is, how do we follow it? We can't very well march back there and ask to see if any of the acolytes have beards."

"They don't," Coeccias said. "Like Uris's, Laomedon's are completely shaven—head as well. Even the Death herself."

Liam did not question the statement; Coeccias had forgotten more about Taralon's gods and the ways of their priests than he had ever known. "And we can't arrest every man with a beard and have Cloten look at them."

"No, we can't," the Aedile said, stroking his own beard. "Some of us would take it ill."

They both sank into their own thoughts; Coeccias doodling absently on another sheet of paper, Liam pacing back and forth in front of the fire. He noticed his friend's sketchings, and wondered at the waste. Truly, white paper was expensive. He thought the Aedile had realized this when, with a puzzled expression, he pushed the paper aside and looked up.

"Think you they would try again?"

"Try what?" Liam asked.

"Whatever it is they were trying in the first place—liberating that gryphon, plundering the treasury—whatever. Might they try again?"

"They might," Liam said, but he did not see that it mattered. "Why?"

"When would they try? Cloten's had a heavy guard mounted since that night, eh? No chance for a repeat." An expectant smile spread across his face; he was waiting for Liam to catch on. "When would they try again? When would the guard be smallest?"

Liam caught on. "During the duel!"

"Truth, it sings, Rhenford. During the duel is right—and so you'll go? You'll answer the new Hierarch's summons?"

It does *sing,* Liam thought, and nodded. It was a slim chance, but it made sense at least for him to be there. He could visit Scaevola, and stay behind after the acolytes left. If necessary, he could even say he was there to protect the treasury, in case the thieves returned.

"It is not foreordained," Coeccias warned. "They may not return, you know. The guilty returning to the scene of their crime is more myth than truth."

"No," Liam agreed, "but it's something to try."

"That it is. But in the meantime? Will you still do this with the ghost?"

He said he would, and mostly because he pitied the lost, mad soul. However, there was something else he was interested in, and he was glad he had told Mother Japh he wanted to corner the ghost for a while.

"I need to go home for a while," he told the Aedile. "I'll be back in a few hours."

"Will you need men tonight?"

He thought about Japer spotting him in the square; a few Guards at his back might be a good thing. At the same time, he did not want to betray the Werewolf, should he come. It did not seem likely, given that they now knew he was in touch with the Aedile, but he did not want to risk it.

"No, only Boult."

"And that, I'll warrant, for that Boult knows to hold of his tongue."

Liam smiled, refusing to be surprised anymore by his friend's quick grasp.

"Exactly. Do you want to eat dinner?"

They agreed to meet at Herlekin's, and then Liam left for the stables.

The traps, if they could be called that, pleased Liam as he rode back to the house on the beach. Holding Duplin's ghost for a few minutes might give him some information, tell him whether a suspicion he was holding was true—and it was an active thing, more than just wandering around asking questions. Waiting in the temple during the duel and hoping the thieves returned was not very active, but at least it would feel like action, and a quiet voice at the back of his head told him it would be worth his while.

The same voice prompted him to go to the library, leaving Diamond tethered by the door, loosening the girth but leaving the horse saddled.

It is strange, Fanuilh thought at him while he scanned the shelves, *that the Death knew those things about you.*

"You think so?" he said absently, his mind and his eyes on the spines of Tarquin's books. He was familiar with most of them, having gone through the library thoroughly over the past two months, but he was not sure which might provide him with the information for which he was searching.

Yes. Could she be right?

Liam pulled his eyes from the books and looked to the doorway, where Fanuilh now sat. "About my accidentally helping the gods? Why not? It's happened before. The question is, which gods? Whose plans am I supposed to further? And, for the philosophers among us, I might ask whether I have any choice."

You do not believe in predestination.

"No, but it doesn't matter what I believe—it's what the gods believe. And if they believe in predestination, then the rest of us just have to go along, don't we?"

I do not know.

"It was a rhetorical question."

The dragon's snout wrinkled, an expression that Liam knew meant it was thinking hard.

Your thoughts are scattered, it told him after a pause.

Liam agreed; he had allowed himself to get caught up in the unresolvable problems of predestination. With a shrug, he returned to the shelves, tapping each spine as he read the title.

The books of fables and travelers' tales would not have what he was interested in, nor would the many history texts. He ignored the thick tomes on magic and wizardry, though they might have something: he knew from paging through them that they were mostly impenetrable, and he did not have the time to check hundreds of pages in hopes of spotting a morsel of intelligible information. That left the philosophies, of which there were over a hundred. Liam frowned, then sighed and started checking their spines.

What are you looking for?

The dragon knew, of course, or could know, if it chose, but Liam was glad to see his familiar upholding the polite fiction.

"I want to know more about the differences between the planes—the ethereal and astral planes, is that what you call them? And the Gray Lands and the real world. You said Tarquin could see into them easily, and I was hoping he might have a book on it."

He does. The bottom shelf, on the right. It is called On the Planes.

"Naturally." The book was where Fanuilh had said it would be, and it stuck to the covers of the volumes beside it, coming free with a leathery rustle. Dust lay thick on its top, a dirty puff when Liam blew on it. "Consulted it often, did he?"

I do not think so, the dragon thought; Liam abandoned the joke and opened the book. The writing inside was tiny, and packed together so tightly that the descenders of one line often overlapped the line below. Cradling the heavy book in the crook of his arm, he flipped randomly through the pages, hoping at the very least for a diagram or illustration, but the book was solid with text from cover to cover.

"I'm not reading this," he said at last, closing the book with a thump and wedging it back onto the shelf. "I don't have a year and a day, and I'd be blind in six months anyway."

I have read it.

Liam looked up, surprised. "You have? How did you read it?" He imagined his familiar, crouched over the open book with its snout close to the words. "How did you turn the pages, with your tail?"

Fanuilh sniffed. *When Master Tanaquil read it, I followed along in his head. He always let me read with him, because I remember everything.*

"Everything?"

Everything.

"So I've been wasting my time here. You could have told me all this."

I did not think—

Liam held up a hand for the dragon to stop. "Never mind. It doesn't matter. Just tell me what I want to know."

You wish to know about the planes.

"Fanuilh!" he shouted, in exasperation. "I know what I want to know, because I don't know it! I want you to help me stop not knowing it."

I was going to, master.

Liam slowly unclenched his fists. "Right. About the planes."

The dragon narrowed its eyes and looked up at him, then shook itself, like a dog shedding water, and started telling him about the planes.

There were four: terrestrial, heavenly, ethereal and astral. The book suggested there might be more, but there was no proof. The terrestrial plane was what Liam had called the real world, and the heavenly was where the gods lived and where the Gray Lands were.

The ethereal and astral planes are not so much places, Fanuilh recalled, *but borders, where the other two planes intersect. The silver cord that binds us can be seen in the ethereal plane, because that plane is attuned to things spiritual.*

"Spiritual, as in spirits? Souls, that sort of thing?"

Yes.

"So that is why the stone gryphons need to walk in the ethereal plane, to guide the souls of dead people to the Gray Lands."

It would seem so. The witchcraft Mother Japh used to show you that Duplin's soul was lost touched the ethereal plane.

"And Tarquin could see this plane at will?"

Yes.

Liam crossed his arms and leaned back against the bookcase, mulling this over. Duplin's ghost should have crossed the ethereal plane to get to the Gray Lands, but it had not. Presumably it was either barred from it, or lost in it. Outside Faius's wineshop, it had said something about being chased by birds and animals, and that it could not help them. Had the stone gryphons come for Duplin when he died? That did not make much sense—the Death had said they only fetched great men, and Duplin was hardly even a good man.

Do you wish to hear about the astral plane?

"Is it relevant?"

Not particularly. It is even less understood than the ethereal plane. It is where magic seems to come from.

"I thought magic came from the gods," Liam said.

Apparently not. According to the book, and Master Tanaquil's own beliefs, it has a source apart from the gods. When I notice magic being performed, it is in the astral plane.

"You can see it?"

It is more like sensing—like heat, a burst of warmth. The dragon paused, and it struck Liam that it was struggling for words. *I cannot explain,* it thought finally, *but it is not seeing.*

"That's all right," Liam said. "As long as you don't think it is relevant. I'm more interested in the fact that Tarquin could see into the ethereal plane. Could he go into it?"

It is not so much a place. He could travel it a little, but it is not like traveling. Again, the dragon paused, but Liam did not leave it hanging.

"Never mind," he said. "He was familiar with it, though?"

Yes, very familiar.

Leaning against the bookcase, Liam was suddenly aware of being tired. He breathed out heavily, letting his shoulders slump.

"Questions, questions, questions. Gods, I hate asking questions."

You should take a nap. If you plan to find the ghost, it will be a late night for you.

The divan he slept on was right in front of him, and he considered it, the soft, cool brocaded fabric, the thick padding. A nap would be a good thing, and with the sunlight from the window in the ceiling, he would be sure not to sleep too long.

"I believe I will do just that, familiar mine."

He slouched over to the divan, noticing how comfortable it was to have his shoulders loose, the tension dissipating even as he let himself down onto the cushions.

I will leave you then. May I fly?

"Yes," Liam murmured, stretched out at full length, one arm over his face. "Just make sure I get up in a couple of hours."

The dragon left, and Liam took a couple of deep breaths to prepare himself for sleep.

It did not come.

His muscles relaxed, knots and cramps he had not recognized fading away, his whole body adjusting itself for sleep. His thoughts started jumping, however, as soon as Fanuilh's padding steps faded away.

"Damn," he murmured.

Fanuilh had once described his thoughts as a flock of startled birds, rising in panicked confusion. They were like birds now, he knew, except that they circled different ideas, randomly lighting on one after another, touching any of a thousand subjects except sleep.

If the dragon could remember everything, why did it have such a hard time explaining certain concepts about the planes? He wondered how its memory worked. It might be eidetic, so that it could quote whole sections of a book, but be unable to explain them to the uninitiated. Then again, it might be entirely different—the mind of a creature as utterly humorless as Fanuilh must be.

Liam let his arm drop away from his face but kept his eyes closed.

Had Duplin been referring to stone gryphons? The Death had suggested that they sometimes came for epople who were unknown, but she had also said they were great people. He doubted that Duplin had been secretly a great person. Of course, it had been fairly obvious that the ghost was unhinged, and its rambling about birds and animals might have been just that, ramblings.

Liam opened his eyes and stared at the ceiling.

What was he supposed to do for Laomedon? When she said he would unwittingly serve the gods, the Death had not specified her own deity, but if it was not him, then why would she have been the one to relay the message? He was wary of the gods, and the fact that they expected his help without telling him directly what they wanted made him uneasy. If he acted wrongly, would they be displeased? *Could* he act wrongly?

He rolled over and pressed his face into the cushions, trying to force sleep.

What had happened in the temple of Bellona? Scaevola called himself a Hierarch, but was apparently Cloten's prisoner—and he would fight at Cloten's command.

"Damn," he said, and sat up. There was no chance he was going to sleep, and as comfortable as the divan was, he could not stand lying there and wallowing in his own questions. Closing his eyes, he sent a thought to Fanuilh.

I am going riding. I will not be back until after tonight.

Should I come to the city tonight? the dragon asked immediately.

Yes, Liam projected, after a moment's thought. *Come to Narrow Lane at nine.*

He imagined a roll in the kitchen, and was munching it as he went outside to get Diamond. From the doorway he could see Fanuilh far out over the slate gray winter ocean, skimming along the whitecaps. He watched it fly, driven by occasional thrusts of its tiny wings, and then went back inside.

When he came back out he had another roll, and his sword at his belt.

■ *15* ■

IT WAS LATE in the afternoon before Liam reentered Southwark by the city gate. He did not take his usual route along the muddy road, but guided Diamond to the north, over the winter-bare fields. There was a thin belt of farmland, which gave way shortly to rolling moors interrupted by rare drainage ditches and the occasional swale.

Houses sometimes huddled in the swales, often sheltered from the sea wind by a screen of hardy trees, and Liam rode along the rough arc they described around the city. Some were the homes of merchants from Southwark, those rich enough to keep a country establishment, but most belonged to the nobility of the Southern Tier. They tended to keep to themselves, apart from the society of the Point, but Liam could tell by the design of their homes that they relied on the city for other things. There were no outbuildings, none of the messy appendages that marked the hold of a Midlands lord and made it self-sufficient; the buildings themselves were defenseless, many windowed and erected in hollows beneath hills.

He counted seventeen structures as he rode in a wide semicircle around the city, crossing their lands with impunity. At one, a man grooming a horse even waved to him. In the Midlands, the man would have mounted and given chase the moment he saw Liam, demanding toll or at least an explanation for his trespass.

To keep his mind from his present business, Liam pretended his ride was a reconnaissance, and planned a siege of Southwark as he went. It could not be in the winter of course, with the ground covered in snow as it was now, and the weather uncertain. Nor in the early spring, when the rains would turn the moors muddy. In the summer, though, the city would be an easy prize, a simple matter of marching straight south. The lords' manors would offer little resistance, and once past them, the artisans' quarters were wide open.

He could see them, the inviting sprawl of Northfield and Auric's Park, the cobbled roads petering out into dirt tracks, completely indefensible. An army could invest Southwark in a single day.

Even if it wasn't invisible, he thought, and started looking for a road into the city. He had tried to avoid the thorny questions awaiting him, but they had followed him into the countryside, and as Diamond trotted southward, he puzzled over his many riddles.

If the situation at Bellona's temple were any indication, the invisible host had done more than just make noise in Temple Street, and the most likely thing was that it had been the sign for which Scaevola had prayed. That fit with his use of the new title, but it did not fit with the fact that he seemed to be Cloten's prisoner.

And it was strange that he was going along with the duel. The Death had insisted that no one was going to die, but what did that mean? She had also said that no one from her temple was involved in the attempted robbery, but he was firmly convinced that whoever the bearded man and his companion were, they were after the stone gryphon, not the treasury. An odd and disturbing thought occurred to him: what did Laomedon look like? There had been no depictions of him in his temple, and Liam did not remember ever hearing any stories that described him.

"He probably has a beard," he said to himself. "And when he comes tomorrow to free his servant, you will have to tell Coeccias that he has to arrest a god for knocking Cloten on the head." It was ridiculous, he knew; if Laomedon himself had been the bearded man, he would not have been deterred by Cloten's doubling the guard on the temple. Who would have been, though?

Diamond found his own way into the city, slowing to a walk as he entered the outskirts of Northfield, and Liam scarcely held the reins as the road became cobbled, the buildings rising higher on either side. Many of the stores were closed, and there were few people in the streets. Word of the strange things in Temple Street must have spread.

If the thieves did return during the duel, who would he find? As sick as he was of looking, he wanted to know the answers. It was like riddles from his childhood: he heard them eagerly, and pondered them avidly for a while, but there was always a gap between giving up and learning the answers, in which his interest in knowing was high but his interest in figuring them out ebbed. He had always spent the interim dutifully mulling over the riddles, knowing that in the end he would have to be given the answers.

Only those were riddles, he thought, *not gods and duels and priests, and I never had to guess how to act before I knew the answer. How am I supposed to know what to do? If they want something from me, I just wish they would ask.*

That was not the gods' way, though, which was one of the reasons he had as little to do with them as possible.

Diamond found the stables on his own as well, and Liam was drawn out of his musings when the horse stopped and looked over his shoulder.

"Are we here, then?"

The horse blew and stamped a hoof.

"It's hardly five yet," he scolded. "You go too fast."

Diamond whickered an apology but refused to move, so Liam dismounted and called for the hostler's boy.

He was half an hour early for his dinner appointment with Coeccias, but he settled himself into a quiet table on the second floor of Herlekin's restaurant, and nursed a mug of beer until the Aedile arrived.

The dinner was slow. Liam did not particularly want to talk, knowing that almost any conversation would turn treacherous, doubling back to pointless speculation on the next day's events. Coeccias seemed to sense his mood, and devoted himself silently to his meal.

They lingered over cups of mulled wine after the serving girl had cleared the table. Liam studied his fingers, drumming them slowly on the tabletop, and Coeccias's eyes roved aimlessly around the near-empty restaurant. Finally, he cleared his throat.

"Truth, we're a gloomy pair." He chuckled, but with little humor.

Liam nodded. "It's been a long week."

"And'll get longer—at least 'til the tomorrow." The Aedile coughed behind his fist, hesitated, then struck out: "I wonder, Rhenford, the time y'unwittingly aided the gods. Would you . . . ?"

"Tell you about it?" Liam frowned. He had promised, not thinking to do it so soon. It had happened when he was much younger, and he had tried not to think about it for years. Still, he could understand his friend's curiosity. Coeccias was much more interested in the gods than he was, and Liam's earlier hint must have caught his imagination.

"Aye, if you've no objection. That is, it can wait, if you'd rather."

Liam spread his hands out on the table. "No, no reason for that. But you must remember, this happened almost twelve years ago. I may not remember it all."

Coeccias pulled his chair closer to the table, and the look on his face and the way he said, "In course, in course," showed that he did not believe that Liam might have forgotten.

If he met a god, Liam thought, *he wouldn't forget a thing.*

"Right. As I said, it was twelve years ago. I was living in Carad Llan—the border city built on the ruins of Auric the Great's fortress—working as a clerk. There were always caravans going north of the King's Range, or coming back south, and plenty of people who could not read or write, so business was good. And one day this mad old noble, Baron Keillie, came into the city with a troop of mercenaries and an ancient map he needed translated."

Liam told the story in broad outlines, leaving out many of the details. Baron Keillie's map had shown the way to a building hidden in a valley deep in the King's Range; the old script indicated that it had belonged to someone named Duke Thunder. Keillie had organized an expedition to find the place, expecting to find either a tomb or an abandoned keep, and hoping, because of certain clues on the map, to find treasure there as well. He brought Liam along because he could read the near-forgotten language with which the map had been inscribed.

It had seemed like a grand adventure at the time, with the promise of riches at the end, but when they reached the valley they found that Duke Thunder still lived there—and that he was no musty Taralonian nobleman, but a god gone mad and made prisoner there by his father, the Storm King.

There were complications Liam chose not to explain, but in the end Thunder had trapped the expedition in the valley, and they had to kill him to get away. Liam's part had been small—he found the weapon, a spike of stone created by the wind spirits Thunder had enslaved—but apart from the captain of Keillie's mercenaries, he was the only survivor.

"I don't see it," Coeccias said, when the story was done. "How did that serve the gods?"

"The Storm King wanted his son killed. Thunder was mad, absolutely mad, like a rabid dog. He was a danger to everyone, gods and men alike, but the King could not kill his own son."

Coeccias shook his head. "But if the Storm King could not kill him, how could you?"

They were questions Liam himself had asked at the time, fleeing the valley with the mercenary captain. "It was not a question of the power to kill him," he explained, "but of the will, and the right. I don't understand it fully myself," he went on, "though the Storm King had tried to make it clear; for some reason Thunder's father could not kill him himself. It had to be someone else, and that was where Keillie and his expedition and I came in."

With a grunt, Coeccias dropped his eyes to his wine, pondering. "I did not know gods could go mad."

"Neither did I," Liam said simply. He could tell his friend was dissatisfied with the story, but then so was he. There were details of the expedition that still puzzled him, and memories that were still troubling. At the time he had shrugged them off, joining up with the mercenary captain to form a troop and later traveling south, where he met Stick; now the questions came back, like dimly remembered wounds aching with the arrival of cold weather.

The bells over the Duke's courts started ringing, and Liam counted along with them up to eight; it had taken longer than he thought to tell the story.

"What time are you to meet Mother Japh?"

"Nine, but I think I will go over there now, and make sure everything is ready."

"Do you really think this necessary? All this with the spirit, that is. Could not Mother Japh see it through? You do not look well, Rhenford."

He was tired, and knew that it showed in his face and the way he kept rubbing his eyes, but the Aedile's voice registered more than just nominal concern.

"I'm fine," he assured him, "and yes, I do think it's necessary. I want to ask Duplin a few questions before Mother Japh does whatever she must for his soul."

"Very well, if y'insist. Only remember you've to meet that Scaevola on the morrow, early."

"I'll be there, don't worry." He wanted to avoid talking about it, so he stood up. "I'm going to see Mother Japh now. Could you send Boult over to the morgue?"

"I can," Coeccias said. "Will he need aught?"

"Aught?"

The Aedile pointed at the sword leaning against Liam's chair. "Aught like that, Rhenford. Arms."

Liam picked up the sword and guiltily buckled it on. "I doubt it— maybe one of those cudgels, just in case. But I doubt it."

"He'll bring one."

"All right. I'll see you tomorrow sometime."

Coeccias nodded and touched his forehead. " 'Til the morrow."
With a wave, Liam strode out of the restaurant.

Mother Japh was waiting in her room in the basement of the Duke's
courts. She opened the door within a second of Liam's knock, pulling
him inside and shutting the door in the sullen porter's face.

"Faith, Liam Rhenford, I thought you'd never come!"

"I am early," he pointed out, but not as sarcastically as he might
have. The old witch's nerves showed plainly on her face, and he was
surprised at how apprehensive she seemed. "Is everything ready?"

"Ready? Oh, aye, all is ready, but I have come to doubt the wisdom
of this."

He did not want to hear it, and laughed to hide his own nervousness.
"What wisdom? We're trying to catch a ghost, Mother Japh. There's no
wisdom involved to doubt."

"It's not catching the ghost that I doubt." She cast a glance toward
the morgue. "It's this with holding him. Showing him his body is right
and good, helping him find peace is all right. But this with holding him
. . . it likes me not the more I think on it. Ghosts are tricksy things,
Liam Rhenford, and of unknown parts. Who knows what he might do if
we present him his body, and then keep him from it? There are strange
things in Southwark these days, and a ghost may not be just a ghost."

She gave the last sentence a strange emphasis, and he frowned.

"What do you mean by that?"

He had never seen her like this: dithering, unsure of herself. She
looked from the door of the morgue to him, then back, then spoke in a
whisper: "I mean, what if this ghost is somehow a part of the troubles in
Temples' Court? What if it's a part with the messengers, and the invisible
host of this morning? What if it's the work of the gods?"

Liam almost laughed, switched to a gentle smile. *You don't understand,* he wanted to say, *I'm doing the work of the gods these days. The
Death told me so.* Instead, he reached out and gently touched her arm.
"Mother Japh, I cannot think of a single reason the gods would want
Duplin's soul to wander the streets without peace. It is only right that he
should be put at rest. And if it makes you feel any better, I promise that
if there is even the slightest indication that we cannot hold him, we won't
try. We will just let him go. All right?"

She pushed lightly at his hand, looked away. "Very well, very well. I
don't know why I should be so skittish. The mood of the city is terrible
just now. It must be wearing on my nerves."

"It wears on everyone's nerves. Now, is there anything we need to do?"

Sniffling, she drew herself upright and shuffled toward the morgue. "Just move the body. I've made the mask ready, and put a shroud on him. Did you think how you would move him?"

Standing at the door, she looked expectantly over her shoulder at him.

"I . . . ," he began, and was saved from admitting that he had not when a knock sounded at the outer door. Boult entered without waiting for an answer, trying to escape the complaints of the porter.

"The courts aren't open," the man was saying, and raised his voice when he saw Mother Japh. "And you know it, woman! There's no call for all this tramping in and out!"

"Go to!" she shouted back, "go to, you rogue! Back to your pot and your couch, for that's all y'are good for! Go to!"

Boult shut the door on the porter's protests, forestalling a shouting match, and grinned doubtfully at Liam.

"Good evening, Quaestor."

"Evening, Boult."

"Good evening, Mother Japh."

"Who's this, Rhenford?" she demanded, looking with disapproval at the crossbow resting on the Guard's shoulder. "Is this the thief's friend?"

"No," Liam said, quickly covering his lapse in planning, "he's going to help me move the body. Aren't you, Boult?"

Grin fading, Boult sketched a mockery of a bow. "In course, Quaestor. I'm at your service. What body did you have in mind?"

Mother Japh harrumphed at his tone, and pushed open the door to the morgue. "This one, Guard."

Liam went into the morgue, Boult at his shoulder, and walked over to the slabe where Duplin's corpse lay. The body was bound in strips of white cloth up to the neck, and a cruved piece of lead lay on the chest, beneath the crossed arms. The two men stood to one side of the slab; Mother Japh went to the other.

"We can bury him as soon as the spirit's recovered," she said, indicating the wrappings, "and the lead should keep the ghost out."

"This is your ghost," Boult said. "Are we moving it to Faius's?"

"Yes," Liam said, prepared to explain, but the Guard merely nodded.

"Very well. Am I to forget this part?"

"This part, no. What comes later, perhaps."

"What is he talking about?" Mother Japh asked.

"I have been in Quaestor Rhenford's service several times," Boult said with a wink, "but I cannot remember any of them. I am in danger of forgetting him entirely." The wink irritated the old woman, but Liam laughed.

"You may wish it all you want, Boult. In the meantime, however, we have to move this"—he pointed at Duplin's body—"down to Narrow Lane."

Boult shrugged. "Very well. Will the porter forget, do you think?"

"Damn that porter," Mother Japh said. "He's a sozzled knave."

Liam had not considered the porter; he did not need a reputation for body snatching added to his one for wizardry. Nor did he want to have to maneuver Duplin's body through the maze of streets leading to Narrow Lane. "Is there any other way than out the front door?"

Mother Japh shook her head, but Boult pointed to the window. "We could lower him out."

To Liam's surprise, the ghost witch did not object. "There's sure to be some rope down the hall, if y'insist on this foolishness." She went off without waiting for his reply, leaving him to exchange amused looks with Boult, and then the two men took hold of Duplin's body.

It was far easier than Liam had expected; the body had none of the stiffness and weight he associated with old corpses, nor any of the smell. Duplin might have been asleep, despite the pinkish stain revealed when they took away the lead plate. They hoisted the limp figure over to a slab near the shuttered window. Boult undid the clasp, shoved the shutter aside, and looked down into the inky blackness of Narrow Lane.

"We could drop him down," he suggested with a straight face. "It's not so far, and he wouldn't feel it in any case."

"You will not drop him down," Mother Japh said angrily, struggling in the doorway with a heavy coil of rope. "How would you feel if it was your corse, Guardsman?"

"It was only a jest," Boult said, so meekly that Liam almost laughed again. He relieved the ghost witch of her burden, and measured out lengths while she berated the sheepish Guard.

" 'It was only a jest,' " she mimicked, waggling a finger at him. "Only a jest, ha! Y'are a rude rascal, Boult of Crosston, and should be ashamed of yourself."

"How did you know where I'm from?"

"Never mind that," Liam said, wondering himself. She had said it as if just remembering it. "Help me get this rope around him."

Wrapped in the shroud and tied with the rope, Duplin's body looked like a bundle of sailcloth, which made it easier for Liam to stomach the idea of lowering it into the black well of Narrow Lane.

"They'd never do this in Crosston, I'd warrant," Mother Japh muttered.

"They've done stranger," Boult countered. "Anyway, we burn our dead there."

"Where is Crosston?" Liam asked. They were all talking just to hear themselves, he could tell, to take the edge off the thing they were doing, like soldiers before a battle.

"Nowhere," Mother Japh offered, helping to guide the bundled body through the window, while Liam and Boult took the strain on the ropes.

"A day's ride north," Boult grunted, easing his rope down so that Duplin's feet dropped below his head.

"At a crossroads," Mother Japh said, with a little sneer. "Can imagine? The town is at a crossroads, so they call it Crosston!"

Duplin's shrouded feet scraped the stones of Narrow Lane; the pressure eased on Boult's rope. Liam paid his out slowly, the muscles of his arms bunching, letting the corpse sink to the ground.

"And Southwark?" Boult asked. "Is that so very clever, Mother?"

"Cleverer than Crosston," she answered, with a toss of her head.

"But not half as clever as the Midlands," Liam said. He could not see the body, sunk in the darkness below. "We can't just leave him there. I'll jump down and wait while you two go around by the street."

Neither Boult nor Mother Japh objected, so he climbed onto the wide windowsill and swung his legs out. Twisting around, he lowered himself down by his arms, legs hanging, and only at the last minute thought of the body below, kicking frantically against the wall to arc out into the street.

It was an ungraceful landing. Liam's heels hit the cobbles—not the body, he realized gratefully—at an awkward angle, and he sprawled backward, arms flailing. He scrambled quickly to his feet, but not before the chill dampness of the street penetrated his cloak.

Boult tied a lantern to a rope and lowered it down to him, and whispered that they would come around to meet him. Liam urged them to hurry, also whispering, though ten o'clock was still far away and there was no one to hear. There was something about standing there, in the meager light of the lantern, looking up at the window in the Duke's courts that made whispering appropriate.

When the Guard had shut the window, Liam tucked his hands into his armpits, prepared to wait, then looked at the bundled corpse and remembered the wetness of his cloak.

Muttering an apology, he stooped and lifted the body, cradling it in his arms and leaning back against the wall for support. The cloth of the shroud was damp and cold. He apologized again to the night air, unwilling to look at where Duplin's head would be. There was an eery stillness all around; he could hear the wind above him, but it was baffled by the height of the surrounding buildings, leaving Narrow Lane a cold, quiet backwater. As at Laomedon's temple, the world seemed to contract, so that there was nothing but the bend in the road, the light of his lantern, the corpse in his arms. He imagined the scene as if from a distance, the strangeness of it.

Like a grave robber, or a ghoul. The shadows beyond the lantern light seemed to shift. *Distractions. Think of something else.* They did not appear to have met before, but Mother Japh knew Boult's name, and where he was from. She knew he was a Guard, just as he knew what her position was—just as they both knew his. The difference was that in his case they were most likely wrong. Boult, thanks undoubtedly to Coeccias, thought he was a human bloodhound, fully deserving his borrowed title of Quaestor. The gods alone knew what Mother Japh thought he was now, but until a few days earlier she had believed him a wizard.

A poor one, but a wizard nonetheless. And Mopsa thinks I am a thief, unless Japer has spread the word, in which case the whole Guild thinks I am an informer. The old man on the docks—Valdas, he recalled—had thought him a rich lord, which was probably the closest guess of them all. *Though my riches are fairly limited, and my estate long burned to the ground,* he qualified. *Still, what can you expect? You're not much of anything, really, are you? Not much of a scholar, not much of a lord, certainly not a wizard or a thief. An apprentice of all trades, and master of none.*

Before he could go further along this maudlin line of thought, Boult and Mother Japh came around the corner, the old woman ordering the Guard to slow down.

"Shh!" Liam said automatically, though there was no real reason to be quiet. Both obliged. He pushed away from the wall and carried the body across the alley to stand in front of Faius's. "Boult, open the door." His arms were beginning to ache, and it was cold. He wanted to be finished.

Faius's door was locked, and no one answered when Boult knocked.

Have I ever been this stupid before? Liam wondered. *What else have I not thought of?*

There was no sound from within, and no light under the door.

"It seems the barkeep has decamped," Boult said.

"Yes." Liam forced the frustration from his voice, trying to sound calm and authoritative. "Break it down."

Boult shrugged, then kicked at the door. There was a small crash and it banged open, rebounding from the inside wall. The interior of the wineshop was dark and empty. The Guard took the lantern and advanced cautiously, his crossbow held in front of him.

"No one here."

"Just as well," Liam said, carrying Duplin's corpse inside and to the back of the shop. There was less litter on the floor there, and he cleared a space before setting his burden down. Then he dusted his hands, and turned to face his two companions. Boult was standing by the door, pointing his crossbow into the street, and Mother Japh was looking around the wineshop and wrinkling her nose.

"Is this where he died?"

"Yes," Liam answered.

"Well then," the old woman said, gathering her skirts around her and squatting against one wall, "there's nothing for it but to wait. At the stroke of ten we'll unveil the corse."

"We should have brought dice," Boult said from the door, "to pass the time."

Liam shrugged. He did not think he would want to game in an abandoned wineshop with a corpse for company. Broken pottery crunching under his boots, he followed Mother Japh's example, squatting against the wall and resigning himself to the wait.

In a dozen wars and hundreds of night watches at sea, Liam had never been able to condition himself to waiting. He hated it, all the more intensely for the vain efforts he made to be patient. Shifting on his haunches, he frowned at the grating noise the movement made, and settled himself once again. The same noise came from the door, where Boult was standing, and it annoyed him. Waiting did that, made him prickly and irritable.

The bells rang nine eventually, and he got up and began pacing. The tolling sounded distant, even though the tower was close by, and somehow mournful. In the wan light of the single lantern, his monstrous shadow paced behind him. The old woman against the wall, the armed Guard at the door, the corpse at the back of the room: the scene was disconcerting, and he had the strange impression that it was not just the wineshop that was abandoned, but all of Southwark, and that they were camping in a dead city.

As he paced he tried to think, running over everything he knew and all the things he did not. The bearded man in Bellona's temple and his impossible escape, Cloten overcome without a scratch, Scaevola and his visions and his new title, the Death and her warnings and assurances. The gods and their plans, into which he was supposed to fit.

He was not sure whether he wanted to know their plans, the better to fit in with them or the better to avoid them. In the back of his mind he held an image, planted by an old teacher, of the gods in the heavens holding strings on which men jumped. He did not like the image.

Master?

The thought in his head brought him up short, and then he projected. *Where are you?*

On top of the Duke's courts.

Come down here.

There was a pause, and Liam looked to the door, expecting the dragon to appear.

You are expecting the princeps.

Yes, he projected, trying to inject some urgency into the thought.

You think he knows you work with the Aedile.

YES. He actually formed the words in capital letters, and instead of projecting them, he shoved them at the dragon. *COME DOWN HERE.*

He may wish to harm you. Perhaps I should wait outside and watch, where I cannot be seen.

Liam blew out a heavy breath and nodded. *That makes sense. I did not think of it.* More, he realized he did not want Boult or Mother Japh to see his familiar. It was difficult enough to convince them he was not a wizard without Fanuilh adding weight to their belief.

"Eh?" Mother Japh looked up at him. "Thinking again?"

"No," he said, smiling wryly. "I just hate waiting."

"Hmph."

I will watch the street then.

That would be good. You can also watch for the ghost.

Mother Japh looked up at him skeptically. "Is this friend of the ghost going to arrive early?"

Liam cleared his throat. "I had arranged two, actually, but one of them seems to have gone. He owned the wineshop. Is a friend absolutely necessary?"

She frowned, waiting a moment before responding: "No, it's not absolutely necessary, but it's best. Y'are not sure of the other, then?"

"No," he admitted, "I am not." Would the Werewolf come? He must know by now about Liam's connection with Coeccias, but if he knew that, he would know that Liam could have turned him in to the Aedile at any

time. And Liam guessed—hoped—that the Werewolf would be curious.
The more he thought about it, the more the hope faded. Curiosity was a
weak thing to put against a spell in the Duke's jails or the loss of a hand,
the common punishment for stealing.

He eventually gave up on trying to figure out whether the Werewolf
would come or not. If it came to that, there would be time enough later
on to deal with the Southwark Guild. He had done such a thing once
before, when a powerful merchant had tried to force him to leave Southwark. With Fanuilh's help, he had convinced the merchant he was a
wizard, and thus not to be fooled with. . . .

*And if Ancus Marcius did not spread the word that you were a wizard,
then those bodyguards of his probably did, you idiot.* He shook his head,
recalling how Fanuilh had put them to sleep, so that he could confront
the merchant. The irony did not escape him, and he appreciated it fully.
So now you are angry that people think you are a wizard, eh?

Mother Japh had her head down and Boult was watching the street
through the half-opened door, so they did not see the smile of self-
derision that crossed Liam's face.

*There is a man on the roof above you, and three approaching the bend
in the road, one from one direction and two from the other.*

Liam's head jerked up. *Are they armed?*

Not with swords. Only knives.

No bows?

No.

"Damn," he muttered aloud. So the Werewolf had come after all. He
went to the door, gesturing for Boult to stand aside. There was nothing
he could see in the street, and nothing to hear, but he knew it nonetheless. The Werewolf had come, and brought friends.

There was no back way out of the wineshop, and they could hold the
front door if necessary. But first he wanted to see if the princeps would
talk.

"Stand here," Liam whispered, placing Boult to his right and behind
him. "If I hold up my hand, step forward and show your crossbow. Aim it
at whoever I am talking to. Do you understand?"

The Guard nodded. Mother Japh stood up stiffly and took a hesitant
step toward the door.

"Is this our corse's friend?"

"I think so. You should step back, and shutter the lantern."

He did not wait to see if she would comply. Opening the door completely, he leaned forward and peered into the street.

How close are they?

You will see the two in a moment. The other is waiting at the corner, hiding, and the man on the roof has not moved. If you wish I can put them to sleep.

Only if I say so. How close are the two?

They have rounded the corner, but they are hiding in the shadows. The light from the lantern does not reach them.

Liam looked at the ground; a weak tongue of light spread from the door a few yards into the street. Taking a moment to gather his wits, he stepped just outside the doorway.

"Avé, princeps."

There was a sharp intake of breath to his left, and he turned that way.

He did not bother any more with chant. "I am glad you could come. I need your help."

The Werewolf's wary voice came from the shadows, and he could sense the man looking around the dark street. "I should think so, Liam Rhenford—or should I say, Quaestor Rhenford?"

Liam appreciated the princeps's flare for the dramatic: he stepped forward as he mentioned the title, placed his fists on his hips and smiled, showing his overlong eyeteeth.

The best defense. "Come now, princeps, you knew I worked with the Aedile when we first met. And you also knew that if I wanted you arrested, I would have managed it that night, instead of coming in and chatting. Have you moved your carad yet?"

It was a bluff, a wild shot in the dark, but it made the Werewolf's smile deepen. "As it happens, we have. And we did. Think you I set Mopsa on you for the promise of a gift? We were passing curious about this attendant of the Addle who could chant, this wizard who sought us out. And it seems we were right to be, eh?"

For just a moment, Liam faltered. It made perfect sense of Mopsa's determination to stay with him. He had thought it was because he was kind to her, when she had been spying on him all along.

Then he rallied: "And yet you did nothing."

"You could have had us that first night, Quaestor, but you didn't. And once we'd moved our carad and were safe, we wanted to know more about you. Y'are a man of parts, Rhenford—chanter, wizard, aide to the Addle. What else can you do?"

He decided not to contradict the part about his being a wizard. "I can tell you that your man on the roof should have a bow, if he is to be of any use."

The Werewolf laughed, but his eyes narrowed, and his mock bow was stiff. "A bow's unhandy on the rooftops, Quaestor. But he can throw a dagger as well as the next, if not better. So you know it would be bloody to try to clap me in here. Now come, what do you want of me?"

"Have you heard of the ghost in the Warren?"

"Aye."

"It's Duplin. He was murdered here a few nights ago. I have his body here. I think he will come back to it and I want to ask him a few questions, but I need someone to be there who knew him. Someone he will listen to."

Suddenly another figure appeared out of the darkness behind the Werewolf.

"I say we kill the bastard," Japer hissed, stopping just behind his chief.

"How many Guards have you got in there, Rhenford?" the Werewolf asked, as if he had not heard Japer's suggestion.

"Just one," Liam said, "and he will forget everything, won't you?" He raised one hand.

"I will," Boult said, "unless I quarrel with it." He stepped forward to show his crossbow, giving the pun meaning, and they were mirrored: Liam and Boult, the princeps and the angry thief.

Japer started to say something, but the Werewolf raised his hand and silenced him. His lips lifted at the corner, turning his smile feral.

"I will come in, then, Quaestor, on your word there'll be no trouble, and that I'll leave unmolested."

"You have it."

The bells started tolling ten as the Werewolf entered the wineshop.

■ *16* ■

BOULT AND JAPER eyed each other like dogs who had not met, distrust plain on their faces and in every line of their bodies. Liam, however, was watching the Werewolf as he walked to Duplin's body. Mother Japh had pulled away the shroud, revealing the dead man's face.

"Aye, that's Duplin," the thief said, crouching down. He took hold of the corpse's chin, moved the face from one side to the other, examining it. Then he pushed the shroud down, looked for a moment at the knife wound, and pulled the cloth back up. "Who took him off?"

"A ship's captain, someone he was working a job with."

"His name?" The Werewolf stood up, and his voice was tight.

"Perelhos, but he has left Southwark."

"He may return."

"He may," Liam conceded. He knew what the other man was thinking. "And if he does, you can have him. In the meantime, Duplin's ghost is wandering the city. We can put him to rest, but I need to ask him some questions first. Will you help?"

"What sort of questions?"

"It has to do with what's going on in Temple Street."

The princeps crossed his fingers. "Well enough. What do I do?"

Liam looked at Mother Japh for help.

"Look, you," the woman said, "when the ghost arrives, speak to it. Reassure it. Show it the corse, and explain, as gentle as you can, that it's dead, and that it must leave this world. Can you do that?"

"Here now," Japer said, "how do we know that the Quaestor didn't take him? This could be a trap! Wolf—"

"Shut it," Boult ordered.

"Yes," the Werewolf said. "Shut it, Japer."

Fuming, Japer shut it.

"I can do that," the Werewolf went on. "Is that all?"

"No. Once you've calmed it, Rhenford'll have his questions. Present him as a friend, point him out. All as gentle as you can, for that ghosts are skittish, confused. And the same for you, Rhenford, go lightly."

The ghost is here.

"It's come," Liam told them. Then Japer cursed and he and Boult both stepped away from the door. The ghost was there, white radiant in the doorway, peering fearfully around the room.

"Faius?" it said.

Mother Japh nudged the Werewolf, whose jaw dropped at the sight of his friend.

"Faius?" the ghost repeated.

At another nudge, the Werewolf spoke, trying to sound soothing. "Faius is not here, Duplin. But it's me, do you see? The Wolf. And Japer's here, too. Remember Japer?"

The other thieves have run away, Fanuilh told Liam.

"Oh, Wolf, look at what they've done to me, the bastards." Duplin gestured at his chest, where the purple stain stood out like a blossom. "They've cut out my heart, Wolf."

"They've killed you, Duplin, I know. But all will be well. We'll take the one who did it. We'll kill him, Duplin, I swear."

"The body," Mother Japh whispered urgently. "Show him the body." She had placed the piece of lead over the corpse's mouth.

"It's bitter cold, Wolf, and I've no heart to keep me warm."

"Don't you worry," the thief said, and Liam was impressed by his composure. "You need to get back into your body, Duplin, and we've brought it for you. It's got a heart, and you'll be warm there."

The ghost stood hesitantly in the doorway, looking unhappily at the Werewolf. Then it began to sob.

"I'm so cold, Wolf, and it's dangerous out here. Can I come in? There's people after me, and animals. Everybody's out for me."

"Come in, Duplin. Look, you, y'are dead, do you see? That Perelhos has killed you, but you've got to see your body. It's warm there. Will you come in?"

"There's people here," the ghost said, sniffling a little and looking around the wineshop.

"All friends," the Werewolf told him. "They all want to help you . . . but you've got to go into your body." He gestured to the back of the room. "Can you see it? It's warm there."

Duplin's ghost walked forward a few feet, then stopped. Liam repressed an urge to shout at it to hurry, but the Werewolf continued in the same soothing tones.

"Come now, Duplin, don't you want to be warm? Don't you want your body? No one can hurt you there. Look at it."

The ghost finally saw its body and went to it, passing Japer, Boult and Liam without noticing them.

"That's me," it whispered, wonderingly. It crouched down by the bundled corpse and touched the cold forehead. "Is that really me?" he asked the Werewolf.

"It is," the live thief said. "Y'are dead."

"What's that on my mouth?"

"It's to protect you," the Werewolf lied, "from anyone who would harm you. Do you see?"

There was a long pause, while Duplin examined himself. "I see," he said at last. "I'm dead, then." He began to sob again, and covered his face with a glowing hand.

"It's all right," the Werewolf said, moving next to his friend. "We're going to make it all right. But there's someone here—someone who's helped you—who has some questions to ask you."

"Who's here?"

"He's a friend."

Mother Japh beckoned Liam forward.

"Hello, Duplin," he said.

The dead thief could not take his eyes off his own face.

"Duplin?" the Werewolf prodded. "This is a friend."

"What's he want? I'm dead."

"I want to know about the animals that were chasing you, Duplin."

The ghost looked at him then, raising its eyes from the body and staring directly into his. "The birds."

"Yes," Liam said gently. "The birds. You said they wanted you to help them, but you couldn't. What did they want you to do?"

"They were giant," Duplin said, and he sounded tired and frightened, and tired of being frightened. "Giant birds with long claws, and they wanted me to help them, but I couldn't."

"That's right. But what did they want you to do?"

Duplin bowed his head, as if trying to remember was difficult. "They wanted my help. They said they'd give me my body, but I didn't know where it was. And I didn't have a heart. How could I help them without a heart?"

"What did they want?" He knew—he was sure he knew—but he wanted the ghost to say it.

"I can't remember."

Forcing patience, Liam coaxed, "Did they want you to go to Temple Street?"

"Yes!" the ghost said eagerly. "That was it! They wanted me to go to Temple Street, and they said they would give me back my body to do it! But my body is here. How did it get here?"

"We brought it for you, Duplin. What did they want you to do in Temple Street?"

"They wanted me to steal a bird. A friend of theirs. But you can't steal anything when you have no heart."

"Your heart is here, Duplin."

Liam nodded to Mother Japh, who reached out and pulled the lead plate away.

Duplin resuming his crying, leaning forward across his body as if to embrace it. Mother Japh stood up and backed away, motioning for Liam and the Werewolf to do the same.

Stroking his body and weeping, Duplin's ghost faded slowly away, dissipating into the air until nothing was left but the corpse.

The ghost witch sighed. "Well and well. That's done. We can send him to Laomedon's temple tomorrow, to prepare him for burial." She looked at Liam. "What was that about Temple Street, eh?"

He let loose the breath he had been holding and shook his head. "I'm not sure. I have to figure it out." He looked at the Werewolf, who was studying his friend's body. His fists were clenched, and he stood rigidly upright.

"We'll take him. We'll bury him."

"As you will," Mother Japh said softly.

The princeps turned to Liam. "I suppose I should thank you, Quaestor."

Liam only half heard him; he was thinking about what Duplin had said, about the birds and the help they wanted in Temple Street. And another thought, an impossible thought.

"That's crazy!" Japer burst out. "I say it's crazy! He killed Duplin, I tell you, and this is a trap!"

"Shut it," the Werewolf ordered.

"No! He's a wizard! He's faked the whole thing!"

Liam looked up just in time to see Japer pull a dagger from his sleeve.

"Quaestor!" Boult shouted.

Fanuilh! Liam projected.

And then Japer stumbled, dropping heavily to the ground, his knife clattering into the trash on the floor. The Werewolf, too, suddenly slumped down, though far more gracefully than his underling. He folded, bending at the knees and then down onto his side.

There was silence for a long moment, and then Mother Japh spoke: "And y'are no wizard, eh, Liam Rhenford?"

They checked the sleeping thieves, to make sure they had not hurt themselves falling down. Japer had a few cuts on his face, but otherwise they were fine.

"We'll leave them here, with the body. When they wake up, they can take it with them," Liam said. The other two only nodded, very pointedly not saying a word. "Boult, will you see Mother Japh home?"

"Yes, Quaestor."

"And what'll you do?" the witch wanted to know.

"I am going to stay here for a moment. I have some things to think about."

"This is to do with that in Temples' Court, doesn't it? I was right, wasn't I?" There was an edge of worry to Mother Japh's voice.

"It does, yes," Liam answered. "But we haven't done anything wrong. Now, please, go home. They will wake up shortly, and I do not think they will be happy."

They left, Mother Japh shooting a glance over her shoulder as she went out the door. Liam did not notice. He was looking down at the Werewolf, thinking furiously.

Duplin's giant birds had to be stone gryphons, and they must have tried to enlist his help in freeing the one slated for sacrifice in Bellona's temple. It made sense; stone gryphons traveled the ethereal plane, and so did ghosts. If they wanted help, they would look there and find Duplin, who had died that night, before his house was robbed and before the break-in at the temple. They had offered him his body back so that he could help them and then, most probably, die properly, but he had refused, or been too deranged by his recent death to be of any use. So who had helped them?

He thought he knew, and the answer bothered him.

On the other hand, he had an idea of what he would do the next day. He mulled it over for a minute, then nodded to himself and started searching the Werewolf. When he did not find what he was looking for, he went through Japer's pockets, and came out with what he wanted: a small set of lock picks. He put a gold coin in Japer's pockets and the picks in his own purse, then left the wineshop and strode hurriedly through the dark streets to the stables.

Fanuilh joined him on the ride back to the beach, perching on the saddle in front of him.

"Does it make sense to you?" he asked.

It is possible.

"Yes, but does it make sense?"

No. Why would the stone gryphons need help? Why would he help them?

They reached the cliff path and started down. The stars were brilliant overhead, and the moon lit up a shining road across the sea.

"There is one way to check, you know."

How?

Liam did not answer at once. He let Diamond plod across the beach, to the door of his shed.

"His grave. We could dig up his grave."

He looked beyond the shed and the house, to the sheltered nook by the cliff base.

And what would you find?

"Nothing," Liam said at last, and then suddenly dismounted and threw open the door of the shed. "Nothing at all. I'm going to bed. Wake me an hour before dawn."

Apart from the message Fanuilh sent to wake him—the dancer from the distant port, banging a drum and shouting "Wake up!"—he had no dreams at all.

As he dragged himself out of bed and into the kitchen for hot water, he wondered if this was a good sign or not. Certainly it indicated how tired he had been, and the grit in his eyes and frequent yawns attested to how tired he still was. Washing and a hot cup of coffee woke him up but he was not happy with the hour, or with his sketchy notions of what he would do in Bellona's temple.

"It should be easy," he told Fanuilh over their coffee. "The cage has to have a door. They can't have built it around the damned thing."

What if it is locked?

"I doubt it is. Why put a lock on a cage for an animal? They don't have hands, after all. And if there is, I have Japer's picks." Over which, he noted with some satisfaction, he felt no guilt at all. The thief was mean, and he had left a coin. If they were difficult to replace—lock picks could not just be bought in the market—that was not his problem.

Yes, but why?

He had no answer for that, but he gave one anyway: "Because it feels right, familiar mine. I never liked the idea of a gryphon in a cage, and now that I know he has friends trying to get him out, I like the idea even less. Plus—and this is important—I can get away with it."

Are you sure?

"Quite sure. And if I cannot, then I won't try."

The dragon dropped its head to its bowl, taking in a deep whiff of coffee smell.

The chair was comfortable, and for a few minutes, Liam toyed with the idea of staying at the beach all day, avoiding Southwark entirely. When he had finished his coffee, however, he got up from the table and went out to the shed. Fanuilh padded after him.

Fresh, cold air drove the last of the sleep from his brain, and he stretched briefly on the stone patio, taking in the predawn blue of the sky, the rustle of waves on the sand. It was a good place to be, and again he wondered if he should go into town.

Diamond snorted in the shed, and he went to it reluctantly, carefully averting his gaze from the spot near the cliff where he had buried Tarquin.

There was a crowd gathering in Temple Street as dawn approached, a fearful group of almost fifty, huddled in the road and exchanging tense whispers. A Guard saw Liam and pointed to the cul-de-sac.

"The Aedile's attending you at the end, Quaestor."

Liam belatedly returned the man's salute and urged Diamond on. The horse pressed through the crowd, people standing aside quickly, as if they were afraid to touch it. He caught sight of Coeccias by the entrance to the cul-de-sac, pacing in front of a row of Guards, all armed and armored, each carrying a torch.

"Rhenford! Good morrow to you!" It was clear the Aedile saw nothing good in it, and he snapped at the Guard he had ordered to take Liam's horse for being to slow about it.

"I see everything is ready." Through the gates of Strife's compound, he could see acolytes in shining chain mail assembling. Bellona's men were massed in front of her temple, equally polished. Guiderius and Alastor stood by the fountain, conferring with an elderly man in a red silk coat with a wheel stitched in gold thread on the back. "This Quaestor business—people saluting, orderlies taking my horse—I must say, I could get used to it."

Coeccias turned from studying the conference by the fountain and offered him a appraising look. "It could be permanent, you know. We'll discuss it later. For now, you should get yourself into the temple. The duel will start any minute."

"I was joking."

"I was not."

He let it drop. "Who is the man in red?"

"The Hierarch of Fortune—note the wheel. He's agreed to officiate. There'll be prayers and the like before the duel itself, but the parties'll have to be here soon, so go to, get into the temple."

Shrugging, Liam started across, then stopped as he heard his name being called. When he turned, he saw Mopsa duck out of the crowd and run up to him.

"Morning, Uncle! What are you doing here?"

"I'm going to pray, and I'm in a hurry. What are you doing here?"

"Practice," the girl said, patting her pocket and grinning at the sound of coins clinking. "Crowd's been here most of an hour. I'll be able to retire soon."

"I'd retire now, pickit. One of those Guards is giving you a look. Now I have to go." He did not want to be rude; he was surprised she was talking to him at all.

"Can I come with you? I want to watch the duel, and I can't see it from here. I'm too short."

"I'll be inside the temple for the whole thing. I won't see it."

"Oh," she said, disappointed.

"Look"—he hesitated, "look, did the Werewolf say anything about last night?"

"About what you did for Duplin? Sure, and he did. That was good on you, Uncle. Everyone said so. Even if you are too close with the Addle."

Which meant neither the Werewolf nor Japer had said anything about being put to sleep. He could understand that; in an organization like a guild, prestige and face were important, but he could not understand why the girl would still associate with him.

"All right," he said hastily, "you can come along. But you'll have to wait outside while I talk to someone, and don't get in the way of the priests. And whatever you do, don't steal anything."

"I've had enough already," she said smugly, and followed closely behind him as he crossed the cul-de-sac, careful not to go too near the fountain, where the three priests were talking. He stopped by the steps of Bellona's temple, behind the silent ranks of Her acolytes, and turned to the girl.

"Wait over there, just around the corner. You should be able to see everything and be out of the way at the same time. If someone tells you to move, move. All right?"

"I'm not a fool, Uncle," she said.

"I have my doubts," he replied, and started up the steps before she could answer. He did indeed have his doubts. She did not seem to hate him, as she could have: he worked with the Aedile, and she was a thief. They should have been enemies. Apparently the Werewolf had spread the word that he had done a good deed for the Guild by helping Duplin.

Not that I didn't have my own reasons for doing it, he thought, but that was beside the point. They had known all along that he was friends with Coeccias, and the Werewolf had brought guards to Narrow Lane, but now he was saying Liam was all right, and had not warned Mopsa off. Did that mean they would not bother him in the future?

No one stopped him until he was inside the doors, when a single guard barred his path with a spear and demanded his name.

"Liam Rhenford. I am here to see Scaevola."

The man's demeanor changed immediately; he was expected. "Hierarch Scaevola is back there." He stressed the title, and pointed to the door by the altar.

Liam thanked him and headed for the door. The temple was dark, lit by only a few candles around the altar. As he crossed the floor he stole a glance up at the dome, where the cage hung. He could just barely make out the stone gryphon, lying listlessly against the bars.

Another guard waited behind the inner door, and when he heard Liam's name he immediately led him down a narrow corridor toward the rear of the temple. They went down a flight of steps and along another hall, past a row of curtained-off cells to the last one, where the curtain was pulled aside. The guard leaned in and gave Liam's name, then went back upstairs.

Liam looked into the cell. Scaevola was standing in front of a straw pallet, his arms raised, allowing an acolyte to buckle on his sword belt. Cloten was leaning against one wall, chewing angrily at his lower lip.

"Good morning, Liam Rhenford," Scaevola said, smiling tiredly.

"Good morning, Hierarch Scaevola. Hierarch Cloten." He deliberately used both titles, and was pleased with Cloten's glower.

"Are they finished up there?"

"Who, Hierarch?" Liam inquired politely.

"Alastor and Fortune's idiot, who else?"

"They were still talking when I came in."

"I had better go and see what's keeping them," Cloten said, leaving the cell, only to stop by Liam and turn. He pointed a finger at Scaevola. "Remember, Hierarch—fight your best. The honor of our goddess is at stake."

Scaevola only nodded, and when Cloten was gone, he signaled for the acolyte to leave. When they were alone, he took off the sword belt and put it back on a different way, with the sword slung on his back, the hilt projecting over his shoulder.

"I am glad you could come," he said, his fingers nimbly adjusting the buckle.

Scaevola sounded as tired as Liam felt—more so, perhaps—and for a moment he searched the cracked skin under the new Hierarch's eyes for signs of shadows, and then remembered that the other man never slept.

"I got your note," he said, rather lamely.

"I wanted to thank you. You were right when you told me to pray. I did—and She answered me."

"You had a sign yesterday," Liam said.

"Yes. We were all in the main hall, at our prayers. I had prayed all night, but I prayed even more than." The sick man's voice grew soft, as if remembering something particularly beautiful. "And then we heard the host, thundering down Temple Street, and they came into the temple, and rode in a circle around me."

"You saw them? No one else saw them?"

"Oh, we saw them," Scaevola said, still awed by the experience, "and they formed a circle around me, and when they doffed their helms to me, they all had low-root. Can you imagine? An army of heroes, all with low-root, bowing to me."

It seemed a fairly unequivocal sign to Liam, but he was glad to hear an edge of humility in Scaevola's tone, as if he still found it hard to believe—not that the host had come, but that they had come for him. "Then why is Cloten still Hierarch? Why aren't you in charge? Why are you fighting this duel?"

Scaevola cocked his head, as if considering a strange idea. "Why shouldn't he be Hierarch? The visit means only that I am blessed by the Lady, not that Cloten has fallen from favor." Liam frowned his disagreement: the host bowing and removing their helms indicated to him that they recognized Scaevola's leadership—and if they did, so certainly should Bellona's mortal servants. But Scaevola was not paying attention, caught by his own thought. "Though he does seem to doubt the truth of what we all saw, which some are taking poorly . . . but as for the duel, it has been contracted in our Lady's name. It must be done."

No one will die today, Liam recalled, and he was trying to think of a way to tell Scaevola this when the other man continued.

"Did you know, Liam Rhenford, that duels such as these can end in draws? Keeper of Arms Alastor told me: if the fight goes on long enough, and neither man is killed or draws blood, honor can be satisfied." He smiled then, a wistful, mature smile that fit his ruined face very well. "I must go now. We will begin soon enough."

Liam followed him out of the cell and up the stairs, staring at his feet all the way.

Scaevola paused in the temple, kneeling at the altar and bowing his head for a moment, then rose in a fluid motion and headed for the door. He stopped when he saw that Liam was not with him.

"Are you not coming?"

"I'm going to stay here," Liam said, standing by the altar. "In case the thieves come back while everyone is outside."

Scaevola digested this, looking pensively into the fire pit. "Of course. Wish me luck, Liam Rhenford."

"Good luck."

The sick man looked up at the dome, then back at Liam. "And good luck to you."

He was not wearing armor, Liam saw, only a light robe of black cloth, which flared as he spun to the door and strode through it.

There was no sign of the guard at the door. *He must have gone out to watch,* Liam thought. *He's probably right there on the steps, just outside.* It would have been better if he was inside. Still, he was alone in the temple.

He jogged quickly to the outer doors just as horns blared in the cul-de-sac. They blew a fanfare, then another, then stopped. He cracked one of the doors just a little, just enough to see, and then Mopsa thrust her head in.

"Aren't you coming? They're starting!"

Liam jumped back, startled, one hand on his chest.

"Gods, girl, don't do that!"

"What? Aren't you going to watch?"

Outside, someone was speaking to the assembled temples. The Hierarch of Fortune, Liam guessed. He did not recognize the voice, and he could not make out the words. Mopsa stared at him.

"Well?"

"No," he said quickly, bending down to take her by the shoulders. "I'm not going to watch. But you are. I want you to stay here by the door and watch everything. If the duel ends, or if anyone comes up those steps, I want you to whistle. Can you whistle?"

"Can I whistle, he says," she joked, as if he had asked if she could walk. "Sure, and I can whistle. What are you going to do?"

"Don't worry about that. Just watch."

He left her by the door and ran back to the altar. He had counted on there being a guard, had prepared Fanuilh for it. The dragon could have taken care of it, and he would have felt safer. A guard would have been a certainty, something to get out of the way, clearing the room. Without one, he could not be sure that someone would not come back to check. He had no choice, though, the girl would have to do.

Fanuilh, he projected. *Where are you?*

On the roof, master. What happened to the Guard?

They didn't leave one. I want you to watch, in case someone comes back. What's happening out there?

Hierarch Cloten is making his accusation to the red priest.

Tell me what happens.

He examined the altar, the shelf behind—the treasury chest, the staple for the chain. He ran his eye along the chain, up the wall, across the ceiling to the dome. It would not be easy, but it would not be as hard as the wall outside.

Kicking off his boots, he climbed up onto the shelf and grabbed the chain. There was no slack, but the links were big enough for handholds. The metal was cold.

Hierarch Guiderius is replying.

Hand over hand; it was not so hard for the first stretch, his fingers fit in the wide links, his toes, too. *Like a lizard, a lizard, a lizard,* he repeated over and over, up the wall, the chain cold and dry, sweat already on his back.

The red priest is speaking, proclaiming the duel.

He reached the second staple and hung there for a moment, putting his weight on his feet and letting his arms rest. *Don't look down, whatever you do. How far is it? Far enough to splatter.*

The chain slanted away, into the dome. That would be the hardest part. He was breathing heavily, waiting too long, putting it off.

"Go," he told himself. "Go."

"Uncle?"

Mopsa called again. "Uncle?"

"Watch the door!" he hissed, looking over his shoulder. It was a mistake. She was standing by the fire pit, miles away. Far enough to splatter.

Another fanfare blew outside, and he shouted: "Watch the door!" He could see her look up in surprise, her jaw drop. Then she shut it and ran back to the door.

Liam grabbed hold of the chain where it angled away from the wall and pulled himself up, flinging his legs over it, clasping with his knees. He was no longer a lizard, but a monkey, clambering upside down along a branch. Sweat poured down his forehead, slicked his fingers, itched on his shins. The lock picks in his purse clanked, and for a sickening moment he was sure they were going to fall out. Had he tied the purse closed? He stopped moving, listening, his eyes shut . . . there was no clatter, the purse must have been closed.

Then he was a monkey again, holding the image in his head—*No monkey would be stupid enough to do this,* he thought, and shoved the thought away—going farther up the chain.

If he tilted his head far enough back he could see the front of the temple, the tops of the doors, the middle of the doors . . . he pulled his head back before he saw the floor; it made him dizzy.

And he was almost there, he was at the edge of the dome, and one hand slipped, reaching for a grip. It dropped down, as if there were a weight attached, and he stared at it, the floor beyond it, amazed by its treachery.

They are squaring off to fight. They are bowing to each other.

Liam grunted and swung his shoulder, forcing the recalcitrant hand back up to the chain, making it grab, pulling again. He passed the lip of the dome, hanging at an even level with the cage. There was a shelf there, where the windows were, within reach, but if he stopped he would never go on, so he kept climbing. The muscles in his arms and legs were quivering, and his thighs hurt from grasping the chain, but he was almost there.

He kept telling himself that—*Almost there, almost there, almost there*—forgetting the monkey, focusing on the length of chain from which the cage hung. He would not need to go all the way to the top—he could reach from the chain he was on to the other, it was not far—

It's not far, just high.

There was more light in the dome. The sun was rising from behind banks of gray clouds in the east.

He reached once and missed, swinging on the chain, but regained his balance and reached again. His fingers slipped through a link, got a firm grip, and then he jumped.

The chain moved just a little, but it set the cage swinging, and he embraced the chain like a lover.

It's not strong enough. It's not strong enough. Gods, let it be strong enough.

It was, but it swung for long seconds while he clung there, gentle arcs that made his stomach turn over. Then it was finished, and he looked down into the cage, into the eyes of the stone gryphon.

They are starting to fight.

The creature was staring at him, settled back on its haunches with its beak open.

"Hello," he said weakly. "I am here to rescue you."

The gryphon squawked curiously, cocking its head.

"Never mind," he said, and let himself down the chain until he was standing on top of the cage. It swayed a little under his feet, but when he lay down, spread-eagled, it stopped. The gryphon imitated him, lying flat but following him with his eyes.

The bars were set close together; he hooked an arm through them and twisted his body around to the edge. The cage tilted, and he slid over the side, pushing his feet between the bars. It tilted more, but the gryphon pushed itself against the far side, trying to balance their weight.

"Thanks," he told it, though the cage was still leaning at an uncomfortable angle. He would be done soon.

There was a lock, and it was indeed locked, but it looked simple. With his free hand—the other was starting to protest its unnatural position—he fumbled open his purse, drew out the largest of the picks.

He took three deep breaths with his eyes closed, then he fit the pick into the lock, jiggled it once, and heard the tumbler click.

Scaevola does not seem to be trying to win.

Liam dropped the pick, ignoring the sound, a second later, of its hitting the floor, and pulled himself away from the door of the cage, letting it swing open. The gryphon tensed, sleek muscles bunching under its gray coat, but it waited.

"Did he tell you I was coming?" Liam asked wearily. He had half expected the creature to leap at the door, knocking him from the cage. "Did he tell you to be so cooperative?"

The creature's tongue, black basalt and thin like a stiletto, flickered over its beak.

Then Liam climbed back up onto the top of the cage and lay there prostrate, exhausted. It hurt to breathe—the cold air in the dome seared his throat—but the bars were cool on his burning face. He heard a noise from behind him, tried to raise his head.

*Scaevola is only playing with Strife's champion. He is not fighting.
Cloten is shouting.*

The noise behind was a window opening in the dome. A gust of
bitterly cold air washed over him.

"Well," said a familiar voice. "Thank you, Rhenford. You seem to
have saved me a great deal of trouble."

Liam forced his head up, looked over his shoulder.

"Hello, Tarquin."

The wizard stood in the window, smiling a little and chewing on a
corner of his mustache. A stone gryphon shoved its head past Tarquin's
waist and squawked at the one in the cage.

■ *17* ■

SITTING ON THE shelf by the altar, Liam pulled on his boots as quickly as he could.

"I really wish you had left the rug where you found it," Tarquin was saying. He had used it to bring them down from the cage, and was now seated on it cross-legged, hovering just in front of Liam. "I had to go all the way back to the house to get it."

Three gryphons sat on the edge of the fire pit, staring impatiently at Tarquin's back, occasionally flaring their wings. Mopsa hung by the side of the altar, her eyes round with wonder. Liam had tried to reassure her, but Tarquin claimed his attention, ignoring the gryphons and speaking quickly.

He could hardly believe the wizard's presence. He had guessed at it the night before, had even considered digging up the grave in which he himself had placed the wizard to confirm it. But it was still amazing.

"I'm sorry about that. I did not know it was you."

"And you threw out all of my things! Cleared the shelves completely! Do you know how expensive dragon's tears are?"

"I did not know you would be coming back for them," Liam said, a little peevishly. "How was I supposed to know? I'm no wizard."

Tarquin regarded him critically. He was wearing the blue robe in which he had been killed, but the tear from the dagger that had killed him was gone.

"No, you are not—that much is certain. Still, I am glad you took care of that lock. There's not much in my spellbook for locks. I had prepared a few spells, but they would have taken far longer than just picking the fool thing. I had no idea you were such an accomplished thief."

"It was a simple lock," Liam said. There were things he wanted to ask, but the wizard was speaking again.

"How do you find the house?" he asked, combing his beard with his fingers.

"It's very comfortable."

"I did not leave it to you, you know. I left no will. Fanuilh faked it."

Liam's jaw dropped, and he stammered for a second.

"I don't object," Tarquin said, raising his hand for silence. "I am happy it has fallen into good hands, and that the little beast has a competent master. I only tell you this because there are some things in it that I wish to give to other people. One other person, really. You will know who I mean when she arrives. She is to have my spellbook, and whatever she likes from the trophy room. The house I bequeath to you."

Liam stammered a little more.

"Do not thank me," Tarquin said, and then hesitated. "It is the least I can do after you . . . avenged me." Gratitude did not become the old wizard; he sounded awkward, and cleared his throat loudly. "I will have to go soon. I have made a list here of apothecary shops, and the things I took from them. I would like you to see that they are paid. I believe that is fair—if you hadn't thrown out all my supplies, I would not have had to rob them. As it was, they had very little that was of any use. Most of my spells were useless. I tried to tell them that"—he gestured toward the stone gryphons, still waiting patiently by the fire pit—"but there was no one else who could help them. That thief would have been perfect, but he was not adjusting well. They can do very few things in this plane, you know. For all of their apparent solidity, they are helpless as babes here, and the iron of that cage completely threw them—it's a base element, after all. They knew me from before I died—I'm sure Fanuilh has told you about my experience in the ethereal plane? It was there I met them—and they were sure I could help. What could I do but try?"

The voice was the same, as were the slightly pompous turns of phrase, but Liam could only stare, slack jawed, at the man who should have been dead.

"Of course, I did not think it would be so difficult. All those guards, and no material components—and no experience as a rescuer of helpless ethereal creatures. I was quite at a loss."

One of the stone gryphons cawed, and Tarquin waved at it.

"Yes, yes, just a moment. In any case, Rhenford, my little adventure is over, and they have to return me to the Gray Lands. I cannot say I have enjoyed my return to life very much, but there you are. I must go, and you must, too. This temple will not long be a place for mortals."

He held out his hand and Liam took it, held it.

"Wait. There are things I want to ask you—"

"You do not want to know what it is like to be dead, Rhenford," the wizard said, gently disengaging his hand. "As for the rest, you can make it up. Aedile Coeccias will believe you implicitly."

He spoke a single, strange word, and the rug started to rise, heading for the dome.

"Wait!"

"You do not want to know," Tarquin repeated, and then the gryphons took flight, shooting up to the dome and out the window. The wizard followed them, angling the rug, and then was gone.

Liam slipped off the shelf, and blew out a heavy breath. "Who cares what it's like to be dead?" The list of apothecaries lay on the altar, along with Tarquin's spellbook; he picked them up, folded the list, and stowed it in the book. A broken link of chain dangled from its spine. "I want to know what he meant about mortals in the temple."

Mopsa came out from behind the altar. "Uncle?"

Liam turned his head, smiled uncertainly. "Well, pickit, what do you think of that?"

She jerked her thumb at the treasury chest. "They say there's a fortune in there."

"There may be," he agreed, "but that wasn't the job. The job was up there"—he pointed to the empty cage—"and as lookout, you are entitled to a tenth of the split, by the Legium. Worse luck for you there is no split. But I will make it up to you. Now stop looking at that, and let's go."

He had to take her by the shoulder to get her away from the altar; as it was, she kept throwing longing glances over her shoulder as they went.

"Who was the old man?"

"A friend of mine," Liam said, and refrained from adding: *Who's been dead for two months.*

"Another wizard?" She did not seem bothered in the least by Tarquin's appearance, or that of the extra stone gryphons. He wondered at her imperturbability.

"No, not another wizard. A real one. I am not a wizard."

"Ha! Y'are not a wizard!"

They were throwing long shadows; they looked like human forms cut from black velvet, stark against the brilliant light emanating from the altar behind them.

Liam stopped, holding Mopsa by the shoulder. He heard a sudden uproar from outside.

"Where's the light—" she began, turning under his hand to look at the altar. "Oh."

Closing his eyes, Liam mouthed a prayer, turned, opened his eyes. Bellona stood on her own altar.

She glowed, but it was not like Duplin. It was as if she were made of diamonds, and all the light of the sun played over her, sparking a thousand random points of golden fire.

He had to squint just to face her, and even then he could not see her face behind the nimbus that coruscated around her. Still, he thought she was smiling.

She stepped off the altar, in a smooth stride, though that should not have been possible. She seemed no taller than he, but as she walked toward them, she reached up and tore the empty cage from the dome. It dwindled in her hand, till it was no more than a bauble. Each step sent a shock through the temple—through Southwark—but Liam and Mopsa were rooted to the spot, frozen by her radiance.

Then she was before them, and Liam slipped to his knees, overcome with terror and awe. He had been in the presence of a god before, and the feeling was the same: shame and exaltation, a foul taste in his mouth for which he was inexplicably grateful. He hung his head before her.

"Liam Rhenford," she said, and it sounded as though a thousand voices were speaking, as echoes flew and broke all around the walls of the temple. "You have done me service. For cleaning my house, I give you this."

She took his hand—the touch burned, but only briefly—and pressed the now-tiny cage into it.

"We do not forget," a thousand voices said, and then she walked past them, each footstep a tremor, and flung open the doors of her home.

Liam turned his head, shading his eyes, and saw her face the crowd in the cul-de-sac. The sky was black, but Bellona was a new sun, bathing the terrified faces in golden light. Her words were like thunder—no, he realized, there was thunder, blazing from the black clouds overhead, but her words rang over it, like the shouting of an army.

His mouth was dry; his hand, where she had touched it, was swollen and puffy, burned brick red.

Mopsa had fainted.

Gods, he thought, *don't let her stay long.*

• • •

Coeccias echoed almost the same sentiment eight hours later. They were sitting in the barracks, drinking from mugs of beer—Herlekin's was closed, everything was closed.

"It'd not like me to have a god walk Southwark every day," he said, without a trace of irony. "There was a riot in the Warren—did I tell you? A riot. A gang of roughs, sure the end of the world was on them, or at least the end of the Duke's law. And the fires as well, but you know of those, eh?"

Liam nodded. He was smudged from head to foot with ashes, his clothes torn. Both of his hands were burned and aching.

Out of the unnatural darkness that had heralded Bellona's arrival, lightning had flared, striking fire to four spots in Temples' Court. In the confusion after her departure, the fires had raged unchecked. He had spent most of his day helping to fight them, hauling buckets from wells, clearing the buildings nearby, tending the burned. Over fifty people had been seriously injured; miraculously, none had died.

"Miraculously," he muttered, and stifled a groan.

"Eh?"

"Nothing."

Mopsa came to a few moments before Bellona disappeared, and ran off at his instruction. Once during the course of the day he had seen Scaevola, carrying an unconscious woman away from a burning building. There had been no time to speak, only to nod and hurry on.

"They are going, you know," Coeccias said.

"Who?"

"Bellona's men. Going north, back to Caernarvon. Not all of them, though. Just that Scaevola, and Cloten, and a small guard. They're leaving Alastor behind, and some men. The damned place'll be a shrine before the month is out."

"What happened?"

"Eh?" Coeccias peered owlishly at him, tired and confused. Then his eyes cleared. "Of course, you were not there. That Scaevola, he was only teasing the other, drawing him on, fighting but not, if you see. And still the grandest display of swordplay I've ever seen. And then the sky went black, and She came out of her temple." He paused, taking a long draw from his mug. "I don't know what She said—it was like a roaring wind, an avalanche, the sea in a frenzy on the Teeth. I could not understand a word. But by the end, Cloten was on his face, begging pardon, and the only person left standing was Scaevola."

They sat silent for a long while, each nursing his own hurts, sunk in a strange, anticlimactic gloom. Then Coeccias chuckled and reached into his pocket, pulling out a crumpled piece of paper. He tossed it at Liam but it fell short, landed on the floor.

"What is it?" He did not want to make the effort to bend over and pick it up.

"Acrasius Saffian's response. The courier brought it during the hurlyburly. It says there's no conceivable way that theurgy could break a wizard's wards. Better late than never, eh?"

The Aedile laughed weakly. Liam made the effort to pick up the paper—and threw it in the fireplace.

"Better never," he said, but he smiled as he said it.

"It was Tarquin Tanaquil, eh? All to free that gryphon?"

Liam had explained as much as he knew already; he could not muster the strength to go over it again. "Yes."

Tarquin, the bearded man that Cloten had seen, who had cast a sleep spell on the Hierarch after a gryphon knocked him down. Tarquin who had broken into the apothecaries' shops, looking for the materials with which to cast the spells that would free the captive gryphon. Tarquin who had broken into Liam's house to steal his own belongings.

"And you were in the temple, weren't you? When She came?"

Liam looked up, met his friend's glance. He thought of the tiny cage in the pouch at his belt.

No, I left before she came. No, I was hiding. No, I fainted as soon as she appeared.

"Yes," he said at last.

"Someday," the Aedile said, standing and groaning as he did so, "someday I'll want the whole tale. All that of Tanaquil and the gryphons, and of what you saw when She came. But there is more to do for me this day, and you should to your bed. Not today, then, or tomorrow. Or the day after. But someday. Will you?"

"I will," Liam promised, and stood as well.

They shook hands on the steps of the barracks, and Coeccias headed off on some unspecified errand.

Diamond was waiting patiently under the eye of a weary Guard. Liam climbed slowly into the saddle and urged the horse toward Auric's Park. He did not want to leave Southwark by the city gate. It was too close to Temple Street.

It began to snow as he trotted onto the road that led to his house, and Fanuilh fluttered down between the flakes, taking up its usual position in front of him.

"Well," Liam said. "Look who's here. The master forger."

I am sorry.

"Sorry? Sorry you gave me a magic house?" He was not annoyed. The house was his now.

I thought you would be displeased. In the days after Master Tanaquil died, it seemed to make sense. Who else would have it?

"Don't worry about it, Fanuilh. I am not displeased. Who else would have it, indeed? And Tarquin did not contest the will. I am just curious how you did it."

A simple spell, an illusion. It made a different will, duly registered, look like one for Master Tanaquil.

"And you cast it?"

Yes. As I told you, it is a simple spell.

They had reached the cliff path.

"Hmm. You'll have to show me one day."

They did not communicate after that; Liam stabled Diamond and trudged into the house in silence. He had brought Tarquin's spellbook from his saddlebags; now he placed it back on the pedestal from which it had been taken.

I cannot say I have been bored, he thought as he took off his dirty clothes in the library. *I have reunited a ghost with its body, and made the acquaintance of a den of thieves. I have stolen a gryphon, met a dead friend, done a service for a goddess. I have tried to convince half a city that I am not a wizard, and ended up convincing the whole city that that is precisely what I am. And I have properly inherited a magical house and a tiny dragon from their previous owner.*

His sleep, when he claimed it, felt richly deserved.

Beggar's Banquet

■ *1* ■

ON THE FIRST day of the holiday week called Beggar's Banquet, Liam
Rhenford woke to an illusory contentment which was quickly dispelled.

The room in which he slept was a library, and the only windows were
in the cupola directly above the divan on which he lay; when he first
opened his eyes he saw by the diffused quality of the light in the room
that there must be a layer of snow on the glass. In the Midlands, where
he had grown up, Beggar's Banquet was called the Feast of Fools, and
snow on the first day of the holiday was considered a good sign.

Smiling sleepily to himself, he rolled over onto his back, stretching a
little beneath his blanket, and peered up at the cupola. A light dusting of
snow, new since he had gone to bed, concealed the sky but allowed light
to filter through, and his smile widened in the pale glow.

Good morning, master. Mage Grantaire is already awake.

The firm thought intruded on his own muddled ones, like a brick
dropped through a cloud of feathers, and he started, hauling himself up
on his elbows and staring down at his familiar. The dragon standing in
the doorway of the library was the size of a small dog, but the intelligent
gleam in its slit-pupilled eyes—and the thought it had just sent into his
head—reminded him that it was considerably more than just a pet. And
the name the creature mentioned quickly overrode his childish contentment at seeing snow on the first day of Beggar's Banquet: he had an
uninvited guest to attend to.

"Good morning, Fanuilh," he said; then, before it could object to his
speaking aloud, he closed his eyes and projected his own thought.

What is she doing?
She is walking on the beach.
Is she far away?
She is some ways down the beach, Fanuilh answered, settling down
onto its haunches and flaring its leathery wings before folding them
neatly across its back.
Can she hear us?
We are not speaking.
You know what I mean, Liam thought, trying to load the thought with
his irritation at the dragon's obtuseness.
I have told you, Master, Fanuilh replied impassively. *No one but us
can understand our projections. A wizard such as Mage Grantaire may be
aware that we are communicating, but she would not know what we
thought.* The dragon had told him that several times, both before and
after Grantaire had arrived, but the fear of being "overheard" nagged at
him.

With a sigh and a small groan, he lay back down on the divan, drew
the blanket over his head and thought about his guest.

Grantaire was a wizard, apparently an old friend of the wizard in
whose house Liam now lived. She had arrived at his door only the night
before as he was getting ready for bed; his first impression of her, seen
through the glass panes of his front door, was that she was some helpless,
well-to-do lady caught out late on the coast road to the nearby city of
Southwark, and that the lights of his house on the beach had led her to
hope for a safe place to spend the night. He had also thought that, with
her cheeks stung to redness by the cold and her hair mussed by the wind,
she was very pretty.

His first impression of helplessness was quickly dispelled: she pushed
brusquely past him into the entrance hall and shuddered once, dropping
a heavy traveling bundle to the floor.

"Gods, it's cold," she said, then unlaced her fur-trimmed cloak and
let it drop to the floor, revealing a fairly short, plain shift that revealed a
disturbing length of leg between the hem and the top of her boots. "But
of course you can count on Tanaquil's house to be too warm," she went
on, rubbing her neck with both hands and sniffing judiciously, as if the
warmth of the house had a smell. Then she had turned to him, frank
appraisal in her glance. "Or should I say, your house? You are Liam
Rhenford?"

"Yes," he confessed, at a complete loss for words in the face of the
woman's self-confident entrance. Tarquin Tanaquil was the wizard from

whom he had inherited the house, and its warmth—along with a number of other things—was an example of the magic with which the wizard had filled it.

"My name is Grantaire. I was a friend of Tanaquil. He told me I could expect to find you here."

"You saw him?" Liam did not know why he had been surprised: he knew that Tarquin had for a brief time returned from the grave. He had seen the wizard himself, and talked with him—but he had not known that Tarquin had talked to anyone else during his return.

A sudden movement of the cloak at their feet made him jump, and then a cat poked its rumpled gray head out and directed a reproachful glare at Grantaire.

"I'm sorry," she told the cat, "but if you insist on being carried, you must sometimes be dropped." As if seeing the cat made her remember, she turned to Liam: "Where is Fanuilh?"

Things had moved very quickly from there, allowing no time for Liam to formulate the proper suspicion, let alone give voice to it. Fanuilh had entered the room and, displaying a complete lack of surprise, had ambled over to Grantaire and allowed her to scratch under its chin.

You know her? Liam had asked, barely maintaining the presence of mind to project the thought instead of speaking. *She is who she says she is?*

Of course, the dragon replied, turning its head a little to redirect her scratching.

Reassured, Liam had prepared Tarquin's old bedroom for her—he would not sleep there, because it was where he had found the wizard's body, but she had no objections.

"I am tired from traveling" was all she had said before closing the bedroom door. "We shall speak in the morning." It had sounded almost like an order.

Now the morning was upon him, and he knew nothing more about her; Fanuilh had only been able to tell him that she really was an old friend of Tarquin, and that she could not understand the thoughts they sent back and forth.

With another groan, Liam sat up, put his feet on the floor and scrubbed briefly at his eyes.

Will you have coffee, master?

"Yes," he grumbled and, forcing himself to his feet, shuffled into the kitchen. He concentrated briefly in the direction of the large oven, closing his eyes; then he opened the oven's metal door and pulled out a bowl and a mug, both steaming. The mug he sipped from himself; the bowl he placed on the other side of the kitchen table.

Fanuilh leapt lightly onto the tabletop and crouched over the bowl, inhaling deeply. It had only drunk coffee once, and hated it, but it enjoyed the smell immensely.

"So," Liam said after a few cautious sips, the coffee warming his stomach and driving the sleep from his head, "you really know nothing more about her?"

She is a great wizard, the dragon answered, without raising its snout from the coffee. *Not as great as Master Tanaquil, but great enough.*

"Yes, but where is she from? Where does she live? Why is she here?"

I imagine she is here to take some of Master Tanaquil's things. The ones you cannot use.

"Because I am not a wizard?"

Yes.

Though he had a familiar, Liam was by no means a wizard. That he was bound to Fanuilh was an accident—one he had at first thought extremely unlucky, but which he had grudgingly come to accept had its benefits.

Tarquin Tanaquil had been murdered, and on the night of his death Liam had happened to come by the house. He had found Fanuilh dying, the part of Tarquin's soul that kept it alive rapidly departing; it bit him, taking part of his soul to keep itself alive, and incidentally binding them as master and familiar.

Strange, he thought to himself, careful not to project, *that I don't notice that part of my soul is missing.* It was not technically missing, he knew, merely residing in Fanuilh, but he found the idea difficult to grasp. *Shouldn't I notice that half of my soul is halfway across the room?*

Another sip of coffee and the sound of footsteps distracted him from this train of thought, and he looked up as Grantaire entered the room.

Her hair was just as disordered as it had been the night before, her cheeks as flushed, and her shift as short; he blushed heavily when he realized he was wearing nothing but a pair of breeches.

"The house is warm, isn't it?" she said without a trace of embarrassment, as if going half-naked in front of a strange woman was merely practical. "But I think you should put on some clothes—there's something on the beach you should see."

"What?" he said, crossing his arms, sticking his hands in his armpits and feeling foolish.

She frowned. "I think you should see it. Get a cloak." She turned and left the kitchen.

"What is it?" he asked Fanuilh, but the dragon only shook its head, then leapt off the table and padded out of the kitchen after the wizard.

Liam followed, stopping only to jump into a pair of boots and throw on a tunic. He did not imagine it could be anything important, or that it would take very long.

Tarquin Tanaquil's villa was long and low in the southern style, with white plaster walls and a red tile roof; it sat on a beach in a sheltered cove, protected by a short breakwater that touched the patio in front and still allowed the cold waves to strike the sand to the west of the house.

They gathered at the edge of the beach, clustered around the dead man, Liam and Fanuilh standing to one side, Grantaire to the other, the gray cat in her arms. Liam shuffled his boots in the sand, beating his arms and blowing on his hands, already wishing he had brought a cloak. It was winter, and the early morning air was cold.

The sea must have been colder. The body sprawled in the sand was white and bloated, the skin heavily pruned. There was seaweed laced in the fingers.

"Well," Liam said at last, "some ship is short a sailor. He must have gone overboard." He was aware of a strange intimacy between them, a set of tacit expectations arising from the dead man at their feet. He doubted she understood it, but he had seen it more than once in his life—a sort of embarrassment around the dead that drew strangers together through the knowledge that something must be done.

Grantaire pushed a wayward strand of red hair out of her eyes and gave him a somewhat contemptuous glance. "Thrown overboard is more likely, don't you think? Look at his neck."

He would rather have looked at her at that moment, not because she was pretty, but because the glance she directed his way intrigued him; it seemed to him that she had weighed him, and found him wanting, simply because he had not examined the corpse's neck. Still, he squatted in the sand by the dead man and reached out to brush away some sodden hair.

"Don't touch him," Grantaire commanded.

He frowned and looked up, suddenly feeling more sure of himself with her than he had since she had arrived. "Why? He's beyond hurt, don't you think?"

She was not listening to him, however; her eyes were closed, and she suddenly opened her arms, the cat dropping with a startled squawk. Her lips moved soundlessly for a moment, her fingers twining in strange patterns—small hands with large knuckles, he saw, the skin much creased—and then she opened her eyes again and pressed her lips tight.

"Too long in the water," she muttered. "Very well—you can move him."

"Thank you," Liam said with a slight sarcastic nod. He reached out again, this time taking the man's shoulder and pushing up, trying to roll him over. Touching the corpse did not bother him, though the skin was cold, but his eyes widened and he gave a low whistle when he saw the thin purple line stretching across the man's throat. Time in the sea had puckered and thinned the wound, but it was clear that the cut had been deep and wide.

A sharp breeze off the sea swept over them, snapping Grantaire's cloak around her heels. Liam gently let the man return to his former position, then stood up and dusted his hands on his breeches.

"Well," he said lamely, "I suppose I will have to take him into town."

"Now?" Grantaire asked, as if it were an inconvenience to her. "I need to speak a bit with you—there are things I must do here."

Liam was silent for a long moment, considering her face, which was set in a businesslike expression. There was something hard about her that set him wondering; though he had touched it without reluctance, the corpse washed out of the sea made him sad and uneasy—but she seemed oblivious to it.

How old is she? he wondered, thinking that she could not be much older than thirty, his own age. *Perhaps less.*

"We can't just leave him here," he said, gesturing at the body. "It wouldn't be right."

"Then drag him up the beach," she suggested. "As you said, he's beyond hurt—and I am pressed for time. Take him into the city later."

Master, Fanuilh thought, *you are forgetting your appointment.*

"What appointment?" he said out loud, and then, remembering: "Mistress Priscian!"

At noon, the dragon prompted.

"What is it?" Grantaire demanded.

"I have to go into Southwark anyway—I have some business."

With the slight arching of an eyebrow, she indicated what she thought of his business. "Can't it wait?"

He found himself compelled to make excuses. "Unfortunately not. It has been set for a long time, and it is fairly important." *To me,* he added silently. Gesturing to the corpse, he went on: "Besides, with him . . . I really should take him into Southwark. I have a friend in the Guard who will know what to do."

Grantaire's lips thinned, and she crossed her arms. "Very well. When will you return?"

"I'm not sure," he confessed. "I'm supposed to meet Mistress Priscian at noon, and it may take about an hour or so."

"Mistress Priscian," she repeated, and the skepticism in her tone annoyed him.

"A merchant—an elderly merchant," he said, irritation slipping into his tone. "I should be back by midafternoon, if that will suit you."

The sarcasm was lost on her, but at least her eyebrows relaxed. "It will have to do," she said, and then spun on her heel and walked off towards the house. Her cat sprang after her.

For a long moment Liam stood in the cold, angry at her and at his own lapse in manners. Despite her rudeness, she was his guest. *Uninvited guest,* he told himself, *but still . . .*

Was she always this . . . certain of herself? he asked Fanuilh, once she had entered the house.

She cannot hear our thoughts, the dragon pointed out again, and then sent another thought quickly. *And yes, Master Tanaquil often spoke of her as very self-confident.*

Liam remembered that Tarquin himself had never been much given to politeness or social niceties, but from him it had seemed an old man's eccentricity. In Grantaire, it seemed like rudeness.

Shaking his head, he set himself to moving the corpse further up the beach, away from the grasping fingers of the sea. A wave soaked his boots in the process, but they were solidly made; he cursed and jumped away from the cold water more from reflex than from a fear of wet feet. When the wave retreated, he grabbed the corpse under the arms and dragged it back from the water's edge, the dead man's feet leaving two parallel swathes in the damp sand. Fanuilh watched the whole process impassively.

Liam was sweating by the time he reached the patio, and he was happy to lay the corpse on the stone there and go back into the house. His hands were cold and clammy, covered with salt and sand that had stuck to the dead man's tattered clothing, and he held them out in front of him, eager to wash. He stopped in the entrance hall.

I will have to pick him up again, he thought with a grimace, *to get him on the horse.*

Turning on his heel, he went back out, the sweat cooling in the chill morning air and making him shiver a little bit. There was a shed on the far side of the house where he stabled his horse, and he opened the door.

"Easy, Diamond," he said, though the horse was perfectly calm, brushing a warm greeting past his ear with its lips.

Fanuilh appeared at the door of the shed as he saddled the horse. *You will take the man to Aedile Coeccias?*

"Yes," Liam said, concentrating on cinching the saddle tight with his fingertips, trying not to get too much sand on the leather. Coeccias was the friend he had mentioned to Grantaire; Aedile was his title, and he was actually in charge of Southwark's Guard, the city's chief constable and representative of the Duke of the Southern Tier. "What else?"

His throat has been cut. He has been murdered. You know what the Aedile will say.

Liam paused, Diamond's bridle hanging in his hands. "I hadn't thought of that," he said after a moment. "But that's ridiculous. He washed up on my beach, that's all. Besides, I have too much to do right now."

Nonetheless, he made no move to bridle his roan. Since coming to Southwark half a year before, he had helped the Aedile solve two crimes, and though he thought their success had been mostly dumb luck, Coeccias had developed an exaggerated idea of Liam's skills as an investigator.

In fact, the Aedile thought so much of Liam's skills that he had offered him a special position with the Guard. Liam had accepted, but only on the condition that it be completely unofficial: he could choose which crimes he would investigate. Thus far it had amounted to little more than occasionally discussing crimes with the Aedile, offering his opinions. Liam had enjoyed it as a sort of academic exercise—an ongoing conversation whose subject was always crime.

This, though, would be different. *He will ask me to figure this out.* Liam could easily imagine Coeccias shrugging his heavy shoulders, scratching his beard and saying, "Truth, Rhenford, why else would the man wash himself up on your beach, if not in the faith that you'd con out his murderer?"

Liam's experiences had taught him to be cautious. There were crimes he could profitably look into, and ones he could not—a distinction it had taken him some time to impress upon Coeccias. His arrangement of unofficial consultation had only been in place for a month, and he guessed that his friend would try to turn the dead man's appearance on his beach into a reason for making the position more official.

" 'Truth, Rhenford,' " Liam muttered to himself. "He's probably a pirate, and his ship a dozen leagues off by now. I couldn't catch them even if I wanted to. And that," he said, leveling a finger at Fanuilh, "is exactly what I will tell Coeccias if he gets any ideas about my looking into this."

The dragon merely blinked at him, and after a determined pause, Liam finished preparing the roan and led it out onto the patio. It was surprisingly calm about the corpse, allowing Liam to hoist the dead man across its rump and lash him in place with only a whicker and a nervous sidestep or two. When it was done, he set Fanuilh to watching Diamond and went back inside to wash up.

Grantaire was sitting in the kitchen, her hands folded neatly on the tabletop, which was bare except for the cold coffee. Liam felt a quick pang of guilt at his poor hospitality.

"I'm sorry—would you like some breakfast? I forgot the oven only works for me."

"Some bread," she said, but she clearly had other things on her mind. "I do need to talk to you today."

"So you said." He went to the oven and imagined fresh bread baking; in a moment the smell filled the kitchen. She had said she needed to talk to him, but he could not imagine what about, and he did not want to miss his meeting with the merchant. "I will be back later in the afternoon, but I have to be in the city soon, and with our visitor, a quick trip now makes all the more sense."

He opened the oven and pulled out two fresh loaves, juggling them for a moment, then put one in front of her. She snorted.

"I tell you, he will keep."

"Yes," he agreed, determined not to let his manners lapse again. "Yes, he will—but unfortunately, Mistress Priscian will not."

"Priscian," the wizard repeated, her eyes narrowing and her face growing thoughtful. "I've heard that name before."

"I mentioned it earlier," Liam said, taking a bite of the hot bread to mask his growing sense that Grantaire was both far more eccentric and far less sociable than Tarquin had ever been.

She waved his comment away, carefully breaking her loaf in two and nibbling a corner of one piece. "No, before you said it. I heard the name before you said it."

"In that case, you've probably heard of their jewel—the Priscian Jewel. It's a little famous, though I have to admit that I never heard of it before coming here."

"A jewel?" Grantaire said doubtfully.

"Yes. It is something of a legend in Southwark. There are all sorts of stories about its provenance, but apparently no one has seen it for hundreds and hundreds of years until it was rediscovered a week or so ago. A niece of the Mistress Priscian I know has been making quite a stir by wearing it around town."

"I don't recall any jewel," Grantaire said. "It was something else. The name is definitely familiar. Perhaps I'll look it up in Tanaquil's library while you're busy in town." She gave a sarcastic twist to the word "busy" which he chose to ignore. "Is that what your business with her is about? Are you trying to buy this jewel?"

"No," Liam laughed. "It's supposed to be beyond price. And if a thing is beyond price, it's also below price, useless in a way."

She frowned, digesting this and picking at her bread. "How long will you be?"

"I don't know," he said honestly. "If I leave now, I should be able to be back before sunset. But I have to clean up first," he said, pointing at a big copper basin just behind her.

Grantaire considered the basin, and for a minute he was afraid she would suggest they talk while he washed, but then she gave a resigned sigh and stood up.

"I will leave you to it," she said, as if it were a serious inconvenience. "I would appreciate it if you would come back as soon as you can."

"But of course," he responded, sketching her a quick bow and restraining an inhospitable urge to tell her not to wait up. When she was gone, he frowned down at the loaf in his hand for a full minute, wondering at her rudeness and at the strange impulse he had to be agreeable.

Why do I feel bad that I cannot stay here all day to talk to a woman who can't take the time to be pleasant? he asked himself. *She's not even that pretty.*

Liam was still trying to answer that question when he left the house half an hour later, having hastily scrubbed himself with hot water and put on his best clothes—a matching dark green tunic and breeches with white piping. Grantaire had been true to her word, and when he went to the door of the library to say goodbye, she hardly looked up from the book she was reading.

Grabbing his cloak and settling it around his shoulders, he left the house.

Fanuilh was perched on Diamond's neck, apparently oblivious to the cold; the roan waited patiently under its double burden of corpse and familiar, only snorting a little at the cold wind off the sea.

You should put something over the body, the dragon told him. *It will look strange if you carry a body into the city.*

Liam nodded and quickly gathered a tarp from the shed, which he tucked around his second uninvited visitor.

At least this one I can get rid of, he thought, then climbed into Diamond's saddle with a little grin. Fanuilh rose off the horse's neck and flew on ahead as Liam slapped the reins.

There was a cliff behind the house, and Liam rode up the narrow path that led to its top with his head sunk down in thought, his long chin resting almost on his chest. At the top of the cliff the wind was stronger, and he pulled his cloak close and kicked Diamond into a trot, still thinking, ignoring the beauty of the fresh mantle of snow that covered the bare fields. The roan located the road that led to the city on its own, and Liam let it have its head.

The red-haired wizard filled his thoughts. *What could she want from me? I'm not a wizard. And why am I worried that my meeting with Mistress Priscian will take too long? Why am I trying to accommodate her? She is pretty, but not* that *pretty, and I hope I am not fool enough to have my head turned that easily.*

Diamond trotted along smartly, happy to be out of its cramped shed and enjoying the brisk wind; they were halfway to Southwark before Liam came up with an answer: he felt guilty about living in Tarquin's house. From what Fanuilh had told him, Grantaire had known the old wizard for a very long time, and would have made a far more appropriate heir than Liam. And even if she did not care about the wizard's bequest, he could not help but feel it would make him uncomfortable to find a stranger living in the house of a friend who had recently died.

Tarquin died three months ago, which isn't that recent, he told himself, *and she certainly isn't making much of her mourning. And anyway, he came back from the Gray Lands less than a month ago and told her to expect me, so she couldn't have been that surprised—or hurt.*

It was not a long ride to Southwark, but he arrived quicker than he had expected, the few spires of Temple Street and the merchants' mansions high on the Point coming into view just as he decided to stop thinking about the wizard and concentrate on his own affairs.

Since I came here, he noted, *I have done exactly nothing, except for helping to find Tarquin's murderer, and getting involved in that mess in Temple Street.*

Those had been short incidents, each lasting hardly more than a week, and lately he had begun to feel more and more that he was idling away his time. The days had weighed heavily on him, and the short hours of daylight had come to seem far too long and empty. His unofficial position with the Guard made him little more than the Aedile's sounding board, listening to evidence and offering suggestions, and he had been careful not to let it get beyond that. There was no point in taking on an investigation just because Coeccias thought he was some kind of human bloodhound. The dead man behind him was a perfect example of the sort of thing he did not want to look into: the Aedile was far better suited to investigating that than he was. *And that is what I will tell him,* Liam decided.

The few things Southwark offered that he felt truly qualified for—posts on a sailing ship, as captain, navigator or even surgeon—required introductions and connections which, until recently, he had not had. Until the Aedile, realizing that Liam was unlikely to take a fulltime position with the Guard, grudgingly introduced him to Mistress Priscian.

She was an elderly merchant, with a fleet of seven ships that were rumored to be in poor shape; rumor, in the form of Coeccias, said that was the result of bad management on the part of the captains and factors she hired. Liam had experience as both captain and factor, and what was more, he had a collection of valuable maps that could turn even seven shoddy ships into a treasure fleet. Gathered in the course of long voyages in distant lands, they were the key to rich cities of which Southwark had never heard. He even had proof: he had sold a few of the maps to two different local merchants, and both had visibly prospered in just the few months since. The Aedile arranged an introduction, portraying Mistress Priscian to Liam as a poor old woman sadly in need of guidance.

Liam had liked Mistress Priscian from the start. Within minutes of ushering him into her home on the Point, she explained that she was not a poor old woman sadly in need of guidance, "as the good Coeccias has no doubt told you. And I doubt y' are a poor scholar, sadly in need of a position. So, how shall we treat?"

They had come to a very simple agreement in only two meetings: with his maps and his practical experience as his investment, they would become partners. He would see to the equipping and manning of the ships, as well as the choosing of routes, and she would handle the accounts and provide the money and the ships.

This third meeting was to be the last of their negotiations; a week before, Liam had given her a proposal for the upcoming trading season, and they were to come to a final agreement on it and their partnership.

And even if she does not like the specifics of the plan, I'm sure we will still have a deal, he told himself, smiling slightly at the idea. At last he would have something to do.

Distant bells began to toll ten as he left the fields, and Diamond's hooves clattered as they passed from the frozen ruts of the coast road to the cobbles of Southwark proper. As always when he entered the city, his familiar left him, rising high into the sky. Liam had made it plain that he did not want its company in Southwark; people had too many reasons to think him a wizard as it was.

Fanuilh! Beaming to himself, he formed the thought into a block and projected it at the diminishing dragon, a small form high in the sky overhead. *We are going to be rich and prosperous merchants!*

Yes, master, came his familiar's reply, *as soon as you give the Aedile the corpse.*

"Spoiler," Liam muttered, but the dragon's laconic thought only made him reduce his smile to a grin. "Corpse or no corpse," he went on under his breath, "I'm going to have something to do at last."

■ 2 ■

WINTER REIGNED IN Southwark, and the bustling crowds of summer were gone, but there were still people in the street, bundled up and moving briskly, intent on the holiday. As usual, occasional passersby displayed an awareness of his presence that made him uncomfortable. He had hoped that it would fade, that the Southwarkers would find something else of more interest at which to stare. They had a weeklong holiday to distract them, but some still eyed him furtively: Liam Rhenford, resident wizard. He pretended not to notice, trying to resign himself to it.

Even a goddess walking their streets only distracted them for a week or so, he reminded himself. There had been a goddess in Southwark recently, a new addition to the pantheon named Bellona. Liam preferred not to think about the event, except for the blessed week after her apparition, when everyone had been too busy discussing her to notice him. Now, though, things were back to normal: the odd whisper, the quickly grabbed arm of a companion, the discreet pointing. Not everyone did it, of course—just enough to make him grit his teeth and breathe a sigh of frustration.

Of course, carrying a corpse along with you won't make them think you any more normal, he thought, self-consciously tucking the tarp a little tighter around the stiffening body.

The thin layer of snow on the city square had been scuffed and kicked and ground into black slush around the edges of the cobbles, and though Liam missed the birdsellers and toy vendors that frequented the place in good weather, the stands selling mulled wine and hot food were surrounded with customers, lending an air of festivity to the place. He threaded Diamond through the crowd, drawing the attention to which he had become accustomed and trying to ignore it.

In honor of Beggar's Banquet, long bundles of boughs had been strung across the imposing front of the Duke's Courts, vivid splashes of green against the stone edifice, wound artfully in and among the rows of windows. Someone, perhaps with a sense of humor, had nailed a few thin branches to the front of the building next door to the courts, a squat, ugly barracks that housed both the Guard and the city's jail.

Liam dismounted by the steps that led up to the jail and addressed the guard who stood at the top, munching on a handful of roasted chestnuts.

"Good morning. Is Aedile Coeccias here?"

"Aye, Quaestor Rhenford," the guard replied, choking down a mouthful and descending the steps. Coeccias had given him that title on the two occasions when they had worked together, and though Liam thought it was supposed to be temporary, it had caught on among the Guard, and they would not let it go. "If you'll in, I'll watch your horse."

Liam handed over the reins with a slight smile. "Watch the package there as well, if you would," he said, gesturing at the corpse. "It's for the Aedile." Then he went up the steps.

Most of the building was a single long room, with roaring hearths at either end and a scattering of benches, cots, kegs of liquor and stacks of weapons. A few Guards lingered near the fireplace farthest from the door, and Coeccias was seated at a cheap table by the other, firelight flickering over his broad back and bent head. A piece of paper lay in front of him, and the Aedile was glaring at it suspiciously, a quill protruding from the depths of his beard.

"Good morning," Liam said, pulling off his riding gloves and dropping them on the table. "And a Happy Banquet."

" 'Merry Banquet,' Rhenford," the Aedile said with a scowl, spitting out the quill. "We say 'Merry Banquet,' not 'Happy Banquet.' "

"And a Merry Banquet to you," Liam replied, taking his friend's bad mood in stride. Coeccias's skin was an unhealthy white against his black beard, and the blurred red of his eyes indicated a hangover. "You have been celebrating it already, I can see."

"There's naught to celebrate, neither for me nor you," the Aedile snapped, then took a deep breath and pushed away from the table. "Truth, Rhenford, some mornings it doesn't pay to rise in this city."

Liam guessed that there was something more to his friend's foul mood than just a hangover. He wanted to mention the corpse, but he hesitated, not wanting to add to the other man's burdens and curious about his inclusion in the list of those with nothing to celebrate.

"What's wrong?"

The Aedile sighed and rubbed gingerly at his temples, his eyes closed. "Y' have an appointment with Mistress Priscian this morning, have you not?"

"Yes," Liam said slowly. "What of it?"

"If I were you," Coeccias said, opening his eyes and fixing Liam with a meaningful glance, "I'd postpone it. There's trouble in the Point, and I won't make you guess whose house it has visited."

"What sort of trouble?" Liam asked, suddenly anxious. "Has she died?" Though she was old, Mistress Priscian had seemed remarkably healthy to him.

Coeccias waved the idea away impatiently. "No, no, none of that. The trouble is this—you know the Priscian Jewel?" Liam nodded impatiently. "It's been stolen."

For a long moment both men were silent; while Coeccias nursed his aching head, Liam digested the new idea. He did not see why it should matter to him—as he had told Grantaire, the Jewel was of almost no value, because no one had enough money to buy it. Its theft should not affect the deal he had worked out with Mistress Priscian.

He was about to say this when he realized how selfish it was, and he reconsidered the Aedile's news. If the Jewel had even a tenth of the value and history that rumor accredited it, its loss would certainly be a major blow to Mistress Priscian, and he could hardly expect her to put her mind to lesser things at a time like this.

"I suppose I had better not go there," he said at last, glad he had not spoken right away. He liked the widow, and the more he thought about it, the worse he felt for her. Another idea occurred to him, however, one tied to his earlier thoughts about the Jewel. "But who would steal it? I mean, why?"

"Why?" the Aedile groaned, raising his head from his hands and staring at Liam from bleary eyes. "Why not? Have you seen it?"

"No."

"I saw it just this week, Rhenford," Coeccias said, a note of awe creeping into his tired voice, "at a feast held up on Goddard's Walk. Mistress Priscian's young niece wore it, and it's as beautiful as a star. No, more beautiful than a star. It's as beautiful as a . . . ." For a few long seconds the Aedile groped for a better word, and then gave up. "Anyone would want it. And I have to con out that anyone."

Entirely forgetting about the corpse on his horse, Liam planted himself in front of the table, eager to make Coeccias see his point. "Yes, anyone might want it, but who would steal it? No one could wear it, at least not in Southwark, not when everyone would know whose it really was. And no thief would steal it—who would buy it? There isn't enough money in the whole city to pay for it; you said so yourself."

Frowning, Coeccias stared up at him. "Y'have a point . . . but then, wanting to have is not necessarily wanting to show, if you take my meaning. A miser does not build a golden house, eh?"

"No, but it still makes no sense," Liam said, intrigued by the problem. "A thief who wanted it for show would be unable to show it, and a thief who wanted it for money wouldn't be able to sell it. It makes no sense."

Coeccias interrupted him, clasping his hands over his ears. "Truth, Rhenford, you make my head ache even more. It does not matter if it makes no sense—it happened. The Jewel is gone, the old woman unhappy, and I'm left to delicately foot my way through a houseful of guests with titles and privileges."

"Sorry," Liam said, a little embarrassed. He had grown used to discussing problems like this with Coeccias, and realized he had been too eager in speculating about what was merely an intellectual problem for him. For his friend, it was important business. The Aedile warily removed his hands from his ears, and Liam said lamely, "But you see what I mean."

"Aye, aye," Coeccias conceded, glumly looking at the paper in front of him. "As could anyone, which makes this even harder." He flicked a fingernail at the offending paper, sending it fluttering to the ground.

Liam bent down, retrieved the paper, and put it back on the table without reading it. "What is it?"

"A letter to one of Mistress Priscian's houseguests—or rather, one of her niece's houseguests. You know the niece?"

Liam shook his head.

"There is some small loss in that, for she's a pretty one—but the point is this: she had a houseful of guests last night, any one of whom could have made off with the Jewel. And the house was locked tight, so it had to be one of them."

The Aedile's glum expression told him that the obvious answer to that—search them all—would not do. He waited for his friend to explain why.

"The niece is a lady, married to the present Lord Oakham, which makes her Lady Oakham, and she keeps high company." Coeccias ticked the names off on his fingers: "Earl Uldericus and his wife, the Countess

Perenelle, the young Baron Quetivel, Master Cimber Furseus and his sister, and Master Rafe Cawood. Do you see now my problem?"

"A little, yes." Liam knew that the Aedile had to be careful in dealing with the Southern Tier's nobility, and with the higher-placed merchants, but had never known specifically why.

"And yet it is clearly one of them—Lady Oakham swears the house was shut tighter than a strongbox, and Lord Oakham warrants it, and the servants as well. Which leaves me to send letters, cringing, fawning, sickly things," Coeccias said, his voice wavering between anger and self-mockery. " 'If it please you, milord, may I beg a moment of your time? This most regrettable crime has obliged me . . .' And on and on. It fair makes me sick, Rhenford."

"That does seem hard," Liam said sympathetically, walking to the hearth behind the Aedile's table and warming his hands. Another idea had struck him, but he wanted a moment or two to think it through. "What will you do if they won't talk?"

"What can I do?" the Aedile said to Liam's back. "I can't compel them, and I can't clap them in on suspicion—it'd be worth my post to offend a peer or a man with the Rights of the Town."

"What are those?" He was not really interested, but he had not pursued his thought to its end, and wanted more time.

With another sigh, the Aedile explained. The Rights of the Town were a provision in Southwark's charter, granted by the Dukes of the Southern Tier when the city was founded almost five hundred years before. The merchants who negotiated the charter agreed to pay a slightly higher tax on certain goods; in return the Duke at that time had agreed that any merchants who met a certain property qualification would not be subject to criminal law, unless a vote of similar property holders agreed to it.

"Which means," Coeccias summed up, "that I cannot clap in Master Rafe Cawood—for he meets and exceeds the qualification at least twice over—until the Council of Rights sits and rules on it. And their interests are not always as close to the Duke's as one might want." He gave the last sentence a sarcastic twist, to indicate that the rich men's interests and the Duke's were most often widely separated.

Liam only half heard the explanation; he was reaching a conclusion to the strange thought that had occurred to him. Earlier in the day he had balked at Fanuilh's suggestion that the Aedile might ask him to look into the death of the man on the beach, but now he was considering offering his help in a different crime.

There were many reasons not to get involved: with Grantaire at his house and his deal in the offing with Mistress Priscian, he had more than enough to keep him busy. Besides, the woman might not like the idea of his interfering, might not like him to mix their partnership with this crime. And finally, there was his own reluctance to get involved in an investigation for which he was not sure he was qualified, something he had tried to make clear to Coeccias many times.

But then, he doesn't call me Milord May-Do-Aught for nothing, Liam thought, remembering the nickname the Aedile had once fixed on him. *Let him think me changeable.*

For there were reasons for him to get involved, despite his normal inclination. Mistress Priscian was as good as his partner, pending a final agreement, and he liked her personally; if there was any good he could do that would help her, it might also cement their business relationship, and he had come to realize that that was important to him. And the nature of the theft—all the suspects being more or less above the law as represented by Coeccias—might make his participation valuable. He had no official standing, and thus could look into things on his own, and no nobleman or rich merchant could cry up the Rights of the Town in the face of a private investigation.

They might send a bodyguard or two after you, he reminded himself ruefully; while searching out Tarquin's murderer, he had run afoul of a merchant who had done just that. He winced a little by the fire, recalling the beating the bodyguards had inflicted on him. *Still. . . . still, it would be interesting,* he admitted to himself, and he also guessed that he might be better than the bluff Aedile at wriggling around the delicate sensibilities of landed gentry and pretentious merchants.

"I wonder," he mused aloud, almost a full minute after Coeccias had finished his explanation of the Rights of the Town, "whether I might not go see Mistress Priscian after all."

He was not prepared for his friend's reaction: the Aedile threw back his chair and turned quickly, hands spread in a nervous gesture. "It would not do, Rhenford, it would not do," he said hastily. "It would not pay to go there just now."

"Why not?"

The Aedile blushed and stammered. "Look you, the widow has strange ideas, and she's like to act on them without consideration."

"What do you mean?" Liam asked, though he had an inkling, and hid a grin behind his hand.

"I may have . . . planted an idea in her," Coeccias said, "when I was crying you up to her as a partner. I may have said too often what a help you had been to me, and what a one you were for solving riddles and searching out misdeeds. For that she has had problems with her factors, and been cheated, and I thought it a recommendation, see you?"

Liam was silent, rubbing his chin to pull down his growing smile, and finally Coeccias said, "And so if you go to see her today, she'll ask you to con out the Jewel, Rhenford. She as much as said so, when I saw her this morning. She said, 'I wonder what young Rhenford would make of this.'"

With a certain perverse pleasure, Liam let his smile show. "I don't know what I will make of it, but it would be interesting to see, don't you think?"

Coeccias's blush faded, and he stopped wringing his hands; a faintly suspicious look crept across his face. "Do you mean you'll take it on?"

"I was thinking about it, yes." Liam's smile grew a little troubled at the expressions warring on his friend's face—confusion mostly, with a touch of exasperation and a small amount of hope. "I don't know what I could do," he added quickly. "I'm not the human bloodhound you always make me out to be, but I think I might give it a try, if you don't mind." The hope bothered him the most; the last thing he wanted was for Coeccias to think the theft solved simply because he had said he would look into it.

"Mind? Truth, Rhenford, it would ease a great load from my mind, to have it solved so neatly."

Liam winced, his smile completely gone. "It's not solved, Coeccias, just because I say I will look into it."

The other man waved the objection away, rising from the table. "As near as makes no difference, once you set yourself to it." He rubbed his hands together briskly, a broad smile now shining through his ill-kempt beard. "Come now—we'll to Mistress Priscian's, and she'll tell you all you need to know."

He strode purposefully past Liam, snatching a jacket from a peg and throwing open the door. "You there," he called to the guard at the door, "watch Quaestor Rhenford's horse! We're off to the Point!"

Liam shook his head at the fire, thinking that he had just made a great mistake. There was no way to dampen the Aedile's enthusiasm, no way to keep him from raising expectations of success in whatever investigation Liam made—particularly Mistress Priscian's expectations.

And what if I fail? he wondered, turning resignedly from the fire and following his friend. *She has agreed to this partnership mostly because of Coeccias's glowing recommendation of me—and if I fail in this, the thing he thinks me best at, what then?*

"Gods!"

The Aedile's shout interrupted his self-doubt and, suddenly remembering the thing that had brought him to the jail in the first place, he ran to the door.

Coeccias was holding the dead man's head by the hair, raising it to inspect the cut throat. The guard stood nearby, gazing with morbid fascination as the wound gaped open; a crowd, drawn by the Aedile's shout, had begun to gather.

"Do you fish now with men as bait, Rhenford?" Coeccias drew a piece of seaweed from the corpse's hair, dropped it with a little grimace of disgust and wiped his hand on his jacket. "Where is this from?"

"I found him on my beach this morning," Liam explained, jumping down the steps and gesturing for the Aedile to keep his voice down. "Washed up. You see his throat?"

"Aye," Coeccias said, stepping back and considering the body. He sucked contemplatively at his teeth for a moment, then dismissed the whole thing with another wave of his hand. "Thrown from a ship, no doubt. Another one for the morgue." He turned to the guard and snapped a series of decisive orders. "See the corpse to Mother Japh's morgue, and have her get the description out. Send a man down to the waterfront—have Balstain go, he'll ask the right questions—see if a ship's missing a man, or if any know this one. And see that the Quaestor's horse is stabled. I'll be back in an hour; mind it's all done by then!"

The Guard saluted loosely and led Diamond away toward the Duke's Courts; the crowd that had gathered parted for him with a whisper of disappointment. They had clearly been expecting something more exciting, and Liam was annoyed, if not surprised, to notice that a few of them aimed their disappointed looks at him, as if he were supposed to provide something more exciting than a man thrown from a ship.

Having disposed of the body, Coeccias took Liam by the arm and steered him across the square, in the direction of the Point. Liam let himself be drawn along, frowning crossly. The Aedile began to describe what Mistress Priscian had told him about the theft, but Liam was not paying attention. He was thinking of the other man's first question, and wondering how many people on the square had heard it.

It sometimes seemed as if everyone he knew and everything he did, no matter how innocent, were conspiring to create an aura of mystery around him, to provide fodder for the city's ridiculous idea that he was a wizard. Riding into town with a corpse behind him was bad enough; then Coeccias had to compound the problem by shouting out nonsense.

I can hear it now, Liam thought. *'You know that wizard on the beach? He fishes for sharks, with live men as bait!'* In every tavern and wineshop

from here to Auric's Park, they will be telling that one for days. Soon enough
children will be crossing their fingers at me, and trying to avoid my shadow.

"Why did you say that, about fishing with men as bait?" he burst out
as they left the square and turned onto one of the roads leading up to the
Point, interrupting the Aedile in mid-sentence.

"Eh?"

The evident confusion on his friend's face mollified him a little.
"Never mind," he said. "What were you saying?"

The two men were an odd pair as they walked through the streets
towards the Point: Liam tall and thin, his blond hair cut short, leather
boots gleaming beneath the hem of his expensive cloak, and the Aedile
short and massive, his unruly hair and beard making him look like a bear
dressed up in a plain quilted jacket.

Southwark went no higher than the Point, in money or elevation, but
the rich who made their homes there had built themselves into a corner.
The area was small, hemmed in on the north and west by less wealthy
neighborhoods and to the south and east by sheer cliffs that descended to
the cold winter sea. Unable to expand, they had gone up, assembling
narrow-fronted stone and brick homes of five and six stories along streets
whose width and straightness made a great contrast to the twisted arter-
ies further down the hill. Liam and Coeccias turned finally onto the last
of these broad, rich streets—the highest in the city and named, appropriately enough, End Street—and headed to one of the last houses in the
row.

Unpretentious for the Point, Mistress Priscian's house would still
have been out of place anywhere else: it had five tall-windowed stories
and an elegantly tapered roof; the bricks were respectably aged and
trimmed with beige stone; and the stairs that led up to the front door
were of the same stone, as were the broad banisters that flanked them.

"Truth," the Aedile said, pausing at the bottom of the steps and
pitching his voice close to a whisper, "you can see that it's trickish: none
in the house but close friends rich and titled, stout locks without, and the
Jewel gone."

"Trickish," Liam agreed impatiently. Throughout their walk, and
Coeccias's retelling of Mistress Priscian's story, he had been assailed by
doubts. It was not too late to back out, certainly—he had said nothing to
Mistress Priscian, and Coeccias was too good-natured to think the worst
of him—but he could not. He saw himself as committed, however impul-
sively, to at least try, and knew that the doubts were natural, second
thoughts a habit with which he should long since have learned to deal.

Let's get this begun, he told himself, and went up the steps, the Aedile behind him.

He had hardly knocked before a servant answered the door; the man nodded somberly at both men and ushered them in. "My lady is in the solarium just now, sirs, with her niece. If you will wait . . ." He did not offer them an option, turning on his heel and disappearing into the depths of the house.

Liam wondered once again at the average southerner's looseness with titles; Mistress Priscian was not noble, and in the Midlands where he had grown up, calling someone a lady who was not would have been considered something of a serious offense. *But then,* he reasoned, *we had no rich merchants, only noblemen and knights and peasants. And no one would call a peasant 'lady.'*

The house was a little gloomy, the walls and floors and furniture of heavy, unreflective wood, with thick hangings in dark colors; Liam and Coeccias waited in an uncomfortable silence for the servant to return, which he did quickly, somewhat flushed. "My lady bids you come in."

"Right in," corrected a voice from further down the dark hallway. "I bid them to come right in, and not be kept standing about the door."

Liam smiled a little and went forward towards the owner of the voice, stepping into the solarium at the far end of the hall. It was a large room at the corner of the house, with tall windows looking out onto a small garden and, beyond, to a breathtaking view of the sea. White-painted walls gathered the meager sunlight, an almost blinding contrast to the dark hall. There were two women; Liam offered bows to both.

Thrasa Priscian was in almost all ways unremarkable—neither tall nor short, with a plain face just beginning to show the wrinkles of age, gray hair pulled back in a loose but tidy bun, a plain smoke-gray dress— yet it was to her, Liam noticed, and not to her considerably younger and far prettier niece, that one's attention was drawn. He thought briefly that it was her eyes, which were sharp and intelligent, or perhaps simply her immobility: in all the solarium, she alone was still. The sea beyond the windows glinted and shifted, the naked limbs of the trees in the garden swayed silently, sunlight rippled along the walls, and her niece twisted and turned in her chair, scarcely acknowledging the two men—but the old woman simply sat on a low divan, more like stone in her dress than smoke, and commanded attention.

"Y' are somewhat early," she observed to Liam, a slight nod and a grim smile adding weight to her comment. "I imagine y' have heard something of our trouble?"

"Yes," he said. "Coeccias told me."

"I see. Duessa, would you leave us for a moment?"

As she obeyed her aunt's politely phrased command, Liam noted that the niece's eyes were red-rimmed and puffy, and her face was extremely pale; she seemed to be taking the theft much harder than her aunt, who calmly motioned the men to the two delicate cane chairs opposite her as soon as her niece had stumbled out, a handkerchief pressed to her mouth.

"I imagine also that Coeccias has told you that I'm interested in what you might have to say about it," Mistress Priscian began as soon as they were seated. "He has made much of you as a solver of mysteries, you know."

Liam smiled and at the same time made a deprecatory gesture with his hands. He liked Mistress Priscian's straightforward manner, and also recognized that she was giving him a chance to set his own terms: he could simply give his opinion, go over the things he had said to Coeccias back at the jail, or he could offer to probe more deeply into the theft.

"First, let me say that Coeccias's idea of my talents is vastly exaggerated." The Aedile snorted loudly, but Mistress Priscian merely gave a noncommittal nod, accepting the statement but reserving judgement. "And I'm not sure that any thoughts I might have to offer—or any help I might give—would be of any use."

"Ha!" Coeccias said.

"Hush!" Mistress Priscian ordered, her attention still on Liam. He found himself sitting on the edge of his seat, with his hands clasped between his knees and his back held uncomfortably straight; it was a position he always adopted around the old woman. He always felt around her as if her were presenting himself to one of his masters at the university in Torquay—a well-liked master, but a master nonetheless.

"That said," he went on, "I must confess that I am interested, and would very much like to help in any way I can."

Coeccias was fairly writhing in his seat, gripping the arms of the chair and shaking his head.

"My only real reservation," Liam continued, searching for the right words to express a delicate idea, "is that I am afraid that my looking into this might damage our business relationship. As far as I can see, anything of this kind requires asking a number of questions, and peering into corners that people might wish . . . unpeered into. Do you see?" He blushed a little at the awkward sentence, but it was the best he could do to explain, without using an example he did not want to bring up. While searching for Tarquin's murderer, he had struck up a friendship with a Southwark merchant and his wife, but the investigation had revealed a number of things about their marriage that made it impossible for the friendship to continue—and he did not want a similar thing to happen to his partnership with Mistress Priscian.

She nodded once, to show she understood. "Ah, Master Rhenford, I would that there were things in my life that would not stand the light of day, but there are not. As for my niece and her household," she went on, her face growing hard, "I have no fear of aught you may discover there, and would be sure not to hold you to blame for any of their dark corners."

It was not quite the answer he had expected, and for a moment he floundered, his hands tapping on his knees and his glance going to Coeccias, who shrugged. Then, with brisk, precise movements, Mistress Priscian stood and walked to a small desk; retrieving a large sheet of heavy paper, she handed it to Liam.

"This, I think, should allay your fears, Master Rhenford. It is our contract, and as you can see, I have put my seal to it."

Pleasantly surprised, Liam glanced over the sheet; beneath the neat, compressed handwriting of a clerk, he found Mistress Priscian's seal, a neat red oval, the edges of the wax evenly trimmed. The space for his own signature, for he had no seal, was empty.

Grinning despite himself, he looked up from the contract, and Mistress Priscian nodded decisively.

"There," she said, "y' have it. When you sign it, we are partners. Now, may we see what can be done about my family's Jewel?"

"Aye," Coeccias burst out, "may we get on with it, Rhenford?"

Liam looked once more at the contract, running his thumb along the crisp edge of the paper, and then folded it carefully and tucked it into his tunic.

"Yes," he said. "Let us see what can be done."

■ *3* ■

"I ASSUME AEDILE Coeccias has told you what he learned this morning?" Mistress Priscian asked.

"Which was precious little," the Aedile pointed out.

"No," the woman agreed, frowning. "I am afraid Duessa was not much help. She was quite . . . excited. She has calmed down a great deal since then."

Liam did not doubt that Mistress Priscian had been the calming agent, and that she might not have been very gentle about it; the way she said "excited" made him think she would not have much patience for hysterics.

"He told me something, but I think it would be better to hear it again."

Mistress Priscian nodded, and quickly outlined the same story Coeccias had told him earlier: the Oakhams had given a party, the guests had stayed the night, and in the morning the Jewel was gone. She named the same guests Coeccias had mentioned—Baron Quetivel, the Furseuses, brother and sister, Earl Uldericus and his wife, the merchant Cawood—but where Coeccias had spoken of them with frustration, because he could not approach them, there was a coldness in the widow's tone as she listed them.

"The thief, of course, is one of those," she said finally. "There are no servants in the house at night, and there are good locks all about."

"And no sign of a break-in," Coeccias supplied sadly, as if he had hoped there would be. "We conned the house entire, and all was tight as a drum."

"I should hope not," Mistress Priscian told him, and then turned to Liam. "I bought the locks, and made sure they were strong. So the Jewel was taken by someone in the house, which means one of my niece's guests. The question then is, which one? And, as Aedile Coeccias has explained to me, how to prove it?"

Liam was silent for a moment, a little lost in admiration for the old woman. She did not act as if she had lost a priceless treasure; she might have been discussing a minor domestic annoyance, a broken dish or a burnt meal. She steepled her hands in her lap and settled a patient look upon him, clearly waiting for him to begin solving the problem.

"Well," he said, clearing his throat, "it is tricky. Since Coeccias cannot question the guests in any official capacity, we thought I might try to talk to them unofficially, as a private person, if you see what I mean."

The old woman nodded approvingly.

"And to do that, I will need to know a great deal more about, well, about everything—the Jewel, each guest, exactly what happened last night, who slept where and that sort of thing. Little details are important, and, as I said, I may ask questions that are not easily answered."

She accepted the warning with another slight frown, and then, straightening in her chair, began to talk.

"The Jewel first, I suppose. It has been in my family for as long as it has been a family. . . ."

The Priscians were old in Southwark, one of the first families to settle there when the city was established. The first Priscian of note had sailed to Alyecir as a soldier of Auric the Great in the Ghost War, and had somehow come out of that conflict with merchant contacts in Alyecir and the Freeports. With those and some luck, he had established a small trading fleet and acquired land on the Point, where he built the house in which they sat. He had two sons, one of whom was unremarkable except in that he continued in his father's footsteps, maintaining the small family fortune and having sons of his own.

The other son, however, was different.

"His name was Eirenaeus," the widow said, "and there are a number of family legends attached to him, most of which I think are ridiculous."

He was supposed to have been, alternately, a goblin cradle-switched with the first Priscian's son, or a normal man who practiced black magic and trafficked with demons. Whichever the case, at some point in his life he acquired the Jewel, and bound it up with the family name in such a way that the two were, in Southwark legend, inseparable.

"You are not from Southwark, Master Rhenford, or you would probably have heard the stories. I flatter myself that they are rather widespread. Currently, the Jewel is considered no more than a priceless stone, but in earlier days, it was believed to be far more than that. My father told me that his father told him it was the crystalized heart of a demon that Eirenaeus had enslaved, though he did not himself believe it." She left unclear which man had not believed it, and her normally composed face grew pensive. "It is not, of course—but it is quite remarkable. I would that I could show you it. I made a grave mistake in bringing it out."

She lapsed into a brooding silence, leaving Liam to snap her out of it with an uncomfortable cough. The rumors about the Jewel were mildly interesting, but irrelevant.

"Perhaps you could explain that—bringing it out, I mean."

The old woman came back to herself with a self-assurance Liam could only envy, and addressed his question directly. "It is the symbol of the house, you know—much like the Goddards' bauble, or Marcius's rising sun. But we Priscians have never been much on show, unlike those two, and so for as long as I can remember it has been locked away in the family crypt. Certainly I can never remember my father taking it out—though of course we could see it, on remembrance days, or when making special prayers to the family fathers. It simply sat in the crypt, on Eirenaeus's tomb. As a child I was very impressed by it, though I never wanted to touch it."

"But you did?"

Mistress Priscian gave a small, bitter sigh. "Yes. There are no men in my family anymore, Master Rhenford, and so, as head of the household, I must perform many of the observances usually reserved for the eldest male." The Aedile nodded sagely, and Liam followed suit, though he was not overly familiar with the southern forms of ancestor worship. He had on occasion made small offerings for his father, but more to ease his conscience than out of any real conviction. The woman directed her comments now to Coeccias. "You will know, Master Aedile, that many families offer thanks to their fathers in the weeks before the Banquet."

"Illustrious ones, certainly," Coeccias agreed, tugging at his beard. "It is common enough," he added, for Liam's benefit.

"In any case," Mistress Priscian went on, completely ignoring the Aedile's compliment, "the time came for the usual offering, but I was slightly indisposed—nothing important, a mere fever—but I was somewhat unsteady on my feet, and so I asked my niece to assist me.

"Duessa is my brother's only child," she said, pursing her mouth a little, "and has suffered all the ill effects one might expect from being raised by an indulgent and weak-willed man. What one might excuse in an older brother, one finds somewhat trying in a child. Oh, she joined me readily enough—I do not fault her there—but it was her first sight of the Jewel, and I had not counted upon her reaction. I had never wanted to touch it, so why should she?"

With a start, Liam remembered that he was not simply listening to an interesting story, though he found it intriguing enough; he was supposed to be gathering information. "How had she never seen it before? You had seen it when you were a child—why hadn't she?"

Mistress Priscian gave another sigh. "My brother would not allow it, would not allow her into the crypt. He thought the sight of so many dead would not be good for her. My brother was a peculiar man, Master Rhenford, and not a very good parent. He considered the girl too high-strung to visit the crypt. And I must confess that I never argued the point with him. Indeed, I would not have asked her there if I had not been sick."

"But if she never saw the crypt," Coeccias said, "how could she carry on with the services?"

Liam shot his friend a discouraging glance—the future of the Priscian family's religious observances was of no interest to them.

"I hope," the woman explained readily, "that my niece will have a child—a boy, preferably—before I am unable to perform the rites. And if not, then there are other possible arrangements. A sum left to the temple of Laomedon will assure remembrance."

"Ah, in course," the Aedile said, as though it should have been obvious. Despite the pointlessness of the question, it brought a strange thought to Liam: that he had learned more about Mistress Priscian and her family in the past half hour than he had in two weeks.

"In any case," he said, returning the discussion to the matter at hand, "she saw the Jewel then?"

"Yes, and was quite taken with it. My brother—a weak-willed man, I have said—never refused her a thing, and I have yet to break her of the habit. And so, once the rites were over and before I could say a word, she took it off Eirenaeus's breast—" She paused at the look of horror that crossed Liam's face, and then shook her head and explained none too patiently: "Not his actual breast, Master Rhenford; it was on his effigy, on the cover of his sarcophagus." She clucked a little at his relieved look. "His effigy, in course. As I have said, Duessa has never been refused a thing, and I was not well. And so I allowed her to convince me that she should wear it. In public! I do not pretend that it was the proper thing—

we are not a family given to show, as I have said. But there it is: I allowed her."

"It was a success, I understand."

"Success!" The Aedile rolled his eyes. "It was bruited all over Southwark! Truth, you could hardly pass a man in the street without a word on the rediscovery of the Priscian Jewel!"

Mistress Priscian sniffed delicately, as if she did not wish to be reminded of the widespread discussion of the Jewel. " 'Rediscovery'! It was never lost! But it should have remained where it was, that is undeniable. We Priscians have no desire to be the talk of the town, I can assure you. Though I must confess that I did not at the time think it necessarily a bad thing." She focused on Liam for a moment. "Given our arrangements, I did think that some word might be spread of the family, to prepare the way for the announcement of our activities. I trust you have no objection?"

"Not at all," he hastened to assure her. A public display of wealth like the Jewel would have made credit easier to obtain—and they would need credit for the voyages he proposed. Again, though, they were straying from the real question, and he attempted to redirect them. "So she wore the Jewel in public?"

"Yes," she replied, with a prim moue of distaste. "It was long ago set in a necklace of gold, so that it might be worn. And wear it she did—to as many balls and feasts and dances as she could."

"So a great many people would have had a chance to see it?"

"All of Southwark," Coeccias threw in, to Mistress Priscian's discomfort, though she did not deny it.

"Yes, all of Southwark, as the Aedile says. Though I do not see that it matters—I have said that the doors and windows were locked. It must have been one of my niece's guests."

Liam held up a hand for patience. "I know, but it is best to be certain that everyone knew of it."

"Oh, they did, Rhenford, they did," Coeccias assured him, drawing another pained look from Mistress Priscian.

"Then we can assume that everyone who was staying here last night was aware that the Jewel was here? Did she wear it last night?"

"I do not think she stopped wearing it," Mistress Priscian said drily. "If I did not know better, I would say she slept with it, though she did not. I insisted that she return it to the crypt each night. I saw to it myself. And I must also say the guests did not stay here. They stayed next door, in my niece's home."

Liam shifted in his chair, leaning forward. "Your niece does not live here?"

"No, she lives next door, as I just said. The original Priscian father built only this house at first, and then added the second for his second son. The two are both mine, since my brother's death. I allow Duessa and her husband to live in the other."

"And where is the crypt?"

Mistress Priscian nodded, as if she had been expecting the question. "It runs underneath the two houses—there are entrances in both cellars. They are always locked, and were still this morning, when Duessa came over to retrieve the Jewel for whatever pointless frolic she had planned for today."

With a look at Coeccias to see if his request was acceptable, Liam asked if they might see the crypt. Before the Aedile could respond, Mistress Priscian did, rising quickly.

"In course, in course. It is as good place to start as any. And after that?"

Liam froze in the middle of rising himself. "After that? I suppose we should talk to your niece, if we may."

The answer seemed to satisfy her: she nodded, and led the way back to the hallway. Taking up a shielded candle, she turned into another hall that went to a large, very neat kitchen. The servant who had let them in stopped his work at the iron stove and faced his mistress with an expectant air.

"I need your keys, Haellus."

Haellus unhooked a large ring from his belt and brought it jingling to Mistress Priscian's waiting hand.

"We will be in the crypt for some time, I expect. I am not in to any callers."

The servant nodded and returned to his work, stoking the stove with coal. There was a door next to the coal bin; Mistress Priscian unlocked it with one of the keys from the ring, paused to light her candle and then descended the steps beyond.

Liam went down after her, trailing one hand along the cold brick of the steep, narrow staircase, ducking his head to avoid the low ceiling. The candle showed a typical storeroom, crates and barrels and bins on all sides. Mistress Priscian went straight to a far corner of the room, where three shallow steps descended to an ancient wooden door with a rounded top. She selected the proper key from the ring and inserted it in the large lock; it turned without a noise.

The hinges of the door creaked only a little when she opened it, revealing a small antechamber with an iron grill at the far end that gave onto a dimly lit space. There were shelves cut into the stone walls on either side of the antechamber, and two primed lanterns waiting on the right shelf. Mistress Priscian lit them both, handing them to the two men and keeping the candle for herself.

A gust of cold wind suddenly blew through the iron grill, setting Liam shivering. Mistress Priscian did not seem to notice it. She unlocked the grill but held it with one hand, turning to the two men.

"I need hardly remind you that this is my family's crypt."

"In course," the Aedile said, bowing his head for a moment, and Liam nodded gravely.

Satisfied with their attitudes, she pushed open the grill and motioned them to follow her in.

The crypt was all stone, a long room with a number of bays opening off either side. Five large sarcophagi lay spaced along the middle of the floor, but what interested Liam most was the spill of light that entered from the left side of the room. His hands clasped respectfully behind his back, he walked past the silent stone coffins and the yawning bays until he reached the center of the room, and looked out on the sea.

There were five bays on the right side of the room, all lined with what looked like tiers of sailor's bunks carved from stone—each bunk containing the shrouded remains of some Priscian—but on the left there were only four; where the middle bay should have been was a short passageway that led to a simple balcony. Another cold, salt-laden breeze met him as he stepped out onto the balcony, resting his hands on the waist-high balustrade. Above him, an overhang of rock formed a pitted roof, and below there was only a long drop into the sea. He could see water boiling at the base of the Point. *No way in here,* he decided.

"A whim of the first Priscian," the woman said from behind him. "He wished always to be able to see the ocean. My father often used to come here to watch for ships, though of course few enough come from the east."

Liam nodded, and allowed her to lead him back into the main part of the crypt. She rested her hand for a moment on the middle sarcophagus, the one that faced the open balcony.

"The first Priscian," she whispered. Her hand laid on the stone fingers of her ancestor's effigy, clasped over the stone chest. The broken haft of a mace protruded above and below the fingers; a foot or so of the handle and the wickedly spiked head lay next to the stone body. "The weapon he carried when he fought for Auric the Great," Mistress Priscian explained. "It's been like that for as long as I can remember." The statue was worn and pitted from centuries of exposure, and Liam resisted the urge to raise his lantern and examine the face; he did not think she would appreciate his purely aesthetic interest in her ancestor's features.

After an appropriate pause, she said, "And this is Eirenaeus," gesturing with her candle at the bay immediately behind the sarcophagus of the first Priscian. There were no bunks in this middle bay, just a single sarcophagus. The effigy on the lid was much larger than that of the first Priscian; close to eight feet long, with massive stone hands almost double the size of Liam's and a broad chest.

"The Jewel rested there," Mistress Priscian said, and this time Liam did raise his lantern, moving along the side of the coffin to get a better look. Shallow grooves an inch wide had been cut in the effigy's shoulders and across its chest; where they met was a slightly deeper depression almost three inches wide. He suppressed a whistle of astonishment.

If that's where the Jewel lay, he thought, *it must be huge.*

He raised his lantern higher and peered at the face of the effigy. If it bore any resemblance to the real Eirenaeus, he had been a cruel-looking man. His lips were thin, compressed in a stern frown, his nose small but obviously broken once. The stone eyes were open, but they did not look unfocused, the way those of most statues did—they seemed to Liam to be attempting to bore holes through the roof of the crypt, and he did not look at them for long.

"I placed it here myself last night," Mistress Priscian said. "My niece being quite . . . carried away by her festivities."

Liam touched the depression where the Jewel had lain; it was cold and slightly damp. He took his finger away quickly and wiped it on his breeches. The wetness did not surprise him; he was only surprised that the rest of the room was not equally damp. He had expected decay and the stench of rottenness, or at the very least mold—but apart from a slight mustiness, and the sea salt, there were no smells.

"And then you locked the crypt?"

"Yes." Her tone left no question about it.

"And gave the keys to Haellus?"

"No," she said, equally firmly. "Haellus left the house yesternight after serving dinner, to celebrate the Banquet with his brother's family. I used my own keys; they were in my bedchamber all night—they are there still."

"And the door into your niece's house?" Coeccias asked, pointing to the far end of the room, where an iron grate stood, a twin of the one through which they had entered.

"It was locked as well. Haellus and I have the only keys to the crypt."
She held up the ring to make her point.

Liam threw Coeccias a questioning glance; the Aedile responded
with a shrug, and the two men walked to the far grate. It swung inward at
Liam's tug.

Mistress Priscian's eyes bulged, but her lips pressed against each
other in a way that reminded Liam of the effigy of Eirenaeus.

"I have not unlocked that door in years!" she said. "I am quite sure
of it!"

Liam looked again at Coeccias, who shrugged again. "We didn't con
this one—with all the outer windows and doors tight, who'd have thought
of it?"

Mistress Priscian protested: "But no one ever enters through here!"

Liam frowned. "Mistress Priscian, if it was one of your niece's guests,
they had to have entered this way—unless the houses are connected
above?"

For the first time, he saw her at a loss—and he did not like it. It did
not seem fair, somehow, that simply because she had had the misfortune
to be robbed, he should be able to observe her at such moments. *Let
alone tour her family crypt,* he added to himself. *How long would we have
been partners before I saw this place?*

Moreover, he did not like pointing out her false assumption: that
because *she* always entered the crypt through her own basement, the
thief would have, too. What bothered him even more was that Coeccias
seemed to have accepted the assumption as well; he knew his friend was
smarter than that. *Probably the hangover,* Liam thought.

She stammered for a moment, then nodded somewhat distractedly.
"No, they are not. In course. Yes, they must have come through here. But
it was locked!"

Liam knelt down next to the grate. "Hold your lantern there," he
told the Aedile, and examined the lock carefully. There were small
scratches on the blacked plate, and scorings around the keyhole itself.
"May I see the key?" Mistress Priscian reluctantly handed it to him, the
rest of the ring dangling heavily from it. There were a number of intricate teeth. He stood, handing back the ring.

"It looks like it has been picked," he said to Coeccias, and then
stepped into the antechamber and pushed at the wooden door there. It
opened, revealing a set of steps and a cellar much like Mistress Priscian's. The second lock revealed some of the same signs. "This one as
well."

The Aedile blew out an angry breath. "What does that tell us,

Rhenford? Only what we already knew—that it was someone in the house. It likes me not—"

"And to think she invited them in!" Mistress Priscian said at the same time.

Liam interrupted them both: "More than that. Think of the people who were staying there. Some noblemen, their wives, a rich merchant? Do you really think they could have picked a lock? Can you pick a lock?"

"In course not!"

"No," the Aedile said, a bit more slowly. "Y' are thinking of something, Rhenford. Unless I miss my guess, y' are thinking of someone else."

"Why not?" It certainly made sense to him, at least: he did not doubt that both entries into the crypt had been locked, and he was equally sure that none of Mistress Priscian's niece's guests could have picked both locks. One might have been luck, but two was out of the question. "We can certainly assume that one of the guests is responsible—but why shouldn't they have outside help? And it gives us another interesting area to explore."

"Aye," Coeccias agreed, catching Liam's reference. "That it does."

Mistress Priscian looked at both of them skeptically. "Say you that someone allowed a common thief into my niece's house? How can you possibly know that?"

The Aedile took the question with a small bow. "We cannot know it, madam, but it seems most likely. I'd not list lockpicking among the guests' many parts, given their eminent station."

" 'Eminent station,' " the woman snorted. "Common thieves!"

"Speaking of which," Liam said, "perhaps we had best see your niece. And her husband, as well."

For a moment, she gave him a strange look, as if he had suggested something scandalous, and then her face cleared. "In course, in course. We may as well go up through the cellar, since it is so *conveniently* open."

The Oakhams' house was built as a mirror of Mistress Priscian's: they emerged from the cellar into a kitchen, but Liam was immediately struck by the differences. Where Haellus had been performing his work in an orderly way, here there was only a mess: dirty dishes piled high, scraps of food on the floor, crates filled with empty wine bottles, and a pair of fat hunting dogs snoring contentedly around the remains of a roast.

Mistress Priscian sniffed with distaste and quickly led the way out.

The hallways were plastered white, and were much brighter than those in the other house. Liam noted that the mess from the kitchen seemed to trail out into the other rooms; there were splashes of wine on one wall, and a plate had been shattered at the entrance to the room where they found Lady Oakham.

It was the equivalent of Mistress Priscian's solarium, except that it looked out on a small terrace instead of a garden, and there were eight divans arranged in a circle, instead of the older woman's simple chairs. Lady Oakham lay on one of the divans, moaning and sobbing quietly, with one arm thrown over her puffy face. A woman knelt at her side, trying to dab at her temples with a wet cloth.

"Becula!" Mistress Priscian commanded, her hands clenched into fists. "That kitchen is filthy. This house is filthy." She took an angry step forward, crunching broken shards of plate underfoot.

The kneeling woman turned sharply, a sneer on her face. "My lady is ill, madam!" As if to confirm this, Lady Oakham groaned and rolled over, trying to hide her face in the cushions of the divan.

"Nonsense. She drank too much, and now she is having hysterics. Go and clean the kitchen."

"My lady is ill," the servant repeated, and resolutely turned her back on Mistress Priscian. Liam and Coeccias shared an uncomfortable glance.

The old woman drew herself up. "Becula!" she barked.

Lady Oakham groaned again. "Oh, do as she says, Becca, please. I can't bear it!"

Becula rose stiffly, tossing the wet cloth down on the divan. "Yes, my lady." She strode grandly out of the room, brushing insolently past Mistress Priscian; Liam and Coeccias hurriedly parted to make room for her.

"Now, Duessa," the old woman said, advancing on the divan. "I have brought the Aedile and Master Rhenford, and you must speak with them."

"Oh, Aunt Thrasa, can't they come back later?" the girl begged, her face still hidden in the cushions. "I can't possibly see them now!"

In turning over, Lady Oakham's sky-blue robe had ridden up, and Liam found he could see all the way up to the backs of her knees. The robe hugged the rest of her body tightly. He flushed and turned to Coeccias, taking the Aedile's arm and angling him away from the divan.

"Perhaps we should come back later," he whispered.

"Aye," the other man agreed nervously. "She was not so distraught earlier."

"Come, Duessa, you are acting like a child," Mistress Priscian chided the girl. "If they cannot talk to you, they cannot find the Jewel!"

"Hang the Jewel," Lady Oakham cried. "I'm going to be sick!"

"Gentlemen," Mistress Priscian began, horror in her voice—but Liam and Coeccias were already heading down the hall.

"Mayhap we can trouble Lord Oakham," Coeccias whispered to Liam.

"We will return at another time," he called over his shoulder.

They hurried out of the house by the front door, followed by the unmistakable sound of Lady Oakham being sick.

■ 4 ■

"OVERMUCH CELEBRATING," THE Aedile said with a wink, once they were safely on the stoop.

"I should think so," Liam said, his grin a little weaker than his friend's. He was thinking more of Mistress Priscian's discomfort than her niece's; it still did not seem fair to him that he should be granted this glimpse into her personal affairs.

It was warm on the stoop, the sun shining brightly high in the sky. The snow from the street and the walks had been swept neatly into banks all along the street, and the two men allowed themselves a few moments to admire the wealthy neighborhood, the large, well-maintained houses. A black carriage with golden scrollwork on the door panels and a team of matching black horses waited outside the house next door.

"The Goddards live there," Coeccias said, pointing out the largest house, a mansion on the northwest corner of End Street. Two well-dressed men were passing by it. "Know you they've their own theater? A true theater, albeit small, in their very house! I ask you, now, what would you do with your own theater?

"Th' Antheurises'," he continued, picking out the larger houses from north to south as he went, "the Cassillevanuses', old Rotcharius's—that's his carriage." He turned and pointed to the first house south of the Oakham's. "That's Clunbrassil's, and on the corner's Apeldoorn, a Free-porter, though no slouch as to spending."

"Freihett Necquer's," Liam said, indicating the second house around the corner on Duke Street, a place he had visited often while looking for Tarquin's murderer.

"Aye, Necquer's. He has not been seen much of late." Coeccias cleared his throat. "Two houses beyond his is Rafe Cawood's. It can't be seen from here," he added, when Liam craned his neck, trying to catch a glimpse. His friend pointed back up towards the Goddards'. "Earl Ulder-icus's is up there, around the corner and a short way down, just near Herione's." Herione's was a brothel the Aedile had taken him to once, in search of information.

"Huh," Liam grunted. "So close."

"Close indeed, though nothing like the Warren, for all that."

"And the Furseuses?"

Coeccias thought for a moment. "Closer to the square, I think. In the neighborhood of the White Grape. The Furseii are not as great a family as they once thought they were."

"What about the other guest? Quetivel?"

"A rural lord, of some account further north. He stays with the Oakhams, I think."

"Well, that at least makes sense."

Coeccias gave him a strange glance. "What does that mean?"

Liam gestured at the neighborhood. "Doesn't it strike you as odd that all those guests, most of whom live nearby, should have stayed the night?"

Rubbing his beard, the Aedile gave it a moment's thought, and then admitted: "Now that you say it, it does seem odd. But then, there's nothing so strange about it, really. It snowed last night, and I cannot imagine any of Lady Oakham's guests trudging home in it. Particularly not if they'd, ah, indulged as much as she seems to have." He pressed a finger over his lips and blew out his cheeks, then laughed.

Liam grabbed his arm. "Watch it."

"What—" the Aedile began, then saw that the two well-dressed men had reached the stoop and were coming up.

"Master Aedile," said the taller of the two men, smiling in welcome. "Have you caught our thief yet?"

"No, Lord Oakham," Coeccias said, bowing. "Though we hope to, we hope to."

Oakham was a handsome man in his late thirties, tall and thin, with glossy black hair trimmed neatly at his shoulders and a slightly curled mustache. He wore well-worn but elegant riding clothes, held a pair of leather gauntlets in one hand, and his eyes danced with good humor as he acknowledged the Aedile's bow with a gracious nod.

"My lord," Coeccias said, indicating Liam, "this is Quaestor Rhenford, who will be looking into the robbery."

Liam bowed, and Lord Oakham gave him a friendly smile, coming up the stairs to stand between them. "Well and well, is this the same Master Rhenford of whom my wife's aunt speaks so highly?"

"The same, my lord," Liam said, bowing again.

Oakham slapped him on the arm. He turned to the man behind him, a youth of no more than twenty, with blond hair so long it was braided. He was wiry and thin, wearing far richer clothes with none of Oakham's easy grace. "Quetivel, this is the man my aunt is doing business with. I hope her faith is well placed," he added, turning back to Liam. He spoke good-naturedly, and smiled all the while, but Liam sensed that he was being weighed in the handsome lord's eyes.

"It obviously was not earlier," interjected Quetivel, shooting a contemptuous glance at Coeccias. "Where I come from, we'd have hung the thief already. How is it that you have not caught the man already, Aedile?"

"Come, Quetivel," Oakham said. "It is not so easy as all that."

"Nonsense! Surely, Aedile, you must know the thieves in your city!"

Liam tensed, noting the anger building up in his friend's shoulders and fists.

"If I knew them, my lord," the Aedile grated through clenched teeth, "I would have clapped them in last night, before the robbery. I'd not have waited til after."

"Sheer incompetence!" the young man proclaimed. "And insolence, too, Aetius! I wouldn't stand for it—this idea that it might be one of your guests!"

"To be fair, Quetivel," Oakham said, "that was my aunt's idea."

"But he subscribes to it!" Quetivel protested, thrusting a finger at Coeccias.

"I am sure no one holds to that idea anymore, Baron Quetivel," Liam interposed quickly, to forestall an angry response from his friend. "We have good reason to believe that someone from outside the house was involved, someone with experience as a thief."

"Eh?" Quetivel said, rounding on Liam.

"I wonder, your grace," Liam went on, addressing himself to Oakham, "if I might have a moment of your time. There are a number of questions I would like to ask you about the robbery."

"Certainly," the tall man said, his lips curling with stifled amusement. "Quetivel, I'm afraid I'll have to ask you t' entertain yourself for a while. Would half an hour do, Master Rhenford?"

Liam bowed graciously. "More than enough, my lord."

"Good, then. Shall we inside?" He turned to the house.

Given the obvious antagonism between Quetivel and Coeccias, Liam paused. "If I might join you in a moment, my lord, I'd like a word with the Aedile."

"In course. Come along, Quetivel." With a nod at Coeccias, Oakham opened the door and went in, followed by the sulking youth.

"See you?" spluttered the Aedile, when Liam had led him down the steps by the elbow. "What an ass! See you why I'm no good at this? Oakham's all well and good—but that Quetivel! And the rest are as noxious as he, if not more! Ah, Rhenford, it likes me to have you on this."

"My pleasure," Liam said sarcastically. *If they are all like Quetivel, this will be harder than I thought.* "Look, can you send some of your men around to the pawnshops? Or better yet, do it yourself. See if anyone has been making any overtures about selling the Jewel. And check jewelers as well. Our thief might have tried to scout out a fence before he did his work."

Coeccias shook his head. "No reason in it, Rhenford—you said it yourself. There's none in Southwark who could afford it, jeweler or broker. Any man who even suggested it would be sent off with a flea in his ear."

"Exactly—and that's why I think we should check. If there were any chance of a fence or a jeweler buying it, there would be no point, because they certainly wouldn't tell you. But since they were all bound to refuse . . ."

A smile grew behind the Aedile's beard. "Truth, it sings! Since they would refuse, they'd have no reason not to tell me, and we might con out our thief not by where he fenced the Jewel, but by where he didn't!"

Liam held up a cautioning hand. "Don't get too excited, now. I still don't think anyone would steal it just to sell it. It is just a possibility."

"Aye, aye," the Aedile agreed, still smiling, "but it's just the thing for me. For I tell you fair, Rhenford, I'm leaving this"—he pointed at the house—"and all this"—he swept his arm around, including the whole of the Point—"to you. Fine lords and ladies like me not, and don't like me either, if you see. I give you free rein. Go to, go to!"

"Thanks," Liam said, and this time his sarcasm was not lost on the Aedile, who gave a loud laugh.

"Y' asked for it, Rhenford, you did. Enjoy!"

Frowning ruefully, Liam spread his hands in surrender. *I suppose I did,* he thought.

They agreed to meet later in the afternoon, and then the Aedile departed, strolling briskly away as if he had not a care in the world.

Liam lingered at the bottom of the stoop, collecting his thoughts. He would have to be more honest with Lord Oakham, and try to convince the man to help him find a way to interview the guests in a way that would not arouse their suspicions. For a brief moment he thought back to how the day started, with a dead man outside his front door and a strange wizard in his bedroom. And now, of his own accord, he had taken upon himself the task of searching out a thief from among a group of people who were practically above the law.

An old proverb from the Midlands sprang to his mind: *Never a lone wolf, but a pack.*

"A very rich pack," he said to himself as he started back up the steps. "But a pack nonetheless."

The maidservant Becula answered his knock with barely suppressed impatience, soapy water dripping from the sleeves of her plain frock.

"What would you?" she demanded. "Were you not just here?"

A little taken aback, Liam said: "I was, and now I am here again. Lord Oakham is waiting for me."

"Huh," she said, as if she did not think it likely, and then turned and walked away, leaving the door open, shouting as she went, "Tasso! Someone for the master!"

Another servant appeared on the stairway that ran off the main hall before Becula had reached the kitchen, a sour-faced man with a pursed mouth and thinning black hair plastered to his skull.

"Master Rhenford," he said, beckoning, "this way, please." Without waiting for a reply, he turned on his heel and went back up the stairs.

Liam stopped for a moment, noting the thick wooden bar leaning in a corner just inside the entrance; at night it would have hung in brackets across the door. Then he went up the stairs, musing a little about the quality of the Oakhams' servants. They had certainly not been chosen for their winning way with visitors. *Though I imagine that Quetivel gets a warm welcome,* he reflected without bitterness. He had known servants with affectations before, and he guessed that a title would have gotten him a far more gracious greeting.

He paused at the landing, having lost sight of the manservant. The second-floor hallway was dark.

I wonder what they would think if they knew that I was once a lord's son, with a chance at inheriting a domain a quarter of the size of the whole Southern Tier?

The "once" being the important part, he reminded himself. *'Once,' and a long time ago.* There was no point in laying claim to a title that had long since been taken from him—and so he only smiled a little when the manservant hissed at him from a dark end of the long landing.

"Hsst! Master Rhenford! Over here!"

Then the man opened the door at which he had been standing, letting light into the hallway. He announced Liam in a solemn manner, and held the door for him.

Casting his eyes down to hide his smile from the suddenly proper servant, Liam strolled past him and into Oakham's study.

Animal skin rugs, worn from long use, covered the floor, racks of antlers adorned the walls, and there were a few simple chairs grouped near the fireplace. Tall, narrow windows offered a view of the houses across the street. Oakham stood by the hearth, warming his hands at the fire and staring up at a tapestry hung over the mantle. It was a hunting scene, and it took Liam only a moment to recognize that the central figure, busily engaged in spearing a stag from horseback, was the lord himself.

Oakham turned, caught Liam's glance, and gestured at the tapestry. "Handsome, eh? A wedding gift from my aunt."

"It is very well done, my lord," Liam said truthfully.

The other man chuckled. "She thinks me vain, is my guess. In any case, we are not here to discuss my aunt's opinion of me, nor her taste in gifts. Tell me—have you really any hope of conning out the thief?"

Whatever the quality of the servants, Liam found himself responding to their master. The lord seemed friendly enough, and there was an earnestness to his question that gave Liam the idea he might have found an ally.

"That depends, my lord."

"On what?" He gestured to a seat. "Sit, please, and tell me. I am anxious to have this solved."

"It depends a great deal on you, my lord," Liam said, acting on his rather sudden liking for the man. Oakham froze in the act of putting his hand on the mantle and stared hard at Liam, who went on quickly: "I was not entirely honest outside, when I said that no one thought the thief might be one of your guests. The simple fact is that someone inside the house was almost of necessity involved."

"How so?" Oakham finished putting his hand on the mantle and leaned there, frowning heavily.

"The locks on the doors of the crypt were picked, your grace, a simple enough piece of work for a trained thief—"

"Well, then . . ." Oakham interrupted, gesturing with his free hand, as if to say: There you have it.

"—simple enough, of course. But the outer door is barred at night, is it not?"

The man at the mantle closed his eyes for a moment, then nodded, grimacing a little. "So y' are saying someone from within the house must have opened the outer door for this trained thief?" He began pacing up and down in front of the fireplace, his hands behind his back.

"Yes, my lord. I understand that this is unpleasant—they are your friends, after all—"

"Give no thought to that," Oakham interrupted. "They are more my wife's friends than mine, and while I like them well enough, I harbor no illusions. A titled man can be as bad as a beggar. Though mind you," he said, pausing in his pacing and leveling a finger at Liam, "I exclude Quetivel. He is my cousin, and a personal friend, and I would trust him with my life and my honor."

"Of course, my lord," Liam said, making a mental note to put Quetivel at the top of his list of suspects. "I will exclude anyone from suspicion that you vouch for."

"I'll warrant Quetivel's innocence only," Oakham said, resuming his walk back and forth. "Now tell me, how does this depend on me?"

"The simple fact is, my lord, that the rest of your guests are either titled or possess the Rights of the Town."

Oakham gestured impatiently: Get to the point.

"That makes it very difficult for us to get any information from them. And information is crucial in something like this." Liam stroked his chin briefly, reflecting. "I have helped the Aedile only twice, my lord, and what help I was able to give him those two times was based entirely on information. Being able to ask questions, to learn things. The more we know about the crime—what was stolen, when it was stolen, where it was stolen from—and the more we know about who might have committed it—why they might have done it, whether they had a chance to do so—the closer we will be to solving it. Does this make sense, my lord?"

Oakham had stopped pacing and was carefully following Liam's words, his eyes narrowed and speculative. After a moment, he spoke.

"I think so. What you want to do is question my guests, but because they are all highly placed, the Aedile cannot do it. I still don't see how this depends on me, however."

Liam cleared his throat. This was the hard part, but he was encouraged by Oakham's earlier comment about his lack of illusions. "I would like it if you could arrange an introduction for me to your guests. A letter, perhaps—asking each to help me as much as they are able, to tell me everything they can remember from last night. You could even introduce me as a friend of your aunt."

There was a long pause, during which Oakham lightly ran the back of one finger under his mustache, smoothing it. The implications of what Liam had asked were clearly not lost on him: his eyes looked troubled, and a small frown tugged at the corners of his mouth.

"It has the complexion of a lie, Master Rhenford."

"The complexion, perhaps, but not the essence. I am a friend of your aunt, and I do wish to help."

"But to say that, and not say that you suspect them—that has the complexion of a lie." Oakham's voice dropped, as if he were thinking of something else, and his eyes were unfocused, as if he were visualizing that thing.

Liam spoke again, but he had the impression that his words went unheard. "Surely they must realize that they are suspected. Who else do they think might have done it?"

With a sudden chuckle, Oakham returned his attention to Liam. "Y' are not much of my wife's set of friends, Master Rhenford, or you would not ask that question. They would never dream that suspicion would fall on them. More, if they did dream it, then they would certainly take my sending you as an extreme insult." He stopped, staring down at the floor for a moment, and then, before Liam could respond, started again. "But come, I have another, better idea. Rather than a letter, why don't I introduce you to them in person? I can arrange things so that it appears under a different, more friendly complexion. No letters, no appeals for help. You might meet them . . . informally, as it were. What do you think?"

It seemed more like a lie to Liam than a simple letter of introduction, but he was not about to let that get in the way. Meeting them in a less than official capacity might make them more open, more prone to let their guards down. And being with Oakham might make him more acceptable; he would be a friend of a friend, instead of an agent of the Duke.

If he can justify it to himself, who am I to argue?

"It sounds like just the thing, my lord. It will certainly make my questions less confrontational, if they do not see me as some kind of inquisitor."

Oakham nodded decisively and resumed his pacing. "Good then. We'll see to this thing together, then. To start with, we can meet Ulder-icus tonight. Quetivel and I were to spend the evening with him; I begged off this morning, but Quetivel is still going, so it will be easy for me to rejoin the party, with you in tow. Cawood will be easy enough—we can visit him at the Staple tomorrow. I often see him there, so it will not be unusual. And if I present you as a friend of my aunt, he'll make no question about it."

For a man who had complained about the appearance of a lie only a few minutes before, Oakham struck Liam as awfully eager to begin what would amount to a deception. But then, he told himself, the niceties of social interactions between southern nobility were beyond him. In the Midlands, the local lords rarely interacted, except on the battlefield. He had grown to the age of eighteen within a day's ride of the nearest lord, and only met him three times—once when the lord came to demand the Rhenfords' surrender, once when his army stormed Rhenford Keep, and the last time when Liam killed him.

If Oakham sees a difference between presenting me by letter and presenting me in person, I have no objections—as long as I am presented.

Still pacing, Oakham stroked his mustache furiously. "The Furseuses, now, will not be so easy. I do not have much to do with them— they are my wife's particular friends. I shall have more on it with her, later; she is indisposed just now. In the meantime, Uldericus and Cawood are a start. Is that sufficient for you?"

"More than sufficient, my lord." Liam rose, inclining his head out of deference. "More than I could have expected."

"Attend a moment!" Oakham said, whirling on Liam. "Y' are not going, are you?"

"I had thought—" Liam began.

"But how will you proceed? What are your plans?" He spoke heatedly, surprising Liam, and then added hastily: "I would know, so that I may be of help. This theft has upset my wife tremendously, and I would see it speedily concluded."

"Of course, my lord," Liam said, blinking a little at Oakham's unexpected eagerness and sitting down again. "Well, as I said, I believe a thief must have been involved, to pick the locks. Coeccias and I will look into that, and try to find the thief."

The tall lord took a seat next to Liam, wearing a rather intense look of curiosity. "You can do that? Find a particular thief, I mean? How?"

"There are ways," Liam replied, and then, realizing how mysterious that sounded, added: "People who, while not thieves themselves, know of them. Pawnbrokers, certain tavernkeepers, some women—we can ask them."

"Pawnbrokers," Oakham repeated, leaning back in his chair while the curiosity faded on his face. "Some women. I see, I see. Then you will be busy, I imagine. It must be more than the work of an hour, to question all those sorts of people."

There was only one person Liam meant to speak with, and she actually was a thief, but he did not want to tell Oakham that. "Yes, my lord. But if I might ask one more thing?"

A little impatiently, Oakham said: "In course, in course."

"I wonder if you might describe your guests for me."

"I don't follow you." He straightened in his chair, a suspicious look on his face.

Liam straightened as well, holding out his hands in an innocent gesture. "Just what they look like, my lord. I know only their names—but the people I will be talking to might not know their names, only their faces."

"Ah," Oakham said, in a tone bordering on enlightenment. The suspicious look faded as quickly as his curiosity. "In course. Well, there is Uldericus. . . ."

It did not take long for Oakham to give Liam descriptions of his guests, but Liam prolonged it as much as he could, trying to read as much as possible into what the lord said. The other did not give much away, restricting himself to simple appearances—though his own feelings did show through once or twice, and Liam made careful note of them. When it finally became clear that, for the moment, there was no more information to gain in the Oakhams' house, he took his leave.

They agreed on a time to meet that evening, and then Oakham called for Tasso to show Liam out.

"Until eight, then," the handsome lord said, thoughtfully tapping his lips with one long forefinger and nodding at the same time.

"Until eight," Liam responded, bowing, and then allowed Tasso to lead him down the stairs and to the front door.

Once they were out of earshot of his master, the servant made little pretense of deference, opening the front door and then shutting it as if he were shooing away an unwelcome dog.

Liam jumped down the steps and then paused on the street, taking a deep breath. He was not at all sure he was proceeding the right way—he thought, for instance, that he ought to have looked around the Oakhams' house a little more, seen the rooms where the guests stayed, tried to talk to Lady Oakham again.

But you didn't, did you? he asked himself, and realized he knew why. He had been put off by Oakham, by his nobility. *You were once nobility,* he chided himself, but it made no difference. Since the sack of his father's keep, he had been a wanderer, both within Taralon and far beyond its borders, and the company he kept had been mostly low. Soldiers and seamen, merchants, factors, spies and caravan masters, thieves and rogues of all descriptions—he was comfortable with them, knew where he stood. But he had been so long out of the company of the class to which he had once belonged that he was a little in awe of them.

And it doesn't make it any easier that Oakham is so aware of his station, he thought. *And his servants, too.* He wondered for a moment how Coeccias stood it, being treated so disrespectfully by Quetivel and even by the servants of the great houses. *It must be galling,* Liam decided, *but I guess he doesn't think about it much. Just accepts it.*

With a shrug and a promise to himself to try to follow his friend's example, he turned right, starting for Mistress Priscian's door—and stopped.

In turning, his eyes rose to the second floor of the house he had just left, and he saw Lord Oakham standing at a window, staring down at him. From his posture and the way he held aside the curtain, it seemed as if he had been watching for some time. When he saw Liam looking up, he smiled and waved once, a regal wave, almost a dismissal.

Liam bowed once again and resumed his walk to Mistress Priscian's door.

Haellus answered the door when Liam knocked, and informed him that Mistress Priscian was unavailable. "Lady Oakham has been taken ill," the servant said, inclining his head meaningfully towards the house next door. "And my mistress must attend her. Would you wait, Master Rhenford?"

"No," Liam decided, "but tell her I will call on her later in the day, if she does not mind."

The other man gave him a deferential nod, waiting until he had turned and started down the stairs to shut the door. On the street, Liam paused, rubbing his hands and thinking.

I will have to have a plan, he realized, *something more specific than just following Oakham around and hoping for a clue.* He would need more information on the guests, preferably from an impartial source, and a set of questions to ask each, as well as a suitable way to present them in a social setting. *Of course,* he joked to himself, *I could just let Oakham introduce me, and start hammering them. 'Good evening, Earl Uldericus. Did you steal the Priscian Jewel?'*

Variations on that theme kept a smile on his face as he walked away from the Priscian houses. He turned onto Duke Street, wondering about the Furseuses' reaction to a direct accusation, and then he remembered Coeccias's roll call of the Point's inhabitants. He knew Freihett Necquer's house well—the Freeporter merchant and his wife were the couple he had befriended while looking for Tarquin's murderer—and the Aedile had said that Rafe Cawood lived two doors down. Slowing his pace a little, he examined the house as he passed.

Simple red brick with a narrow front and modest gables, it did not detract from the neighborhood's aura of quiet wealth, though it stood between two far larger homes. It seemed merely a pause, a comma in a long sentence of larger words, over which the eye slid without much notice.

Snapped at by a cold breeze, Liam gave a small shrug and moved on. *Does he dream of a bigger house?* he wondered. *With his own theater, maybe?* There was no way the Jewel could be sold in Southwark, or the proceeds spent there. It was simply too small a town, and a merchant's profits were common gossip, easily tallied even by strangers. So what would a thief gain?

Simple possession, perhaps. Liam had known men to become obsessed with something they did not have—a woman, a ship, a kingdom. And as Coeccias had said, a miser did not necessarily build a golden house.

The theft of the Jewel, a symbol of the Priscian family, might have been a form of revenge, or an attempt to put them at a disadvantage in trading, but that seemed highly unlikely: he could not imagine Thrasa Priscian having such enemies, and her share of Southwark's trade was very small. And in any case, symbols such as the Jewel were much less important in Southwark than in the Freeports, where they were equated with great political power as well as wealth.

The houses grew smaller, the street narrowed; Liam descended from the Point into the middle-class neighborhoods of the city, mulling over motives. Without really thinking about it, he turned off Duke Street a block before it passed the temple of the Storm King, and headed inland, towards the city square.

Cawood's modest house stayed in his mind. If the merchant had stolen the Jewel, he could not simply sell it and start spending money. He would have to make up a source for the sudden wealth, as, indeed, would any of the other guests. It might be easier for Uldericus or Quetivel, who presumably had lands somewhere else in the duchy and could claim them as sources of revenue. But then, where would they sell it?

There was not enough private money in Southwark, of that Liam was sure. Some of the treasuries on Temple Street would have enough, of course, but no temple would deal in stolen goods. It would have to be sold in a larger city, a Freeport or Harcourt or Torquay, and that would require contacts in one of those cities. Cawood might be presumed to have those—but would any of the others? They were Southern Tier aristocracy, and from what little he had seen of that breed, he knew they were not great travelers. During his time as a student in Torquay, he had never met a single person from the Southern Tier, though the duchy was relatively close to the capital, and the scholars there drew students from all over Taralon.

So if it was stolen for money, Cawood is probably the one, Liam decided, and then shook his head. He was jumping to conclusions, and getting far ahead of himself. That sort of speculation would have to wait until he knew more about the guests; in the meantime, he would have to look in other directions.

■ 5 ■

THE FESTIVE AIR of the square was even more pronounced when Liam entered it; the booths selling hot wine were crowded, and music drifted from the taverns and restaurants lining the eastern side. It surprised him: concentrating on the theft, he had forgotten that few other people had such unpleasant preoccupations. A day that brought most everyone else only thoughts of the week of celebration to come had brought him a corpse on his doorstep and consideration of the possible motives for theft among friends.

How does Coeccias stand it? Liam asked himself, going to the counter of a booth selling roasted chestnuts. *Always knowing the worst, and having to solve it, or clean it up.* The man behind the counter took his coin and scooped a handful of nuts into his cupped palm, with a "Merry Banquet" and an open smile. Liam nodded back and stepped away from the stall, juggling the hot chestnuts from hand to hand.

The chestnut man knew nothing about stolen jewels or sailors with their throats cut; he knew it was Beggar's Banquet, and time to sell as many chestnuts as he could. What Liam knew gave him a feeling of distance from the people around him, a sense, almost, of superiority. *They do not know what has happened,* he thought, *and I do.* He realized too that it was foolish, that what he knew did not make him superior. Even what he did about it, if anything, would not make him so. Coeccias could feel superior, because he had to deal with the city's problems all the time, day in and day out, and had somehow managed to avoid becoming jaded or bitter. For Liam it was no more than a lark, really, a game with a potentially positive outcome, but still a game.

Except that it is not a game to Mistress Priscian, he scolded himself, *nor to that sailor.* The sailor was not his problem; the stolen Jewel, however, was, and he resumed his thinking while gingerly biting into the first of his chestnuts. It burned the roof of his mouth a little, but he swallowed it quickly and took a second one.

There was nothing he could do about the guests at the moment; that would have to wait for his introductions from Lord Oakham. The Aedile was checking into the possibility of someone having tried to fence the Jewel, or at least to seek out a fence. A remote chance at best, Liam knew, but worth looking at—he had learned more than once to leave no stone unturned. That left him with one direction to explore, one which neither Coeccias nor Oakham could help him with: the thief who had picked the crypt lock.

Which means Mopsa and the Werewolf.

In his years of travel, Liam had been many things, from clerk to sellsword, surgeon to ship's captain—and, briefly, apprentice thief. More by accident than design, he had fallen in with a legendary thief from Harcourt, who had taken him under his wing and taught him the craft. Chances to practice had never really come his way, but Liam remembered enough of the lore so that, when someone broke into his house a month or so earlier, he had been able to find the Southwark Thieves' Guild and convince them that he was a retired "chanter," as they called themselves.

The Southwark Guild was not an impressive thing, hardly more than a gang, and they had not been responsible for the break-in, but he had maintained a fair amount of contact with them. And he had also done them a service, laying to rest the soul of a thief named Duplin who had been murdered, so Liam thought they would be responsive to him. The only thief he knew well was an apprentice, a young girl named Mopsa who had been assigned to help him look for his things. All he had to do was seek her out and arrange an appointment with the Werewolf, the head of the Guild.

If you can find her, he thought. Since there was no guildhouse he could apply to, and the one hideout he knew of had been abandoned, his only option was to wander the streets and hope that he could find the girl.

Sighing resignedly, he tossed the last chestnut, now cold, into his mouth, dusted his hands, and set off for the Warren.

•   •   •

The Warren was not the lowest point in Southwark—the docks and the warehouse district were a little lower—but it was certainly the dirtiest and, in winter, the darkest. With the sun perpetually low on the southern horizon, even in the middle of the day the neighborhood lay in the shadow of the Teeth, the jagged fence of rock that guarded the city's harbor from the sea. Walking down Harbor Street from the city square, Liam could actually see a dark dividing line across the road, a visible border between neighborhoods, as if the people of the Warren could not afford sunlight.

Shops were open along Harbor Street, hung with ribbons and greenery and offering up holiday fare—fat plucked geese, barrels of oysters, bushels of giant lobsters—but Liam paid them no mind, pushing through the dense crowds of shoppers, his boots slipping occasionally on the slick cobbles. The shops grew fewer and farther between as he approached the zone of shadow that marked the beginning of the Warren, the buildings growing shabbier, as often as not with boarded-up doors and gaping, empty windows. Once he entered the shadow, pulling his cloak close about him against the sudden chill, even the humped piles of snow by the side of the road looked dirtier, more soot-encrusted, and the few attempts at holiday decoration seemed somehow sad to him.

He had no definite destination, just the vague idea of wandering around the Warren until he ran into Mopsa or darkness fell. His good clothes brought him a great deal of covert attention, whispers and pointing, but, sunk in his own gloomy thoughts, he paid them no mind, simply going where his feet led him.

The buildings here were mostly wooden, the rare brick or stone construction a dilapidated monument to better times, all of them rising in tottering stories high above the street. Sometimes the buildings met, overhanging floors reaching out across narrow alleys and throwing deep shadows; he hurried past these.

Once he interrupted a group of children at a game and asked them if they had ever heard of Mopsa, but they only stared at his boots and mumbled, unused to being addressed by anyone so well dressed. Liam hurried away from them as well.

After nearly an hour of pointless searching, he suddenly stopped, closed his eyes, and cursed and smiled at the same time.

Fool, he berated himself. *In a holiday week, with people out buying, why would she be in the Warren?* And a moment later, inspiration following on inspiration, he thought of Fanuilh.

• • •

I was wondering when you would call me, the dragon thought to him, as Liam looked down through its eyes at the Arcade of Scribes.

Of all the benefits conferred by their bond as master and familiar, seeing with Fanuilh's eyes was the one Liam liked the least. It often made him dizzy, and he had noticed a slight distortion in the dragon's eyesight that gave him headaches if he looked too long.

You might have suggested it before, Liam projected back grumpily. *Move a little to your left.*

His field of vision shifted—Fanuilh must have been perched on a rooftop opposite the Arcade—and he could see the professional letter-writers lined up behind the arches, some squatting by small wooden secretaries, others seated behind broad tables, and all with samples of their work pinned to boards close at hand. Some of the scribes had braziers nearby, to keep their hands and inks warm; others were bundled up, hands thrust under their armpits or deep in their pockets. There were more people than usual waiting, anxious to buy the gaily drawn Banquet messages, some done in as many as five different color inks.

He had sent Fanuilh flying over Harbor Street and the city square with no result, strolling leisurely after it, pausing when the dragon was in position. Shading his own eyes, he had shifted to the dragon's sight, but both street and square, though busy, held no sign of the young thief. A brief flight over Temple Street, where people with fat purses were going to make offerings, had proven equally fruitless. As a last chance, he had sent Fanuilh to the Arcade.

There she is.

He recognized her first by her lank, dull brown hair; she was lounging against one of the arches, looking for all the world like some innocent waiting for her parents. She still wore the clothes Liam had bought for her a month before, although the jacket was dirtier and the hem of the dress had been taken up so that it did not drag at her heels. New was the glint of steel that peeked from her clenched fist. Her gaze rested on a man on line for the nearest scribe; he was third from the front of the line, wearing an expensive red cloak that he had flipped back from his belt to expose the pouch tied there.

Liam snapped back to his own eyesight, aware of a dull ache in the back of his head, and hurried the three blocks to the Arcade. By the time he arrived, the man in the red cloak was at the front of the line, and he could see Mopsa tensing. He edged his way up next to her and, before she knew he was there, leaned back against the arch and tapped her arm.

"Avé, pickit," he whispered, and then grabbed her arm as she tried to bolt.

For a moment, seeing the fear on her face as she found herself caught, he regretted the trick, but then her look of relief made him laugh.

"You are not careful enough," he began, letting go of her arm.

"Don't do that!" she hissed. "You near frighted me to death!"

He let go of her arm. "Well, you aren't careful enough. What if I had been someone else?"

Mopsa whipped her head around, scanning the crowd, suddenly nervous. "Are there any here?"

"No," Liam assured her, "but if there had been, they might have seen your friend. I did." He tapped the hand that held her knife. "Now come on, I need to talk to you."

The girl frowned at him. "Can't. I'm working." She cast a glance over her shoulder at the man in the red cloak, who was ordering a number of Banquet greetings in various colors.

"Too late," Liam said. "He will have spent it all before you can get to him—and you couldn't cut both strings without him noticing. Come on."

"I could," she said, pouting.

He shook his head. "Come on. It's important." He gestured for her to precede him, but she hung back, suspicious.

"How important?"

"Important enough for lunch," he sighed.

Grumbling, she agreed, discreetly tucking her knife back up her sleeve. "Where will we eat?"

There was a stall selling sausages and bread nearby. "There," Liam said, pointing, and with a quick grin Mopsa darted away, shouting an order as she went. Before he could reach her, she had ordered three.

"My uncle'll pay," she was saying as he arrived, and the sausage-seller's look of skepticism faded when she saw Liam. She gave him a half-curtsy and drew three sausages from her little grill.

"And one for myself, and bread if you have any."

"Mine on bread too!" Mopsa demanded, and grabbed the first two sandwiches that the woman laid on the counter and thrust them into her jacket. The third she snatched and started gobbling.

"Hungry child," the sausage-seller noted.

"I haven't fed her for a week," Liam said, counting out his money. "It's too expensive." Dropping a few coins on the counter, he took his own sandwich, gave the woman a bright smile, and steered Mopsa away from the stand with a hand on her head.

"Over there." He nudged her toward a relatively isolated corner at the end of the Arcade. The girl went willingly, engrossed in her meal. By the time they reached the spot, she was already starting on her second sausage. Liam took a bite of his own, then grimaced: the bread was stale, and the sausage was mostly gristle and fat. Shaking his head, he handed it to Mopsa, who stowed it in her jacket without comment and without interrupting her steady eating.

Not for the first time, Liam wondered how old she was. *Twelve? Certainly not more than fourteen.* Her clothes were considerably dirtier than when he had given them to her. *But she does not look too bad, otherwise. She doesn't smell as bad, and she isn't starving.* She was skinny but not emaciated, and her face looked full enough, though there were dark circles under her eyes.

"Well," she said, finishing the second sausage and licking her fingers, "what would you?"

"I need to see the Werewolf."

"And why?" she asked, folding her arms across her chest, more a gesture of curiosity than suspicion.

"To tell him how much I love him."

She laughed and clapped her hands. "That'll set him running, sure! Honest, now—why?"

"None of your business. Just tell him that I want to see him."

"And he's to come running, like a dog to heel? I can't go to him with that!"

He had to admit that she had a point. He was not in a position to order the Werewolf to come to him—and the thief was not much given to casual meetings. "Right. Just tell him that something has gone free in the Point, and I would like to see him about it. At his convenience."

"To reslave it?"

They were slipping into thief slang, something Liam did not want to do on a public street.

"Not necessarily. Possibly, but not necessarily. I may just want some information. In any case, I'd like to meet with him, as soon as possible. Can you tell him that?"

Mopsa gave him a little sneer. "See you, I'm not a messenger boy."

"No," he agreed, "but you are eating my sausages. And I will make you a deal—if you promise to deliver the message and return with the answer, I will get you a Banquet gift."

Her eyes lit up, half wary and half excited. "What sort of gift?"

Liam gestured mysteriously, covering up the fact that he had no idea what sort of gift. "Something grand."

Mopsa's eyes narrowed. "How much will you spend?"

He snorted his astonishment. "I forgot what a little weasel you are, Mopsa. You don't ask how much someone is going to spend on a gift."

"You do if they're only gifting you so you do them a service."

Leaning forward, he poked her in the shoulder with one long finger. "Listen, pickit, if you don't deliver my message, and return with the answer, not only will you not get a gift, but I can guarantee that the Werewolf will make your life very unpleasant for a very long time."

"Go to, go to!" She knocked away his finger and massaged her shoulder, though he knew he had not poked her hard. "I'll tell him, I will. There's no call for rudeness. Gods."

Satisfied, Liam nodded. "When you have his answer, leave it at Herlekin's. You know the place?" Herlekin's was a tavern on the city square, opposite the Guard barracks and the Duke's Courts.

"Aye, I know it," she said, a little sullenly. "But it may not be today, for that the Wolf is sleeping. It may be tomorrow."

"Tomorrow morning, then. Leave word with Herlekin."

"When will I get my gift?"

"Gods, you are a greedy one! You'll get your gift after I have seen the Werewolf. Fair enough?"

She agreed with ill grace and, without another word, headed off to the west, down the hill and in the general direction of the Warren.

Liam remained behind a minute, shaking his head and smiling ruefully. When he could no longer see her, he turned to go himself, stopping when a particularly gaily colored Banquet greeting caught his eye. He stepped up to the board to examine it. About a foot wide and half that tall, it had a twisting border of greenery punctuated with bright red berries; the scene showed a group of impossibly fat and happy beggars in multicolored clothes singing against a background that he recognized as Temple Street.

For a moment, he was tempted—*Would she . . . ?*—and then he came to his senses. *She would hate that. Maybe a new knife?*

With a last shake of his head, he left the Arcade and headed for the city square, trying to figure out what sort of gift he would get the apprentice thief.

The noon bells had rung while Liam was looking for Mopsa, and by the time he reached the Guard barracks he realized he was hungry.

Coeccias was hunched over the same table, laboriously scratching away at a piece of paper. When he saw Liam at the door he barked a happy laugh, crumpled the paper, and tossed it over his shoulder into the fire.

"It likes me to see you, Rhenford—I was just leaving you a note."

"Have you eaten?"

"I have, for that I didn't expect you so early; I thought we'd dine, not lunch. But I can send a man for something, if y' are hungry—" The Aedile half rose, but Liam waved him back to his seat.

"No need." He brought a stool over to the table and sat facing his friend. "What was the note about?"

Coeccias sat again, leaning back and scrubbing at his cheek thoughtfully. "An interesting thing I've conned out, passing interesting. Look you, after we parted, I set straight about looking up fences, but as I happened to go by way of the Alley of Riches—do you know it? There are the most of our jewelers and goldsmiths and whatnot—and I bethought me of how much the Priscian Jewel could fetch, and how a fence might not afford it, but a jeweler might. So I stopped in. Now there are not so many, six or seven in all, and look you, there's a Yezidi there, much the richest of all of them, and he told me a man had been in asking in particular about the Priscian Jewel!"

"Trying to sell it?" Liam asked eagerly, unable to believe their luck. "What did he look like?"

Coeccias held up a hand. "Now this is where it passes merely interesting, Rhenford. He was not asking if he could *sell* the Jewel—but if he could *buy* it!"

"What?"

"Here's more on it," the Aedile went on gravely. "Our Yezidi friend swears up and down that his questioner was a wizard."

"Wait a moment, wait. What do you mean, buy the Jewel?"

"Just that! He waited on the Yezidi yesterday morning, and asked him what he knew of the Priscian Jewel. The jeweler told him what he knew, which is what everyone knows, and then this man asked if he thought the Priscians would sell it!"

Liam frowned and stared at the floor. "But that makes no sense. . . ."

"Give me news, Rhenford; I know that. But that is what happened, or so the Yezidi swears."

"What did he say?"

"About whether they'd sell? He said no, that it was the family symbol, that it was priceless and so on. And then the man left. That's all. But a wizard, now? And asking after the Jewel? It must connect with our theft."

A thought struck Liam. "Are you sure the Yezidi said it was a man?"

"Aye. He gave his particulars—unless women wizards grow beards. Why?"

Liam gave a shrug. "There is a wizard, a woman, at my house now. Now that I think of it, though, she had not heard of the Jewel until today." *Or had she?* he wondered.

Surprisingly, Coeccias winked. "At your house now, is she? Attending your return? Rhenford, your wonders never cease."

"It's nothing like that," he said, scowling a little. "She was a friend of Tarquin's, and he left her some things." The Aedile's knowing smile stayed firm, so he hurried on. "That's not important now. What did he look like, and when did the jeweler see him?"

To be honest, he was not sure what to make of Coeccias's information. It should have been a thief, someone who could pick locks, who approached the Yezidi jeweler, not a wizard—but he listened carefully to the description anyway. A man of medium height, with an odd accent and a red beard that only partially covered a purplish mark on his cheek. He had visited the jeweler the morning before the theft, which meant he had to be considered a suspect.

"With such as that," the Aedile summed up happily, "the mark and the beard, he should not be hard to con out. I'll send a man around to the better inns, and with luck we can clap him in soon."

Liam frowned, disconcerted as much by his friend's smile as by the strange appearance of the wizard. "He might not be staying at an inn. He could be staying with someone he knows. If he opened the door to the crypt, he might be staying with the person who let him into Oakham's house. He could be anywhere in the city."

Taking the hint, Coeccias dimmed his smile a bit, but did not let it go entirely. "True enough—but anywhere is also somewhere, and there is nothing for it but to look where we may. Now tell me, how was it with Lord Oakham? Did he tell you anything of note?"

"Not precisely," Liam said, and explained his appointment for later in the evening. "I think he hopes I can question his friends without looking like I'm questioning them. It's rather a fine line."

"Very fine," Coeccias agreed. "These are prickly, Rhenford, these lords and ladies. I'm not sure it's well conceived. They could easily take offense at the simplest of questions—and y' are known to be associated with me."

"What else can we do? It seems better than just knocking on their doors. In any case, I will try it tonight with Uldericus, and if it doesn't work, we can try knocking."

They left it at that, each mulling over his own uncomfortable

thoughts. Liam was reconsidering the whole plan he had worked out with
Lord Oakham; in the light Coeccias had put on it, it seemed chancy at
best—but then, what choice did he have? It had to be better than simply
knocking on each guest's door. In fact, he was more concerned about the
addition of the unknown wizard to the situation. What would a wizard
want with the Jewel? *I might ask Grantaire,* he thought, and even as he
did, he remembered his promise to return in the afternoon and speak
with her. He stood quickly, pulling on his cloak.

"I have to go. I have to meet someone."

"Is it to do with the Jewel?"

"No," he said hastily, "it's my guest. I promised her some time this
afternoon." Seeing Coeccias's incipient wink, he cut it off with: "I think
she wants to hear about how Tarquin died. And come to think of it, I will
ask her if she knows of any other wizards in Southwark at the moment. It
might save your man a round of the inns."

The wink did not appear, but the knowing smile refused to go away.
"In course, in course. Shall we meet tomorrow?"

They agreed on a time, early in the morning, and then Liam left,
shaking his head at the way Coeccias could misconstrue the simplest
situations.

Diamond was restive; Liam had to restrain the horse in the narrow
streets of the city. Past the city gate he loosened the reins a little, but only
enough for Diamond to reach a smart trot. A cold wind was blowing
from the east, and Liam did not fancy galloping face-first into it; besides,
he wanted a little time to think before reaching the house on the beach.

What could Grantaire possibly want to talk with him about? He was
no wizard; he knew little more of magic than most. What could they have
to discuss?

Maybe she wants to exchange tips on how to handle unruly familiars, he
thought, spotting Fanuilh in a field off to his left, waiting for him. They
were a safe distance from the city, so he beckoned and projected: *And
speak of the Dark. Do you want to ride?*

The dragon bounded into the air, gave a lazy flap of its wings and
then two more powerful ones to counter the easterly wind. In a remarkably graceful swoop it landed on Diamond's neck, its back to Liam. The
roan gave a snort.

"Nicely done," Liam commented. "Have you been practicing?"

I do not see why I cannot go into the city with you. Why must I hide?

For a moment, Liam had no answer. He had simply assumed that
being seen in Southwark with his familiar would be bad, but he had never

examined why he felt that way. There was no reason, really, except that
he did not want to be thought a wizard.

"Did Tarquin ever take you into the city?" he asked finally.

No.

That was a relief, an easy answer. "So why should I?"

*Master Tanaquil rarely left the beach, and when he did, it was for simple
errands. He did not need me.*

Liam laughed. "And I do?"

I found the girl.

"True," he said slowly, "but you did not have to be at my side to do
that. And besides, how do you think the good people of Southwark
would feel about having a dragon running rampant through the streets?"

Fanuilh's back was to him, so he could not see its face, but he imagined it might have borne a disdainful expression.

I am a very small dragon, it projected. *And I would not run rampant.*

"I'm not convinced of that," Liam said with a smile. "Who knows
what trouble you might get up to? You might fall in with low companions, be led astray, visit wineshops and brothels—you could be pressed,
and spend the rest of your days chained to an oar in an Alyeciran galley.
I would hate to think of you as a galley slave."

When he first was bonded to Fanuilh, he had seemed to Liam that
the dragon had no emotions, but he had long since learned that it had at
least one, a combination of primness and old-maidish disgust. It shot that
at him now, bending its long neck to peer at him over its shoulder. That
drew a laugh from him, at which he could have sworn it gave a little sniff
before turning its attention back to Diamond's mane.

You should project, it thought at him.

"You always say that when you don't have an answer," he chuckled,
then grew a little more serious. "I will think about it. I promise nothing,
but I will think about it. Now there is something more important I want
to ask you about. Have you noticed any magic in Southwark recently?"

To a certain extent, Fanuilh could detect the use of magic, could
sense it, like a burst of light or heat. There were limitations—it could not
tell what the magic was being used for, or who was casting it—but if the
unknown wizard were really a wizard, and had been active, the dragon
would know.

*Mage Grantaire cast a few small spells. Nothing very large. Apart from
that, there has been nothing. Is there another wizard in Southwark?*

Liam explained about the Yezidi jeweler and his strange visitor. "According to Coeccias, he swore up and down that the man was a wizard,
though come to think of it, I didn't ask why he was so sure. After all,

people think I'm a wizard. The real question is, what would a wizard want with the Jewel?"

Mage Grantaire might know.

"Huh," Liam grunted, and sank into silence, considering the suddenly large list of demands on his time. He had to try to see all of the Oakhams' guests, arrange a meeting with the Werewolf, and give Grantaire however much time she needed, to ask questions at which he could not even begin to guess. And given the contract tucked in his tunic, he really ought to begin planning the spring trading season in earnest.

You have definitely bitten off more than you can chew, he told himself, and then noticed that Diamond had stopped, waiting at the top of the cliff path. Shaking his head to clear it, he nudged the horse with his heels and started down to the beach.

■ *6* ■

GRANTAIRE WAS WAITING at the door, arms crossed, and even though the sun was still well above the western horizon, Liam felt an unreasonable pang of guilt.

"I have many questions for you," she said as soon as he came in, but he could not tell if she was angry, impatient or merely eager to have her questions answered. She stood in his way, though, as if she meant to keep him in the doorway until they were.

A little flustered, he resorted to sarcasm, offering a deep bow. "I am at your service, my lady. I apologize profusely for the delay."

She gave him a startled, suspicious look, as if this was the last thing she had expected, and then turned and walked into the kitchen. The shift she wore was a different color from the one of the day before, but of the same cut, and as he followed her, he carefully kept his eyes on the back of her head.

"Can I get you something?" he asked, tossing his cloak on the kitchen table, but she shook her head impatiently and took a seat.

"I found out where I had heard the name Priscian before," she said briskly, while he went to the stove and imagined a large mug of coffee. "There was an Eirenaeus Priscian once, a wizard. He was mentioned in one of Tanaquil's books."

Liam had opened the oven, but he stopped his hand an inch from the steaming mug. "He was? That's strange—I saw his tomb today."

"His tomb is here?"

He pulled the mug from the oven, surprised at the eagerness of her voice. "It's in the family crypt in Southwark. The Mistress Priscian I had to meet today is a descendant of his." He sat opposite her, blowing on his coffee to cool it.

"I must see it," she said immediately. "Does she have any of his books, his papers? I must see them as well. You will arrange it?"

Liam got the impression that she was not really asking *if* he would arrange it, but *when* he would arrange it. He let that pass, however, because he was more interested in her excitement.

"I can ask Mistress Priscian, but why? He died hundreds of years ago."

"He left no records for the Guild," she said heatedly, "none of his notes or researches. If there is a chance of recovering them, I must try."

"But why?" Liam repeated, beginning to grow a little annoyed. It was as if she could not answer a straightforward question. "Who cares about his researches?"

"He was one of the most powerful wizards of his day," she snapped. "Everyone cares about them!"

So much so that you could not remember his name earlier today, he thought, and kept the thought to himself. Instead he cleared his throat. "I see. I don't know if Mistress Priscian has any of his notes—but he did leave something else. That Jewel I mentioned to you this morning?"

"That was his?" Her eyes widened, and Liam decided that if she were not so rude, she would be very pretty. "I must see that as well! I must see that!"

"Hold on a moment," he said carefully. "Notes and books I can understand, but why the Jewel? How can that be important?"

She rolled her eyes at him and took a deep breath, as if she were dealing with a particularly idiotic child and needed all the patience she could muster. "Do you understand the difference between soul and spirit?"

"Not at all. Should I?"

"These things are elemental," she said, glaring. "Did Tanaquil teach you nothing?"

"Actually, no—"

She went on, ignoring his answer. "Soul and spirit are two major divisions within—never mind. Priscian experimented extensively with spirit, and was thought at one time to have attained the answers to certain fundamental problems. I say 'thought' because no one was ever sure. When he died, he took his work to the grave with him."

"This was all in Tarquin's book?"

Grantaire gave him another frown, and he began to feel like the idiotic child she seemed to be addressing. "He is mentioned in passing in two of them—but only mentioned. He never shared his work, and as a consequence was . . . banned from the Guild." For some reason she blushed, apple-red blooms on both white cheeks.

"And the Jewel was important to his work?"

She frowned instantly, the blush fading. *The idiot child strikes again,* he thought.

"It could be important," she explained, displaying what she clearly thought was immense patience. "Some sort of physical object, something enduring like a gem or forged metal or stone, is always associated with spirit."

The mention of stone stirred a memory in the back of his head, but he put it aside for the moment, concentrating on the point he had been trying to lead up to. "So it would be of interest to any wizard? I mean, if the Jewel was associated with Priscian's work, it might be useful? Valuable?"

"Of course!"

"For research only?"

She gave him a suspicious look. "For research definitely. But also, potentially, as a source of power. It is too complicated to explain. Why do you ask?"

Why don't you finish your sentences? he wondered. *'Too complicated to explain to an idiot' is what you mean. . . .*

"It seems," he said, choosing his words with care, "that there is another wizard in Southwark at the moment, and he has been asking questions about the Jewel."

Before he had even finished his sentence, Grantaire was on her feet, looming over him.

"Who?" She was practically shouting. "Who is here?"

Liam gaped up at her, trying to master his amazement. "We don't know his name," he stammered. "He has a red beard and a mark on his face."

"Desiderius," she said, sounding relieved. Her hand strayed to her chin and stroked it in a curiously masculine gesture. "Desiderius." Her eyes unfocused, as if she were seeing the other wizard's face somewhere above Liam's head.

"You know him?" he asked. Though her initial shock had passed, he could not help but notice the way she trembled under her shift.

Stop that! he told himself.

"Yes," she answered after a pause. "I know him." With an effort, she forced her attention back to him. "Now leave me. I must think."

Liam bridled at her rude dismissal, but stood nonetheless. "There is something else you may want to know—the Jewel was stolen last night." He cringed slightly, expecting another angry outburst, but she only stroked her chin and nodded, more to herself than to him.

"Perhaps he is only here for that. Stealing, though," she muttered. "What will they not sink to?"

Liam hesitated by his chair, unwilling to bother her; she took her seat again, her hand now a fist pressed tight against her mouth, thinking furiously and completely oblivious to his presence.

I suppose my questions can wait, he thought ruefully, and backed out of the kitchen.

Fanuilh lay in the entrance hall, its head between its paws, staring at the sea through the glass panes of the front door. Beside it sat Grantaire's cat, grooming itself with studied dips of its head, pausing between licks to consider the view.

"Very cosy," Liam muttered, and then projected: *Fanuilh, come here. I have some stupid questions for you.*

The dragon lifted its head, shared a glance with the cat, and then lazily rose to its feet and shuffled after him into the library.

He lay at full length on the divan, staring up at the cupola, and waited for Fanuilh to arrange itself satisfactorily, nose to tail, on the floor.

Comfortable? he asked.

Yes, master.

Good. He had not yet figured out how to give his projected thoughts a sarcastic edge—was not, in fact, sure that the dragon would even be able to interpret that—so he put aside some of the comments that sprang to mind. *Good. Now, in simple terms, terms even an idiot can understand, explain the difference between soul and spirit.*

For some reason, Liam found it easier to project with his eyes closed; he could see the shapes of the words in his head, and could envision pushing them away from himself, towards his familiar. He did so now, resting one hand on his brow while the dragon explained, interjecting questions from time to time.

Soul, Fanuilh began, *is the individual essence of a person.* Spirit, on the other hand, was the life, the motive force that allowed an individual to be an individual. No two souls were alike, but spirit was roughly the same for everyone. *Consider spirit as fuel, and soul as fire. Two logs may be identical, but they never burn the same. The fire is different.*

But no two logs are ever identical, Liam countered. *And fire is still fire.*

The analogy limps, it conceded, and suggested another: *Consider spirit as food. All people eat, but none are alike.* When Liam grunted his acceptance, it went on: *A person may have no soul, but still have spirit.* This, it seemed, was one of the primary purposes of familiars—to separate a wizard's soul, rendering it less liable to attack. Without a soul, a person was left open to many forms of wizardry, in particular various forms of enslavement.

Simply to exist, however, required spirit; spirit animated the body and allowed the soul to inhabit it. While centuries of practice and research had allowed wizards to discover effective methods of protecting their souls, very little progress had been made in extending the length of time during which a body could sustain spirit.

Wizards can live almost double the length of time that a normal man can, it said. *Master Tanaquil was almost 120 years old.* Liam whistled, impressed, but the flow of thoughts did not stop. *Much beyond that, however, and the body simply begins to wear out. There are spells that allow a wizard to rejuvenate his body, but even so, the maximum length of time is considered somewhere between a century and a century and a half. No amount of rejuvenation will sustain a body beyond that.*

There was a way to step around that, however: stealing the bodies of other people—but that was cause for expulsion from the Guild.

"And not much appreciated by the population at large," Liam commented.

No, Fanuilh agreed, as usual missing the irony. *Wizards who take other bodies are usually hunted down and exterminated by the Guild.* Other methods of extending the lifetime of a body had been sought, but nothing reliable found. The usual method, apparently, involved constructing an object in which spirit could be stored and from which it could be drawn, without its actually entering the body. *Consider it gaining nourishment,* the dragon elaborated, *without having to consume food.*

"Aha!" Liam said, thrusting his index finger at the skylight.

A thought appeared quickly in his head: *I am aware that that analogy limps as well . . .*

"That's not what I mean," he said aloud, but the flow of thoughts did not stop.

. . . because it is not actually a question of the food being consumed, but of the food having to pass into the body. Consider a jug that wears out because it is continually filled . . .

"Fanuilh."

. . . with water. Each successive filling abrades some of the surface of the jug . . .

"Fanuilh."

. . . until eventually there is nothing left. If you could find a way to pour water without abrading the jug—

"Fanuilh!" Liam sat up and stamped one foot on the floor. The dragon's thoughts stopped instantly. "You may stop considering me an idiot. I think I understand. What I want to know now is, could the Jewel be an object like you described? An outside source of spirit?"

A long moment passed while the dragon considered the question. *Quite possibly,* it projected at last, with a tentative feel to the thought. *Master Tanaquil did not go into spirit much, but it was considered a given that the best receptacles for spirit would be durable items—stone, metal and, of course, gems. Diamonds were thought best.*

The mention of stone again stirred the memory that Grantaire had dislodged, and he ordered the story in his head before telling it.

"Some time ago," he began, when he was sure he was remembering correctly, "about eleven or twelve years, I was traveling north of the King's Range, and I came by chance to the house of a wizard who was supposed to have died hundreds of years before, after turning his entire household to stone. At least, there were statues of them all in the house—courtiers and servants and so on, including one imposing statue that was supposed to be the wizard himself—caught in the most lifelike poses you can imagine. I had to spend the night, alone, and I dreamed I was in another place, one that looked just like the place where the statues were, except that all the statues were alive. And I met the wizard, the one who was supposed to have been dead for hundreds of years, and all of his servants and friends were there as well."

The dream wizard said that he removed his household to another plane of existence in order to escape the machinations of his enemies at court; the king whose court he meant had died three centuries before Liam was born. He questioned Liam closely about the new state of the kingdom, and decided that the time had come to return. "I realize that's not very clear, but does it sound like something to do with spirit?"

Again, Fanuilh's response was tentative; the thought seemed to waver in his head, as if it had come from a great distance: *That, too, is quite possible. The statues could well have been conduits for spirit from the material plane that the wizard and his household required to exist in the other plane; on the other hand, they might simply have been placeholders, a connection with the real world that the wizard required to mark the way back. I could not say for sure. What happened to them?*

Liam blew air between compressed lips, remembering the scene. "I woke up, and everything was back to normal. The house was abandoned. And then I heard a scream, so I ran to find out where it was coming from. His statue—the wizard's—was in a room where the windows were broken. The winters that far north are very harsh, and I suppose the locals had done some damage; anyway, his statue was broken as well. There was an arm missing, and the foot was broken and . . . well, the face was . . . was rubbed away. Exposure and wind, I would guess. He cast the spell that was supposed to return them to this world and . . . I'm not sure. He died. There was a great deal of blood."

A heavy silence descended on the room, Liam brooding over his memory. He had never understood what happened. Though damaged, the wizard's statue had been standing when he first saw it; after the spell was cast, he had found it fallen over in a wide pool of blood, but still a statue, still stone. The other statues remained exactly the way they were when he first saw them; perhaps the wizard had decided to return alone.

"I heard him scream," he whispered, and then shook his head. "That's not important. I am more concerned with the Jewel now. I suppose we can take it for granted that a wizard would want it, assuming that a wizard would assume that it was a relic of Eirenaeus's research into spirit?"

The dragon bobbed its head in agreement. *If he was researching spirit, then yes, most definitely. Though Master Tanaquil was never much interested, many wizards find spirit an endlessly fascinating subject, despite the immense danger associated with it.*

Liam lifted his head, drawn away from his unpleasant memory. "Danger?"

If the wizard in your story was working with spirit, it would be an excellent indication. Spirit is a fragile thing, much more so than the soul. Liam's soul, for instance, could be split so that part resided in Fanuilh— but spirit could never be so divided. Moreover, the link between soul, body and spirit was complicated and poorly understood. *Master Tanaquil once said that more wizards were killed attempting to protect or prolong their spirits than from any other cause. Others go mad or . . . change. Some think that vampires originated from experiments in spirit gone awry. You know vampires?*

"Not personally, but I am familiar with the concept."

There are recorded cases of wizards receiving too much spirit. It is called blasting. They become . . . less than human. It is hard to explain. From the moment they are blasted, they require much more spirit than normal; it is similar to vampirism, but they do not drink blood. They are called liches.

"And people wonder that I do not want to be a wizard. Why don't these people become scribes or cobblers or blacksmiths? If you make a horseshoe and it goes badly, you end up with a bad horseshoe. It doesn't steal your soul and drive you mad."

Fanuilh offered him an inquiring gaze. *Is there anything else you wish to know?*

Smiling at his own joke, Liam shook his head. "No, I think that will do. What time is it?"

An hour or so before sunset.

Their conversation had taken longer than he expected, but it still left him a few hours before he had to be back in Southwark. He frowned irritably; waiting annoyed him immensely, and he was eager to get on with all the different tasks he had taken upon himself. There was so much to do, but none of it could be done right away. With an angry grunt he lay back down on the divan and began ordering his tasks in his head, as much searching for something to do immediately as actively planning.

First off there was Grantaire; he had promised her he would ask Mistress Priscian if Eireneaus had left any papers, and whether the wizard might look at them. *Did I actually promise her?* he wondered, thinking how awkward the asking might be. The man had been dead for hundreds of years; what chance was there that anything of his would be left? Moreover, how would Mistress Priscian feel about having another person digging into her family's affairs? Bad enough to have thieves, Aediles, and amateur investigators wandering around their private matters—wizards would hardly be a positive addition.

Nonetheless, he had as good as promised, and he knew that the sooner he asked, the easier it would be for him. The longer he waited, the more it would weigh on him, and the more chances he would have to imagine the different ways she could take offense at the question.

He toyed with the idea of doing it right away, and then rejected it. For some reason he imagined Mistress Priscian as an early diner; he pictured her, in fact, as someone who did everything early. "Early awake a fortune makes," he recited, a rhyme he had heard in the Freeports and one he could easily imagine on Mistress Priscian's lips; "Early to sleep a fortune keeps." The last thing he wanted to do was interrupt her at her evening meal with an intrusive request. As if in confirmation of his decision to postpone asking, he remembered that Haellus left the house every evening; he guessed that she probably shut up the house and retired after her servant's departure.

No, he corrected himself, *she said he left to celebrate the Banquet.* But then she had said there were no servants in the house at night. She must have meant the Oakhams' house.

"Odd," he muttered, tugging at his lower lip. Duessa Oakham did not strike him as likely to give up the services of her maid at any time. It must have been just for the night, he thought, maybe in honor of Beggar's Banquet, but it still seemed strange.

Certainly worth asking about, he decided, making a vague mental note of it; one of the guests might have suggested letting the servants go for the night.

There was nothing he could do about the Jewel at the moment. The few times he had helped Coeccias investigate crimes, he had found that one of the most useful things he could do was simply think about the crime, mulling over motives and opportunities, raising hypotheses and striking them down. That, however, required knowing something about the circumstances and the people involved, and as yet he knew very little. Once he had met some of the Oakhams' guests and spoken with the Werewolf, he might be able to begin conjecturing. But until then he was useless.

The bearded wizard waited temptingly at the back of his head, but Liam dismissed him temporarily; he was there solely because he was the only suspect who had a motive Liam could believe. If the Jewel were some sort of magical relic, that would be a reason to steal it: it could not be readily sold for coin, and he had difficulty imagining the kind of envy that would prompt someone to steal something they could not display.

"A miser does not build a house of gold," he reminded himself, but still found it too strange to grasp.

His thoughts leapt fruitlessly back and forth between the few things he knew, and after several minutes he sat up on the divan, muttering: "No point to this. None at all." He stood and stretched, hearing his bones crack. A glance at the cupola told him he had killed a fair amount of time, but there was still plenty to go before his appointment. With a sigh he looked around the library, hoping for inspiration.

His eye lit on a leather writing case tucked into one of the lower shelves, and in a single step he was on it, unclasping the lid. A neat stack of maps lay inside, his maps, the key to his partnership with Mistress Priscian. There was plenty of work there, Liam knew: he could flesh out the trading plan for the upcoming season. Courses to chart, timetables to be considered, cargo lists to draw up—there was work for weeks in cargo lists alone. What would sell in one place would rot on the docks in another, and an idea of what they would need would provide an excellent excuse for his visit to the merchant Cawood at the Staple the next day.

The paper of the maps rustled happily as he closed the lid and tucked the case under his arm. He could spread them out on the tables in Tarquin's old workroom and draw up the cargo lists until the time came to leave for his appointment with Lord Oakham. Grinning to himself, he turned to the door of the library and faltered when he saw Grantaire standing there.

They both bowed slightly; Liam almost smiled at the mirroring, and then he noticed the wizard's face. Lower lip firmly gripped by her teeth, she appeared almost hesitant, and the expression was so much the opposite of her usual one that it looked like she was in pain.

"Hello," Liam said, drawing the word out carefully, as if he were talking to a strange dog, or a potentially violent madman.

"I must apologize," she said, ignoring his wary greeting. The fingers of her right hand were wrapped around the wrist of her left arm, as if to restrain it; the words came slowly. "I have not been . . . honest with you, and I think I must be."

Liam sensed that she rarely apologized, and that it was difficult for her. "There is no need—"

"No," she interrupted firmly. "I will explain. Otherwise you will wonder."

I have enough to wonder about, he groaned inwardly; aloud, he said: "I'm thirsty, and there aren't enough chairs here. . . ." He gestured to the kitchen, and after a moment she nodded and preceded him.

The jug by the stove was beaded with condensation even before Liam grabbed it. Grantaire took the cup he offered without really noticing it, and began talking and pacing even as he sat.

"This mage you have heard about—his name is Desiderius, and he is a representative of the Guild from Harcourt. It is possible that he has been sent to look for me. It is also possible that he is here in search of Eirenaeus Priscian's Jewel. It is equally possible that he is here on some other business entirely, but the Jewel caught his attention. All these things are possible."

She stopped speaking but continued pacing, the fingers of both hands laced tightly around the cup from which she had yet to drink. Liam did not speak; he did not think she had finished, and after a long pause she spoke again.

"I cannot, however, discount the idea that he may be looking for me. At the very least he may come here, knowing that this was Tanaquil's home, and that he and I were friends. If he does, it is crucial that he not know I am here."

If she knew that he was there, Liam could not tell it: she seemed to be speaking to herself.

"I am no longer a member of the Guild. They have labeled me Gray, as they had Tanaquil, but when he was so named it meant less. The distinction is political. It means nothing—less than nothing. At least I don't practice black magic, which is more than can be said for some of them."

Liam shivered for no perceptible reason. Again, there was the feeling that she was not aware of his presence, and that she was rehearsing some private soliloquy.

"If Desiderius finds me, he may try to bring me back. With Tanaquil's spellbooks, his library, his enchantments, I can prevent that. And if he does not try to bring me back, or kill me, he must still not be allowed to bring word back. They cannot know where I am."

Then, for the first time, she looked directly at him, registering his presence. In that look, he sensed the whole of their relationship changing. It was as if she were seeing him for the first time, and knew she needed him. *She may not be so rude from now on,* he thought with a grim, silent laugh, *but what does she need?*

She told him.

"I am sure he will come here. He may or may not ask about me, but he will come. He may demand Tanaquil's things, but you must not give them to him. When he died, Tanaquil was not a member of the Guild, and it has no claim on him. If he asks about me, you must say that you never saw me."

Easy enough, Liam thought, and realized that now he might speak. "I certainly won't give up any of Tarquin's things. And if you do not want him to know you are here, I will not tell him. But I would like to know why the Guild wants you."

He had tried to sound as indifferent as he could, but still Grantaire stiffened, clearly about to tell him that it was none of his business. She held herself in, though, and slowly nodded.

"I killed two Guild mages in Harcourt. It is complicated. They kidnapped my apprentice to draw me into the city. They let her loose in a crowd, a riot, and she was trampled. When I tried to save her, they prevented me, and she was killed. So I killed them."

"Ah," Liam said, trying to compress sympathy and comprehension into one syllable. The sympathy was genuine, but he was miles from comprehension.

"You do not understand," she said immediately, and he blushed. "They were not attacking me, and the girl was already dead. I should not have killed them. But then, I suppose, they would have turned me over to the Magister anyway, in which case I would have been killed."

To a certain extent, Liam thought he understood revenge; there had been no question of self-defense when he killed his father's murderer. "Why would you have been killed?"

Irritation flashed in her eyes but was quickly suppressed, and he knew for sure that he was in charge when she began explaining.

"At the same time I was labeled Gray, the Magister in Harcourt declared all Grays anathema. The distinction, as I said, is political, but it has been made a Guild policy, and is being spread around the kingdom as a fact. Unless I miss my guess, various atrocities will soon be laid at the feet of prominent Grays, and the Whites of the Guild will take action."

Each sentence left Liam even more confused. Reluctantly, with some prodding, Grantaire cleared up his questions until he thought he understood.

The Mages Guild was not decentralized, she said, like those of weavers or carters, or even thieves. When she mentioned the last, Liam squirmed a little in his seat, but she did not notice. The Guild was a united body, each city's chapter headed by a Magister who belonged to the ruling Senate. By custom, the Magister of Torquay headed the Senate, but in recent years the power of Torquay had declined, and the current Magister of Harcourt had taken advantage of that to raise himself to effective control. He had promulgated the division between White and Gray, first as an informal distinction and later as an official label.

Loosely speaking, Whites believed in a more disciplined Guild, each wizard ranked and subordinated to a strict hierarchy. They also favored direct intervention in worldly affairs, some going so far as to encourage the actual seizure of temporal power.

Liam frowned at that. "I thought wizards were forbidden power. Isn't that in your Guild charter? They have been excluded from state affairs since the Seventeen Houses first came to Taralon."

Grantaire glared at him, as if resenting the interruption.

"The charter is supposed to forbid it," she admitted grudgingly, "but the wording is vague, and can be twisted. In any case, that is what the Whites want."

Grays, on the other hand, favored a more relaxed Guild. They were, on the whole, far fewer in number, but vastly more powerful. "Tanaquil was a Gray long before the name was devised. There have always been Grays, in that sense—solitary mages, who prefer their own company and their own researches. They leave the petty Guild politics to mages with less talent and more ambition. For obvious reasons, they tend to live in the countryside, or in places like Southwark, where the Guild has no chapter houses."

For as long as history recorded, it had been like that, with some wizards keeping only the weakest ties with the Guild, and most others more or less its servants. The prohibition against political action and a general lack of interest had kept the Guild from any attempt to grow stronger. "In Torquay then there was a real king, and the Torquay Magister was his man. But now—let us be honest, the king is king in name only. He can scarcely rule his own capital, let alone all of Taralon. As he has weakened, so has the Torquay Magister. So Harcourt has risen, and he has the power and the will to change the Guild, to make it a political power. The Grays, whether labeled or not, would not allow that for very long, however, and he knows that. So he strikes against them. To call them Blacks would be too obvious—but Gray, it implies. It hints. Who will trust a Gray mage, when they can turn to a White? And with no true king in Torquay, and most local lords weak or busy squabbling among themselves, will not people look to the strong?"

It was certainly plausible; Liam had to admit that. And he had no reason to doubt her, though he had no reason to believe her. That, however, did not matter; what mattered was what she needed from him.

"If this Desiderius comes, I won't tell him you are here, and I definitely won't give him any of Tarquin's things. But is that all you need?"

She laughed harshly. "Not unless you can put a true king in Torquay, and root the Magister out of Harcourt."

Despite its harshness, her answer was a relief to him. He did not need any more responsibilities. "He may be gone by now. Desiderius, I mean. The Jewel was stolen; maybe he has gone with it."

"Stolen by force, or stealth?"

"Stealth."

Grantaire shook her head, sure of herself. "Then no, he has not left with it. If he were to steal, it would be by force. Harcourt's creatures are arrogant." Her mouth tensed and her eyes narrowed, as if she were remembering. "They would buy it or rip it from the owner's neck, but they would not sneak in the night."

Over an hour had passed. The kitchen window showed darkening shadows in the strip between the back of the house and the cliff.

"I have to go into the city tonight," Liam said. "I may be back late. Tomorrow I will ask Mistress Priscian if she has any of Eirenaeus's papers. Do you need anything in the meantime?"

"No." She sounded exhausted. For the first time, she drank from her cup, a long gulp that made her throat and shoulders move as if she were sobbing.

■ *7* ■

DRESSED IN THE same clothes he had worn earlier in the day, but freshly bathed and shaved, Liam rode back into Southwark. The sun had already set in the west, leaving an infinite blackness beneath the deep blue bowl of the sky. Later, when the stars were out and the moon had risen, their light would shine off the snow in the fields; for now, Liam shivered and pulled his cloak closer, turning his head rapidly from side to side, staring into the blackness and seeing nothing. Diamond, however, jogged along nonchalantly.

Fanuilh? Liam projected. He did not even want to whisper in the darkness.

Yes, master?

In the Midlands, they say that the Black Hunter rides out on nights like this, and catches unwary travelers.

Does he?

Liam rolled his eyes. *No.* He wished he could accent his thoughts to indicate exasperation.

Soon enough Southwark appeared in the distance, a cheering orange glow. Ordinarily the city was much darker at night, but he guessed that the Banquet festivities would probably keep it lit up later and later as the week went on. He spurred Diamond into a trot, and Fanuilh flew off into the darkness.

The streets by the city gate were not crowded, though Liam passed the occasional reveler. As he came closer to the city square he found more and more, so many that he had to force Diamond through thick knots of people, some going about their usual business, but most with the special shine to their faces that indicated celebrations to come.

And something to drink, he thought, as Diamond shied to one side of a congested street, avoiding a surge of boys from a wineshop, none older than sixteen and many wearing holiday masks.

There were fewer people in the city square than he had expected, though the inns and taverns that lined it, including Herlekin's, were full and noisy. He left his horse with the guard at the barracks, explaining that he would be back in a moment, and ducked across the cobbles to Herlekin's.

Heat and song blasted out of the door when he opened it, but he took a deep breath and plunged in. Each table seemed bent on outsinging all the others, and people milled in the spaces between tables, shouting encouragement or singing on their own. Many were already drunk, and Liam had to bob and weave around a steady stream of sweating serving men and women—Herlekin usually had only women serving, but he had pressed his tapsters into service for the large crowd. Liam found the fat innkeeper near the back of the common room, bowing obsequiously to a one-legged man wrapped in a tattered blanket and perched on the dais where musicians sometimes played.

"Your pleasure, master?" the innkeeper bellowed, and the beggar peered down in a good imitation of lordly snobbery. Just then a pair of men burst from the crowd, one holding a piece of some kind of cake and the other a jug. They thrust Herlekin aside and bowed unsteadily to the beggar, holding each other up and presenting their gifts. The innkeeper stepped away, smiling good-naturedly and mopping at his brow with a corner of his apron. Liam tugged at his elbow.

"Master Herlekin," he shouted, trying to make himself heard.

"Sir Liam," Herlekin shouted, bowing deeply. He spread his hands to indicate the noise and, giving an apologetic smile, led Liam through a nearby door into a dim hallway. The roaring of the holiday crowd was slightly less there, but Liam still had to raise his voice to be heard.

"Has anyone left a message for me?"

Herlekin smiled eagerly and began drywashing his hands. "Indeed, Sir Liam, a young whelp did bring you a word. She said when the bells toll nine tomorrow morning to be at the Arcade of Scribes. A most ill-mannered girl, Sir Liam."

"Yes, she is. Thank you."

A tapster came down the corridor, rolling a barrel, and Liam used the opportunity to slip back into the crowd. Coeccias had introduced him to the innkeeper with the warning that, unless stopped, he would talk forever.

Liam pressed through the crowd again, keeping a tight hold on his cloak. Near the door a woman in a low-cut gown with heavily rouged cheeks staggered into him; she whirled around to face him, a high-pitched laugh on her lips, but it died when she saw his face. She muttered something and backed away with a small curtsy. Her fingers were crossed.

Frowning, Liam left the inn. The cold air was a blessing, washing away the smell of smoke and sweat. He was sweating himself, and he walked slowly across the square, allowing the night wind to dry him.

Why did she do that? he wondered. Crossed fingers in Southwark, he knew, were the same as forked fingers in the Midlands—proof against curses or the Evil Eye. *Why would she do that?*

The answer, when he realized it, made him pause on the steps of the barracks and curse. The guard on duty flinched. "Quaestor?" he asked.

Do not trouble me, Liam thought. *I am a deadly wizard of tremendous power.*

"Never mind," he muttered, and stomped into the barracks.

Stupid, he thought, scolding himself. *Stupid, stupid.* He knew he was not a wizard, and so he often forgot that for most of Southwark that was exactly what he was, because he had been friends with a wizard and now lived in a wizard's house. And if a whore in a tavern recognized him and thought him worth crossed fingers, then any wizard from Harcourt could ask a few questions and hear the same thing.

Coeccias was not in, but Liam had not expected him to be. He could have gone to the Aedile's house—there was time, the bells in the Duke's Courts having only just tolled seven—but he chose not to. One of the off-duty guards gathered around the liquor barrel in the middle of the room found him paper, quill and ink. He hastily wrote a note, mentioning the red-haired wizard's name and asking Coeccias not to do anything regarding him until they could talk. He wrote that he would stop by sometime the next morning, and signed his name. The same guard promised to see that the Aedile received the letter, which Liam had folded but not bothered to seal.

Who would read the mail of a wizard?

Shaking his head, he left the barracks and led Diamond to a nearby ostler, who promised that his boy would be in the stables all night.

A sour mood lay heavily on him, and he could feel his shoulders sagging as he trudged away from the ostler's towards the Point. The woman's crossed fingers had annoyed him, not just because he did not want people thinking he was a wizard, but also because it had made him realize his mistake. He had practically promised Grantaire that he would have nothing to do with the other wizard, not recognizing that he would have to investigate him in connection with the Jewel. He could conceivably leave that part to Coeccias, but that would entail lengthy explanations and, he had to admit, he was not entirely sure he wanted to leave it to his friend. In many respects he admired the Aedile and thought he handled the immensely difficult job of keeping order in Southwark very well, but secretly he did not believe that the gruff man would be much of a match for a wizard. At the same time, he thought that Coeccias's estimation of his own skills was vastly overrated—and if that was a contradiction, he knew and accepted it.

So you are unsure of yourself and *obnoxiously proud,* he told himself. *So be it.* He smiled a little, an old, self-directed smile of derision with which he was well familiar. *So be it,* he thought again, and squared his sagging shoulders. There was no point in worrying about the wizard; at the moment he had to concentrate on his evening with Lord Oakham.

There was almost an hour before he was expected, so he forced himself to a slower pace, wandering leisurely on a route that would eventually bring him to the end of the Point and the Oakhams'.

Fewer revelers wandered the streets of the Point, but many of the houses were gaily decorated. Candles burned in most of the windows, and greenery festooned the gables of brick and stone, sometimes in elaborate patterns, and sometimes with colored lanterns worked in. At two he saw beggars being given food, and remembered the beggar enthroned at Herlekin's. It seemed Southwarkers took the name of their holiday seriously.

There was a group of five or six being fed outside a building he knew, the brothel owned by Coeccias's acquaintance Herione. The brothel had a long portico and enormous double doors carved with erotic bas-reliefs; in front of one door a stout woman was ladling soup from a steaming pot into bowls and handing them out.

"All well and good, mistress," one of the beggars was saying as Liam passed, "but y' have other things inside that a man needs above food."

"Go to!" the woman said, rapping the beggar's knuckles with her ladle and drawing a laugh from his companions, who were both male and female. "It's the Banquet, not the Bedding!"

Laughter trailing him, smiling himself, Liam strolled up the street, beginning to feel a little of the holiday spirit.

The brothel stood on the north side of the Point's northernmost street; only a few hundred feet further on it connected with End Street, where Mistress Priscian and the Oakhams lived. Liam had planned to wander the rich neighborhood until the time came for him to meet Lord Oakham, but now he saw a large gathering at the corner that drew his steps in that direction.

If he remembered Coeccias's list correctly, the crowd was assembled outside the Goddards' house, a five-story mansion easily three times the size of any other building on the Point. The crowd waiting to go in was equally impressive, a far cry from the ragged bunch outside Herione's; richly dressed men and heavily bejeweled women formed a long line that spilled into the street. Servants in what Liam assumed was Goddard livery wandered about with trays, dispensing hot wine in silver goblets; the guests chattered noisily amongst themselves and awaited their chance to present their invitations to another liveried servant standing beneath a two-story arch. He was flanked by two halberdiers in silver-plated armor, who stood to attention as each guest was admitted. Liam wondered whether they would use the halberds on someone who tried to get in without an invitation.

Settling himself against the wall of a building across the street, he crossed his arms and watched the parade of guests with an amused smile. For a while he tried to gauge which woman was wearing the most makeup and which man's stock was tightest around his neck. The odd thing was that the woman with the whitest face was usually accompanied by the man with the reddest. He silently awarded the prize to a purple-faced man who was talking loudly about how few people there were compared to previous years.

Liam found that hard to believe: he had been watching for at least ten minutes, the guests were moving into the courtyard at a good pace, and yet the line showed no sign of diminishing. If anything it was increasing, as more people in fancy attire came up the road, most walking but some riding, usually with servants in tow. When they reached the line, they dismounted and handed the reins over to their servants. At one point a coach rattled up at high speed, scattering the tail end of the line and provoking a storm of shouts from the men and squeals from the women, until the occupant of the carriage emerged. Apparently he was a favorite; the shouts turned friendly and the man was quickly absorbed into the line.

So much money, Liam thought, surveying the mass of party-goers in their finery, steaming silver goblets in their hands, gold and jewels at their throats and on their fingers, furs and fine woolens and silks all around. *So many fools.* The rich in the Freeports were better, he decided, less given to show. *They have sumptuary laws to keep it that way, of course, but still . . .*

The qualifier was still lingering in his head when a polite cough interrupted him. He jumped a little, and saw Mistress Priscian beside him.

"Good evening," he said, beginning to bow. She restrained him with a gloved hand on his arm.

"Good evening to you, Master Rhenford. You are going to my niece's?" She was wearing no makeup, though the bun of hair at the back of her head was tight and neatly arranged. A stout cloak of good blue wool was pulled close around her, so he could not tell what she was wearing, but he imagined it was eminently sensible.

"Yes. Lord Oakham has arranged for me to meet some of his guests."

"I know," she said, angling her head back and frowning up at him. "He told me. A surprisingly sensible suggestion, from him. I did not think he would have the courage to stand at your side while you question his friends."

Liam coughed, unsure what Oakham had told her. "The hope, I think, is that perhaps I can disguise my questions a little."

She waved this aside. "Even so, it is more than I expected."

An uncomfortable silence ensued; Liam was thinking about Grantaire's request, a small voice at the back of his head telling him to ask right then, and a louder voice telling him to wait.

"Are you going to the Goddards'?"

She frowned down at the gilt-edged card in her hand. "Once again, yes. Every year. I suppose it is a wonderful party, if you enjoy noise and drunkards and food that is too rich to eat. I am invited every year, and I always go, to pay my respects to Master Goddard. The Goddards also make ships, you know," she said, tapping his arm with the card. "And he is an old friend. We may need ships, you and I."

Liam did not think they would need more than the small Priscian fleet; he was more concerned about money for goods to trade, but he merely nodded.

"Not immediately," she went on, turning her gaze on the guest line. "But someday. By that time, in course, you will be receiving an invitation as well."

"Will I?" he laughed. "That will be nice. I like noise and drunkards and food too rich to eat."

"Then you will be very happy," she said placidly, still examining the line. "You will probably stay at these far later than I do. I always leave early. Early to wake a fortune makes—"

"—and early to sleep a fortune keeps," he finished.

She looked back at him and nodded judiciously, a smile of approval on her lips. "Just so. When are you expected at my niece's?"

"At eight o'clock."

"Then perhaps you will keep me company. I do not wish to go in just yet, and in any case the line is too long. I am not cold," she added, as if he had asked, "though I imagine she is." With one arched eyebrow she indicated a woman who had just emerged from a coach wearing a bright yellow gown with short sleeves and a very low neckline.

Liam nodded solemnly. "Very cold."

Another silence ensued, more comfortable this time. Mistress Priscian stood upright, tapping her invitation against the palm of her hand and studying the shifting line of guests with a sort of regal indifference that made Liam want to laugh. His promise to Grantaire repeated itself in the back of his head, however, and after a few minutes he finally brought himself to ask.

"Mistress Priscian, I wonder if I might ask a question."

She stopped tapping the invitation. "In course, Master Rhenford."

"I have a guest, an old acquaintance of Tarquin Tanaquil—I live in his home, you know, he left it to me—and this guest has an interest in your ancestor. Eirenaeus Priscian, I mean. My guest is a wizard, you see—an old acquaintance of Tarquin Tanaquil—and apparently he is mentioned in several books as having been a wizard. My guest was wondering if, perhaps, Eirenaeus had left any papers, and if he had, if you might allow . . . of course, there may be no papers, but if there were . . ." He trailed off lamely, trying to guess from her impassive face what her reaction was.

"Is your guest a woman, Master Rhenford?"

He blushed, and hoped that it was too dark for her to notice. "Yes."

"And a wizard?"

"Yes, an old acquaintance of Tarquin Tanaquil." Liam still could not guess her reaction. She reminded him again of one of his university masters.

"I see. She would like to examine his papers. I do not know if there are any."

"Of course," he began, but she interrupted him.

"If there are any papers, and if you will vouch for this wizard, I see no reason that she should not see them. Since I do not know of any, they are clearly of no use to me. I will look tomorrow. Will that be soon enough?"

"Oh, I'm sure," he stammered. "That would be fine, thank you."

"I promise nothing," she said, holding up a warning finger. "And now I think I had best go." She pointed to the line, which had shrunk perceptibly. Turning, she paused; Liam, belatedly recognizing a cue, offered her his arm. They crossed the street together, and exchanged goodbyes even as Mistress Priscian had to present her invitation to the liveried servants. Liam sketched a hasty bow and backed away, certain that the two halberdiers were eyeing him suspiciously. Up close they looked less ornamental, their breastplates shining in the torchlight but their faces decidedly menacing. Grinning sheepishly, he walked away at a brisk pace.

It was foolish, Liam knew, but he hated being early almost as much as he hated being late, so he deliberately slowed his pace once he rounded the corner onto End Street. The windows of the Goddard mansion were unshuttered on this side, and multicolored oblongs of light lay across the cobblestones, crisscrossed by a hundred flitting shadows. Muffled music and laughter seeped out, and he crossed to the far side of the street, the better to look in.

He slowly passed the windows, each showing a different variation on the same theme of dancing, drinking people beneath enormous chandeliers, the candles of which burned blue, red and green, as well as the normal yellow.

"That had to cost something," Liam said appreciatively. "How many beggars in there, I wonder?"

There was only so long, however, that he could envy someone else's party, so he moved along, doing his best to imitate a man of leisure with no particular place to go. It was cold, though, and he wished he could walk faster, but that would have left him on the Oakhams' doorstep waiting for the bells to toll eight—which they did even as he thought of it. He hurried the rest of the way, jumping up the stoop before the bells had finished.

To his surprise, Quetivel answered the door, a cup in his hand and a snarl on his face.

"At last," he snapped, the last toll of eight still shivering in the air. "Now we can go. Oakham!" he shouted over his shoulder. "Let's to it!"

Oakham came bustling down the corridor, throwing a cloak around his shoulders.

"Good evening, Master Rhenford." He took Quetivel's cup with a wink and downed it in one gulp, then handed it back empty. "Y' are ready?" He looked Liam up and down, nodding his approval. Quetivel, meanwhile, frowned at his empty cup, then dropped it.

"Come, let's to it!" the young baron said.

Liam took a step or two down the stoop, expecting them to follow, but Oakham did not move. Eyebrows raised, he looked from the fallen cup to Quetivel and back. The baron grunted, then bent and retrieved the cup. Shaking his head so that his braids whipped around, he stalked back down the corridor.

Oakham sighed and came down the steps, putting a hand on Liam's shoulder and drawing him into the street.

"These border lords have a number of rough edges—he is still surprised that there are no rushes on the floor to soak up his messes. Now, Master Rhenford, y' are ready?"

"I think so, my lord."

"Use my name," Oakham said, smiling. "I think it will serve better." Liam nodded his assent. "Be as discreet as you may, Rhenford. Quetivel knows your purpose—I trust him implicitly—but I would that, insofar as you may, you keep it from the others."

"I will try." He could not bring himself to add the man's name, though it should not have been a problem. Many of his fellow students in Torquay had been noble, and he had been on a first-name basis with them. *You were noble too, once,* he chided himself yet again. Still, it would feel odd; it had been many years since he had had reason to think of his background, much less spend time with anyone of rank.

Quetivel emerged from the house, sulking, and as they set off down End Street, he put himself between Liam and Oakham. The young lord was far shorter than the other two men, and with his pout and long braids he seemed more like a little girl than a man out for a night of . . . *Of what?* Liam wondered. *Where are we going?* He would not ask Quetivel, though, and he did not want to talk over the shorter man's head, so he stayed silent. Oakham strode briskly, whistling a holiday song; Liam kept pace with him easily, but Quetivel had to scurry to stay abreast of them, and his scowl darkened.

Oakham stopped abruptly by the first of the Goddards' windows and peered in, brushing at his mustache. "Quite a party," he said.

"Merchants," Quetivel sniffed, and continued walking.

"Oh, I don't know," Oakham said, with a wink at Liam. "They have their points." He started walking again, though it seemed to Liam that he went more slowly, forcing Quetivel to drop back and join them.

They turned off End Street in silence, passing the Goddards' gate, where the halberdiers still stood at attention, though the liveried door-man was sipping from a chased goblet and chatting with another servant.

Oakham led them to Herione's, where the stout woman still stood by her cauldron of soup. She curtsied as they walked up the steps. "Merry Banquet, masters."

"And to you," Oakham smiled back; Liam echoed him, but Quetivel only scowled anew, tugged at the large doors, and disappeared inside. Oakham stopped Liam with a touch on the arm and chuckled. "You should look at the doors."

"They are . . . interesting, aren't they?" He was a little surprised that this was where they were to meet Uldericus, but he did not want to seem "rough at the edges," and he had, in fact, been to Herione's before. "I am always surprised that no one objects to them. Out on the street as they are," he added.

"A point," the lord said quietly, giving Liam a strange look before ushering him in.

It was mostly as he remembered—the sweeping staircase along the back wall, lined with niches containing erotic statuary, the fountain with its larger and even more explicit statue—but where before the room had been filled with bright summer flowers, now it was dressed for the Banquet, with wreaths of greenery everywhere and colored lanterns scattered about. The main difference, however, was the people. The last and only time he had visited had been during the day, and the room had been empty. Now it was almost full of young women in surprisingly modest dresses, all of the same cut, waiting on men of all ages and styles of dress. A sober-looking group of middle-aged men were talking amongst them-selves in one corner, while two or three young men in half-masks whirled women around the fountain to the music provided by a trio of musicians near the stairs.

Herione was as Liam remembered, a tall, statuesque woman with an elaborately coiffed headdress of black hair. She finished cautioning one of the young men to dance a little slower and dropped a deep curtsy to the three men at the door.

"Is Uldericus here?" Quetivel demanded.

"Good evening, Baron Quetivel," she said smoothly, ignoring his rudeness. "Earl Uldericus attends you in his usual room. Good evening, Lord Oakham, Master Rhenford." She said his name without missing a beat—even as Quetivel shouldered past her—and Liam smiled and bowed in return. A good memory for names must have been a requisite, given her work, but he was still impressed. *Particularly since you spent no money,* he thought. Even better, Oakham was directing another assessing look his way, and Liam guessed he had just gone up another notch in the man's estimation.

Which is ridiculous, he added to himself. *Because the madame of an expensive brothel knows my name. . . .*

"Alethe will show you the way, my lords." She snapped her fingers, called the girl's name. Alethe detached herself from one of the dancing boys and rushed over. "Show Lord Oakham and Master Rhenford to the Red Chamber. Merry Banquet, my lords."

Herione turned majestically away, drifting towards the group of middle-aged men. Alethe gave a deep curtsy. "If you'll attend me, my lords?" She led them past the fountain and up the marble stairs.

"Uldericus has his own room?" Liam asked.

"He gives Herione a great deal of custom," Oakham said absently. He was watching Alethe mount the steps, his eyes focused on the narrow waist of her dress and the movement of the cloth below.

"Really?"

Oakham tore his eyes away from the girl. "You would scarcely credit it, when you see his wife. She's a passing beauty. But then, I don't think he comes here to bed, if you take me."

The stairs came to a landing, off which two hallways sprinkled with doors led to left and right. Alethe led them to the right.

"Herione's girls are most talented," Oakham went on. "They sing like larks, foot it like nymphs, and keep counsel like priests. Isn't that so, Alethe?" He reached forward and goosed the girl, who whirled around, at the same time blushing furiously and managing a sweet smile.

"As my lord says," she murmured, and then indicated a nearby door. "The Red Chamber." She opened the door and ushered them in, again with a deep curtsy.

The Red Chamber lived up to its name. Walls, floor, ceiling and furniture were all done in varying shades of red, from near-orange to almost-purple. Red shades around the few candles completed the effect, which Liam found a little uncomfortable. There were too many shadows, and everything in the room seemed a little blurry, including Uldericus, who was lounging on a low couch on the far side of the room. A woman knelt next to him, draping his forehead with a wet cloth, while another sat at his feet with a closed book; both were fully dressed. Quetivel was sitting on another couch opposite the earl, looking exasperated.

"More poetry," he exclaimed, turning to Oakham for help. "He is listening to poetry again!"

"Yes," Uldericus groaned, pulling himself up to a sitting position on the couch. He kept the wet cloth on his forehead. "Poetry again. It soothes away the cares of the day, Quetivel, and the aches in my head. What's more, the girl has a lovely voice." Wearily, he dropped the cloth in his lap and clapped his hands. The two women stood, curtsied and hurried out. "Now I warrant you want a game, is that it?"

The earl was as unprepossessing a man as Liam had ever seen: thin, of medium height, with short-cut gray hair. His neck was long and his ears a little too large for his head, but otherwise his face was average-looking. He wore a simple tunic and breeches of gray, and his feet were bare.

And he likes poetry, Liam thought. *How many thieves like poetry?*

Oakham chuckled. "Some wine betimes," he said, "and some talk, and then a game. I am not as eager as Quetivel to lose. And I brought a friend—an acquaintance of my aunt's. Master Liam Rhenford."

For the first time the earl noticed him, and Liam was sure the man's eyes widened a little at his name. Liam bowed.

"My lord."

"Master Rhenford. Merry Banquet. Quetivel, there is wine in the cupboard—pour us some, if you will."

The young baron went to a red-painted cupboard and began filling cups, grumbling all the while.

"Seat yourselves, gentlemen," Uldericus said, and they occupied the couch Quetivel had just left. "An acquaintance of Mistress Priscian, eh?"

"Yes, my lord."

"Y' are in trade?"

"I dabble, my lord. It passes the time." He remembered Quetivel's sneer at merchants.

"Ah."

"Does your head still ache, Uldericus?" Oakham asked, a little smile on his lips.

"The poetry was helping," the earl said, taking up his cloth and scrubbing at his temples. "I would task you for it, and your ample supplies of bad wine, but y' have trouble enough. Has the Duke's man clapped in the knave?"

Liam's mind raced, searching for a way to exploit the turn in the conversation. Quetivel handed around the cups to the seated men, but remained standing himself.

"No," Oakham replied. "There is little enough he can do. The thief was passing clever."

"What amazes me," Liam put in, "is that the man had the nerve to enter the house with all of you in it." Both Uldericus and Quetivel turned quickly to him, and he went on smoothly: "I met Mistress Priscian this evening, and she explained it all to me. It is strange—did you hear noth-ing?" He directed the last question to Oakham, who took it up smoothly.

"Not a thing. I was far into my cups," he said, and laughed ruefully.

Putting on his most innocent face, Liam turned to their host. "And you, Earl Uldericus? Not a thing?"

"I sleep very soundly," the man said, and then, inexplicably, shot a glance at Quetivel. "And so does my wife."

The baron said, "I heard nothing."

"I had the strangest dream, though," Uldericus said, as if it had just occurred to him. "I wonder if it was a sign. I dreamed I was a wolfhound rounding a henhouse, and a sly fox kept pattering on quiet feet, conning out an entrance. How does that like you?"

"Strange," murmured Oakham. Quetivel maintained a tight-lipped silence, gripping his cup tightly.

"It might be an omen," Liam admitted. "Or perhaps you heard the thief's steps, and they entered your dreams. Every time it rains, I dream that I'm at sea."

Quetivel burst out: "Nonsense! Dreams are dreams, no more."

Uldericus ignored him, staring thoughtfully at Liam. "There may be something in that, Master Rhenford. Who knows what makes our dreams? But what of it? I did not dream the knave's visage, and could not even tell the hour when I dreamed his footsteps."

"I would that you had," Oakham said, with a wry smile.

"What I most wonder, though," Liam said into the silence that fol-lowed, "is why steal the Jewel in the first place? There is not enough money in all of Southwark to pay for it—and who would buy it?"

Uldericus answered, but he was looking at Oakham. "A fool. Only a fool would buy it."

"Buy, sell, buy, sell," sneered Quetivel. "Not all things have a price, Rhenford, and the value of some is not measured in coins."

Liam smiled equably. "You are quite right, Baron Quetivel. You cannot buy happiness, for instance, or love—but a jewel? It *is* money." He had chosen his examples because they were cliches, but they seemed to strike home with Quetivel, who paled and looked down at his feet.

Now that's strange, Liam thought, and then turned back to Uldericus. Quetivel could wait; there would be plenty of chances to sound him out, but this might be his only meeting with the earl.

"I ask you, Earl Uldericus, if you were a thief, and knew you could not sell the Jewel, would you steal it?"

It was a little strong, Liam knew, too open a question, but he was worried about how much he would be able to dig, and since they were on the subject, he wanted to press ahead. The earl took his time about answering, rubbing his forehead with the cloth and looking at the rug between his feet.

"It passes my understanding, Master Rhenford," he said at last, and then looked up. "But I think we worry this subject to death. I am sure Aetius is ill with it, and it only reminds me how large a cup I crawled into yesternight." There was a bellpull by his couch; he reached out and tugged at it.

"Come, sirs, let us have a game."

■ *8* ■

THE WOMEN WHO had been attending the earl before responded to the bellpull, and Uldericus sent them off for plain lights and a table. It must have been a frequent request, because they returned only a few moments later, followed by two manservants carrying a small table with four stools stacked on top of it. The men quickly moved the couches away and set up the table, arranging the stools; one of the women hung an ordinary lantern from a convenient hook and removed the colored shades from the candles. The room brightened considerably, and Liam began to like it more.

The other woman had brought two decks of cards and a lacquered box, in which were neatly stacked wooden counters painted in blue, red and white. As soon as the stools were in place Uldericus sat and began deftly shuffling the decks, seven times each.

"Come, sirs, come," he said. "What game shall it be?"

"Alliances," Quetivel said, taking a seat and dropping a heavy sack on the table.

"In course," Oakham said, doing the same. "For what stakes, though?"

Liam sat as well, disturbed for no reason he could name. He knew how to play Alliances, and before leaving the house on the beach he had filled his purse with a fair number of coins, just as a precaution. When Uldericus announced the stakes, he breathed a mental sigh of relief. But the unease remained.

"Whites a silver, reds five, and blues a crown. Agreed?"

The other men readily agreed, and Liam opened his own purse, reaching in for a handful of coins.

"Rhenford, I think I may have not mentioned this to you," Oakham said, concern in his voice. "I can advance you a stake—"

This drew an arched eyebrow from Uldericus and a snort from Quetivel, but Liam merely smiled and shook his head, drawing a handful of gold coins from his pouch.

"Not at all, Oakham. I am always prepared." He stacked the coins on the table in front of him, and was happy to see that Uldericus nodded approvingly.

"A happy state," the earl said. "And do you know the game?"

That, Liam realized, was why he was not entirely comfortable. "I do," he said, which was true. He knew the rules, which were fairly complicated—he knew the rules for many card games. The problem was that he was no good at them. Cards were, he had long since decided, a combination of good memory and luck. He had a good memory, but for some reason could not bring it to bear on remembering all the cards in a deck; he also had good luck, in most things, but it had never extended to games of chance. So he said: "I have played from time to time, but I must warn you that I am far from the good."

Oakham smiled good-naturedly. "No matter. Quetivel isn't either."

The young baron frowned and tossed one of his braids over his shoulder. "I will trounce you all." There was nothing friendly in the way he said it.

Uldericus took their coins, stacking them neatly in the lacquered box and replacing them with the colored chips. Then he started dealing.

Alliances—and Generals, a version for three players—was popular in the Freeports, where there were entire taverns devoted to it; Liam had learned it there, between voyages. There were two decks, the first of which was dealt out, while the second was left in the center of the table for drawing. From the thirteen cards originally dealt them, each player was supposed to field an army, laying it out face up. An army had to be led by a king or queen, called generals, and be composed of at least three cards from the same suit. At the beginning of each turn, a player drew an extra card from the second deck, and at the end threw a card to the dead pile. In between, they could attack the other players' armies. A general could lead an extra army out of the player's hand, as it could for the player attacked, while existing armies could be reinforced. The rules of engagement were fairly simple—after reinforcing, the cards in each army were counted up and the player with the most powerful army took the loser's army. Later, if the loser was forced out of play, all of the armies he had lost could be bought into the hands of the winners. More important than winning cards, Liam knew, was that each action cost money.

Keeping an army out cost a red chip each turn; drawing a card cost a white; each card brought out to reinforce an army not under attack cost a white; an army under attack could be reinforced with one card for free, but each additional card cost a red; one army with a general could be laid out each turn for free, but to lay out an additional army on the same turn cost a blue. A player could pay to draw extra cards, or to avoid discarding, or to proclaim himself neutral for a number of turns, or even to ransom armies lost in an attack—in short a player could pay, and pay, and pay, and pay.

When Liam had learned in the Freeports, the game had not seemed so expensive. *You were playing with sailors,* he told himself, *for coppers.* He could not remember ever having put more than a few silvers into the warchest over the course of an entire game.

The idea was to force other players out, by attacking them until they could no longer field armies, either because they had no generals to lead or not enough cards of the general's suit to back them up. With three players, the game continued until only one was left; with four, the last two players left usually broke the warchest into shares equaling the number of armies left in play, each taking the same number of shares as they had armies.

It was not a fast game.

In the first of the five hands they played, much to his surprise, Liam split the warchest with Uldericus, taking two shares to the earl's seven. In the second, Liam drew a poor hand and Quetivel attacked him relentlessly, weakening himself so that Oakham and Uldericus split. The third was called a truce, because Liam had no generals on the deal, and could field no armies. Quetivel, with the strongest hand, took the meager warchest, a white ante chip from each player and a red indemnity from Liam for not being able to field.

The fourth hand was longer than the first three combined. No one seemed willing to attack, building up their armies slowly and husbanding their strength. Liam had the weakest position on the field and very little in his hand to reinforce with; when the attacks finally began, they were centered on him. He was forced to buy heavily to defend himself, but eventually, after a long, drawnout and expensive series of defenses, he was put out of the game and left with a tiny pile of chips. Uldericus declared himself neutral for three turns, paying three blues for the right, and in the flush of victory over Liam, Quetivel turned on Oakham and put him out of the game.

"Alliance?" Uldericus asked. His forces were untouched, and his smile seemed to indicate that he had a strong hand in reserve. Quetivel, though, had most of Liam's and Oakham's armies; for a heavy fee he could field them and try to take the whole warchest himself.

He hesitated, swaying in his chair a little. He had filled and emptied his cup more times than the other three men put together. Screwing up his eyes, he surveyed the table, inspecting the armies Uldericus had laid out, the discard pile and the hands Liam and Oakham had laid out after their defeats, as if he were searching for something.

"Alliance," he mumbled at last, and stumbled away to refill his cup. Liam and Oakham stood as well, stretching, while Uldericus split the warchest into shares.

"Shall we try a final hand?" the earl asked, eyes still on the pile of chips.

"Yes!" Quetivel shouted from the far side of the room. "Another!"

"I'll venture," Oakham said. "Rhenford?"

Liam shook his head and waved a hand at his tiny stake. "No. I can hardly field an army."

Oakham smiled. "Come, I'll vouch for you. You can repay me tomorrow."

Uldericus looked up, frowning. "Y' are not doing so well yourself, Aetius."

"I have enough for another hand—and I'll vouch for Rhenford. What say you?"

Oakham was looking at him, but Liam waited for Uldericus, who looked back and forth between the two standing men. The earl thought for a moment, one finger tapping his chin, and then drew the lacquered box towards him.

"Thirty?" He started counting out chips.

"Thirty to start," Oakham said with a bright smile. "And ten for me, if it please you. You and Quetivel can't have all the luck."

"I hope not," Liam said, taking his seat and accepting the new chips Uldericus sent his way. Borrowing the money did not bother him, because he knew he had more than enough at home to repay Oakham; besides, he was having fun.

Enjoy your losses all you want, he scolded himself, *but are you learning anything?*

He was learning things, in fact, but nothing that was of any use. Early on he had tried to start a conversation, but his comments had fallen flat, the other three men concentrating solely on the game at hand. He gave up trying to start them talking, and focused on their playing.

Oakham was bold but careless, laying his armies out in full strength, with very little in the way of reserves. He attacked Liam and Quetivel recklessly, laughing when he won, laughing even louder when he lost. He bought very little, however, relying mainly on the strength of the cards he was dealt and what he drew, so that even though he had lost twice, it had not hurt his pile too much.

Quetivel, on the other hand, made a great show of trying to be canny, carefully examining all the armies laid out and making an effort to remember all the cards in the discard pile and those held prisoner. He kept large reserves, paying heavily to bring them in when attacking and defending. In the first two hands he had only attacked when someone was weakened by previous attacks from other players, and then only Liam and Oakham. In the fourth, though, emboldened perhaps by the wine, he had attacked almost as often as Oakham, though still maintaining reserves. Still, he avoided fighting the earl, though he frequently shot calculating glares at the man. Even with his share of the fourth warchest, it was clear that he has lost money.

Uldericus was the only consistent winner. His pile of chips was much bigger than anyone else's, despite the fact that he almost never attacked. He had bought neutrality for himself in the fourth hand, but Liam could not see why: neither Oakham nor Quetivel had ever attacked the earl, and Liam had only done so in the first hand, when he had the strength. At first Liam had worried that the other two men might have been refraining from engaging the earl out of deference, but Uldericus had taken no offense at his attacks, so he put it down to fear of the man's pile of chips, with which he could afford to buy enormous reserves.

Quetivel came back to the table with another cup of wine and brilliant red spots on each pale cheek. "I shall trounce you all," he announced, as if he had a grudge against them, and sat. Uldericus began dealing the fifth hand.

From the moment he picked up his cards, Liam knew he was going to lose. He had only one general, a queen, and the rest mostly low cards scattered among the suits. Oakham and Uldericus arranged their cards in silence and with blank expressions; Quetivel sneered happily at his and immediately, before it was his turn, laid out an army. The earl frowned and laid out his first army, Liam and Oakham following, skipping Quetivel's turn.

The play started even slower than in the hand before. Oakham and Uldericus drew normally and laid out no more armies, Quetivel fielded a general each turn until he had four, and Liam brought extra cards, hoping for another general. He drew neither kings nor queens, but managed to get a few decent reserve cards, including one of the two dragons in the deck.

Thus it went around the table for several rounds, with Liam's pile of chips steadily dwindling as he sought vainly for generals. Both Oakham and Uldericus had laid out extra armies and then, suddenly, Oakham attacked, laying out a third army and directing it at Liam. Led by a king and with high cards to back it up, it easily beat both what Liam had showing and his reserve cards—except for the dragon.

The dragon was an expensive card to play, but he had little choice. Oakham called for his defense with a small smile. Liam payed out the equivalent of five blue chips, which left him with only ten white chips and two reds, and played the dragon.

Oakham's jaw dropped. The army he had attacked with, his strongest, went to the dead pile, as did the dragon, and Liam was allowed to counterattack. He chose the lord's weakest army, reinforcing his queen-led army with two high cards and paying the fee into the warchest.

"I have nothing," Oakham stammered, and watched Liam scoop up his weakest army.

It was Uldericus's turn. With a sour look at Oakham, he bought neutrality for two rounds. Quetivel was champing at the bit, and as soon as the earl had paid his fee, he paid the upkeep fees on the four armies he had, laid out a fifth, and attacked both Liam and Oakham.

Without reserves, Oakham handed his last army over. Liam stayed in a little longer, using his last three whites to buy in strong cards to support his queen, and the last red to field the army he had taken from Oakham. Quetivel, though, had strong reserves as well, and when he bought them in, he took both.

Liam nodded graciously, impressed by the quick move, and handed his armies over. Quetivel snapped them up.

"It seems I bought neutrality to no purpose," Uldericus said, a hint of bitterness in his voice. "Alliance?" He reached forward to split the warchest. Quetivel reached out unsteadily and stopped the earl's hand.

"No. No alliance." His voice was husky, wavering, and he cleared his throat. "No alliance. I'll trounce you all."

There was something in his tone that made Liam lean forward, a feeling that Quetivel's words had some significance he could not catch. Oakham did not seem to understand the young lord's meaning either; he watched both Quetivel and Uldericus with an expression that combined confusion and anxiety.

"Well enough," the earl said at last, pulling his hand from underneath Quetivel's. "My draw, then."

He paid his fee, drew, and paid another to avoid discarding. Quetivel paid, drew, paid to lay out another army, and discarded a low card. There was a sudden tension around the table, and Liam found he was holding his breath. He let it out slowly between his teeth; after all, he had already lost all of his money. *Oakham is out too,* he thought, *but he is as nervous as I am.* It was true: the lord's handsome face was pale, his glance flickering back and forth between the remaining players.

Quetivel glared at his opponent, his eyes narrowed to slits; his head jerked forward from time to time in rapid pecks, and he rubbed his lips together hungrily. Uldericus appeared not to notice, nonchalantly paying the proper fees to draw and lay out a strong army. Then he paid for three reserve cards, the most he could draw in a turn, and discarded one of them, a red two.

"It is not too late to call Alliance," Uldericus said, but Quetivel ignored him, drawing and starting to field all of his armies. He had five led by kings and three by queens, and even though he had fumbled a great deal with his hand to lay them out, he still had an impressive spread of reserves.

"Trounce," he said, with a mean and happy smile. He attacked with all his armies. There could only be sixteen armies in the field—eight kings and eight queens. Quetivel held eight, and one of Oakham's was in the dead pile, untouchable, which meant that Uldericus could only field seven.

With a wry smile, the earl laid out seven armies. "It would like me to play this out," he said.

"If y' enjoy a slow trouncing," Quetivel said with a flourish of his free hand. "Go to."

Uldericus placed his seven armies in order against Quetivel's eight. "Reinforce?"

Quetivel swayed forward and blinked deliberately, studying which armies had been placed against which, and then reinforced the first. Sudden beads of sweat stood out on his brow and cheeks, obstinately refusing to run. Uldericus laid out enough reserves on his first to make the two armies equal—and they went to the dead pile. The second and third armies for both men went the same way, tied and discarded, and Liam began to see the earl's strategy. He was husbanding his strength, using cards just strong enough to match and leaving his highest reserve cards in his hand.

Oakham licked his lips nervously and left the table for a cup of wine. Three more armies went to the dead pile, and Uldericus had only one left, his strongest, matched against Quetivel's strongest. Quetivel's eighth lay unopposed, and the young baron laughed. "Trounced!"

"Would you reinforce?" Uldericus asked pleasantly.

"Why?" Quetivel demanded. "Even if you take it, it cannot be fielded until your next turn, leaving mine the only army in play. No, I'll not reinforce! Take it, if you will—the warchest is mine."

"Unless the only army left is unfielded," Uldericus said. Paying and reinforcing his seventh army, he took Quetivel's, then threw five blues into the warchest and played a dragon against the last army on the field. "And that army is now mine." With a satisfied smile he sat back.

Quetivel stood, knocking over his stool, and planted his fists heavily on the table, leaning over the wreckage of his game. "Impossible!" he shouted. "No!" He threw his head back and practically howled. "Oakham! It's impossible!"

Leveling a stern glance at the angry baron, Uldericus called out: "Aetius, I think our young friend needs some air."

"No!" Quetivel cried, and he would have lunged across the table if Oakham had not caught him by the shoulders and pulled him back. The wiry baron struggled briefly, but Oakham easily caught him around the waist and carried him out of the room. Liam would have thought it funny—Quetivel kicked and shouted like a child—if Uldericus had not been staring so thoughtfully at the departing pair. When they were gone, he stood and stretched, then went and shut the door behind them.

"Well and well," he said, rubbing his chin. "He should neither drink nor game, I think. He should learn to lose from you, Master Rhenford."

"I am very good at losing," Liam said with a wry smile. "I do it much quicker than anyone I know."

Uldericus waved the sarcasm away. "I mean the squalling. It ill becomes a man." He found a pair of boots and began pulling them on. There was a precision to his movements that interested Liam, a neatness and economy to each action that suggested they had all been planned in advance. His dealing had been the same—deliberate and careful.

"I suppose I should go," Liam said, looking about for his cloak. He had learned a little, though nowhere near as much as he would have liked.

"Nonsense," the earl said. "It likes me to leave, but only for another place. Accompany me—for that y' are a man who can lose and smile. And if y' are out of pocket," he gestured at the large pile in front of his seat, "you will be my guest." He finished pulling on his boots, blousing his long gray breeches just so, and fished a matching gray cloak out of one of the cupboards.

Liam bowed his thanks and found his own cloak lying on one of the divans. He did not particularly wish to stay out longer—it had been a long day, and his eyes had begun to feel gritty—and he was not entirely sure he liked Uldericus, or the offhand manner with which he had assumed Liam would stay out longer simply because that was what the earl wanted. Still, he was not asleep on his feet, and he hoped that a chance might present itself to get more information about the previous night.

So they left the Red Chamber together, Uldericus pausing for a moment to study the table at which they had played, and went downstairs. The masked youths were gone, but most of the middle-aged men were still there, though now comfortably seated and very closely attended by the modestly-dressed young women. Herione stood by the fountain, her lips pressed thin, directing a servant in mopping up a puddle.

"Madame," Uldericus called, striding across the marble floor, "we have concluded. If you would see to the room, and the money there—and I'll tell you, I know it to the coin. See that it is all accounted for when next I'm here."

Herione curtsied deeply, murmuring, "In course, my lord," but Liam could see she held her head down to hide an angry blush at the insult.

"Coming, Rhenford?" The earl walked on to the doors and began rummaging through a tall basket tucked in one corner. Liam hung back, waiting for Herione to rise, offering her a bow and an apologetic smile when she did.

"Merry Banquet," he said.

She nodded, an answering smile gradually draining the anger from her face. "And to you, Master Rhenford."

No harm in being polite, he told himself, going on to the door where Uldericus waited. *Besides, she may be able to answer a few questions. . . .*

Uldericus held up a heavy walking stick as Liam approached. "See you this?" He swung it two or three times through the air, smiling at the whistling sound it made. "A life preserver. An uncommonly useful thing, with all these knaves about. Go to." He pushed the door open with the head of the life preserver and gestured for Liam to precede him.

Oakham leaned against a pillar, arms folded across his chest, watching a servant slop water over the steps. Uldericus stopped in the doorway, the stick over one shoulder, and gave a sharp sniff.

"Our young baron is much taken with the customs of the Banquet," he said to no one in particular. "He shares my wine with everyone, it seems."

The servant sloshed more water on the steps, emptying his bucket.

"I ducked him in the fountain," Oakham said, "and he seemed the better for it, and quieter, but when I got him outside—well." He nodded at the servant and the mess he was trying to wash away. "Then he ran off, to Pet Radday's, unless I miss my guess."

Liam circled around the servant, avoiding the stains. Uldericus let the door close with a snort. "Radday's, eh? Will there be baiting, then?"

The night was clear and cold, with no moon; once his eyes adjusted, Liam could see the dim outlines of the street by the stars' faint light. He had not drunk much, trying to concentrate on the game and the players, but the fresh air felt good and cleared his head a great deal.

"It's likely," Oakham said doubtfully. "But will Quetivel like company?"

Uldericus laughed and set off down the street, away from the Point. "Damn him—I want to see the baiting."

Liam and Oakham followed him in silence. It was too dark to see the lord's face, but Liam could tell that he was concerned. The situation reminded him of his university days in Torquay—the pointlessly complex play of hierarchy in friendship. *Oakham wants to play with Uldericus,* he thought, *but feels responsible for Quetivel. And Quetivel refuses to play nicely.* Drinking too much and throwing up on the steps of a brothel was not behavior calculated to endear—and the baron had come dangerously close to calling Uldericus a cheat. And there was that strange exchange about the earl's dream, how his wife slept soundly, sly foxes and guarding the henhouse. What did that mean? *I would try to keep them apart too.*

Uldericus walked briskly, completely at east in the dark streets, tapping the life preserver on the cobbles in time to his steps. They headed north, towards Auric's Park, passing the entrance to Temple Street, still brightly lit despite the late hour. Apart from the occasional late stroller, and one or two parties of torch-bearing holiday-makers, they had the streets to themselves.

Liam wondered about Quetivel's near-accusation. Had Uldericus cheated? He had certainly done very well—Liam had lost the forty-odd crowns he had brought with him, as well as the thirty he borrowed. Oakham was down whatever he brought with him along with most of the ten he had borrowed. There was no guessing at Quetivel's losses, but he had thrown huge sums into the last warchest. Uldericus had split three warchests and taken the last all for himself. They had used his cards, in his room, where Quetivel had apparently lost before.

Don't get carried away, Liam thought. *You played badly. You always play badly, so of course you lost.* Oakham had not played well, either—but Quetivel had. Still, there had been nothing unusual about the game, and the baron was drunk. *And a rude brat as well,* Liam added, surprised at how much he disliked the young man. *He is, though. An obnoxious little lordling. He deserved to lose.*

"Have you been baiting, Master Rhenford?" Uldericus was speaking to him. Liam begged his pardon, and the earl repeated his question.

"No, my lord."

They had been walking for almost twenty minutes, and were far into Auric's Park, approaching Northfield, where Southwark straggled loosely into the countryside. The streets were wider, the houses set farther apart, and the road they were on had turned from cobbles to dirt.

"Radday's the best—they say he sends to the Midlands for his animals, and he's ever open, though not always with baiting. Cockfights, ratcatching, wrestling, boxing, he always has some sport."

Liam made a noncommittal noise; he had never been baiting because he had no interest in blood sports. Even while growing up in the Midlands, he had disliked the formalized aspect of the hunt, though at least there they ate what they killed. Staking a bear or a boar in a pit with a pack of dogs and watching them kill each other seemed vicious to him.

"And there it is," the earl said, pointing out a strange building standing alone in a large lot. It was long and low, a roof of wood raised up on thick posts with canvas walls. Two rows of smoking torches led to the entrance. Uldericus led them in, paying three silver pieces to the large and unfriendly men who guarded the door. Liam ducked through the flap in the canvas with the others, but almost immediately wished he had not. The space was filled to bursting with a strange mix of classes—from men as well dressed as Uldericus or Oakham, some even better, down to the most ragged beggars—all talking, shoving and jostling over the dirt floor and churning it into mud. A few more torches were fixed over the pit in the center, a good fifteen feet deep and walled with heavy logs; the air was thick with smoke and an eyewatering smell, animals and unwashed men packed too close, cheap torches and fresh blood.

Uldericus shouldered his way right into the crowd, straight for the pit, Oakham in his wake; Liam pushed in the opposite direction, putting his back to the canvas and sliding along the wall. There would be no chance for questions here, but since he had come all this way he decided he might as well wait, and hope for an opportunity on the way out.

An animal roar rose suddenly over the noise of the men, drowning and finally silencing it; then the crowd was shouting, men calling out bets, others acknowledging them, markers passing back and forth. Hands and heads flashed around Liam; as far back into the canvas as he pressed, he was surrounded by the crazed mob of men, jostled and pushed back and forth.

"Six dogs," a man near him cried. "That one'll take down six! Who's got six?"

Another man asked, "How many's Radday loosing tonight?"

"Sport," Liam muttered angrily, and began to shove back, making a way for himself towards the back of the room, where it looked like there was more room. The roar came again—a bear, he guessed—and dogs began to bark and howl. The crowd grew frenzied.

He kept pushing, and then, suddenly, he was through, in a canvas corner of the room that was almost empty, and face to face with Quetivel.

The young baron was filthy, stains across the front of his tunic, the hem and much of the rest of his cloak clotted with mud. He leaned bonelessly against the corner post, a tall jar of wine dangling by its neck from one hand. His face was gray, studded by the same obstinate beads of sweat, but his eyes lost some of their glassiness, focusing weakly on Liam. He mumbled something.

"Baron Quetivel," Liam shouted, "are you all right?"

The barking and roaring from the pit were continuous now, punctuated by cheers and cries from the crowd. Quetivel straightened a little, gestured vaguely with the jar. "How does it like you to be cheated?"

He really is an ass, Liam thought. "You are drunk, my lord—come outside!"

Quetivel shoved aside Liam's offered hand. "Cheated," he repeated, his voice rising. "Cheated! By a man who can't keep a wife!"

Liam goggled; involuntarily he turned his head, hoping not to see— Uldericus, a grim look on his face, the life preserver on his shoulder. Oakham stood behind him, pale and fearful. Liam whirled back to the drunken baron.

"Come on!" he shouted, pulling at Quetivel's arm. The crowd was howling now; a high-pitched yelp of pain tore through the noise.

"Where's your wife?" Quetivel shouted at Uldericus. "You goddamned cheat!"

Even over the noise of the crowd Liam heard the crunch, though he had not seen the life preserver leave the earl's shoulder. Quetivel crumbled, his nose spurting blood and lying at an ugly angle to the rest of his face.

For a long moment no one moved: Uldericus held the stick just where it had hit Quetivel, Liam gaped in shock, and Oakham cursed. Then the lord took hold of Uldericus's arm and tugged him gently away; the earl let himself be led, a grim smile forming on his lips.

Liam was left to look after Quetivel, who lay moaning incoherently in the mud.

A quarter of an hour later, Liam had managed to haul the baron to his feet, stanch the flow of blood, and half carry him out of Radday's. The sounds from the pit followed him out into the night, even when the canvas flap shut—the weakening roars of the bear, the deep-chested barking of those dogs still on their feet, the high yelps of the hurt.

The cold air seemed to do Quetivel good: he stirred groggily and opened his eyes. "What—" he murmured, then groaned.

Oakham hurried to help, propping the baron up from the other side. Together they brought him out to the street. Uldericus waited there, the life preserver held across his chest, parallel to the ground. Torch-shadows flickered over his face. He was not smiling anymore.

"I'll have satisfaction," the earl said. "When he is recovered, we'll meet. Master Rhenford, you witnessed all—you'll be my second. Attend me tomorrow noon, at my home." Without another word, before Liam could respond, he turned on his heel and stalked off into the darkness.

A few seconds later, Liam cursed and stamped his foot. "Ah, gods! As if I haven't enough to do!"

Oakham spat bitterly. "Count yourself lucky. I'll end as his second." He nodded at Quetivel, who was slowly regaining control of his legs. They got the baron a few more steps before he started straining against them, groaning and muttering.

"Come," Oakham said at last. "This is foolishness. We need a horse. Yours is at a stable?"

"Yes." He mentioned the ostler's name.

"Well enough—I know the man. Fetch yours, and have them send one to me. I'll watch the boy."

Liam quickly agreed, slipping out from underneath the baron's arm. He hesitated a moment, having seen the results of blows to the head a number of times. "Keep him walking until the horse comes, and make sure he sits up. When you put him to bed, keep him sitting up. And if he vomits, do not let him go to sleep. Do you understand?"

Oakham nodded impatiently. "Go to, go to."

He hesitated again, staring the lord in the face. "I think there are some things we should talk about, Oakham." He stressed the name. "I do not think this will work the way we are going about it. You must tell me more about your guests."

"Aye, aye, I see that now," the lord said, sighing wearily. "Come tomorrow in the morning. Near ten or so. We'll go to see Cawood, and we'll talk."

Liam waited a moment, trying to read Oakham's face, and then gave up. He left the two men in the torchlight and walked off into the darkened streets. After a few minutes, when the torches outside Radday's were mere pinpoints of light in the distance, he stopped and projected.

Fanuilh!

Yes, master?

Are you nearby?

I will be with you in a few minutes.

"Good," Liam said to himself. He was angry, angry at the things Oakham had obviously not told him, at Uldericus's imperious manner, at Quetivel's rash and obnoxious stupidity, but beneath the thin layer of anger was a deeper current of exhaustion. It had been a very, very long day. Tired, and distracted by his anger, he did not want to walk the streets alone. *It would be just the thing,* he thought, *after losing almost eighty crowns, being dragged into a bear-baiting pit and a duel, to be knocked on the head by robbers.*

He heard more than saw Fanuilh's descent, the flapping of its leathery wings. It was a black shape blotting out the stars in front of him, hovering with slow wingbeats.

Master.

"Ride on my shoulder," Liam said. "Keep me company."

The dragon leapt into position, landing so lightly that he barely felt its claws. It seemed to weigh nothing. He started walking again.

The stableboy brought Diamond out in record time and began saddling a second horse before Liam had even finished asking for it. Exhaustion had overwhelmed anger on the long walk. His feet, hands and nose were cold; all he could think of was his bed.

"You know Radday's?" he asked.

"The baiting pit," the boy stammered, and Liam suddenly realized that the boy was not looking at him, but at Fanuilh.

Too late to do anything about that, he thought, too tired to care much.

"Go quickly, boy." He fished the last silver piece out of his purse and tossed it. The boy instinctively caught the coin, and then juggled it as if it were hot.

Liam grinned tiredly and swung up onto Diamond's back. He guided the horse as far as the city gate and then let it find the way home.

"Well," he said, "you have made your first appearance in Southwark, and scared the wits out of a stableboy. Happy?"

He will recover.

Liam laughed, a small, happy chuckle that eventually trailed off to a sigh. They traveled the rest of the way in silence, Diamond instinctively heading for home. Huddling in his cloak to escape the cold, Liam could only think of how miserable he was, and even when the horse started picking its way carefully down the cliff path, his only thought was: *Bed.*

■ *9* ■

THE HOUSE WAS ablaze with light, and as Liam led Diamond across the patio to the shed, he guessed that Grantaire was still awake.

He grumbled to himself, sure that there was no way he was going to get to sleep soon. Fumbling the saddle off the roan, he gave the animal a barely adequate currying and trudged back to the house through the cold, exaggerating his own weariness.

She will want to talk, he whined to himself, *and talk and talk and talk.* Once on the patio, though, he hung his head for a moment, composing what he hoped was a cheerful-but-not-interested-in-extended-conversation face—*She is my guest, after all*—and entered the house, Fanuilh at his heels.

Grantaire was in what Tarquin had called his trophy room; Liam called out, "Good evening," hung his cloak on a convenient peg and, hoping to forestall conversation as much as possible, went to stand in the doorway. He could not have gone much further, in any case.

The trophy room was dominated by a set of waist-high cabinets with glass lids, in which Tarquin had stored a collection of wands, flasks and various pieces of jewelry, all of which Fanuilh had assured Liam had magical properties. The walls were hung with enchanted items as well, including a sword and shield, what appeared to be a stringless lute, and a rug which flew.

Grantaire had taken everything out of the cases and off the walls, and arrayed it on the floor. She sat cross-legged in the midst of it all, the gray cat in her lap.

"Good evening," she said, looking up at him innocently.

Liam took the room in at a glance, leaning against the doorjamb with his arms folded across his chest. "You've been busy," he said, as nonchalantly as he could.

"I don't know how Tanaquil expected me to find anything," she said sourly. "There was no way to identify all of this." She gestured at the mess around her.

"Fanuilh knows what it all is," Liam said. "I'm sure he would be happy to explain."

"Well, neither of you was here, so I did it myself. I've figured them all out—I'll be taking most of them with me, but there are a few things I will leave for you."

Liam nodded and cleared his throat, still a little taken aback by the mess she had made. She stood then, a smooth, graceful motion, and dusted off the back of her shift.

"I wonder, would you mind making me some dinner?"

He started guiltily. *Some host,* he thought. *The oven will not work for her.* "Oh—yes, yes, I'm sorry. Come on." He led the way to the kitchen and asked her what she wanted. She had no preferences, though, and left to his own devices, he imagined a typical Southwark sea pie.

"They eat these a lot around here," he explained as he laid the dish in front of her. "It's mostly fish."

She nodded her approval and cut into the pie, nodding more at the fishy smell that spread through the room. She ate quickly, with little ceremony, but he found himself fascinated by her movements, even the way she picked out a piece of fish and fed it to the cat. He knew he was staring, but he could not help it; he was tired, and the effort of moving his eyes away seemed too much for him.

When she was finished, she pushed the half-eaten pie towards the cat and sat back, closing her eyes with a look of contentment. "That was very good," she murmured. "I haven't had fish in a long time." Her throat was firm and smooth; Liam shook his head, forced himself to move. He paced a little, and then remembered:

"I spoke to Mistress Priscian about those papers you were interested in," he said. "She said she would look and see if there were any this morning."

"Wonderful! And she said I might see them?" She sat up straight, genuinely pleased, her mouth open a little, expectantly, eyes wide and hopeful. Her lower lip was fuller than the top, and Liam thought the way her hair just brushed her shoulders, auburn against the white skin, was very pretty. He stirred himself. *What are you thinking?*

"Yes," he said, "but she was very clear that she did not expect to find anything. He lived—and died—quite some time ago."

"Life and death mean much less to mages," she pointed out, "and if there were anything . . ."

"Also," he went on, looking away from her, "she is a very proper woman. I mean, a little formal, if you know what I mean."

Annoyance briefly wrinkled Grantaire's face; then she forced it down, and plucked at the shoulder strap of her shift. "I think you mean this. I will certainly wear something more appropriate, and I shall bow and be polite. Mistress Priscian will have no cause to regret my acquaintance—if she has anything to show me."

"You understand, I hope," Liam said, feeling vaguely as if he had insulted her. "She is an old woman, a little prim, I mean, but I like her, and we are partners. It's all right around here, on the beach."

"Is it, though?" Grantaire wondered, and then said lightly: "Every time you see me, Liam Rhenford, you blush. This is not what I expected from Tanaquil's diary."

Predictably and quite involuntarily, Liam blushed, then tried to move the conversation away from Grantaire's clothes. "Tarquin kept a diary? You've read it?"

"It is in the library. It is really more of a record of his experiments, but on occasion he included little personal notes. He mentioned you more than once."

"Did he?" Was that why her attitude towards him had changed? "I'd like to see that."

She shook her head. "I do not think you should. He said a number of complimentary things, but he was also a scrupulously honest man. There were one or two things that might sting."

Liam chuckled. "Those are exactly the things I want to read." Of all things, he hated this sort of teasing worst; he knew that for a long time he would wonder what Tarquin had written about him.

"In any case, I will be taking those books with me. Most of it would be of no use to you anyway."

Suddenly he realized that he was quite happy to talk to her, that he was not ready for the conversation to end. He went to the table and took a seat opposite her.

"Tell me something—why is it that you haven't asked me about Tarquin's death? I mean, you have traveled half the length of Taralon to be here, but you haven't asked about that."

"He told me about it," she said. "I told you that he appeared to me."

"Ah," Liam said lamely, "of course."

To his delight, she went on: "What I do want to know, though, is why he came back at all. He said he had business in Southwark. Do you know what it was?"

He did, but he did not want to talk—he wanted to listen to her. As quickly as he could, he outlined what had brought Tarquin back. "It was Laomedon, or his servants. They needed his help freeing one of the god's servants, a gryphon. There is a new goddess now, named Bellona; some of her worshippers had captured the gryphon and were going to sacrifice it."

"Bellona," she said. "I've heard the name. All the way south people were saying that she had appeared here." Liam confirmed that she had, and Grantaire digested this for a moment, eyebrows raised. "It is not every day that a new goddess appears, or that one walks the earth. And you were there?"

"Yes," Liam said hesitantly. "I was helping Tarquin."

She nodded, as if this was what she had expected, and then rose. "I think I'll go to bed, now. It has been a long day."

Not just for you, he thought sourly, irritated that the conversation was at an end. He rose, though, and smiled. "Yes, it has."

They started out of the kitchen, Grantaire in front, and then she stopped short and turned to him, holding out her hand so that her fingertips just touched his chest.

"Tell me—the gryphon was freed?"

"Yes." His throat was inexplicably dry.

"And who freed it, you or Tanaquil?"

For a moment, he recalled hanging from the roof of Bellona's temple, picking the lock of the gryphon's cage. "We both did."

He was terribly aware of how close they were, but he did not step back. Neither did she.

"Tanaquil told me you found the woman who killed him. Is that true?"

Liam nodded, and then stammered, "It was luck, mostly. I am very lucky."

She nodded, her eyes fixed on his. He was much taller, and she had to crane her neck to do it, but she gave no indication that it was awkward. Her eyes were green, he noticed.

Her hand just rested on his chest, but there was nothing sensual about it; she was merely holding him in place. And her face was completely blank, unreadable; her lips were parted, but her teeth met behind them. There was nothing inviting about her, but he was quite sure that he could kiss her. *I could kiss her now,* he thought, somewhat surprised. *I could.*

More important, he did not think she would object.

It was an amazing moment to him, so amazing that he thought again, *I could kiss her!* and he paused too long, trying to grasp what, to him, was the enormity of his realization. *I could kiss her.*

Liam waited too long, reveling in the idea; she dropped her hand and turned away.

"Good night, Liam," she called, turning down the corridor to her bedroom.

For a long minute he stood in the entrance hall, his eyes wide with disappointment. Then he closed them and tilted his head back, stifling a groan in the back of his throat.

Fanuilh trotted into the entrance hall from the trophy room and paused, cocking its head at Liam's strange posture.

Master? Are you all right?

He let his head drop to his chest and trudged heavily into the library.

The dragon followed, and watched as he undressed and crawled onto the divan.

Are you all right? it asked again.

Liam sat up suddenly, a disgruntled look on his face. He formed the thought and shoved it at the dragon: *Did you see that? In the entrance hall?*

Fanuilh sat back on its haunches and peered quizzically up at him. *What, master?*

"Oh, never mind," Liam said, and let himself slump down on the divan. He was asleep before he knew it.

However long Liam had been asleep—he could not remember what time he had come home—it was not enough. The sockets of his eyes were filled with sand, his mouth tasted foul, and he was in no way ready for the long list of tasks that lay ahead of him. He sat on the edge of the divan, head in his hands, and groaned twice.

It is almost half past the hour, master.

Fanuilh had woken him at seven, and he had lain there since, "resting his eyes" and muzzily dreading his day.

"I'm getting up," Liam said, and dragged himself from the divan, pulling on his breeches and undershirt from the day before. He slouched out to the kitchen, Fanuilh at his heels. Grantaire sat at the kitchen table; he wished her a good morning and went to the stove. With the image of his breakfast fixed firmly in his head, he poured a handful of water from the jug and splashed it on his face, then opened the stove and pulled out a platter. He parceled out plates and cups on the table: mugs of coffee for himself and Grantaire, a bowl for Fanuilh, and a plate of hot sweet rolls. The dragon hopped up onto the table.

"Good morning," Grantaire said, an odd smile on her face. Her cat stepped from her lap onto the table and sidled over to Fanuilh's bowl. With a dainty sniff, it inspected the coffee. The dragon sat back on its haunches and looked at Liam.

Perhaps the cat would like a bowl of his own.

"Mm," Liam said, his mouth full of honeyed roll. He swallowed. "Does your cat want something? Milk? A dead mouse? A gutted sparrow?" While he did not dislike cats, he did not much appreciate their eating habits.

"Milk, I think."

Stuffing down another roll, Liam went back to the oven and imagined up a bowl of milk, which he set down before the cat. It left Fanuilh's bowl, and the dragon took over, breathing deep.

"Why is his so dark?" Grantaire pointed at the dragon's bowl.

"He likes it that way," Liam said. Coffee was not drunk in Taralon; he had encountered it in the course of his travels. "It's better with milk and sugar, but then, he does not drink his. Do you want yours plain?"

She shook her head and reached out for a roll. "No, it's good as it is. The smell is nice."

The change in their relationship that he had felt the night before was still there, an easing of tension. She also seemed to have gotten over her panic on learning about the other wizard in the city—but she gave no indication of what she thought about that moment in the entrance hall.

For a few minutes they sat and ate, Liam eating each roll whole, Grantaire tearing hers into shreds, chewing and swallowing each piece separately. When he had finished five, he leaned back, nursing his coffee in little sips. She was still wearing the same shift as she had the night before; her shoulders were pure white, and he thought they would be soft to touch. He vividly remembered the scene in the entrance hall, and he picked over it, wondering what he had missed. *Should I have kissed her?* He tried to imagine what would have happened if he had.

"Rhenford," she said suddenly, waving a hand in front of his face, "you're staring." It was not an accusation at all—she might have been pointing out that he had spilled some coffee—but he jumped guiltily.

"Excuse me," he blurted, averting his eyes and hiding his embarrassment in his mug. Searching for a way to change the conversation, he remembered suddenly that it was possible he and Coeccias might be meeting Desiderius later in the day. "I have to go into the city soon—this thing with the Jewel is going to keep me busy. But I will see Mistress Priscian this morning, and let you know if she has anything for you. There is another thing though, something I forgot yesterday."

"Yes?"

"The wizard, Desiderius—he was asking about the Jewel before it was stolen. You said that sneaking it away was not like him."

"No. He is too proud for that."

"We'll take that for granted. Now, what if someone tried to sell it to him? You see," he said, holding up a finger for her to wait while he explained, "I can't see what anyone would do with it in Southwark. Where would they sell it? Who would buy it here? There isn't enough money in the town. But a wizard might have the money—or be able to get it."

"So?" She seemed to have completely forgotten his staring, and he was not sure if he was relieved or disappointed.

"So, the thief may try to sell it to him. It's a long reach, I know—a thief who wanted money would be more likely to try to sell it elsewhere, in Torquay or Harcourt, even the Freeports. On the other hand, wizards rarely go unnoticed, particularly in a city the size of Southwark. And who knows what people might remember of the Jewel, or Eirenaeus? He has been dead for centuries, but you know how legends like that can grow. So the thief might approach Desiderius."

"You are working up to something," she said suspiciously.

"I am," he admitted. "Coeccias—the Duke's man here, a friend of mine—already knows there is a wizard here who was asking about the Jewel. He told me about it. And he will naturally want to find this wizard. What I'm wondering is if you think it will be dangerous for me to approach Desiderius."

She thought carefully before answering, gently biting the tip of her thumb. "I cannot say. I do not know why he is here. If he is looking for you, he could easily find you here, so there is no secret lost there."

"I wouldn't mention you, of course."

"No," she said, shaking her head absently, as if the possibility had never occurred to her. "He must not know I am here. If he is looking for you, your approaching him might take him by surprise. He might not press whatever claims he has as hard."

"And if he is looking for you, I might be able to throw him off the track."

"Subtly, of course. Desiderius is very subtle. And if he is not here on account of either of us, there can be no harm in it. You should be careful, but no, I cannot say that it would necessarily be dangerous. So you know where he is?"

Color came to Liam's cheeks again, and he cursed to himself. *When did I start blushing so much?* "Actually, no, but Coeccias—the Duke's man—is looking. He should not be hard to find."

"No. He will not be hiding."

There was a great deal to do. Liam rose and started gathering the dishes, putting them all on the platter and returning them to the oven.

"I will be in the city most of the day, but if Mistress Priscian has anything for you, I will send Fanuilh to let you know."

Grantaire nodded her approval, sinking into some internal reverie even as he left the kitchen to wash and dress.

Liam was on the road to Southwark less than half an hour later, huddled in his cloak and trying to plan his day. He had to be at the Arcade of Scribes at nine, and then he wanted to see Mistress Priscian and Oakham, and he needed to stop at the Guard barracks and talk to Coeccias. Uldericus had practically ordered him to come at noon, but he was not sure if he would. Dueling was high on his list of foolish things, along with bear-baiting and love poetry. It was not a moral objection, but a practical one: the idea of the field of honor was flawed. He had never known a case where the injured man won simply because his cause was just—duels always went to the better fighter. Being better with a sword was no proof of virtue.

Granted, Quetivel had thrown out some serious insults, but he had been drunk, and why Uldericus could not take satisfaction from what he had already done to the baron was beyond Liam. It made him wince just to think of the sound of the life preserver crushing Quetivel's nose.

Finally, he knew that the real reason he did not want to wait on the earl was that he objected to being ordered around. Had his father ever been as arrogant as Uldericus? Had he ever been as irresponsible as Quetivel? No. Even when there was still a Rhenford Keep for him to inherit, he did not think he had been so high-handed. And if being noble naturally led to that sort of behavior, perhaps he was lucky to no longer *be* noble.

Worry about that later, he told himself. *Concentrate.* There were too many things to do for him to race off on tangents. He needed to meet Cawood and the other two guests, the Furseuses; he had never had a chance to talk with Lady Oakham. There was the wizard, and his meeting with the Werewolf. Too much, far too much.

Most important, he still could not imagine a real reason for stealing the Jewel. There were reasons, of course—money, mere greed, or even, according to Grantaire and Fanuilh, magic—but none of them rang true, at least so far. If Grantaire was right, magic was unlikely, since this Desiderius would not resort to theft. Neither Quetivel nor Uldericus had struck him as the covetous sort, and they both seemed well supplied with money.

"My money," Liam said ruefully, his hand straying to his purse. He had shoveled enough into it to pay his debt from the night before. There had to be a better way to interview the Oakhams' guests than losing money to them.

Cawood and the Furseuses might turn out to be desperately poor, but that still left the question of disposing of the Jewel. After visits from the Guard, no fence or jeweler in Southwark would touch it, and selling it in another city would require contacts.

His stomach grumbled. "What?" he demanded, but he knew the answer. He had eaten nothing the night before, and the rolls, though good, were small. There were places near the Arcade to get food, and he promised himself another breakfast.

Southwark was mostly asleep when he passed the city gate, an indulgence only explained by the Banquet. Quetivel was not the only one with an aching head, Liam knew, but at least the others had done it to themselves. A few people were wandering down Temple Street as he rode by, carrying offerings from temple to temple, but apart from the devout, the streets were empty and more than half of the shops were closed.

He left his horse at the stables, waking the boy from the night before. Hay in his hair and awe on his face, the boy treated Diamond with a respect bordering on fear, handling the reins gingerly and even, once, bowing to the horse.

I should bring Fanuilh with me more often, Liam thought, chuckling to himself and setting off on foot. When he reached the Arcade there were only a few scribes in place, and even they were just setting up their tables and booths. The stand where Mopsa had bought her awful sausages was, unfortunately, the only place open that sold food; he bought two in rolls and settled himself on the steps of the arcade. He shook the sausages into the gutter and contented himself with the grease-soaked bread, which was not quite as stale as the day before.

Licking his fingers and brushing crumbs from his tunic, he turned his face to the meager sun, closed his eyes, and waited.

The bells began tolling nine, and he opened his eyes, scanning the Arcade and the street. There was no sign of Mopsa. He stood, rubbing some warmth into the seat of his pants, and started walking the length of the Arcade, examining the few displays. He walked and examined for about five minutes, drawing a few curious stares from the scribes, and once or twice the beginning of a sales pitch, which he cut off politely. Then he saw the Werewolf coming down the street.

Liam had expected Mopsa to come, to lead him to someplace secret; the Werewolf had once boasted to him that he never went out in the daylight. Still, there the man was, eyes narrowed balefully, darting glances left and right as if he expected an ambush. Liam stepped into the street as the man approached.

"This'll not do," the head of the Southwark Guild growled. "We'll walk." Liam nodded agreement and the two stepped away from the Arcade, heading down the hill toward the Warren. As always when he saw the Werewolf, Liam wondered which had come first, his nickname or his appearance: a grizzled black and gray beard welled up from his chest, over his chin and cheeks, ending in sharp points beneath his eyes, which were a disturbingly bright green, and his canine teeth were pronounced. Ordinarily he made a point of showing them in a feral grin, but now his mouth was tightly closed.

"This'll not do," he repeated, keeping his voice low. The shoulders of his much-patched coat kept rising and falling, and his fists punched at the insides of his pockets. "I know what you would, Rhenford, and I cannot help you."

Liam stopped, touching the Werewolf's elbow. "What do you mean? How do you know what I want?"

The other man scowled and walked on, forcing Liam to keep up. "What else would it be, but this damned Jewel? I told him no commissions, but he'd not listen—and now's dead. So I cannot help you."

"Wait, wait, wait," Liam said. "It was one of yours who stole it?"

The Wolf shot him a withering glance. "In course it was—that lock cried out for one. But I tell you now, if I'd known you would concern yourself, I'd have made good the ban. Not that I'd need to. Soon as he heard you were on it, he fair soiled himself, so sure he was you'd con him out."

Frustrated with the man's cryptic talk, Liam demanded: "Who? Who are you talking about?"

"Japer," the Werewolf said. "Japer picked it. On commission from another." For a moment, Liam's heart leapt; it must have shown on his face, though, because the other man quickly said: "But I know not who, Japer wouldn't say."

"All right, wait a moment. Start over. Start from the beginning." He knew who Japer was—a sour, stupid thief who had hit Mopsa one too many times for Liam's liking—but otherwise his frustration was growing.

"No games, Rhenford," the Werewolf said, glaring at him. "I've things to do, and you know enough."

"I know nothing," Liam said, grabbing the man's arm and forcing him to stop. "And I want you to tell me everything, from the beginning, now."

The Werewolf shook off Liam's hand, but he stayed still, breathing out a long sigh. "Well and well. In fine: Mopsa brought your word yesterday, and I was vexed, for we'd done nothing I knew of to interest you. But Japer did, and was sore frighted, and all came out. He'd taken a commission to pick that lock. I'd have taken him up for it, but he was near wooden with fear. Said a beggar had brought him the job, one we know, named Malskat. Said Malskat brought him to the house, and this man let them in, but then there was a quarrel."

"Wait—did they get the Jewel?"

"Aye, or the man did who let them in. Japer knew him not, said he was noble. There was a quarrel, though, in that tomb, and the man killed Malskat, cut his throat and pitched him from a window to the sea."

Thus the corpse on my beach, Liam realized, but put the thought aside as near useless. "He let Japer go?"

"Aye, and when Mopsa said you were asking questions, he told all. So I sent him to the beggars, and they took him off." The Werewolf's voice was full of remorse.

"Why did you send him to the beggars?"

"For to tell them that we'd nothing to do with it," the other man said incredulously. "Why else?"

"And now he's dead?"

"Aye," the Werewolf said heavily, then snarled: "They killed him for that Malskat, and I sent him there!"

Liam shushed him, and started them walking again. "You are sure he is dead?"

"We found him in the Warren, not two hours ago, Rhenford: I'm sure he's dead."

"Are you sure the beggars killed him?" Liam asked, feeling his way cautiously. He thought it more likely that it was someone else.

"Who else, then? I sent him there, he left us to go to them, and that was the last of him. Until this morning. Where do you go with this?"

Liam shrugged. "I would think it was the man who commissioned him."

The Werewolf snorted bitterly. "I think not. If you'd seen Japer—he was as frighted of him as he was of you. Would say nothing of him, how he looked, his name, naught. In any case, it matters not. Look you, Japer is dead, and I've told all, so there is nothing in it for you to bother us."

"No," Liam said, his mind racing to conclusions. "I suppose you are right." His steps slowed as he tried to arrange what he had learned.

"I came only to tell you this, for that you did for Duplin. It was good in you."

Liam stirred himself, putting away his conjectures for a moment. With two of his thieves killed in the space of a single month, it was clearly a hard time for the Werewolf. Liam watched the other man's mouth work angrily, and his shoulders bunch, and felt a pang of sympathy. "I am sorry about Japer."

"The fool," the Werewolf grated harshly. "The fool. I told him no commissions. But we'll make it good."

Liam cocked his head at the dangerous words. "What are you going to do?"

"What think you?" As if the answer were obvious.

"You don't know the beggars killed him."

The Werewolf said nothing, staring hard into Liam's eyes.

"You don't know."

Still the other man said nothing.

"Look," Liam said desperately. "Look, just wait on it." The simple theft he had agreed to investigate was suddenly growing bloody. Two deaths had already come out of it, and Uldericus's challenge would probably lead to another. He did not want some sort of vendetta added. "I cannot believe it was the beggars. Give me a chance to find the man. That's why I asked to meet you—I want to find the man, and the Jewel. Wait until I find him."

The silence dragged on, as did the Werewolf's luminous green stare. Liam returned it as strongly as he could. At last the thief relented.

"If you find him, what then?"

"We find out if he killed Japer."

"And if he did?"

Liam shrugged uncertainly. "I don't know. Give him to the Aedile."

"No good." The Werewolf set his jaw stubbornly.

The last of Liam's patience fled. "Good enough," he said angrily, raising his voice, "and all you are going to get. If he killed Japer, the Aedile deals with him. And you avoid a feud with the beggars. If you kill one of theirs, do you think they will let it go? You cannot risk that when you cannot be sure they did it. And if you do risk it, and then find they did not kill Japer, what then? Wait, I say!"

The Werewolf flinched a little, backing up a step.

"Will you wait?" Liam demanded.

The thief's mouth moved silently, then he brought out: "Until to-morrow night. I'll send Mopsa to you." Before Liam could agree he turned, walked three steps, and then started running.

Liam raised a hand and began to call out to him, then let his hand fall to his side and muttered a mild curse. He started back up the hill, in the opposite direction from that the Werewolf had taken, heading for the city square and the Guard barracks.

Today is going to be even longer than yesterday.

Liam never felt completely comfortable in the barracks. The guards all knew him, called him Quaestor, and let him in without question whether Coeccias was there or not, but he still felt like an outsider. Though they gave him a title, he was not really one of them; they tolerated him because he was the Aedile's friend.

He warmed himself by one of the fires, waiting while Coeccias gave orders to a number of guards, two of whom had bloodstains on their hands and clothes.

"You two," the Aedile was saying to the bloody men, "report to the Sergeant of the Day, then scrub up and take you home. Sergeant, split the rest, keep the half here, and send the others home, to report back this evening for night patrols. We'll go light on days for the rest of the Banquet, and I want the men walking through the night, Sergeant; pass it on, if you please. Constant patrols. And look you, tell all the men of those two children—the boy and the maid."

The sergeant dismissed the men, and then he and the Aedile discussed the added patrols for a few minutes. Not for the first time, Liam was impressed by the range of Coeccias's responsibilities. He watched the burly man talk with the sergeant, rattling off street names and neighborhoods, hours and the number of men for each patrol. When the sergeant had repeated everything to his satisfaction, he came over to the hearth where Liam stood.

"Truth, Rhenford, I hope you've good news. Your note said you knew this wizard?"

"Just his name," Liam said, then hesitated. What he had learned from the Werewolf made the wizard a dead end, since the man who hired Japer had been inside the house. It also ruled out the two women, he realized. That made his task a little easier, but presented the problem of how to relate the information to the Aedile. He could not just say that he had met with the head of the Thieves' Guild.

"I do not think we need to concern ourselves with him," he began, feeling his way cautiously. "I heard some things this morning. There was a thief involved, a professional, and he was let in by one of the Oakhams' guests."

He stopped, waiting for the Aedile's reaction. The other man gave him a searching look from beneath lowered eyebrows, but said nothing.

Liam cleared his throat, fixed his eyes on the fire, and went on: "Someone killed the thief last night. It's complicated, though, because the person in the house met the thief through a beggar, and the beggar was murdered, too."

"Ah," Coeccias interrupted, "that I know. We found him this morning, though we did not know the why."

"What?" Liam asked sharply.

The Aedile frowned at his tone. "The beggar—we found him this morning."

"No," Liam said slowly, "I found him yesterday. The man I brought in yesterday morning. He was the beggar. His name is Malskat. Was Malskat," he corrected himself. "Who are you talking about?"

Coeccias rolled his eyes to the ceiling. "And here I'd hoped you'd solved it all. We found a beggar this morning in the street. His head was fair crushed, most vicious. For that I made the night patrols stronger. You say this isn't your beggar?"

"No," Liam said, horrified, wondering for an instant if the Guild had already acted—and then dismissed the idea. The Werewolf had spoken only of future action. "The man I brought in yesterday was Malskat. He was killed by one of Oakham's guests and thrown out of the crypt. You remember the balcony? And that was two nights ago. The thief who picked the lock was killed last night. The person I spoke with thought it was the beggars, because of Malskat. But I think it was probably the man who killed Malskat."

"Aye, aye, I doubt the other. The beggars are not so forward. I know their chief, and for all he's a rogue, he'd see through to the right of it. So the man is a murderer twice over, eh?" He did not sound in the least bit happy about it.

"Probably. At least once. It limits where we have to look—the wizard is out, and the women, too. Which leaves just the four men, Cawood, Furseus, Quetivel and Uldericus. I'm going to meet Cawood this afternoon, and I have to arrange about Furseus. But I saw the others last night."

He narrated the events of the previous evening, including what happened at Pet Radday's and the subsequent challenge. "Uldericus was very quick with the life preserver," he finished up.

"No stranger to blood, then, eh? It hangs together—but it is not enough to clap in a peer."

"No," Liam said. "But why would he want the Jewel? Besides, I'm not sure Quetivel would have any qualms about killing a beggar or a thief. He lost a great deal of money last night, and I gather he has done it once or twice before. Perhaps he is deep in debt, deep enough to consider desperate measures. Though where he would sell it is still beyond me."

"Truth, it is a pretty riddle. You must sound out the other two before we can go further."

"I will." He nodded absently, staring into the fire. Pine boughs had been hung on the mantle; he braced his hands on the stone and leaned forward, feeling the heat from the fire on his chest, smelling the scent of the needles. The single large log was slowly breaking apart into glowing chunks. A hazy idea came to him amid the crackling of the fire.

There was no place to sell the Jewel in Southwark, he was sure of that. Moreover, knowing that the guest who had arranged the theft had then killed two people, he could not believe that it had been done solely for possession. No one would kill to have a bauble they could never show in public, would they? He refused to believe it. So it must have been done for money, and that meant selling the Jewel in another city, which would take time and contacts. *But if they thought they could sell it in Southwark . . .*

"Have you found the wizard?" he asked.

Coeccias grunted, taken by surprise. He had been gazing into the fire too, his heavy eyebrows knit together in a furry bunch. "The wizard? Not as yet. I've a man on it, but there're a lot of inns."

"If you can spare more men, have them look." The idea Liam was toying with was still rough, but if it was even to be considered, knowing where Desiderius was would be important.

Sketching a deep bow, Coeccias said: "As you wish, Milord May-Do-Aught." He had given Liam the name while they were investigating Tarquin's murder; it meant that he would never be surprised by anything Liam did.

"And if you can, don't let him know that you are looking."

"As you wish," Coeccias repeated, bowing low again. When he rose, though, there was no humor in his face. "That still leaves me with the second beggar. Rathkael'll tax me with that." Seeing Liam's questioning look, he went on: "The chief of the beggars. He'll tax me with the beggar's death."

"I thought you said he was not 'forward'?" Sometimes the southern dialect left Liam wondering if he fully understood anyone.

"Not in that way, no. He'd not take off the thief until he was sure he had the right of it. He's patient, but a grudge-holder—more a poison than a sword, if you take me. I suppose a beggar must be. This, though, he'll tax me with, for that the streets aren't safe. And I confess," the Aedile said with a sigh, "that he'll be right, in a way. Even beggars shouldn't be taken off in the streets, most especially during their own feast."

Liam thought of the Werewolf, and his threat. He was not sure whether he should tell Coeccias about it. If he could find the Jewel by the end of the next day, he would not need to; and from what the Aedile said of Rathkael, the beggar chief would not make any rash moves. On the other hand, he could not be sure that the Werewolf could control the Guild. After all, if he had been able to enforce the ban on commissions, the Jewel might never have been stolen. *And if you had only met with the Werewolf last night, Japer might not be dead today.*

There were simply too many ifs. He cleared his throat again. "If you do see this Rathkael, you might tell him what we know about Malskat and the thief. You might tell him to warn his people to be careful tonight."

"Why?" Coeccias asked, genuinely puzzled.

"Well, you could tell him that you have it on good authority that the Guild thinks the beggars are responsible for the thief's death." The complex constructions were becoming awkward, but he held to them. "You could also tell him that they have done nothing about it, and will not, and that the second beggar is not their work."

Speaking slowly, fixing Liamwith his stare, the Aedile said: "I could say that, but I would need good authority. Do I truly have it?"

"Yes." *I hope so.*

"Truth, Rhenford, I hope so. I do not need a war in these streets during the Banquet, or at any other time. Southwark is just growing normal again, after all that with Bellona. Can you vouch for the Guild?"

"I can," Liam said, almost completely sure that he could.

"Then I'll do my best with Rathkael. I am glad you told me this, Rhenford. I can at least say who did not kill his beggar, and the rest will give him something to worry on."

The bells in the Duke's Courts started ringing ten; Coeccias heard the sound and shook his head, while Liam stepped away from the fire, counting the hours. If he wanted to see Oakham alone, then visit Cawood with him, and go to Uldericus's by noon—he had still not decided whether he would obey the earl's command or not—he would have to move quickly.

"I should go," he said. "It's going to be a very busy day."

"It already is," Coeccias countered. "I've to con out who took off this other beggar, and gather up some lost children."

"Children?"

Coeccias made a noise of disgust in the back of his throat. "It is nothing—a boy and a maid from up the Point, out masking and caroling too late. Their parents fear they've run off together. More likely they're hiding at a friend's, bussing and spooning like innocents. It is nothing. Look you, will you dine with me?"

"Not lunch," Liam said from the door, "but perhaps dinner. Are you free?"

"Leave word here," the Aedile said, waving him off. "Go to, y' are busy. Dinner can wait. I've work of my own."

Liam left.

■ *10* ■

LIAM WALKED QUICKLY, eating up the cobbled street with long strides. There were many things he needed to know, and Oakham was going to have to tell him most of them. The others he could find out in different ways—among other things, he thought a talk with Herione might prove worthwhile; the brothelkeeper had given him and Coeccias valuable information before. But Oakham would have to provide most of it.

And he will, too, Liam promised himself. He needed to know more about the guests, much more than he could learn in a social setting. The idea had been a bad one, and he should not have agreed to it. All it had done was cost him a pile of crowns and embroil him in a duel.

He was still undecided about whether the fact of the duel told him anything. Though it was premature, he thought Uldericus the most likely suspect, primarily because of the way he had lashed out at Quetivel. The earl did not need the money, as far as he could see, but the two murders had almost overtaken the theft in his mind. *One proven murder,* he corrected, *and one assumed.*

Quetivel, on the other hand, was certainly quarrelsome enough to have started the argument in the crypt, and arrogant enough to have thought nothing of killing a beggar and a thief; the size of his pocket was a mystery.

Still, Liam was putting his money on Uldericus.

"For now," he said firmly, "I'll wait on Cawood and Furseus." He could not allow himself to jump to conclusions; he needed information, and soon.

He deliberately avoided the most direct route to End Street because it led past Uldericus's house, choosing instead to go up Duke Street and come from the south. The maidservant he had seen attending Lady Oakham the day before was kneeling on the stoop, scrubbing the steps.

"Good morning," Liam said. "Is Lord Oakham in?"

"I wouldn't know," Becula replied in a surly tone, dipping her rag in a bucket of water, wringing it out and scrubbing at some rusty stains. "You'll have to ask inside."

"That might work better if you splashed some water from the bucket right onto the steps," Liam suggested.

The girl flipped the hair out of her eyes and stared hard at him. "It would work better if certain ones wouldn't go bleeding all over the stairs." Her look clearly challenged him to come back at that; he declined.

"And a good day to you," he murmured behind a smile, and went up the steps.

Tasso answered the door, offering him a very slight bow. "Lord Oakham is in the study; he said to bring you up."

The Oakhams have bad taste in houseguests and *servants,* Liam thought. "Lead away, then, and let the trumpets sound."

Tasso repeated his slight bow even more stiffly, and went up the stairs. At the door of Oakham's study, he called out Liam's name in the same solemn way as before and held the door open for him, the picture of the respectful and unobtrusive servant. Liam resisted the urge to kick him as he passed into the room.

Oakham was standing by the fireplace, head down beneath the tapestry of himself hunting. He chewed his underlip anxiously.

"I am glad y' are here, Rhenford," he said, signing for Tasso to shut the door.

"Oh?" Liam stayed by the door after the servant closed it. He was afraid he sounded too cold, but he wanted to make sure that Oakham understood things were going to change.

"Aye," the other man said, starting to pace, throwing a look across the room from time to time. "I wonder, how much longer do you think this will take? How long before the Jewel will be returned?"

"I do not know," Liam said, quite honestly. "I hope to finish it by tomorrow evening." Just how, he was not sure—but he wanted to keep the Werewolf in check. At the very least he needed to be able to show some real evidence of progress.

"Tomorrow? Gods!" Oakham's face was a comic mask of surprise. "So soon?"

"I hope so. Again, though, it depends on you."

"How so?" The lord sounded defensive, so Liam pressed.

"I mentioned last night that things were going to change—and they will, if I am ever to find the Jewel. I need information, and you must provide it for me. I need to ask you questions, and you must answer them, or . . ."

Oakham raised his chin, bridling. "Or what?"

"Or I will not be able to find the Jewel, and it will be lost to your family forever."

A long moment passed, Oakham glaring down his nose at Liam, Liam returning the stare impassively. Oakham gave first, turning to the mantle and crossing his arms behind his back.

"Very well," he said quietly. "What would you know?"

Liam became brisk and businesslike. "First, how long ago did you invite your guests? And did they know they would be staying the night?"

The guests had been invited a week earlier, Oakham told him, and spending the night had been understood from the first. The Jewel had made its first appearance at about the same time, but it was still plenty of time to arrange the theft, Liam knew.

"And had all the guests been in your house before at some time?"

They all had; the Furseuses visited often, Cawood and Uldericus had come to dinner once or twice, and Quetivel had been staying at the house for almost two weeks.

"Did they all know where the Jewel was kept?"

Oakham was sure that they must have; his wife had told the story of its "discovery" in the crypt any number of times.

"Those were all simple questions," Liam said, "with no harm in them. Now, however, I am afraid I must be specific. I hope you understand—I simply cannot learn enough doing things the way we did them last night. You will have to tell me something."

Oakham stiffened, but he did not turn around. "Go to."

Liam nodded, gathering his thoughts. "Do you know if any of your guests have money problems? Debts they cannot pay?"

"Debts?" Oakham's voice came out a little strangled.

"For instance, gambling debts," Liam said quickly. "For instance, Quetivel—he lost quite a bit to Uldericus last night. Has he been gambling much since he came here? Losing a great deal?"

"It is not Quetivel!" Oakham snapped over his shoulder.

Liam waited for a moment. When he spoke at last, he made his voice as quiet and firm as he could: "I will tell you something I learned this morning, Oakham. I know for a fact that it was a man who let the thief into your house. I also know who the thief was—but Aedile Coeccias cannot arrest him, because he is dead. The man who let him into your house killed him. He has also killed another man, an accomplice. So this is no longer just about the Jewel. One of your guests killed two men, and he cannot get away with it. Do you see that?"

Oakham had spun around when Liam said that the thief was dead, his face a pale mask of shock. Now he groped his way to a chair and sank into it, one hand fluttering feebly at his forehead.

"Two men, you say? How can you know this?"

Liam waved the question away. "That is not important. I know it. What is important is that we catch the man who did it. Your reticence is honorable, Lord Oakham, but dangerous, and underserved by at least one of your guests. As for the others—I promise you that nothing I learn from you will go beyond these walls. You can trust me."

"Yes, yes," Oakham said, covering his eyes with his hand. "Ask."

Masking a small, grim smile of triumph, Liam took a deep breath. "Do you know for a fact that Quetivel did not do it? I mean, can you prove it? Are you absolutely sure?"

"He is my cousin." It sounded like a plea.

"I know that, but are you absolutely sure of him? I have known men to betray far more than a cousin over far less than this Jewel."

"No," Oakham whispered. "I am not sure."

"Then does he have any debts that you know of?"

The answer came slowly. "He gambles a great deal, but I have never seen him give a marker. He loses often, though . . . more than I think he can have."

"Always to Uldericus?"

Apparently not. Oakham had known him to drop large sums at Pet Radday's, in tavern games, even at one or two horse races.

"And Uldericus? I cannot imagine that he has any problems with money."

Oakham knew of none. He also knew nothing of Cawood's finances; as far as he knew, the man was a fairly successful merchant, with his own fleet of four ships. "The Furseuses are not rich," he said, hastening to add: "But they live very modestly. Their father was a knight in the Duke's service, pensioned off with a living, something in the courts. They collect that. I have never known them to live beyond their means, and they are my wife's oldest friends."

So Quetivel and the Furseuses might be interested in the Jewel for its value, Liam decided. Cawood had money, and Uldericus had too much—*Seventy-five crowns too much*, he thought—to need the Jewel. Greed could not be discounted, he told himself, but he was beginning to wonder.

"This question will be more difficult," Liam said. "Did anyone ever say anything about the Jewel? Express any interest in it?" He sought for the right word: "Covet it? Did anyone covet it?"

"Everyone did," Oakham said, very quickly. "I forget—you have not seen it. It was . . . wonderful." Awe softened his voice. "Ah, Rhenford, anyone would covet it."

This was not what Liam wanted to hear. "So it would seem, Lord Oakham, but that does me no good. Did anyone covet it any more than everyone else? Cawood, for instance. A merchant. Did he ever ask how much it was worth?"

"No," Oakham said miserably. "He knows something of stones. *He* told *me* how much it was worth."

"He did?" That was interesting.

"Aye. He said it was worth nothing, or everything."

Liam smiled grimly; it was his own thought. "Anyone else?"

Oakham took a deep breath. "Poena Furseus admired it extremely, but she admires everything extremely. As I said, she and her brother live most modestly. Countess Perenelle also . . . admired it. I believe she and my wife had some words about it. The countess wished to borrow it, and Duessa quite rightly refused. They quarreled, but they had made it up by that night. It was over."

Neither woman interested Liam; it had been a man, after all, who cut Malskat's throat. But what Oakham said next caught his attention completely.

"Earl Uldericus." He paused, rubbing his hands on his knees. "Earl Uldericus asked to buy it from me."

That was something. That was something indeed. Liam tried to keep the eagerness from his voice. "And you refused?"

"In course!" Oakham exclaimed indignantly. "It was not mine to sell!"

"How did he take your refusal?"

The other man's indignation deflated. "He was most vexed. He doubled his offer—an amazing offer, in truth—and when I refused again, stormed off. He was . . . most vexed."

Careful, Liam warned himself, trying to control his excitement. *Be thorough.* "When did he make the offer? Did he ever mention it again?"

"Four or perhaps five days ago. The day escapes me. And he never repeated the offer."

"Did he say why he wanted it?"

He had not, according to Oakham, who looked as if he wished he had never brought the whole thing up. Liam felt sorry for him; the sort of delicacy and sense of honor that would make a man keep such things to himself in the face of a great loss were rare. *And it has to kill him that one of his guests does not deserve it.*

The whole thing began to point strongly in Uldericus's direction, though Liam had to admit that money could not be a motivation. If he had been prepared to pay for it, that meant he wanted the Jewel for itself.

"Do you have any idea why he might want it?"

"No," Oakham said, standing suddenly, brisk now. "As I said, no one who saw it could help but desire it. It was magnificent, Rhenford."

"Hm. So you said."

Pacing again, Oakham waved his hands, trying to indicate the Jewel's attraction. "It glows, unlike any diamond I have ever seen, and its depths . . . there are no words. Anyone would want it."

"I have one other question, for now. It will seem foolish, but . . . well, do any of your guests have an interest in magic?"

"Magic?"

"Yes. The Jewel was Eirenaeus Priscian's, after all, and there are the legends about him—wizardry, sorcery, that sort of thing."

Oakham laughed weakly, but with genuine humor. "Gods, no! Why-ever they may have coveted it, it was not for any magic it could do, I assure you."

That's good news. Liam smiled. *It only leaves money and pure covetousness.* For some reason the word appealed to him, something about the sibilance. *Covetousness.* "I think that is all for now. I need to meet Master Cawood and the Furseuses. I know we were supposed to go to see Master Cawood now, but I have to see your aunt, and I would like to speak with your wife, and then I have to go somewhere at noon. Can we go to the Staple afterwards?"

"I am at your service," Oakham said, then started to say something else, but stopped himself.

"Is it inconvenient? Is he waiting?"

"No, no," the lord said hurriedly, clasping his hands firmly together. *To keep from wringing them,* Liam guessed. "We can see Cawood at any time. It is my wife. I wonder, Rhenford—"

"I promise you," Liam interrupted, with what he hoped was a suitably earnest expression. "I will be far more . . . delicate with her."

"Thank you," Oakham breathed. "We are men, in the end, and can stand things. Duessa is not, is not . . ."

"I understand. I do not have many questions for her, and you can join us, if you wish."

Oakham shook his head, insisting that that was not necessary, that he trusted Liam completely, and he only asked that Liam not mention the murders. "You will be delicate, I know. She is with her aunt now, next door."

Offering a final assurance that he would, indeed, be delicate, Liam started for the door. "I will come back some time this afternoon, around one o'clock, I hope."

Following after him, Oakham asked: "Are you attending Earl Uldericus?"

"Yes," Liam said, and both men frowned. They went down the stairs together, and Oakham opened the door for him.

"Quetivel will be abed for at least another day, I fear. His nose was, well—you saw. I pray you, see if you can't get Uldericus to drop this. There has been quite enough blood. And, Rhenford—I am sorry you have been dragged into this."

"Not to worry," Liam said, starting down the steps to the street. "I will come back around one, I hope." In fact, he was guiltily grateful for the duel: he wanted another chance to talk with the earl.

Mistress Priscian was in and expecting him, her servant told him at the door. Haellus took his cloak and said, "If you will follow me?" Without waiting he turned back into the house and walked down the main hall, the cloak folded neatly over his arm.

They went to the solarium, the servant announcing "Master Rhenford" and slipping unobtrusively away. *She should choose her niece's servants,* Liam thought, and then saw that the niece was there, as well as a man and woman he did not know.

"Master Rhenford," Mistress Priscian said, nodding graciously to him. "Y' are well come." He bowed, hearing the way she separated the words, and once again noticing that she commanded attention by stillness. Her niece fidgeted in her chair, half twisting to shoot a glance at the woman beside her, who was perching her plump body on the edge of her seat, straining towards him. The man rose fussily.

Mistress Priscian made the introductions: Lady Oakham he had met;

the man was Cimber Furseus, the woman his sister Poena. Liam offered them each a bow, taking in details.

"Oh, Master Rhenford," Poena Furseus said breathily, "speak of the Dark! Lady Oakham was fresh from telling us of you, and you appear! Come, tell us, will you catch this low caitiff?" She was a pleasant-seeming woman, fat in a matronly way but with a young, eager and very plain face. In her plain linen dress and her snood, she looked more like Lady Oakham's governess than her friend, though she could not have been more than three years older.

"Do say, Master Rhenford," her brother piped in, and Liam instantly ruled him out as a suspect. He had his sister's dull brown hair, and large horselike teeth that he bared in what Liam imagined was supposed to be an encouraging smile. He was also considerably plumper than his sister, and he wheezed when he rose. Japer had been a big man, well muscled, and even the beggar Malskat would not have fallen to Cimber Furseus. "It sounds passing exciting! Lady Oakham has told us everything!"

"Yes, she has," Mistress Priscian commented drily.

"It is not really exciting at all, I am afraid," Liam said. He was not sure what Lady Oakham knew, or whom she knew it from, but he was annoyed that she had been talking. She seemed to sense it, too, or perhaps she was merely responding to her aunt's tone: she sat stiffly in her chair, straightening the pleats of her dress, her chin in the air and a little defiance in her eyes.

"Come, Master Rhenford," she said, accenting "master" in a condescending way, "surely it is. This can be no ordinary theft." Recovered from her hangover, she was pretty in a fragile, doll-like way. Blue-black ringlets framed her porcelain face.

"I am no expert on theft," Liam said, "but I think it is." For some reason he had taken an instant dislike to Lady Oakham. How could she be so stupid as to tell the Furseuses about his involvement with the theft? She did not know that it was a man who had let Japer into the house, and she did not know that that man had to have been stronger and far more agile than Cimber Furseus. Not to mention more threatening. *What is she thinking? Is she thinking?* "And I wonder if I might ask you a few questions—I think they will prove just how unexciting it is."

"In course," Lady Oakham said, as if she were granting a boon. "Would you excuse us?" She swept the others with an imperious gaze, faltering only when she reached her aunt, who gave no evidence of noticing it.

The Furseuses started bustling, but Liam held up his hands. "Actually, it would be good if you could stay. You may be able to help." Since she had chosen to tell them "everything," they might as well stay, and hear what he had to ask. A very small part of him whispered that he was forgetting his promise of delicacy to Lord Oakham, and that he was also being petty.

The siblings were more than happy to stay; Cimber settled himself back into his chair with an excited wheeze. Mistress Priscian offered Liam a chair, which he took gratefully, using the time to settle his conscience and discard all the rude questions that had sprung to his mind. *She is just a merchant's daughter who married well,* he reminded himself. *Let her have her airs.*

So he did not start by saying how glad he was that she had gotten over her indisposition of the previous day; ladies did not drink too much and throw up the next day, and if they did it was impolite to refer to it. But he wanted to.

"First," he said, "do any of you know anyone who might have expressed a special interest in the Jewel?"

Lady Oakham held her head cocked primly to one side, and spoke very patiently. "Everyone expressed an interest in it, Master Rhenford. It is a passing thing."

Liam gave a very wide smile. "So I understand, Lady Oakham. But what I meant was, did any of your friends express a special interest in *having* it. For instance, I know Earl Uldericus was quite taken with it."

One of the Furseuses snorted; Liam was not sure which one, because Lady Oakham suddenly uncocked her head and raised her voice. Little spots of red appeared as if by magic on each cheek. "I do not know what you can intend by that, Master Rhenford. If y' are implying that the earl had aught to do with this—"

"Come, Duessa," Mistress Priscian said, none too gently, "this is given. We have discussed it."

"No, Aunt Thrasa, I will not have it! Some thieving knave breaks my house and steals my Jewel, and you accuse my friends! I say I will not have it!" She stamped her foot, most of the effect lost because she was sitting. This time Liam caught the Furseuses' expression: identical wide-open mouths and eyes. Poena leaned over and touched her friend's arm.

"Duessa, is this true? Are we accused?"

"Gods," Cimber wheezed. "Gods! Me, a thief!"

Lady Oakham shot to her feet, her arms rigid at her sides and her fists clenched. "No! No, I tell you! I will not hear it!" Then she put her fists to her ears and stormed out of the solarium, leaving a deafening silence in her wake.

Poor Oakham, Liam thought.

Mistress Priscian broke the silence at last. "I am sure you two are not accused of anything," she said to the siblings, and to Liam it sounded less like an assurance than a condemnation.

He quickly agreed: "Oh, yes. You are completely in the clear. . . ." He trailed off, unsure how to address them.

The Furseuses seemed disappointed by their innocence.

"Damn," Cimber said with a chuckle. "It rather liked me to be thought a thief. A cunning, desperate rogue." He mimed a few passes with a sword.

"To think, we ate with a very thief," Poena said, wonder in her voice. "I wonder who it was? I'll wager money it was that Quetivel."

"The servants," Cimber guessed. "That Tasso has more than a touch of the hungry dog."

"No, he was out of the house," Poena said.

Cimber conceded that this was quite true. "Still, it happens so often. You remember the silver plate Antheuris lost?"

They began to remind each other of thieving servant stories they knew, completely oblivious of Mistress Priscian and Liam, and he took the chance to ask the older woman for a moment alone.

"Certainly," she said, gathering herself up from her chair. "We'll talk in the kitchen."

Liam stood, and the Furseuses noticed. "Oh, do excuse us, Mistress Priscian; we are quite rude. We should go."

"No, please," Liam said quickly, "stay just a moment. I have a few questions."

They settled back in their chairs, puzzled but willing, and Liam went with Mistress Priscian to the kitchen. They stood by the worktable.

"I assume you meant it when you said the Furseuses were . . . 'in the clear'?" she asked. Liam nodded. "That is to the good. They are the best of Duessa's lot, and they had a good father. What do you want of them?"

"I hope they can answer some of the questions Lady Oakham would not."

"Ah. My niece is—" She paused, searching, then gave up. "As I said, she was brought up strangely. But the Furseuses should do admirably. They love talk." She rubbed her hands together then, as if ridding them of previous business. "I assume you wish to know if I have found anything for your friend."

"Yes. If you haven't, it is not important."

"I have, though I do not know if it was what she sought. There are some books with his name in them, which I presume are his work. They were deep in the attic, and in passing good condition, given their age. I do not wish them to leave the house, so she may look at them here. There is a very quiet study upstairs that she may use. The light is good. When will she call?"

"Whenever is convenient," Liam said, "and thank you very much. I believe she thinks this is important."

"I could make nothing of them. She may come this afternoon, if she wishes, and during the day for as long as she needs. You will bring her?"

"Yes," Liam said, thankful and eager. "This afternoon, I think. She was very interested in anything you might have. And thank you again."

"It is nothing," she said. "I will expect you later in the afternoon, then. You can tell me what progress has been made. I am anxious to know."

She did not seem anxious, Liam thought, but he promised to give her a full report. She started briskly out of the kitchen. "And now I think we have kept the Furseuses waiting too long."

The Furseuses were waiting in the hall, cloaked and hooded. They explained that they did not wish to impose on Mistress Priscian anymore, and should in any case be returning home; but if Master Rhenford chose to accompany them . . .

"Of course," Liam said, and before he could ask, Haellus was behind him, helping him into his cloak.

Once outside, they surrounded him, each taking an arm, complaining cheerfully about the cold.

"Have you known a winter like this?" Cimber said, though he was heavily bundled up. He panted as they walked.

"It is the very coldest," Poena threw in, from behind a long, thick scarf wrapped three times around her neck. Liam did not think it was particularly cold, but he meant to agree; the Furseuses, however, did not give him a chance. They were already discussing Mistress Priscian, leaning in front of him a little as they walked down End Street.

"Aunt Thrasa seemed most displeased with Duessa, didn't you think?"

"Passing displeased," Poena agreed, and then added for Liam's benefit: "We call her aunt, though she is not: she is an old friend of our dear father's, though somewhat fierce. Don't you find her so?"

"When we were young," Cimber said, while Liam was still trying to open his mouth, "we were sore frighted of her. And I think we still are!"

"She is most kind, though, on further acqaintance; I'm sure you'll find her so," Poena said soothingly, patting Liam's arm.

"Oh, I already do," he said quickly. "I admire her a great deal. But there are those questions. . . ."

"Quetivel," Cimber said, allowing no doubt. "Baron Quetivel is your man."

"And what of Earl Uldericus?" Poena asked. "He would want it for the same reason."

"Yes, but Quetivel is the younger man—the juices of passion flow more strongly in him!"

"Oh, juices," his sister said disparagingly. "What do you know of juices? And what do you mean by them? Baron Quetivel is shallow, unpersevering, he lacks sap. The earl hopes to revive his marriage. It is self-evident."

They turned off End Street, heading down past the Goddard mansion and towards the center of the city.

Cimber countered, "The baron is hot-blooded, and young. I believe the earl has quite given up. Does he not pass all his evenings there?" He nodded at Herione's, just a few yards down.

Liam took advantage of the pause to yank gently on their arms, as if he were reining in a team of runaway horses. He was getting dizzy from trying to follow their conversation. "Please, I am not sure I understand. Why would both Quetivel and Uldericus want the Jewel?"

The siblings shared a look of surprise, and then launched into an explanation. Countess Perenelle, apparently, was quite enamored of the Jewel. Poena described the "quarrel" Oakham had mentioned as more of a brawl. After that, the countess had made no secret of how much she wanted the Jewel, and how she would give anything to have it—though never in front of Lady Oakham.

Now, they explained carefully, it was common knowledge that all was not well in the earl's home; Uldericus spent most of his evenings unhappily at Herione's, and there were rumors—Cimber stressed the word "rumors" in such a way that Liam guessed they were more than rumors—that his wife was receiving visitors at home. Furthermore, it was plain that Quetivel wished to be one of these visitors.

"In fine," Poena summed up, "whoever has the Jewel has the countess's heart."

"And welcome to it," her brother added, still puffing a little, though they had stopped walking. "For all of me, she is not worth it."

"Not everyone thinks that," Poena warned. "Many men would gladly steal more than the Jewel for but one kiss."

They rambled on a little more, but Liam was not paying much attention. He should have thought it all through before—Quetivel's comment before the game about some things being worth more than money, Uldericus's odd dream and the way he had looked at the baron after recounting it. And, of course, the insults that lead to the duel. It should have been obvious, he thought, but refused to scold himself. He had been right, in a sense: neither Uldericus nor Quetivel wanted the Jewel for itself or for money, or for the magic it was supposed to possess. They wanted it because it was the key to possessing the countess.

Her wanting it is ridiculous, he judged, *but* their *wanting it* . . . He would have to see her in person to decide about that.

"Is it true?" Cimber said, interrupting Liam's train of thought. Brother and sister were staring at him with expectant eyes.

"What?" He had not been listening to their chatter.

"That the earl and the baron will duel, in course!"

"Ah," Liam said. "Ah. No challenge has been given yet." He wondered how long it was before noon; Uldericus's house was nearby. It would be worthwhile to get a look at the earl's wife.

"There will be," Poena said, wagging a finger at the two men, and wearing a knowing smile that said she looked forward to the event. "Mark me, I'll warrant it."

Liam gently disengaged himself from their clutches. "You remind me of something. I have an appointment with Earl Uldericus very shortly. His house is near here, isn't it?"

"Over there." Cimber pointed it out, a narrow-fronted building three doors up from Herione's. "Is it about the duel?"

"Will you dissuade him from it?" Poena asked.

Cimber snorted and flapped a hand at his sister. "Who could dissuade him? Or Quetivel, for all that?"

"Oh I wish we could have spied his nose!"

"Oakham's Tasso said it was quite flat," Cimber giggled. They began to wonder gleefully whether Quetivel would be permanently disfigured.

Liam took a step backward, bowing. "Thank you very much for talking with me," he said. "I really must go." He took another step backward, and to his relief, they hardly noticed him, caught up in their speculations.

Turning, he trotted off to the house Cimber had pointed out.

THOUGH THE PLACE was undistinguished on the outside, the inside of Uldericus's house laid to rest any lingering questions Liam may have had about the earl needing money. A servant let him in the front door, took his name, and disappeared up a grand staircase, leaving him alone in the entrance hall. There was money everywhere, in the intricate patterns of the rugs that muffled the servant's footsteps, the gilt-framed portraits on the walls, the gleaming brass fittings of the tiled fireplace. To his left, double doors opened on a dining room, a sideboard laden with silver plate, a long oak table flanked by matching chairs, legs and arms carved and turned elegantly, and an enormous chandelier of crystal.

As if he needed my money, Liam thought. *Probably had to hire an extra servant just to polish the plate.*

The servant returned. "Earl Uldericus is not in; he is not expected until noon. The countess will receive you in her sitting room."

Liam allowed himself a small smile as he followed the servant up the grand staircase. He had expected Uldericus to be at home, but hoped that his early arrival might gain him just a glimpse of the earl's wife, a chance to judge how much of an incentive to theft she was—and now he would get to speak with her. The question, of course, was, what would he say?

The countess's sitting room was on the second floor, the first room off the stairs; the servant announced him and then left them alone. Liam bowed, keeping his gaze on her face to avoid staring at the room's furnishings, a vague impression of crystal, gold and silk crowded around a low divan much like the one in his library. Hers, though, had gilded legs, and the upholstery was laced with gold and silver threads in an elaborate pattern of birds and flowers; beside it stood a water pipe of brass and purple glass and a delicate lacquered table with a golden plate of sweetmeats.

"Master Rhenford," she said, "do come in." She had been lying back on the divan; now she swung herself around to sit on the edge.

Liam smiled blandly, narrowing his eyes until all he could see was her face. *I would steal the Jewel for her.* Countess Perenelle was quite possibly the most beautiful woman he had ever seen. It was undeniable, though he knew that a great deal of it was artifice and attitude—the studied grace with which she swung her legs over the edge of the divan, the subtle bend at the waist that emphasized the strain on the upper part of her dress, the makeup that delicately enhanced her natural pallor and made her lips so red. Her voice was high but soft, her face composed and curious. A sweet, flowery scent radiated from her direction. Liam tried not to think about her dress. He wanted to whistle.

"Excuse me for disturbing you, my lady," he said with a bow. "I was hoping to see your husband."

Her eyes trailed languidly over him, a slow sweep from boots to head. He fought an urge to square his shoulders and throw out his chest.

"We expect him shortly. Can I offer you something while you wait?" Her knees shifted minutely.

One of those, Liam thought. He was not entirely sure what he meant by "those," but the image of a predatory cat came to mind.

"No, thank you."

"I imagine it is to do with this challenge?" Her lips curled into what might have been a smile.

"Yes," he said regretfully. "It is an unfortunate thing."

"I am not so sure." She began to busy herself with the water pipe, filling it with quick, deft gestures. "It is a little flattering. A lady's honor must be upheld."

She smiled sweetly at him, and he decided he did not like her. *So many unpleasant people,* he thought. *And this one wants men to fight over her.*

"Certainly," he agreed. He was at a loss; if Uldericus or Quetivel had stolen the Jewel, would they have given it to her already? She wore no jewelry, but that meant nothing, because she could not wear it in front of strangers. And anyway, if either suitor had stolen the Jewel, they would hardly have spent the previous night gambling—the man who had it would have run right to her with it.

The countess finished priming and lighting the pipe, put the mouthpiece to her lips and puffed gently. She was looking at him.

Liam closed his eyes and thought. Might the thief have waited? What would be the point? When he opened his eyes, she was examining him again, a smile quirking her lips around the mouthpiece. She was not drawing on the pipe.

"Still," he said, clearing his throat. "I hope the duel might be avoided. Baron Quetivel was drunk."

She seemed to find this funny; she giggled, putting the mouthpiece down on the table. Smoke curled lazily around her, its odor mixing with her own sweet smell. A dreamy haze stole across her face. "Think you he'll apologize?"

"I hope so." Why wait to present her the Jewel? She was beautiful, leaning back now on the divan, drawing her legs up under her. *Enough to steal for?* Liam did not like her, her casual attitude towards the duel, her obvious self-absorption. *Perhaps.*

It was complicated. To suspect Quetivel and Uldericus, he had to assume that the countess was their motive. But neither of them, as far as he could see, had claimed their prize. Did that mean they had not stolen the Jewel, or were they waiting? If they were waiting, what for?

There was still Cawood to consider; he might be the thief. Liam found himself hoping that would prove the case.

"I don't," Lady Uldericus said, putting a hand to her mouth and yawning behind it. Liam had to admit that he had never seen a yawn more perfectly executed. "It will clear the air."

"My lady?" Had she really just said that?

"My husband," she said, closing her eyes, and Liam heard footsteps on the stairs.

Uldericus entered a moment later, stopping in the doorway. His face was cold. Liam bowed.

"Master Rhenford." He paused, taking in the scene. Then he gestured to the hallway. "If you will attend me." He let Liam go before him, and shut the door firmly behind them. "We will speak in my sitting room. Y' are early."

"I was in the Point on other business, my lord, and finished early. I thought you would be at home."

"My wife does not receive visitors," Uldericus said, scowling. "You should have come at noon."

"My apologies," Liam said, though he wanted to say something else entirely. *Easy,* he counseled himself. *You do not want to be involved in a duel yourself.* Instead, he smiled innocently. "Your sitting room?"

The earl grunted and led the way a little down the hallway, to a room half the size of his wife's but just as expensively furnished. He seated himself behind a massive desk, its top a single sheet of polished wood, in the surface of which Uldericus was blurrily reflected. He did not offer Liam a seat.

"I propose that as soon as Baron Quetivel is recovered, we should meet. I will accept no apologies. He may choose the weapons. I believe that is clear enough."

"Perfectly clear," Liam said, heaving a sad sigh. "But are you sure you wish to refuse apologies? The baron was not himself; he was drunk."

"There will be no apologies."

"But he may—"

Uldericus pounded his fist once on the desktop. "Master Rhenford! Y' are not here to offer advice! He may make his apologies, but I'll not accept them! Is that clear?"

Once again, Liam put aside his instinctive response. "Perfectly," he said. Then, a beat later, responding to a whim whose origin he was unsure of, he went on: "And of course, there is this rumor about Quetivel and the Priscian Jewel. It would be good to put an end to that, I suppose."

Uldericus's head snapped up. "What rumor?"

"It is nothing." Liam waved a hand dismissively. "I should not have brought it up—and please do not mention it to Lord Oakham. It would upset him a great deal."

"Do they say Quetivel stole the Jewel?" the earl demanded, his mouth set in a tight line, fists clenched on the table. Liam immediately regretted his whim. He could practically hear the other man's mind racing, reaching certain conclusions.

"It is just a rumor," Liam hastily put in. "I don't believe it myself. What good would it do him?" The instant he spoke the words he realized that they, too, were a mistake.

"No good at all," Uldericus said, the words hissing out between his teeth. Bright red spots appeared on his cheeks, the cords of his neck standing out like taut rigging. "Deliver the challenge, Master Rhenford. I'll expect a response."

He rose and stalked to the door.

"You can show yourself out."

Liam stepped out of the room to let him pass, then went to the head of the stairs. Uldericus, trembling, took a deep breath at the door of his wife's sitting room, then shoved the door open and went inside. After a moment, Liam went down the stairs, staring at his feet and shaking his head.

Well, what did that tell you?

The answer, he thought, was absolutely nothing—but he would have to think about it.

The servant who had let him in was waiting by the front door. He bowed at Liam's approach and silently held out a folded piece of paper. Liam took it with a nod and stepped out into the street.

The note could wait. It smelled faintly of perfume, and at the moment he was more interested in organizing what he had learned—if anything—than in whatever the predatory countess might have to say. He walked slowly down the street, stopping outside Herione's.

Uldericus thought having the Jewel would do Quetivel no good, Liam reflected. The way he had said it was ambiguous, though.

The earl must have known how his wife felt about the Jewel—that she had promised "anything" for it—and thanks to Liam he now probably guessed that Quetivel knew as well. But he had said that the Jewel would be of no use to the baron, which made no sense to Liam. Did it mean that Uldericus could prevent his wife from fulfilling her promise, or that he could prevent Quetivel from using it? Liam feared he would never know which.

Of course, it did show the lengths to which the earl would go. His barely controlled rage had not been faked, and Liam guessed that he would not flinch at killing a thief and a common beggar.

It seemed unlikely, though, that Uldericus had the Jewel; if he did, why had he spent the night at Herione's? He should have been home claiming his prize. The same held true for Quetivel.

The steps of the brothel were swept clean; he gathered his cloak underneath him and sat down, closing his ears to the noise of the street and trying to concentrate.

He needed something else. The idea he had had in mind when he asked Coeccias to find Desiderius would not work. Simply put, he had hoped to let the guests know that there was a wizard in the city willing to buy the Jewel. Beyond that, the idea had been vague—putting someone in an inn, as far from the one where Desiderius was staying as possible, and luring the thief there. But since neither Uldericus nor Quetivel would have stolen the Jewel for money, it was no longer a plan worth considering.

Unless it could be applied to Cawood. *Gods, let him be in debt,* Liam prayed. The trap was the only solution he had at the moment, and he could think of no way to differentiate between Uldericus and Quetivel. If it was either of those two, he would need to come up with another plan entirely.

Further thought was pointless, he decided. He had to sound out Cawood, and talk to Oakham. *Coeccias, too.* The Aedile might well be able to shed some light on the question, or come up with another plan. For that matter, discussing it with Fanuilh could be valuable. In the three months or so that they had been linked, he had found the dragon an excellent sounding board.

Thinking of Fanuilh reminded him of Grantaire, waiting at the house on the beach. He leaned back against the stone steps and closed his eyes.

Fanuilh! he projected.

Yes, master? The response was almost instant.

Please tell Grantaire that she can come see Mistress Priscian this afternoon. She should leave soon.

Liam had already begun to form his next thought when the dragon replied: *I cannot, master.* He cleared his throat and closed his eyes even tighter.

What do you mean, you cannot?

I cannot give Mage Grantaire a message.

In his head, Liam's thought was capitalized and very large: *WHY NOT?*

I cannot speak.

"Oh," Liam said aloud, a moment later. "Right." Growling to himself, he sent a final message: *Fine, forget it. I will come out.* He opened his eyes and got to his feet, brushing behind him, where the seat of his pants was cold despite the cloak.

The piece of paper Uldericus's servant had given him was still in his hand, neatly folded and sealed with a perfect circle of purple wax. The paper crackled as he opened it.

Master Rhenford, it read. *Come to me this evening at eight bells—my husband will be away.*

It was not signed, but there was no question whom it was from. He held the note to his nose and inhaled. No question.

What does she *want?*

He folded the paper and tucked it inside his tunic, starting to walk down out of the Point.

By the time he had reached the stables, he had decided that what Countess Perenelle wanted was beside the point. He could guess, though an inborn modesty made him laugh at the idea. "How bored can she be?" he chuckled to himself. Still, it did not matter: what mattered was what he could learn from the meeting, and cuckolding the earl was not on his list at all. Was there any information to be gotten from her? If either of her suitors had given her the Jewel, he could hardly expect her to confess, and in any case he did not think either had. Otherwise, why would she be making assignations with him?

"It may not be an assignation," he said to himself, "much as that may hurt your pride, my boy." But if not that, then what? He assumed she did not know that he was looking for the Jewel, so it was doubtful that she wanted to give him information.

Out of the Point, he passed a shop selling mirrors and glassware. He stopped and examined himself briefly in a large mirror in the shop window. Tall, close-cropped blond hair, a youthful face with a long, narrow nose. He ran a finger down the length of that nose, first trying what he thought might be a seductive expression, then grinning at his own reflection.

Liam Rhenford, lady-killer, he thought. *She must be* very *bored. How do I turn that boredom to good use?*

Liam was still considering the question, pulling it back and forth in his head and getting nowhere, when he arrived at the beach. He had pushed Diamond hard, and the cold wind had numbed the tip of his nose and blasted his face red. He left Diamond saddled on the sand and ran quickly to the door.

Fanuilh was waiting just inside.

Hello, master.

The cold ride and his frustration at the course of his investigation had put Liam in a bad mood. "You," he said, aiming a finger at the dragon, "you I do not want to talk to. Why didn't you tell me you could not give her a message?"

You did not ask, his familiar responded, *and I did not know you wanted me to.* It flared its wings once. Liam closed his eyes and started to count to ten. Grantaire spoke when he was at five.

"Good afternoon. Have you spoken with Mistress Priscian?"

He opened his eyes. "Yes, I have. She is expecting you this afternoon." She stood in the library door, wearing a gray, ankle-length dress with long sleeves and a high neck.

"Will this do?" She indicated the dress, tugging at the tight collar. Liam grinned at her discomfort.

"Perfectly. You will make a good impression. But can you leave now?"

"Of course. A cloak." She went into the bedroom and returned a moment later, drawing on her fur-trimmed cloak. Liam explained Mistress Priscian's conditions, to which she had no objections, and they went outside.

She followed him to Diamond, and he realized that she had no horse. *How did she get out here?*

"I suppose you will have to ride behind me," he said hesitantly, and she said, "Yes," as if it were nothing. He mounted, and she climbed up behind with ease, sitting sidesaddle and wrapping her arms around his waist.

Liam set Diamond going at an easy pace, mindful of Grantaire's position—and her hands, snug around him—though he was anxious to be back in the city. There was so much to do, so much to figure out. He wanted to sit down with Coeccias, perhaps over dinner—the Aedile thought best over meals—and go over what he had found out. Quetivel and Uldericus were his main problem. If either was the thief, he could think of no way short of searching them to find the Jewel.

Near the city gates Grantaire pulled the hood of her cloak down so that it obscured most of her face.

"We will take the shortest route there?"

"Of course," Liam said, remembering that she would be worried about meeting Desiderius. He should have thought of that earlier. "I will introduce you to Mistress Priscian, and then there are some things I must take care of. I'll come back for you later."

They passed through Temple's Court and turned up the Point's northernmost street, riding past Herione's and the Uldericuses' to End Street. Grantaire jumped lightly off when he stopped outside Mistress Priscian's; Liam dismounted and tied Diamond's reins to the hitching ring discreetly bolted to the stoop.

"This is it," he said, and they went up the stairs together.

Haellus let them in and led them directly to the solarium. There was not much sunlight, but Mistress Priscian was standing by the windows, staring out to sea.

"Good afternoon, Master Rhenford," she said, turning from the view.

"Mistress Priscian, this is the friend I mentioned—Mage Grantaire." He was not sure if that was the proper way to introduce her, but it was what Fanuilh called her, and he figured the dragon would know. He was vaguely aware that true wizards preferred the more arcane "mage," but he had never known why. In any case, she did not object, dropping a very creditable curtsy at the older woman.

"Allow me to thank you for this opportunity, Mistress Priscian. It is a great privilege."

The older woman nodded, as if this was only proper. "There are a fair number of papers and two books to examine. I imagine it will take some time."

"I hope not to inconvenience you," Grantaire murmured.

Mistress Priscian laid a hand on her chest. "It is no inconvenience to me," she said. "But come, Master Rhenford grows restless. I am sure he must have pressing business."

Liam had not thought his restlessness was obvious, but he nodded. "There are some things I must see to. I will leave you to it, if I may."

"Certainly," Grantaire said.

"In course," Mistress Priscian said at the same time.

He promised to return by five, and left the two women alone.

Tasso let him into the Oakhams' and led him to the rear room on the first floor. It had been cleaned up since the last time Liam saw it, some of the padded couches removed, the remaining ones grouped by the fireplace. Oakham was lying on one, but he sat up as soon as he saw Liam.

"Y' are back." There was a cloak folded over the end of his couch; he gathered it up and stood. "We'll to the Staple, then." He spoke heavily, as if it were a duty he would rather not fulfill, but knew he must.

"I saw Earl Uldericus a little while ago," Liam said, unsure of the etiquette surrounding duels. "He gave me a challenge for Baron Quetivel."

Oakham paused with his hands on his hips, grimacing. Then he shook his head. "There is no point, just yet. He's in no condition to receive it—can scarcely think straight. I think it'll keep."

Liam agreed. "I suppose it will. Has he eaten?"

"He has, and's kept all down. I'll warrant his health, if he's given a day or so." He clapped his hands together, as if bracing himself for a hard job. "Come, the Staple."

They walked down Duke Street, Liam leading Diamond. There was a stable on the way. He was thinking about the rest of his afternoon—after the Staple, he wanted to sit down with Coeccias. Would it be worth his while to stop by Herione's? She had offered him good information before; he would ask the Aedile about that.

He stole a glance at the lord beside him. Oakham walked slowly, his head down, studying his feet. He was chewing one end of his mustache, and a heavy vertical line creased his forehead.

This is getting to him, Liam thought. *And why should it not? It was not even his, and one of his friends stole it.* Thinking of Oakham's friends reminded him of something. He drew his purse from his belt.

"I forgot, my lord." He started to count out crowns, looping Diamond's reins awkwardly around his arm. "It was thirty, wasn't it?"

"What's that?" Liam had meant to distract Oakham from his brooding, but the man was acting as if he had been offered a live snake. "That's not for me." He shook his head, rejecting the money. "That's Uldericus's. You'll pay him."

"But you vouched for me," Liam said slowly. "I thought—"

"The money is Uldericus's," Oakham repeated, sharply this time. "We'll have no more on it."

Liam slipped the money back into his purse, wondering at the other man's attitude. Duke Street bent at a right angle, and they passed the temple of the Storm King.

"Perhaps you can tell me something about Master Cawood," Liam said, determined not to be put off by Oakham's bad mood.

With an exasperated sigh, the lord told him what he already knew: that Cawood was a merchant, with several ships.

"Yes, I know that," Liam said patiently. Oakham refused to meet his eye, looking anywhere on the street but at his companion. "I was hoping you might tell me something else. For instance, how did you meet?" Cawood was the only guest who had no social rank—even the Furseuses were the children of a knight.

"At the baths," Oakham said. "He enjoys sparring, as I do."

Liam was vaguely aware that the southerners did more at their baths than just get clean. They held debates, races, contests of strength, wrestling and boxing matches—almost anything that could be done indoors.

"Sparring? With swords?"

"No," Oakham said, sighing heavily, clearly resigning himself to Liam's questions. "Boxing, you might name it, with helmets and padded gloves."

"Ah. Is he good?" He was trying to imagine boxers wearing helmets. Even with padded gloves, he would not want to smash his fist into a war helmet.

"Yes, he is very good." Oakham tugged the end of his mustache out of his mouth and smoothed it. "I see your direction, Rhenford." He sighed bitterly.

"What direction is that?" Liam asked, genuinely ignorant.

The other man finally met his eye. "You wish to know if he could have killed the thief. That I can't tell you. I only know that he's a good boxer."

I wish that had been my direction, Liam admitted to himself. However, there was no reason for Oakham to know it was not, and it allowed him to ask some other questions.

"What about Earl Uldericus? And Baron Quetivel?"

Once more fixing his eyes on the ground, Oakham spoke reluctantly, weighing each word. Uldericus was not a soldier, but was known as good with a blade. He had a private tutor, and had from time to time participated with success in practice matches at one of the more exclusive baths.

"These parts do not sum up a murderer," Oakham cautioned, and Liam agreed.

They had turned off Duke Street and reached the stables; Liam arranged for Diamond to spend the afternoon, not bothering to haggle with the ostler. He hurried back to the street. They headed for Harbor Street, Oakham resuming his talk.

Quetivel was from the northern parts of the duchy, bordering partly on the Midlands and partly on the wild mountains around Caernarvon. Noblemen there were bred to fighting, particularly on horseback. "He is partly in Southwark now to pay obeisance to that new Bellona. He's made an offering and said prayers at her fane."

Liam raised an eyebrow at this: Bellona's worship in the Southern Tier was only a month old, and though the goddess had actually appeared in the city, he did not think word would have spread so fast. More, though, he could not reconcile his image of Quetivel as a gambler and a rakehell with the idea of the baron praying and making offerings.

"I am sure he can couch a lance and draw a bow," Oakham went on. "On the marches, every man is a warrior, and from a young age. But again, that does not sum him up a murderer."

That was certainly true, Liam knew. A man could do things in the heat of battle that he would never consider in cold blood. Moreover, the sort of skills Oakham had described were meaningless—Japer and the beggar had not been run through with lances or beaten to death with padded gloves. Their throats had been slit.

"I note you do not ask after Cimber Furseus," Oakham said.

Liam shook his head. "No. I met him this afternoon, and I saw both the men who were killed. Furseus could not have done it."

"Y'are sure? Even a strong man can be taken by surprise, and it is but the work of a second to cut a throat."

One moment information had to be dragged from the man, the next he wanted to implicate another man. *Does he want to find the Jewel or not?* "No," Liam said insistently, "it was not Furseus."

They passed off Harbor Street onto straight, narrow streets running between the high walls of warehouses. Winter was slow for Southwark's merchants, and with the Banquet in progress, there were even fewer people than usual in the neighborhood. Gull screams from the nearby docks echoed off the warehouses, as did the men's footsteps.

"Rhenford, do you still think you can recover the Jewel by tomorrow?"

Liam could not read the other man's tone, but it was as if he had read his mind. He had just been thinking that he had vastly underestimated the amount of time he would need. If Countess Perenelle was really the cause of the theft, he could imagine no way to find the Jewel. *If we could just search them—all of them! The gods know there's reason enough to suspect them.*

That was out of the question, though: gossip, however close to the truth, was not cause enough for accusing noblemen of theft. Even the truth was not enough, for that matter. He would have to have proof, concrete proof. It was no wonder that Coeccias had been eager to hand the investigation over to him. Still, there was no sense burdening Oakham any more. The lord looked worn down by his cares.

"I hope so. At the very least I hope to know who did it. Proving it will be harder, but once we know who it is, we can figure out a way to prove it." *No sense raising his hopes too much. . . .*

Oakham nodded, as if this confirmed his own thinking. "If that's the case, there is something I'll tell you. I wish to leave Southwark. This affair has put a great strain on Lady Oakham—and on me, for all that. I have family in Torquay, and it would like me to pass some time there."

"I can imagine." It was hardly strange, though Liam was a little surprised that Oakham would tell him about it.

"I have booked a passage for us on a ship, the *Sourberry*. It parts Southwark in three days."

"That soon?" Liam blurted. He was by no means sure he could have the Jewel back by then.

Oakham nodded grimly. "The city oppresses me, Rhenford, but I think most of my wife. This has been passing hard on her."

"Of course" was the only thing Liam could think to say, but he felt panic rising inside him. There was no way he could have the Jewel back in three days, not at the rate he was going. He might know who had stolen it—would have to know who had stolen it, he reminded himself, to satisfy the Werewolf—but having it back was another thing entirely.

"I have not told my wife or my aunt," Oakham added, "and I would consider it a kindness if you would not mention it to them just yet. It is a delicate thing, and I wish to do it myself."

"Of course." It was still the only thing he could think to say. Three days seemed a very short time.

In a solemn silence, they walked on past the warehouses.

■ *12* ■

THE STAPLE WAS out of place in the warehouse district, a rectangular building neatly plastered and painted a delicate blue. Large windows marched down its sides, clean white shutters framing each broad expanse of glass. A tall tower rose above the gently sloped roof of gray tile, topped by a gilded statue of a woman shading her eyes with one hand to gaze out to sea, and holding a piece of paper in the other. The building fronted on a small square, more a fortuitous gap between the surrounding warehouses than a planned space, and two shallow flights of steps met in a broad landing in front of the entrance. The whole effect was surprising, a strange apparition of grace among the squatting brick and wood shells all around it.

Liam had seen it once or twice, in rambling walks around the city, and the week before, when it had begun to seem as if his partnership with Mistress Priscian might really materialize, he asked Coeccias about it. It was little different from similar constructions in the Freeports and Harcourt, a place for merchants to meet and arrange cargos, to exchange goods they could not sell for those they could, to barter and to cheat. The name was odd, but Coeccias had explained that; the Duke held a monopoly on wool in the Southern Tier, and to ship a bale of it out of the city, the bale had to be marked with a staple, a foot-long red wicket. Originally, it had been a warehouse full of wool and red staples, from which the Duke's agents would sell the bales. The trade had long since grown too big to operate out of a single building, and when the old warehouse had burned down some fifty years ago, the merchants of Southwark had

erected the present building, providing offices for the Duke's wool agents
and booths and a trading floor for themselves. No goods actually moved
through the Staple now, just invoices and bills of lading, but if it had not
been for the deals made there, most of Southwark's ships would have
sailed empty.

They went up the stairs and through the entrance, through a small
vestibule and down onto the trading floor. Literally down, because the
floor was sunken, three steps down to stone flags that stretched across
almost the entire first story. Massive white posts rose every so often,
branching out into braces and struts supporting the ceiling beams; on
three sides wooden dividers reached from the outermost posts to the
walls, creating stalls for individual merchants. Many were empty, at others single men sat alone, waiting for business, and at a few there were
groups of men. It was only slightly warmer inside the building than out,
and all of the occupied stalls had braziers. There were a few groups of
men in cloaks or heavy coats scattered around the trading floor itself,
though they did not seem to be working hard. A wine jug was being
passed around one group, and another was laughing at some joke just
told. Liam was sure he recognized one of the laughing men from Herione's. At the western end of the room, a uniformed guard sat on a broad
flight of steps leading to the second floor, his pike leaning against the
banister.

"I do not spy him," Oakham announced after scanning the room.
"We'll visit Denby—he'll know of Cawood."

Frowning, Liam followed the other man across the trading floor. He
should have guessed that Cawood might not be there—it was winter,
after all, and the trading season did not begin for another few months—
but he had assumed Oakham was sure of the man's whereabouts. The
lord was unconcerned, however; the anxious look he had worn on the
street dropped away, replaced by a light smile, as he walked towards one
of the stalls manned by a lone merchant.

"Master Denby," he called, jumping up the three steps, "how are
you keeping?"

Tall, thin and stooped, Denby unfolded himself from his chair and
offered a bow as if he were falling over. "My Lord Oakham."

"Master Lons Denby," Oakham said, "Master Liam Rhenford. Master Rhenford is joining with my aunt in a venture."

Denby blinked mildly and offered his hopes that it would be profitable.

Liam thanked him. "With luck it will be."

"Tell us, Master Denby, have you seen Rafe Cawood? I had hoped he might show Master Rhenford the Staple."

"There is not so much to see," Denby said, blinking again and digging solemnly at his ear. "Nor would Master Cawood be the man to show it. Not this day."

"And why not?" Oakham asked with a pleasant smile.

"For that he's there," Denby said, pausing in his digging long enough to point at the stairs, "with the wool agents."

"Are they so terrible?"

Denby shrugged, blinked. "No, they're not." He blinded again. "But he's two cargos to pay for, and the ships not in."

Liam's heart leapt, but he tried to hide his eagerness. "Not in?"

"Not in," Denby agreed, nodding slowly. "And the Duke's agents can be fierce with those who can't pay."

"Surely it is a mere gap," Oakham said, practically pleading. "A temporary shortfall. When the ships are in . . ."

"The Duke is not patient," Denby responded solemnly, as if he were a judge passing sentence. "And the ships are more than a month out. The agents'll guess them lost." He said the last as if the consequences were obvious, and Liam thought they were, at least as far as he was concerned. If the agents assumed the ships were not coming back—had sunk, or been taken by pirates—they would call in Cawood's debt for his wool. That meant he would need money, and if he needed money, he had a reason to steal the Jewel. Most important, it was a reason Liam could understand, and one he could work with.

"He may be down shortly," Denby went on, digging in his ear again. "Though he may not be in the mood to take Master Rhenford on the rounds of the Staple. Such as it is."

"Will he be long?" Liam asked. "I was hoping he could answer a few of my questions."

Denby shrugged. "Who can say? He may be coming down presently, or not for hours. But it may be that I can answer your questions."

"I don't think so, Master Denby," Oakham said. The news about Cawood had not pleased him, and once again he refused to meet Liam's eyes. "We had hoped to speak with him directly."

"We can wait a bit, Lord Oakham," Liam said, a little annoyed at the other man. "And Master Denby may be able to answer some of my less specific questions."

He was, and he and Liam spent a few minutes discussing the way the Staple functioned, as well as trade in general. Denby, it turned out, was a sort of general factor, dealing in tapestries produced by the peasants of a

Midlands lord, wine from Alyecir, and ore from some small mines near
Caernarvon, among other things. Liam was particularly interested in the
mines—one of the ports to which he wanted to send Mistress Priscian's
ships needed metals of all sorts.

Oakham fretted the whole time, folding and unfolding his arms, tugging at the ends of his mustache, but refusing to participate in the discussion.

"Perhaps we can walk around ourselves," the lord burst in at last.
"We don't want to keep Master Denby from his tasks." It was a transpar-
ent lie, since no one had come anywhere near the stall since they arrived,
but Denby accepted it, shrugging and blinking.

"As you will, my lord."

Liam cast a sharp glance at Oakham. "I would like to speak with you
some more," he told Denby. "Are you here often?"

In a tone that clearly wondered where else he might be, the merchant said he was there every day, and bid the two men good day as they
turned away.

"I am sorry, Rhenford," Oakham said, as soon as they were out of
earshot. "I cannot listen to such pratings. I've too much on my mind."

Liam waved the apology away. As much as Oakham's scruples annoyed him, as much as they made his investigation more difficult, the loss
was still Oakham's, and the lord's problems were far more serious than
any Liam faced. He should have remembered that. "It doesn't matter.
What does matter is that we know Cawood is having money problems."

"He never told me." There was sorrow in Oakham's voice. "He has
never told me much of his business, in course, but such a blow! Two
ships!"

"Yes, but the Jewel would more than make up for that," Liam
pointed out, wanting to make sure that Oakham understood. "It puts
suspicion strongly on him."

Oakham admitted as much with a heavy sigh, then stiffened, his eyes
fixed on the stairs at the far end of the trading floor. The guard was
scrambling to his feet to make way for someone to descend. A man came
into view a second later, dressed in a jerkin and plain hose, a short cape
over his shoulders. A floppy cloth hat was balled up in his fists, and his
face was red with anger.

"Cawood," Oakham whispered, pointing.

"Speak to him," Liam urged, taking the other man's elbow and propelling him gently towards the stairs. "Arrange a meeting with him later
today or early tomorrow, just the two of you."

"Why?"

"Just do it, please." Liam said, pushing harder. Cawood had reached the bottom of the steps, and Oakham, with an angry glance at Liam, raised his voice and hailed his friend.

Cawood heard, and stopped, but he made no move to meet them, waiting while they hurried over.

"Cawood," Oakham said, "how are you keeping?"

"Not well," the merchant growled. He was tall and thickly muscled; his head seemed to grow from his shoulders, with no intervening neck. His lower jaw was large but rounded, and he jutted it at them now. "You'll excuse me, Aetius, but I'm not fit company."

Liam put on a suitably sorrowful face as Oakham said, "We've heard of your troubles. It's a sad pass."

"Aye." Cawood clearly did not want to talk.

"Cawood, this is Liam Rhenford, an acquaintance of my aunt."

Cawood bowed stiffly. "Master Rhenford." Liam returned the bow.

"I had hoped you might show Rhenford around the Staple, but you've got worries of your own. It can wait."

"It must, I fear." Cawood twisted his hat, eager to be gone.

"I understand," Oakham went on, "but look you, Rafe, perhaps we can meet later. At the baths—a round with the gloves might be just the remedy."

He shook his head, apparently about to refuse, then took a deep breath. "Y'are right, Aetius. A round might be the thing. Though I cannot vouch for your health if you stand against me."

Oakham laughed sympathetically. "I'll wear two helmets," he promised. "This evening?"

"Later, though," Cawood said, then added grimly, "I have business to tend to."

They agreed to meet at eight, and Oakham expressed his sympathy again. Then Cawood took his leave, his bow to Liam less stiff this time. Once he was gone, the two men started walking slowly towards the door. Oakham waited to speak until they were out on the street again. He could just see Cawood, going out of sight around a corner.

"What is this meeting for, Rhenford?" His voice was low, almost dangerous.

"You will not like it," Liam said.

"Go to, Rhenford."

Hearing the mounting anger in the other man's voice, Liam took a deep breath. "I want you to tell him, as casually as you can, that there is a wizard in Southwark who wants to buy the Jewel. You must make it sound like gossip you have heard, and I'll give you the name of an inn where he is supposed to be staying."

"You would have me trap him!"

"Lord Oakham," Liam said, summoning his patience, "it will only be a trap if he stole the Jewel. And if he stole the Jewel, he is not your friend. If he did not do it, then it will be just a piece of harmless gossip."

"Why didn't you do it, then?" Oakham asked. "He was there—with us! You could have set your own trap!"

Liam shook his head. "No. I do not know what inn to use yet, and I could hardly ask to meet him again just to tell him that."

Sputtering, the lord grabbed his arm and stopped him. "You don't know what inn? What does it matter? Pick one!"

"I cannot. The point of the trap is that no one but a wizard would have enough money to buy the Jewel—or at least, no one would think so. The problem is that there really is a wizard in Southwark who wants to buy the Jewel."

The color drained out of Oakham's face in an alarming way. "What?" He sounded strangled.

Without mentioning Grantaire, Liam explained what he knew of Desiderius, including the wizard's visits to jewelers. "So I have to be sure what inn not to use, you see? And I do not know where he is yet—Coeccias is looking into it."

None of this reassured Oakham. He grew frantic, grabbing Liam by the shoulders. "How can you be sure he is still in Southwark?" he demanded. "He might have parted already! You must find him, find him now!"

"The Aedile is looking for him even now," Liam assured him, speaking gently. "He does not have the Jewel." A small, mean part of Liam's mind reminded him that, for all he knew, Desiderius might have the Jewel, but he could not help that. He did not promise that the wizard had not left Southwark. "We will find the inn he is staying at, and then choose another one for the trap. Now come, I must see the Aedile now."

He managed to get Oakham moving, though he was chewing the ends of his mustache furiously, roughly knuckling the middle part of it. "Gods, Rhenford," he muttered, "gods. If this wizard should buy the Jewel . . ."

Oakham was still shaken when they parted near the city square, though he had regained much of his composure. Liam felt bad leaving him, but he very much wanted to speak with Coeccias—and he was also uncomfortable with the lord. He had promised Mistress Priscian that whatever dark secrets he uncovered would go no further than his own ears, but even the simplest of facts were painful to Oakham. There was only so much of his unhappiness that Liam could take.

Small stabs of guilt needled him on the way to the square, heightened by his relief at being rid of Oakham. He had enough to worry about, he told himself, without being overly sensitive to other people's distress. It was not his fault that the Oakhams chose their guests poorly, or that they had thieves among their acquaintances.

Recognizing how unfair his thoughts were, he forced them in another, more specific direction, trying to order what he knew. There were facts and there were suspicions, guesses, hints and rumors, but it seemed to him as if there was not enough of anything on which to base any useful speculation. And he knew that was his strength, or at least the tool he had used most successfully in the past: speculation, potentially elaborate games of "What if?" and "Why?" in which the point was to try to assume a different perspective on the information he had.

The information, though, refused to cooperate, slipping around inside his head, unwilling to point out profitable avenues for his imagination. His frustration mounted as he entered the square by the barracks.

Coeccias was in, and though it was past three, too late for lunch and too early for dinner, he leapt to his feet, grabbed a coat and suggested they go across to Herlekin's.

"Truth, Rhenford, I'm sick to death of this place. I need air, and something hot."

Liam did not argue, and they crossed to the tavern, Coeccias pausing in the middle to take three or four deep breaths, rubbing his chest with both hands and commenting on how good it felt. Even then, though, Liam noticed that the Aedile's eyes scanned the crowd, an almost automatic movement. His look of satisfaction seemed to stem as much from the quietness and placidity of the square as from the cold air in his lungs.

For a moment, Liam gained a sense of perspective: Coeccias looked after an entire city, thousands of people and all their concomitant problems, worries and troubles. What was his own search for the Jewel compared to that?

All the tables on Herlekin's ground floor were occupied, but there was none of the claustrophobic crowding Liam had met the night before, and the customers were much better behaved. Herlekin himself came forward, a clean apron spread across his wide belly, and led them to a fairly secluded table on the second floor.

"Does he never sleep?" Liam asked, when the innkeeper had bustled away to fetch a serving girl.

"Eh?"

"It seems that, no matter what time we come in, he is always here."

Coeccias smiled and leaned across the table. "I'll give you a secret, Rhenford. Did you see his apron? Clean, eh?"

"Yes."

"He's just woken. When we leave, it'll be so spattered you'll swear he's been here an age. He does it himself in the kitchen. I have seen him take a leg off the fire and rub it on an apron as pure white as the snow, and his wife crying rivers." They laughed at the idea, and the serving girl who appeared smiled with them.

"Y' are merry, sirs; would you dine?"

Liam said he would, and ordered a sea pie and beer; Coeccias said he had eaten already, and ordered the same.

"Aye, it's rare that Herlekin does any work," he went on, "but he gives the appearance of it. But y' are not here to fathom his arts, Rhenford; you wore a world of care on your face when you came into the barracks. This with the Jewel is not going well?"

Liam shook his head shortly, choosing to ignore his friend's comment on how his face looked. "No, not at all. I have an idea or two, but . . ."

"But they don't satisfy?" Coeccias said helpfully.

"No, not at all."

The serving girl brought their drinks and, sensing the change in the mood of the table, solemnly promised that their pies would be ready shortly.

When she was gone, Liam glanced around the room—half of the tables were full, but Herlekin had seated them at a window far away from the other customers—and then put his elbows on the table, leaned forward, and started talking.

He laid out what he knew first: that someone inside the house had let Japer in on the night of the theft, and presumably Malskat as well. In any case, Japer had picked the lock, the Jewel had been stolen, and whichever guest had let them in slit the beggar's throat.

"We know it was a man, and I think we can assume it was a big man, both because he was able to kill Malskat and because the lockpicker was afraid of him." He did not mention Japer by name, but Coeccias made no comment; instead, he nodded.

"Aye, it would follow."

He described Cimber Furseus, and the Aedile agreed that he could be safely dismissed from suspicion.

"But that still leaves three—Master Cawood, Earl Uldericus and Baron Quetivel. What know you of them?"

"That's my problem. I'm stuck between them. Neither Quetivel nor Uldericus has any money troubles that I know of. Uldericus certainly doesn't." He briefly described Uldericus's house, and then explained the game of Alliances. "Quetivel played with his own money the whole evening. Oakham says that he has lost a great deal since coming here, but he still seems to have coin—and I think he was more upset at losing the game than at losing the money, if you see what I mean."

"It may have been his last."

The serving girl appeared with their pies; they sat in silence while she put them on the table and waited until she was gone before talking again.

"I don't think so; and anyway, I cannot see stealing something so large because you were out of pocket. If you had large debts, perhaps."

"But not for that you lacked the ready; go to, I see where you lead. You do not think much of the earl or the baron, then." Coeccias spread his hands as if the answer were obvious. "It must be Cawood, then. I'll warrant he has debts, eh?"

"As a matter of fact, he does," Liam admitted. "Some ships of his are long overdue, and apparently the Duke's wool agents are pressing him hard. So he certainly has debts, and large enough ones that the Jewel makes sense."

The other man raised an eyebrow, though his hands were busy manipulating knife and fork. "Truth, Rhenford, there is more. You don't put much credit in Cawood, but I can't see why not."

"Oh, I put credit in him. He's as likely as the others—and that's the problem. They are all equally likely." He took a bite of his pie, and realized that he was very hungry. Around mouthfuls he outlined Countess Perenelle's reaction to the Jewel, how much she admired it, the argument she had had with Lady Oakham, and what she had said she would do for the man who brought it to her.

"Anything," he repeated, putting down his beer and emphasizing the word. "Have you met her?" Coeccias shook his head. "She is the kind of woman whose 'anything' would make many men do anything in return."

"And that puts Uldericus under a cloud again?"

"Apparently he tried to buy the Jewel from Oakham. But it also puts Quetivel under as well."

Coeccias stopped eating long enough to raise a bushy, questioning eyebrow. Liam nodded, and told about the young baron's reported obsession, the countess's rumored indiscretions, and the comments that had led to the duel.

"A duel, eh?" The news did not seem to bother him; the Duke fully approved of the field of honor, and the Aedile rarely saw reason to disagree with his master. "It's a shame, but Quetivel's words would sting. Still, that does put them both back under a cloud."

Liam sighed. "Exactly." Both the earl and the baron appeared to have a reason to steal the Jewel; however, he explained, that was not the real problem, as far as he saw it. The problem was that neither man seemed to have produced the Jewel and claimed the prize. "Both spent the night gambling with Oakham and me. If one of them had taken the Jewel, wouldn't he have gone straight to her?" He did not mention the note the servant had given him, but it more than anything else convinced him that the countess had not yet surrendered her "anything."

To his surprise, the Aedile laughed, a deep, happy bark. "Truth, y' are wooden, Rhenford! If neither has claimed the prize, then neither stole the Jewel! It is as plain as your nose!"

Listening to his friend chuckling, Liam realized that he was probably right. He had been trying to think of a reason why Uldericus or Quetivel might put off giving the countess the Jewel, never considering that the most likely reason was that neither had it. It was a simple answer, so simple he had not thought of it—and so simple he mistrusted it. *Nothing is ever simple,* he told himself.

Coeccias, though, was beaming with pleasure. "It needs must be Master Cawood, then. Look you—he has a reason, in his debts, and the same chance as the others. In fine, all that's left is proving it. With proof, we can get round the Rights of the Town, and the other merchants'll be quick to let us have him. Nothing puts a man down in their eyes like a failure in business, whether it can be helped or no. So, how do we prove it?"

Liam put aside his doubts concerning the other two suspects, and addressed himself to the question at hand. "I have an idea about how we might do that. With the wool agents pressing him, Cawood would want money quickly. No one in Southwark has enough money to buy the Jewel for anything near its real worth, correct?"

"Aye—the Goddards might, if they marshaled all their wealth, but they would not. So say no one."

"And no one would buy it, even if they could, except Uldericus or Quetivel, but forget them for a moment. My idea is that if someone were desperate enough to steal the Jewel for money, they would want the money as soon as possible. Now, if there were someone in Southwark they thought could buy it, wouldn't they jump at the chance?"

"Y' are thinking of the wizard," Coeccias said doubtfully.

"In a sense. Not Desiderius himself, but a wizard. Someone claiming to be a wizard, and offering to buy the Jewel. If we can let Cawood know there's a wizard in the city who would buy, I think he will try to sell. All we have to do is be there."

The beaming smile returned to Coeccias's face. "It likes me, Rhenford, it likes me. It is a sweet trap. Now I see why you wanted me to find this Desiderius—so that we can make sure our trap is nowhere near him."

"Have you found him?"

"Not yet." He gestured negligently. "A little later this afternoon. I've a man going round the inns. If he's still here, we'll know where by dinner. My question is, how do you let Cawood know of our wizard without making him prickle? And who will our wizard be?"

Liam explained the meeting Oakham had arranged at his urging. "I hope he can drop the hint without giving it away. As for who our wizard will be, I'm not sure yet. I had thought I might do it myself, since everyone in Southwark seems to think I'm a wizard, but then people know I'm associated with you, which might scare him off. I have someone else in mind, but it may end up having to be one of your men in disguise."

"You'll ask your guest?"

As always, the Aedile surprised him with his insight. "I would like to. She would give an air of authenticity to the whole thing."

"Aye, that she would, but if she'll not, one of my men can. Truth, it seems finished to me!"

Liam picked uneasily at his pie. "I suppose."

With a mouthful of pie, Coeccias still managed an incredulous laugh. "Y' have not given up on Countess Perenelle, have you?" he accused good-naturedly.

Blushing, Liam admitted that he had not. "It just seems too simple. At first I didn't think that there could be any good reason for stealing the Jewel. But I have seen Quetivel and Uldericus do so many strange things, and I have this feeling that neither would hesitate a second over killing the lockpicker or the beggar." Which, he knew, was a product simply of having spent more time with them than with Cawood. For all he knew, the merchant might spend his spare time sharpening a dagger specifically meant for beggars and thieves. Still, despite his earlier inability to believe any motive, he now could not rid himself of the suspicion.

"Look you," Coeccias said, more serious now, "what does it matter? We try this with Master Cawood. If it works, and he's the thief, all is well. If he is not, and the Jewel is with Uldericus or Quetivel—well, at least it does not part Southwark, and we can search it out in some other way. Does that satisfy?"

"Yes, yes. I'm just worrying. It may be that I don't like putting all our eggs in one basket."

"There is that," the Aedile allowed. "Then go on with the other. Seek out Countess Perenelle. Press the Furseuses for more. Go see Herione—she'll know something of Uldericus, and the others as well. She casts her net wide, and'll part with news for that y' are with me."

Liam nodded, not mentioning that he had already planned to. Coeccias was right: if either of the other two men had stolen the Jewel, then it was unlikely that it would leave Southwark. That was small comfort—he had promised he would know who had killed Japer by the next night—but it was still comfort. And he could do no more than the Aedile had suggested.

He took a few more bites of his pie. Coeccias had long since cleaned his own plate, and held his mug in both hands, studying Liam over the rim.

"I had the right of it about Rathkael," he said at last.

"Eh?"

"He tasked me hard—at first. Your good authority, though, stopped him fairly quick. He grew thoughtful of a sudden, and said he'd mind it." He peered nonchalantly into his mug, then asked, with apparent indifference: "That will hold, eh? Your good authority?"

"Yes." *As long as the Guild does nothing—and as long as I can find the Jewel.*

Coeccias nodded, as if this was exactly what he had expected.

Liam wanted to change the subject. "When do you think you will know about Desiderius?"

"If he's lodged in a public house, then in an hour, two at the most. I could only spare a single man, for that I've doubled the night patrols, and I had to send another man out looking for those maskers."

"Maskers?"

"The boy and the maid," Coeccias said. "Their parents taxed me almost as much as Rathkael."

"Ah," Liam said, vaguely remembering the Aedile's other problem.

They fell silent, moodily nursing their beers and their problems. The bells in the tower across the square started tolling four o'clock. Liam found himself counting each hour. As four shivered in the air, a thought formed in his head.

Master, there is magic near you.

Despite himself, he jumped, nearly knocking over his beer. He grabbed wildly at the mug, righted it. Coeccias stared at him.

"What?"

"Nothing—someone on my grave." He shook his head; the Aedile shrugged and turned to the window, looking out over the square.

Liam focused and projected. *What do you mean?*

The thought came instantly: *Someone is performing magic near you.*

Grantaire, Liam replied.

No, Fanuilh sent back. *It is not in the Point—and it is not just near you, master. It is directed at you.*

Liam stood hastily, pulling coins from his purse and dropping them on the table with fingers suddenly gone clumsy.

"I have to go," he said, and grabbed his cloak.

■ *13* ■

LIAM FOUGHT AGAINST panic, thinking, even as he reached the stairs, that he was overreacting. He felt nothing, no magic, no spell—nothing. Could that be right? Could you have magic directed at you and not feel it? And if you could not feel it, could it harm you?

Where are you? he projected, walking into the firstfloor common room. His eyes tracked uneasily around the customers, though he had no idea what he was looking for—unless it was a red beard and purple mark.

I am on the roof of the courts, master. The magic has stopped.

Where was it? Who did it? What was it?

He was moving quickly, threading through the tables, but he brought himself up short by the door, even as he projected his last question. Once before he had gone bolting out of Herlekin's, and it had landed him in the middle of a battle between the devotees of two different war gods.

Now he stopped, one hand on the doorknob, waiting for Fanuilh's reply.

It was in the square, the dragon told him. *I would imagine it was Mage Desiderius, but I do not know what he was casting.*

His arm was shaking, and he realized the doorknob was cutting into his hand. He let go, debating whether or not he should open it. If Desiderius meant to harm him, he would be harmed already.

The door swung open; Liam jumped back, and two men he had never seen before entered, glanced warily at him and pushed right by, heading for the table from which friends called to them.

"Idiot," Liam muttered. "You look like an idiot." Sheer embarrassment made him take the few steps out the door, but he flattened himself against the outside of the inn and started scanning the crowd.

Can you see him?

No, master. I am too high up.

He was overreacting, he told himself, repeating the thought over and over again. Grantaire had said that Desiderius might seek him out, and if the wizard meant to harm him . . .

"I know, I know," he muttered through grinding teeth. He saw no red beards, but the sun was lowering on the far horizon, half its bulk hidden behind the roof of the courts. Most of the square was in shadow; he had never noticed how quickly it could become dark there.

It was cold, too, and he held his cloak bunched in one hand. Slowly, trying to keep his eyes on all parts of the square at once, he pulled it on, shrugging it onto his shoulders and tying it loosely at the neck.

Beside him, a voice spoke up: "Mage Rhenford?"

Liam's head snapped towards the voice, and he knew that his face was a mask of fright. Deliberately, he closed his eyes and gave a long sigh of relief.

"Gods, you startled me," he said, and was pleased that his voice obeyed him.

Liam stood much taller than the wizard, but he sensed no advantage from the fact. From beneath a broad triangle of a hood, Desiderius offered him a polite smile.

"My apologies," the wizard said. His beard was merely red, but the mark that covered the entire left side of his face was a vivid, unnatural purple, a fascinating color. Liam found his eyes tracing the border between the mark and normal skin. "I did not mean to startle you, Mage Rhenford, but I have been meaning to speak with you since I arrived in Southwark."

Fanuilh, Liam projected, *let me know the instant you notice magic.* He smiled back at the wizard, masking the dryness of his mouth. "Really?" He tried to feign embarrassment. "I am afraid I don't—have we met?"

The other man chuckled. "No, but I have heard of you. My name is Mage Desiderius. I come from Guild Magister Escanes." His smile was confident, as if that explained everything.

His mind racing, Liam tried to stall. "Did you say 'Mage Desiderius'? Are you a wizard?"

"A mage, much like yourself," Desiderius said, with a polite inclination of his head.

"Oh, I'm not a wizard," Liam said, and held up a hand when the other man raised his eyebrows. "I know everyone in Southwark thinks I am, but I am not, really." The white of Desiderius's left eye seemed particularly bright against the purple of his skin. The man's manner was not threatening, but Liam still felt nervous. "Did you say you were from the Guild?"

"Yes." His smile shifted slightly, a tinge of disbelief shading his confidence. "We have heard of Mage Tanaquil's death, and I was sent to look into it. You were his apprentice, no?"

Liam faked a laugh. "No, no, no. Just a friend. He left me his house, and so a great deal of foolish talk has spread around, but I am definitely not a wizard."

The disbelief grew more marked, the wizard cocking his head as if to say they both knew better. "Come now, Mage Rhenford—apprentices are supposed to be registered with the Guild, but it is no crime. Mage Tanaquil was forgetful."

What would I say to him if I had never heard of him? Liam dropped his smile and grew earnest. "Honestly, Mage Desiderius, I am not a wizard. Please take my word for it—I am not a wizard, have never been a wizard, and never will be a wizard." His nervousness grew. He did not like the way the conversation was working; he felt a little as if he were being judged, and he wanted more control. *Coeccias can help.* "But it is cold here—why don't we go inside?" He jerked a thumb towards the door of the inn. "We can have something hot to drink, and discuss this."

"Very well."

With a bright smile, Liam held the door for the wizard. "I cannot tell you how often people make this mistake, Mage Desiderius. People are forever coming to the house, begging spells and potions and so on." He walked behind, steering the other man with gentle taps on the shoulder. "We will go upstairs, if you do not mind—it's much less crowded."

Desiderius made no objection, walking ahead of him and pausing to look around the second floor room. Liam peered over his shoulder and saw Coeccias still sitting where he had left him. The table had been cleared.

"Aedile Coeccias!" he called happily. To Desiderius, he said: "A friend—I am sure he can clear all this up." He led the way to the table and introduced the two men, using their full titles. "Coeccias is the Duke's man in Southwark. Mage Desiderius is from the Guild." He gave the Aedile a broad warning smile, hoping he would play along.

"Good day to you, Mage," Coeccias said, rising from his seat. "You'll have something to drink?"

Desiderius said he would, and sat at the table, completely at ease.

Coeccias found the serving girl, ordered, and returned to the table, sitting opposite Liam and the wizard.

"Mage Desiderius has been misled," Liam began. "The same old story about my being a wizard."

To his relief, Coeccias chuckled convincingly. "Truth, have you not laid that to rest? Look you," he went on, addressing Desiderius in a friendly tone, "Quaestor Rhenford is no more a wizard than I am. It amazes, how these rumors breed. My house was once a shoemaker's, but am I a shoemaker?"

The serving girl arrived and handed out goblets of mulled wine. Desiderius sipped appreciatively at his, closed his eyes for a moment with a gentle smile. When he opened them, his smile turned sad. "Ah, well—it seems we were mistaken. I hope you will accept my apologies, Quaestor Rhenford. It is important for the Guild to keep track of those who practice magic. It is a question of proper control."

"Not at all," Liam said magnanimously. "I understand completely. I am just glad you believe me. Now, if you could just convince every heartsick girl who wants a love potion . . ."

Desiderius gave a polite laugh. "There I must leave you to your own devices, I am afraid." He grew serious then. "However, there is something else I would like to ask you about. Mage Tanaquil had a number of, shall we say, artifacts. Items of power, magical power. They would be of no interest to you, and the Guild would very much like to have them. I wonder—"

Liam had thought about this. He grimaced, as if he had bad news, and interrupted the wizard. "I am afraid I have to disappoint you, Mage Desiderius. As you say, they were of no interest to me—so I sold them."

The other man's eyes widened slightly. "Sold them?"

"I am afraid so," Liam said. "I had no idea someone would come for them."

The wizard's voice was calm, but it was clear he considered it a blunder. "Who to?"

"A merchant from Torquay," Liam lied. He paused, searching his memory for an appropriate name. "His name was Hincmar. He seemed to think he could get something for them, and I had no use for them. There were some books, as well, but I could make neither head nor tail of them. I sent them to an old tutor of mine, Master Bahorel. You may have heard of him?" Bahorel actually existed, and had been Liam's tutor; he had also been considered an expert on old books.

"The name sounds familiar, though I am not often in Torquay. You say he has Mage Tanaquil's books?" Liam nodded, trying to appear as remorseful as possible. "And this Hincmar—he was from Torquay as well?" Liam nodded again. Desiderius frowned, then forced a wry grin. "Well, I think my journey will be a little longer than I thought. Torquay is not so far off, I suppose."

For an instant—a very short instant—Liam felt sorry for the wizard. Then he remembered what Grantaire had said about him, and the fact that he himself was lying. *What is wrong with you?*

Through the same instant, no one else spoke. Then Coeccias cleared his throat, and began hesitantly: "Mage Desiderius, I wonder if you might not help us with a matter."

What's he doing? Liam wondered, suddenly nervous.

"Concerning what?" Desiderius's face was open and affable.

"As Quaestor Rhenford said, I am the Duke's man in Southwark. As such, I needs must see to the resolution of all the varied crimes committed within the city. Quaestor Rhenford is an invaluable help in this. Of late there has been an incident that has exercised us a great deal."

It was rare for Coeccias to produce anything like a polished statement, and whenever he did Liam was always impressed. This time, though, he was more concerned about where his friend was heading.

"Go on," the wizard said, pulling closer to the table and giving Coeccias his full attention.

"One of the local merchant families has lost an invaluable treasure— a stone of passing beauty and worth. In fine, it has been stolen. It is called the Priscian Jewel." The Aedile paused, wiped some wine from his mustache, and looked up at the ceiling, as if weighing his words.

"I have heard of the Priscian Jewel," Desiderius said shortly. His face had gone blank.

Coeccias smiled. "Ah—did you perhaps visit several jewelers just a few days ago, inquiring about it?"

"And if I did?" The wizard spoke warily, looking back and forth between Liam and the Aedile.

Liam laid a soothing hand on his shoulder. "Oh, please, Mage Desiderius—you must not think the Aedile is accusing you of anything. Not at all. We know for a fact that you were not involved." He turned to Coeccias. "I was so surprised at meeting him that I didn't even think of that."

"It only just occurred to me," the Aedile said, and then addressed the wizard: "As Quaestor Rhenford says, we know you were not involved. The matter I was curious about was why you took an interest in the Jewel."

"You see," Liam put in, "we have narrowed down the number of people we suspect, but we are unsure of their motives. If you could shed any light on the matter, we would greatly appreciate it."

Though he was not sure where Coeccias was taking them, Liam preferred the way the conversation was going. He was not in control, but at least his friend was—and Desiderius looked off balance, his eyes moving back and forth. He was on his guard.

"It is of no use to anyone but a mage," he said. "It has certain . . . *properties* that would make it interesting as an object of study. But only for a mage." He stopped, letting that sink in, then asked suddenly: "Is one of the people you suspect a wizard?"

Liam shook his head sadly. "No, unfortunately not. That might make it easier."

"How?" The question was snapped out suspiciously.

"It would give our suspects different parts," Coeccias said after a beat. "As it stands, they are as alike as peas, all wanting the Jewel for money."

The answer seemed to satisfy Desiderius, but he did not let his guard down. "Is there something else I can help you with? It seems I must now arrange a journey to Torquay."

"Actually, there is," Liam said, looking a question at Coeccias. The other man shrugged. "Since all our suspects are interested in money, we believe they may try to sell the Jewel somewhere. It is priceless, though, so buyers are few and far between."

Coeccias nodded. "To put it bluntly, none in Southwark could part with enough for it. Whoever stole it would have to know that. They might, however, think that a wizard could."

The wizard's eyebrows shot up, but before he could speak, Liam did: "It is possible that the thief might approach you, and try to sell it. Southwark is a small city, and we do not get many wizards here. So word of your presence might spread."

"And the thief may hear of you, and try to sell you the Jewel," Coeccias said.

"And if he does?" It was practically a challenge.

Liam and Coeccias shared a glance. "We would appreciate it no end if you would inform us," the Aedile said.

"Ah." Desiderius took a deep breath, let it out with a nod. "Of course. I would be happy to."

"It would be a very lucky thing for us," Liam said, sounding—even to himself—remarkably grateful.

Desiderius shrugged. "It would be nothing. I should report it in any case."

"That is a sentiment I would we heard more often," Coeccias joked. "And tell me, Mage Desiderius, if we should have any more questions, are you lodging somewhere convenient?"

Liam wanted to applaud: the question had come out completely naturally—and the wizard answered after only a moment's consideration. He was staying at the Three Foxes. Liam did not know it, but Coeccias nodded.

"Well and good, well and good," the Aedile said. "I imagine that is all. Our thanks for your aid, Mage Desiderius. I do not wish to keep you, and Quaestor Rhenford and I have pressing business to attend to." He stood.

That, Liam thought, *was a little much,* but the wizard took the near-dismissal in stride, staying in his seat and regarding the Aedile with cool eyes.

"I must prepare for my journey to Torquay," he said, "but if I might, I would have a word with Quaestor Rhenford, in private."

"In course," Coeccias said. "I will leave you for a moment." He stepped away to another table out of earshot and slid heavily into a seat.

The good feeling that had kept Liam going through the conversation suddenly left him. Desiderius turned his seat so that he was facing Liam, less than a few feet away. He licked his lips once, his eyes gone cold. He spoke with odd pauses between the phrases, and with extreme clarity.

"Someone may visit you, a woman named Grantaire. She will call herself a mage, but she is not. The Guild has expelled her. She has murdered two people, and if we catch her, we will kill her."

Liam nodded, unsure what to say.

"If she comes to you, do not listen to her. Do not help her. She may want some of Mage Tanaquil's things. Tell her the same story you told me." When Liam started to protest, Desiderius cut him off fiercely: "Be still! You have Tanaquil's things. You may have killed him yourself, for all I know or care. But if we find you have helped this woman, we will come for you, Mage Rhenford. Do you understand that? The entire Guild will come down for you."

"But I am not a—" Liam began, stammering.

"Hush," Desiderius said softly, rising. "Good day to you, Mage Rhenford."

Leaving Liam speechless in his wake, the wizard walked to the stairs, giving Coeccias at his separate table a friendly wave.

Liam did not see Coeccias rejoin him; he had the heels of his palms pressed firmly to his eyes, and was groaning in the back of his throat.

"That went ill, I take it," the Aedile said.

Liam let his hands drop to the table. "Ill? I suppose being threatened by the entire Mages Guild could be called 'ill.' Yes, I think so."

Coeccias' head jerked up. "Threatened? How so?"

"They don't like my guest—the one I told you about. They parted on bad terms."

"They cannot threaten you. I'll not have it. Shall I pay a visit to the Three Foxes?"

Liam shook his head quickly. "No. Definitely not." He did not think Desiderius would do anything to Coeccias, but he did not want to stir the wizard's suspicions. With Grantaire actually in his house, he did not want to draw any more attention to himself, as much for her sake as for his own. "I don't think anything will come of it—just bluster." That was untrue; he had a feeling that he had let himself in for far more trouble than he wanted. How hard would it be for the Guild to find out that Grantaire had visited him? More importantly, would they really follow through on Desiderius's threat?

If you have to make enemies, he told himself, *why make any but the best?*

"The real question is," he went on aloud, "do we really believe that he would tell us anything?"

"Not for a moment," Coeccias said immediately. "He'd never. So we put a man on him?"

"Can you?"

He thought, counting on his fingers, then: "I think it can be done. But then, do we still go on with your trap?"

"I don't know. I'm tempted to turn Desiderius into our trap, but that would be dangerous. So, no, I don't think so. Have a man watch the Three Foxes, and keep track of him if he goes out. See if he gets any messages. I doubt he will, but just in case."

"Well and good. In the meantime, you'll continue with the trap? And you'll see Herione?"

"Yes. Probably tomorrow morning, though. There are a few other things I have to do tonight." He needed to see Oakham again, and arrange to take Grantaire back to the house, and then there was his appointment with Countess Perenelle. He wondered if he ought to go to Mistress Priscian's right away, to let Grantaire know about Desiderius—and then discarded the idea. For all he knew, the wizard might be watching him, and he did not want to lead him right to her. Instead, he formed a thought and sent it to Fanuilh.

If you notice any more magic, let me know immediately.

Yes, master.

Any magic, anywhere.

Yes, master.

"It is curious," Coeccias said, then stopped.

"What?" He thought he knew what was coming.

The Aedile toyed diffidently with his wine. "It is curious," he repeated, "how you of a sudden have to leave, but come back in a moment with the wizard himself. Happenstance, I'd wager." His expression showed that he doubted it.

He already knows about Fanuilh, Liam reflected. "No," he said, drawing out the word. "Not happenstance. He was looking for me, using magic. Fanuilh warned me."

"For all y' are not a wizard, Rhenford, y' act as one. You know that?"

"I know," Liam said miserably. "But I'm not, I swear." *Depending on your definition,* he added silently. Living in a shoemaker's house did not make Coeccias a shoemaker, but then he did not get his meals by making shoes, and his closest companion was not . . . Liam cursed the limp analogy, but knew the basic sense of it was true. He lived in a magic house, ate from a magic oven, and his closest companion was a miniature dragon that could cast spells and send its thoughts into his head. He used magic every day—and what was a wizard but someone who used magic?

Coeccias was grinning at him. "Truth, Rhenford, when I think of the charlatans and knaves who spend their breath trying to convince the world that they are wizards, and see you fighting tooth and nail to convince that y' are not, it likes me enormously."

"Laugh," Liam said, standing up with a sardonic grimace. "Laugh away. But think about this—wizards have notoriously poor senses of humor. I might just turn you into a toad." Coeccias cringed in mock fear, and Liam had to laugh himself. "Failing that, I will perform a very simple piece of magic: disappearing and leaving you to pay."

Ignoring the Aedile's protests, he strolled out.

His amusement faded shortly after he left Herlekin's, as Liam realized he did not know where to go. He wandered aimlessly through the square, at a loss. It was near five o'clock, so Grantaire might conceivably be finished—and Mistress Priscian would probably want her to go soon anyway. He imagined the older woman throwing out not-so-subtle hints about the lateness of the hour, and the younger one blithely oblivious to them, deep into some musty paper or other. He smiled a little at the idea.

The sun was already sunk beneath the roof of the courts, and the winter night was coming on fast. If he picked up Grantaire, it would mean making the trip out to the house immediately, and he wanted to be sure that there was nothing else he could do in the city before dinner-time. It was a little late to visit Herione; she would be preparing for the evening already. And though he was plagued by a premonition that he was forgetting something important—omitting some crucial and proba-bly obvious step—he could think of nothing that needed doing right then.

With a frown, he started off for the stables.

"Tramp, tramp, tramp," he muttered to himself. He seemed to spend a great deal of time walking, and wondered if anyone else in Southwark covered as much of the city as he did. Coeccias certainly, and the Guard, but were their walks as pointless as his seemed to be?

Stop that! he scolded. It was ridiculous to depress himself, when everything around him conspired to do so already. He tried instead to concentrate on the town around him. As night fell, holiday candles were lit in many of the windows he passed. There were wreaths of pine boughs on many doors and colorful ribbons, mostly red, hung from practically every other gable and windowsill. In the courtyard between the stables where he had left Diamond and the inn it belonged to, he saw a group of servants—the women wore white aprons and mobcaps, the men heavier aprons of brown, all cut the same way—gathered around a small bonfire.

With tremendous enthusiasm, they sang a song he did not know, passing a jug, oblivious to the cold. As he watched, two or three of the women and one of the men left the group and went into the inn; a minute later three different women came out and demanded a chance at the jug. They were granted their wish amid a storm of laughter and the beginning of a new song.

Reluctantly, he called the stableboy away from the bonfire and asked for Diamond. The boy brought it in record time, hardly waiting for his tip before dashing back to the fun. Liam would have liked to ask about the songs they were singing, but he could not bring himself to interrupt again.

Instead, he swung himself into the saddle, took a last look at the happy group, and set Diamond to an easy pace towards the Point. He breathed deeply of the cold air, noting with a sudden pleasure the ex-pressions of the people he passed—all variations on happiness, from the simplest contentment to the most extravagant joy. A lone boy tramped along beside him for a few steps, shouting one of the songs Liam had heard at the inn, and when he turned off onto a different street, Liam was tempted to follow him.

In the midst of his own worries, it had been easy to forget that

Southwark was celebrating—and in the midst of the celebrating, he knew it would be easy to forget the dark business he was investigating.

He rode up Duke Street, surrendering himself to the beauty of the houses dressed for the holiday. The further up the street he went, the more candles shone in windows, the more greenery and decorations festooned the homes. A house three down from the Necquers' was covered from cornerstone to rooftop in red ribbons that had not been there earlier in the afternoon, when he passed with Oakham. Even the house that Coeccias had identified as Cawood's was brightly lit, candles in all the windows, lanterns and wreaths around the door.

End Street was a little more subdued; though he could still see candles in almost every window—the Goddard mansion spilled such pools of orange light onto the street that it looked as if it were a furnace—there were fewer boughs and no ribbons.

Nonetheless, he was in a good mood as he looped Diamond's reins through the hitching ring on the Oakhams' steps. They had candles lit like the rest of Southwark, and he went up the steps lightly. Even Tasso's sneering welcome could not shake him, and he wished the sour-faced servant a very Merry Banquet.

"And to you, I'm sure," Tasso muttered, and disappeared down the front hall. A few seconds later, Oakham came to the door.

"Good evening, Rhenford." He was not happy to see Liam. "I'm with Quetivel now. Have you learned anything?"

"Is he awake?" Liam asked. He had never delivered Uldericus's challenge, but he guessed from Oakham's wince that it was not a good time for that.

"But barely," the lord said quietly. "And in no condition for this business with the earl. It'll have to wait. Have you found the wizard?"

"Yes. He's at an inn called the Three Foxes, down the hill from the city square."

Oakham nodded. "I know it."

"What's the Three Foxes?" a peevish voice behind him said. "And what knave's at the door, Aetius?"

Quetivel loomed out of the corridor like a ghost. The top of his head was wrapped completely in linen strips, so that only his bruised and swollen eyes showed above his lips. His braids had been cut off.

"Is it that Rhenford?" He put a hand to his head, swaying a little, unsteady on his feet.

"Come, coz," Oakham said gently. "You should not be up."

"It is!" he exclaimed, jabbing a wobbly finger at Liam. "Y' have news for me," he accused.

"Now is not the time," Oakham interrupted, laying a gentle hand on the younger man's shoulder. Quetivel brushed it off weakly and lurched forward a step or two.

"I say it is, and if Uldericus's whining dog has something to say, let him speak his piece!"

Liam's good mood lay shredded at his feet, but he kept still.

"Well?" Quetivel demanded.

"Coz!"

"Coward!" the baron shouted, and then swayed on his feet and pitched forward. Oakham just barely caught him, and struggled with the dead weight for a moment before Liam stepped forward and helped. They caught him up between them and carried him back to the first floor sitting room.

"My thanks," Oakham said, when they had arranged Quetivel on one of the couches. With a groan, the wounded man stirred and flung one arm out.

"Does he know about the challenge?"

Oakham frowned. "One of the servants' needs must have told him. It likes me not—he should not think on such things now. It was a shrewd blow."

"I can see." Beneath the linen, Quetivel's nose was a misshapen lump, too far over beneath one eye. As Liam looked, the baron's eyes flickered open briefly, then shut firmly.

"The challenge will keep," Oakham said, gesturing for Liam to lower his voice. "What of this wizard in the Three Foxes?"

"Let me see." Liam was silent for a moment, pretending to collect his thoughts. He was listening to Quetivel's breathing—except the young lord was not breathing. "I met him this afternoon." Liam frowned and lowered his head, looking at the couch from out of the corner of his eye. "He was indeed interested in the Jewel, but only as an object of study."

There. Quetivel's chest rose shallowly. His eyes were half-lidded. *He's listening,* Liam thought. *Why?*

A possibility occurred to him. "He said he had come here all the way from Harcourt in the hope of buying the Jewel. He even said he could cast a spell that would create a replica, so that you could have the appearance of the Jewel while he studied it."

"So my aunt could have the appearance," Oakham corrected carefully.

Liam accepted the correction with impatience. He hoped Quetivel was hearing all this. "Yes, yes, your aunt. He seemed very disappointed that it was stolen—said his trip was wasted, no profit in it at all." He broke off, because Oakham was giving him a curious look. "Never mind—it is not important."

"Strange, though," the lord mused. "So much interest in the Jewel, just now. What did you say the man's name was?"

"Desiderius," Liam replied. He forbore mentioning that he suspected the wizard's interest in the Jewel was secondary. *He was looking for me,* Liam thought with an inward shudder, *and for Grantaire.* "It is strange, but not really relevant."

Oakham turned away, pensive. "Stay a moment. It is so strange. The Jewel is found, and presently this wizard comes to Southwark for to see it." He turned back to Liam, but his eyes were still a little dreamy. "Do you believe in Fate, Rhenford?"

"No. It is a coincidence, no more." *And not even that,* he thought. "The Jewel was not even really lost, Oakham. Mistress Priscian knew where it was all along."

"That is true," the other man admitted, and roused himself from his reverie. "And not to the point, as you say. What do I tell Cawood?"

"Tell him that there is a wizard in Southwark who has expressed interest in the Jewel. You can tell him that Aedile Coeccias told you, and that the man has a great deal of money with him. Also, that he is leaving the day after tomorrow." He added the name of the inn where he had seen the servants singing. It was on the opposite side of the city square from the Three Foxes. "Make sure he knows that the wizard is leaving the day after tomorrow," Liam said.

"What of the real wizard? Does he stay in Southwark long?"

"I am not sure," Liam said, which was the truth. He did not put much faith in Desiderius's story about going on to Torquay. For what he hoped was Quetivel's benefit, though, he mentioned it. "I gathered he might be leaving tomorrow or the day after."

Oakham nodded absently, and suddenly Quetivel groaned loudly, giving what Liam thought was a convincing portrayal of awakening from a faint. "Aetius?"

"I'll go," Liam said before Oakham could say anything. "Do your best to be convincing with Cawood."

"I'll try," the lord said, not bothering to hide his distaste at deceiving a friend. He went and knelt by his cousin's side, uttered a few soothing words, then led Liam to the front door.

"How long will you be with Cawood?" Liam asked.

Oakham shrugged. "We meet at eight—perhaps an hour or two."

"I may be back in the city at eight, for an appointment. If you don't mind, it might be good if we could talk afterwards."

The lord frowned for a moment. "I don't know. I'll be very tired." There was more, Liam could tell: the man simply did not wish to see him. "Look you, come by after your appointment. I put the candles out when I go to bed—if they're still lit, knock. Else, and I'll see you in the morning."

It sounded like the best he would get, so Liam accepted. He began to think he had pushed the lord too far.

But what else could I do? he wondered, alone on the stoop after Oakham had shut the door. *What else?*

▪ *14* ▪

HAELLUS ANSWERED THE door at Mistress Priscian's, and when Liam wished him a Merry Banquet, he returned the wish happily.

"Mistress Priscian and Mage Grantaire are in the study, Master Rhenford," he added as he led Liam up the stairs. The houseplan was the same as the Oakhams'; Haellus rapped respectful knuckles on the door that corresponded to Oakham's study.

"Come," Mistress Priscian called, and the servant opened the door for him.

The room was well lit, filled with heavy, dark furniture. Mistress Priscian sat at a massive trestle table of unfinished wood, a tidy stack of paper at either hand, an open ledger before her and an inkstand just beyond that. Grantaire sat at an identical table just opposite the older woman, with a similar arrangement of papers and inkstand, though she was reading from a folio-sized leather book, not a ledger. Both looked at the door with nearly identical expressions and postures: patiently expectant, bodies forward and heads cocked to the door.

Liam almost laughed at the mirroring—they might have been mother and daughter, or some allegory of age and youth—but he did not think they would appreciate the observation. He bowed instead, and wished them a good evening.

Both women nodded their acknowledgement at the same time.

"Good evening," Mistress Priscian said. "Have you had a successful day?" She indicated a vacant chair. Liam perched on the edge of it.

"More successful in some ways than others. Mostly it has just been confusing."

She sniffed. "Lord Oakham had the foolish idea that you would have the Jewel recovered by tomorrow."

Wincing, Liam shifted uncomfortably in his chair. "I am afraid I gave him that idea. There is a chance, but I think I was overhasty."

There was a riffle of paper, and Grantaire closed her book with great care. Mistress Priscian looked in her direction, her mouth twisting between a smile and a frown.

"Mage Grantaire believes she has learned some interesting particulars about the Jewel. And about my ancestor, it seems."

The younger woman's hands were pressed flat on the cover of the book, as if there were something inside that might spring out if she let up the pressure. She was chewing her underlip, but out of thoughtfulness, not embarrassment.

"Yes, I think I have. Eirenaeus was a genius."

"And a monster," Mistress Priscian said, her tone an odd mix of hauteur and pride, as if Grantaire had suggested something improper but nonetheless impressive.

"That too." The wizard looked at Liam, tapping the book. "The things he writes here are . . . amazing."

Liam craned his neck to look at the book, but it still seemed like an ordinary folio volume, significantly aged but normal. "What is it?"

"His notebook. There is a code, but it is relatively simple. Still, the things here . . ." Words failed her, and she made an expressive gesture: the book had made a tremendous impression on her. "He has laid out everything so very simply, and solved problems with ease and a sort of style that have eluded the Guild for centuries."

"But he's a monster?"

"He was studying black magic," Mistress Priscian confided, as if she were relating the naughty antics of a favorite grandchild.

"Not exactly black magic," Grantaire corrected, and Liam was a little annoyed to notice that she did it gently, with none of the patronizing tone she had once used with him. She turned to him. "Do you remember when I said he studied spirit?"

"Yes."

"His work on spirit is all it was rumored to be, and more."

Mistress Priscian interrupted. "Tell of the Jewel."

Grantaire nodded. "The Jewel was the focus of his work—he wanted it to be a source of spirit."

"So that he could draw spirit without his body having to sustain it?"

The wizard tilted her head, regarding him with curiosity and surprise. "Yes. Exactly." She shook her head, and Liam silently promised to
be nicer to Fanuilh. "He made the Jewel in such a way that it could hold
and supply spirit to a body indefinitely. According to his notes, he
seemed to think it would work. I have not finished the book, but from
some of these other documents"—she ruffled the pile to her left—"I
think he could not solve the last real problem."

"Where to get the extra spirit," Liam guessed, and was rewarded by
another curious glance.

"Yes." She flipped carefully through the pile, and withdrew an ancient parchment. She held it by the edges and placed it delicately on the
end of the table nearest Liam.

He stood and crossed to the table. The paper was browned and the
ink had faded, but he could see that it was an official document: there
were three cracked seals at the bottom and a number of signatures.

"It is his expulsion from the Guild," Grantaire explained. "In a very
wordy way it says he was stealing spirit from people."

Liam had just reached that part: " '. . . this most heinous and vam-
piric practice,' " he read aloud. "So he did it."

Both women nodded. "The Guild thought so," Grantaire said, and
tapped the pile on her left again. "There is an order in here authorizing a
reward for the death or capture of the vampire thought to be plaguing
the city then. It is dated a few months after the Guild order—and the
interesting thing is that he signed it. Eirenaeus, I mean, along with a
group of merchants."

Mistress Priscian shuddered. "As I said—a monster." All trace of
pride was gone.

Liam thought Eirenaeus's signature on an order calling for his own
death indicated a certain twisted sense of humor, but he did not think
Mistress Priscian would agree. He scratched his chin, thinking of Desiderius.

"Interesting, interesting. You say you have only gone partway
through his notebook?"

"You must finish," Mistress Priscian insisted immediately, her voice
a little thin.

"That would be good," Grantaire said simply. "May I come tomorrow?"

"By all means. What time shall I expect you?"

Grantaire looked at Liam. "Master Rhenford?"

"I need to be in the city in the morning. Would nine o'clock be too
early?"

The older woman snorted, as if nine were ridiculously late, and they agreed that Grantaire would come at eight. When they left her, Mistress Priscian was standing by Grantaire's table, chin clamped firmly in one hand, squinting balefully at Eirenaeus's book.

Once again uncomfortably aware of Grantaire's arms tight around his waist, Liam guided Diamond out of the Point at a smart trot. He had told Grantaire to pull her hood close around her face, and she had done so without objection.

The stars were out already, the cold winter night wide open around them. At any other time of the year Liam would never had made Diamond go at anything above a leisurely walk, but the candles in the windows gave him enough light to see and avoid passersby.

Fanuilh, he projected.

Yes, master?

Would a wizard know if you were watching him?

Not unless he looked, master.

Where are you?

Above you.

Liam stifled an involuntary impulse to look. *Are you cold?*

No, master.

Not at all?

No.

He told the dragon where to find the Three Foxes. *Go there, find a place to watch from. Let me know if Desiderius comes or goes.* Coeccias would certainly have put a man there—but he wanted to be sure.

Yes, master.

Wait, he thought, and brought to mind the faces of Oakham's guests. *Look at these.* Through their link, Fanuilh had access to Liam's memories—could ransack them at will, in fact, though Liam had made it clear that the dragon was not to do so unless invited. *Can you see them?*

Yes.

Good. Let me know if any of them arrive—particularly the men.

As you wish, master.

Outside the city Liam pulled Grantaire's arms even closer around him and touched Diamond lightly on the ribs; the horse broke into a swift, exhilarating gallop. He wanted to explain about Desiderius, to ask her a number of questions—but he wanted to ask in the house. In the three months that he had lived there, he had come to view the house as a sort of ultimate sanctuary, a place apart from the world. He felt more secure there than he would have in a fortress.

Grantaire waited on the patio while he put Diamond away, and they went into the kitchen together. He left his cloak in the entrance hall; she dropped hers on the kitchen table, unhooking the high collar of her dress.

"Do you want something to eat?" He had only eaten part of the pie at Herlekin's, and thought that the news about Desiderius could wait at least until they were eating.

"Something small," she said. "Mistress Priscian gave me lunch. She is not at all what I expected." She stood by the table, one arm tucked under the other, her free hand barely caressing her neck. He went to the stove and imagined a meal, aware of the appraising gaze she bent on him and wondering what it portended.

"How do you mean?"

The oven produced two bowl of soup, an oily brown stock thick with onions, and a loaf of bread. He laid the meal out on the table.

"You painted her an ogre of propriety. She was very pleasant."

They sat at the same time.

"You wore the right dress," he pointed out. He broke the loaf and handed her half. "You . . . dunk it." The soup was from Alyecir, and not well known in Taralon.

"And I was very proper and respectful," she assured him sarcastically. Looking at him over her spoon, she continued in a more neutral tone: "She told me a number of interesting things about you."

"Really?"

"Things the Aedile had told her. She is very impressed with you. Were you really the first to greet Bellona when she appeared?"

Liam choked on his soup. "That was an accident," he said, when he had regained control of himself and wiped off his chin. "I was in the wrong place at the wrong time."

She made a noncommittal noise, as if she were reserving judgement. "And have you been all the other places she says you have?"

"Yes. Most of them at least." He considered his travels differently from his experience with Bellona. The former had been his choice, a conscious accomplishment in which he took a little pride, if only because he knew no one as well travelled. Meeting Bellona had really been an accident, completely unintentional and not entirely pleasant. "Where did she say I had been?"

"Everywhere."

"Ah. Well, I haven't been everywhere. I may have been everywhere that matters, though." He chuckled at his own joke, but Grantaire made no response, turning her attention to her soup.

They ate in a silence only broken by the purring of her cat, who wandered in and started rubbing at their ankles. Liam dipped a piece of bread in his soup and offered it, but the cat made a disdainful face and slunk up into Grantaire's lap.

The wizard ate on, rubbing a piece of bread around the inside of her bowl and licking her fingers to get the last of the soup.

"That was very good," she said. "I like onions."

Somehow that did not surprise Liam. He gathered up the bowls and put them back in the oven, then imagined two mugs of coffee and a bowl of milk.

He set the milk on the floor, and the cat leapt from Grantaire's lap. Then he got the coffee.

"I met Desiderius today," he said, and put a mug in front of her. He was gratified to see that she did not jump, though he could see her tense, her arms grow rigid on the tabletop. She pulled the mug closer, blew on it.

"When?"

He recounted the whole story, down to the wizard's parting threat. "So I think we can safely say he is here to look for you."

She pushed her mug away and ran a hand through her hair. "Yes."

"Now I need to know some things. If he got the Jewel, would he be dangerous?"

"No more than he already is," she said bitterly. "Which to you is too dangerous. You should not have spoken with him."

Liam waved that away. "I had no choice. Would he be more dangerous to you?"

"No." Her lips were pressed together in a thin, unhappy line. "No. Now that I have Tanaquil's spells and his things, he is not really dangerous to me at all. I could face him. The Jewel does not change that. It is merely a repository of spirit, an inert thing. He might use it to live longer, that is all."

That was good to know. "I have set Fanuilh to watch him, so we will know if he tries anything. Do you think he will?"

"Not here." She gestured around her, at the house. "Tanaquil has warded this place well. It would take something very powerful to pierce his spells." Then her voice grew harder, and she seemed to shake off a certain apathy. "Still, he must not be allowed to have the Jewel. If he should have it, or give it to Escanes . . ."

"Escanes? That's the Magister? What does it matter if he gets it?"

"I have not given you the correct impression of him," Grantaire said, fixing him with a stern glance. "If Escanes were to get the Jewel, he would be practically immortal."

Liam let out a little, incredulous laugh. "But you said the Jewel wouldn't work without spirit from—" He cut himself off, and began to realize he had made a great mistake.

"He would do it. Just imagine what that would mean—a man who would achieve immortality that way, what would he not do? And with the power of the Guild behind him? He could tear Taralon in two."

It was, strangely, a prospect Liam could easily imagine. In his mind's eye he saw the kingdom as an Alyeciran slave galley, its progress across a stormy sea marked by the crack of whips and the screams of the rowers. But the picture palled beside his growing realization of what he had done.

The hints he had dropped in Quetivel's hearing had been meant as a test. At the time, he vaguely imagined that they might force the young baron to some sudden action, and that from the results he might learn something. Just what, he was not now sure. He had tried to slant the story so that Quetivel might imagine he could buy a replica of the Jewel; if he went to see Desiderius, that would show that he had not stolen the Jewel.

Looking back on it, however, Liam saw that he had bungled that: his words might inspire the baron to visit the wizard whether he had the Jewel or not. If he had the Jewel, Desiderius would get it; if he did not, and found that the wizard had no replicas, he would undoubtedly reveal who had given him the information. And that, Liam imagined, would draw the wizard's attention to him in a very, very unfriendly way.

Why did you do that? he demanded of himself, knowing full well that mostly he had been angry, stung by Quetivel's insults, and moved to an ill-conceived action by his own dislike.

He cursed, suddenly and with great feeling.

"Rhenford!" Grantaire exclaimed. "What is it? You look sick."

"I feel sick," he said, though he did not. There was a sort of electric tingle all over his body, but his arms and back felt strangely limp. *What have I done? What do I do?*

He groped for his mug, then checked his hand and shook himself. He would simply have to fix it—make sure that Quetivel would not go to Desiderius.

Grantaire reached across the table and slapped his hand. "What is it?" she demanded.

His mind raced. "I told Oakham about Desiderius. I was going to set a trap for someone."

Her jaw dropped. "With Desiderius? Are you mad?"

"No," he snapped. "Of course not. In a different inn, with one of Coeccias's men posing as a wizard. I had to explain about Desiderius to Oakham, so he would be careful." Now that he thought about it, there had been no real reason to tell about the wizard, but that did not matter. Grantaire's face was a mask of incredulity and confusion.

"Wait. Oakham is Mistress Priscian's nephew?"

"Yes, her niece's husband. He is helping me look for the Jewel—introducing me to the guests who might have stolen it." Her confusion was deepening, but he plowed on. "I had to explain, but Oakham is not the problem. When I told him, one of the guests was there, a baron named Quetivel. He has been . . . ill, and might have been asleep, but—"

"He might have heard." She stood suddenly, her chair scraping back harshly. "And he might have the Jewel, and he might go to Desiderius."

"He might go even if he doesn't have the Jewel," Liam said. Much as he wanted one, he could not think of a lie to explain why Quetivel would seek out Desiderius. "I didn't think he was asleep. I let him hear, because I thought I might be able to trap him, too." As briefly as he could, wincing at her occasional exclamations of dismay and disgust, he told about the countess's promise. It was a not very coherent account, but Grantaire understood enough.

"So now he'll go—to sell the Jewel or to try to buy a replica. Gods, Rhenford, what were you thinking?"

Thankfully, she did not seem to expect an answer. Pacing the kitchen, she continued: "If he sells Desiderius the Jewel, then Escanes gets it. If he does not, then Desiderius will seek you out and demand an explanation. Mark me," she said, "he will. I know Desiderius, and he will not take this sort of thing lightly. Particularly after his threat of this afternoon."

Liam cleared his throat. Watching her grow more agitated, he had gradually calmed down. "Now wait, let's not get carried away. I will simply have to make sure Quetivel does not go to visit him."

"And how will you do that?"

He bridled at her tone, at the way she implied he could not do it. "I'll tell him the truth, or whatever convenient lie comes to hand. And if that fails, I'll knock him out and tie him to his bed. I'll think of something." What he would do, he realized suddenly, was talk to Oakham. Oakham might be able to manage it.

He stood. "I'll go now. Oakham has to go out at eight, but I might be able to catch him."

"It's not Oakham that—never mind." She picked up her cloak and started putting it on. "I'll go with you. I need to make sure of this."

Liam did not object; secretly, he was relieved not to have to go alone.

Tramp, tramp, tramp, Liam thought to himself, though Diamond was far from tramping. Grantaire had her face buried in the back of his cloak, and he was half-blind with tears from the wind, his cheeks numb and his nose aching. The bundle Grantaire had insisted on bringing—an odd assortment of things from the trophy room and a small satchel of her own—dug into the small of his back.

He was completely calm, almost unconcerned; they had almost certainly overreacted. Quetivel was in no condition to go out looking for wizards, and Liam thought it unlikely that he would go at night. Not that he thought they should not be rushing into Southwark: it was he who urged Diamond faster, not Grantaire. It was his mess, after all, his responsibility.

And even as he shook his head at his own stupidity, he wondered if there was a way to turnt the situation to his advantage.

Fanuilh!

Yes, master?

Has anything happened there? Messengers or anyone we know shown up?

No. Mage Desiderius has been here for the past few hours, and has not gone out. Some people have gone in, but they have stayed.

Good. Are you cold?

No.

Hungry?

I have eaten.

Liam almost asked what, but stopped himself, obliterating the thought in his head. He did not want to know. Then an idea struck him. *Go to Oakham's and watch there. You can find it?*

Yes.

Good. Let me know if anyone leaves or enters—particularly any messengers.

He could not imagine that Quetivel would go himself, not if he wished to keep up the pretense of being seriously wounded. Liam considered it just that—a pretense, probably to put off Uldericus's challenge. *And he called me a coward!*

They had reached the city gate when Fanuilh's next thought appeared in his head.

Master, Lord Oakham has come out.

Liam cursed. Oakham had gone to meet Cawood. He considered not going to the house—Fanuilh could watch, and he did not much relish the idea of having to talk to Quetivel alone—but he did not think Grantaire would accept it, so he urged Diamond on. The bells started tolling eight as they turned onto End Street.

The candles were out in Mistress Priscian's house, but next door they still blazed. When they had dismounted, Liam held the reins out to Grantaire.

"Stay here. I will go in and see to Quetivel." She started to protest, but he held up an imperious hand. "I will take care of it. If I need you, I'll come back out." He could not see her expression, but she took the reins with a jerk.

He turned with a nod and went up the steps.

Lady Oakham answered his knock, opening the door only partway. Her face turned hard when she saw who it was. *Servants gone,* Liam noted, as well as the fact that her expression robbed her of her limited beauty.

"Lord Oakham is not in," she said coldly.

"I know, Lady Oakham." She took offense at his knowledge, drawing herself up for some stining comment; he hurried on. "Actually, I was hoping to speak with Baron Quetivel. Is he in?"

She blinked once, and then all of her features conspired to produce one of the most remarkable expressions of disgust Liam had ever seen. "In?" she shrilled. "In course he is in! He's in his couch, where he has lain this last day, his head near broken in!"

Poor, poor Oakham. "If I could, I need to speak with him," he said, as mildly as he could. "It is a matter of some importance."

She goggled at him, astounded by his effrontery. "Y' are mad!" she stammered at last.

"Has he sent any messages to anyone?" Liam asked quickly.

"No! How could he? He is sore hurt, and asleep, and I for one have had enough and too much of you!" She slammed the door in his face.

"Merry Banquet," Liam said to the brass knocker, and turned and trudged wearily back to Grantaire. Her voice was a hiss in the night.

"That was impressive."

"Baron Quetivel is asleep, and has sent no messages," he said, taking the reins. "Fanuilh will watch the house—if anyone comes or goes, we will know. We will be fine for the next hour or so, and then I can see Oakham. With him I can make sure Quetivel does nothing."

"Rhenford," she said, grabbing his arm fiercely. "I don't think you understand how important this is."

His arm twitched underneath her hand, but he stilled it, and made himself speak calmly. "I think I do. But what would you have me do— knock the woman over? Quetivel will keep for now. And if he doesn't, remember that I'm the one Desiderius will come for first. Now, there is something I need to do. Will you let go of my arm and let me do it?"

He heard her take in a hissing, angry breath, and then she let go of his arm.

"Very well. What are we doing?"

Liam swung up into the saddle and offered her his arm. "I am going to visit Countess Perenelle, to have little talk." About what he had no idea, but he would think of that later. Probably on her doorstep, in between knocks. "I'm not sure what you are going to do—we'll have to figure that out."

"This is the countess who will do anything for the Jewel?" she asked, and it seemed to him that she pulled harder on his arm than she needed to to get herself up behind him.

"The same."

"And my presence would undoubtedly spoil the atmosphere of your little tryst."

He stiffened, then turned awkwardly. "Do you want to walk?"

"What?"

"I asked if you wanted to walk." A sudden wave of anger rushed over him, the uprush of two frustrating days. "It is a holiday here, Grantaire. The past two days have been a holiday here. Do you know how I have spent them? I have spent them in the company of people who sneer at me, running all over this damned city to prove to a decent man that one of his friends is not just a thief, but a murderer as well. I am trying to find a man who cuts throats for fun, and I am not doing very well. I am making mistakes—I am aware of that—but I will do my best to mend them. And to add to all my fun, I have had the pleasure of entertaining you, for which pleasure the Mages Guild has threatened me with death." He paused, out of breath. "So I ask you if you want to walk, because I do not particularly wish to ride with you."

"I am sorry," she whispered after a moment, and his anger deflated at once: there were tears in her voice. "Sorry to have brought this on you." She started to climb off, and he grabbed her hand brusquely.

"Don't be stupid." He kicked Diamond and the horse started walking. He regretted his outburst intensely. *How fair was that?* Having the entire Guild as an enemy was only a threat for him, but for her it was a reality. And it had been his choice to investigate the theft of the Jewel. His troubles seemed small in comparison to hers.

As they turned off End Street, she quietly asked him where they were going.

"To the Aedile's house." He did not want to leave her at an inn or a tavern, and Coeccias lived fairly close by. "He won't mind letting you stay for a little while."

She said nothing, but her hands tightened a little around his waist.

Coeccias was not at home, but his servant let them in with a broad smile.

"Quaestor Rhenford! A Merry Banquet to you!"

"And you, Burrus. Burrus, I have to attend to a little business— official business—and I wonder if Mage Grantaire might stay here for an hour or so."

Burrus swept a grand bow in Grantaire's direction. His head, entirely bald, reflected the myriad candles in the windows. "In course, in course. I'm sure Coeccias wouldn't mind. He's seeing to extra rounds just now, but he'll be back presently."

"Thank you, Burrus." Liam shook the other man's hand briefly. "I'll leave Diamond by the door, if I may, and be back in an hour."

"No hurry, Quaestor. I am just brewing something for the holiday; Mage Grantaire can help me test it, if she will."

Grantaire nodded gravely at the man's happy smile.

"An hour," Liam said, and left.

An hour would be more than enough time. Coeccias lived on the edge of the Point, where it mingled with less wealthy neighborhoods, and the earl's house was less than five minutes away.

Liam walked quickly, rubbing his arms against the cold and berating himself. *Why can't you keep your mouth shut?* What he had done with Quetivel was an enormous mistake, but it had been pure meanness to lash out at Grantaire. Her situation was bad enough—alone, in a strange city, with the Guild after her. *Why can't you think before you speak?*

Two days gone by, and what had he accomplished? Nothing. Exactly nothing. He had made Oakham lie to his friends, had become party to a duel, and had potentially made an enemy of the Guild. Noblewomen slammed doors in his face, and he was nowhere near to finding the Jewel. He stopped short of blaming himself for Japer's death, but he wondered if he could have prevented it. *If you had gone to the Werewolf earlier,* he thought.

Then he cut the thought off: that way was madness. He could only do what he could do, and the first thing would be to pay more attention to his words, to think before he spoke, before he acted.

Vowing to do that, he strode past Herione's, and a voice called his name. He checked his stride, quickly scanning the portico. There were no candles in the brothel's windows—there were no windows—but lit torches had been set in brackets all along the wall. He could see the stout woman with the pot, serving out bowls to two silent beggars; a few feet further, two men came down the steps towards him.

"Master Rhenford," Earl Uldericus called again in a stern voice. "Whence this headlong rush?"

Going to see your wife, Liam thought wildly, and then he recognized the man with Uldericus.

"You're supposed to be with Oakham," he said accusingly.

"Have you seen him?" Cawood asked. "I attended him at the bath for a while, but he never arrived."

For a long moment Liam simply stared, unable to think. Then he managed to say: "How long did you wait?"

"Long enough, in faith," Cawood said. "I gave him up for lost only a few moments ago, and was on my way to his house to rate him for his absentmindedness, when I chanced on Earl Uldericus."

"Come inside, Master Rhenford," the earl said. "You can tell me how the baron took my challenge, and then we'll have a game."

Liam still could not think. Where had Oakham gone? Had he decided not to go through with it? *What is that idiot thinking?* He knew the two men were staring at him, thinking him the idiot, with his jaw on the ground.

Pull yourself together, he demanded. A stray thought came to him, and he started fumbling with his purse. "A game—no. No, thank you. I have an appointment. But I believe I owe you some money from yesterday evening." He started counting out coins with numb fingers.

"Come, you'll have a game with us, proper Generals, and perhaps you can win it back."

Liam scarcely heard him. Why would Oakham miss the appointment? He reached the right sum and handed it to Uldericus, who dropped it negligently into his own purse.

"Well," he said, "I wish all debtors paid so quickly. Oakham could learn something from you, Master Rhenford."

Oakham, yes. Oakham. Where is he? His words to Grantaire came back to him: *I am trying to find a man who cuts throats for fun.* Oakham had said something on the way to the Staple, something about it not necessarily being difficult to cut a throat—that anyone might do it. He had been trying to dissuade Liam from completely discounting Cimber Furseus as a suspect.

"Master Rhenford?" Cawood sounded cautiously concerned. "Are you ill?"

Liam mouthed the words to himself: *I never told him the beggar's throat was cut.* He gulped, trying to bring some moisture to his arid mouth.

"Does he owe you money?"

"I beg your pardon?" Uldericus sounded offended.

Damn that, Liam thought. "Money!" he snapped. "Does he owe you money?"

"I don't think—" the earl began, stiffening dangerously.

"How much?" He was shouting.

"Master Rhenford!" Cawood exclaimed, sounding shocked.

Uldericus's voice was a low growl. "I will not be spoken to in that tone."

Liam uttered a strangled curse, whirled, and started running to Coeccias's house.

■ 15 ■

LIAM RAN, HIS cloak spread behind him like wings, wanting to stop, to pound his chest, to kick something, to beat his head against a wall. He settled for pounding his feet, slamming them down on the cobbles with unnecessary force. A mad rage had settled into his head, a whirlwind of curses and evil desires. He wanted to pound Oakham, to kick the man, to beat *his* head against a wall.

He watched me! He put himself at my side! That bastard!

Coeccias's house was just a street away, and he slowed his pace, stopped, bending over and groaning out his frustration. He could not go in just yet. He stood straight and started pacing. His run in the cold had burned his lungs ragged, but he hardly noticed. A hot flush suffused his face.

All that time he watched me, and knew where I was going. He told me not to suspect Quetivel, and knew that I would. And then he let me, oh so unwillingly. Gods!

Liam's anger did not cool, but he gained control of it. He began to think clearly.

Oakham had been brilliant. Brilliant! There was no other word for it. He had doled out damaging information about his friends, always at just the right moment, always with just the right degree of reluctance— Uldericus's attempt to buy the Jewel, his wife's promise, Quetivel's gambling losses. Cawood's debts he had not revealed, but he must have known of them, and he must have known they would be mentioned at the Staple. The loss of a fortune would not go unremarked.

Gods, Liam thought, gritting his teeth. *How he must have laughed!* A muscle jumped over his eye, and he erased the thought, refusing it consideration. However much of a fool he had been, brooding now would not help him. He concentrated on Oakham.

There had to be debts, he knew. Uldericus had not said so, but he had not said no, and to Liam that was as damning as a full list of losses. Would it be gambling? Those stories he told about Quetivel—the money lost at horse races, at Pet Radday's, in the Red Chamber at Herione's—were those really his own stories?

The Oakhams' house belonged to Mistress Priscian. She could afford to have a live-in servant, but the Oakhams could not. He had borrowed money from Uldericus when they played cards.

An electric shudder ran through Liam. "He cheated!" he said aloud. Cheated—but not for himself. He had attacked and attacked, recklessly, carelessly, squandering his own forces and weakening everyone but Uldericus. And in each hand, the earl had come in at the end and split the pot.

Liam stopped that thought, too. There was no proof of that, and it was not to the point.

The point . . . the point reached through his anger, chilling it, leaving him aghast in the dark.

Oakham had the Jewel, he wanted money, and he knew all about Desiderius.

Fanuilh! he projected desperately. *Go to the Three Foxes! Go now!*

Yes, master. The answer, as calm and precise as any of the dragon's thoughts, went a long way towards keeping Liam from panic. He stopped pacing and took three deep breaths, squaring his shoulders. He knew where Oakham was going—was sure of it. That was not the point. The point was, what would he do about it?

Burrus had put a blanket on Diamond, Liam noticed, and he stopped on the doorstep, absently stroking the horse's nose. Then he squared his shoulders again and went in without knocking.

Coeccias and Grantaire stood by the hearth, cups in their hands, talking in low voices. Both looked up when he entered.

"Rhenford, what news?" The Aedile nodded in Grantaire's direction. "Mistress Grantaire tells me something about Baron Quetivel and that wizard of this afternoon. Is it true?"

Grantaire did not notice the incorrect title. "I had to explain," she said to Liam, as if she had revealed a secret and wanted forgiveness.

"Fine," Liam said briskly. "But Quetivel is not the problem. The problem is Oakham." As coherently as he could—new thoughts kept coming to him, half-remembered shreds of Oakham's conversation and behavior—he told what he thought. Spoken aloud, it sounded unconvincing to him, a mass of speculation, open to different interpretations. Uldericus had not actually said that Oakham owed him money; the hints and rumors Oakham had supplied him might not have been meant to be misleading; even the lord's comment about cut throats was ambiguous: could Liam be sure he had not mentioned it?

Liam knew it was true, though, felt it as deeply as he did the urgent need for immediate action. It made sense, more sense than anything else, and as he watched Coeccias and Grantaire digest the news, he felt his earlier rage rising again.

The only decent one of them, he sneered at himself. *How could I have thought that? One and all, a set of . . .* There was no word strong enough, and that insufficiency brought him back to the room, to the other two.

Grantaire was pensive, clearly not prepared to judge. She looked expectantly at the Aedile, who found a chair and sat heavily, expelling a long, whistling breath. He moved his head from side to side, but he was not denying Liam's argument, just trying to express his shock.

"Aye," he said at last, "aye. It makes sense."

"I am not sure I understand," Grantaire said hesitantly. "Why would he steal the Jewel? It is his, is it not?"

"No," Liam explained patiently. "It belongs to Mistress Priscian, to the Priscian family. I suppose it would eventually come down to him, through his wife—but he must have needed the money now. He talked about going to Torquay, said that the stress had been too much for him and his wife. He probably planned to sell it there—but I think now that he means to sell it to Desiderius." An unimportant thought strayed across his mind and was gone: *How many passages did he take for Torquay?* Liam was willing to bet there was only one.

"We must stop him, then," Grantaire announced. "Desiderius cannot have that Jewel."

"No," Coeccias said, drawing the word out. "No. It would not do." He stood and looked at Liam. "What would you do?"

"That depends." He frowned, not liking his own tentative plan but unable to think of another. "I think he has gone to Desiderius now. We'll know shortly—from your man or from Fanuilh. If he has, then we can try to arrest them."

Grantaire objected. "You won't find Desiderius easy to arrest."

"I know. If we can, we want to avoid confronting him. The real question, though, is whether Oakham has taken the Jewel with him or not. I would guess not."

"Not if he has any wit at all," Coeccias said. "He knows that this wizard knows the Jewel was stolen. He'll bargain. And if he does not have it with him, our arrest is wasted."

"Exactly. So we can wait until they part. When they do, we can take Oakham. For that, we should wait until he gets home, I think."

"And do what?" Grantaire wanted to know, a little lost in the back-and-forth between Liam and the Aedile.

"Confront him," Liam said. "I'll do that." He did not know just exactly how, but neither Coeccias nor Grantaire asked him. "And that will be that."

There was an uncomfortable silence, and finally Grantaire broached the topic no one wanted to address. "And what if he has given the Jewel to Desiderius already?"

Liam glanced significantly at the bundle of things from the trophy room. "Do you still think you can face him?"

She laughed, a harsh bark with no humor in it. "I can, but I do not want to."

"With any luck it won't come to that. I will go to him and explain that we have Oakham—which we will—and that we are sure he was unaware that he was sold stolen goods. I will give him back whatever he gave Oakham. Then, if he refuses, it will be up to you. But remember, he doesn't know you are in Southwark. You will be able to surprise him."

"There is that," she allowed; then, not as if she were troubled by the idea but rather as if she were seeking permission, she asked: "But you understand that I will have to kill him?"

"You had better," Liam said.

Coeccias said nothing, his face grim.

"What do we do now?"

"Wait," Liam told them, and took the chair next to the Aedile's.

Burrus had come with cups of some hot drink and, sensing the mood of the room, quickly withdrew. Liam held his cup absently, not drinking, staring at the floor between his feet.

What if he was wrong? What if Oakham had not gone to the Three Foxes? *Then the wait is for nothing,* he told himself, but he did not think it would be. He had no doubt where the lord was. There had been more than enough time between when Fanuilh had seen him leave his house and when Liam had ordered the dragon back to the inn. Oakham was there. The question was, what was he doing, and when would he leave?

It was an effort not to pester Fanuilh with questions, but Liam restrained himself, confident that his familiar, at least, would make no mistakes.

Burrus came back with a steaming pot to refill their cups. Coeccias alone had drunk his, but he waved the pot away. The servant was going into the kitchen when the thought came into Liam's head.

Lord Oakham is coming out of the Three Foxes.

Liam closed his eyes and mouthed a silent prayer of thanks.

"Oakham is leaving the Three Foxes," he told the others. Coeccias half rose from his seat, but Liam waved him back down. "We will wait until he gets home."

Coeccias stood anyway. "I'm thinking of putting another man on the Three Foxes, and I needs must check in at the barracks in any case. I'll return before he gets there."

As he left, Liam projected: *Fanuilh, follow Lord Oakham home. Let me know the moment he arrives.*

Yes, master.

He held the thought in his mind. Why could he not be more like Fanuilh? More logical, more competent. *More humorless.* Perhaps he did not want to be completely like Fanuilh.

It was strange, how at ease he was. Ordinarily he hated waiting more than anything else. Now, though, he felt only a calm eagerness, if such a thing could exist. He had mastered his anger, and was enjoying it in a strange way. With a self-conscious laziness he rose and strolled to the fire, rubbing his hands slowly before it.

Grantaire was sitting on a low stool by the hearth. She turned her face up to him, and he was surprised to discover that she was scrutinizing him, an abstracted, assessing expression in her eyes.

"What?" He laughed a little, but it sounded nervous, so he stopped.

"I am wondering what you will do when you see this Oakham."

"Spank him soundly and send him right to bed," Liam replied. This time when he laughed, it sounded normal to him. Grantaire shook her head impatiently.

"No. I wonder."

He was wondering too, but about something different. *Should I bring something? No.* Oakham had used a knife; a knife was not much, after all, and he would be on his guard. He was sure the beggar had not been— and the Werewolf had said Japer was nearly beside himself with fear. *Besides, I might kill him.*

That surprised him, and his eyebrows drew together as he stared into the fire. *Would I?* He dismissed the idea immediately. Wounded pride, no doubt, and there was nothing to be gained from that. It would be much more satisfying to see Oakham tried—and hanged. The prospect of Oakham at the end of a rope gave him a certain grim pleasure, but he dismissed it, too, a little reluctantly. There was no guarantee of it, after all: Oakham was titled, and a beggar and a thief did not count for much against that.

At that, who knew why he had killed them? Thieves quarreled, Liam knew, and though the quarrels rarely escalated into violence, Japer had been a hothead. And the beggar—who knew? Oakham had laid himself open to all sorts of threats.

Liam shook his head. Whatever came of that, there was still the theft itself, and at the very least the lord would be disgraced.

In a gust of cold air, Coeccias returned; the extra man to watch the Three Foxes had been arranged. "And the oddest little girl was waiting on you, Rhenford. Filthy as a frozen midden—she's outside."

It was Mopsa, about as dirty as Coeccias had said, patting Diamond's foreleg nervously. Liam squatted down beside her, shivering—he had left his cloak inside.

"What are you doing here?"

"The Wolf sent me," she said, "and for that I'm ruined!"

"What are you talking about?"

"I'm ruined!" she wailed. "If the whole Guard doesn't know me by now, they will in the morning—and the Addle himself!"

Liam had no time for this. "What does he want?"

"To know what y' have found," she said, sulking. "And to say we're attending your results. It's beyond me why he couldn't just wait—or why he couldn't send someone else. Why me? And now they all know me!"

"Mopsa," Liam interrupted, "shut up. Go to the Werewolf and tell him I know who did it, and it's not the beggars." She was still moping, so he caught her by the shoulders. "This is important! Tell him it was not the beggars, and that I will have the man shortly. Can you remember that?"

"Of course I can." She wrenched free from his grip. "Small lot you care, if I'm ruined! Some chanter! I can't work crowds now, do you see?"

He did see; he understood that she thought herself compromised. "I know—but there is nothing I can do about that. And you have to tell the Wolf what I said."

"Huh."

"And tell him I will come to him when I can, to explain. Will you do that?"

Mopsa scowled, barely mollified, and finally nodded. "I'll tell him," she muttered, and then burst out: "And what of my gift?"

Liam winced; he had forgotten. "You will get it," he promised, "but you must go to the Werewolf now."

She glared suspiciously at him for a moment—he strove to look trustworthy—and then she stalked off into the night without a word.

Liam shivered once, all over, and went back inside.

"That was my good authority," he told Coeccias, knowing that he might be compromising her even more. *I will make it up to her,* he promised himself. "We will be able to wrap that up tonight, too."

Before the Aedile could do more than nod, Fanuilh's thought came: *Lord Oakham has come home.*

A cold smile lit Liam's face. "Lord Oakham has returned home, and will see us now."

They stopped at the end of Duke Street. The Oakhams' house was just visible around the corner; a single candle burned in one of the first-floor windows.

"He's expecting me," Liam told the others. "He said he would leave a candle burning if he was still awake." In fact, he was surprised to see the signal; when they had parted earlier Oakham had given Liam the impression that he would have been happy never to see him again—and given the business the lord had presumably just transacted, the signal seemed doubly unlikely. Nonetheless, there it was, winking at him, shedding a yellow glow on the sill and the mullions, the edge of the light just barely illuminating the front door.

"Well," he said, rubbing his hands together, "there's nothing for it."

"Rhenford, this is wooden," Coeccias said, waving a shuttered lantern at the house. "Why don't we both go?"

"This will be trickish," Liam said, using the Aedile's word. "Count to ten thousand, and if I'm not out by then, come after me. I want him alone for a little while." *If I'm lucky, I may get to hit him—just once.*

He threw a smile at them and started across the street, fast enough that he only heard the Aedile begin to mutter something about having to stay out in the cold.

Jumping up the steps two at a time, he put his hand to the knocker, thought better of it, and rapped gently with his knuckles.

Oakham opened the door almost at once, a lantern raised above his head. His handsome face was pale and strained; he grabbed Liam's arm and pulled him through the doorway.

"Gods, Rhenford, y' are well come. Something passing strange has happened!"

Liam allowed himself to be pulled along a few steps without resisting, completely taken aback. This was not the greeting he had expected at all. They were halfway down the corridor before he dug in his heels and forced Oakham to stop.

"Come along!"

"What is it?" Apart from the lantern, the hall was dark; their shadows stretched behind them, grotesque monsters.

"The Jewel!" Oakham whispered. "It has returned! Come along!"

The lord tugged at him again, and Liam allowed himself to be led, out of the main hallway, down the white-plastered corridor towards the kitchen.

This was not right; this was not the way it was supposed to be at all. He stopped again, forcing Oakham to face him in the doorway of the kitchen.

"Oakham, where are we going?"

"The crypt! It's there!" He hurried into the kitchen alone, disappearing through the door to the cellar.

The light from the lantern faded almost immediately, and Liam had to hurry after or be left in the dark. He followed the light down the stairs, always just at its edge, hearing Oakham urge him to hurry, not to dawdle so.

A box crept out of the shadows and caught Liam's shin a shrewd blow; he stifled a curse and went on, to the end of the cellar, the entrance to the crypt vestibule.

"It's here!" Oakham was standing at the far end of the anteroom, one hand on the iron gate, the other holding his lantern. Another lantern burned somewhere beyond him, deep in the crypt.

Liam took two steps into the anteroom, then stopped, deeply regretting the weapon he had not brought. *Wasn't I going to think before I acted?* Still, he was on his guard, and Oakham had entered the house alone.

Two steps more brought him to Oakham's shoulder, and he gestured for the lord to precede him.

"Show the way," he said. Oakham nodded eagerly and walked into the room, holding his lantern high.

"It's amazing," he said, then turned around, a puzzled look on his face. "Aren't you coming?"

"Yes," Liam said softly, wary, his uncertainty growing every minute. He took three steps into the room, looked around. The second lantern whose light he had seen was perched on the central sarcophagus. Oakham stood next to it, beckoning Liam on.

"It's here! It's where it's meant to be!" He was practically dancing with excitement, the lantern bobbing in his hand and throwing his shadow over the stone walls, the great bulks of the sarcophagi. Whistling in the narrow hallway from the balcony, a cold wind snaked into the room, coiling around Liam's ankles.

He went to Oakham, his eyes jumping around the room, his boots grating on the floor. His arms hung loose and ready at his sides, fists clenched.

"Rhenford! Come along," the other man said, exasperation drawing out his words.

Liam came, stopping at the edge of the bay that held Eirenaeus's tomb, uncomfortably aware of the shadowed recess at his back, the thick blackness that filled the other bays. Oakham stepped back, holding the lantern higher.

"Look," he commanded, nodding his head towards the bay.

For a long second Liam stared at him, trying to puzzle out this strange behavior, trying to figure out what was going on. He could not; slowly, unwillingly, he turned to look at Eirenaeus's coffin.

Movement flickered in the corner of his eye—Oakham's free hand darting to his waist—and Liam jumped back with a loud shout, a burst of fear and energy exploding through his body. For a moment, his feet tangled beneath him, he was going to fall.

He caught at the wall, righted himself, lurched forward.

Oakham had shouted as well, skipped back a step, and now he stood tall, the lantern in one hand, a thin piece of wood clenched in the other. Liam froze, staring at the piece of wood, and distinctly heard the other man take two ragged breaths.

With his eyes locked on Liam, Oakham brought his thumb against the wood and pressed, bending the sliver over, almost double, and then it snapped.

For another long second, neither man moved; then Liam started cautiously advancing, knees bent in a fighting crouch. He remembered the broken mace head from the first Priscian's effigy, and spared a glance. It was no longer there.

No matter, he thought, and his lips twisted in a small smile of anticipation. Whatever the stick had meant, it would not stop him from taking Oakham.

"Stay where you are," the lord commanded, holding out a hand, palm out. "Not one more step."

Liam let his lips part, his smile widening. He flexed his hands.

Master! Fanuilh was in his head. *There is magic down the hill.*

He froze again, cocking his head. *What—*

The thought was only partially formed when he saw the shimmer, an insubstantial gleam, like light reflecting from a spiderweb. He blinked, and Desiderius was there, standing at the far end of the first Priscian's sarcophagus. His arms were thrust out, fists clenched, his face in shadow.

"Take him!" Oakham shouted.

A *trap,* Liam thought, dazed, terrible realization sapping the strength from his knees. *They set a trap for me!*

"It is not so easy," Desiderius snapped, and then, almost hesitantly, he opened his fists, flicking his fingers in Liam's direction.

A visible wind sprang from his fingertips, mottled white ribbons of cloud that melded together and barreled at Liam, wrapping his legs, his waist, his shoulders. He was encased in the ribbons; they flowed ceaselessly from his toes to his shoulders. He pushed against them, but it was like being wrapped in a wet carpet. He could twist a little, and wiggle his fingers, but nothing else.

Master, there is magic with you now!

"I know," he whispered, staring fearfully at the wizard. Desiderius let his arms drop, staring back, a curious expression on his face. After a moment, a happy smile split his piebald face, a flash of white teeth in the unnatural purple.

"You really aren't a wizard! You really aren't!"

"Kill him!" Oakham shouted.

Desiderius held up a single, commanding finger. "A moment. He isn't a wizard!" He put his fists on his hips, savoring the words, an ugly pleasure sliding across his face.

Master—

FANUILH! Liam interrupted the dragon's thought, obliterating it in his head with his own thought. *GET COECCIAS! GET COECCIAS!*

"Kill him!" Oakham repeated. "The thief said he was a wizard!"

Liam licked his lips and fixed his eyes on Desiderius. "I told you I wasn't a wizard."

"Oh yes, yes, you did," the wizard agreed with a chuckle. "Sometimes I am too clever by half."

"But the thief said—" Oakham began, and Liam cut him off with a snarl:

"Is that why you killed him?"

"He wanted to give the Jewel back!" The lord came forward till he was right next to Liam, peering intently into his face. "He said you were a wizard, that you could see men's souls."

"Which he clearly cannot," Desiderius said, enjoying himself immensely. "I would have thought Mage Tanaquil could do better."

Deliberately casual, Liam cursed him, in no uncertain terms, and then prayed: *Let them get here soon.*

"This is interesting," Desiderius said, his smile gone. "I wonder, now. I did not believe you were not a wizard, but I did believe you had not seen Grantaire. Could I have been wrong both times?" He gave a gesture, and the ribbons of cloud tightened suddenly, crushing Liam's arms to his side and grinding his knees together. "Could I?"

Liam gave a startled cry, but the pain was negligible, only a hint.

Over the wizard's shoulder, he imagined he saw a shadow in the hallway to the balcony.

He screamed then, as loud as he could, making it last as long as he could. Desiderius's face twisted in an angry grimace, and Oakham jumped forward, clamping his fingers over Liam's mouth. Liam bit down as hard as he could, catching a fold of flesh in his teeth. He spat it out and screamed again, as if he were being murdered. Oakham drew his arm back and punched him hard on the side of the head.

His head snapped to one side. Where was Fanuilh? Squirming sparks of gold swam in his vision, and suddenly Oakham was gone from his field of vision, and he could see one of the sparks, glowing in the middle of Desiderius's chest. The wizard was staring down at the glowing mote, his cupped hands framing it. He looked up from the spark, straight at Liam.

"You—" The word was the beginning of an accusation, but he did not finish it.

Other sparks appeared, on his legs and shoulders, on his hands. He opened his mouth to speak again, and there were sparks on his tongue, sparks everywhere. He was like a congregation of fireflies, and then he was a solid mass of glowing gold, back arched in pain but silent except for a low crackling sound.

The mottled ribbons faded to nothing, and Liam stumbled, suddenly free. He spun from the molten mass that was the wizard, and saw Oakham pressed back against the far wall, eyes wide in horror.

Liam did not see the sparks brighten suddenly, and then collapse like a broken log. He did not see the cinders float to the ground and go out, leaving only a thin scattering of ash.

He only hit Oakham once—but it was enough.

▪ *16* ▪

THE CRYPT FILLED up quickly: Liam's screaming woke both houses. Mistress Priscian arrived first, stern and tight-lipped, Haellus's incredulous face peeping over her shoulder. Quetivel came in a moment later from the opposite entrance, propelled from behind by Lady Oakham. Catching sight of her husband lying at Liam's feet, she shoved both Quetivel and Coeccias aside and bolted across the room, oblivious to Grantaire, who was stirring all that remained of Desiderius with the toe of her boot.

With a wild cry, Lady Oakham threw herself down beside her husband and began stroking his forehead and chafing his hands.

"They've killed you!" she wailed, over and over again, with minor variations.

Just before her spectacular entrance, Liam had made sure the man was still breathing—in reeling from Liam's punch, Oakham had managed to clip his head against the wall—and now he turned away and met Mistress Priscian's inquisitorial eye. With a nod at Lady Oakham, he moved her aunt back into the antechamber. Haellus disappeared into the cellar, and Coeccias joined them.

"This all has some meaning, I'm sure," Mistress Priscian said, her head held high. She was wearing a nightdress, and her unbound hair fell in gray strips down her back, but she still reminded Liam of his university master.

"It does," he assured her. "I wish it could have been done in a more discreet manner, but the Aedile and I have to arrest Lord Oakham for the theft of the Jewel."

She turned to Coeccias, seeking confirmation. He looked extraordinarily uncomfortable, but he nodded and managed to meet her eyes.

"Aye, it's true. We'll need to clap him in."

She nodded thoughtfully. "You have proof?" It was not a challenge, only a request for information. Coeccias directed the question to Liam.

"He admitted it."

"I see. It is very strange, but not altogether out of character. Very well—arrest him. I will see to my niece."

This caught both men unawares; Liam had expected some sort of protest. Evidently, Coeccias had too: "Y' are sure? I mean, you could extend him the Rights of the Town—he's a relation—"

"I will do no such thing," she interrupted sternly. "Please remove him presently." She swept past them, back into the crypt.

They drifted after her, sharing a look of surprise, and found her kneeling by her niece, holding her firmly by the shoulders.

"Come along, Duessa. The gentlemen have some business with Lord Oakham."

"Look on him," the young woman wailed. Oakham's eyes fluttered weakly, and he mumbled something.

"He will be fine," Mistress Priscian said. "Now come with me. Y' are overexcited." She rose, drawing her niece, suddenly compliant, with her, and steered the young woman towards the door.

"What will they do with him?" Duessa asked.

"Hush, child," Mistress Priscian counseled, and they were gone.

Coeccias looked embarrassed, but Liam, strangely, felt nothing but satisfaction. He knew he should feel sorry for Lady Oakham, but he simply could not bring himself to do so. He motioned to the Aedile, and between them they brought Oakham to his feet. The lord shook his head groggily, as unresisting as his wife, and they started helping him to the far end of the crypt.

Suddenly Quetivel was before them, trying to sound firm but licking his lips nervously.

"Now, what is this all about?"

His bandages were askew, showing the stubble of his shaven scalp in places, and Liam fought down an urge to laugh—not just at the ridiculous-looking baron, but at everything. The side of his head throbbed where he had been hit, and his limbs felt hollow, scoured out by fear and nervous energy, but it was done. *Done!*

"Lord Oakham is under arrest for the theft of the Priscian Jewel," he said. "And for two murders."

"As well as attempting the life of one of the Duke's officers," Coeccias added. "I think perhaps you might go with Mistress Priscian, my lord. Lady Oakham will be sorely distressed." His tone was hard, indicating that the most important thing was that Quetivel get out of their way.

Licking his lips again, Quetivel shot a glance at Oakham, lolling drunkenly between Liam and Coeccias, then hurried after the two women.

Liam and Coeccias moved Oakham along at a brisk pace, with Grantaire walking behind, Fanuilh on her shoulder and a lantern in one hand.

The dragon had alerted them, Grantaire told Liam, dropping out of the sky onto the street in front of them. When they did not take its meaning quick enough, it flew behind them and nipped the Aedile, which had induced them to enter the house.

"By then, though, my cat had told me about magic in the house," Grantaire explained, "so we were somewhat prepared."

"Somewhat," the Aedile grumbled.

You bit Coeccias? Liam projected.

He would not move. I did not draw blood.

"He is very sorry," Liam told his friend, privately amused. "He won't do it again."

Coeccias grunted sourly. "It likes me not that we did not guess their purpose. That could have been dangerous."

"Could have been?"

"Not a simple spell," Grantaire mused. "Matter transferral is never easy. He must have guessed we were watching him."

"Wait," Liam protested, remembering the way the ribbons of cloud had tightened, *"could* have been dangerous? *Could?"*

"There is still the Jewel," Grantaire reminded them, ignoring Liam. "We must find it."

"He hasn't got it with him," Liam said. He had checked Oakham's pockets along with his breathing.

"But he'll know," Coeccias said. "I doubt me he'd already given it to the wizard, but if he has, we can search the Three Foxes. Unless I miss my guess, though, it'll be somewhere in the house."

This satisfied Grantaire, and they walked down Duke Street in silence. As they went further down the hill, they began to pass people, small parties and occasional individuals, many masked, many drunk. After one particularly sodden youth tried to pet Fanuilh, Liam suggested that the dragon make itself less conspicuous—which it did by taking flight from Grantaire's shoulder in full view of a wagonload of drunken farmers.

Watching their panicked faces, he sent an inadequately ironic thought after the dragon: *You have just made this their most memorable Banquet ever.*

Fanuilh did not deign to respond.

With his familiar gone, Liam realized that they blended in quite well with the growing crowds—just another group laden with a drunk. Oakham began to come around as they entered the square, getting his feet under himself and taking a few stumbling steps.

Holidaymakers seemed to fill the square, but they were loosely packed, the cobbles covered and uncovered in swirls and eddies of laughing, singing people. They plowed easily through, a little confused by the sounds and the constant shifting movement, bumped and jostled from time to time; a drunk in jester's motley erupted into raucous greetings when he saw them, then quickly subsided when he recognized the Aedile's bearded face, and ducked into a concealing group.

They washed up on the steps of the barracks, where a frantic guard leapt down on them.

"Aedile Coeccias, there's something," he panted, "something—something!"

Coeccias rolled his eyes. "Aye, aye, Taenus, in a moment. Let us get this in."

The man balked, trying to stammer out his message, but Coeccias cut him short.

"Let us get this in," he repeated, bulling forward, dragging Oakham and Liam with him. The guard jumped out of the way. "I'll talk with the Sergeant of the Night."

The guard followed them up the steps, still stammering. "But the Sergeant's not there, Aedile Coeccias, for that he's gone to this, this thing!"

Liam pitied the poor man, trying to get his meaning across to the Aedile's unresponsive back, but Oakham had begun to stir and protest, dragging his feet a little, and he wanted the lord behind bars as soon as possible.

The barracks was almost empty, with an air of having been hastily abandoned—stools were overturned, and a poker lay half in and half out of one hearth, its tip beginning to glow. Mopsa stood at the liquor barrel in the center of the room, sniffing cautiously at the contents of a tin cup.

"Away from there!" Coeccias roared; the girl dropped the cup and skipped backward, a defiant sneer quickly replacing her look of drop-jawed surprise. "Taenus! Can't you even keep a child out of a barrel?"

"Come on," Liam said, wondering what had possessed the apprentice thief to return to the barracks. "Let's get him in a cell, and then you can find out what is going on."

He had never seen more of the barracks than the main room; a single heavy door in the rear wall led to the cells, he knew, but he had never been there. At Coeccias's command, Taenus found a ring of keys and opened the door, fretting and fumbling, and then ran ahead of them to find an empty cell.

The door opened on the middle of a long corridor, the far wall of which was lined with bays in what was, to Liam at least, an eerie echo of the Priscian crypt. The bays were barred off, and there were far more of them—eight that he could see, and a staircase at the right-hand end of the corridor might lead to more—but they were almost exactly the same size, and in the uneven glare of a pair of fitful torches, they made him shudder.

The three nearest the door were full, and their occupants erupted into drunken shouting at Taenus's entrance. In one, four masked young men began serenading the guard with a filthy version of a Banquet carol; they broke off when Grantaire entered, and one of them offered her a slurred apology and attempted a low bow, which ended with his head clanging against the bars.

Grantaire pursed her lips and suggested a cell farther away.

They eventually settled Oakham in the cell closest to the stairs, letting him slide to the ground in a graceless huddle. For a moment they all stared at him: Coeccias with a satisfied nod, Grantaire with an air of impatience, as if he were secondary to the actual recovery of the Jewel, and Liam with a faint sense of wonder. With his hands flopping ineffectually at his hair and his legs sprawled out before him, Oakham cut a pathetic figure, and Liam found it unbelievable that he could have stolen the Jewel, and then killed two men and kept up a masterful two-day charade to keep it.

And let's not forget that he tried to kill you, he reminded himself. That, too, was unbelievable. *How much did he take off the price of the Jewel to get Desiderius to do that? Or did he just throw it in for free?*

He clapped his hands, assuming an attitude of briskness to block out the thought. "We will need some water, I think."

"Aedile Coeccias," Taenus began desperately. "This thing . . ."

Coeccias turned to him wearily. "Aye, aye, I'm with you. Rhenford, you'll do this?" He pointed at Oakham. "Search out the Jewel? Master Taenus'll burst if I do not hear him out. I'll join you in a minute. Now, Master Taenus, unburden yourself." He started out of the cell.

The guard's voice was quickly lost in a renewed burst of song from the young men's cell, and Liam offered Grantaire a shrug.

"I imagine they must be busy all throughout the Banquet."

She nodded at Oakham. "I think you hit him too hard." The lord was rocking his head back and forth now, cradling it in his hands.

"Not hard enought," Liam corrected her. "A little water will bring him around." His conscience stirred a little, though: it had been an unfair punch. "I'll get some." He left the cell and went back down the corridor, ignoring the rowdy men in the middle cells.

Mopsa was back at the liquor barrel, sipping from the cup. Liam hurried over and took the cup away. "What are you doing? And what are you doing here?"

"What's it to you?" she sneered. "If I'm ruined, and'll never chant again . . ."

"Well, why did you come? They would never have thought twice about you!"

"I didn't mean to come," she whined, "not the first time. I was just attending you, out of the way, quiet, and that damned guard caught my eye and demanded my business! Well, I had to tell him, didn't I? And when they heard it was you I was laying for, it was 'Quaestor Rhenford this' and 'Quaestor Rhenford that,' and nothing would do but that I wait inside by the fire, and the Addle—the Addle himself!—pats me on the head!" Her shoulders slumped, and she looked truly miserable. "And for that I'm ruined!"

Liam raised his hands, helpless. "Mopsa, I am sorry. The Werewolf should never have sent you—"

"Too right," she muttered.

"—but why did you come back?"

She spat on the floor. "The Wolf made me. For that he says he must see you, tonight."

Liam shook his head. "I cannot. Tell him I will come when I can— sometime tomorrow. Meet me at the Arcade tomorrow, at noon. I will bring you your gift." When this did not cheer her up, he started ushering her to the door. "Now go—and keep a low profile for a while. The guards will forget you soon enough." He believed it, almost, and she let him steer her out the door.

Taenus was standing on the steps, a halberd in his hand, watching the milling crowds in the square. He gave Mopsa only the briefest of glances.

"Where's the Aedile?" Liam asked, as much to find out as to distract the other man from Mopsa's forlorn departure.

"Gone to see," the guard said. "It's a murther!" The southern slur irritated Liam.

"A mur-der, eh?" He deliberately split the word, emphasizing the "d." "Will he be back soon?"

Taenus shook his head emphatically. He was young, hardly more than sixteen. "I doubt it, Quaestor. The Sergeant said it was most frightful."

Liam grunted sourly and went back inside. It was not his business, though it would not surprise him if Coeccias tried to make it that. *I'm finished,* he told himself. It had been a long two days.

There was no water to be found in the main room, and he guessed it was probably kept in the cellar. He was still holding the cup of liquor Mopsa had been drinking. With a shrug, he went back to the cells.

A very long two days, he thought. He was tired, but the tension he had felt earlier was gone. Walking down the cell corridor with the cup in his hand, he felt quiet, walled off from the shouts and songs, quite alone. There were only a few things left to do.

Grantaire was standing over Oakham, arms folded, listening. The lord, his eyes clear and his head bent back to look up at her, was saying something about his study. Liam paused at the entrance.

". . . a tapestry. It's behind that."

The wizard nodded curtly.

"There was no water," Liam said, as if he had just returned. "But it looks as if he doesn't need it."

"I woke him," she said with a shrug. "He says the Jewel is in his study, behind a tapestry. Do you know where that is?"

Liam glanced back and forth between the two. Oakham was staring fixedly at the wizard, his mouth working soundlessly. "What did you do to him?"

She looked annoyed. "Nothing—I just woke him up, and cleared his head for him."

"Hm." He squatted by the lord's side and held out the cup.

"Perhaps he is remembering Desiderius," Grantaire suggested.

Oakham's hands trembled around the cup, but he managed to raise it to his lips without spilling any. He sipped cautiously, his eyes now roving between Grantaire and Liam.

"Can we get the Jewel now?"

"In a moment, in a moment. I want to ask him some things." He ignored Grantaire's exasperated sigh and focused on Oakham. "If Desiderius hadn't been here, what were you going to do with it?"

A spasm of anger flashed across the lord's face. He looked up at Liam and cursed him in a low whisper, then glanced fearfully at Grantaire as if awaiting her reaction.

Liam sucked on his teeth for a moment. "All right. It will all come out in the end."

"Can we go now?"

"Yes." He stood. "Good night, Lord Oakham." Oakham did not respond, only let his head sink down onto his chest. Liam motioned for Grantaire to precede him out.

The key was still in the lock, and as he closed and locked the cell, Liam realized that he had no idea what came next. Returning the Jewel, obviously, but what about Oakham? Would there be a trial? Would he have to confess, or would Liam's word be enough? The Jewel itself would be damning evidence, but then there were the murders, for which he had no physical proof.

He walked slowly down the cell corridor, oblivious to the racket and Grantaire's impatient stare. There were judges in Southwark—he had heard Coeccias name one or two of them—but he did not know how they worked. The Duke's Courts were next door, but he had never seen a trial there; he had only visited the first floor and the basement, which were taken up with administrative offices and a place called the morgue, where unclaimed bodies were stored, under the supervision of a witch named Mother Japh.

Justice in the Midlands was a rough sort of thing; his father had held "court" whenever and wherever necessary—in Rhenford Keep, in a barn, in a field. Issues were brought before him, and he simply decided. That could not be the case in Southwark, Liam knew. The Duke was too far away, and the duchy was too large. Hence the judges Coeccias had mentioned—but he still had no idea how the process worked.

Grantaire made another impatient noise, waiting for him at the door to the main room. "Come along, Rhenford! I won't rest easy until that thing is safely locked away!"

Her anxiety puzzled him, but he quickened his step anyway, pulling the door closed behind him and locking it hastily. "Who do you think is going to take it?" He nodded at the locked door. "Oakham is back there, and Desiderius is dead, and we are the only people who know where it's hidden."

She scowled, but did not answer.

"Exactly," Liam said, as if her silence were an admission. "No one.

But we will go anyway—because we should restore it to Mistress Priscian. All right?"

"Whyever, Rhenford, as long as we see it safely locked away." She went to the door and out.

Liam rolled his eyes, wondering at her insistence. *Why is she so nervous about this?* And then he thought about Desiderius's end—had she winced when he mentioned that the wizard was dead? That could well be it: he had known only a few people who could kill and think nothing of it. *And I didn't like any of them.*

So it was a way of coping, he decided, like a soldier he had known once who, after every encounter, spent hours cleaning himself, his weapons, his armor—all of his equipment, even things he had not taken into battle. It had been a harmless mania. *We'll lock the Jewel in the crypt, and then get some sleep, and she will feel fine in the morning.*

And all he would have to do was buy Mopsa a gift and talk to the Werewolf. Both ideas bothered him; he knew he should have arranged to see the thief that night, but he was just too tired, too fed up with all the things he had to do. *My word ought to be good enough,* he thought. *He doesn't need to see me in person.*

As for Mopsa, it would have to be a large gift. It was not exactly his fault that she had been seen by the guards—the Werewolf should never have sent her to the barracks—and he really did not think it would make much of a difference, as long as she was careful. But she was taking it very hard, and he felt bad for her.

"A very large gift," he said, shook his head, and went outside.

The crowd in the square was thinning; it was growing late, and the revelers had begun to break up.

Liam took a deep breath, enjoying it, reveling in the knowledge that he was done. *Tomorrow night I'll be out there,* he promised himself, eyeing a group of young women, half-masked, kicking their legs high in a ragged dance just in front of Herlekin's. A cheering, clapping crowd had gathered around them. *Right in front.*

Then Grantaire called his name from the bottom of the steps.

"Coming, coming," he said, and joined her.

"Rhenford, can't I make you see that this is important?"

"No," he said, grinning. He took her arm and started across the square. She started to pull away, then stopped and let her arm hang limply in his, muttering something he did not catch.

They had only gone a few steps before the crowd parted and a furious Coeccias appeared before them, flanked by two guards.

"Rhenford!" he barked. "We've a problem."

"What?" Liam snapped back, letting go of Grantaire's arm. The Aedile's tone annoyed him.

"Come with me," was all Coeccias would say, grabbing him by the shoulder.

Liam went, dragging his feet a little. *Haven't I done enough?* he grumbled to himself. Aloud, he said: "What is it?"

Coeccias pulled him close and hissed in his ear. "Three beggars, Rhenford, dead. Where's your good authority now?"

He jerked away in surprise. "Where?"

Grantaire thrust herself forward. "What is it?" she demanded.

"In the Point," Coeccias said, ignoring her. "Will you see?"

"Is it—was it thieves? Do you know?"

"Who else?" Coeccias growled, pushing Liam along by the shoulder.

Two more guards with lanterns marked the entrance to the alley, a narrow lane between the high, blank walls of two modest houses in the middle of the Point. They had walked in silence, the Aedile's grim and angry, Liam's fearful.

"In there," Coeccias said. "Take a lantern." Liam could see a spill of light farther down the alley, but he did as his friend said, taking the lantern the guard held out to him. Then he closed his eyes briefly, shook his head, and started in.

Behind him, he heard Coeccias begin to speak, and Grantaire cut him off.

"I should think not," she said, and a moment later she was behind Liam, almost on his heels, one hand tentatively holding his elbow for guidance.

A wind Liam had not really noticed cut off as they moved down the alley, the walls rising around them, enclosing them; it felt almost perceptibly warmer, though he could still see his breath. They came to a bend, a jog where the first alley twisted and expanded to meet another alley coming from the far street, where the light was.

It was a ghoulish scene: an old woman shrouded in black, a lantern held high above her head, bending to examine the shattered corpses, three of them, sprawled around the little space like discarded dolls in a toybox. The blood that splashed the walls glistened black in the lantern light, and Liam stopped, hoping he had not walked too far. The men had not been dead long; the blood had not even begun to freeze.

The old woman looked up at their approach.

"Good evening, Liam Rhenford," she said, and he recognized her.

"And to you, Mother Japh," he answered. They both let their eyes drift to the wreckage around them, mutually acknowledging the horror of the scene.

"See you," Coeccias said from just behind him, and Liam could hear the frustration in his voice, a thin layer just underneath the anger. "Three of them."

"I see," Liam said, meaning to say more but unable to think. He knew what the Aedile was thinking, and was thinking it himself: that the Werewolf had done this, despite his promise. From their clothes, the men were clearly beggars, and what had drawn them to the little alley—the way it cut off the wind, the two entrances—had made it an easy place for an ambush.

So, Liam thought, squatting carefully, bunching his cloak up to keep it off the ground, *this is my fault. Japer was not, but this . . .*

He heard Grantaire ask, "You know who did this?" and Coeccias replied, a terrible accusation: "Rhenford does."

He could tell it had been brutal, the way the blood had splashed, the terrible wounds. The man nearest him was lying propped against the wall, as if he had been thrown there, and most of his jaw was missing. The second's arm hung at his side, bone showing at shoulder and elbow; he lay face down, a deep indentation at the back of his head mostly covered by matted hair. Mother Japh was between him and the third man, but an odd thought had occurred to Liam.

"Did anyone see it? Or hear anything?" He rose, stepping over the first two men and joining Mother Japh by the third. She was shaking her head, clucking sadly.

"No," Coeccias answered shortly; Liam heard the unspoken addition, that it did not matter, since they both knew who had done it. Then the Aedile did add something: "They used clubs."

Liam shook his head, wondering about his odd thought. "I don't think so." He closed his eyes, trying to remember, picturing the blood-soaked aftermath of a battle, and a surgeon taking him through the tent where the wounded groaned and screamed, or sometimes lay silent. The surgeon pointing out wounds, telling what had made each and how he would treat it.

The third man's face had been battered unrecognizable.

"It looks like maces, or ball-and-chains. Morning stars. Why would they use those?" He had addressed the question to himself; Coeccias grunted, but Mother Japh touched Liam lightly on the arm. They had met a few times; he liked her, and believed she liked him. *Of course, she doesn't know this is my fault.*

She frowned quizzically up at him. "How can you know that?"

"The wounds, the . . . holes. They are too precise, too small. The spikes have cut through the skin, as well. Clubs don't mangle like that." He pointed at the third man, the missing face.

"Maces, morning stars or three-masted caravels," Coeccias said with disgust, "the how does not merit attention. It is the who—and where to find them."

Liam ignored the Aedile for the moment, frowning down at the third man without really seeing him. He had thought about a mace earlier, had wanted one. "Priscian's," he muttered, and remembered the broken piece of statuary. *So?* he asked himself; he could think of no reason why it would be important. *Unless Mistress Priscian is using it to massacre beggars.* The sarcasm tasted sour; there was nothing funny in the alley.

"These are just like the other," Mother Japh said to Coeccias, and Liam turned fast enough to see the Aedile nod.

"Aye—vicious."

"What other?" Liam asked, and then answered his own question: "The beggar from the other night." A dim spark of hope flashed in a corner of his mind. "It was the same as this?"

"The wounds, aye," said Mother Japh, clucking again. "Terrible things. And you know who did this?"

"No," Liam said, straightening up and facing the Aedile. "No, I do not. Not if it is the same as that other one." The Werewolf said he had taken no action after the beggar was killed, and Liam believed him. *And he still hasn't done anything.*

Coeccias exploded. "That's ridiculous!" he shouted. "You know whose work this is—and y' are going to find them, and bring them to me!"

"Coeccias, listen: I don't think it's them. They promised—and they know we have caught the man. I sent them a message hours ago." Which was not quite true, but close enough.

The Aedile glared, restraining himself, his whole body quivering, and then he turned on his heel and stomped away down the alley through which they had entered. Grantaire stepped forward to Liam.

"You do not know who did this?"

"No," he said, confident now. Little things occurred to him: the thieves would only have killed one man, and Mopsa's words about how they were "attending his results." *And they would never use maces—how would you hide a mace? Or climb across rooftops with it in the dark?*

So . . . who did this? He looked around the little space, at the slaughter. It was like a frozen abattoir.

Grantaire took a deep breath with a hitch in the middle of it. "You said something earlier, about maces. Something I did not catch. What was it?"

He looked blankly at her, shaking his head.

"It sounded like 'Priscian,' " she said.

"Oh, that." He waved it away. "I was thinking of maces. There was one in the Priscian crypt."

"I didn't see it," she said anxiously. "Where was it?"

"It's gone. Mistress Priscian pointed it out to us when she first showed us the crypt. It was part of one of the sarcophagi, but it was broken. She must have taken it." He realized that she was not merely curious, that she was hugging herself; he poked her shoulder. "You are thinking of something. What is it?" How many times had Coeccias asked him that?

She spoke too quickly, avoiding his eyes. "Nothing, nothing. Listen, Rhenford—you stay here. I'm going to get the Jewel and return it." Before he could say anything she was running down the alley. He stumbled after.

"Wait!" He slipped, horribly aware of what he had slipped on, almost fell, and recovered by windmilling his arms wildly. The lantern swung in wide arcs, pieces of slaughter swinging in and out of the light.

▪ *17* ▪

WHEN LIAM WAS steady, he decided it was too late to go after Grantaire—and he did not think Coeccias would let him go anyway. He heard the Aedile coming down the alley.

"Truth," the big man said, "what brought her to such a hurry?"

"I don't know," Liam replied, puzzled by her sudden departure. It was not the mania he had imagined in the barracks; her questions had not been prompted by some desire to avoid thinking of what she had done to Desiderius. She was worried about something, and remembering himself what she had done to the wizard, he could not imagine anything that would worry her.

It had to do with the Jewel, and the news of the missing piece of statuary had set her off. If Desiderius had not been able to match her, what was she afraid of? He was the only wizard in the city, and he was dead. *And if she's going to be afraid of dead wizards, why not add Tarquin and Eirenaeus. . . .*

The name hung in his mind, taking on substance and weight like one of Fanuilh's thoughts.

"Ridiculous," he said aloud, but the name would not dissipate in his head, his other thoughts trying to roll around it.

Tarquin came back from the dead, but he was brought back, brought back by the gods. It's ridiculous. How could he come back? And why now?

The Jewel had been moved, the Jewel that sealed his tomb, but Liam refused to accept that. It was gone for a week; why would he have come out tonight? The name disappeared as he built this strange train of thought, piecing it together as he went. *He didn't come out tonight, he came out two nights ago, and killed the beggar. He would need spirit after those centuries in the dark; so he killed the beggar. And the two children, the maskers that had disappeared, what about them?*

Liam frowned, shaking his head. Just because Grantaire took it seriously was no reason for him to; she was jittery because she had killed a man, and he could think it through clearly.

She was a wizard, though, and she had read Eirenaeus's book; she knew what he might be capable of.

He was tired suddenly, bone tired, exhausted, and thinking was too difficult for him. He turned to Mother Japh. She called herself a ghost witch; he knew there was a vast difference between wizardry and witchcraft, but he did not think that would change what had to be basic things.

"Do you know the difference between spirit and soul?"

She cocked her head at him, as if she had not heard him right and said, tentatively, "Yes. . . ."

There was a trick she had done once for him, proving to him that a body in her morgue belonged to a ghost then haunting Southwark. He reminded her of it. "You said the soul was gone, that it always was when there was a ghost." She nodded. "If the spirit had been taken, would the result be the same? I mean, if you did the same thing with these"—he swept his arm out, indicating the dead men around them—"would you be able to tell if they had any spirit?"

Her lips twitched while she considered the question. "It is possible," she said at last. "What you saw was the soul guttering; it has the form of a flame as a symbol, if you see. It is the soul breaking the last of its ties to the body, expending the last of the spirit. A ghost is a soul and spirit without the flesh; a ghost has no flame, for that the spirit and the soul have been bundled, tied together for some reason outside the flesh. So— aye, aye, no flame, no spirit, though it is the soul that interests us most."

"Can you do it here? For them?"

"Rhenford," the Aedile said, "what are you thinking?"

Liam noticed that the anger had faded from his friend's voice, replaced by his usual wary curiosity, but he ignored it. He was trying to make himself think, to concentrate on the problem at hand—*The new problem,* he thought with weary disgust—and he knew that if he thought at all of Coeccias, it would be with anger of his own.

He repeated his question to Mother Japh, and the old woman shrugged.

"If you wish," she said, as if it did not matter to her in the least.

She held out her right hand and slowly opened the fingers wide; a small ball of pure blue flame rested on her palm, floating an inch above the skin. As she drew her slightly cupped fingers down, the circle expanded, stretching out to become a plane.

Liam had seen this before, in the morgue beneath the Duke's Courts, but he still held in his stomach and his breath when the shimmering blue broke around his waist, circling him and spreading beyond to Coeccias. He heard the Aedile gasp, and then the plane filled the little space, and it was like they were deep in a glowing blue well. He even noticed that there was a meniscus along the walls, where the blue light curled up slightly against the stone.

"This is not so easy," Mother Japh said, her lips twitching again, and then she brought her hand out from underneath the field of blue, turning it palm down and pressing, fingers still cupped.

In the morgue, the bodies were laid on stone slabs, all at the same height, and the shimmering plane had remained flat; it billowed now, as she pressed, like a sheet thrown out over a bed, drifting towards the ground. Soundlessly it settled, touching the ground at Liam's feet, shrouding the head of the first man, propped against the wall, folding and dipping to touch the mouths of the two others, face down and face up. It was like a landscape of blue, hillocks and valleys, and coming through it were the faces of the dead.

Nothing stirred; there should have been flames burning over the mouths of the dead men. There were none.

Mother Japh closed her hand, tucking her fingers into her palm, and the blue landscape shredded like mist. They were left blinking, the two lanterns suddenly insufficient. The ghost witch cleared her throat, looking expectantly at Liam.

"One, even two lacking might be, but all three—it's unnatural."

Liam nodded absently, his eyes fixed on the face of the first man, where the flame had failed to appear. *So it might be.* He played with that thought, repeating it in his head three times over. After the third time, he turned his head slowly from the corpse, blew out a long breath, and rubbed at his face.

"All right," he said to Coeccias. "I have to go to Oakham's. You should go back to the square, and try to find that girl—the one who brought me the message." He would find Grantaire and see if he had guessed correctly about what was worrying her, but he could not ignore the fact that he might be wrong, that the Werewolf and his men might be responsible. And if he was wrong, he would prefer to find out about it alone. "Find her if you can, and tell her I need to see her friend. Mother

Japh, there should be two other beggars in the morgue—please check them as well."

"Think you I'll find the same?"

"Probably." He turned back to Coeccias. "I will come to the barracks as soon as possible. Find the girl if you can." Then he turned and started past Mother Japh, down the opposite alley, the one by which they had not entered.

"Rhenford—"

Liam called back, "I won't be long," and forced himself to a trot, the lantern tossing back and forth.

Better to be wrong alone, he thought.

Once out of the far alley, Liam slowed to a walk, feeling fatigue in every limb. He was complaining, too, silently, scowling wearily as he walked. Coeccias was not being fair, not fair at all. He could hardly be held responsible for the Werewolf's broken promise—if, indeed, he had broken his promise—but Coeccias had acted as if Liam had killed the beggars himself.

If he gets blamed for something, it's 'Oh, they tax me with everything,' and 'What am I supposed to do?' but when something might possibly be my fault, he jumps on it with both feet. And it's not even my responsibility! It's his city, not mine!

The alley gave out on a cross street just a short distance from Duke Street. Liam turned that way, heading up the Point, indulging his sense that he had been wronged, wallowing in self-justification. Tired as he was, long as his day had been, it felt good to tell himself that he did not have to do this. That he could have stayed home, that he could even go home, right now, but he would not, he would see it through.

He had almost reached End Street before doubts began to creep in—beginning with his usual reflection that Coeccias had so much to worry about, such a heavy load of responsibility—and by the time he stood before the Oakhams' house, he was shaking his head at his own complaints.

You would have been angry too, he told himself, and further knew that, as much as he wanted to, he could not go home just then. He had taken the responsibility on himself, however unwittingly, and knew that he would not be able to live with himself if he did not see it through.

No lights shone at the Oakhams', the windows black and lifeless. There was nothing frightening about it, just a house shut up for the night, but there was something that held him, staring at it. The cold pried at his cloak but he did not mind it, trying to figure out what it was that kept him there, looking at the blank facade.

And then he knew: it was the very normality of the house, the quiet respectability that fit in so nicely with the rest of the street. *Who would know?* he thought. *Who would walk by and say, 'Bad things have happened here'?* Liam had known places that you could not see without sensing the evil that had gone on within—black castles, ruins, temples devoted to hideous rites—and he had known places that gave that impression but belied it inside. Like the temple of Laomedon, an evil-looking building a few streets away in Temple's Court, behind whose high, foreboding walls the priests smiled cheerily and tended beautiful gardens.

The Oakhams' house, though, showed nothing; to Liam it was a smiling mask facing the street, with a bloody knife behind its back—and a mace, he imagined now, striped with gore.

He shook himself and trotted over to Mistress Priscian's, where a light was showing.

Haellus answered his knock, much disheveled and hardly his usual polite self.

"Master Rhenford," he said, as if he had been expecting Liam, "come—they're in the study." The servant practically ran up the stairs, Liam in tow, and began announcing Liam's arrival even before they reached the study.

Grantaire was sitting where she had earlier, the enormous folio open to her left and another, smaller book before her. Her finger traced her reading, darting up and down the pages; she read with impossible speed and complete concentration—she did not even look up when Liam came in. Mistress Priscian, though, standing by the door, turned anxiously to him.

"Oh, Master Rhenford, it likes me to see you here!"

"I'm sorry to disturb you so late," he began, but she went on, taking his arm and propelling him to Grantaire's side.

"It matters not. If what she says is true . . ." The voice of the older woman trailed off; she was unable to imagine the consequences.

"Well?" Liam asked the wizard. "Is it?"

She did not answer, holding up a hand for silence, her finger moving faster down the pages of the small book. It was a diary, Liam saw from over her shoulder, neatly written in fading ink. The pages crackled as she turned them; the binding was coming apart, and many of the pages were entirely loose. Grantaire handled them carefully, turning them over as if they were still attached.

The sound of her breathing reached Liam's ear; it came out between her working lips, matching the cadence of her finger as she read to herself. He tried to follow along, but she was hunched over the book and he could only catch glimpses of the page. He saw the name "Eirenaeus," and gave up; he had guessed correctly.

Right, he thought, taking a step back. She was worried about Eirenaeus, but was she right to be? And if she were right, what would that mean? He thought of asking Fanuilh, but he did not think the dragon would know; besides, Grantaire was stirring, closing the diary on her finger and reaching over to turn to the last pages of the large folio, then reopening the diary, as if checking the two against each other.

Whatever she had checked apparently was enough for her; she closed the diary with a snap and pushed it decisively away from her.

"Well?" Liam said anxiously. "Is it Eirenaeus?"

"It could be," she said, not at all surprised at his question. "I would have thought of it earlier if I had read all of his book." She tapped the folio, her lips twisting ruefully. "It is clear that the Jewel did not really work as he wanted it to. It allowed him to store his spirit, but it had to be 'primed'—his word—supplied with spirit from some other source, and even then he could only use a fraction of what went into it."

Liam was aware of Mistress Priscian standing at his elbow, listening to the wizard's explanation; he wondered briefly if she should hear it, but Grantaire continued without a pause, stroking the folio absently with her fingertips. It struck him that her recital was as much for herself as for him and Mistress Priscian, as if she was working it out aloud.

"He writes that the Jewel took spirit from him, draining him, and that the more he was exposed to it, the more it took. By the end, he had to feed the Jewel two or even three lives a week to get enough spirit just to live. The Jewel was a sort of parasite, taking all the spirit he stole and only returning a small amount of it; but because he had made it, and tuned it to himself, he could not destroy it without doing himself tremendous damage." She spoke with a calmness that was strange to Liam, as if she were describing nothing more serious than a recipe gone wrong.

"Grantaire," Liam interrupted, "I don't mean to be rude—but what does all this mean? Are you assuming that Eirenaeus is back from the dead, that he killed those beggars?"

She stood, shaking her head impatiently. "He is not back from the dead, Rhenford," she said, as if that should have been obvious. "He never died. Now come, let's deal with this."

•   •   •

Grantaire brought the diary with her, and a small sack that had apparently lain in her lap while she read. Mistress Priscian followed her without question, falling in behind her before Liam could begin to ask the many questions that sprang to mind. Foremost among them was just what the wizard thought she was going to do. He grabbed his lantern, still lit, and hurried after them.

She marched straight downstairs and into the kitchen, as if it were her own home. Mistress Priscian hurried to open the cellar door, producing a ring from a pocket of her dress and searching for the proper key. Liam took advantage of the pause to ask his question.

"Why, seal him up again," Grantaire said, irritatingly sure of herself. She held up the diary. "It is all here. His brother kept this. Eirenaeus feared the Jewel as much as he needed it—he kept it at a distance, in one of the family warehouses. The brother—"

"Dorstenius," Mistress Priscian supplied in a troubled whisper, gesturing to the open door. Grantaire took Liam's lantern and started down the steps, speaking over her shoulder to him.

"—The brother discovered that Eirenaeus was behind the murders, and used the Jewel to stop him. The closer the Jewel was, the weaker Eirenaeus grew, so the brother forced him into the sarcophagus and sealed it with the Jewel. Without a source of spirit, he was helpless, drained completely by the Jewel."

They passed through the cellar, Liam feeling as he were being pulled along, barely keeping up, and quite sure that whatever Grantaire was doing was not safe.

"The Jewel is proof against him," she was saying, waiting by the door to the crypt while Mistress Priscian unlocked it. To Liam it sounded as if the keys jingled a great deal, and he knew her hands were shaking, though her back was to them. "With it, we can force him back into his tomb."

"Then we need the Jewel," Liam said, not wanting to go into the crypt again, his conviction growing that Grantaire was being careless.

"I have it," she responded, and swept through the open door into the antechamber. Liam hurried up behind her and put a hand on her shoulder. The gate before her was closed.

"Grantaire," he whispered, aware in a frightened way of the black crypt beyond the gate, "this is not safe."

"Don't be simple, Rhenford," she said, but he noticed that she was whispering. She noticed it herself and raised her voice. "Mistress Priscian, if you will?"

"Wait," Liam said. "Let's think a little bit more about this. If it is Eirenaeus, how do we know what he can do?"

Grantaire held up the sack. "We know what he can't do, Rhenford, and he can't stand against this. All we have to do is wait until he returns. Now, Mistress Priscian?" She swung the sack in the direction of the lock. The older woman hung back for a moment, her gaze darting from Liam to Grantaire, and then she stepped forward, the gate key already in her hand, and put it in the lock.

The gate swung away on its own, after a few long seconds clanking against the inside wall. Grantaire held up her lantern, throwing light as far as the middle of the crypt; then, satisfied, she threw Liam a triumphant look and went in.

Despite her apparent nonchalance, Liam was happy to see that she walked along the left-hand bays, approaching Eirenaeus's sarcophagus circuitously, the sack with the Jewel in it raised as high as the lantern. He followed her, whispering.

"Are you sure that will stop him?" Without understanding why, he was suddenly convinced that Eirenaeus had come back, that he had killed the beggars, that he was waiting by his sarcophagus for them now.

Grantaire refused to whisper. "Quite sure. The only reason he could come out at all was because the Jewel was removed—and even then, it was only Oakham killing the beggar that allowed him the spirit to actually rise." She sounded sure, but Liam crept close, warily peering into the bays they passed. *One loud noise,* he thought, *and I will explode.*

She slowed as they approached the sarcophagus of the first Priscian; a slow draught of air swept around them, and Liam smelled the sea. Grantaire held up the lantern and waved it towards Eirenaeus's bay.

The sarcophagus stood undisturbed.

For some reason this relaxed Liam; the tension flooded away. His shoulders slumped a little, and he shook his head. To compensate for his nervousness, he walked forward to stand by the sarcophagus, resting one hand on the stone foot of Eirenaeus's effigy.

"So we just put the Jewel back, and then he can't come out?"

Grantaire joined him. "He may not be there," she said, handing him the lantern.

"And if he isn't?" It occurred to him that there was no reason for Eirenaeus to return at all. Why did they assume he would come back? *If I had been kept in a tomb for hundreds of years, I would never come near it.*

"He will return—this is his home, his place of refuge. And when he returns, we can use the Jewel to keep him here. Now please be quiet." She handed him the sack as well, and gestured for him to back away from the sarcophagus. When he had, she laid both hands on the stone and bowed her head, mumbling under her breath.

Liam could not make out any of the words, and as he stood listening, his nervousness began to return. Mistress Priscian had followed them, and stood now at the foot of the first Priscian's sarcophagus, her back to the balcony corridor.

His nervousness grew, but it was fueled now by logical thought. If Eirenaeus had indeed come back, they should be looking for him out in the city, not in the crypt. Why should he come there? Who was to say that he was not killing someone else right that very minute, stealing their spirit? Liam supposed that he might return, because the crypt was a safe place from which to go forth to kill, but would he return with the Jewel there? Grantaire had said that the closer it was to Eirenaeus, the weaker he was—surely he would avoid it.

His eyes fell to the bag in his hand. The Jewel was inside, the thing he had spent two days looking for, for which two men had died and for which he himself had almost been killed. Curiosity overcame him; he put the lantern down by his foot, opened the drawstring—and stopped, his fingers just inside the soft leather mouth.

Something from beyond the far gate, the one that led to the Oakhams', had made a noise. His mouth went dry, an instant dessication, and then he heard it again, a quick, chittering squeak.

A rat. Liam let out a pent-up breath, then walked over to the Oakhams' gate, the sack still in his hand. He pulled at the bars and the gate moved towards him, unlocked. If Eirenaeus returned, he assumed, that was how he would come, and Liam was not sure he could stand it— stand waiting in the crypt. At the very least he should tell Coeccias what was going on.

Fingers still touching the gate, he closed his eyes and projected. *Fanuilh, are you far from here?*

As always, the dragon responded immediately. *No, master.*

I want you to watch the Oakhams' front door. If anyone comes, I want to know immediately.

Yes, master.

"He is not there," Grantaire said from behind him, satisfaction audible in her voice. Liam turned.

"How can you be sure?" *How can you be so calm?*

"A spell." She shrugged and then held out her hand. "The sarcophagus is empty. Give me the Jewel."

Liam brought it to her, still in the bag, all of his questions bubbling out. "Are you sure this will work? Are you sure he will come back? What if he doesn't? Won't the presence of the Jewel warn him? Won't he be able to sense it?"

She snatched the Jewel from him, but once she had it she answered his questions thoughtfully, almost as if she were convincing herself. "He will come back. This is his home, after all, and for the moment the safest place. It will take a great number of lives for him to regain his former strength, and in any case he will not want to be too far from the Jewel. Not too close, but not too far. He will come back," she said, nodding firmly.

Liam was not convinced. "He kept the Jewel in a warehouse, Grantaire. What does he care where it is?"

"He let the Jewel get away from him once," she countered, "and Dorstenius used it against him. He will want to know where it is now. Besides, we don't need to wait here—we can wait upstairs. Fanuilh can hide down here, and let us know when he arrives."

"Oh, no he can't," Liam started to say—he was certainly not going to expose the dragon to that sort of danger—but Mistress Priscian's faint cry stopped him. Both he and Grantaire turned to the older woman, and the thing that stood behind her.

For Liam, there was a terrible familiarity to the scene, as if time had doubled on itself. For the second time that evening, he faced someone across the first Priscian's sarcophagus, and for the second time, he wished he had a weapon.

It was impossible to see any resemblance between the creature behind Mistress Priscian and the stone effigy behind Liam, but he had no doubt it was Eirenaeus, and that it had been hiding on the balcony, listening to them—had returned from its spirit-hunting before they came down to the cellar, in fact, and then been trapped there by the proximity of the Jewel. The thing was tall, towering over the old woman, around whose neck it had thrown one of its arms, so that her chin rested on its bony elbow. Its height accentuated the terrible thinness of its limbs; the arm it raised above Mistress Priscian's head was thinner than the handle of the mace it held, and its body was completely hidden by the woman's thin form.

Grantaire reacted faster, yanking the Jewel from the sack, but Eirenaeus gestured threateningly with the mace, letting it dip just a little. The movement reminded Liam oddly of a drummer hesitating before a stroke.

"Let her go," Grantaire commanded, cold and self-assured. Out of the corner of his eye he saw her hold up the Jewel, a spot of pure white in the shadowy crypt, dangling from her hand by a gold chain, but the sight of Eirenaeus held him facing forward.

He can't be alive, Liam marveled, watching Eirenaeus try to speak. Its neck was a rotten branch, a bundle of bone-dry twigs that seemed more likely to snap than move, but move they did, and a dry cough whispered out. Its eyes had sunk so deep the sockets looked empty, except for the bright sparks far within; sparse black hair hung in wisps down either side of the skull-like head.

It coughed again, and a puff of dust dribbled out and onto Mistress Priscian's head. She stared pleadingly at Liam.

". . . get away . . ." Eirenaeus managed, barely audible.

"No," Grantaire said firmly, advancing a step with the Jewel held high. Liam tensed, readying himself to jump forward. *Why isn't he weaker?* "Let her go," Grantaire said again.

Atrophied over centuries, Eirenaeus's voice sent a literal shiver down Liam's spine; he gritted his teeth, helpless and horrified.

"It is mine. . . . Leave it . . . and go." With slow majesty, it leveled the mace, pointing at Grantaire, and then drew it back up, back behind its head, and Liam was sure it was going to come down on Mistress Priscian's head.

Grantaire must have thought so, too; she shouted, "No!" and started forward, and then Eirenaeus threw the mace.

Even before it hit Grantaire, the long-dead wizard had pushed Mistress Priscian aside; Liam, though, hardly noticed this. He only saw Grantaire spin away, the Jewel flashing past him, and then she fell.

He jerked away, as if he had been hit himself, and heard the Jewel fall somewhere behind him, by the Oakhams' gate, and Eirenaeus was clambering over the first Priscian's sarcophagus like an obscene spider, crouching amid its own long limbs. For a nightmarish moment it stared at Liam, head sunk to the level of its knees, long stick-fingers curled around the edge of the stone.

And then Liam was turning and running, two steps only, and he saw the Jewel gleaming, a white star in the gloom just beyond the bars, and he leapt, hitting the ground hard, grinding his hip into the stone. The bars were not far; his hand went between them, grasping the Jewel. He had expected it to burn, it glowed so, but it did not hurt; it fit his hand perfectly.

Eirenaeus landed on him, and it was like being trampled by horses, most of the weight on his right thigh, and the snap that echoed in Liam's mind, a bone, his bone, another foot coming down in the small of his back, driving the air from his lungs, his chin into the stone, the Jewel from his hand.

He could not breathe; he bucked, more a reaction to the abuse than a thought-out offensive, and Eirenaeus tottered. The weight on his back lifted for a moment, descending on his thigh, on the broken bone there. The pain was a jolt through his entire body, from his toes through his head and up to his grasping hand. It seemed to terminate in the Jewel, just beyond his reach, the bright white physical manifestation of his incredible pain, and he dragged it back into the crypt by the necklace of gold to which it was attached.

The Jewel seemed to bring breath back with it; air came into his lungs and he twisted on the floor, unaware of his own howling. The Jewel followed his twisting, arcing up from the floor, and he followed it in the long second as it flew—of its own volition, it seemed to him—flew up at Eirenaeus, the terrible stick-thing crouching over him.

In the even longer second as the Jewel struck, he saw the face, the permanent grin, flesh dried and stretched taut around the jawbone, the evil flicker of the deep-sunk eyes.

And then the Jewel struck, and Liam shut his eyes a second too late, the silent white flash lancing through into his brain.

The last thing he knew was that someone was screaming, but he was not sure who.

LIAM DREAMED, CONVOLUTED visions that drifted imperceptibly from the nightmarish to the merely confusing. He drifted with the dreams, helpless and to a certain extent apathetic, as if the things he saw were of no concern to him personally, even though many of them happened to him. He felt a curious detachment, so that kissing Countess Perenelle meant as little to him as opening Eirenaeus Priscian's sarcophagus and placing his father inside. He just watched, floating.

Eirenaeus, a pyre of burning twigs, sat beside him in a temple, tearing pages from a book and tossing them, flames licking at their edges, at Grantaire; he climbed a long, black curtain just below Oakham, the other man's boots continually grinding on his head, and when the curtain fell, he swept out over the sea, flying with frightening speed in long, arcing loops. His legs were on fire, burning while he patted at them in amazement. Once again he walked through the ruined villa north of the King's Range, Mistress Priscian at his side, and the old woman identified each statue; the statues crumbled at her touch, and he wearily tried to support them, handfuls of gritty dust that trickled through his fingers, always too much until he gave up.

There were more peaceful dreams, long interludes of sunshine and warmth, and occasionally Fanuilh sat by his side. It was during one of these interludes that he kissed the countess, ten or a dozen languid, almost passionless kisses.

After that there was Eirenaeus again, crouching on the first Priscian's sarcophagus, talking and talking and talking in a vicious little whisper. Liam could not hear him, but he did not want to go closer, though the other man continually curled his long fingers in a come-here gesture.

And then there was Grantaire, bending over him, her hand cool and firm against his cheek, better than a pillow. He leaned into it, closing his eyes, and slept.

Then there were no more dreams for a while.

When Liam was awake and knew it, he lay still, unwilling to open his eyes. He was in a strange bed, softer than the divan in the library, but it was comfortable, and he could feel sunshine on his hands where they rested on the blankets. His right leg ached, but not too much.

He lay there for a long time, the bed too perfect a nest to leave. Even the scratching of claws somewhere out in the room did not make him open his eyes; but when he felt a weight suddenly land on the bed, stretching the blankets tighter over his stomach, he grunted and forced his lids up.

Fanuilh stood on the bed beside him, staring at him. It was shaking a little bit, a gentle quivering in its legs.

You are awake.

"Not for long," he mumbled, and raised a weak hand to pat clumsily at the dragon's head. It flopped down next to him, snug against his side.

It was not a room he knew; there was a window, but all he could see was blue sky. He assumed it was Mistress Priscian's house, and he was vaguely happy that it had not burned down; his last impression had been of intense heat.

He closed his eyes, letting his hand lie on the soft, clothlike scales of his familiar's back. The steady rhythm of its breathing lulled him back to sleep.

When Liam woke the second time, his head was much clearer. A great flood of moonlight lay across the foot of his bed. He stirred, trying to raise himself up, but a twinge in his leg warned him and he fell back.

His movement woke Fanuilh, though; the dragon raised its head. The moon silvered its black scales, but its face was dark.

You are awake.

"Again," Liam whispered. "We're in Mistress Priscian's house?"

Yes.

"How long have I been here?"

Five days.

He blew out a long breath, lacing his hands together behind his head.

Mage Grantaire is gone.

That brought his head back up with a jerk.

"Gone? When?"

This morning. When she was sure you were well.

"Where did she go?"

She did not say. She left a letter with Mistress Priscian. She stayed with you while you were ill. The Aedile has been to visit you many times as well.

His neck ached from the awkward position; he laid his head back, staring up at the ceiling.

"What was wrong with me?"

Your leg is broken.

"I know that," he said. He could feel the splint, holding the leg rigid. The foot below it was numb. "Why was I asleep for five days?"

The dragon's thought was hesitant. *Eirenaeus . . . exploded . . . over you. Mage Grantaire said there was a backlash of magic. In a sense, you were blasted.*

"So am I lich, then? Something hideous, less than human? A monster all right-thinking people will run away from?"

No, you are not a lich. As usual, Fanuilh had missed his attempt at humor; Liam smiled to himself and closed his eyes. After a while he felt the dragon lower its head.

They slept again.

Liam was awake the next morning when Haellus came in with a pitcher and a cloth.

"Master Rhenford, y' are with us again!"

"Yes," Liam said, smiling. He had managed to pull himself up to a sitting position with only a little pain from his leg. "And glad to be so."

The servant held up his pitcher. "I am come to wash you, on which score Mage Grantaire was plain."

"I think I can wash myself." He had looked himself over on waking, surprised to find just how clean he was. The shirt he was wearing had been fresh the day before, as were his linen smallclothes. Knowing that Haellus had been responsible relieved him.

"Ah," the servant said, "Mage Grantaire warned that you'd essay that, and expressly forbade it. Y' are not to stir from the bed for a week entire—for that your leg may heal."

"I don't need to get up to wash," Liam said patiently, and in any case, the leg looked very well to him. He had seen enough broken limbs to know that his could never have healed as much as it had in five days. It would not do to walk on it for a while, even with a crutch—but he was sure Grantaire had done something magical for it.

Haellus was stubborn, but after several minutes of haggling it was agreed that Liam could wash himself, provided he did not move too much.

"Your back'll wait," the servant said, putting the pitcher and the cloth on a stand by the bed. "I'll see to it later, if you wish; you mustn't do it for yourself. Absolutely mustn't: Mage Grantaire was most clear. And I'll get you a bite, and Mistress Priscian'll wish to see you, when y' are ready."

Liam agreed to all this, particularly the food—he was starving. When Haellus finally left the room, he threw back the covers and hastily scrubbed those places he could reach, careful not to jar his leg or strain himself. Even so, he was tired when he was done, and he was slumped wearily on his pillows when the servant returned with a tray.

There was broth and bread, and he ate too much, refusing Haellus's many offers of help. Liam would never have suspected that the servant had such a nannying streak in him.

"Look—not a drop spilled," he said at last, but the other man still eyed him critically, finally giving a grudging nod and collecting the tray.

"If y' are well enough, Mistress Priscian earnestly desires a moment. But only if y' are well enough," he said.

"I am well enough," Liam said. "Please tell her I would be happy to see her."

Mistress Priscian inquired immediately about his health, and appeared greatly relieved when he told her he felt very well. Greatly relieved, but not entirely relieved; Liam noticed the way she clasped her hands before her, holding them tight as if she had no idea what they might do.

He frowned unhappily at her hands, and then she burst out: "Master Rhenford, I offer you my apologies. I can only plead that I could never have guessed the danger involved."

Liam goggled for a moment. The apology had come out almost defiantly, but he did not doubt the woman's sincerity; he was simply amazed that she was apologizing to him. He had meant to apologize to her.

"What—what for?"

It was her turn to goggle; for a moment, she was speechless, as if this was not at all what she had planned. Her hands flew apart, one to her ear, the other out to wave in his direction.

"Why, for all of this. Your leg, your . . . illness. That wizard." He was not sure which wizard she meant, but she went on in a low, mournful tone. "Mage Grantaire and the Aedile have told me everything, and as I said, I can only plead my woeful ignorance."

Liam could think of nothing to say. He really had meant to apologize to her—he had arrested her niece's husband, after all—but he could not ignore the relief he himself felt.

"You must not . . ." he stammered at last. "Really, I should apologize. I mean, Lord Oakham—"

"Nonsense," Mistress Priscian said firmly. "You quite rightly warned me that I should expect unpleasantness. And I must say that his low character is not entirely surprising to me. The Aedile informs me he will be taken before the Duke and tried for murder, and I for one think it quite right."

She had regained control of her hands, Liam was happy to see; she folded them complacently at her waist and gave a little nod. Liam could not help but wonder about Lady Oakham, but he did not want to say anything that might spoil her composure.

"Well, there is nothing you need to apologize for," he assured her.

"Hmmph. When y' are up and walking, we'll see about that. For the moment, there is this for you." She produced a thick sheaf of paper, triple-folded, from her pocket and placed it on the bed near his hand. "Mage Grantaire left it, with her apologies as well. Pressing business took her from Southwark, or she'd have attended your recovery. As it was, she sat with you from morning till night."

"Yes, so I heard," Liam murmured, holding up the letter. His name was on the outermost sheet, visible where it was folded. She had misspelled it: LIAM WRENFORD. *At least she got the first name right,* he thought.

"I'll leave you to it," Mistress Priscian said quietly. "If there's aught you need, call Haellus." She slipped out the door before he could respond, and he turned his attention to the letter, eager and curious.

It was five pages long, all but the last written on both sides; Grantaire's letters were so compressed the words looked like series of slashes, but he found that he could puzzle it out after a few lines.

Wrenford, it began, *please forgive my leaving before you were well, but it is not safe for me to stay here, and you will be well soon in any case. I have seen to that. The leg will heal cleanly, and there will be no permanent damage from the Jewel.*

The first three pages were an extraordinarily detailed explanation of Eirenaeus's return and his eventual destruction. A great deal of it went over Liam's head—she sprinkled the description liberally with quotes from Eirenaeus's notebook and Dorstenius Priscian's diary, as well as a number of references to the work of other magicians—but he managed to grasp the general outline, with Fanuilh's help.

The Jewel had, in effect, blasted Eirenaeus; he was nearly immortal, but he had to provide himself with vast amounts of spirit, since the Jewel continually drained him. And the closer it was to him, the more it drained; in explaining this, Grantaire had included a long series of what Liam assumed were mathematical formulae, but he could make neither heads nor tails of them, so he skipped them.

There was a point of equilibrium, where the Jewel stopped draining him but left him completely incapacitated. When, at the head of an angry band of townsmen, Dorstenius Priscian had entombed his brother, Eirenaeus and the Jewel had been at that point. Grantaire was quite sure that the brother had not known he was condemning his brother to life eternal in a stone box—his diary made it quite clear that he fervently hoped his brother would die shortly. She was less sure what the intervening centuries had been like for Eirenaeus, though she entertained a few gruesome conjectures.

Liam skipped those as well. "She certainly flinches from nothing," he commented to Fanuilh, a hint of admiration in his voice.

There is no way to be sure, the dragon replied, peering over the edge of the paper.

Liam rolled his eyes.

The removal of the Jewel for Duessa Oakham to wear had only set the stage for Eirenaeus's resurrection; it was the murder of Malskat that had allowed it to happen. Oakham had apparently confessed to cutting the beggar's throat directly over the sarcophagus, but Grantaire stated that she did not think such proximity was strictly necessary. Anywhere in the crypt would have done, she wrote. The sarcophagus, it seemed, had been designed by Eirenaeus himself, sometime after he enchanted the Jewel. At the back there was a hidden exit; Grantaire seemed impressed by this, calling it "extremely clever, and well hidden." Apparently Eirenaeus believed in preparing for all eventualities.

The rest, she thought, was obvious: the gradual series of murders— the second beggar, the two maskers, then the three beggars together—as a way of building up his strength. A single life would have provided him enough spirit for a day or two, but she speculated that he would have required more to work any magic.

She dedicated a full page to explaining what she called "his final and irrevocable demise," but the simple fact seemed to be that bringing the Jewel directly into contact with him had allowed it to completely drain him of spirit. The reason for the explosion—which had apparently done no damage at all to the crypt, only to Eirenaeus and Liam—was beyond her, but Liam had his own ideas about it.

"If a single life gives off a flame," he said to Fanuilh, "wouldn't the three or four he had stolen give off a much larger flame?" He was thinking of Mother Japh's blue plane.

The dragon cocked its head at him. *I do not think so. The flame is more of a symbol.*

Liam waved his familiar's skepticism away; the idea appealed to him. It seemed appropriate that Eirenaeus and his Jewel and his stolen spirit should mix explosively. "I like it," he said, grinning at the dragon, "and you will not disagree with me. I am sick."

You are not very sick.

"Sick enough," Liam said. "Don't contradict me."

Fanuilh gave up on the letter, and Liam read on alone.

The fourth page was a brief, maddeningly cryptic description of the events of the past five days. She referred to the two maskers twice, but did not explain how they had been connected to Eirenaeus, and she spoke of Oakham's confession without mentioning any of the details. Lady Oakham had "taken it badly," but Grantaire would not say how. She mentioned Quetivel's departure and a visit by Earl Uldericus, but nothing about the duel. There was a great deal of praise for Mistress Priscian, her calmness and good nature.

All in all it frustrated him, raising more questions than it answered— he wished she was there to answer. And somehow, he had expected more, something . . . personal, he realized. The moment when he had thought he might kiss her recurred to him. The letter gave no hint that she remembered that. *She might as well be writing to her brother,* he thought. Had he imagined the whole thing? He was turning to the fifth page with a sour expression when Haellus poked his head in the door and announced the Aedile.

"Come," Coeccias chided, standing at the end of the bed with a broad grin, "y' are too lazy here, Rhenford. Waited on hand and foot, and for what? A scratch!"

"How else can I relax? If I had known that breaking a leg would keep you away for five days, I would have done it long ago."

The Aedile chuckled, but his expression quickly grew serious. "Truth,

Rhenford, it likes me to see you well. Aye, it likes me well. It was nearly a bad end to the whole affair."

Liam was not sure if he thought that was a vast understatement, but decided to give Coeccias the benefit of the doubt. He rattled the letter. "Grantaire says Oakham confessed."

The Aedile's face lit up. "Truth, confessed isn't the word for it! He fair drew us a map of his evils, from the Jewel through the beggar and the thief to that Desiderius. He's gone up to Deepenmoor these two days, for trial before the Duke. For that he's a peer, he must go before the Duke, but I don't doubt the outcome. He'll be hanged, not least for attempting your life."

Strangely, the thought gave Liam little satisfaction; he certainly did not object, but he was surprised to find that he was mostly indifferent to Oakham's fate.

"The Jewel, in course," the Aedile continued, "was destroyed—but then, I'm not sure that isn't for the best."

"Destroyed? Grantaire didn't mention that."

"In your bonfire, Rhenford. There was as little left as there is at the bottom of a tipster's bottle—a fine powder was all. Not that Mistress Priscian took it poorly. She is a fine woman, not given to airs. Unlike some," he said, leaning over and dropping his voice confidentially. "That Lady Oakham, for an example. It is well that she took herself off to Deepenmoor, or I'd have had to post a man at your door. I imagine after the hanging it'll be a temple of seclusion for her."

Liam could think of worse things than temple life, and he could manage no sympathy for the spoiled girl.

"And what about those maskers? Grantaire says it was Eirenaeus."

The Aedile grimaced. "Aye, it was. We only found them two nights past, in an old cistern. A beggar found them, to be fair—I'd naught to do with it." He hung his head sorrowfully. "The same wounds, and no spirit. They were but children—no more than twelve. They should never've been let out."

There was a long silence while Liam digested this, imagining Coeccias telling the parents. He knew the Aedile would have done it himself. *And to think I thought my responsibilities were too much. . . .*

After a while the silence grew lighter, and Liam ventured another question: "What about Uldericus and Quetivel? Was there a duel?"

Heavily at first, and later with growing relish, Coeccias described the earl's arrival a few days before at Mistress Priscian's door, bearing a fistful of papers that he claimed were Oakham's debts to him. "He tried to come all over the gallant, and offered them to her, saying that he would not trouble her in her sorrowful time, and that she might destroy the markers at her convenience, but that he must see Quetivel, who was dancing attendance on the distraught Lady Oakham at the time."

Mistress Priscian had told him off in no uncertain terms; according to Coeccias she had threatened him with a poker, the thought of which set the Aedile laughing. "She packed Quetivel off that very afternoon, and brought the markers to me. I had a quiet word with the earl—he was much annoyed, but finally saw sense. Most especially after I told him that Oakham had confessed to cheating for him, so that he could take Quetivel for greater sums."

"Ha!" Liam shouted. "I knew it!" *There was no way I could be that bad at Alliances.*

"Aye, they had a scheme—Uldericus forgave a fraction of his debt, and Oakham did something for him. I doubt not that y' understand it better than I; I don't game much. And then there's this: Uldericus never asked to buy the Jewel. It seems Oakham offered it to him, in return for his markers. The earl refused, quite rightly. I can only think that he must have guessed that Oakham was responsible—but there's no proof, and it's not a crime, though it should be. In fine, though, Oakham was still as far in debt to the earl as we could have hoped." He named a sum, and Liam blinked, appropriately impressed.

"You could raise a fleet on that," he said.

Coeccias agreed. "Aye, but it was only the half of what he said Desiderius was going to give him for the Jewel. Can imagine? And here's more—the ship he booked passage on, the *Sourberry?* He had only booked one. I've told Mistress Priscian, but she asked me to keep it dark."

"I imagine she wants to tell her niece herself."

"Aye, there's that. She was most surprised, for that it seems he has no family in Torquay."

They considered this in silence, Liam gazing out the window. Then a different thought occurred to him: he had been in bed for five days.

"I have missed the whole Banquet," he said.

"Y' have, y' have," Coeccias said sadly, and then snapped his fingers. "I near forgot—there was a message for you. That maid, the one you sent me after. I never found her that night, but she came around the next day. She asked that you remember her gift. Does that signify? She was a rude little thing."

Liam laughed, amazed at Mopsa's audacity. *Does she call that keeping a low profile?* "I will have to think about that," he said, refusing to answer the question implicit in the Aedile's raised eyebrow.

When it was clear that no explanations would be forthcoming, Coeccias coughed into his fist. "Well and well; I should leave you to regain your strength. It would like me, though . . . truth, I needs must—well, there is this, Rhenford: I am sorry for that with the beggars, and that I doubted you."

The Aedile's blush appalled Liam; was everyone going to apologize to him today? He had forgotten his anger with his friend, had explained it away to himself in that walk up the Point.

"Forget it," he said, and then repeated himself more forcefully. When Coeccias still appeared uncomfortable, he held out his hand. "Shake, and we will both forget it. Doubting me is never a bad thing."

The Aedile took his hand and pumped it twice. "It ran through my mind when I saw you in the crypt, that my last words to you were angry. I would not have us part that way." He seemed more comfortable now, but the sentiments embarrassed Liam a little.

"Forget it," he said again.

"I will," Coeccias promised with a smile, "and I will leave you now. This lazing about can't last."

"It will last as long as I can make it last," Liam called after him, and to prove it he sank himself down into the pillows, even as the door closed behind the Aedile.

Liam sat up a little later and finished the rest of Grantaire's letter. There was only one more page, but it was very different from what had gone before. From the very first sentence it seemed much less assured, a complete departure from the dry, almost scholarly tone of the first four pages. Even the letters were different: they were easier to read, better formed, as if she had spent more time tracing each letter, using the time to think about what she was writing.

> *I should thank you for letting me stay in the house,* she wrote.
> *It has been over a year since I stayed in a house. I have stayed at Mistress Priscian's for the last three days; it is very comfortable and she is a fine woman. But I think I like your house better—you are a better cook than Haellus.*

He laughed at this, and then wondered if she meant it as a joke. As far as he could remember, he had never seen her smile.

> *Tanaquil was right about you. When he came to me, I was in Carad Llan. (The Guild chapter house there is very small.) He told*

me to go to Southwark and take his things, but he also said I should meet you. He said you could be trusted, that you might be a useful friend. I must admit that on my journey here I did not think much about it; you are not a mage, after all, and it has been a long time since I have dealt with anything but. But he was right.

There are things I have to do now, people I must visit. Other mages, mostly. Harcourt represents a serious danger, and they must be warned. It may be that from time to time mages may come to Southwark—that I may send them here. The Guild has no presence in the Southern Tier, and the closest chapter house is Torquay, which is so disorganized as to present no danger. I may give them your name, and I hope you will be as kind to them as you were to me.

Liam frowned, torn by the last sentence. He did not think he had been overly kind to her, but it was exactly the kind of personal sentiment for which he had been looking. On the other hand, he was not sure he wanted to be drawn into a conflict between wizards. He shook his head; Grantaire had only said she might give out his name—he would worry about it if another wizard arrived on his doorstep.

I would like to come back sometime, if I get a chance. In the summer, I think. Tanaquil said you used to swim in the ocean from his beach, that was how he first mentioned you: "A man who used to swim from my beach." I have never been in the ocean—I think it would be very cold.

However, I do not think it will be for some time. I have a great many things to do, and I must leave today.

There was a line across the page, as if to mark off separate thoughts.

It is very early in the morning. I have been watching you sleep—you will recover today or tomorrow, I am sure. You look very lonely when you are asleep. I think you are like me, Wrenford.

Rif says he thinks you were going to kiss me, that night when we talked in the kitchen. I don't think so, but he is quite sure. Were you?

I wonder what would have happened if you did?

She signed her name below that, a large, sprawling signature. There were two names, and he thought the second one was Fauve, or Fauvel.

He puzzled over it for a minute, trying to work it out, then gave up and reread the last three paragraphs again.

"Fanuilh, what was Grantaire's cat's name?"

The dragon raised its head from the blanket. *Rif, master.*

Liam nodded ruefully. "Smart cat." *I should have kissed her,* he thought, but then his conviction wavered a little. If she wondered what would have happened, that probably meant that she was uninterested in being kissed.

And what did she mean about his being like her? *She doesn't mean she looks lonely when she sleeps,* he thought. *Does she think I'm lonely?*

"Fanuilh, am I lonely?"

Master?

"I'm not lonely, am I?"

You are not alone, the dragon thought, after a long moment of consideration. *I am always here. And Aedile Coeccias is your friend.*

"Right," Liam said, but he wondered—not about Coeccias or Fanuilh, but about whether she might mean a different kind of loneliness. Exactly what kind, he was not sure, but he thought that was what she meant.

The letter lying facedown on his stomach, he turned to the window to think about it. He remembered then the feel of her hand on his cheek, and how it had helped him sleep.

Much later, he turned from the window and called Haellus's name as loudly as he could without shouting. The servant must have been waiting, because he arrived only a few seconds later.

"Is there something you need, Master Rhenford?"

"Yes," Liam said. "I need to buy a Banquet gift."

"But the Banquet is over," Haellus said, puzzled.

"I know that, but I need one anyway." When the servant looked at him as if he had lost his mind, Liam pointed to his leg and added: "I meant to get it earlier, but I didn't have a chance."

"Ah," Haellus said, comprehension dawning. "In course, Master Rhenford. What will you need?"

Liam frowned. His thoughts had turned to the two children killed by Eirenaeus, how they were no older than Mopsa, and he had decided that he would have to do something to help her, something permanent. It would have to wait until he was back on his feet; in the meantime, all he could do was remember his promise.

"Something big," he said, and then he waited for Haellus's suggestions.